House of Smoke

"So good it makes the heart leap."   —*Time*

"Intriguing . . . distinctive." —*Washington Post Book World*

"A gritty, gripping sins-of-the-fathers tale . . . with two irresistible women."   —*Kirkus Reviews*

"Vivid . . . wealth, promiscuity, and violence."
                    —*Chicago Tribune*

"Top-notch . . . smart and fast-moving . . . an exciting modern thriller with a classic feel . . . rewarding on all levels."
                    —*Publishers Weekly*

"An excellent crime novel in the Ross MacDonald tradition . . . Kate Blanchard is a fascinating new detective."   —*Booklist*

"A dandy thriller of many layers, textures, and characters with depth . . . if only it didn't have to end."
                    —*St. Petersburg Times*

Against the Wind

"Gritty, vivid courtroom thriller ... sexually provocative, superior suspense." —*New York Times Book Review*

"A ripsnorting, full-throttle ... high-octane blast that makes *Presumed Innocent* look tame by comparison. A compulsively readable tale of crime and punishment that kept me up late into the night." —Stephen King

"A powerhouse thriller ... the narrative's storm surge of courtroom duels, gritty crime action, twisty plotting, and technicolor characters irrevocably sweeps the reader up." —*Kirkus Reviews*

"Sexy, nasty, head-knocking ... a real grabber!" —Philip Friedman, bestselling author of *Grand Jury*

"Provocative ... delivers irresistible legal wranglings and entertaining lawyerly theatrics." —*Publishers Weekly*

J. F. FREEDMAN

KEY WITNESS

A SIGNET BOOK

For David A. Freedman

SIGNET
Published by the Penguin Group
Penguin Putnam Inc., 375 Hudson Street,
New York, New York 10014, U.S.A.
Penguin Books Ltd, 27 Wrights Lane,
London W8 5TZ, England
Penguin Books Australia Ltd,
Ringwood, Victoria, Australia
Penguin Books Canada Ltd, 10 Alcorn Avenue,
Toronto, Ontario, Canada M4V 3B2
Penguin Books (N.Z.) Ltd, 182–190 Wairau Road,
Auckland 10, New Zealand

Penguin Books Ltd, Registered Offices:
Harmondsworth, Middlesex, England

Published by Signet, an imprint of Dutton NAL,
a member of Penguin Putnam Inc.
Previously appeared in a Dutton edition.

First Signet Printing, October, 1998
10 9 8 7 6 5 4 3 2 1

There were things which he stretched,
but mainly he told the truth.

—Mark Twain,
The Adventures of Huckleberry Finn

PART
ONE

EARLY dark, time suspended between sunset and true night, the barest sliver of dying sunlight fading on the western horizon, flickering dull yellow-vermilion patches visible through the thick clusters of trees that bracket the narrow two-lane road.

Wyatt Matthews was running. Five strides to a breath, deep inhale, then out, resisting the urge, late in the run, to breathe more quickly. T-shirt soaked across the chest and under the armpits, feeling a slickness on his forearms, forehead, neck. Driving himself, sweating out all the crap.

He had been running almost forty minutes, just under five miles. He was forty-eight years old, a tick under six feet tall, and his weight—173 pounds—was the same it had been the day he'd graduated law school. No matter how far he ran—three miles or ten or any distance in between—he ran the last mile with the same cadence, the same timing as the first. His daily run was almost as fast as it had been ten, even twenty years earlier.

Wyatt ran for exercise; more important he ran for the high it gave him. Running, sweating, feeling his heart beating faster, was commonsense good health; on a deeper, more important level, running helped clear his head.

Tonight, though, the fatigue, the sweating, the physical depletion, couldn't blow the shit out. The more he tried not to think, the more a crazy-quilt jumble of ideas, images, and scenarios flashed across his mind. Stuff from the firm, especially residual stuff from his last case, which he had worked on for over three years and had finally concluded a month ago in triumph.

More than anything, what Wyatt was thinking about, what he had been agonizing over almost from when the trial was over, was why he didn't feel better about it. Part of it was the normal letdown after such a long, arduous struggle. That always happened, he knew that, he knew the size and shape of it and how to deal with it.

This was something different. Something deeper, heavier. This was ambivalence and life-crisis chaos on a major scale. In runner's terms, he had hit the wall. The problem was, he didn't know what the wall was. How big, what it was made of. Anything.

His run was almost over. Another third of a mile to go and he'd be at the entrance to his driveway, and then it was the last hundred yards to the front of his house.

Wyatt's home was like all the houses in this section of the township—large, expensive, exclusive. The lots were an acre or more, each secluded from view by thick stands of old-growth maple, ash, and hickory. Rich people's houses—people who had made it. Privacy and security were valued—if you didn't live here, or weren't visiting someone who did, you had no reason to be in the area. Gardeners, maids, day workers, they came and went, but they didn't leave lasting footprints.

Except for the sounds of his footsteps and breathing, the only noise Wyatt had been conscious of was the wind in the trees; but now, suddenly, rising out of the darkness, he heard the shrill scream of a siren, and then it was two sirens he was hearing, and as he turned, startled, and looked back over his shoulder, he saw flashing lights, the vehicles coming up loud and fast behind him.

The road was dark. There were no streetlights. He moved far enough off the asphalt onto the shoulder to make sure he was well clear of the approaching vehicles, because wherever they were going, they weren't watching for runners.

A police car sped past him. Right behind it was an ambulance.

There weren't many houses up ahead—just his and a couple others.

He panicked—what were cops and ambulances doing here? Had something happened at his house while he'd been running? When he'd gone out the front door, his wife had been starting to dress for dinner, and his daughter had been doing homework. Had something turned wrong in that short a space of time?

Instant adrenaline rush kicked in, he was sprinting for home.

It wasn't his house. It was his neighbor's, the closest house to his own, the two properties separated by a large shared lawn bisected by a natural fence line of elms.

Wyatt stopped, catching his breath in deep gulps, grateful that it wasn't his house, it wasn't his family. He could see the police car and the ambulance parked in front, the lights still flashing. Outside floodlights had been turned on—the front of the house was as bright as daytime.

The cops and paramedics were out of their vehicles, talking to the Spragues, his neighbors. They were in their mid-sixties—Ted Sprague had been president of Radmill, one of the largest auto-parts companies in the country. He'd retired last year. The Spragues were supposed to be out of the country until this weekend, vacationing in Paris.

Wyatt jogged up the driveway. "Ted," he called out as he approached, "are you all right? What's going on?"

"We've been robbed, that's what's been going on. Enid was shot."

Wyatt rushed over. He put a comforting hand on the other's forearm. "Jesus!" he exclaimed. "Is she . . ."

"I'm all right." He heard a woman's shaky voice.

Enid Sprague was lying awkwardly on the front steps. A female paramedic was cutting off part of her dress around her waist. The dress was soaked with blood.

"What are you . . . ?" Wyatt turned to the paramedic who was tending to Mrs. Sprague's wound. "Is she all right? What happened?"

The paramedic, wearing latex gloves, finished cutting away the bloody dress, revealing the wound underneath. A red, ugly blotch along the rib line, blood oozing out. She wiped away the blood so she could see the wound.

"Didn't hit any arteries or vital organs," the paramedic told Enid Sprague in a practiced, reassuring voice. She swiveled around to look at the husband. "I'm sure she's going to be all right."

The man staggered next to his wife.

Wyatt hovered over him. "Ted. What happened?"

Sprague shook his head. "We walked into the house," he said, his voice full of astonishment, "the lights were all out, which was logical since we weren't home, and all the curtains were drawn—we'd sealed the house up before we'd left. It was black as a tomb in there, believe me. We're about to turn the front lights on, and we see a beam of light coming from under the study door, at the rear of the house. Like a flashlight." He took his wife's hand in his. "How do you feel? Are you all right?"

"It feels like somebody took a tooth out without Novocain," she told him, "all of them at the same time. Try not to worry," she said, her voice coming in a gasp.

"How can I not worry?"

Enid Sprague looked up at Wyatt. "We walked right in on the bastards," she told him, her voice indignant even through the pain, "surprised the hell out of them. We could see they were robbing us—silverware, my jewelry, they must have known we weren't in town. They had everything they were going to take in neat piles on the floor, we could see it from their flashlights."

"We got back a day earlier than we were supposed to," Ted interjected.

"I asked them what the hell they were doing," Enid said.

Wyatt smiled. Enid was a tough cookie; nobody screwed her around.

"So they shot her," Ted said, shuddering.

"They shot you," one of the policemen echoed. "Did they both have guns? Or just the one who shot you?"

Ted Sprague looked away.

"Did you notice if the other one had a gun as well?" the young officer asked again. He was being polite. These people were old enough to be his parents, almost old enough to be his grandparents.

Ted Sprague shook his head. "The other one didn't have a gun." He hesitated. "Neither one of them had a gun. That we could see," he added.

Enid flinched as the paramedic applied antiseptic to her side, placed a gauze pad over the injured area, and began bandaging it. "We're going to the hospital now," she said. "Do you feel steady enough to stand up and walk over to the ambulance? We can put you on the gurney if you'd rather."

"I think I'm okay," Enid stated. "Help me up."

Each paramedic took an arm and helped Enid to her feet. Ted hovered at her side.

"I'll ride in with you," he said. "Can I do that?" he asked.

"Certainly," the paramedic told him.

"The gun," the policeman said a third time. "I misunderstood you. You said neither one . . . or which . . ."

"It was my gun." Enid turned to the policeman. "He used my gun to shoot me."

"He was stealing your gun as well?" the officer asked. "Where in the house did you keep it?"

She shook her head. Her husband put a protective arm around her shoulder, the side that hadn't been shot. "He took it away from her," Ted said flatly, avoiding the officer's question.

"You got your pistol out from somewhere in the house, where you kept it for emergencies, and you brought it into the room with you," the policeman said, putting it together. "Which you assumed would give you some protection, but it didn't because he took it away from you. I see the picture now," he concluded.

"He was walking at me," she said. The color was rapidly draining from her face, her voice coming out in airy, wheezing gasps, like she'd had a tracheotomy. She shook her head. "I couldn't pull the trigger. He took it right out of my hand."

"And then shot you with it," the policeman confirmed.

"I tried to take it back away from him once he'd taken it. That's when it went off."

You're lucky it didn't go off in your chest, Wyatt thought. Two inches to the left and we wouldn't be standing here talking like this.

"At least they didn't get anything," Enid added defiantly, almost gloating. "As soon as that gun went off they ran like scared rabbits."

A woman suddenly materialized, running up the driveway. "What happened?" Moira, Wyatt's wife, asked. "Oh!" she gasped, seeing the blood seeping through the bandage on Enid Sprague's rib cage.

"Burglars," Wyatt explained. "Enid tried to stop them and they took the gun away from her, and it went off in the struggle."

"Oh, my God! You poor thing! What can we do?" Moira was wearing a black cocktail dress, but she had no shoes on and no makeup.

"I need to go to the hospital," Enid said.

"Of course." Moira was chagrined.

The paramedics lifted Enid into the ambulance.

"Before you go, sir," the officer asked Ted Sprague, "can you give me a description of them? Did you get a decent look at them? Either of them, or both?" He had his notepad out.

"Well, it was dark, like I said," Ted began. "Pitch-black, except for their flashlights. All we could really see were silhouettes."

"They had stocking caps pulled down low over their faces," Enid interrupted from the back of the ambulance. "And they were wearing gloves." She pointed at the paramedic's hands. "Like hers." She lay down inside, on the gurney.

"They were black," Ted told the cops. "They were black men, both of them."

The lead cop, who was white, cocked his head quizzically. "If it was pitch-black, how could you tell?" he asked.

Ted Sprague turned from helping his wife into the ambulance to face the cop. "I didn't fall out of the tree this morning, son. It could've been black as the inside of hell in there, but I can tell a black man when I hear his voice. I heard them both talk, and they were both black men. Of that I am certain."

"All right, then." The officer made some notes. "Did they seem young or old, or in between?"

"Young." Ted was as firm as concrete. "From gangs, I'd bet my life on it."

"We're going to check the house over," the officer told Ted, "and we'll leave someone here until you get back. These people won't be back," he said, looking at Wyatt and Moira as well as the Spragues. "They're likely a dozen miles away from here by now, but you might want to let your security service know what happened. They'll send someone out to keep an eye on things."

The ambulance took off down the driveway, disappearing into the street. The cops went into the house to assess the damage further.

It was quiet again, only the sounds of night in the country, but Wyatt felt like he was standing in a war zone. He put an arm around Moira's waist. She was shaking.

"Let's go home," he said comfortingly. "It's over here."

She looked up at him. "I never thought something like that could happen here. Nothing's safe anymore," she stated, her voice flat.

"That's not true," he countered.

"Of course it is. You just saw it."

He shook his head. "This was a professional, planned burglary. The men who did this knew the Spragues were out of town. It was dumb bad luck for everyone that they came back early."

"You don't know that," Moira said. "And they shot Enid."

"They didn't have guns." He wanted her to understand the truth of the situation so she could put it in its proper perspective. "It was *her* gun. It went off by accident. People get robbed, honey. It doesn't mean gangbangers are coming out here and threatening us."

She thought about that for a moment. "It's the world. Nothing is safe anymore," she proclaimed a second time with a shudder.

"Camels."

Normal, everyday purchase, nothing suspicious.

The owner, a squat statue behind the counter, barely looked at him, singsong: "Regular or filters? Kings or lights?" One sideways glance then away, the black narrow eyes opaque marbles. Like he was a dog turd stinking up the pavement.

The gun hung heavy in the right-hand pocket of his jacket. A compact automatic, like the hit men use. He didn't know any hit men, he'd heard that from his homie, who swore he'd stolen it from some Italian guy's house.

He could kill this motherfucker and sleep like a baby afterward. Take the gun out and shoot this prick right in his face.

"Change that—make it Marlboros," he managed to respond as the short man, almost as wide as he was tall, was reaching up on his tiptoes for the pack of smokes high on the shelf behind the counter. You asshole, you're so dumb you don't keep the cigarettes someplace where you can reach them easy, you deserve having to stretch your short fat arm up there—the owner's shirt coming out from where he'd neatly tucked it into his pants, which were belted halfway up his chest.

Then he noticed that there were packs closer down, easier to reach. Son of a bitch was trying to foist a stale pack off on him. Save the fresh ones for his regular customers.

You're on my list, he thought to himself, eyes burning at the owner's back.

He hated when people pulled shit like that. Like he was some fool back in school, didn't know the answer, teacher trying to ridicule him. Fumbling, tongue-tied. "Yeah, Marlboros," he said again. "Hard box." It threw him, being asked a dumb-ass question like that. And trying to sell him stale goods, that really burned his ass.

Not that it actually mattered. He didn't smoke tobacco. One brand was the same as the other, far as he was concerned. Camels had been the first brand that had popped into his mind, because of that Joe Camel character you saw everywhere, on the billboards and in the subways, a takeoff of an ultracool dude, shooting pool and scoring the bitches.

Tobacco was a plot: evil, enslaving, you saw that message plastered on the signs in the buses, the billboards all through the south side—sometimes plastered right over that Joe Camel's jive-ass face: a picture of a skeleton handing a lit cigarette to an innocent little black kid. Little girl in pigtails, face all clean and shiny. Big shit-eating grin on the deathhead's skull-face.

Pass on tobacco. Smoke weed, or he would mix up some crack with Valium that was part of the contents of some old bitch's purse he'd grabbed off the seat of her car where she had left it while she was putting coins in a parking meter. Deserve the bitch right, leave her purse on the seat with the window wide open.

Doing drugs on a regular basis was expensive, too much for him, especially where he was at these days. The only good thing about not having money he could think of.

He wasn't going to have a habit—ever. Habits were for losers. Like they say on the street, if you have a regular habit that's all you have. You *deal* shit, you don't use it, unless you're dealing it and taking a taste for yourself. Preferably you sell it to white people, 'cause they paid top dollar. They want to score and get the fuck out of his neighborhood, scared shitless, you could smell the fear on them.

Score dope and cheap pussy, blow jobs in their expensive cars, that's all they came down to his neighborhood for.

Mostly, though, it was his own people who copped. Where you live is where you do business. But you got to be careful, you're gonna do a lot of prison time if you get caught dealing if you're black. Black dealer goes to prison, white dealer goes on parole. Check it out, Dexter had told him once.

It was true. Still, as the saying goes, selling drugs is a living. Mighty fine one.

Getting into dealing was going to be his next move. He was already desperate thinking about it, about the life he was missing out on. Cars, jewelry, clothes. Bitches.

His best friend, Dexter—like a brother: blood, almost, born four days apart. Their mamas sitting out on the stoops, side by side, legs spread against the August humidity, drinking Cokes out of the bottle, baby boys bouncing on their knees. That's how far back. Dexter Lewis and Marvin White, from the cradle. Dexter four days older, he'd pulled rank all their lives. And still did.

Dexter was a dealer, a legitimate high roller, not some street hustler selling dime bags. Just turned eighteen and he's a lieutenant in the city's drug syndicate, run from the state prison by bloods: a multimillion-dollar business.

Dexter was a prime example of how good you could do if you were willing to take chances, hang tough, be a hard-nosed businessman. Dexter had started dealing barely a year ago, and already he's driving a Jeep Grand Cherokee, the Orvis model, top of the line—leather on leather, two car phones, CD player, he's buying his suits three, four at a time at the most expensive men's stores in the city. Ralph Lauren, Dexter's very buttoned-down, nothing flashy. Rolex on his wrist, a real one, not one of those jive knockoffs. The Navigator model, understated chrome, good down to fifty fathoms. The watch cost Dexter $3,500, Dexter pays for it in cash, hundred-dollar bills, crisp like he'd printed them up himself. Whipping out his roll, peeling them off, laying them down on the jewelry-store counter. The salesman, pasty-faced middle-aged white asshole, his eyeballs bulging, checking it out, shit-eating grin on his face. "Very good, sir, is there anything else I can show you today, sir?" Salesman thinking, eighteen-year-old nigger drug dealer, pimp, I hope you

choke on that watch, you socially worthless piece of shit,
smiling, "an excellent selection, sir, you have excellent
taste." You could read that motherfucker's mind like he had
a window in his forehead.

Standing there next to Dexter, watching. With less than
five dollars in his own damn pocket. About as useful as a
second asshole.

This being-poor shit was going to end, and soon. Get out
of the projects, get his mother off her knees.

Six months. A year, tops. He'd be peeling off the hundreds, just like Dexter.

Look around the Korean's store. Take your time. Check it
out. Play it cool, play it slow. Don't rush it, it ain't going
nowhere.

This store was a little gold mine. He'd been checking it
out for months, from when he'd been a delivery boy. The
block the store was located on had been part of his route, he
had walked by it every day, five days a week. Once or twice
he'd gone inside and bought a soda, and that was when he'd
seen how much money was coming in.

The store owner slapped a pack of Marlboros—hard box,
like he'd asked for—down on the counter.

Lay his money down, nice and polite, pocket his change,
cigarettes, walk out. Casual, no big thing. Owner not even
looking at him, he could've been a spaceman from Mars.

Violet Waleska's feet were killing her. Her ankles, her
calves, her knees. Some days it felt like she'd been beaten
with a baseball bat from the waist down. She had been
standing on the rock-hard concrete floor, slippery from being constantly hosed down, for her entire shift, ten miserable hours, only breaking for lunch and the bathroom—but
she was going out tonight and aching legs weren't going to
stop her.

She peeled off her white pants and smock that the company furnished daily, freshly laundered and deodorized,
continued stripping down to her underwear, off came her
Dr. Scholl's support hose, it all went into the big canvas
laundry basket. Everything was soaking wet with her sweat
and stinking to high hell; they could wash these uniforms in

boiling water forever and the smell would still stick—the smell of dead, burning pigs.

She was naked but she could care less about modesty. They were all women, over two dozen of them, old, young, short, tall, skinny, fat, black, white, and they knew each other intimately. Killing, cutting, gutting, rendering, ten hours a day, year in and year out—it formed a bond among them.

The stench of burnt hair and rendered pigskin hung in the air like a mushroom cloud. Five acres under one roof, thousands of pigs butchered daily. They moved up the conveyor belt, four hundred pounds of sheer squealing terror, each hog's ten pounds of watery shit running on the floor like blood, the hose washing everything away. But not the smell of death, the awful decay.

It never went away, despite the air conditioners and industrial fans that blew twenty-four hours a day, and the quantities of lemon oil and deodorant, also provided by the company. The women lathered the stuff on at the end of every shift, after scrubbing themselves raw in the scalding showers. But it never went away.

She stood under the shower of near-boiling needles, the steam rising up and filling the room. Standing there until the muscles in her neck and back began to stop aching, the tension flowing away like the water flowing down the drain. She had a strong, full figure—a womanly woman, nothing weak. Washing her hair, she eased herself to the floor, the water flowing under her butt, under her legs, lying on the floor of the shower on her back and elevating her legs, feeling the circulation coming back.

She dried off with her own towels she'd brought from home, nice thick terries. When you worked this hard you had to pamper yourself. That's why, despite the ache in her calves and ankles and feet that would outlast a two-hour professional massage, she was going to dress up in a sexy outfit and go out dancing. She was meeting a couple of girlfriends, Peggy and Paula, they'd dance with each other like teenagers, drink some margaritas, act up. And maybe she'd meet a cute guy, dance with him—some slow ones. Not that anything would ever come of it—it never did, not someone you met dancing in a bar—but a girl has to dream.

She still had time, but not an infinite amount anymore,

not very much at all. She had turned forty on her last birthday, a month ago. The dreaded *four-o*.

She wanted a family, a husband: every girl's dream, was that so much to ask for?

She was beginning to give up hope. But not completely; it would flare up when she least expected it. Tonight she was going to go dancing with her two best friends, and she was going to get wild. Within bounds, of course. She was more wild in thought than deed. She was an officer in her union, and she had worked too hard to get to where she was to act like someone who was like what she had come from.

They brought Dwayne Thompson down to the city under supertight security.

Two veteran guards rousted him in his cell, waking him from a bad dream. All his dreams were bad. You didn't have any other kind in here.

"Rise and shine, bright eyes."

"What the fuck?" He'd barely been asleep an hour, so he was discombobulated, disoriented. His cell was windowless. It could have been high noon or the middle of the night, he didn't know. Six of one, half a dozen the other, like he could give a shit.

The one guard reached down and grabbed him roughly by the neck of his T-shirt, jerking him off his bunk. He had been in isolation for two weeks for breaking some chickenshit rule, he couldn't even remember now what it had been. The prison system had a million bogus rules, and over time he'd broken his share of them. So what—what could they do to him they hadn't done already?

"Grab your shit."

They led him down the long concrete corridor that connected his wing of the prison to the central control area. Four guards flanked him. He had a small ditty bag in his hand, everything he would take with him. It was early nighttime—he could see the sky turning as he looked out the barred windows.

Two state marshals were waiting. His escorts. Tough old

boys, ex-marines, they'd as soon break your arm or leg you gave them any shit.

"Prisoner been to the can?" one of the marshals asked the prison guards. "Four hours' drive, and there ain't gonna be any pit stops. Don't wanna hear no whining about his weak bladder or whatever."

"He's done his duty," the guard said.

"I've been having the runs lately," Dwayne ventured. "Can't control my bowels."

The marshal shrugged. "Worse things in the world than shitting your drawers. Last fella couldn't wait, we made him eat it."

"Least I'd have a hot meal," Dwayne answered.

The marshals grinned at each other. "This could be fun," the other said.

"Just don't play country-western, that's all I ask," Dwayne went on. "That definitely qualifies under the cruel-and-unusual clause."

They shackled him from head to foot—waist chains connected to handcuffs, connected to heavy leg-irons—standard procedure for transporting a felon like Dwayne. The marshals double-checked the locks on his irons and signed the release forms.

"Be careful with this one," the deputy warden on duty warned the marshals as he handed over the keys to Dwayne's irons. "He's got no conscience whatsoever."

"We hear you," the lead marshal replied.

Dwayne showed no emotion at hearing this. He'd heard it before, countless times.

Dwayne Thompson didn't look particularly dangerous. In his late thirties, he was about average height and build, rough-handsome like the photos you see of authentic cowboys. Blond hair almost white, milk blue eyes the color of a dry sky. A woman had once told him he looked like Robert Redford, the actor, but he attributed that to drunkenness and wishful thinking.

His most distinctive feature was the dozens of tattoos all over his body: up and down his arms, all across his chest, his legs, his back. They were real works of art—some of the most famous tattoo artists in the country had made their contribution to Dwayne Thompson's needle-inflicted flesh. The most outrageous tattoo, also the largest, covered his entire back, neck to ass crack. It was a reproduction of Michelangelo's Sistine Chapel, in stunning color and detail. Except that Satan, finger extended, took the place of God.

Dwayne's body was tight. He kept superbly fit by doing sit-ups, push-ups, and chin-ups by the hundreds in his cell. He didn't use the weights in the yard because he didn't do much of anything that would put him in close contact with other prisoners. He went his way and everyone left him alone.

At the main entrance, after clearing final security, the marshals were handed back their side arms, 9-mm automatics that could seriously hurt. They strapped the guns into their holsters and escorted their prisoner out the gates of Durban State Penitentiary, the number one maximum-security prison in the state system. They don't sentence you to do your stretch at Durban unless you are a really bad guy with a lot of hard time to do.

Dwayne qualified on both counts.

He had a jacket several inches thick. Armed robbery, assault with intent to kill, forgery, rape, strong-arm coercion— you name it, he'd done it. He'd also, some years back, murdered two men in cold blood that no one except him and one other man knew about, and that man would take his secret to the grave. Of that Dwayne was certain, because he had the goods on that guy for shit he'd done, crimes that were as bad as any Dwayne had committed. So although this current stretch was a long one, Dwayne wasn't doing life without parole.

Except that when he finished doing this stretch there was a pending case he was going to be tried on, another felony assault—if he had a specialty, that would be it. And under the newly enacted three-strikes law in the state, if he was convicted on that one, he would be a lifer for sure.

For now he wasn't sweating that. When his release date came closer, he'd start thinking about it, how to work it, beat it. Right now, since he was already in, why worry about something he couldn't control anyway?

The marshals were moving their prisoner in a plain-wrap Ford Taurus station wagon with regular tags, a nice comfortable vehicle nobody notices. They didn't want to attract attention, hence the unmarked car instead of one bearing state tags and door ID, or a prison bus. It's easier driving at night, less traffic, you make better time, and there is less chance of a foul-up with the prisoner. Not that they had any worries about him trying to escape—with the quantity of metal he had on his body and the small amount of play in the leg-irons, he couldn't run a hundred yards in five minutes. And he couldn't go for one of their guns because his hands and arms had virtually no mobility, and anyway, he was in the security cage in the backseat, locked in. They were in the front.

The only problem would be if they got into an accident. He could be trapped, unable to escape. The gas tank blew up, he'd be roasted.

The odds on that were about ten thousand to one. Acceptable.

They rode in silence except for the Garth Brooks tapes one of the marshals had brought. Dwayne hadn't said anything when they started playing them. "Either of you have any cigarettes?" was the only thing he'd asked, shortly after they hit the interstate. They drove at a comfortable sixty-five. Outside it was overcast, the stars obscured by cloud cover.

"Don't smoke," the driver had informed him.

"Can we stop and get a pack?" Dwayne asked. "I'll pay for them."

All the prisons and jails had gone to No Smoking for over three years now. It made cigarettes as valuable a commodity as marijuana or cocaine. A single cigarette could go for five bucks, a full pack for a hundred. Men in Dwayne's cellblock had been severely beaten, and worse, over a disputed pack of contraband Pall Malls.

The shotgun rider shook his head. "No can do."

They had food and water in the car, in a small hamper under the shotgun rider's feet. After about an hour he looked back over his shoulder at Dwayne. "You want something to eat?"

"What do you got?"

"Ham and cheese, and turkey. And some Hershey bars. There's water, also."

"Which one doesn't have mayo? I don't feature mayo."

The one who wasn't driving pulled a couple of sandwiches out of the hamper and unwrapped them. "They both do. Mustard and mayo both."

"Well, shit. All right, fuck it, give me a turkey. And some water. And one of the Hershey's. With nuts if you got it."

The marshal passed the sandwich back through the narrow slot in the bulletproof divider that separated the front seat from the rear. Then he handed back a small dental-office-sized paper cup of water, spilling some on the floor at Dwayne's feet.

"Sorry 'bout that."

"Can I have the Hershey bar too?"

"Not unless you eat up all your dinner first." Both marshals laughed. Then the one who wasn't driving passed back a candy bar.

"Gracias," Dwayne said.

"You're welcome," the marshal replied. He unwrapped a sandwich for himself, and another for the driver. "Let me know if you want me to drive at some point," he told his partner.

"I'm fine."

The tape finished playing. They ate in silence. The road passed under their wheels.

"Are you sure you still want to go out?" Wyatt asked, rubbing his hair vigorously after his shower. They were upstairs, in their bedroom.

"Well . . ." Moira held two different earrings up to her face, trying to decide which one went better with her dress.

"What about Michaela? Maybe we shouldn't leave her here alone tonight."

Michaela was their daughter. An only child, she was a junior in prep school. Like many only children, she was the sun and the stars to her parents.

"No burglar's going to come within a million miles of here tonight—isn't that what the policeman promised us?" she said with a mocking edge to her voice, a tone he wasn't used to hearing from her. "Anyway, in case you didn't notice, Michaela isn't here. She's over at Nancy Goodwin's working on a science project. We'd be home long before her. In fact, we could swing by and pick her up on our way back."

She settled on a pair of earrings. Then she sat on the edge

of the bed and pulled on her panty hose, revealing a flash of dark pubic hair under sheer underpants.

Wyatt watched her as she dressed. She looked good tonight; she always looked good, she was a great-looking woman, but when she got all dressed she could really get heads turning.

Moira was tall, almost five-ten, with long, long legs. In heels, standing next to him, they were of identical height. She had a prototypical Audrey Hepburn kind of model's figure of the sixties that clothes hung perfectly on—slim boyish hips, small breasts. Gamine-cut jet-black hair, large hazel eyes. Her face didn't show much age—someone looking at her would never figure her for forty-six.

"Okay," he agreed readily. "Getting out for a couple hours will help get rid of the bad taste."

She started applying mascara. "We need better security, Wyatt."

"We have a good system already. If that had happened here the police would've been here in five minutes. Less." He began dressing—sports coat and slacks would be formal enough—he wore a suit and tie all day long at the office.

"So how come they weren't at the Spragues?"

"Maybe their system doesn't work as well." He paused. "Or maybe it was an inside job," he reluctantly ventured—he had been thinking about that since the Spragues had told them what had happened.

"That's comforting. Anyway, five minutes could be forever. You could be dead in a lot less than five minutes."

"So what do you want to do? Build a moat? Put up electric fencing? The yard would be littered with dead birds."

She applied lipstick, blotted with a tissue. "We could get a dog. A big one. Or better yet, a gun."

He froze in place. "You're kidding."

She turned to him. "No, Wyatt. I am not kidding."

"So an intruder could take it and use it on you? Like what happened to Enid?"

"That wouldn't happen to me."

He finished getting dressed. "Forget it," he told her. "We are not going to have a gun in this house. That's how people get killed."

"Maybe some people deserve it," she answered back.

He thought before speaking. "Maybe some people do," he agreed. "But that's not for us to decide. Not like that."

She came close to him. "If someone was threatening your life . . . or mine, or Michaela's, you couldn't kill them? If it was us or them?"

"I'm sure I could. I hope I never have to make that choice." He took her hand. "Come on—this is getting too grim. Let's have some fun."

As they were leaving the house—Wyatt double-checked the door to make sure it was locked, and that the alarm system was on—Moira turned to him. "Enid should've pulled the trigger," she said.

Was she serious? "Would you have?" he asked, trying to keep the alarm out of his voice. More than alarm: fear.

"If I owned a gun, and it was me standing there, and some intruder was coming at me? Who might rape or kill me? Yes—I would have pulled the trigger."

"**T**his band is *hot*."

"They are *great*. Didn't I tell you?"

They were at *Teddy's,* one of the city's primo dance bars—three women dancing with each other, bodies pressed against them from all sides. Hot, sweaty, loud.

The band was fronted by a woman singer, a local favorite. They were playing classic bluesy rock 'n' roll: Van Morrison, Otis Redding, Janis Joplin.

"We're going to close this place down tonight!" one of them shouted. The dance bar was basically a big old barn, you had to yell pretty loud to be heard over the din.

"Unless we get lucky." One of the women laughed, a deep alto vibrato. She was black, the other two were white. She was the youngest, the prettiest, the sexiest.

"You let a man from here pick you up and take you home, you've got to be crazy."

"Beggars can't be choosers," the laughing woman shot back over the music.

"Who you calling a beggar?"

"Three ladies in their prime, without a man between them, out dancing with each other, what would you call us?"

"We're choosy."

All three of them laughed. Violet and her two best friends, Peggy and Paula. Peggy was a nurse, a friend from the old days at the hospital. Paula was a coworker on the slaughterhouse floor.

Both of the other women were divorced. Peggy for a long time, Paula recently, less than a year. Paula still wasn't comfortable—or at least accepting—of her status as a single woman. All the stuff that goes with being with a man—feeling his bulk up against yours when you're sleeping, his sweat from the heat, lovemaking on a regular and frequent basis, cooking him up a good meal, a shared bottle of wine, laughing, fighting, the whole nine yards—all those things were essential to her, almost as basic as eating and sleeping.

Paula dated more than the other two did, more being a relative term. She was less discriminating about whom she went out with than they were, and she was more openly accessible, easier. Her vibe said, "Yes." Violet's and Peggy's said, "Let's check this out first."

They all were looking for the one right man. None of them were finding him. They talked about it. Sometimes talking about it helped. Sometimes it didn't.

The band finished an up-tempo rendition of "Dock of the Bay." "Here's one for all you lovers out there!" the singer, a heavyset, exuberant woman, yelled out over the microphone. "Two, three, four!"

They segued into a mournful version of "Unchain My Heart."

Violet and her friends drifted off the dance floor and flopped into their chairs at their table, over near the wall, at the edge of the action. They watched as couples paired off and started slow-dancing, bodies melting into each other.

Paula fanned herself with a menu. "Damn, it is hot in here." She was provocatively dressed; her skirt was a mini; she had the legs for it, and the ass, too. Paula knew that she had the prototypical black woman's butt. You could balance a dinner plate on it and still have room for rolls and dessert, as her mother would say.

"You look like one of those hookers out there on Farraguet Avenue," Peggy had joked to Paula when they'd met up earlier for dinner. "You'd better be careful some guy cruising by in his Mercedes doesn't hit on you for a quickie."

"What model Mercedes?" Paula had answered, deadpan.

Paula was proud of her flowering tush; men followed behinds like hers. Right into her bed, she hoped—but only if he was the right man.

The trouble was, as they all knew from experience, you couldn't know if he was the right man or not until long after that, and by then, when you found out he wasn't, it was too late.

Just then a man approached their table. He looked them over, then leaned down to Violet, whose dress, moist with sweat, was clinging to her voluptuous figure. "Can I have this dance?" he asked politely.

Startled, she looked up at him. He was rail thin, looking like someone whose forever-heroes were James Dean and Jerry Lee Lewis: hair greased in a fifties-style pompadour, sideburns halfway down his cheeks, short-sleeved western shirt, jeans, cowboy boots. Interesting-looking in a way, like a scorpion is interesting: deadly—you don't get near someone like this.

"Thanks, but I'm taking a break," she told him, politely but distantly.

"You sure?" There was a cockiness in his voice. He was devouring her body with his eyes. She was used to that.

Firmly: "Yes, I'm sure."

He took a step back, as if the rebuff had been unexpected. Then he smiled at her. His teeth were long and canine, like a wild dog's.

"Maybe later," he said, his voice holding out hope, while at the same time mocking her.

She looked away. This man had no attraction for her.

His smile faded. He stood there, hovering over her one more moment to be sure, then walked away and was swallowed up in the crowd.

"You blew it, girl," Paula teased her.

"Yeah, my dumb luck," Violet answered.

"That guy was creepy," Peggy said.

Violet nodded her agreement. Being held by a man like that, even for three minutes out on a dance floor, was not in her plans.

The song ended with a crescendo of drum brush. "We're

gonna take a break!" the singer announced over the cacophony of voices. "Won't be long, so don't y'all be leaving, hear?" A flourish of drumroll. "We *shall* return!"

Violet felt a sudden moistness between her legs. "Damn!"

"What is it?" Peggy asked.

"I'm getting my period. Son of a gun!"

Peggy and Paula moaned in sympathetic unison.

"I don't have anything on me," Peggy said, rummaging in her purse.

"Me, neither," Paula echoed. "They've got a dispenser in the ladies' room."

"I've got my own tampons in the trunk of my car," Violet said. "I'll be right back."

She checked her dress as she walked toward the exit. The flow had just started—the dancing had brought it on prematurely. She could feel that her underpants were wet, but it hadn't soaked through to the dress, thank God. She could put in a tampon in the ladies' room, discard her panties, and everything would be fine. The heaviness of her flow wouldn't start until tomorrow.

As she approached her car, which was parked at the far edge of the lot, she saw a man standing near it, looking in the side window as if he was checking to see whether or not it was locked. A young man, tall. Black. He had a strong, athletic, sexy body, and he was handsome, almost beautiful. He looked to be a teenager, she could tell that from a distance, but definitely a man—the kind of young inner-city man, particularly minority men, who are men by the time they're twelve.

He wasn't aware that she was approaching. He took a step toward her car.

"Hey!" she called out. "That's my car. What are you doing?"

He turned and looked at her, his face devoid of intention.

She ran toward the car. Be careful, she thought, he could be dangerous—but she wasn't about to watch some street punk break into her car.

"Get away from there!" she yelled at him.

He stepped back.

Eyes stared into eyes. His were dead eyes, eyes that masked feeling. She felt a shiver as he looked at her.

Time was suspended for a moment. Then he turned his

back on her and strolled away, turning the corner and disappearing in the shadows.

She unlocked the trunk of her car and took out a couple of tampons from the box she kept there for such emergencies as this. Locking the trunk up again, she took a last cautionary look over her shoulder and walked back inside.

As Violet sat down at the table (detouring first to the ladies' room), Paula stood up. "It's stuffy. I'm going to get some air." She grabbed her purse.

"I'll watch your purse for you," Violet volunteered.

"I'll take it, just in case I get lucky." She laughed, the low alto voice humming up from her throat.

"Don't even think about it," Violet cautioned her.

"Don't worry, girl, that was a joke. I might be foolish, but I ain't stupid."

Paula slung her beaded purse over her shoulder and walked across the floor toward the back entrance. "Order me another vodka tonic," she called back over her shoulder. "Extra slice of lime."

As she saw her friend leave it flashed on Violet that she should have said something about that kid she'd encountered, just to let Paula know. She should get up and follow Paula out, she thought—but immediately she decided not to. The parking lot was well lit, there were people coming in and out, and Paula could handle herself.

It was hot outside, too, but not as hot as it was in the bar. Paula had been afraid that one of her friends would come out with her. She wanted to cool off from the heat, that was true, but more than that, she wanted a cigarette. She was supposed to have quit three months ago; and she had. For two weeks. Then the temptation had been too strong, and she'd started up again. But she kept it a secret, she snuck them on breaks at work and when she was alone at home. It wasn't that she felt that she had to apologize—she was a grown woman, she could do as she damn well pleased—but she knew her friends would get on her case something awful, and she didn't need any more disapproval or moralizing.

Anyway, she was going to quit again, this time for good. A week; two, tops. She just needed a little more time to work up to it.

In the parking lot out back, among the cars, she snapped

open her purse and rummaged around the contents for her Virginia Slims. The crumpled pack was at the bottom, crushed under her wallet, compact, lipstick, other necessities. Binaca to cover the smoke-breath. She really ought to give this purse a spring-cleaning, she thought; there could be God knows what festering in it. Almost as bad as her car, which was overdue for a cleaning out, too.

The pack was empty. Damn! She was sure there had been one or two left from lunch. Or had she smoked the last one while she was getting dressed for tonight?

She really wanted a smoke. Being in a bar, having a drink, dancing, you needed a cigarette to complement all that.

At the edge of the parking lot, where it ended in an access alley that ran between rows of buildings on either side, a man was standing alone, leaning against one of the old brick structures. Standing there, casually leaning, the position of his body that of someone with no agenda, no time frame. Paula couldn't see his face; it was dark outside except for where the lights lit up the parking lot, and he was past that area. She couldn't tell if he was old or young, rich or poor, handsome or ugly, nice or cruel. She could only tell one thing—he was smoking. A thin plume of smoke drifted up out of the shadows above his head, forming a shimmery nimbus in the light from the parking lot that was bouncing off the wall behind him.

She could cadge a cigarette off him. One smoke and a light, that's all. The thought relieved her smoker's anxiety. She walked across the lot, her high heels clicking off a staccato drum-shot as they struck the asphalt. Crossing the space, she realized there was no one else out here. Just her and the man leaning against the wall, whose face she still couldn't see.

The light on the overhead pole caught her as she walked and cast her shadow into the alley, a long sinuous projection. It was an attractive shadow, like from an old black-and-white cartoon, long legs, an elongated, willowy figure (the kind she'd always secretly wanted), the miniskirt ridiculously, almost obscenely short in this greatly exaggerated layout.

"Excuse me," she called out when she was about a dozen paces from him. "Can I bum one of your cigarettes?"

She felt he was looking at her. To see who was suddenly intruding on his space.

She smiled to try to put him at ease, and moved closer.

Wyatt and Moira's dinner companions were the Fairchilds and the Dugans. They went to L'Angleterre. It was Gault-Milleu rated the best restaurant (and the most expensive) in the region ten years running, but if you could afford it, it was worth it for the wine list alone.

Dennis and Marybeth Fairchild and Rod and Cissy Dugan were among their closest friends, going on two decades. Like Wyatt, Dennis and Marybeth were both high-powered attorneys, partners in different firms, and Rod was executive vice president and treasurer for Baldwin Aircraft. The net worth of the six people sitting at the table tonight, who had called ahead to have two bottles of '85 Chateau Leoville Las Cases opened to have with their dinner, was deep into eight figures.

"I want to propose a toast." Marybeth raised her glass.

"Hear, hear!" All glasses were raised. "To Wyatt Matthews, the man who brought Uncle Sam to his knees. To his *knees!*" Marybeth crowed. "Who got his own profile in *Time.*"

"Not to mention *Forbes* and *Business Week,*" Rod added. They clicked glasses and drank.

"Thank you," Wyatt smiled, "and shut up."

"Shut up baloney," Dennis said. "You the man, Wyatt. You kicked the government's ass in one of the biggest cases of this decade, man. That is no small thing. Anyone who can take on the SEC, the Justice Department, and Common Cause at the same time and bring them to their knees is a player, palsie."

"Thanks," Wyatt said, feeling uncomfortable. "Now let's drop it, okay?"

As they looked over their menus Cissy turned to Moira. "I think I found a location for our store that would be perfect," she said, excited. "I'm meeting the Prudential agent tomorrow at ten. Can you come? You need to see it; you'll fall in love with it."

Moira glanced at Wyatt. "I think I can."

Under the table, he put his hand on her knee and squeezed gently. "Go for it," he encouraged her.

She put her hand on his and squeezed back.

Moira and Cissy had never worked. College educated, both women had married early, but instead of going into the workforce, they had stayed at home in the role of mothers and homemakers and supporters of their men and kids. Old-fashioned women, in today's terms.

But now their kids were suddenly older, leaving the nest; they'd gone from toddlers to teenagers with frightening speed. Moira didn't want to be one of those women who grow old on the golf course, eating three-hour lunches and sitting around gossiping and getting drunk. Cissy didn't, either; so a few months ago they'd decided to go into business together. Something small and manageable, and, if possible, with an artistic touch. Making money wasn't the issue; they had money. They wanted to have fun and be their own persons, even if the scale was small and local.

They envisioned a bookstore. Or a music store. Or a combination; sort of a vest-pocket Borders. With a cappuccino bar, of course. Maybe a fireplace, a focal area for readings and music.

They even had a name picked out: Lucy & Ethel's.

"So what's happening in everyone's world?" Marybeth adroitly changed the subject. "Anything new and exciting?"

"Our next-door neighbors were robbed," Moira told her.

"When?" Cissy asked.

"About two hours ago."

Dennis said, "You're kidding."

"I wish I was."

Dennis turned to Wyatt. "Were you there? Did you see anything?" he asked.

"I saw the aftermath."

"The woman was shot," Moira continued, unable to contain herself. "A sixty-six-year-old woman. Shot in her own house by robbers."

"Did the police catch them?"

"No. Not yet, anyway."

"Did they get a description?"

"Two black men. Gang members, according to the man."

"Who knows nothing at all about gangs," Wyatt said

dismissively. "They don't know what they saw, there weren't any lights on."

"They were young and black," Moira insisted. "The Spragues were sure of that."

Cissy turned to Moira. "How badly was the woman shot?"

"She got hit in her side. She should be all right."

"Thank God for that." The women nodded in supportive female agreement.

"She should have had her own gun," Rod declared.

"She did," Wyatt told him.

"She should have used it, then," Rod said. "That's why you have a gun."

"Well, since they took it away from her," Wyatt answered with anger, "she wasn't able to. They were pros and she wasn't, so the inevitable happened."

"You don't have to be a professional to shoot someone in your own home. You're crazy if you don't," Rod said.

Wyatt was taken aback. "Do you have a gun?" he asked, surprised. "A pistol?"

"Two. Mine and hers." He looked at Cissy.

"You have to be able to defend yourself," Cissy said unapologetically.

Wyatt looked at them. "I wouldn't think of you two as having guns around the house. Doesn't the idea of an accident scare you?"

"The alternative scares me more," Cissy answered.

From across the table: "I've had a gun for five years," Marybeth threw in.

"Five years?" Wyatt was incredulous.

"And a concealed permit for three," she added. As he looked at her in disbelief: "I'm alone on the street at night, after a dinner meeting or whatever, I have to have protection, Wyatt." She turned to Moira. "You've never felt you had to be armed? At least in your house?"

"I thought about it tonight," Moira added, looking at Wyatt.

He shook his head forcefully. "We are not having guns in our house. That's how people get killed. Especially with kids around."

"Well, to each his own," Cissy said. "I can see your point—it took me a long time to get okay with the idea, and

I still don't like it, but I want to feel secure." She turned to Moira. "I take lessons at the range once a month. You could come with me next week if you want to."

Moira looked at her husband—she knew how strongly he felt about this subject. Then she turned to Cissy. "Maybe I will," she said. "Call me when you're going."

Marvin stood across the street, in shadow. Looking into the front window, he could see the owner posted stoically behind the counter, making change for the lone customer. An old white lady, even from this distance Marvin could see how her veins were broken in her face, especially her nose, and on her legs, her old legs were black and blue from bad circulation.

The old lady left the store, holding the plastic bag pressed up tight against her bony, sagging chest, scurrying along the sidewalk, head down for fear of looking somebody in the eye. He knew that feeling, how if you felt bad about yourself you thought people could see it in your eyes, so you didn't let them look. You looked away, you didn't ever let them look you right in the eye.

He glanced up and down the block. No one was coming. One last look, to make certain. Then he was out of the shadows and walking across the street.

The store was a little gold mine, but not because of the eighteen-hour days the owner put in behind the counter, occasionally assisted by his wife, who would come down from their apartment on the floor above. This store was a numbers drop run by the main Thai gang, one of the biggest and toughest gangs in the city, as big as any of the black or Latino gangs. Marvin had seen the action with his own eyes. All day long, around the clock practically, Asians of all nationalities came in with little slips of paper and handed their selections and dollar bills—or fives or tens or twenties—across the counter to the owner, who would write their code numbers and amounts in a little black ledger he kept under the register. The money wouldn't go into the register—the Korean stashed it in a canvas bank bag that he kept locked up in a cabinet. Housewives, businessmen, kids, even cops—he'd seen two beat cops, white dudes, slip the owner some bills after taking a couple of sodas and a package of beef jerky, which Marvin knew they didn't pay for (compliments of the house, so the cops would leave the owner alone). Of course, the Thai gang was paying the police off, that was a given, but at a higher level, lieutenants and captains.

Mondays and Fridays were the payoff days. The numbers would come out, a combination in the newspaper, and if you had the right three numbers, you were rich. Problem was, the odds were thousands to one.

His own mother played. A dollar a week, the same three numbers for years. She'd never hit, not once, and she never would. Fifty-two dollars a year down the toilet—by the time she was dead she'd have lost hundreds to it, thousands.

It was a racket, like everything else. But it meant that the people who were running them, the big-timers and the local store-owner drop shops, like this Korean, were sitting on a mountain of cash money most of the time, because the pick-ups were twice a week. Five thousand dollars, at least, sitting in the cabinet right behind the owner's back. Every Sunday and Thursday night.

Tonight was Thursday.

For months Marvin had been thinking about doing this store. It would be so easy, as close to a sure thing as he would ever come across. The money was right there, just sitting in that cabinet. And the owner couldn't go to the cops because the money was illegal and the police were on the take.

No one from around here knew him. This was an Asian neighborhood, not a black one. Where he lived was more than five miles away; another country. To these slant-eyed bastards he was one more dumb nigger, a race of people who all looked alike. He'd actually heard that once, this store owner talking to one of his customers, a Korean like himself. "They all look alike to me," the owner had said. "And smell alike," the customer had said back.

They had both laughed.

He'd been standing right next to them. But since he was black he was invisible.

The only reason he came on this street at all was because it was on his delivery route. Had been. He didn't have that job anymore. He'd been fired three weeks ago. It wasn't his fault he couldn't always get there on time, he had to take two buses to get to work, and the first bus was always running behind schedule, and then he'd miss the transfer to the second bus and that would make him late.

His boss had forearms on him like Popeye, that guy in the Saturday morning cartoons. A giant Lithuanian who stank from the garlicky herring he was always eating, he would put a fatherly arm around Marvin's shoulders and tell him to catch an earlier bus, then he wouldn't be late so much of the time. The boss's breath would knock him over.

To be honest, his boss wasn't so bad. Sometimes there would be an extra five- or ten-dollar bill in Marvin's pay envelope. And he would joke with Marvin, asking about his girlfriends, telling him a big handsome kid like you must be beating the girls off with a stick.

Truth be told, girls did like him; he was big and good-looking, he knew that. Kind of like that Denzel Washington dude from the movies. But that didn't mean jack shit, because what girls really liked was money—they wanted to be with a man who could buy them whatever shit they wanted. Being a delivery boy for minimum wage didn't cut it.

On the other hand, there were older ladies on his delivery route who didn't care how much money he made. Middle-aged horny white ladies. Fucking him in the middle of the day, like they'd never had it so good before. Which was probably the truth. Sometimes they'd give him money. Other times they wouldn't, as if fucking a flabby middle-aged white lady was part of the job, as long as she was a customer of his boss.

He never said no to any of them, but there were times when he would leave their places and feel like a piece of meat. There were times when he felt like punching one of the bitches out, break half the bones in her goddamn face, teach her a lesson.

Stealing from his boss had been wrong, he knew that. He just couldn't help it, skimming a little here and there from his delivery receipts. It wasn't that much. Except that his boss caught him stealing, red-handed—he had called a long-time customer and had cursed the man out for not paying his bill in total, and the customer had cursed him back and sworn that he had, and so the boss had been forced to set a trap for Marvin, and Marvin had walked right into it, and the boss had made him empty his pockets right there on the spot. Marvin was big and strong but his boss had lifted him up clear off his feet like he was a ten-pound sack of potatoes and jammed his back up against the wall, practically breaking Marvin's bones, he'd slammed him into the wall so hard.

"I treated you good, didn't I, *schvartzer*?" the boss had yelled into his face, holding him up against the wall like a rag doll. "And this is how you repay me!"

He was fired on the spot. Not even bus fare home—he had to walk the whole seven miles.

His mother had gone through the roof. "After all what people have done for you!" she'd screamed. Screaming and crying at the same time. "You think I work my ass to the bone so you can pull that kind of shit? Mr. Livonius was good to you, he gave you a good job even though you ain't got no high school diploma or nothin', and this is how you repay him!"

"It wasn't no big deal," he had argued back, trying to blunt her rage. "He can afford it."

"That's not the point!" she'd raved. "You stole from the man. That makes you a thief. Ain't no thief living under my roof, not one who ain't got no job, you are eighteen years old now and you are on your own, Marvin. As of this very minute."

She kicked him out, right out into the street. Hardly gave him time to pack a bag. "When you get yourself another job you can move back in. And not one minute before."

He'd slept on the street that night. It was warm out, he was in shock from what his mother had done to him. She had always treated him like a little king, always coddled him.

That was three weeks ago. After that first night he slept with friends, a night here, a couple nights there.

He was about out of friends to spend the night with.

But in less than an hour he'd be checking into a nice hotel with clean sheets and hot water in the shower, scalding water, for as long as he wanted. And soft, fluffy towels. Then tomorrow, first thing, he'd buy some new clothes, quality merchandise. And after a short time, when he was set up in business, making it like Dexter, he'd come back and throw a bunch of money in his mother's lap and watch her eyes get all wide. She would cry in his arms and forgive him. Then they would move out into a nice apartment in a decent neighborhood, where you aren't so scared that you hit the floor every time there's a sudden loud noise outside on the street.

He caressed the pistol through the material of his jacket. It felt alive, like a grenade ready to explode. A nice little piece, a .32 Berreta, small enough to handle easy but plenty big enough to blow somebody's brains out, if it had to come to that. Not one of them crappy Saturday night specials that could as easily blow up in your hand as in some chump's face. This was the real article—his buddy Raymond, a professional thief, had scored it during a burglary in the north side of town, took it out of some rich woman's nightstand.

You had to have a burglar's guts to walk into someone's house, right into their bedroom where they were sleeping. Marvin didn't feature that kind of dumb bravado. You don't put your life on the line so you can boast about being cool to the men in the 'hood.

But that didn't mean he couldn't take care of business. Like robbing this store.

The ice was melting in Paula's drink.

Violet and Peggy came off the dance floor. They'd been dancing steadily without taking a break, one fast song after another, and hadn't been paying attention to whether Paula was sitting at the table or not. The floor was crowded with bodies, everybody pressed up against each other, and the lights were dim, to promote that down-and-dirty sexy feeling, and everyone, with or without a partner of the opposite sex, was in their own space, their own thoughts.

Peggy dropped into her chair. "I'd say I was sweating like a pig, but I wouldn't want to offend anyone you know." She waved her hand to get the waitress's attention. "I've got to get some fluids into my body pronto or I am going to pass out from dehydration, and passing out in a bar of this caliber would be too mortifying for words." She looked around. "Where's Paula?"

Paula's drink hadn't been touched. The ice had melted; the slice of lime was floating on the top of the glass like a dead goldfish.

"I haven't seen her," Violet said. How long had it been since Paula had gone outside? She had lost track of the time.

"She hasn't come back inside?"

Violet shrugged. "I don't know if she's come back or not. I haven't seen her, that's all I know."

"Maybe she came back in and went out again. It really is hot as blazes in here tonight."

Violet pointed to the limp drink. "I don't think so."

Peggy nodded in agreement. "She wouldn't let a drink go flat. Not our Paula. Not when it's on her tab."

Violet pushed herself to her feet. "I'm going to go out and look for her. Maybe she got sick. She had at least three vodka tonics by my count, and I don't think she'd had anything to eat before we came."

"Leave it to that girl. Nothing in moderation, that's her motto." Peggy stood also. "I'll come with you." She shook her head, half in exasperation, half with envy. "You don't think . . ."

"She found someone? She's impulsive, but she isn't dumb."

Grabbing their purses, they pushed their way through the crowd, which was pressing in on all sides, from the edges of the dance floor to the long bars against the walls, and went out the same door Paula had earlier used. After the heat and body humidity inside, the relative coolness of the nighttime breeze momentarily took their breath away.

Peggy sucked in a lungful of moist air. "What a relief."

"Do you see her?" Violet asked, craning her neck to try to peer over the roofs of the parked cars.

"No, not yet."

Violet looked around. Here and there she could see couples making out in the shadows. None of the women was Paula, she could tell that from a glance. "She wouldn't have left without telling us," she ventured.

"No, of course not."

They both laughed: nervous relief.

"The hell she wouldn't. You or me, but not Paula."

Violet thought about it. "You know, she was casing the place out the whole time we were inside. If she'd seen someone that attracted her, even a little bit, she would have broadcast the news."

"This is true." Peggy hesitated. "Unless there was somebody out here she hadn't seen, and she got carried away in the moment."

Violet frowned. "She's done it before."

"And been sorry the next morning. She carries protection, doesn't she?"

"That woman carries protection when she's taking out the garbage."

They had been wandering through the lot as they talked, looking up and down and around the spaces between the cars. They reached the area where Paula had earlier seen the man in the shadows smoking his cigarette.

Paula was nowhere to be seen.

"I don't feel like hanging around out here," Violet said, turning away as she caught a glimpse of yet another man and woman making out like bandits in the backseat of a nearby parked car.

"Me, neither."

They started walking back across the lot, toward the bar.

"She'd better be inside," Violet stated, feeling more anger than she realized she had.

"Hey, you're not her mother. Lighten up."

"I'm talking about courtesy, not responsibility."

"I hear you there."

Paula's chair was empty.

"Well," Violet said, "I guess she got lucky after all."

"Let's hope that's what she got," Peggy replied. "Or she is going to be pissed at herself in the morning. Royally."

"No more than I'm pissed at her right now. You don't walk out on your friends without at least saying good-bye."

"Maybe things happened too fast, and she didn't have the time."

Marvin stood outside the entrance to the store, angled away from the door so the owner couldn't see him if he happened to look that way. His fingers were all tingling, like how it is when your legs go to sleep and then you stand up suddenly. And he had major cotton-mouth, dry as a bone, he should've had something to drink, get the bad taste out.

He had the jitters, but that was to be expected. Earlier, when he'd gone away from the store, killing time while waiting for any last-minute shoppers to clear out, he'd opened the pack of cigarettes he'd bought earlier and lit one up to have something to do with his hands, which had developed a life of their own. One inhale and he almost coughed his lungs out, so he'd just stood there where he'd wound up, a couple of blocks away, the cigarette burning down in his fingers. Made his hands and breath smell bad.

He wished he had something to drink. Something sweet, like a Pepsi.

In a little while he'd have so much money on him he could buy a case of Pepsis. A pallet-load, if that's what he felt like.

His fingers curled around the butt of the gun in his pocket. Now was the time. He took one last, deep breath.

The Korean's back was to him. He was writing something down on a notepad. Korean-looking writing, Marvin could see over the short man's shoulder as he leaned in toward the counter. The owner had heard Marvin come in—there was a bell above the door that tinkled whenever a customer went in or out—but he wasn't going to turn around until he was ready, Marvin realized.

Fuck this, he'd been planning on this stickup for months, he wasn't about to wait on this asshole one minute longer.

"Turn around." His voice was low, calm.

The storekeeper glanced at Marvin over his shoulder, started to turn back to his writing, then froze as he saw the gun in Marvin's hand.

"And hold your hands out in front of you, where I can see them. Both of them."

His gun hand was pretty steady. A little bit of a shake, but hell, whose wouldn't be? He was doing good, he was handling this like a pro.

The Korean pivoted on his heels so that he was facing Marvin across the counter, standing in the middle of the small aisle between the counter and the cabinets in back of him.

"What you want?" the Korean asked in that singsong voice of his. Flat, no feeling to it. Marvin hated that voice, it sounded like it was coming out of a robot instead of a human being.

"Your money, man. What the fuck do you think I want?"

Just stay calm, man, this chump is pigeon bait. "You speak English plenty good, don't be pulling no dumb show on me."

The storekeeper stared at him impassively.

"Hey, man, come on, I ain't got all night. Open up the damn register!"

The man stood rooted to the floor. Silent.

Marvin raised the gun up and pointed it right in the owner's face, two inches away from the absurdly small mushroom-shaped nose. The man's whole damn nose was the size of one of his own nostrils. "Open up the register right fucking now or I will bust a cap right into the middle of your face. Ain't no difference to me, one way or the other."

He was sweating. Under his arms, down his chest, his crotch. He took a quick look behind to make sure nobody was coming in.

The coast was still clear.

The Korean stared at him a moment longer. Then he reached over and punched open the cash register.

Marvin felt the muscles surrounding his ass relax. "Now you're acting smart." With his free hand he pulled a small plastic trash bag out of his pocket, held it up to the store-keeper. "Just the bills," he commanded, "no coins."

Slowly, methodically, the owner started emptying out his register, drawer by drawer—twenties, tens, fives, ones. Marvin watched him like a hawk. There looked to be about three, four hundred dollars in bills.

"Don't forget what's underneath," he said, indicating for the owner to lift the drawer, to get to the larger bills that were stashed underneath.

The owner glared at him, but did as he was told.

There was a small stack of fifties and a couple of hundreds hidden underneath, held together by a paper clip. The owner picked them up and stuck them into the plastic bag with the rest of the evening's take. He held the bag up to Marvin.

Marvin indicated with his head. "The rest."

The Korean stared blankly at him. "No more. You see yourself." He pointed to the empty register.

"The money you keep in the cabinet," Marvin told him. "Behind your back. In the bank bag."

The storekeeper's eyes narrowed.

So he's human after all, Marvin thought. Finally. He fought back a smile.

"The bank bag in the cabinet," Marvin repeated. "You know what I'm talking about."

The man was staring at him, as if trying to see through his eyes into his brain. Then he took a step back. "No."

Marvin twitched visibly. "What the fuck did you say? Did I hear you correct?"

"No." The man spoke the word again, this time with more force.

Marvin could feel his heart pounding in his chest like a jet airplane taking off. " 'No' ain't an option," he said back to the man.

"No." A third time.

He was sweating like a bandit. "Don't you get it, man? If you don't give me that money *I will shoot you!*"

The storekeeper didn't move. Not a muscle. He stood there, staring into Marvin's eyes with his own black marble eyes.

He was going to have to shoot this fucker for the money. "Give me the goddamn money, it ain't no sweat off your ass. Come on, man! Don't make me kill you, you dumb Jap!"

Yet again; flat, emotionless: "No."

He lunged forward to snatch the bag out of the man's hand but the storekeeper, surprisingly nimble, hopped a quick step back and he caught nothing but air. His hip bounced hard against the counter—he ricocheted off and then he had his pistol in the fucker's face. Right against the Korean's forehead.

He'd crossed the line. The future was now—no turning back.

He pulled the trigger, flinching from the expected explosion of sound, of blood and cartilage and hair spraying across the walls.

The gun clicked.

What the fuck!

He pulled the trigger again. This time there wasn't even a click. The mechanism was frozen right in his hand. It was useless.

That motherfucker Raymond, with his "professional" gun.

He'd paid Raymond good money for this worthless piece of shit.

The store owner was bending down behind the counter. Marvin knew what that meant—he was going to die.

Pure animal survival instinct got him running to the door. This was a nightmare—if he could have willed himself to vanish into thin air he would have. It felt like he was running in slow motion, the entrance receding from him, farther and farther.

Then he was finally jerking the door open and catching a mouthful of moist night air, and as he took the first step outside to the safety of darkness there was this incredibly loud roar, like a cannon going off underneath him.

His ass and legs were on fire. It felt like a bucket of nails that had been heated to white-hot intensity in burning oil had been blasted onto him. All the air was instantaneously sucked out of his lungs, the force of the blow was so strong and unexpected.

His mind went black and he pitched face forward, slamming in a heap onto the sidewalk.

The marshals and their prisoner were on schedule. They had called ahead every half hour, giving a progress report. Everything had gone smoothly, no screwups.

They flashed their IDs at the gate. The guard in charge, a sergeant who had been sent down for the express purpose of helping facilitate this transfer, radioed upstairs to the main check-in floor.

"I got the two marshals and their charge from Durban State here."

"Copy that. Send them in."

The sergeant pressed the button that swung the gate open and they drove down into the basement underneath the jail, passing through two more locked gates. The second gate didn't start to open until the first gate had slammed shut, the echo reverberating loudly in the hot stillness.

Dwayne looked out the windows. He had been here before, he knew the drill. Same way it had been every other time he'd been taken into a lockup, jail, or prison.

The jail was huge, and it was old. A WPA project, built in

1935 at the height of the depression, it had been obsolete for decades. It felt more like a prison than a jail. The form was essentially that of a wheel; a center core extended from the basement to the roof, divided into floors two stories high. Each level was its own command center, where deputies' lockers, information counters, and administrative were contained. Radiating out like spokes were the two-tiered cellblocks that housed the inmates. In the center of each cellblock was a corridor onto which all the cells opened.

The marshals parked the car by the reinforced metal entrance door and unlocked the back door and helped their prisoner out. They showed their badges once again through the small barred window that was next to the entrance door. Then they unbuckled their automatics and took them out of the holsters that rode low on their hips and passed them through to the officer, who put them in a small secure locker and locked it. The jail deputy swung the door open so they could enter.

The door clanged shut behind them with solid authoritative finality. Dwayne raised his shackled hands in the lead marshal's face.

"Soon," he was told.

They rode up on the elevator to the third floor. The elevator creaked slowly in fits and jerks. The doors wheezed open and the marshals led their prisoner into the two-story rotunda that was the central booking area.

The place was busy with activity. Over two dozen men and a few women were seated on the benches, waiting to go through the procession and enter the system. They had all gotten to this sorry place for the same old reasons—get fucked up on drugs and liquor, act out festering grudges that have been building up. Or they committed straightforward serious crimes, nighttime is the right time. Domestic violence. Gang shit. Drug deals—more drug stuff than everything else put together. Most of the women, like those slouching on the scarred wooden benches, bored, numbed-out expressions on their overly made-up faces, were in for prostitution. Blow jobs in cars, not two-thousand-dollar nights in high-priced hotel rooms. A smattering of the male arrestees, openly gay, lounged together on their own bench, away from the others.

The half dozen deputies on duty stopped what they were doing and turned to look as Dwayne, wearing his penitentiary-issued clothes and metal chain on his person, walked out of the elevator and was escorted by his marshal transporters to the booking desk.

The lead marshal pulled a folder out of a manila envelope. "We are hereby officially transferring custody to you of Dwayne Thompson, inmate #3694, Durban State Penitentiary," he told the sergeant in charge. "Sign here."

The sergeant signed the documents and handed them back. "He's all yours," the marshal said.

Dwayne was patiently waiting with his hands outstretched. The other marshal unlocked the shackles from Dwayne's waist, then the handcuffs. Dwayne stepped out of the pile of metal at his feet, rubbed his wrists to start the circulation going again.

The marshal slipped the cuffs onto his belt loop and scooped the shackles off the floor, cradling them in his arms. "See you in a couple weeks, old son," he told Dwayne. "Don't fuck up too bad."

Dwayne looked at him sideways. The marshals got back on the elevator, and the doors closed behind them.

"You've been here before," the sergeant said to Dwayne as he led him where he would begin to be processed in. It was a statement, not a question.

"Couple times."

"How long since it's been?"

"Four years." And four months, twenty-three days. He knew how much time he had done—to the day, and in which prisons and jails—and how much he had left to do. There was more left to do than had been done already. Not counting the other stretches he'd done over the years.

"Nothing's changed much," the sergeant told him. "The roaches are bigger and bolder, is about all."

"That's comforting."

"Do I need to cuff you?" the sergeant asked. "While we're checking you into our fair establishment?"

"I'd prefer you didn't."

"Then until you give me cause, I won't."

"Thanks."

He stood passively at the counter while a female clerk-deputy made up a housing card for him, copying down his vital information from the transfer papers. They lined him up against the wall and took a Polaroid, stapled the picture to the card. Then the sergeant led him out of the rotunda into a smaller room adjacent to it, where the formal processing took place. A complete set of fingerprints was taken, both in the computer and in traditional ink. If he had just been arrested they would have run the computer prints through the FBI in Washington, but in this case that wasn't necessary. The ink prints were for their own records. After that, he stripped out of his prison clothes down to his shorts and faced the medical examiner, who was a male nurse. Most of the nurses in the jail were men.

"Healthy set of pictures," the examiner commented, meaning the tattoos.

Dwayne didn't reply—it was all bullshit.

They took body Polaroids of him, front and back.

"Any current problems, sickness? Open sores, chronic diseases? You wear glasses, a hearing aid, anything like that?"

"No."

"Venereal disease. HIV-positive, AIDS, clap, herpes, whatever?"

"Nothing."

"You aren't gay, are you?"

If someone on the outside had asked Dwayne that question, Dwayne would have torn the offender's head off. In here it was SOP, no offense meant. Which didn't mean he liked being asked. Sexual orientation inside prison had a whole different context than it did in the free world. Dwayne's criterion was that if he had a choice of fucking a man or fucking a woman, he'd fuck a woman, every time.

If he had a choice.

He was escorted into a small cubicle with a classifications officer. Because of who he was, and what he was here for, Dwayne's interviewer was a lieutenant, who'd stayed on after his shift had ended earlier in the evening. The lieutenant leafed through Dwayne's prison documents. "You've been a good enough soldier," he commented, mildly surprised. "Not many bad marks, considering how much time you've done."

"I stay out of people's ways, they stay out of mine."

"Good policy." The lieutenant picked some dinner crud out

of his teeth with a paper clip. "Regulations say you should be housed in protective custody. For your own safety, which I'm sure you can appreciate."

"I don't want that. I've been taking care of myself for years without any problems. In tougher places than this."

"I know you don't. But we've got our own interests to watch out for. You wind up with a knife stuck in your back we're up shit's creek." The lieutenant paused for a moment. "No one in population knows why you're in here. Not even most of the guards, just a handful in administration."

"They won't be knowing from me."

The lieutenant kicked back. "This trial you're testifying in, it's moving slower than the proverbial glacier. They should've delayed transferring you down here, but the orders had already been cut. You could be with us a couple, three weeks."

"Time's time. Here or Durban, it's still time."

"That's a fact."

Dwayne put his hands on the lieutenant's desk. "I'm here to do the state a favor," he said bluntly. "And since I'm doing the state a favor, I think the state should treat me nice."

The lieutenant looked at Dwayne. "Like how?"

"You've got an infirmary here. I want to work in it."

"So you can get your hands on drugs? Forget it."

"I don't do drugs. It's the best work in the place, and I've been working infirmary duty at Durban."

The lieutenant was skeptical. "I don't know . . ."

Dwayne leaned in toward the man. "This is no skin off my ass, you hear what I'm saying? You treat me good, I do the same. Otherwise I'll call the district attorney up tomorrow, tell him I've changed my mind about testifying, they can ship me back upstate." He leaned back. "I'm not going to make you look bad. But I want my stay down here to be as comfortable as possible—it's a small perk but it means a lot to me."

The lieutenant thought about it for a moment. "All right. But if you fuck up, you'll do the rest of your stay in isolation."

"I hear you."

The lieutenant looked at his watch. "We'll house you in a protective cell tonight and transfer you into the general population tomorrow." He stood—the interview was over. "So's we understand each other."

"We understand each other."

They gave him the customary delousing shower. His prison garments were put away for when he would be taken back to Durban. Regulation jail clothes were issued—green T-shirt, green sweatpants, boxer shorts, sweat socks. He was allowed to keep his own shoes, Nike cross-trainers he'd bought in the Durban commissary.

He collected his mattress, bedroll, and toiletries, and was escorted by one of the guards into the bowels of the jail.

Wyatt and Moira picked Michaela up on the way home.

"Oh, that's terrible," she commented when they told her what had happened earlier in the evening. "Poor old Mrs. Sprague. Do the police know who did it?"

Moira stared at her daughter, wanting to make a statement. "Ted Sprague said they were young black males who looked like gang members to him. Those were his exact words," she said pointedly, as if daring Wyatt to contradict her.

He wasn't in the mood to get into a fight. Later on, when everyone's passions had cooled, they would talk about it rationally.

"I thought the Spragues were in Europe," Michaela said from the backseat.

"Yes, they were," her mother confirmed.

"Then how come they didn't have their alarm on?" Michaela queried. "Don't you remember last year, when Mrs. Sprague set it off by accident at three in the morning? It woke us all up, remember? We were all running outside in our nightgowns and everything, wondering what was happening, and then the police came, and Mrs. Sprague had to make them coffee and apologize, and the people from her security company came, too, and everybody was so pissed off at her. Don't you remember, Mom?"

"Yes, I remember," Moira answered. "They must have forgotten to set it."

Or it was an inside job, Wyatt thought to himself again,

inwardly seething, but remaining quiet about it. He was going to look into that, first thing in the morning. They used the same security company—Alarms Unlimited—as the Spragues did; most of the neighbors used them. If there was a breach of security in the company, they'd better find out ASAP.

He pulled into their driveway and parked the car in the garage.

"I've got more homework to do," Michaela told them. "I'll finish in my room." She kissed both parents good night and disappeared behind her door.

"I'm going to bed," Moira told Wyatt, sloughing her shoes as she climbed the stairs to their bedroom. "I'm beat."

"I'm still too wound up to sleep," he said. He kissed her good night.

"Maybe I'll still be up when you're ready," she said invitingly.

Wyatt went out the back door, skirted the swimming pool, the water dark, still, rippling with light coming from the rising moon and the lamps that were on inside the house, and let himself into the small pool house on the far side of the pool.

His trombone, a Bach tenor, stood on its stand in the corner. Apart from the main stuff—family, work, friends—running and music were the two constants in Wyatt's life. Music was great therapy—it made all the bullshit and pettiness of the day melt away into the ozone.

He usually worked on classic trombone pieces, Arthur Pryor solos, and Marine Corps virtuoso stuff, but when he got tired from what he was practicing, or stuck, he'd improvise jazz riffs, closing his eyes and playing à la J. J. Johnson, Jimmy Knepper, Bill Watrous.

Jazz was his passion. He had every album J.J. had ever cut; de rigueur for a trombonist—plus all of Miles, Coltrane, Monk, just about everyone, starting with Bird—thousands of old LPs and CDs. Whenever he was in New York on business he would hit all the big-name jazz clubs—the Blue Note, Village Vanguard—wherever there was someone good.

Wyatt's secret fantasy, nurtured from Jack Kerouac books and forbidden trips to local clubs when he was still in high school (underage and using a friend's stolen draft card to get in), was to live in some funky apartment in the Village and play jazz trombone professionally. It was an indulgent pipe dream. He knew that the life of a jazz musician was impossible—no money, scant recognition in relationship to your worth as an artist. And he was white—how many whites made it in jazz?

He picked up his horn and started blowing, warming up for a minute with long tones. For the past few weeks he had been working on a difficult eight-bar section, a series of 64th-note triplets that were all written above high D. The piece was by Pryor—"Blue Bells of Scotland," one of the trombone master's most famous numbers. It would take Wyatt about eight months to work through the intricate work, note by single note sometimes, from start to finish, until he reached the point where he would be comfortable enough with his technique and understanding to play it all the way through, nonstop.

Tonight he wasn't playing for enjoyment, as he usually did. Tonight he was playing because he had hit a wall, and losing himself in music was the best way he knew to stop agonizing over it. Compounding his free-form anxiety was the incident next door and then, worse than that actual incident, how his closest friends had reacted to it. The latent racism and bunker mentality, the hostility and fear, had been chilling. Jesus Christ, he thought, is everybody in this country armed except me?

He knew he'd been burning out for a long time, but he had been unable—unwilling was more to the truth of it—to admit it to himself. He was fighting the feeling like a warrior, but it was a fight he knew he wasn't winning.

He closed the cover on the Pryor piece. Then he played the opening notes of "On Green Dolphin Street," glissed down from B flat to sixth-position F, secured the slide lock, and set the trombone on its stand. He fastidiously wiped a finger smudge from the bell with a chamois and turned off the light over the stand.

The paramedics and the cops arrived at the scene of the botched crime at the same time. A crowd had gathered, forming a loose circle around Marvin, who was lying half in the street and half on the sidewalk. He was obviously no threat to anyone, so there wasn't any tension. It felt like a block party—a couple of the male onlookers were drinking beer out of cans, while mingled sounds of radios, televisions, and ghetto blasters came from nearby open apartment windows and passing cars.

The store owner hovered in the entrance of his shop, his face a stone.

After giving Marvin a cursory check to make sure he wasn't in immediate danger of dying, the paramedics loaded him into their wagon and took him, sirens wailing, to Memorial Hospital, the city's main public facility, a couple miles away. One of the responding officers rode in the ambulance with him, while the other stayed behind to take the store owner's statement.

The officer in the ambulance Mirandized Marvin, who was lying on his stomach, one hand cuffed to the gurney. There were about two dozen pellets in his ass and the backs of his upper legs. Number-four bird shot, pheasant load, a little smaller than a BB. His pants were shredded and he was bleeding good; there had been a trail of blood on the sidewalk, from where he'd been hit to where he had landed. He had regained consciousness before the police had arrived.

Marvin moaned loudly. He knew he sounded weak, but he couldn't help it. "This is killing me! Give me something for it, it hurts like hell!"

The paramedic felt his pulse and checked the flow of the IV he had inserted into his arm to keep him from dehydrating and going into shock. "Can't help you there," he told Marvin. "You'll have to wait for the doctor to examine you first."

"It's killing me," he moaned again.

"Hey, shut the fuck up," the cop ordered him. A veteran, a black man like Marvin, his face pocked with craters from years of shaving with a can of Magic and a butter knife. "Be a man—if you know how."

"It hurts." Softly, a wounded dog's whimper.

It took the ER intern over an hour to pick the individual pellets out of Marvin's ass and legs. He had to probe with tweezers, and every time he pushed against one of the open sores Marvin screamed. They didn't give him any painkillers—he was going directly to jail from here and he couldn't be admitted with drugs in his system.

Wyatt and Moira sat in the kitchen. Wyatt, bare chested, had on a pair of boxer shorts. Moira wore her old thin cotton nightgown that she'd bought years ago in Paris, on their second honeymoon. He poured himself a glass of white wine out of the refrigerator left over from the night before's dinner.

"So . . . ?" she prompted him.

"I can't keep doing this anymore. I mean . . . I don't want to." He stared at her.

She held his look firmly, without judgment, but said nothing. For one thing, she didn't know what he was referring to. "I thought you were upset about what happened tonight."

"I was, but it's deeper than that, Moira. It's about me. This isn't why I became a lawyer." His arm waved a vague all-encompassing motion.

Moira pulled her legs up onto her chair and wrapped her arms around her knees to anchor herself. "What isn't?" she asked.

"What I'm doing."

She got up and poured herself a glass of orange juice, sat down again.

"This is not original, what I'm talking about. Everybody in the world seems to go through it. Everybody that can afford the luxury of thinking about it."

"Everyone goes through periods of self-doubt, Wyatt," she said, trying to soothe him.

"I don't have any self-doubt," he corrected her. "Not personally. It's the work."

"With you they're the same thing."

He shook his head. "That's not true anymore. It used to be that way, I used to think that was true, but it isn't. My work, the firm, it's part of me but it isn't me, like playing trombone is part of me, and running is part of me. And being your husband, and Michaela's father. They're all part of me, but they aren't who I am."

"I know," she said, "but still . . ."

"Still . . . what still?"

"If somebody asks you who you are you don't say I'm a trombone player or a runner. Or a husband or a father, for that matter. You say you're a lawyer. That's what it says in *Who's Who,* in the *American Bar Directory,* in your college newsletters. You're a famous attorney who wins important cases all over the world."

"And makes a lot of money," he added pointedly.

"That, too," she agreed.

"So what does that mean?"

"It means you're successful."

"So?"

She got up and stood in front of him, taking his head in her hands. "Something's troubling you besides whatever this is," she said. "So tell me whatever that is so we can go to bed."

He looked up at her. "I'm burned out, babe."

"You're tired. You've been through a grueling case. You always feel down after a big long case; it's inevitable. And what happened tonight didn't help. We should go somewhere for a couple of weeks," she declared. "We're overdue for some time off."

"You're right, we should." He paused. "But that's still not what I'm talking about."

"Okay," she said. She massaged his temples. "But let's put some distance in this. For perspective."

He shook his head doggedly. "I don't need perspective to see what's wrong with this picture." He took hold of her hands and stood up. "There's a basic phoniness to all this and I can't not look at it any longer."

"Phoniness where? With me, Michaela? I don't think so, Wyatt. I know that isn't so."

"No, not that. It's about why I'm a lawyer. Why I wanted to practice law in the first place."

He'd been all fired up as a young man. *Ask not what your country can do for you, but what you can do for your country.* He was going to be Ramsey Clark, William Kunstler. Instead, he had become one of the most important and sought-after corporate lawyers in the country. It was tremendous power and awesome money, but it wasn't the stuff of his dreams. "I haven't defended an actual human being in ten years—only corporations. And I'm almost never actually in the courtroom."

"I thought that was good. You've always said you don't ever want to go to trial with your clients."

"Because juries hate clients like mine. Nobody feels very sympathetic toward multibillion-dollar corporations."

"I'm calling the travel agency tomorrow."

"I could retire tomorrow. We could afford it."

"Not the way we live now."

"We don't have to live the way we live now," he said. "We could live fine with much less money."

She turned to him. "You're too young to retire, you're decades away from even thinking about it, it's not an option. Now enough for tonight. I really am tired—come on to bed."

"You're right," he admitted. "Quitting isn't what I want."

She leaned against his body in relief.

"**W**hat happened to this one?" the duty officer inquired. He glanced over his shoulder at the clock on the wall: 3:25, dead of night. A few stragglers were sitting on the benches waiting to be booked, but the main surge of arrests had abated.

"Got shot in the ass." The arresting officer chortled.

A couple of jail deputies, watching the arrival of the prisoner who was being transported from the local ER, laughed along with the cop. Marvin, still in a hospital gown, his exposed ass wrapped in bandages, grimaced, trying to become invisible.

That's who he was now—a joke. A chump who ran away from a simple holdup.

The pain was pulsing through his body. "I'm gonna throw up," he cried out.

"Not on my floor!" the duty officer shouted. "Get him in there," he bellowed, pointed to a bathroom across the dirty linoleum-covered floor.

Marvin had to get down on his knees and hang his head over the edge of the bowl. The toilet was old and superfunky—the overwhelming smell of human waste invaded his nostrils and made him throw up more, dry heaves.

He was taken through the booking procedures, his personal effects inventoried. Besides the gun, which had been confiscated and would be used as evidence (the fact that it was a stolen, unregistered weapon would be an additional factor against him), there were a few dollars in bills and change, a pack of cigarettes, a driver's license, and a Swiss Army knife.

When that was done he was examined by a doctor, who checked and rebandaged his wounds and then finally, mercifully, gave him a fifteen milligram shot of morphine.

His entire body relaxed almost instantaneously. This shit was good. His last thought, as they were taking him to the infirmary, where he would stay for a few days until his condition stabilized, was that when he got out of here and started out dealing, he'd have to get ahold of some of this stuff.

The tank-sized disposal vehicle rumbled slowly down the alley behind the dance bar where Violet and her friends had been partying the night before. The driver set the brake and jumped down from his cab, joining his partner, who was rolling a large orange cart on wheels down the asphalt. The two men (Portuguese, the Portuguese had the monopoly on the city's waste-disposal contracts) worked opposite sides of the alley, grabbing the garbage cans that were lined up against the building walls, lifting and dumping them into the large orange one, which they wheeled to the back of the truck, where they heaved the entire contents—garbage, trash, whatever—into the open jaws that shut down and crunched everything it was fed into shreds.

The two men covered the block quickly and methodically, twenty 25-gallon garbage cans emptied into the bowels of their truck in less than two minutes.

"Give me a hand over here," the partner called, wrestling with the last can in the row. "This one's heavy as a bitch."

The driver crossed the alley. Each man grabbed a handle and lifted.

"Jesus, somebody must've dumped a load of bricks in this one," the driver groused. "Wait a second, save your back. I'll pull the truck down so we can dump it right in."

He drove down the alley a hundred feet and parked right

next to the can that was particularly heavy. He climbed down; each man grabbed a handle.

"One, two, three." They lifted the heavy metal can to the lip of the opening, tilted up the bottom, and emptied the contents into the belly of the disposal truck. The driver returned to the cab and started the mechanism that mashed and chewed and crunched everything into a tight, compact mass.

The jaws started closing. The last load of garbage began rolling down the slope of the truck inside, turning and folding on itself.

"Hey! Stop the motor!" The second man sprinted to the door of the cab. "Stop it. There's something in there! Open it back up."

The driver hit the grinding gears. The back door reopened, the jaws lifted. The driver got out of the cab again and joined his partner at the back of their truck.

They looked inside. All they could see was one foot and ankle. The rest of the body was buried under a load of trash.

"Oh, Jesus!"

They reached in and brushed the trash to the sides, clearing off enough so the body could be seen. A woman. Black. She was wearing a dress, but most of it had been ripped away, exposing her. She was a big woman, and when she was alive she had been attractive.

The sixteen senior partners who made up the firm's executive committee sat around a large oval table in their conference room. Twelve were men, four women. Two were African Americans, one was Latino, the rest white. A quarter were Jewish. An unremarkable assortment demographically, but all very powerful, capable, important lawyers.

It was the beginning of the workday. Coffee and pastries were available at a side buffet.

There were 168 lawyers in Wyatt's firm: Waskie, Turner, Liebman, Schultz, Carter, & Matthews. These sixteen owned the firm. One was a former secretary of commerce. Two others had been deputy attorneys general.

Wyatt was the youngest partner and newest who had his name on the door. He got the distinction four years ago, when as lead attorney overseeing hundreds of other lawyers he had won the first billion-dollar case in the firm's history.

Over the past five years Wyatt had become the most important lawyer in the firm. He had brought in more money than any other partner. He was the lead attorney in all of the huge antitrust cases the firm handled, where the profits or damages could run into hundreds of millions of dollars, and the fees into tens of millions. If for any reason he were to leave, their revenues could drop as much as twenty-five percent, which would be catastrophic. That knowledge gave him extraordinary power; he was extremely cautious about how he used it.

Ben Turner, at eighty-one the only founding partner still active, sat at the head of the table. He ran these meetings and he was brisk about it. Information was exchanged, cases were discussed—the progress of ongoing work, and the decisions about what new cases should be accepted. Generally, if a partner had something he or she wanted to take on it was a done deal, unless there was a conflict with an existing case or client; most of their work came from clients who had long-standing, ongoing arrangements with the firm.

"Let's get on with it, ladies and gentlemen," Turner said. "We haven't all gotten together in one room since Mr. Matthews and his crack team won the Larchmont case, which is going to help make this the most profitable year this firm has ever had, not to mention the future work it will bring. Congratulations, big boy," he said, turning to Wyatt, who was seated a few chairs down the table.

Sitting next to Wyatt, Darryl Davis, the firm's top criminal-defense litigator, offered his huge palm. Wyatt high-fived him. Wyatt had brought Darryl into the upper echelons of the firm, the first African American to achieve that status. Darryl, four years younger than Wyatt, was terrific in the courtroom, spellbinding in front of a jury. Other members of the firm would come and observe during his summations. Despite Darryl's individual brilliance, however, criminal defense was the smallest division at Waskie, Turner. Darryl was the only prominent attorney in it.

Turner called the meeting to order and in less than half an hour he'd covered all the bases. "Any new business before we go back to work?"

"I do," Darryl spoke up. "I talked to Lucien Walcott at the

Public Defender's office last week about our ongoing pro bono commitment. We've had two probationary people, Morris Estead and Lucille Walton, doing this for the past twelve months. They've finished their apprenticeship with him and will be coming in as associate members of the firm, so we're going to have to assign two new people to that program. I've been interviewing applicants but so far I've only come up with one. She had a full scholarship to Michigan Law, clerked for Justice Stevens a couple terms back. I'd like to start her next month. She'll be working out of the PD's office and the firm will be picking up her salary, our normal SOP."

"It's your division, Darryl," Turner said. "What about the other intern we've committed to?"

Waskie, Turner had an ongoing commitment to supply two lawyers a year to the Public Defender's office, which was how they worked off their obligation to do pro bono defense work, a burden undertaken by most of the large law firms in the city.

"Haven't found one yet," Darryl said. "We're not known as a criminal-defense firm, so we don't get the cream of that crop."

"I'll take the job."

It wasn't the way Wyatt had planned to make his announcement, but it would have to do.

A couple of the other partners sitting around him turned to look at him, not believing what they'd heard. Darryl grinned broadly at Wyatt. "What a trooper. Anything for the firm. It's okay, big fella, I'll come up with someone. I think we need you right where you are."

Turner got up from his chair. "That wraps it up."

"I'll take the job. I want it."

It took a moment for what Wyatt had said to sink in. Then everyone turned to look at him, fifteen heads moving in disbelieving unison.

"I want to do criminal defense." He looked at Turner. "I'm serious, Ben."

Turner stared at him in disbelief. "What's this all about, Wyatt?"

"I intended to tell you that I was going to take a leave of absence from the firm, starting right away."

"What . . ." Turner paused, collecting his thoughts. "I don't get it," he said. "You just won the biggest money case in this firm's history. Your bonus is going to be over three million dollars off that one case alone. You can't be serious about walking away."

"Maybe this is the time to walk away—while I am on top."

Turner came around the table so that he and Wyatt were face-to-face. "There's no delicate way of putting this, Wyatt, so I won't try to. This firm needs you." He paused. "What's the matter, Wyatt?"

Wyatt took a deep breath. "I'm volunteering for this public-defense work, Ben, because if I don't do something different in my life, right now, I won't have a choice."

"Where is this coming from?" Turner asked.

"I don't know, Ben. I just won a case against the government of the United States, and I'm not convinced right now that justice was served by my winning. And I'm not happy about that."

"What on God's earth are you talking about? Justice is subjective, Wyatt. Juries decide what justice is. You handled the case brilliantly from start to finish. What do you think it was, a fluke?"

"I know it wasn't a fluke. That's the problem! Some poor innocent schmucks are going to be ruined because I won that case. I'm a million-dollar lawyer going up against a seventy-five-thousand-dollar lawyer. It's David versus Goliath. And nobody likes Goliath."

Turner put a fatherly hand on Wyatt's shoulder. "I understand you," he sympathized. "I've been in the same position myself. You work like mad on a case that goes on forever, it's finally over, and there's this incredible letdown."

Wyatt was silent.

"You need a vacation," Turner continued. "Away from the office, away from all of it. Go to Tahiti with Moira, lie in the sun, drink mai tais and look at beautiful women."

That's what he'd envisioned, initially, when he had started thinking this way. Not Tahiti, that wasn't his style. More like a lot of fly-fishing, golf, sleeping in late. Reading fiction, going around the country and hitting the great jazz clubs.

He wanted to do all those things; and he would, someday. But that wasn't the answer to this problem.

"No." He turned and faced his partners. "I'm burned out, and a fancy vacation won't cure what I need. I want a moratorium from defending huge multinational conglomerates. I need to look at the law in a different way, a fresh perspective."

Turner looked at him. "What *do* you want to do?"

"I want to practice criminal defense. For poor people who need a good lawyer, not some kid fresh out of law school." He turned and faced his partners, who were slack-jawed, staring at him. "I want to work the right side of the street for a while, or I won't be able to live with myself."

Turner shook his head in frustration. "You're not some wild-eyed idealist who's going to change the world, Wyatt. We don't change the world. No one does. It's one of those things you learn as you get older. And our clients are big, yes—small fry can't afford us, that's the way life goes."

It was Wyatt's turn to put a comforting hand on the older man's shoulder. "Haven't all of you, at one time or another, felt like you had to get out of this rat race?"

No one answered him. Most of them weren't even looking at him. It was as if he had announced he had some communicable disease.

"Public Defender law," Turner muttered. "For how long?"

"I don't know. Six months, a year." He turned to Darryl. "Am I crazy?"

"Yes, but it doesn't matter."

"We can't afford to have you out of the loop for a year," Turner stated flatly. "Six months, we could survive that, I guess." The color was coming back into his Irish cheeks. "This might not be so bad. Maybe we can use it to our advantage."

"I'm not doing this for publicity."

"You do it for whatever you want to do it for. Save the dolphins, work alongside Mother Teresa, whatever you want to do. I've got our reputation to worry about. The firm's biggest star is leaving the lucrative field of corporate law to practice criminal defense, and not only criminal defense, but public criminal defense, the lowest of the low. We are such a civic-minded law firm that we give our best and most important lawyer to the people—for a while."

"You make it sound so calculating," Wyatt protested.

"It is what it is. Besides, what counts is action and results, not words, right?"

"Yes."

"Then it's settled," Turner declared. "Six months." He turned to Darryl. "You've got a new pro bono lawyer in your division. And this meeting is adjourned," he stated as he turned on his heel and left the room.

Violet got the call at home. The ringing startled her out of a dark morning dream. Her hand fumbled toward the night table and reached for the phone, knocking it off the cradle onto the floor.

"Hello?" she answered, once she managed to grab hold of the receiver and bring it to her mouth, her voice thick with sleep. She hadn't drunk so much last night, but that last vodka tonic was two more ounces of alcohol than was good for her. She smelled of cigarette smoke—it was in her hair, on the clothes that lay in a heap on the floor. She'd been so wiped out when she got home, from the exhaustion of work, dance, and drink, that she had dropped everything on the floor, item by item, where she stood.

She would do a load of laundry before she went to work. Get the acrid smoke smell out of her clothes. Wash her hair.

Before falling into bed she had remembered to put in a Super Tampax, and had worn a pad as well, but she had still soaked through, staining the sheet underneath her.

"Yes?" she managed into the phone, swinging her legs to the side and sitting up on the edge of the bed. Her feet scrounged underneath for her shower clogs.

"What?" She listened for a moment. Breathlessly: "When?"

Another brief moment went by. She felt a chill coming on suddenly, and a numbness in her fingers and toes, spreading up into her arms and legs.

"Yes. I'm coming in. Right now."

She hung up. For a short while she sat motionless on the bed. Then she got up and staggered into the bathroom.

Already, her face was dripping wet, the tears flowing down her cheeks. She didn't know when she had started crying.

The police were at the slaughterhouse when she arrived. Peggy was, too. Violet still smelled of cigarette smoke in her hair—she hadn't showered, or put on any makeup. In a trance she had splashed cold water on her face, put in a fresh tampon, thrown on jeans and a sweatshirt, and driven down.

Her face was puffy from crying. Peggy's was, too. The two women fell into each other's arms. The tears came again.

The police detective interviewed her and Peggy in her supervisor's cubicle. On the other side of the partition, her fellow employees looked at them through the glass half windows.

"I'd say about . . . ten-thirty?" Peggy said, answering the detective's question. She looked at Violet, who nodded in agreement.

It was assumed that they had been the last people to see Paula alive. Except for whoever killed her.

"How long was she gone before you noticed she was missing?" the detective asked them. He was an old pro, his people a couple generations removed from somewhere in Eastern Europe, Violet guessed, in his late middle age. Comfortably rumpled. He had introduced himself but his name hadn't registered with her, she'd been too distraught. "Ten minutes, fifteen?" he went on. "Longer?"

"I'm not sure," Violet answered for both of them. "We were dancing, talking. You know. You don't keep track of time."

He nodded. They were the victim's contemporaries: friends, not parents.

"It could have been as much as half an hour," Peggy said. "Like Violet told you, we were up dancing, several numbers in a row. When we sat back down she wasn't there. The ice was melted in her drink, I remember that. How long does that take?"

Long enough to get murdered. They all knew that—it didn't have to be said out loud.

"Was there anyone there she knew?" the detective asked, keeping his interrogation as gentle and low-key as he could. "Any man, especially?"

They looked at each other, shook their heads.

"Did she meet anyone? A man, I'm talking. Out of the ordinary, strange? Funny—funny odd, not humorous."

"There's always oddballs at places like that," Peggy answered. "Strange guys that ask you to dance, then rub up against you. Just strange guys."

"Did she dance with any strangers? Or get asked to, and turn them down?"

"No." Violet paused. "I did."

"Danced with a man who you didn't know?" He started to flip his notepad open.

"No. A man asked me, but I didn't."

"White or black? The man."

"White."

"Did he do anything? Other than ask you?"

"No. We were all sitting at our table, he asked me, I turned him down, he went away."

"Did you see him later that evening?"

She thought for a second. "No, I didn't."

"How long was that before your friend went outside?"

"I don't know. Not right before."

He laid the notepad back down on his knee without writing on it. "If you can think of anything else," he said, "I'd appreciate it if you'd give me a call." He took two of his cards out of his wallet, handed one to each of them.

Violet glanced at his card: *Joseph Pulaski. Detective-sergeant.*

She was half Polack herself—her mother, God rest her soul. Her instinct about him had been right, not that it mattered. She slipped the card into her back pocket.

In a corner of her mind, something jiggled.

"There is one thing that happened," she spoke up, remembering what it was. "It was kind of upsetting, at the moment."

He leaned forward in his chair, the notepad again at the ready. "What was that?"

"I went outside before Paula did, to the parking lot," she said, feeling a slight blush coming on. "I . . . my period started, unexpectedly. I had to go out to my car to get a Tampax out of my car trunk."

"Uh-huh." He had no reaction to the mention of her female troubles.

"There was this kid near my car," she continued. "This young black kid. I mean a man, a young man, he was older than a kid."

"How old?"

"Late teens, I'd guess. It was dark, not real dark, I got a decent look at him, but he was a man, not a kid."

"How tall?"

"Oh, pretty tall, over six feet, easy. He had a good build, what I could see, I mean he looked strong. I wasn't paying that much attention to what he looked like," she went on, talking faster than she wanted to, she didn't want this cop to think she'd been checking this kid out—not a kid, a man—"I was more worried that he might be thinking about breaking into my car. He was standing near it and looking in the rear window like he might be thinking about breaking in."

The detective wrote something in his notepad. "What happened?" he asked. "What did you do?"

"I told him to get away from my car."

"Okay. Then what?"

"He stepped back. He looked at me for a minute. He didn't seem scared, or shook up or anything, so then I thought I'd misread what was happening, that he hadn't been thinking about breaking into it, he was just hanging around like young guys do."

"So . . . and then?" he prodded.

"He walked away. He left—walked down the street, went away." She turned to Peggy. "I didn't say anything to you guys because it didn't seem like anything." She turned back to the detective. "Do you think . . . ?"

"He might've been the one who killed her?" he finished. "No. If this was the same man who's been committing these murders he wouldn't have drawn attention to himself by hanging around someone's car suspiciously."

"But what if it had been him, and I hadn't warned her?" Violet fretted.

"Don't beat yourself up about that," the detective assured her quickly. "The one had nothing to do with the other, I'm sure of it." He looked from one to the other. "Is there anything else? Anything that might help us?"

"She was looking for a man," Peggy told him, her voice breaking. "She was hoping to meet someone."

"That's the problem," the detective said, folding up his notepad and putting it in his jacket pocket. "She did."

After breakfast, a steam-table meal of powdered scrambled eggs, toast, juice, and coffee, which was served off carts that rolled down the cellblocks and was served into the individual cells—like most high-volume jails, they had stopped using the common eating area years ago; it was easier to maintain control by feeding the inmates in their living space—Dwayne was escorted downstairs to the visiting area, where his lawyer, Edwin Galeygos, was waiting for him. Galeygos was a short dark-complexioned man who dressed in padded-shoulder western-cut suits, wore bolo ties with turquoise tie holders, and slicked his hair back with Brylcreem. He got his cowboy boots mail-order from Tony Lama in El Paso, but he had never been there; he had only been in the state of Texas a couple of times, having to do with his legal work.

In the hierarchy of lawyers Galeygos was of that breed known as "trash-can lawyers," attorneys who take out ads on public trash cans and above the seats of city buses. He did, in fact, show up at hospitals and funerals, offering his services as a personal-injury lawyer, and he also hung around the courthouse, trolling for accused people who were without counsel and were cowed and bewildered by the whole system, people who had been brainwashed into believing that any privately hired lawyer, no matter how pathetic his credentials, was better than a government-appointed one, a fear that lawyers like Galeygos were quick to exploit. Quite a few of his clients came to him that way.

He would never fit into a big, respectable law firm—not that any large establishment would ever make him an offer. He didn't have the polish. But he knew his way around the courtrooms, and the entire criminal-defense system in general, because that's where he lived.

Dwayne and Galeygos sat across a scarred wooden table in one of the small windowless conference rooms off the visiting area. In prison, when Dwayne talked to anyone from the outside, including a lawyer, it was over a telephone, the parties separated by plate glass. This old jail, perenially underfunded, still hadn't converted all their attorney-client meeting rooms into separate warrens.

"You don't look all that bad," Galeygos backhand-complimented Dwayne by way of introduction. "Considering how long you've been living in a hole this time."

"I'm getting by."

"You're good at that. About one of the few things you are good at."

Both men had known each other a long time. There was no reason for Galeygos to try to pump Dwayne's hopes or expectations up—they both knew where Dwayne had been and where he was headed.

"Their trial got fucked up so you're going to be bunking here awhile. You're going to be the last witness the prosecution puts on the stand."

Dwayne shrugged. "I figured as much." He sat up straighter. "I'm the strongest part of their case, you always save the best for last."

"Don't be coming on too cocky," Galeygos admonished him. "They want your testimony, that's true, but they have a decent case without you this time, so they're not going to be cutting any kind of killer deal."

"Then maybe I should call the whole damn thing off. If there ain't something worthwhile in it for me."

Galeygos shook his head. "You can't do that, it's too late. You fuck them over now, they'll stick it so far up you you'll choke to death."

"So what're they offering?"

"Another year shortened on top of your good-behavior time."

Dwayne stared at him. "Come on, Galeygos, you've got to be shitting me."

"I wouldn't shit you, Dwayne, you're my favorite turd." He chuckled at the hoary joke. "But seriously. You're not their whole case this time, so they don't have to deal as much. But I can probably get you another year off, on top of the one. That'll put you back on the street in what, less than three years now. That's not so bad."

"Except for one thing," Dwayne rejoined. "The day I finish my time on this one I go up on trial again on the other case. And they won't give me bail on it, either, so I won't spend day one out in the free world."

"We'll deal with that when the time comes," Galeygos said. "I've got a few tricks up my sleeve there." He glanced at his watch. "I've got to run, I'm due in court in fifteen minutes. Now here—the DA's going to want to start talking to you, commencing tomorrow. So your testimony is iron-tight. He's already been embarrassed in this case and he doesn't want his chain getting pulled anymore. I can be there with you if you want—I don't think it's necessary, but it's up to you."

Dwayne shook his head. "I don't need you for that. I need you to get that next case against me dropped, is what I need you for."

"You need God for that, or at least his only begotten son, not a single practitioner with a shared part-time secretary and a busted fax machine."

"That case'll be my third strike," Dwayne reminded his lawyer. "I don't want to die in prison."

"We'll deal with that case when it comes up," Galeygos said again. "The state's got to try it and convict you, and I think we have a good chance of whipping their tails."

"That's what you said the last time."

Galeygos steepled his fingers, peered over them at Dwayne. "I'm going to bring you in a washcloth the next time I come, so you can clean out your ears. You aren't listening to me, Dwayne, and that is dangerous for you, buddy. They aren't going to cut you that deal, not what you want, not remotely close. Your testimony on this case here isn't worth it. And that is all she wrote, man."

He stood up, stuffing Dwayne's files into his briefcase.

"If you want something that big from them, man, you're going to have to give them something equally big or bigger in return. You're going to have to give them something they need so bad that they won't care what happens to you. And that, my friend, is something that you don't have—I know where all your bodies are buried."

He walked to the door and knocked for the guard to let

him out. "Pray for a miracle, Dwayne," he advised his client. "Because that's about all you've got left."

"**H**ow much criminal-defense law have you practiced?"

"None. But I'm a quick study."

They sat in Wyatt's office: Wyatt, Darryl, and Lucien Walcott, head of the Public Defender's office. To make the meeting less formal and try to put Walcott at ease, Wyatt had suggested they doff their jackets, so they were sitting in shirtsleeves.

Despite Wyatt's hospitality, Walcott seemed uncomfortable, or perhaps he was awed. Wyatt had a corner office. It was like a salon, large and richly appointed, with views over the entire city to the south. There was good original regional art on the walls from Wyatt's personal collection, as well as a small Frankenthaler. Fifty-four floors below, the river bisected its way downstream, and the crisscross of traffic was so small and distanced from this aerie as to be almost inconsequential, irrelevant.

"We all have to start somewhere," Walcott joked. He leaned forward, trying to get comfortable—he wasn't used to parking his ass in leather of this quality. "I'm curious, though—why someone in your position would want to do this."

"Because he wants to suffer," Darryl kicked in, answering for Wyatt.

"I want to do trial work," Wyatt explained for himself, ignoring Darryl's jibe. "And I want to help people who need it."

"How long will you be with us?" Walcott asked.

"My commitment is for six months."

"Six months isn't much time," Walcott said, with some skepticism. "It takes about that to figure things out."

"He's a quick study," Darryl reminded Walcott, grinning at Wyatt.

Darryl had started his career where Walcott was now: in the Public Defender's office. They had come up together, even sharing a cubicle for a while. Darryl had moved out as fast as he could, winding up in the seat of power he presently occupied; Walcott had stayed, grinding his way up the ladder rung by rung, eventually getting the top job.

Walcott was a good lawyer; Wyatt knew that—word gets around. But he wasn't a risk taker. He needed the security of the sure thing that a civil-service job offered.

"Let me explain how we work," Walcott said, pulling the meeting together. "We handle both misdemeanors and felonies. The majority are misdemeanors, of course. And this may come as a shock, but we don't do much trial work—we do as little as we can. We plea-bargain almost everything—it works better for us and for the prosecutor's office, too. The system's too clogged. And unlike crime shows on TV, ninety-five percent of our clients are guilty as charged. Going to trial doesn't do them any good; in most cases it prolongs the agony, because we can always plea a better deal than they'll get from a jury. The prosecutor is always willing to take half a loaf, and in most cases they're happy with a slice or two."

"It sounds as cynical as what I've been doing," Wyatt noted.

"No," Walcott corrected him, "it may be as cynical, but it has no relationship to the kind of law and the kind of clients you deal with. It's life on the bottom floor, the subbasement. And these people you'll be defending, they may be guilty of what they've done and a lot more as well, but they've been handed the shitty end of the stick, and we're their last and only line of defense."

Wyatt liked hearing that. It was a hard world, low-rent criminal defense, he understood that that was no myth. The criminal litigators he knew—even Darryl, up here on this lofty perch with him—affected a tough attitude. You had to, because your clients were tough, and expected you to be.

"However." Walcott put up a hand, like a stop sign. "If you're convinced one of your clients is innocent, and they won't offer you a deal, we *will* go to trial, no ifs, ands, or buts."

"Good." That felt better to Wyatt.

"Don't get dreamy-eyed about the reality of what goes on," Walcott continued. "Your clients won't thank you, and most of the time they'll shit on you, because they don't know any better."

"Sounds like a barrel of laughs."

"No—but it can be damn rewarding," Walcott said. "You can make a difference."

"That's what I wanted to hear."

"Good. Now about money—"

Wyatt interrupted him. "This is strictly pro bono work. You won't be paying me."

He knew how much Walcott made; he'd looked it up: $105,000. The head of the entire Public Defender's office, supervising sixty lawyers, and he barely made six figures— and that was after twenty years on the job. No one else in that office, even senior lawyers who did the biggest trials in the county—murders, rapes, other capital crimes—pulled down six figures.

Wyatt's own annual draw was a million dollars, before bonuses. This year he'd made more than this man, whom he was going to be taking orders from for the next six months, would make in his entire life.

It was a sobering thought.

"So," Walcott said, rubbing his hands together briskly, "we'll see you Monday morning?"

"Eight a.m.," Wyatt said, standing as Walcott did.

"You know where we're located?"

"Yes."

"It's a shame, not being able to use this nice office," Walcott commented, taking it in one last time, "but the clients you'll be representing wouldn't appreciate it."

"It wouldn't be appropriate," Wyatt agreed as he opened the door for his new boss. "Thanks for the opportunity," he said, meaning it.

"We'll see if you thank me in six months," Walcott rejoined.

At five o'clock in the afternoon the mayor, flanked by the chief of police and the district attorney, held a news conference on the steps of city hall.

"We have reason to believe that the victim found this morning was murdered by the so-called Alley Slasher, the same person who killed the previous six," he announced, his voice rising with agitation and indignation. "The circumstances were roughly the same, and so was the manner in which the killing was committed." He paused, glanced at some notes he was holding. "However, there was one major difference."

He looked out at the dozens of reporters, television and print, who lined the steps of the building, spilling down into the street.

"Unlike the previous eight," he said, "this victim . . . this woman . . . was not a prostitute. We know that conclusively. She was a workingwoman with a solid job and no criminal history whatsoever."

This was new and unexpected; the clamor and hubbub from the gathered reporters rose like a cloud into the air.

"Does this mean the police are going to work harder at finding the killer?" one of the reporters called out audaciously.

"The police are working as hard as they can," the mayor spat back, his anger rising. "That's not the issue." He took a deep breath to calm himself—he couldn't afford a show of temper, not now, although there were many times when he would love to punch out every one of these vultures.

"The issue is simply this," he explained. "Up until now we could concentrate our energy in one specific direction. We could pinpoint our focus; and we have, and we thought we were getting results. There haven't been as many streetwalkers out after dark, arrests have been down, and the killer hasn't struck for several months, we think because of these efforts, at least partially; there could have been other reasons: he could have been biding his time, or been out of town, or maybe he was in jail for some other reason.

"But now he's struck again," he went on. "And this time it wasn't a prostitute he killed, but a person who simply was in the wrong place at the wrong time."

"What happens now?" a reporter called out.

The mayor looked out, a practiced eye finding the television cameras. "If you have any ideas who this vicious person might be, no matter how far-fetched you might think they are, call the police. We've set up a special hot line that will be open twenty-four hours a day. The number is 555-4321, an easy number to remember. Write it down, carry it with you." He paused. "We're going to get this bastard. We promise you that."

"**D**wayne Thompson. Fancy meeting you here." It was a low, husky woman's voice, the tone a nervous mixture of sarcasm, superiority, loathing, and intense desire.

Dwayne looked up. "Hello, Sergeant Blake," he said to the woman, who was wearing the unisex jumpsuit uniform of the sheriff's jail cadre.

"It's Lieutenant now," she corrected him, her fingers flicking the bars on her collar. Lowering her voice, she added, "But you can still call me Doris."

Or desperate, or lonely, or horny, he thought. Especially horny.

They were in the jail's small law library. Dwayne had been granted permission to go there to prepare for his upcoming testimony. He needed a quiet place to think, and as an important witness for the prosecution he could request such perks.

There were only a couple others in the library, trustee inmates who kept the place in good order.

"I was wondering what had happened to you," he said smoothly.

"Life's what happened. Like you."

They checked each other out. She could feel the flush rising up her neck. He was one of the few men she'd ever known who looked at her like a woman.

"You're down to testify in a trial?" she asked. She was uncomfortable with silence between them.

He nodded.

"Snitching for the state again?"

"I'm doing the right thing," he said calmly, not rising to the bait, which was transparent and pathetic.

"Don't you ever worry somebody might retaliate against you, the amount of men you've turned evidence against over the years?"

He shrugged. "It's a chance you take. To get something for yourself in return. So far I've survived okay."

"What're they promising you this time?" she asked, now genuinely curious.

"An all-expenses-paid Caribbean cruise for two, a set of graphite-shafted golf clubs, and a new Porsche convertible waiting outside the Durban gates for me the day I get out," he deadpanned.

She laughed. "It's good to see you've still got a sense of humor."

"Better'n sitting around day after day feeling sorry for yourself. Which I do enough of, the time I've got to put in yet."

"I know how you feel." She touched his wrist with her fingertips, a quick touch. "I wish I could help you. You know that, don't you?"

"I guess."

"I do. I mean it." Her voice was taking on a clingingness. She gathered herself together. "Really—what will you get out of testifying at this trial that makes it worth the risk?"

"Two years' reduction in time. It'll kick me out in less than eighteen months."

"That's good," she commented. She hesitated; then, unable to stop herself: "You could have a life outside. A real life." She looked around to make sure nobody was eavesdropping on them. "I could help you—if you'd let me."

"Yeah, that would be nice," he said blandly. "The only problem with that is, there's this other charge hanging over me I'm going to have to stand for, after I do this time. So the chances of a life on the outside are about slim to none right now."

She frowned. "That's a shame."

"That's life, ain't it." Changing the subject: "So what've you been up to the last three, four years? Which is it, three or four?"

"Coming up on four." She smiled, almost shyly. "You've got a good memory."

"For things that matter." He could charm her off a tree without half trying; he knew that from their past encounters.

"I . . ." She was going to say, "I'm glad I was important enough for you to remember," but she caught herself. She had to maintain her position, especially with a man like Dwayne Thompson. "I've been going to law school," she told him with pride in her voice. "That's why I left Durban and went to work down here, even though the money isn't as good."

"That's ambitious. Congratulations. When do you graduate?"

"I already did. Last fall."

"Have you taken the bar exam yet?"

"Two weeks ago."

"So how did you do?" he asked.

"I don't know yet," she answered. "They haven't posted the scores."

"You probably aced them. Knowing you, you worked real hard at it."

She shook her head. "I don't think so." She bit her lip. "I think I blew it," she said morosely.

He looked at her. "When will they post them?" he asked. "Officially?"

"A few months. You know how slow these bureaucratic things go."

This time he was the one who looked around to make sure no one was watching them. He leaned in close, his lips almost touching her ear. She could feel his exhalation; it almost took her breath away.

"I could find out for you," he said.

She stared at him. "How?" she asked incredulously.

"Do you have a computer?" he asked. "A laptop? With a modem?"

"Yes," she nodded.

"Bring it in tomorrow. We'll see what's up." He glanced around the room. "Is there someplace we can be tomorrow night by ourselves?"

She caught his drift immediately. "I could get us in here. They close up at five. I have a key," she added.

"Is there a phone we can use that's safe?" was his next question.

"We can use one of the pay phones," she said. "They're clean."

All the telephones in the jail were supposed to be tapped, for security reasons, but they didn't have the funds for that, so they only tapped the ones the prisoners used in the cell-blocks.

"Then we should be okay," he assured her; and himself.

She nodded slowly. "Is this . . . will this, whatever you're going to do . . . be legal?"

"Nobody'll catch on, if that's what's worrying you." His

smile was meant to be reassuring, but there was an obviously cynical undertone to it. Doris had seen that look on him before—she knew it well.

. She didn't have to think twice about her decision. "Okay." Her fingers touched his wrist again. "What can I do for you in return?" she asked tenderly.

"We'll talk about it tomorrow," he answered, his mind already in another gear. "After we see what I can do for you."

"**H**ere's your office." Josephine DiStefano, the paralegal, a cup of coffee in one hand and half a bagel in the other, nudged the door open with her hip. They had met ten minutes earlier. "You share it with Max Strauss. He's already in court this morning."

The office he had been assigned was a partitioned cubicle about ten feet square, half the size of the bathroom in his own office. No windows—one wall was battleship gray concrete, and the other three were particleboard at the bottom with a half-glass top that went up about eight feet. There were about twenty offices on the floor just like it, none of which had any privacy.

Two government-issue battle-scarred metal desks facing each other, partner-style, took up most of the space, along with their desk chairs and another straight-back chair alongside for interviews, again metal. He hadn't seen furniture this ugly since his stint in the Peace Corps in the early seventies, working in a hospital in Zaire. Up against one wall were some ancient legal-sized file cabinets, and leaning in the corner diagonally from the entrance was a wooden clothes tree, from which hung a set of sweats, assorted jackets and rain gear, and a racquetball racket in a case.

In deference to his new job he had worn an old suit to work, a navy blue Brooks that had been languishing in the back of his closet for years. It was heavier than the svelte lightweight Armanis he was used to—already he felt uncomfortably hot. There was no air-conditioning on the floor that he was aware of, and the windows, which were open, offered little cooling.

Laying his briefcase on top of his newly assigned desk, he

shrugged off his suit coat, glancing toward the clothes tree for a hanger.

"If you want a hanger for your jacket," Josephine instructed him, reading his mind, "you'll have to bring in your own. Our budget doesn't cover the necessities, let alone something fancy like a wooden coat hanger." She smiled at him. "Not exactly what you're used to?"

"It'll do," he said with a shrug. "I'm here to work, not worry about appearances."

"Good attitude to have," she said, polishing off the last bite of bagel. "You'll need it." Having dispensed with the formalities: "Lucien wanted me to bring you up to his office as soon as you were settled in. I'd say you're as settled as you're going to get, so follow me."

Chucking the rest of her coffee in a trash can, she led him through a rabbit-warren maze of cubicles similar to his, corridors that bisected them, and open bullpen areas, where people were talking on the phones, banging away at typewriters and computers, or having their morning coffee with the paper. He figured her for her late twenties, unmistakably Italian, given the name DiStefano. Her long black hair was teased above her head, and her skirt was tighter than those worn by the women who worked in his firm. Waskie, Turner didn't have a dress code, but there were unwritten rules.

Against the far wall there were a few larger offices, which had real walls, solid, that went all the way to the ceiling, and windows with a view. Josephine knocked on a half-open door, then stuck her head in. "Mr. Matthews," she announced.

"Come on in," Walcott sang out.

"I'll catch up to you later," Josephine told him as he entered Walcott's office. "I'll be your eyes and ears for a few days, help you find your way around. My space is right near yours."

"I appreciate that," Wyatt said. "I'm sure I'll need all the help I can get."

"Sit down." Walcott indicated a chair across from his desk. "You want coffee?"

"Thanks."

"What do you take?"

"A little milk."

There was a Mr. Coffee on a credenza in the corner. Walcott poured a cup for Wyatt. "All we've got is the powdered stuff."

"Black, then."

They sat across the desk from each other. Walcott leaned back, his fingers laced, stretching his arms over his head.

"So. Are you ready to jump right in?"

"If you feel comfortable with that, yes."

"Good. I'd like to break you in gently, but I don't have that luxury. We've got three lawyers out with the flu, and a stack of cases to the ceiling." He picked up a handful of files from the top of a two-foot-high pile on his desk and rifled through them. "This is from over the weekend—simple felonies. Every one of these is someone who's going to be charged and bound over within the next forty-eight hours, or earlier. None of them have a lawyer, none of them have met with a lawyer yet. We have to be their lawyer, and we might not meet with some of them until a half hour before they go up before the judge."

"Sounds hectic." Wyatt sipped at the coffee. It was terrible. He made a mental note to bring in his own thermos, starting tomorrow.

Walcott took three files off the top of the pile. "Here's your first three cases." He handed them across the desk to Wyatt.

"What are they?" Wyatt asked.

"I don't know the particulars, I haven't read them." He pointed to the edges of the files. "They're color-coded, that's how you know. Green for nonviolent, meaning no weapons or force, and red for violent felonies. Juveniles would be yellow, but another office handles them."

Wyatt glanced at his folders. He had two greens and a red.

"Josephine'll help you," Walcott said. "She's a better lawyer than most of the lawyers. She'll hold your hand till you catch on."

Walcott stood up, glancing at his watch. "You're due in court in an hour and twenty-five minutes. Trial by fire."

Wyatt felt a surge pulse through him—part exhilaration, and considerable nervousness.

"Don't worry," Walcott said calmly, a smile playing over his lips. "The obvious losers you try to cut the best deal you can, the rest you finesse. The judges always grant one continuance, at least."

"So this is how the law works in the public sector."

"Every day of the year."

Dwayne and Lieutenant Doris Blake sat side by side at the guard's desk in the law library. It was after hours—the facility was closed. They were the only ones there, she'd made sure of that.

Dwayne connected her small computer to the wall plug and turned it on. It hummed to life.

"What do you have, sixteen megabytes of RAM?"

"Thirty-two. It's a Pentium two hundred." She didn't know if that was important, but the salesman had told her it was.

"Bitchin'. Plenty of power and speed."

He played around with the computer for a few minutes, checking out the various options. "Okay, baby," he said to the screen, clicking the track ball onto a cursor, "show me everything you've got."

Besides the extraordinary artwork on his body, Dwayne Thompson was famous for two things. He had an uncanny knack for getting people to talk to him, to open up and bare their souls, which was why he was a good snitch. During the years he had spent in the state prison system, which was over half his adult life, three men had been convicted and sentenced for serious crimes because of his testimony in court against them. Each time he had helped send somebody up one or more charges against him had been dropped completely or reduced to time already served. Considering all the terrible shit he had done (not counting the crimes he had committed but hadn't been caught at), he would have been a lifer several times over by now if they hadn't.

The other thing that Dwayne was famous for was as a computer wizard. He had taken advantage of the system and gone to college on a Pell grant inside the walls, receiving a B.S. in computer science, cum laude. He was acknowledged as being the best hacker in the entire state prison system, which was why he had been denied official access to a computer at Durban the last three years, since they'd realized how dangerous he could be.

Until he had been shut down he had done legitimate work

in the warden's office. He had also, from time to time, done some off-the-record, not entirely kosher work for various prison officials. For that he was rewarded with cushy jobs, better food and living accommodations, canteen privileges, and extra good-behavior marks. He didn't live like a Colombian drug lord, or anything close—that's impossible in the American prison system—but for a guy in jail, he didn't do badly.

Working rapidly now, Dwayne scrolled through the myriad applications. Doris sat close to him, legs and hips touching. He ignored it, but she was acutely tuned in to every inch of bodily contact.

He checked to confirm that her modem was working. "Make sure the door's locked," he said. "This is going to take some time, and if we got caught we'd be fucked royally."

Getting royally fucked was precisely what she wanted from him, but this wasn't the time to bring that up. She walked to the door at the end of the room and locked it. Then she walked back and sat next to him again.

Dwayne connected one end of the telephone cord into her computer. Then he took the other end to the pay telephone that was attached to the wall, which the prisoners used to make calls to their lawyers. Unscrewing the receiver, he took it off the cradle, revealing the wiring underneath, and looked it over. Then he moved some wires aside and inserted the other end of the telephone cord.

"Aha!" He clicked onto a particular item, brought the information up onto the screen. "Take a look," he told her.

On the screen, it read: STATE BAR EXAMINATION RESULTS, SPRING 1997.

"How did you do that?" she gasped. She looked at the screen again. "There's no closing date," she commented.

"That's because it isn't complete yet," he explained.

"So every bar exam result is on this?" she asked.

He nodded and typed some instructions onto the screen. "What was the date you took the exam? The exact date, and the location."

She gave him the information. He typed the details into the machine.

They waited a moment, watching the screen together. Nothing came up.

She sagged. "That means I didn't pass, doesn't it."

He smiled, a deadhead grin. "Not necessarily. It could mean that your group's test scores haven't been recorded yet, like you thought. They give the test in dozens of locations all over the state at the same time," he explained, "since they only do it twice a year. Then they have to collate them all, and grade them, and then go back through to check for mistakes. It takes time. Months."

"So we can't find out how I did."

"I didn't say that."

She looked at him. "How can you . . . ?"

He started typing. On the screen there was a flurry of activity: then a program came up.

Dwayne smiled—the cat that ate the canary. "We're in," he told her.

"In what?" she whispered.

"Their computer. The one that has your test score record in it."

"We're going to be able to find out how I did? Before it's posted?"

"We're going to try." He looked down at the information on the screen. "It shouldn't be too hard."

He sat down at her computer again and started typing in some instruction, combinations of words and numbers. She hovered over him, watching.

"Don't crowd me." His fingers flew over the keys.

She backed off. She was having a hard time breathing.

"Come on, baby. Don't fuck with the kid." He tried another combination, then another.

A code flashed onto the screen and held. "All fucking right!" he whooped.

She looked around nervously to make sure there wasn't anyone else in earshot. The door was still locked—they were the only people in there.

"What?" she asked. She was shaking, she was so nervous.

He typed in a command. The computer hesitated a moment as it processed the information: then a series of names came onto the screen.

"Everybody who took the bar exam the day you did, in alphabetical order," he said, pointing. "And how they did." He read the date at the top. "We're lucky. They're not going to post these for a while—probably still waiting on results from other, more out-of-the-way locations."

He typed in her name: BLAKE, DORIS. The screen scrolled down to the middle of the B's, faster than the eye could read the names.

Blake, Doris, came up. 66. The word "Fail" was next to it. "Oh, shit!"

His look to her almost had some compassion in it. "Sorry, babe. I mean Lieutenant."

"I knew it. I knew it. I can't take tests."

The tears started. She couldn't stop them, and she didn't care now.

"I get so scared when I have to take these fucking tests. I clutch. Oh, shit. Son of a bitch!"

"You can take it again in six months," he said. "Now that you know what it's like, you'll do better. You only missed by a few points."

She shook her head. "I'm forty-one years old," she sniffled. "I'll be too old to start practicing law." She wiped her runny nose on her uniform sleeve. "I'm going to be a god-damn jail sheriff for the rest of my life."

"Maybe," he said. And then, enigmatically: "Maybe not."

She looked at him through red scrunched-up eyes. "What do you mean?"

"Watch this."

He highlighted the 6 on the screen next to her name, punched the delete key, and typed in a 7.

She stared at the screen in disbelief. It read, Blake, Doris. 76. The word "Fail" flashed, then automatically converted to "Pass."

"Congratulations," he told her. "You are now a member of the state bar, with all the privileges that come with it."

"I . . . how . . ." For a moment she was speechless. "Won't they catch it?" she asked when she found her voice.

"Not unless somebody was to go back in and reread your test book. The odds on that are conservatively a thousand to one."

He worked his way out of the program, exiting everything. The screen went blank, except for the blinking C:prompt. He disconnected the telephone cord from the receiver, arranged the wiring back the way it had been, rescrewed the mouthpiece cup on, and hung the phone back up on the wall. Then he exited the program and turned off the computer.

Blake stared slack-jawed at the blank screen, as if the entire episode had been a dream.

"You're sure . . . ?"

"I'm sure."

She looked down at him. "How can I make this up to you?" she asked, beginning to regain her composure. "I owe you so much, Dwayne."

"There is one small thing you could do for me," he said.

"Anything." She started crying again.

"They've got me sleeping in the general population. It's shit up there. No way to get your thoughts together. I'd like to bunk down in the infirmary, where I'm going to be working. It would make my life a whole lot more pleasant." He hesitated. "And it would be easier for us to . . . you know, spend time together."

She thought for a moment. "I might be able to do that. Since you're already working there."

"That's great, Doris. I'd really appreciate it." He touched her face again, a feather-light touch.

She was all over him, devouring him, her mouth on his, her hand down his pants.

He returned the embrace with equal ardor.

Doris Blake was large, over six feet tall, and weighed well over two hundred pounds. There was no beauty in her face, and her body was lumpy, a woman lumberjack. It would have been easier for her if she had been a lesbian, but she was aggressively heterosexual. She had never been married; she could count the dates in her lifetime on the fingers of one hand. Until she'd met Dwayne she had been a virgin.

She was horny, lonely, desperately sad. She would fuck anyone who would fuck her, even a prisoner, even though the penalty for getting caught would be losing her job and maybe going to jail herself. She didn't care.

The first time Dwayne had laid eyes on her, up in Durban, he'd known everything there was to know about her. He'd played her like a Stradivarius—not that he'd had to work hard at it. They had become lovers less than two weeks after they met.

They had fucked wherever they could, anytime they had a free moment together.

No one ever suspected. No one ever looked at her like a woman, except him.

He used her to get all kinds of goodies. She knew that. She didn't care.

She almost hadn't left Durban because of him. But she'd had to, eventually; sooner or later they would have been caught. And she needed a life, something more than being a prison guard.

Now she was with him again.

There was no foreplay. Her jumpsuit came down around her knees, his pants dropped. Bending her over, both hands gripping her huge, marbled, pasty white thighs, he entered doggie-style, the way he best knew how.

He thrust hard, two fingers simultaneously massaging her clitoris. She bit down on her wrist to stop from screaming.

He had known this was going to happen. He had jacked off this morning, twice. Otherwise he would have come as soon as he entered her, and he wanted this to last. It had been four years.

She was a beast; maybe not the ugliest woman he'd ever seen, but close; but she was a woman, she had a pussy that was hot and wet and tight enough. A vagina, not a butthole.

She was a beast: but when he closed his eyes, she was a woman.

The corridor outside the courtroom was a beehive of activity: accused, their families, cops, lawyers, reporters, assorted hangers-on. With Josephine DiStefano sitting reassuringly nearby, Wyatt huddled on a bench with his first client, a middle-aged Latino who was accused of stealing a dozen wallets from the gym where he worked as a janitor. The wallets had all belonged to women, and the man, whose name was Fernando—clearly not a woman's name—had tried to use one of the credit cards from the wallets to buy a new thirty-two-inch Sony television from Sears. He'd been nabbed before he could get out of the store, and a search of his apartment by the police had turned up the other wallets and most of their contents.

"It was a mistake, man," Fernando was telling Wyatt in

a low, slurred voice. "I thought it was my own card I was using."

The morning's still young and he's already drunk, Wyatt thought. Or high. There was a strong stench coming off his client, but Wyatt wasn't sure if it was his breath or general unwashed BO.

Before he could think of a plausible way to rebut that statement, Josephine broke in. "You don't own any credit cards," she said curtly. "You don't have a bank account and you're three months behind on your rent. Your landlord's already given you thirty days."

"So?" His voice had the whiny air of the wounded accused.

"So cut the bullshit."

Wyatt, seated between them, turned from one to the other. I've got a few things to learn, he thought. I'm glad she's with me.

"Who is representing the accused?" the judge asked from the bench.

They were in Judge Arcaro's courtroom. Arcaro was a wizened old man with an acerbic temper, one of the few remaining of the Italian-Irish-Jewish tribe of male judges appointed decades ago, when the conservative Democratic machine had a deathgrip on the city. Almost all the newer judges were minorities or women.

Wyatt stood at the defense table. "The Public Defender's office, Your Honor."

From his perch on the bench Arcaro peered down at him over his bifocals. He was a small man who had a thick pad on his chair and still had to stretch to look over his desk.

"I haven't seen you before," Arcaro squinted. Even though he wore glasses he was nearsighted. "Are you licensed to practice law in this state?" He cackled at his bad joke; his bailiff and the court stenographer chuckled dutifully, by rote.

"I haven't had the privilege of being in your court, Your Honor," Wyatt smiled pleasantly. "And yes, I do have my license."

Arcaro's bailiff walked to the bench and whispered into the judge's ear. Arcaro leaned over, listening.

He looked up. "You're Wyatt Matthews?"

"Yes, Your Honor."

A murmur went up in the courtroom, particularly among the other lawyers who hadn't been paying attention; they all had their own problems to deal with.

Arcaro gaveled for quiet, leaned back in his high chair. He looked down at the docket sheet in front of him. "Is there more to this defendant than I think there is?"

"I don't know what you think he is, Your Honor. He's being defended by the office of the Public Defender, who I'm working for."

The judge leaned forward. "I'll be damned." He shook his head. "What is a man of your status and reputation doing working for the PD, if I may ask?"

"My firm has an ongoing commitment to do pro bono work through the Public Defender's office," Wyatt answered smoothly, "and we decided it was time someone other than a new associate ate at the public trough. Since I've been wanting to try my hand at criminal-defense law, I volunteered."

"Well, you sure picked the right place to do it," the judge said, laughing nasally. "It's refreshing to see an attorney of your stature getting his hands dirty, although I suspect it's a vanity move and you'll be back where you belong sooner than you expected. But in any case, good luck, son."

You're wrong, you old fart. You're going to see so much of me you'll get sick of my face.

"Thank you, Your Honor."

The second case Wyatt had been given was possession with intent to sell. He asked for and received a seventy-two-hour continuance so he could go over the case with his client and review the charges.

"You're not doing too bad," Josephine backhand-complimented him as they sat in the hallway, waiting for the third case to come up. It was still before lunch.

"Thanks." Needling and put-down seemed to be the way everyone dealt with each other around here. "Did you expect I wouldn't?"

"I didn't know what to expect."

"I'm not here on an ego trip."

She studied his face for a minute. "Most lawyers spend their whole lives trying to get to where you are," she told him. "And almost none of them make it. How come you're doing this?"

"You can get tired of anything. Even champagne and lobster would get old if you ate them every day."

"If you say so. But I'd be happy to try."

"You'll get your chance someday."

She shook her head. "That's not where I'm going. I can't afford to think that way."

"What kind of mentality is that?" He was already liking her; this defeatist attitude upset him.

"A realistic one. Look, I might get it together and become a lawyer someday, but the odds are against it. I'm already the first woman in my family to go to college, let alone graduate. But if I ever do become a lawyer I'll be a good one," she added defiantly. "I've seen enough lame attorneys to know I could do better."

"You've certainly impressed me."

"Thanks. Glad to be of help." She stuck her head into the courtroom, came back out. "You're up next."

"Your Honor," Wyatt addressed the court, "I've been informed that my client"—he glanced at the arrest sheet—"Marvin White, is in the infirmary at the county jail, recovering from wounds he sustained during his alleged crime."

"Have you had a chance to meet with him yet?"

"No, Your Honor. I got the case this morning and I've been in court all that time. I'm planning to interview him at the jail as soon as I'm freed up here."

"You do that," the judge told him. He flipped through his calendar. "Report to this court by Thursday morning as to his condition and when he'll be able to appear." He banged his gavel down, hard. "Next case."

Because Marvin was still laid up, his ass swaddled in bandages, Wyatt couldn't meet with him in a regular attorney-client room, so the jail authorities agreed for them to meet in the infirmary, after lunch. Wyatt went alone—Josephine had to go back to the office, where she had a mountain of work for her other lawyers.

While he was waiting to be cleared and sent down, Wyatt glanced at a summary report on Marvin's juvenile record. He'd read the entire file later, when he had a few free hours. It was depressing reading.

Dropped out of school in tenth grade, having been kept back twice. IQ 95, within the normal range, but with severe learning disabilities, particularly dyslexia—for all intents and purposes functionally illiterate. Black. Father unknown. Grew up in the projects. First arrested when in third grade—shoplifting. A few years later committed arson (set fire to his classroom with the teacher inside—young Marvin had locked her in. She'd had to jump from a second-story window, and broke both ankles—that was the end of her teaching days, and brought with it an additional charge of battery).

At seventeen Marvin White had seven arrests, three convictions, done time in the county work camp, juvenile hall, the state reform school.

"Follow me."

Wyatt looked up from his seat in the waiting room. A guard was beckoning him. He went inside the bars.

The main area of the infirmary was busy with inmates getting treated for various ailments, but Marvin was the only bed patient. A significant number were openly homosexual, Wyatt noticed—some of them aggressively so. If he hadn't known they were all men (female prisoners had their own facility, two floors up), he would have sworn some of them were women. Their problems were almost exclusively drug and AIDS related—some were openly dying; you could see the life draining out of them right before your eyes.

Wyatt felt a sense of uneasiness around all these inmates. Despite all his experience, this was a side of the law and of life he'd rarely been exposed to.

He sat on the bed next to Marvin's. The curtains had been drawn to give the appearance of privacy; but if anyone had wanted to listen in, they could.

"My name's Wyatt Matthews," he said by way of introduction. "I'm going to be your lawyer."

"My mother hire you?" the boy asked suspiciously, looking up at Wyatt through veiled eyes. The kid was eighteen, legally a man—in the eyes of the law a man who would be tried as an adult and sent to prison if convicted. To Wyatt's eye, however, this was a boy, only a little older than his daughter.

"No. The city appointed me. Is there a particular lawyer your mother would want to hire for you? Have you talked with her about this?"

"Fuck, no." Marvin turned his eyes away from Wyatt and stared up at the ceiling. "What you want to talk to me about?" His eyes darted to Wyatt for a second, then resumed their blank upward stare.

"The crime you're accused of would be a good start, for openers." He felt a surge of annoyance—you got your ass in a sling, kid, and I'm trying to help you, so don't come on so salty with me. "This is a serious accusation, Marvin. You could go to jail for several years if you're convicted. I'm going to try to keep you out of prison, if I can. But if you're not willing to help me, then I'm not going to be much good for you."

The kid looked away, as if conducting an inner debate. Then he turned and faced Wyatt, propping himself on his elbows, grimacing as he shifted his weight.

"What you want to know?"

"Let's start with the basics. What's your name?"

"Marvin. White."

"Any middle name?"

"No."

"You're eighteen? You just had your birthday?"

"Yeah."

"And you live at home?"

Marvin fidgeted.

"You *don't* live at home? Are you living somewhere else? With a friend, a girlfriend? On the streets? Where?"

"Here and there." The answer was low, almost a whisper.

Wyatt had a hunch. "Your mother doesn't know about your being arrested yet, does she? You haven't talked to her since this happened, have you?"

"She knows. The police told her. When I was up at the hospital."

"So she saw you in the hospital? Before they brought you here?"

Marvin turned to him again. "They *called* her. She didn't come. She ain't gonna come."

"Why won't she come to see you?"

" 'Cause she don't truck with no lawbreakers," Marvin stated defiantly.

He was going to have to meet the mother. Find out what she knew, what was going on with her son in general, and enlist her to support Marvin. A strong family front would help with his defense.

"Have you ever been arrested before?" The file only contained Marvin's juvenile offenses, nothing as an adult.

"Shit, yes."

"As an adult, not a juvenile."

"How could I be? I just turned eighteen, you already know that. What difference does it make?"

"If you have no record as an adult, that works in our favor."

Marvin nodded. "This was my first one. As a adult," he added.

"Tell me about it," Wyatt said. "From the beginning."

Marvin looked at him. "From the beginning like how?"

"Everything that happened from the time you decided to do it until the time you were caught." He paused—was he supposed to ask whether or not Marvin had tried to rob the store? In his own practice he never directly asked his clients if they were guilty because he wanted to conduct the most aggressive defense he could, and knowing a client was guilty hurt the cause—ethically you couldn't put him on the stand to say he didn't do it. But he didn't know how that worked in this field.

He wished Josephine was here now, so he could quiz her. He'd better save that question for later.

Marvin broke his chain of thought. "Like when I first started thinking about it, or when I set out to actually do it?"

That statement in itself was a quasi admission of guilt, Wyatt thought. "Let me put it another way," he said. "Tell me about what happened that day—from the time you first went by that store."

Marvin's brow furrowed. Whether he was trying to recall what had happened, or, on the other hand, deciding whether or not to confide in this strange man who had all of a sudden shown up and said he was his lawyer, Wyatt couldn't tell. "You a private lawyer?" Marvin asked.

"Yes." Wyatt explained: "I'm working for the Public Defender's office. Private lawyers do that, because there aren't enough staff public defenders to handle all the clients—like you."

Marvin's face lit up. "Why didn't you say so in the first place?"

"I didn't think of it. Does it matter?"

"Hell yes, it matters!" His smile broadened. "I got me a private lawyer. All right!"

"Does that mean you'll talk to me now? Tell me what happened?"

"Yeah, man. I'll talk to you."

Marvin began laying out what happened, from when he had first noticed the store, on his delivery route. That had been about a year and a half ago, when he'd begun his job. How it looked like a busy little store, with shitty security. And then later, when he'd figured out it was a numbers drop and that the cops on the beat were in on that, they knew it was going down and they let it ride, even played a number themselves from time to time, and ate free.

This is good, Wyatt thought, writing it all down. If this was true and he could document it, it could be embarrassing to the police and the prosecutor's office, and help in structuring a good deal with the DA.

He hadn't thought anything about it for a long time, Marvin went on, because he didn't have a weapon to use, and also because it was right in the middle of his delivery job and he could get spotted in the neighborhood. But then his homie had given him the stolen gun, and he had been fired from his job. A bullshit firing—he had done right by his boss, his boss had scapegoated him because he—the boss—had fucked up, and he needed to blame someone, and Marvin was low man on the totem pole.

Wyatt jotted a note to find out about the gun, which was now in police custody. And he would interview Marvin's former boss to get his side of the story to see if the boss had anything good to say about Marvin.

So now he had a gun, and he wasn't going to be in that neighborhood anymore, it wasn't his territory, he didn't like it around there, too many damn Asians with shitty attitudes. Do the deed and vanish into the crowd.

"So I checked it out," Marvin said, "and I figured the best day to do it. Night, I had to do it at night, when it wasn't crowded and I could get away easier. So then I went down there and looked it over again, to make certain. You got to have a plan with shit like this, you can't just go running in someplace and start waving a gun around."

A plan, Wyatt thought. Pretty sad plan if this is how it ended up.

"Okay," he prodded. "Go on."

"I went in and bought a pack of smokes, checking it out inside one more time. It was more crowded than I wanted, I didn't want nobody in there, 'cause I didn't want nobody to get hurt. Except the Korean behind the counter, and I didn't want to hurt him, either. But if he made a play, then I was prepared to."

"If it was too crowded, then why did you try it?" Wyatt asked.

"I didn't—right then. I paid for my merchandise and walked away."

"Where did you go?"

"Walked away a couple blocks. So I wouldn't be loitering right outside the store and get the guy suspicious."

"So you smoked a couple of cigarettes. How long did that take?"

"I smoked one cigarette, man. Didn't even finish that. I don't smoke tobacco, it was something to buy, so's he wouldn't get suspicious. I only lit that one up so I'd have something to do with my hands."

"You were scared."

Marvin flared. "Fuck, no, I wasn't scared. Scared of some jive-ass Korean? No. I was nervous. There's a big difference. You want to be a little nervous when you do a job, so you're on your toes."

Wyatt was making notes. "Keep going," he said.

So Marvin went back, and this time the store was empty of customers, and it was time to do or die. He went in, showed his weapon, told the storekeeper it was a robbery, and got him to take the money out of the register.

So much for worrying about his guilt or innocence. He's laying it all out—for the prosecution.

It was certain now that this case would never go to trial. He couldn't put Marvin on the stand. If they were lucky, they could make him a halfway acceptable deal with the DA.

"And then?" he asked. "How is it he came to shoot you, if you were holding a gun on him?"

"I told him I wanted the numbers money he kept hidden. He wouldn't give it up. It was like if I didn't shoot him for it, I wasn't going to get it."

"So you turned and ran."

Marvin shot up in his bed. "Fuck, no! My piece jammed. I'd've done that motherfucker in a heartbeat!"

"Shh," Wyatt cautioned him. "Keep your voice down. When did he fire his shotgun?"

"How should I know, man? I was running for my sorry-ass life. I never did see it." He paused, then grimaced. "I heard it, and felt it. But I never did see it." He rolled his eyes toward Wyatt. "I should've done the fucker. The next time, I'll have me a gun that works."

Count your blessings, Wyatt thought as he packed up his notes. A load of shot in the ass is a lot easier to recover from than a charge of murder.

Dwayne exchanged his jail issue for hospital whites. Immediately, he felt better. He looked good in white.

"You've done hospital work before, I assume?" the head nurse, a civilian, peevishly asked Dwayne. The head nurse was a pencil-mustached prissy little twerp who ran a tight ship. He didn't like the idea that some new inmate, who was only going to be with them for a couple of weeks anyway, had not only been assigned to "his" infirmary, but would be sleeping in it. But he wasn't about to buck Lieutenant Blake's orders. He was physically afraid of her, as were many others, inmates and deputies alike.

"Yes," Dwayne answered calmly, not responding to the gibe. "I was a lab tech in the army."

"Have you been trained to change dressings? Clean infected wounds?"

Dwayne nodded.

"Well, I guess we can find some use for you," the head nurse grudgingly allowed. "Make sure you stay out of the pharmaceutical supplies," he warned Dwayne. "I run a tight inventory. If anything is unaccounted for, I'll know it."

"I'm clean there," Dwayne assured him.

For the next hour, wearing latex gloves and a facial mask, Dwayne swabbed cuts, sores, and abrasions from sick inmates and transferred them to petri dishes, two to a dish. He also made cultures from sputum and sperm. Containing the spread of VD (HIV being the most deadly, along with common clap, herpes, and syphilis) was one of the jail's primary health missions.

"You're okay with cleaning and changing an open wound?" the head nurse asked Dwayne again, after the last of the cultures had been finished and put in the refrigerator.

"No problem," Dwayne answered.

"There's one in the back who needs changing," the head nurse smirked. "You'll find the supplies you need in the cabinet over the sink."

Dwayne got a package of sterile bandages, some cotton swabs, a tube of salve, and a bottle of antiseptic from the cabinet and walked to the back, the bed ward. The lone inmate, a young black kid, was lying propped up in bed, watching a Roadrunner cartoon on the small black-and-white television that was bolted high on the wall.

"Afternoon, stud," he said to the kid. "Time to change your dressing."

Marvin looked up at him, startled at the intrusion. He loved the wily roadrunner and that dumb-ass coyote; it was one of his favorite cartoons.

"It don't hurt. I don't need no changing," he protested.

He wasn't afraid of the physical act of having his dressing removed and the wounds cleaned—there wasn't much pain anymore. It was a man touching him on the ass, the possibility of hands grazing his pecker, that he didn't like. He especially didn't like the looks of this honky. Whiter than white, he looked like he drank bleach. Tattoos all up and down his arms, even coming out from the top of his T-shirt onto his neck. And his eyes—they looked like a snake's eyes, a rattlesnake or a cobra.

"Doctor's orders," Dwayne told him. "It ain't my decision, I do what the man tells me to do, and when. I'm an inmate here like you, so don't cause me grief. Roll over."

Reluctantly, Marvin turned onto his stomach. Dwayne

pulled the sheet down below Marvin's knees, exposing the bandages that covered him from midthigh to the small of his back. Putting on a fresh pair of sterile gloves, he deftly cut away the bandages, revealing the raw flesh underneath.

"You really caught a load," he commented.

Marvin twisted on the sheets, trying to keep his johnson under his leg so it wouldn't hang out. Dwayne took notice of the kid's squeamish modesty and laughed to himself. Modesty was a luxury you gave up fast, once you were inside. This kid had some painful lessons to learn, if he got convicted.

Pouring antiseptic onto a gauze pad, he cleaned the wounded area thoroughly, gently prodding the pinpoint reddish holes to make sure there weren't any pockets of pus forming.

Marvin squirmed in discomfort. "Shit, man, not so hard."

Dwayne continued the steady probing. You better hope they don't send you to some hard-core joint like Durban, he thought. The boys there would eat you for lunch and wipe their ass with the remains, especially with a pecker the size of yours.

"Your wound looks pretty good," he said as he finished his cleaning. "You're healing up okay." He patted them dry with a clean pad. "How did you wind up with your ass shot full of bird shot?" he asked casually.

"Gun jammed," Marvin grunted.

"How did you get shot if the gun wasn't working?"

"*My* gun. There was two guns, mine and his. His worked fine."

"That's a bitch," Dwayne commiserated. He spread salve on the infected area, preparatory to bandaging. "What happened?"

Marvin looked at Dwayne over his shoulder. "How come you asking so many questions?"

"Friendly, that's all. You got to make friends in here, pal, or it's a long, lonely ride."

"Yeah?" He thought for a moment. "What're you in for?"

"Murder," Dwayne answered flatly.

Marvin's eyes widened. He flicked his lips with his tongue. "No shit."

"No shit." Dwayne laid cotton pads on the wounds, started bandaging over them.

"Where?" Marvin asked, unable to hold back his curiosity, even though he knew that wasn't cool. "When?"

"Six years ago. Downstate. No big thing."

"Jezuss!" Marvin whistled. He thought for a second. "How's come you're in here? Don't murderers do their time in the state pens?"

"I am," Dwayne said. "Durban."

Marvin nodded respectfully. This fucker had to be pretty bad if he was doing his time at Durban. Only the toughest hard-core felons were sent there. A few gangbangers from his hood had been sent up to Durban. Nobody had heard from them in a long time. "Why are you down here?"

"I'm a witness in a trial." Dwayne didn't elaborate.

Murder. Marvin chewed that over in his head.

"I've never killed anyone—yet," he confided to Dwayne, trying to impress this big-time con, pump up his own status. "But I would have, if that motherfuckin' gun hadn't jammed up on me."

"Yeah, that's too bad. Who was it you were going to shoot?"

Marvin told him his story of the botched robbery, skewed to make him look good—as good as he could. He described how cool he was, how scared the storekeeper was, how the storekeeper was begging him to spare his life. When he got to the climactic part he really laid it on thick, how his gun had jammed and the storekeeper had pulled out his shotgun and blasted him. Even so, with a humongous shotgun pointed at his stomach, he had almost managed to pull the weapon out of the owner's hands, but the owner had lucked out and managed to pull the trigger just before he could wrestle it away from him.

You don't get shot in the back if you're fighting over a gun, Dwayne thought. He kept the thought to himself.

He finished rebandaging Marvin's ass. "You're all set."

"Thanks, man." He carefully rolled over onto his back.

On the TV the Roadrunner had been replaced by Deputy Dog. "Do you mind if I change the channel?" Dwayne asked. "I like to keep up with the news."

Marvin liked Deputy Dog almost as much as he liked the Roadrunner, and he didn't give a shit about the news; he had never read a newspaper in his life, and the only time he saw the news on TV was when it was about something hot like the O. J. Simpson trial—but he wasn't about to say no to someone of Dwayne's stature. "Nah, I don't mind. I like to keep up with the news my own self."

Dwayne reached up and flipped through the channels (there was no remote control; such loose objects that could be used as weapons were verboten) until he came to one that had a local newscast in progress.

A woman field reporter was standing in the alley where Paula's body had been found. She was looking into the camera, talking to the anchors back at the station. Behind her there was a flurry of police activity.

"As you can see, Don and Lisa, the police are pulling out all the stops," the newscaster said, indicating the officers and detectives milling in a clusterfuck behind her. "The city is in an absolute panic over this latest killing because, as you noted, this victim doesn't fit the profile of the previous seven, although the method that was used clearly points to the Alley Slasher."

A police detective, his ID hanging from a chain around his neck, walked into the picture and stood next to the reporter.

"Joining me is Detective Dudley Marlow, who has been one of the lead detectives on this series of murders. What can you tell us about this one, Detective?"

"The victim has been identified as Paula Briggs," Marlow said. "She was last seen by two friends leaving the club here to get some air. That was the last anyone saw of her until the body was found this morning."

"Is this case the work of the Alley Slasher?" the reporter asked.

"Yes. There's no question."

A second detective came up and whispered in Marlow's ear.

"I have to get back there," Marlow told the reporter. He walked away.

A snapshot of Paula came up on the screen. She was smiling, posing for the camera. It looked like it was taken at a family barbecue, or on a hike. The newscaster spoke over the freeze-frame of the photo. "Paula Briggs was an employee of Marcus Meat Packing, and had been divorced for a year. Her ex-husband was unavailable for comment, but he is not a suspect. What we do know, which the police have conclusively established, is that she was not a prostitute. She had no criminal record, not even an outstanding traffic ticket."

Paula's picture was faded out, and the newscaster reappeared on the screen.

"This latest murder, the first one by the so-called Alley Slasher in five months, escalates these killings into another sphere."

One of the anchor's voices, a man's, spoke over the screen. "Is it possible that the killer mistook her for a prostitute?" he asked. "What was she wearing?"

"It's possible, yes," the field woman answered. "She was wearing an attractive dress. But if every woman who is dressed nicely, or even provocatively, is now fair game, that makes two-thirds of the women in this city eligible victims, and that's what has the authorities so concerned." She struck a serious pose. "From live at the murder site, back to you."

Marvin had been staring at the screen. "I know where that is," he said. "Where that lady was killed."

Dwayne turned to him. "How's that?"

"My old job was in that neighborhood," Marvin explained. "Shit, that store I tried to rob was only about two blocks away. I had to pass by that alley earlier that night to get to it."

Dwayne's curiosity was piqued. "You happen to see her?" he asked.

Marvin shook his head forcefully. "Fuck, no. I didn't see her. I didn't see nobody. I wasn't paying no attention to no bitches, I had a job of work to do."

That was a lie. He had seen one woman—the good-looking older bitch who had caught him checking out her car in the parking lot, the same parking lot where the murder took place.

He wasn't about to cop to that, though. Anyway, the woman he'd seen was white; the murdered one was black.

He was in enough trouble as it was. He wasn't about to admit that he knew anything about any murders that everyone in the city was all crazy about.

Wyatt sat in Walcott's office, recounting the events of his first day on the job. Josephine had joined them.

"Sounds like you had a busy day," Walcott commented dryly. "How do you feel?"

"Good," Wyatt answered. "I hate to admit that I have anything about the law to learn, but I do. Certainly this stuff. It's definitely a different life."

"I've been doing this over twenty years," Walcott said, "and I learn new things every case." He turned to Josephine. "How did he do?"

"He did fine." She smiled at Wyatt.

Wyatt picked up Marvin's file. "This armed robbery. There's something about it that doesn't seem right to me."

"You said he admitted to it."

"Yes, but—"

"Where are your extenuating circumstances?" Walcott interrupted.

"His age. It's his first adult offense. And he did get shot in the backside."

"Yes, that is something." Walcott paused.

"The other cases you've given me are cut-and-dried," Wyatt continued, pressing the issue. "I'd like to look deeper into this one."

Walcott nodded. "Okay. See if there's anything to bargain with. You'll help him out, won't you," he said to Josephine.

"I'll be glad to," she replied, smiling at Wyatt again.

Walcott stood, shook Wyatt's hand. "Welcome to the jungle."

Michaela had gone to Burger King and then the library to study with some friends, so Wyatt and Moira had dinner alone. It was a casual meal—Cloris, their longtime housekeeper, who did most of the cooking, had been given the night off, so Moira had prepared a simple dinner herself— grilled swordfish, baked potatoes, salad, a decent bottle of wine.

They hadn't talked about his first day on the new job. He'd come home, had a quick Scotch, and taken a shower. Then he'd sat alone in his study for half an hour, outlining his thoughts in preparation for this defense in front of him, the kid who had bungled a robbery so badly that he'd gotten himself shot in the ass. He'd stayed in the fading light, doodling free-form on a legal pad, until Moira stuck her head in and announced that dinner was on the table.

They sat across the rough-hewn pine dining table from each other. Two candles threw off soft diffuse light. Breaking the ice as she poured herself a small glass of wine, Moira asked in a calm, deliberate voice, "So how did it go?"

"It was a whole other world from anything I've known or lived in years."

She took a bite of swordfish. A little dry—she'd left it on the grill about a minute too long. Next time she'd do better.

"You read about this stuff in the paper, see it on the tube—the news, I mean, not those lawyer dramas, although you see it on them, too. . . ." He forked in a mouthful of fish, chewed, swallowed. He could have been eating anything; it didn't matter, he wasn't tasting it. He was somewhere else.

Moira felt a pang, a little pinging in her chest. It was a simple meal, but she'd put some time into it.

". . . but to be in it, it's really different, it's hovering, like being in a bazaar in Pakistan or something. All these people, talking a bunch of different languages." A gulp of wine, another hearty bite. He looked down at the plate. "This is good. Where did Cloris come up with"—he pointed to the dill butter, sitting in a little silver butter dish in the center of the table, halfway between them—"this?" He took another bite, this time chewing more slowly, with enjoyment and awareness. "Cloris didn't cook this, did she? You did."

She nodded. The pinging stopped.

He smiled at her, continuing where he'd left off. "So anyway, I felt—not like a real lawyer, I am a real lawyer, I'm as real a lawyer as you can find—engaged. That's the word."

"What did you do, exactly?"

"I plea-bargained a man down from multiple counts of grand theft to a single charge of possession of stolen goods. Instead of doing three years to five in state prison, minimum, I got him six months on the county farm." He beamed, flush with the memory of his first successful venture in his newly chosen arena.

Moira frowned. "Is that good? Wasn't the man guilty?"

"As hell!"

"Then why is that good?"

He stared at her. "What do you mean?"

"This man you defended . . ." She backed up, to make sure her thought process was clear. "What did he steal?"

"A bunch of purses from the lockers of the women's gym he works at."

"Purses?"

He nodded. "Credit cards, cash, driver's licenses, God knows what. It was a goodly haul—he didn't deal in halves."

"What if one of the wallets had been mine?" she asked after a moment's hesitation. "Or your daughter's?"

"It would've been lousy," he admitted, "but the stuff was recovered, and we are insured, like those women were. It's the price you pay for living in the end of the twentieth century, unless you want to move to North Dakota or wherever." He went at the meal with gusto: the work he had done today had created quite an appetite.

She laid her knife and fork on her plate—her own appetite had vanished. "He had their driver's licenses. He knew where they lived."

"I guess he did. I hadn't thought of that."

"He could have broken into their houses. He could have hurt them. Or even killed them. Like what happened next door," she said with agitation.

He hesitated in midbite, looked at her across the table. "Isn't that pushing it a little, honey?"

The pinging in her chest started up again. "Another woman was murdered downtown, a couple nights ago," she told him. "Did you know that?"

"Of course I knew." He'd read about it in the paper, seen a few clips on television, heard fragments of excited conversation. It hadn't registered as much as it normally might have—he was too wired with his own new stuff.

"This woman that was murdered," she continued. "What if that had happened to her?"

"What if what happened?"

"Some creep had stolen her wallet and found out where she lived and stalked her and killed her."

"I don't think it happened that way, Moira," he answered. He put his utensils down, too.

"It could have," she retaliated. "The point is—"

"The point is you don't think I should have defended this scumbag. Is that the point?"

She looked at him. Where were they, all of a sudden?

"Is that the point?" he asked her again. He brought his voice down several notches in volume.

"You said he was guilty," she managed to answer.

"Does that mean he doesn't deserve a defense?"

She didn't say anything.

"Only innocent people should be defended?"

She kept quiet.

"Sometimes it's hard to tell in advance," he reminded her.

She stood. "Let's not anymore, okay?" Her knees were shaking. She pressed them together.

"Babe, I'm not—"

"Let's not." She started to clear the table. He took her wrist, firmly but gently.

"Did I do something wrong?" he asked. "What did I do wrong?"

She put the dishes down. "Why are you doing this?"

"Doing what?"

"You know what."

"This kind of law?"

She sat down in the chair next to his. "Somebody out there is killing women, Wyatt. In this city."

"I know that. I told you, I saw the story."

"Maybe it's someone who knows them."

He shook his head. "They were prostitutes, that was the only thing any of them had in common."

"How do you know that? Anyway, that isn't true. They all knew this man, whoever he was that murdered them."

"Not necessarily." He didn't like the direction this conversation was taking. "The killer might have taken them completely by surprise."

"But he *might* have known them," she came back. "Or where they lived. Like this man you defended so well today."

He asked again: "Are you saying I shouldn't have defended him?"

"There are a lot of lawyers out there, you've said that yourself, they're reproducing like rabbits, that's your exact quote. It could have been me that was murdered, or Michaela, who is out there"—she pointed toward the window behind her—"in the dark. Right now."

*   *   *

He sat in the pool house, his legal pad on his lap. The trombone rested on its stand. He hadn't played it today, not one note.

Their conversation, discussion, argument—call it what you will—was still in his head. What could she want from him?

Was it the race thing? Moira came from a wealthy, conservative environment. When they had been young, the two of them starting out dating, she had gone to jazz clubs with him. It was exciting, foreign, strange to her, but she'd never developed the feeling for it that he had.

They hadn't gone to a jazz club together for decades.

Wyatt had always had an affinity for the black world. It came from his love of jazz, that was obvious. That love had led him to look at things with an open eye, which turned out to be a good thing, he'd always thought. Integration for him wasn't cerebral and abstract, it was essential and visceral. In a closed-off society, the way things were going today, he would have been denied that which he loved the most—the music. When he was young, in college and law school, he would go to jazz bars in black neighborhoods. Sometimes he'd be the only white person in the club, but he never felt uncomfortable or threatened.

He hadn't been to that kind of jazz club in years. He wasn't sure he'd be comfortable doing that anymore.

He picked up his trombone and sprayed some water on the slide. "Blue Bells of Scotland" was on the music stand, but he didn't feel like playing that kind of music tonight. Instead, he put a CD on the player, the Thelonius Monk quintet, an old Blue Note recording. As the master and his group swung into "Straight, No Chaser" he joined in, for the moment leaving the cares of the world behind.

The jailhouse doctor, a genial hack, made his rounds in the morning. He was a private physician who couldn't sustain a normal practice if it was handed to him on a silver platter, so he worked on contract to the city and various insurance companies, drank his lunch, and was useless for the rest of the day.

He peeled Marvin's bandages off and peered at his backside. "You're healing up fine," he pronounced after giving the wounds a cursory glance. "We'll be able to send you into the general population tomorrow." He took Marvin's temperature, pulse, and blood pressure, scribbled some indecipherable notes on the chart at the foot of the bed, and promptly left, leaving the rebandaging to the staff, which was Dwayne again.

The tattooed man applied fresh unguent to Marvin's pitted flesh, laid gauze strips over it, and secured them with adhesive bandages. The overhead television was tuned to a local news and talk show, talking heads droning on, the sound turned down to where it was barely audible. He glanced up at the TV as he worked. They were talking about the murder from two nights ago. The city really has a wild hare up their ass about this shit, he thought. So some fucking cooze got offed—big fucking deal. So she was another victim of some crazy serial killer. So what? Serial killers had been around forever.

Then he had another thought. Leaving the bandaging unfinished for a moment, he turned the TV up loud enough to hear. A remote shot of the alley—the murder site—came on the screen.

"You were there, were you?" Dwayne inquired of Marvin, pointing up to the set.

"Yeah. I was there."

He didn't like the way this dude was bandaging his behind. The way his hands moved, it was too friendly; you don't bandage someone and try to stroke their ass at the same time.

"Where is that, anyway?" Dwayne continued.

"It's back behind this bar, dance hall kind of place. The Happy Joker, it's called. Half a block off the corner of Braverly and Farraguet, over on the west side. Lot of hookers hang out in that neighborhood."

Dwayne paused. There hadn't been any mention of those streets on the news. The bar hadn't been identified, either. He was sure of that—it was the kind of specific detail he'd remember. He had a near-photographic memory for particulars like those: he used them when he took the stand in his testimonies at the various trials. Judges and juries were impressed with crap like that. He had spent years honing his mind that way, to advance his interests.

He fitted the last strip of bandage over the corner of a gauze pad. "You're all set," he told Marvin.

Marvin rolled over and sat up. "Thanks, man."

"You don't want to go into the population with a red ass," Dwayne told Marvin. "Might give some of them fellows the wrong idea 'bout you. Some of those clowns up there don't have any scruples whatsoever."

Marvin nodded. That was exactly what he was afraid of.

"One of the guards is a friend of mine, from prison," Dwayne said. "I'll put in a word for you."

Marvin regarded him with suspicion. "What do you want to do that for?"

"You've never been in jail before, have you? For real, in a regular jail, not in juvie or some such petty shit."

A glib, jive, tough answer started to roll off Marvin's tongue: he stopped it before it got out of his mouth. You don't bullshit this kind of heavy-duty character, he knew that much.

"Nah, I ain't," he admitted. "That's 'cause I ain't never been caught yet. As a adult," he clarified. "I have done some evil shit as a youth, but they can't use none of it against you in regular court."

"Which is lucky for you, I bet," Dwayne said. He glanced up at the TV again. "They're making one big stink about that."

"Seven women murdered. I guess so."

"And you were there."

"Yeah, I was." He looked up at the screen, where Dwayne was pointing. "Shit, man, I've been all over that part of town. I've been where every one of them bitches been killed," he bragged, trying to build up his stature, to give Dwayne a better feeling about him—that he wasn't just some young inexperienced punk, but closer to an equal, a force to be reckoned with. Not that anything he had ever done or could embellish would come close to someone who was doing his time for committing murder; but a force nonetheless.

"Oh?"

"I had this delivery route?"

Marvin knew that he was going to lie, that the words were going to come sliding out of his mouth like syrup from a bottle, smooth and easy, that he shouldn't be talking trash to this man, because no matter what he said, this one sitting here with him had done it and bettered it, a thousand times. But he couldn't help it, he had to brag on himself, status is everything, if you don't have some you're dead.

"This delivery route," he repeated. "It was all over the west side, from the river clear on out to the Jefferson Freeway."

"That's a lot of territory. How'd you get around—you have your own wheels?"

"Drove a delivery truck," he mumbled. Wearing a uniform that made him look like a damn UPS delivery man. He hated that fucking uniform, he always changed out of it before going home. Quickly changing the subject: "I know shit about those killings that nobody except the cops know. Shit you didn't never see on TV or newspapers."

"I'd keep that under my hat if I were you," Dwayne counseled. "You don't want the wrong people hearing you say things like that."

"Hey, I hear you." Marvin looked around to make sure no one was watching them. No one was—they were alone. "The deal was, this delivery route was just so I could have a legitimate reason to be there in those places, you hear what I'm saying? 'Cause I needed something to shield me from what I was really doing, you dig?"

Dwayne shook his head. "Doing what?"

"Dealin', man. What do you think?"

"Ah!" Dwayne waggled a "naughty-naughty" finger at Marvin.

"See, this delivery gig, that was chump change, man. I was making more damn coin in one minute dealing than in a whole week of delivering." His voice was rising in pitch as he got into his dream. "Thousands, man. I couldn't spend it fast enough. I got me a Rolex watch, the Navigator model, you ever seen it? It's pressurized down to a hundred and fifty fathoms."

"Must be pretty."

"It is, man, it truly is. And just last week I walked into this car dealer, Jeeps, ordered me up a Grand Cherokee, the Orvis model, leather on leather, car phone, CD, every damn thing. It's supposed to be coming in two weeks. I hope I'm out by then," he added forlornly.

"You'd better hope you've got a good lawyer."

"He seems good," Marvin said, recalling Wyatt. The lawyer had looked good; he was wearing an expensive suit, an expensive watch. "I only have met him one time so far."

Dwayne nodded. "Do you mind if I ask you a question that's kind of personal?"

"Like what?" Marvin said suspiciously.

"What's a major drug dealer who's pulling down thousands of dollars a week doing robbing a mom-and-pop convenience store?"

"Shit, man." Marvin came on indignant. "That wasn't no damn little store. That was a Mafia store. The Thai Mafia used that store as a numbers drop, there was over fifty thousand dollars in that store," he bragged, wildly inflating the illegal take. "You think I was going to rob some nickel-and-dime joint? Fuck no! This was major!"

A numbers drop, Dwayne thought. Could be—stranger things have happened. Look at what had happened for him, coming across Doris Blake like that. This was getting interesting. "You'd better hope the Thai Mafia doesn't have any members in here," he warned Marvin.

Marvin had had that very thought himself, ever since he'd awakened to find himself in the jail infirmary.

"This delivery route you had," Dwayne said, steering the conversation back to their earlier topic. "How long did you say you had that job? A year and a half?"

"Almost two. Started it right after I turned sixteen. I didn't want to have to go to my mama for spending money no more. That was before I got into making real money," he added hastily.

"Right," Dwayne agreed, massaging Marvin's ego. "It sounds like right after you started working those women started getting dead, in the same general area."

"This is true," Marvin said with a touch of braggadocio. "Actually," he added, dropping his voice conspiratorially, "I was right where some of those killings happened, right *when* they happened."

Egging the kid on: "You serious?"

"Shit yes, I'm serious!"

"Name one," Dwayne challenged him. "Unless you're bullshitting me, ace."

Marvin bristled. "You want to hear about one?" he asked, rising to the bait as Dwayne had known he would. "The third woman that was killed? I'll tell you something about her that wasn't in no newspapers, or on the TV, either. *She* was a *he*."

"A cross-dresser?" Dwayne was taken by surprise. This was a fresh twist.

"Full-blown transvestite, titties and everything. But she still had a cock. She was saving up to go in for the sex-change operation thing."

"How did you find out about that?" Dwayne asked.

"I heard some cops talking about it. Joking."

There was more Marvin knew—a lot more. It never ceased to amaze Dwayne how much people on the street knew that was never reported. Cops were always talking to people, trying to get information, dropping their own tidbits in return.

They talked for quite a while: Marvin did the talking; Dwayne listened and asked questions. He didn't have to probe much—the kid wanted to talk, to show off. He had good ears, and a strong memory for details.

"I wouldn't let these jailer folks in on how much of that stuff you know," Dwayne counseled Marvin. "Between what you've told me, and your being near that alley where this last one was done, you could be in for some serious grief."

"Don't worry, I ain't gonna. Besides, I wasn't around for most of them killings. I was with my friends—they'd stand up for me if anyone ever wanted to fuck me over about that shit."

"Well, you're clean then."

"Clean as a baby's ass."

Marvin lay back on his pillow. Between having a private lawyer who wore an expensive watch, and this badass in his corner, he was beginning to feel better.

Wyatt drove by himself to the scene of the crime. Josephine had been set to accompany him, but at the last minute she'd gotten bogged down with one of the other lawyers she serviced. The ratio in the Public Defender's office was one paralegal to fifteen lawyers—a 180-degree turnaround from his own firm, where the split was two assistants to each lawyer.

Normally an investigator would have done this kind of basic legwork. There were cases his firm handled—corporate espionage, allegations of massive fraud or money laundering, for example—in which the fees from the detective agencies alone would run over a million dollars. There were six investigators assigned to the Public Defender's office in total, not nearly enough to handle the massive caseload, and cuts in the city's budget were about to reduce that number to four.

Besides, he needed to get his hands dirty. Feel things firsthand.

He found a parking spot half a block from the store and locked his car with the remote. He was driving the Mercedes. Except for a couple of Japanese compacts it was the only foreign car on the block—everything else was solid working-class American sedans.

As he walked along the street he checked out the dingy little storefronts, at least a third of them boarded up and vacant. At one time a cozy old ethnic middle European neighborhood, the German, Yiddish, and Italian voices that rang through the streets with such authority and verve had long since given way to Spanish, Korean, Cantonese, and other tongues foreign to his experience.

Wyatt had grown up in the city. He didn't remember this particular street, but he most likely had been on it before, when he was a boy.

A bell over the door rang when he stepped inside the doorway, heralding his arrival. Anything you could buy here could be purchased cheaper at a supermarket, but the nearest supermarket was eight blocks away. For people who didn't have a car—a large percentage in this kind of neighborhood—or were older, eight blocks was too far away. Even people who did their big shopping at the large markets would stop in here when they needed four or five quick items—a loaf of bread, a quart of milk, a box of Tide—because it was fast and easy.

There were half a dozen customers in the store. All women, most of them Asian of one ethnicity or another. Wyatt meandered around, taking mental inventory.

As his roving eye looked up at the water-stained ceiling he noticed a video surveillance camera high on the back wall, tucked away in a corner. There was no light on to signify that it was recording, but it looked like the lens was contracting and expanding.

"Help you?" the Korean man behind the counter asked as Wyatt finally made his way to the register. Wyatt noticed that his accent was very strong.

"Do you have . . . Chap Stick?" Wyatt asked. He had to buy something, otherwise he'd be suspicious.

The man pointed to a bin nearby, where lip balms of various flavors were displayed. Wyatt picked up a strawberry-flavored tube.

"Anything else you want?"

Wyatt shook his head, dug into his pocket for his money clip. "This is a nice store," he commented pleasantly. "Are you the owner?"

The man grunted something unintelligible. "One eight-five," he quoted the price.

He was the owner, the one who had fired the shotgun. The description fit.

He handed the man a couple of singles. "Is this the store that was robbed the other night?" he asked offhandedly as he waited for the man to make change.

The owner looked up suspiciously. "Why you ask that?"

Wyatt shrugged. "It was on the late-night news. I was curious."

"Store not robbed," the man said, puffing out his chest. "I shoot robber."

"That took guts," Wyatt said admiringly.

"Not guts," the owner corrected him. "Brain." He pointed a finger to his temple. "No nigger boy rob me of my money."

"Good for you," Wyatt commended the man. It was time to go—he'd seen what he needed to see, and hearing this confirmed the suspicions that had come up when he had read the police reports. He glanced up at the video camera again—unless someone happened to see it by accident, as he had, it was almost impossible to notice. "Too bad your camera isn't working," he said. "You could've sold the footage to one of those reality shows on TV. You'd be a hero."

"No hero," the man shook his head. "No want to be on television." For a fast part of a second his lips cracked, almost in smile. "But camera work fine. Keep it where robber not know it there. Keep record if anyone else try to rob me and I can't stop them."

He turned away from Wyatt dismissively, giving his attention to a customer who had approached the counter with her shopping items.

"There's a surveillance camera?" Walcott asked. "That isn't in any of the police notes, is it?"

"No," Wyatt answered. "Which means the police don't know about it."

"Or they've seen it and there's nothing on it that serves their cause. In either case, it's good work." Walcott chucked Wyatt on the shoulder.

"I'm sure it would be exculpatory." Wyatt laid a rudimentary hand-drawn layout of the store on Walcott's desk. "Take a look at this floor plan I made." He traced his finger along the path from the front door to the counter. "I counted the steps from here to here. Eleven paces—that's over ten yards. A cannon couldn't blow someone Marvin's size that far, let alone a shotgun firing bird-shot pellets."

"The kid was running away when he was shot," Walcott said, getting the implication.

Wyatt nodded. "And here's the backup for that theory: there were no bloodstains anywhere inside the store. Not on the floor or on any of the counters. The only blood was outside, from where the kid landed on the sidewalk."

"Might be a good idea to subpoena those tapes," Walcott mused. "You don't think there's anything on them that could backfire on us, do you?"

"What difference would it make? He's going to be found guilty as things stand now; if these make us look bad we haven't lost anything, and if they help, they help."

Walcott turned to Josephine. "Type up a subpoena for the tapes from that evening, if there are any."

"Instead of just that evening, why don't we ask for a week of tapes?" Wyatt suggested. "If this really is a numbers drop, like our client claims it to be, that could be a nice negotiating chip."

Walcott smiled. "I like your style, Counselor."

The subpoena for the videotapes caught the prosecutor's office flatfooted. Walcott broke his best investigator free to accompany Wyatt and Josephine and ensure that the tapes didn't mysteriously become misplaced or erased. By the time a representative from the DA's office had arrived on the scene the location had been secured.

The deputy DA, a cynical middle-aged black woman, looked over the subpoena, shaking her head in displeasure. "Do what it says," she ordered the storekeeper sharply.

The Korean pulled the DA aside. They huddled away from Wyatt and his crew, talking animatedly. Wyatt watched as the deputy DA threw her hands up in disgust. "Do as it says," she told the store owner again, leaving the store with unseemly haste. "Exactly what it says—don't think about getting cute with anything." She shot Wyatt a murderous glance as she left.

They found the tapes in a storage room at the rear of the store, neatly lined up on shelves and labeled as to the date. Four to a day—the week for which the subpoena was certified covered thirty-two tapes in all. The detective stacked them neatly in a large cardboard box he had brought with him for that purpose, sealed the box, wrote out a detailed inventory of what they were taking, and gave it to the owner. They would be returned when the Public Defender's office was done with them; he couldn't say when.

Wyatt called Moira from his car to tell her he'd be working late and wouldn't be home for dinner. It was after seven when he led Josephine down the long, thickly carpeted hallway to his office. Over his shoulder he carried the heavy box of videotapes like a sack of potatoes. A few of his colleagues were still working, and he waved and smiled as he passed their open doors, but the place was pretty empty.

He had assumed they would be looking at the tapes at the PD's compound, but both video players were out of commission, so he moved the parade to his own office. That he was taking a temporary leave didn't mean he gave up his privileges. Besides, they could work more comfortably up here.

"This be it," he motioned, unlocking his office door and ushering her inside. Setting the box of tapes down next to a stressed pine cabinet that was situated against the far wall, he opened the doors to reveal a thirty-five-inch Sony and a host of equipment, including two VCRs, a laser-disc player, and a full CD stereo system on which he played his large in-town collection of jazz albums.

"Where's the sauna?" she cracked, pivoting to take in the full office and the views below.

"A floor above, where the gym is. Do you need a break?" he asked solicitously. "I was about to order in some dinner, so if you want to, go ahead. I'll let you in. We have steam, too, and a Jacuzzi. Whatever you like."

He was serious, she realized. Her attitude had gone right over his head.

"I forgot my bathing suit," she replied. "Next time."

"Anytime. It's open to everyone that works here, so it might as well get used."

He knew she felt she was out of her league. He'd only known her a short time and he was already fond of her. She was smart, feisty, attractive—very attractive, in an earthy, gutsy way—and he was sure she would make a first-rate lawyer.

He brought in a few menus from his reception area outside, tossed them to her. "Deli, pizza, Chinese. Your call. The deli isn't bad."

They ordered in dinner—she had gone for Chinese—and opened the box of tapes. "Here we go," she said, pulling out the tape that had the correct date and time of day on it and handing it to him. "You'd better run it—this machine is more complicated than the ones I'm used to back in steerage."

"I'll bet you're smart enough to figure it out once you've watched me do it," he parried, slipping the tape in and turning it on.

The tableau they began watching was shot with the one fixed camera, with a fish-eye lens that took in the entire store. No sound. Most of the time nothing happened. The store was empty except for the Korean owner, stoically standing behind his counter. Then a customer, an older Asian woman, came in and started walking around the aisles, dropping items into a shopping basket. A second Asian woman came in shortly after, doing the same thing. The women didn't acknowledge each other. The first paid for her items, the owner bagged them, made her change, she left. Same thing with the second. The most crowded the store got at any one time was less than a dozen customers.

Josephine pointed. "There's our boy!"

The camera looked down on Marvin walking into the store, peering furtively over his shoulder.

"Brimming with confidence," Josephine remarked, jotting down the time-code number for future reference.

There were two other people at the counter ahead of Marvin, who patiently waited in line while they finished their transactions. As they watched, the Korean slapped a pack of cigarettes on the counter in front of Marvin, hesitated, then replaced it with a different pack from the rack behind him.

"I'll bet that owner's motto is 'The customer is never right,'" Josephine said. "Especially when the customer is black."

Wyatt nodded. On the screen the Korean gave Marvin his change. Marvin left the store, looking around as he did—obviously checking it out.

"Well, we know he was there," Josephine commented dryly.

"More than once. Not good. That implies planning—criminal intent."

"Yes," she answered soberly.

He fast-forwarded the tape. The people in the store moved around like actors in silent movies, everything herky-jerky. The intercom buzzed. He put the tape machine on hold, picked up the telephone. "Yes, that's ours. Send him up."

The delivery boy deposited the bags of food on the coffee table. Wyatt went to his secretary's station and brought in plates, napkins, and silverware, signed for the food, and tipped the boy in cash. "Drinks in there," he told her, pointing to a cabinet on the far wall. "Refrigerator behind the door. I'll drink whatever's there, as long as it's nonalcoholic."

When they worked this late at the Public Defender's office they drank beer, courtesy of Joe Taxpayer, whose interests they were defending. She took out a couple Snapples. There had been beer in the refrigerator, Beck's and Urquell, and some bottles of white wine that looked expensive. When you have an office like this, she thought, you don't drink the cheap stuff.

They loaded up their plates while watching the screen. With the tape speeded up it didn't take long for Marvin to make his next entrance.

Suddenly, they put their plates down and got serious: the gun was out of Marvin's pocket, pointing in the owner's face.

They viewed the incident all the way through, then rewound the tape and looked at it again. Then a third time. As the owner fired his shotgun, Wyatt put the recorder on pause.

"He had his gun to the man's head," Josephine commented. "You can't deny that."

"But you can't even see Marvin White," Wyatt countered; "he's so far away he isn't even in the picture." He got up and walked to the television, bending over to get a closer look. "I had a sense that the owner was lying. The kid was out the door, turned away from him." He pointed to the set. "This proves it, in living black and white."

"You're right," Josephine said. "Although I don't know how a jury would feel, seeing a young kid pointing his gun at an older man."

"We need to make a copy of this for protection."

"I'll get it done first thing tomorrow morning," she promised. Then she expressed a thought: "Why isn't that video camera in plain sight? The point is supposed to be to discourage people like Marvin from robbing you. If the camera isn't visible, it isn't doing its job. Is it?"

Wyatt snapped his fingers—the puzzle was coming into focus. "You are a smart lady," he praised her. "Self-defense is why that owner shot Marvin, all right," he mused, "but not from some scared kid who's hightailing it out the door." He crouched down at the box containing the tapes, looked at the times and dates on the end labels.

"What're you looking for now?" she asked.

"The kid said the store was a numbers drop. Mondays and Fridays are the days the winners are paid off, so if that's true

they'd collect on Sunday and Thursday, probably at night."
He pulled another tape out. "Here's the previous Thursday
night, nine until one in the morning, closing time."

They ran the tape on fast-forward. The scene was similar
to what they'd been watching, minus Marvin White.

About halfway through, a piece of business caught Wyatt's eye. He slowed the tape to regular speed.

Two uniformed cops came into the store, waved to the
owner in greeting, and went over to the drink cooler, taking out a six-pack of root beer. Then they helped themselves
to a couple of premade sandwiches, an assortment of fruit,
and finally a carton of cigarettes, one of the cops reaching
around the owner to get them from behind the counter. They
talked for a few moments with the man, who nodded,
shrugged, shook the hand of one of them, and gave them a
paper bag to put their stuff in. They sauntered out without
paying.

"Interesting," Wyatt commented.

"So they helped themselves to a few freebies," Josephine
said. "It's no big deal."

"It's against the law."

"So's jaywalking. You want to go to jail for crossing
against the light?"

"That's not the point," Wyatt said. "You met that
owner—he wouldn't comp his mother a bag of potato chips,
let alone give twenty-five dollars of free merchandise to a
couple of beat cops."

"So why is he?"

"To look the other way, maybe." He set the machine to
fast-forward again.

They didn't find what they were looking for until near the
end of the tape.

"Back up!" Josephine said excitedly, spotting the action.

Wyatt rewound the tape and slowed it to normal. They
watched the screen intently, leaning forward.

The store was empty. Then the two cops who'd been in
earlier walked through the door, followed a moment later
by a young man of Asian origin, wearing the street uniform
of white T-shirt, khakis, combat boots, and an Oakland
Raiders cap turned backward. He shut the door behind him
and rotated the sign on it from Open to Closed, while the

cops took positions near the windows, to keep an eye on the street.

As the Asian approached the counter the Korean owner was already opening the back cabinet and taking out a manila envelope and a canvas bank bag, the kind that has a lock built into it. The young bagman opened the envelope and looked at the slips while the Korean was unlocking the bank bag. He handed the bag to the courier, who reached in, pulled out a handful of bills, rifled through them with his thumb, put them back.

The men exchanged a few words; something the bagman said made the owner laugh.

"Gee, he's human after all," Josephine remarked.

On the screen, the two men had finished their transaction. The bagman gave the cops some bills, and they left. He waited a couple minutes; then he, too, exited the store, helping himself to a Coke on the way out.

After he was gone the owner locked and bolted the door, shut off the lights, and left the room.

Wyatt ejected the tape and shut the set off. "By the balls," he crowed. "And with the city's finest riding shotgun!"

"Why would they tape their own illegal actions?" Josephine asked.

"Quality control. Make sure there's no skimming." Quickly crossing the office, he picked up the phone, speed-dialed. "Hi," he said after a beat, "did I wake you? I'm sorry, babe, I got involved, I lost track of the time." He listened. "On a case." Another moment. "No, by myself," he said, glancing in Josephine's direction, who was studiously looking out the window at the lights far below. "You, too. Good night." He hung up. "I don't like her worrying," he told Josephine's back. "Come on. I'll walk you downstairs."

The car-service Buick was waiting at the curb. The driver hopped out and opened the passenger-side back door.

"What's this?" she asked.

"Your ride."

"Are you paying for this?"

"Company policy. A woman works past seven-thirty, we give her a ride home."

"I don't work for your company."

"You're working with me. This is the way I work."

"You're going to spoil me," she said.

"Is that so bad?" He smiled at her, to try to put her at ease.

"In six months you'll be a memory as far as the Public Defender's office is concerned and this nice car will turn into a pumpkin again."

He hadn't been thinking along those lines. "Let's get through the rest of this week," he soothed her. "Six months is a long time from now."

She slid into the car, looked up at him. "Thank you."

"You're more than welcome. See you mañana."

The driver closed the door, got behind the wheel, and headed off down the street. Wyatt watched from the curb until the car was out of sight.

"**I** scratch your back, you scratch mine, no?" Dwayne asked Doris Blake.

They were in the infirmary. It was night.

An idea had come to Dwayne that afternoon, which he needed to act on while he could. In a couple more days he'd be testifying at trial, and as soon as he was done they'd ship him back to Durban.

"I'll scratch your back anytime," she purred.

They had already fucked. Half-dressed, they sat in the shadows, on the bed that had been Marvin's. His back was against the wall; she rested against his chest. In the dim light his tattoos radiated off him like phosphorescent holograms.

Whenever possible, Dwayne kept the lights off when he was with Doris Blake—the less he actually looked at her, the better. When he was screwing her he could close his eyes and imagine the sexiest, most erotic women in the world; but when that was over he had to open them and look at what was real, which right now wasn't the most appetizing of pictures.

From Blake's standpoint, being caught flagrante delicto with an inmate would be ruinous. It was a chance, though, that she was willing to take; once they were in actual copulation nothing else mattered.

"Do me a favor?" he asked her casually.

"You know I will."

"Do you have your computer with you?"

"It's in my office."

"I need to use it tonight. You can come get it in the morning."

"What do you want it for?" she asked, warning bells going off inside her head.

"I need to access some information on this case I'm down here testifying for," he told her. "This chickenshit law library doesn't have hardly anything I need."

"You aren't going to do anything . . . *illegal* . . . are you?"

"I'm not going to do anything that'll get you in trouble, if that's what you're worried about," he told her bluntly. "And it's late in the day to be worrying about the consequences of our actions, isn't it?"

"I . . ."

"I don't mean this," he said, a hand cupping her ponderous breast, his fingers feathering the wrinkled nipple, which immediately began stiffening. He leaned forward and lightly bit the back of her neck, which caused spasms and shivering all up and down her body. "We're talking about two people who care for each other and want to help each other, that's all." The hand on her breast was moving down her body, past her waist to her turgid pussy. He stuck one finger in, then another. "You do care about me, don't you? You do want to help me."

She moaned, her behind wriggling on the bed in rhythm with the movement of his hand inside her.

"Yes," she breathed. "I want to help you."

Thelma Fuller, the deputy DA Wyatt had encountered in the store, sat next to him in one of the two chairs facing Walcott's desk. Her expression was grim. The three had just come from watching the incriminating videos in the Public Defender office's conference room—Wyatt had commandeered a VCR from his own office to run the tapes.

"What's your pitch?" Fuller asked Walcott, pointedly ignoring Wyatt.

Walcott extended his arm to Wyatt. "Mr. Matthews is the

attorney in this case. Talk to him." He leaned back in his chair, arms behind his head, a grin lighting up his face.

The woman looked at Wyatt. "I'm listening."

"You've got a middle-aged Asian immigrant who shoots a young African American in the back. The kid has no record, and he had his back to the shooter. You saw that with your own two eyes."

"Are you planning on playing a race card here?" she asked, her voice rising in anger.

"These are facts," he retorted. "And the larger community does come into play, let's not pretend it doesn't. We have an illegal gambling operation captured on film. And it's their own film, there's no sting involved, they stung themselves. And we have cops taking bribes, also on film."

"Let's cut to the chase," Fuller said.

"We don't file suit for wrongful assault, police Internal Affairs can deal with their own people, and you've got the tapes to prosecute on the numbers stuff. Hey, you threaten to deport this guy, he might give up the heavies he works for."

"What do we give you in return?"

"You drop the charges."

Fuller came out of her chair. "Never in a million years! Marvin White stuck a loaded gun in a man's face. It goes off, we're talking murder one. I can't let that slide."

"Okay. Try this, then. A year's probation, a hundred hours of community service, and he has to go back and finish high school."

"A year on the honor farm, two hundred hours, plus the high school diploma," she parried.

"Two years probation, a hundred hours, high school. No jail time beyond what he's already served."

"The kid's a scumbag," Fuller protested. "He has to do some time. Sober him up, show him what he has to look forward to the rest of his life if he keeps going down this path."

Wyatt shook his head. "You're not his mother, his shrink, or his priest. No jail."

"You want to come out of the gate hot, don't you? That's what this is all about."

He smiled at her. "You've got a guilty plea. Save the taxpayers some money. Take it."

She snatched her purse up off the floor. "I'll check this

out with the powers that be and get back to you." She walked out the door, slamming it behind her.

"And a pleasant day to you, too," Wyatt called after her.

"**T**his is Detective Dudley Marlow, homicide division." Dwayne remembered the name on the news, from where they'd found that last body. If this guy was heavy enough to honcho that case, he'd have access to every file in the police department.

"Yes, Detective. What can I do for you?" The woman's voice at the other end indicated to Dwayne that she knew who Marlow was, and that he was important.

"I need to review some files," Dwayne said over the telephone, camouflaging his voice. "I'll access them over the line here, into my computer. Would you set that up for me, please?"

"Yes sir. It'll just take a few minutes. I'll need your badge number for verification."

The cop had only been on the television screen for a few seconds, but that had been long enough for Dwayne to have locked the badge number into his brain.

He gave her the badge number. There was a moment of silence, then she said, "Thank you, Detective Marlow. What files were you looking for?"

He told her. A few moments later, he began downloading the files.

Dwayne was a thorough worker. It was almost dawn when he was finished reviewing the material to his satisfaction, so that it was indelibly burned into his memory. Then he very carefully hid the information in a program he knew Blake would never use. There was a bit of danger to that, but he wanted to keep the stuff available, in case he'd ever need to refresh his memory on a particular detail.

Blake slipped into the infirmary before seven. "Did you get the information you were looking for?" she asked.

"Everything I needed."

"You didn't do anything that could get me into trouble, did you?" she asked fretfully, slinging the computer over her shoulder.

He shook his head. "Not to worry—protecting you protects me. We're partners, Doris." He gave her a friendly smooch on her cheek, patted her ass. "Better get going—you shouldn't be seen down here alone with me this early in the morning."

"I'll come down later," she told him. "When I'm done work."

"I'll be waiting," he smiled. "I ain't going nowhere."

The blackboard on the wall of the visitors' waiting area had the rules posted in English and Spanish. Wyatt read them.

VISITING AREA RULES
1) No physical contact.
2) No passing of objects.
3) No food or drinks.
4) Prisoners sit across from visitors.
5) No objects on the table.
6) Hands must stay on top of table.
7) Children must remain seated on lap.
8) Violations may lead to loss of visit rights and more jail time.
9) All rooms are on camera.

He was there to meet Marvin's mother, Jonnie Rae Richards. After he talked with her they'd both meet with Marvin. He wouldn't discuss anything with his client that could breach the attorney-client privilege, but he wanted to see them together, get a feeling for their dynamic.

It was Saturday morning, and the place was packed. Almost all the visitors were women, and most of them had two, three, or more young children in tow, the kids running around the large central waiting room, playing with toys, crayons, and coloring books that the jail provided. It was noisy as hell, everyone talking, yelling, laughing, complaining. Most of the women were black, he noticed, with a good smattering of Latinas. The few white women were rough-looking blue-collar types, biker mamas and Southern redneck ladies. If there were any white-collar inmates, they weren't being visited by their friends and families.

There was a big hand-lettered warning posted over the door through which all visitors passed. Three lines: NO GANG CLOTHING. NO SIGN-THROWING. NO FIGHTING. Wyatt noticed a few males, young adults, in the mixture. Except for two Latinos and one white, who wore biker colors in defiance of the regs, they were black.

He'd driven in from home, and since it was the weekend he was dressed casually, although he wore a sports coat, which was more dressed than he would have been if he'd been meeting a corporate client. He wanted the boy and his mother to know they were getting decent representation, not being shuffled around in the system.

As a lawyer with an appointment, Wyatt had priority—they met in one of the rooms reserved for lawyers, where they could talk freely. It was an open secret that conversations in the regular visiting rooms were taped. He guessed the woman's age to be under thirty-five.

"I'm Mr. Matthews, Mrs. Richards," he said, introducing himself and shaking her hand. "I'm Marvin's lawyer." She was starchy-overweight, but she had a pretty face. She was alone.

She took a good, hard look at him. "How bad is it for that boy?"

"Not as bad as I originally expected it would be. He isn't going to have to go to jail."

"Not go to jail?" She clearly didn't believe him.

"We agreed on an appropriate punishment, the district attorney's office and I," Wyatt explained. "He will be on probation for two years, and he'll be assigned community service, and most importantly, he'll have to finish high school and get his diploma. If he doesn't, they can pull the offer and then he will have to do his time, so he'll have plenty of incentive to stay in school and finish up there. And he can't hang out with any of his buddies who are shady characters."

"I don't see none of that happening," she said, looking him square in the face.

"Why not? It sounds reasonable to me."

"That boy is a gangbanger, Mr. Lawyer. He don't know nobody that ain't no shady character."

"If he goes back to school he can make new friends," Wyatt argued. "One of the conditions of his probation is that he lives with you and stays clean."

"I've already kicked his sorry ass out," she informed him.

"I know. He told me. But if the alternative is jail, won't you take him back in? Give him another chance?"

"Another chance? You know how many chances I've given this boy?"

"More than a few, I'm sure. But this time the stakes are higher, he has more reason . . ." He was going to say "incentive," then caught himself; maybe she wouldn't know that word, and immediately he chastised himself inwardly. Why did he think that, except that she was poor and black? Continuing: ". . . more incentive to do good."

"You should have let him go to jail," she said. "Made a man of him."

He felt a prick of displeasure—what had he worked so hard for if it wasn't appreciated?

She picked up on his distress. "I'm running my mouth too much, that what you think? I got three younger ones at home, Mr. Lawyer, and I'm working two jobs to keep us off welfare and I ain't got no time to baby-sit no eighteen-year-old whose only ambition in life is to be dealing crack and driving some fancy car."

The jail-side door opened before Wyatt could come up with a suitable reply. A deputy escorted Marvin in, exited, and locked the door behind him. Marvin slouched into his chair.

"Hello, son. How they treating you?" Mrs. Richards asked brusquely.

Marvin shrugged. "Good enough."

"Mr. Matthews here tells me you ain't gonna have to serve any time. He did good by you, Marvin."

"Yeah, I know."

"I hope you appreciate what he's worked out for you."

"Yeah, I do." His eyes were looking down at the floor, unable to meet her own.

Wyatt explained what was going to happen. They were going to court on Monday morning. Marvin would plead guilty to a single count of robbery, but the armed part of it was being dropped. The DA's office would present their plea bargain to the judge, and Marvin would walk out of the court and go home.

"And if you fuck up, you'll find your ass right back in here," his mother said emphatically, leaning toward Marvin across the table.

"He isn't going to mess up," Wyatt said. "Are you?"

"Nah."

"You're going back to school, get a new job, and help your mother out."

"Yeah. That's what I'm gonna do."

He'd say whatever he had to. Once he was out, that was another story.

Two visitation rooms over, Dwayne was meeting with Galeygos, his lawyer. "I hope this is good," Galeygos said. "I'm passing up a free lunch with a client who has actual cash dollars to pay me."

Dwayne was sitting perfectly still and yet he seemed to be vibrating, his aura was so strong. Allowing himself a tight, controlled smile, he asked his lawyer, "What we were talking about before—what I have to do to get them to knock down what I'm serving, forget what's ahead, and let me walk out a free man?"

"Yeah?" Galeygos was already rueing his decision to pass up that free lunch. There would have been a couple of premium bourbons to go with it.

"You said solving the crime of the century would probably do it? You remember saying that?"

"Yes." Galeygos was salivating, thinking about that lost lunch. He could wrap this up now and call that other client, still make the lunch date.

Dwayne leaned forward and kept his voice low, in case the deputies were monitoring the conversation, even though it was against the law to, and they told you they didn't: "Listen up careful to what I'm about to tell you, and then you can decide where we go with it."

"Before we begin," Galeygos said, puffing up like a peacock, "I want to lay out some ground rules."

He and Dwayne were in an interview room in Alex Pagano's suite of offices on a Sunday afternoon. Alex Pagano was the district attorney. Pagano was an ambitious man—it was an open secret that he was going to run for the House next year, and eventually for either the Senate or the governorship.

Galeygos and Dwayne were with the man himself and his chief aide, the number-one deputy DA. Since Pagano was a politician, his assistant ran the office on a day-to-day basis. Pagano did the heavy lifting: press conferences, approving and strategizing on major cases, getting reelected.

Galeygos had been his usual skeptical self as he had listened to Dwayne the day before; but after spending a couple of hours with his client the lawyer had gotten on the phone and browbeaten Pagano's office into meeting with them.

Dwayne, wearing his hospital whites, had been transported from the jail across the street. He wasn't handcuffed, but two sheriff's deputies were standing right outside the door.

"Go ahead," Pagano said, eyeballing Dwayne.

"All pending and outstanding charges against my client will be dropped," Galeygos stated. "His present sentence will be commuted to time served. He will be put in the Witness Protection Program, his records will be sealed, and he will be given one hundred thousand dollars, which he will use to start up his new life."

He handed his list of demands to Pagano, who passed it to his assistant without reading it. "How about a Rolls-Royce and a villa in the south of France, as long as we're asking for the moon?" the DA deadpanned.

"Do we have a deal or do we not?" Galeygos asked belligerently.

"We could give him early release and have any pending state charges dropped," Pagano said, looking to his assistant, who nodded in agreement. "The rest of it I have to coordinate with the Justice Department. You have my assurance we will act in good faith and do the best we can."

Galeygos looked to Dwayne.

"If the man here tells me he'll do his best, that's good enough for me," Dwayne said airily.

"That's *if*—I want to emphasize the word *if*—what you tell us leads *directly*—emphasize that word, too—to a grand jury indictment and a trial," the deputy DA cautioned. He looked to his boss, who nodded his agreement.

"Fair enough," Galeygos told him.

Monday morning. Wyatt was up, showered, dressed, and out of the house by 6:15, long before Moira and Michaela were awake. Even though the Marvin White case was all settled, he still had great anticipation, and he couldn't help relishing the sense of satisfaction he felt over the way he'd discovered the incriminating tapes. He might be new at this forum, but good lawyering was good lawyering, regardless of the specific arena.

He stopped downtown at his favorite Greek deli for coffee and a bagel and arrived at the courthouse a little after seven. Court went into session at nine. He had the morning paper with him—he was going to finish the sports and financial sections and reread his motions once, to make sure there were no last-minute glitches.

It was almost empty outside the courtroom; a few other earlier arrivals were scattered the long length of the corridor. He sat on an empty bench and took the motion out of his briefcase.

"Hey, sport. Fancy meeting you here."

Wyatt looked up from his paperwork in surprise. "Hello, Alex," he said.

"What is this cockamamy crap I'm hearing?" Alex Pagano teased Wyatt, plunking down next to him. Pagano was wearing one of his $2,200 custom-fitted Hickey-Freeman pinstripes—he was always prepared to look good for a camera. "Since when did you become a defense lawyer for the downtrodden?" he asked. "Saving corporate America from themselves isn't a big enough arena for you?"

Wyatt smiled without answering. Alex and he were social acquaintances; both were powerful players in their respective arenas, and occasionally served together on various blue-ribbon ABA ventures. "What's going on to warrant your showing up at twenty after seven on a Monday morning?" he asked Alex.

"Pursuing justice, of course. Wherever and however it might rear its benighted head." He cuffed Wyatt lightly on the shoulder. "Watch where you're stepping in these hallowed halls. It gets slimy down here. You wouldn't want to slip and fall on your million-dollar ass."

Wyatt looked at him with a bemused expression, but didn't respond to that gibe, either. Pagano stood up, made a show of checking the time, then walked away around the corner.

Wyatt watched him. What was that all about? he thought. Alex Pagano hadn't run into him in an empty courthouse corridor at 7:15 in the morning by accident. Alex was a devious conniver—there was a purpose to every move he made. And why the mocking, the empty words of warning?

Nine o'clock. The courtroom was full. Wyatt sat with Marvin's mother. Other lawyers and defendants' families were scattered around the room, waiting for their cases to be called.

He'd gone over the deal carefully. Everything was in order. The woman had been nervous, which was to be expected. Even though she knew her son had done what he was accused of, she was still his mother. She still had hope for him.

In the back of the chamber, half a dozen young black men and a couple of girls, all Marvin's age, had congregated. Jonnie Rae pointed them out to Wyatt.

"His so-called entourage," she commented with scorn. "Bunch of damn fools, just like him."

Wyatt looked them over. Tough-looking kids. He didn't know what gang clothing or colors were, but they all looked like they were in some kind of informal uniform—long sagging shorts and pants, high-top Nikes, red-checked handkerchiefs tied around their heads à la Deion Sanders. Both girls wore tight hip-huggers and tank tops, and were braless. One girl had at least a dozen earrings in her ears and nose, and through her thin top he could see the outline of another earring in a nipple. A couple of the boys waved greetings to Jonnie Rae, who pointedly ignored them.

He should bring Michaela down here, he thought as he watched them giggling and grab-assing. She should know how the rest of the world lives; seeing this side of life firsthand, instead of viewing it through the safe prism of a television set, would be beneficial in some undefinable but meaningful way. She might even enjoy it, watching her dad in action. She had no real idea of his work—it was too complicated; even he found it boring and unfathomable when he tried to explain a case to Moira. But this stuff, down in the trenches, that they could understand and appreciate, even enjoy.

A side door opened. A bailiff led the morning's defendants into the courtroom. Officially innocent until proven otherwise, they were nevertheless in orange jail-issue jumpsuits, joined in a line to each other by light waist chains so that one deputy could wrangle the entire herd.

Marvin was situated in the center of the pack. As he saw his friends in the back of the room he raised a hand and flashed a sign. Immediately, a deputy sheriff stepped over to him and said something in his ear. Marvin nodded and dropped his hand; but he was smiling.

The court deputies removed the chains that bound the prisoners together. They were seated shoulder to shoulder in the front row behind the lawyers' tables.

Wyatt glanced around. The kids were grinning, like they were members of a secret society. He realized with a start that they were, and that he didn't know anything about it.

It would be good for Michaela to bring her down here, yes; but he was the one that really needed the education. He was going to be representing clients who lived in a world that was completely alien to him, and if he was going to do the proper job for them he had to know and understand that world.

First things first. Put this case to bed. Go to school later on.

As he looked more closely at Marvin's friends he saw that one of them—a boy roughly Marvin's age—was with the group, but not of it. He was standing as far apart from the others as possible while still being in the same space.

He was interesting looking. Unlike the others, he wasn't big and tough-looking. He was, in fact, rather small, almost diminutive. He was wearing an expensive conservative suit, what a rich Ivy League professor or Wall Street colleague of Wyatt's would wear. Unlike the Wall Streeter or professor, however, this kid had three or four garish rings on his fingers, each studded with a large authentic-looking stone. A large emerald glittered in his left ear. Paper-thin-soled Italian shoes, a bespoke English broadcloth white-on-white dress shirt, and a silk tie that had to have cost at least $150 rounded out his wardrobe. He lounged with his back to the wall, casually looking over the proceedings with a comfortable air.

He's got to be a dealer or a pimp, Wyatt figured. No eighteen-year-old kid dresses and acts like this otherwise.

"All rise. This court is now in session, the honorable Alfonse Arcaro presiding."

The aged jurist laboriously climbed up onto his chair. "Call the first case," he rasped.

Wyatt had checked the morning's docket earlier. They were fourth up. The first three cases were simple; they would be finished and out of here in less than an hour.

As the third case was being settled, Thelma Fuller, the assistant DA handling the case, whom Wyatt had met earlier, came into the courtroom and took a seat at the prosecution table. As she passed Wyatt, seated on the aisle in the spectators' section, she gave him a fleeting, almost mocking smile.

Alex Pagano entered on her heels, accompanied by his chief deputy and another official-looking man. They strode up the center aisle, passed through the gate separating participants from spectators, and sat down next to Fuller.

A low buzz went up in the room. Judge Arcaro looked down from his perch, interrupting the case in progress.

"Good morning, sir," he greeted Pagano cheerily. "It's nice to see you this morning."

"Always a pleasure to be in your distinguished courtroom," Pagano replied. He turned and looked back at Wyatt for a moment, making sure they made eye contact. Then he directed his attention to the front of the room.

An alarm instantly went off inside Wyatt's head: something is wrong. And somehow, it involved him.

The case ahead of them was concluded.

"Call the next case," Arcaro said.

"People versus Marvin White," read the clerk of the court.

Wyatt walked forward and took the vacated seat of the lawyer ahead of him. He took the proper documents from his briefcase and laid them neatly on the table in front of him. He remained standing. The bailiff led Marvin to the table, where he stood next to Wyatt.

Across the two-foot divide, Fuller stood in place. There was nothing in front of her—no documentation, nothing.

"Are you ready to proceed?" Arcaro asked.

"Yes, Your Honor," Wyatt responded. He turned to Fuller—since they had agreed upon a plea bargain, it was her responsibility to introduce it to the judge.

She didn't say anything; instead, Pagano stood up next to her. "We have a complication in this particular case," he stated, glancing over at Wyatt. "We ask that the defendant be bound over for another forty-eight hours."

Wyatt responded like he'd been shot out of a cannon. "On what charge? The prosecution and the defense have agreed upon a resolution of this case, Your Honor. They've given us no cause to agree to any extension. In fact, this is the first I've heard of it."

Pagano ignored him, focusing on the bench. "As defense counsel knows, this situation involves potential implications and charges that could be far-reaching and consequential," he said. "We may have need of this defendant in the next two days. It's important that he be immediately available to us."

"Your Honor, I strongly object to this. The prosecution gave us their word on a plea and now they want to change it around, and they haven't explained their request."

Arcaro cocked an eye at Pagano.

"Some new evidence just came to us, Your Honor," Pagano said smoothly. "We will be happy to share it with defense counsel; we haven't had the time yet, we're still sorting it out."

"That is absolutely—" Wyatt began.

Arcaro cut him off: "Objection overruled," he decreed. "The defendant will be bound over until Wednesday morning at this time." He peered down at Pagano, a bantam eagle on his perch. "You'd better have your ducks lined up, sir."

"We will, Your Honor. Or we'll abide by our previous agreement, to the letter."

"Request immediately release on personal recognizance," Wyatt demanded.

The judge nodded. "Any objections?" he asked Pagano.

"Yes, Your Honor. The defendant has a lengthy juvenile record, and he is at this time unemployed. In addition, he presently has no permanent address, as he has been kicked out of his house by his responsible parent. We ask bail should stay at what it was originally set."

"Objection!" Wyatt called out again.

"Overruled!" Arcaro answered, equally loud. "Bail will remain set at twenty thousand dollars." He banged his gavel down, hard. "Next case."

Fuming, Wyatt watched as Marvin was led out to be returned to the jail.

"Don't worry," he told Marvin. "You'll be out of here the day after tomorrow."

He didn't bring up the issue of bail. Twenty grand—two thousand to the bondsman. They might as well have asked for a million.

"What was that all about?" Jonnie Rae Richards asked in bewilderment as Wyatt escorted her from the courtroom. "You said it was all taken care of."

"There's a problem with the police," he told her. He had to be careful; she couldn't know of the existence of the tapes—that information couldn't go out into the community; it was too inflammatory. "Marvin might have to be a witness."

"But why does he have to stay in jail then?"

"Given his history, they're afraid he'd get scared and take off. Don't worry—he's walking out of that courtroom on Wednesday morning. You have my word on that."

He watched as she got on the elevator to leave. Then he went looking for Pagano. The DA was waiting for him outside the courtroom.

"What are you trying to pull?" Wyatt demanded of him.

"Calm down, Wyatt."

"Calm down my rosy-red. We had a deal."

"Step into my office." Pagano put a hand on Wyatt's arm and led him around the corner into the well of the staircase, looking around to make sure no one was watching them. "Something heavy's come up. I need for you to play ball with us on this. I have to keep him on ice for another forty-eight hours."

"What's different all of a sudden?"

"Give me forty-eight hours." Pagano leaned in. "If I don't have what I'm looking for, he walks out as agreed. On the square. But I can't let him go; not right away."

"Is this about the numbers stuff? Cops on the take? My guy isn't involved in any of that. You want to prosecute there, fine, that's not up to me. But cut my client loose. A deal's a deal, and I expect you to honor that."

"There's more to this than meets the eye," Pagano repeated, deliberately evasive.

"Why didn't you bring this stuff up then? This isn't the way lawyers I'm used to dealing with treat each other," he added, reminding Pagano of the level at which he practiced.

"You want to fight this," Pagano answered stiffly, "go get a writ—if you can. We'll contest it and by the time the smoke is cleared the forty-eight hours will have passed." He paused. "You're a good man, Wyatt. Not many in your position would do what you're doing. I wish you well—and I don't want to see you fall into a barrel of shit."

He started walking away down the long corridor.

Wyatt called after him. "I have copies of those tapes," he reminded Pagano's retreating back. "Ten o'clock Wednesday morning, if my client hasn't walked you'll be watching me in front of your television set. And I'll bet the state bar committee on ethics would be interested, too."

Pagano hesitated in his stride for a moment; then he continued on his way without a backward glance.

"Don't ask me to understand the machinations of the district attorney's office," Walcott frowned. "They have no rhyme or reason—although you can bet there's politics involved, there always is." He sat back in his chair, contemplating the pattern of water-damage stains on the ceiling. "You ruffled quite a few feathers with the cops and numbers stuff. This could be the surface of a very large pool and they need to use the kid." He handed Wyatt a thick stack of folders. "In the meantime, the grass is growing."

"**D**o you swear to tell the truth, the whole truth, and nothing but the truth, so help you God?"

"I do."

"State your name for the members of the grand jury, please."

"Dwayne Thompson."

"What is your legal address?"

"Durban State Penitentiary."

"You are at the present time in temporary custody at this county's main jail facility?"

"Yes."

"For what purpose?"

"To give testimony in a case that's in trial right now."

"You are a witness for the prosecution?"

"That is correct."

"And you've been in custody at the county jail for a week?"

"About a week, yeah."

"For the record—did the state, in any way, directly or indirectly, offer you anything tangible in exchange for whatever help you could give them?"

"Reduction in time on my current sentence."

"All right." The assistant DA conducting the questioning looked at some papers for a moment. "Now regarding this information you are bringing forward today. Did anyone from our office, or any other law-enforcement agency—city, county, state, or federal—approach you for your help?"

"No. I came to you."

"Of your own volition? Nobody coerced you?"

"I did it on my own, that's right."

"Okay. That's established, on the record. Next question—did the district attorney's office make any warranties or guarantees regarding the information you brought to our attention in this matter?"

"If what I tell you helps get a conviction I'll get some easing on my current sentence or my pending case, something on those lines."

"Did anyone from my office or any law-enforcement agency help you develop this information, feed you information, or in any way give you information regarding the testimony you are going to give today to this grand jury?"

"No."

"All the information came from a source or sources you pursued and developed yourself?"

"Yes."

"All right." The assistant DA stepped back, leaving Dwayne center stage. "Tell the members of the grand jury what you know about a series of killings that have been referred to in the press as the 'Alley Slasher Murders.' "

"I was down there, starting to work in the infirmary," Dwayne began, "which they had assigned to me, since I have experience doing that, and they're shorthanded. There was this patient in there who'd been shot up during a robbery, and I had to change his bandages. And they were playing the news on the TV, about this serial killer they call the Alley Slasher, and this guy and I started talking about it. He knew the area where all the killings had happened real good—he worked there, his job took him all over where these women had been murdered. And as we were talking— not that one time only, but whenever I had to change his dressings, and other times, too, most of the time we were the only two men in there, when it wasn't hospital hours, since he was the only inpatient in the infirmary—as we were talking I could tell he had things he needed to talk to someone about. Things that were troubling him that he needed to talk about, share with someone. It's like going to confession— people that've done something bad need to get it off their chests, 'cause it's too heavy a burden to live with by yourself. And the thing about me is, people find it easy to talk to me. 'Cause I'm a good listener, probably. I know what it's like, being on the wrong side of the law myself at times, I've got sympathy for someone in a similar situation that a regular person on the outside, a police officer or a priest or whatever, just can't have, 'cause they ain't never walked in those shoes, you know what I mean? So what I did was, I listened to this prisoner, Marvin White is his name, and he started talking to me, more and more, I couldn't shut him up he wanted to talk to someone so bad about what he'd done. And before I knew it he'd told me his whole story, everything that had been going on with him over the last two years. And what had been going on with him was, he'd been doing some very terrible things."

Violet Waleska was on her way out the door when the phone rang. She was running late for work; she was a punctual person and prided herself on her punctuality, but in the days since Paula had been killed she hadn't been able to keep to a schedule. For a moment she debated letting the answering machine take the call, but she was unable to let a phone ring without answering it unless it was something completely inconvenient, like making love—not that she'd had any occasion such as that in recent memory.

"Hello?" She listened. "Yes, this is she."

"This is Sergeant Pulaski," the voice on the other end of the line said. "Do you remember me?"

"Yes, I remember you."

"I hate to bother you, but something's come up that we need help on. Would it be possible for you to come down to police headquarters today?" he asked politely.

"What is it?" she asked. Her throat was instantly constricting; she could barely swallow. "Have you found out who killed Paula?"

"This is all preliminary, ma'am. But you might be able to help us."

She was in a dimly lit viewing room, facing a wall that was all glass. On the other side of the glass was the lineup room. It featured bright fluorescent lights, a platform raised about three feet, lines marking height on the wall behind. Numbers on the front of the platform were spaced out for people to stand behind.

In the room with her and Sergeant Pulaski was a man who identified himself as a representative of the district attorney's office, a police stenographer, and two other people, a man and a woman, whom Pulaski introduced as police detectives.

"We're going to bring some men in," Pulaski told her. "They'll stand against the wall and look straight out. You look at them and tell us if you've ever seen any of them before. This is one-way glass"—he rapped his knuckles on it—"so they can't see you, they don't know you're here. They don't know who's in here, or even if there is anyone or not. We do some of these identifications on tape now," he explained, "without anyone present, but in this case we think a firsthand ID would be better. We're taping it, too, for backup."

He escorted her to the middle seat of the front row and sat down next to her. The deputy DA took a seat one row behind them.

The female police officer stood at a small podium that had a microphone attached to it. "Bring in group A," she announced over the mike.

A uniformed officer inside the lineup room opened a door at the side of the platform and six black men entered. They were dressed in civilian clothes. The men mounted the platform, each man standing in front of a number.

"Recognize anyone?" Pulaski asked.

She looked at them. "No."

"You sure?"

"Yes. I've never seen any of these men."

"Take your time. If there's anyone you want to get a better look at we can ask him to step forward."

"I'm sure."

Pulaski nodded to the detective at the podium. "Thank you, gentlemen," the detective announced. "Next group."

The lineup-room officer led the group out. A second group of six came in.

Violet looked them over, shook her head. "No."

"You sure?"

"Yes."

Pulaski nodded, glancing over his shoulder at the assistant DA, who shrugged. The podium detective dismissed the group and asked that the third set of men be brought in.

She recognized him. The fourth one in, third from the left. She leaned forward, staring intently through the glass, her heart pounding.

"You recognize one of them?" Pulaski asked, keeping his voice calm.

"The young, tall one."

"Have each man step out in turn," Pulaski instructed the detective with the microphone, "stand there for five seconds, and return."

The detective called the men out, starting from the right. When the man she had ID'd stepped forward, Violet jerked back in her seat.

"That's him," she said, her voice quivering with fear and excitement. "That's the man I saw."

"You're absolutely sure." Pulaski exchanged another quick look with the DA, who was on the edge of his own seat, his arms on the back of Pulaski's.

"Would you be willing to swear to that, under oath?"

"Yes," she said with rock-solid conviction. "That is the man."

Some of the men in those lineups were prisoners. The rest of them were cops, or civilians who worked the jail complex—cooks, janitors, computer operators, etc. The cops and day-giggers went back to their jobs; the prisoners were returned to their cells.

Except for Marvin. Two jail deputies took him to a special wing on the top floor: the maximum-security unit, where prisoners under indictment for the most serious crimes were kept in individual cells, under twenty-four-hour-a-day watch. Men accused of capital crimes, for which the death penalty is a definite option, often the preferred one.

Most of the cells on the floor were empty. It was a bitch keeping prisoners in this unit. The expense was three times that of maintaining a normal inmate. One man to a cell, no exceptions. No contact with any other prisoners, which meant they each exercised separately, showered separately, were fed in their cells. Inmates had to stay in their nine-by-six-foot space except for exercise time, shower time, and when they had visitors—family members or, more commonly, their lawyers.

"What's going on?" Marvin asked as the elevator groaned past the floor he'd been staying on.

The guards didn't answer him.

"Where we going?" he asked.

"Your new home," one of them answered, giving him a small break.

"What new home?"

"They didn't tell you?" The same jail deputy. The older one.

"Nobody's told me shit."

They exited the elevator and entered the high-security ward, passing through three separate sets of locked doors. It was scary, being in such a quiet cellblock after the deafening noises of where he'd been. There had been comfort in that noise: you were one of many there; if you stayed out of other people's ways you could get lost, sort of. Up here, it was like a tomb.

"When?" he asked. "Will they tell me?"

"Sooner or later."

They put him in a cell at the far end, as far away from the elevators as they could. His meager array of personal effects—toothbrush, toothpaste, bar of soap, hand towel, deodorant—was already there on the freshly made bunk, waiting for him.

The cell door slid shut behind him, clanging loudly. From where he was, looking out through the heavy bars of his door, he couldn't see a soul.

"Hey!" he called out. "Hey! What am I doing here?"

His voice echoed up and down the long corridor. All the walls and flooring were concrete: sound carried and reverberated over and over, loud and hollow. *Hey hey hey hey hey!*

Nobody answered him. The guards on this floor were cocooned in a sealed control booth that had video surveillance of everything, in every cell.

"Hey!" Marvin shouted. "I ain't supposed to be here. I'm getting out tomorrow!"

The only sound that returned was the echo of his voice. It had a mocking ring to it.

Wyatt ditched work at the stroke of five. He didn't run, or practice his trombone—instead, he took Moira to an early dinner at Edgemont, their golf club, an easy twenty-minute drive from their house. The food was good for what it was, and Moira enjoyed the comfortable ambience, where she knew everybody and there was no stress. Her parents had been members for over forty years; her father had sponsored Wyatt, two decades ago.

"What's the special occasion?" she asked.

"Us," he replied. She was taking his midlife crisis hard. This was a way of showing her things hadn't really changed.

"I like that," she purred.

Black waiters in white coats, bow ties, and dark slacks glided around the room, greeting each patron with familiar deference. The service was unobtrusively soothing; it hadn't changed an iota since long before Wyatt had first started coming, he thought, and it would go on like this long after he departed. There were black waiters and black caddies at Edgemont, but the only blacks (or Latinos or any other "minorities"—they had finally admitted a handful of token Jews a few years back) out on the golf course or eating in the dining room were guests of members. Wyatt thought the attitude was retro but he rationalized his part in it by ignoring it, a minor glitch in his moral makeup.

Moira leaned across the table and kissed the tip of his nose. "You're not so bad, as husbands go," she told him.

They were done with coffee and home by nine-thirty. Michaela was in her room, studying for midterms. This was an important semester for her—she was sending in her college applications, and she wanted high grades. Wyatt wasn't worried about her—she was going to do well in life. Unlike the poor bastard he was currently representing.

"How was dinner?" she asked, poking her head out her door to greet them.

"Romantic," her mother told her, kicking off her heels and beginning to unfasten her dress.

Wyatt checked the messages on his private line. There were none, a good sign. A simple dinner with his wife had reminded him how much he appreciated his life: the past few days, dealing with people he normally never came in touch with, amplified that appreciation. Not just the Marvin Whites of this world, but people like Josephine, who had been bowled over by a car-service ride home.

Michaela retreated to her room. Wyatt locked the house up, set the alarm, and followed Moira up to their bedroom.

She was already under the covers. Her dress, bra, underpants, and panty hose were neatly folded on a chair in the corner. He undressed, turned out the lights, slid into bed next to her. They came into each other's arms, hands and mouths fondling bodies. They knew where to touch to give pleasure; they had been lovers for twenty-five years.

Their foreplay was slow, mutually generous. When she was ready she grabbed hold of him, pulling him close to her, already pumping as he entered her, feeling her orgasm coming, ready to explode.

The phone rang next to their heads, as loud and disconcerting as a fire-alarm. Startled, she started to reach for it.

He grabbed her wrist. "Let the service get it," he whispered in her ear, still moving inside her.

"No one would call this late unless it was an emergency," she said, still fearful from the burglary next door.

"Shit." He stayed in her, maintaining his hardness. The phone kept ringing.

She reached over and pulled the receiver to her. "Hello?" She listened for a moment. "It's for you," she said. "A woman," she added, looking at him querulously.

He took the phone. "Hello?"

It was Josephine. "I got you at a bad time, didn't I?"

"No, it's all right," he said. With his free hand he caressed Moira's breast—she wasn't happy with this unexpected intrusion from a female voice she didn't know.

"I'm sorry, but I couldn't help calling, even though it's late." Her voice was shrill, almost out of control.

"What is it?" Cupping a hand over the speaker, he mouthed "The office" to Moira.

"You aren't watching TV, are you?" Josephine asked over the line.

"No."

"You'd better turn it on! Channel eight." There was a quick pause. "I'm flipping through, it's on all the channels!" She was shouting.

He hung up and slid out off Moira. Grabbing the remote from the bedside table, he clicked it at the television set and sat on the edge of the bed.

"What is it?" Moira asked, not trying to mask her frustration.

"That was the office. Something on the TV they need me to see. I don't know. . . ." He stopped talking as the picture faded up on the screen.

The broadcast was a live feed from the mayor's office. The mayor was standing in front of a bank of microphones. At his side was Alex Pagano, his shirt as freshly starched as if it were eight in the morning. He changed for this newscast, Wyatt thought to himself. Once a politician . . .

". . . the serial killer," the mayor was saying.

Reporters were firing questions at him. "When did you find out?" a reporter asked from off camera.

"I'm going to let the district attorney answer those questions," the mayor stated. He stepped to one side, and Pagano took center stage.

"We presented our evidence to the grand jury earlier today," Pagano said, "and they immediately handed down an indictment, which should assure any doubters that we're not shooting at clay targets. To be doubly certain, however, we also held a lineup. An eyewitness who was present at the time of last week's murder placed the suspect at the scene of the crime, within minutes of when it occurred."

Moira sat up next to Wyatt. The coitus interruptus was forgotten. "The Alley Slasher," she gasped. "They've caught him."

"Sounds like it."

"Thank God," she breathed.

"Yes." He was as happy, as relieved as she was. Then the thought rose up—how did this relate to why Josephine had called him?

Another reporter shouted from behind the cameras: "You're positive that you have the right man?"

"We're sure of it," Pagano answered. "One hundred percent."

"Where is he now?" came a voice.

"He's in custody," Pagano said, answering the second question first, "and we can tell you his name. He's from this city, and although he's young, he has an extensive juvenile record, which points clearly to his having committed these heinous crimes. We have a picture of him, taken earlier today from the lineup." He pointed offscreen.

The camera panned over to an easel that had an eight-by-ten photo mounted on it. The camera began zooming in on the picture.

Wyatt sat bolt upright. He stared at the face in disbelief. "Jesus fucking Christ!"

"What?" Moira cried in alarm. "What is it?"

The close-up of the Alley Slasher filled the screen: the man they were accusing of raping and killing seven women and turning the entire city into a frightened and revenge-bent mob.

Marvin White wasn't walking out of that courtroom tomorrow morning. No matter what his million-dollar lawyer had promised him and his mother.

PART
TWO

ALEX Pagano formally introduced his case at a mob-scene press conference that afternoon in the large rotunda on the first floor of the courthouse. He stood in front of a bank of microphones—at least two dozen of them—with the mayor, the chief of police, every member of the city council, and his own senior deputy DAs standing behind him. He was smiling grimly and shaking his head as he watched the media fighting and jockeying for position, thinking what a bunch of damn fools these people are, they want blood, they want their daily ration of blood.

He held up his hands for silence. Slowly the bedlam became less clamorous. Dozens of microphones on extension poles were thrust into the air to suck up his remarks.

Pagano felt his power. It was large, it filled him, he could feel his own expansion. Even this gradual silence was power, real power. They were all here for one reason—to hear what he had to tell them about the killer who was in his jail, even though any trial was months away and not a shred of specific information had been made public.

"We have identified the killer you have named the Alley Slasher," he began.

Reporters, unable to restrain themselves, started firing questions at him. Christ, sometimes this is like being inside an insane asylum, he thought. He almost laughed out loud at the thought: wasn't that, at the core, what his job was all about? Making sure the inmates didn't take over the asylum?

He answered a few questions nonspecifically but boldly, forcefully, conveying the confidence of the strong professional who does his job well and without undue and unnecessary fanfare. The strong professional who was going to put this murderer on death row, and by doing so begin the drive to put himself into the governor's chair.

The offices the district attorney's division worked out of were conformably bland—the equivalent of a midlevel motel chain, all components interchangeable and indistinguishable, bought by some unknown purchasing agent who was careful with the taxpayers' dollars. The only signs that individual human beings occupied these spaces were photos, diplomas, a potted plant, or special coffee cup. This was work space, where egos were subordinated (in theory) to the common goal. They occupied the fifth and sixth floors of the Hall of Justice, the main city courthouse. Courtrooms took up the first four floors, a few big, most of them small, dispensing justice nine hours a day, five days a week.

There was only one personalized office upstairs. Alex Pagano's sixth-floor corner office was ultrastark and spartan. The floors and walls were bare, painted industrial white. Pagano's desk was a slab of rock, his chair a draftsman's stool; the space was like an artist's loft, but without any humanizing colors. This office, in its absolute simplicity, massive emptiness, and lack of warmth, exuded power. It added to the man's stature.

In the center of his room sat a big black conference table with canvas tube chairs around it. Six people sat at it—four men and two women, Pagano's senior trial attorneys. Thelma Fuller, the original deputy on the case, wasn't one of them. This was above her, way above.

In the corner, Pagano's trusted senior deputy, Cy Lofton, the man who had been with him when they'd met with Dwayne Thompson, sat watching. He would take notes and check pulses.

"Well, boys and girls," Pagano commented, stating the obvious, "this is a juicy one."

The six senior deputies stirred in their chairs. They knew that for a fact. They also knew this would be the biggest case to be tried in the city in decades, a career case.

"So . . . who wants it?"

Six hands shot up, six voices rang out. "Chief, it's my turn." "This is exactly my kind of case, Alex." And so forth.

Pagano, in his shirtsleeves at the head of the table, sat back and watched the fury. There are a lot of ways to play God, he thought gleefully. This was one of the most enjoyable ones. Pagano loved doing this—pitting them against each other. He only did it a couple times a year, when passion for the cause was of major importance. It was like setting fighting cocks in a ring—only the strongest one would survive.

He put up a hand for quiet. "Okay. I'm going to give each of you two minutes to tell me why this should be your case instead of anyone else's."

"Shit," one of them muttered. They could all feel the rumblings in their stomachs, the beginnings of the acid wash.

They went clockwise around the table. Talking about experience, preparation, presentation, talent, each touting personal strengths, not so subtly belittling the others' shortcomings.

Pagano leaned back in his chair, shooting his cuffs, listening and watching. He had tentatively made his choice, in his gut; but he needed to hear all this. More importantly, he needed to hear what his choice had to say, to make sure that his instincts were right. This trial, almost certainly, would be the make-or-break benchmark of his administration. If they won—especially if it was a big, juicy win—it could propel him into the stratosphere. If—God forbid—they lost, it would be a quick ride back to private practice, and a lifetime of anonymity and recriminations.

Helena Abramowitz, sitting to his immediate right, was the last to speak. In her late thirties, Abramowitz was Sephardic-dark, brooding, flamboyant, aggressive. She had tried and won over half a dozen capital cases. She stood up, looked at each of them in turn briefly, then turned to Pagano and fixed his gaze with hers.

"It should be a woman," she began, "because these are crimes against women, the worst nightmare a woman has, outside of losing a child. The person who tries this will be speaking for every woman in this city, in this state. From the heart, the gut, the soul. Only a woman can truly speak for another woman, can make her feel that she, the millions of *shes* out there, are truly being taken care of, nurtured, shielded. Which leaves me and Betsy," she said, nodding to the other woman deputy, seated across the table from her.

An attractive woman, about her age. Her physical opposite—
tall, blond, with a sunny disposition and great legs.

"That is utter bullshit!" one of the man sang out. "Gender
is irrelevant here. These have been crimes against the entire
community."

Helena looked at her associate, smiling slightly. Then she
turned to Pagano. "Normally I'd agree," she answered, "but
not this time. This time, chief," she said directly to Pagano,
"gender is everything. And when you think about it, you'll
know it, you'll feel it in your bones. I know you, chief—
you've got great instincts for this kind of thing."

Pagano watched her, his face a noncommittal mask.

"So," Helena went on. "Me or Betsy. We both have the
experience, we both have the talent, we both have the fire
in our bellies." She paused, as if giving an important part
of a summation. "There's only one thing Betsy has that
I don't. And most of the time I envy her for it, but in this
case a great husband and two wonderful little kids are an
impediment. This is going to be a twenty-four-hour-a-day,
seven-day-a-week case." She turned to Betsy. "Marcia Clark
almost lost custody of her son in a situation like this. You
don't want that to happen to you."

"Marcia Clark was divorced," Betsy shot back. "My
situation is different." She appealed to Pagano. "I resent this
kind of gutter politicking, chief," she said with heat. "It's
uncalled for, and personally insulting. I'll do whatever it
takes to win. You know I will." She smiled at him, a charged
smile.

Pagano nodded. "Duly noted," he said mildly. He looked
at Helena. "Is there anything more you want to add?"

"No. There's nothing more that's necessary." She sat down.

Pagano looked at his senior deputies in turn, making brief
eye contact with each one. "You're all good," he said.
"That's why you're sitting here and two hundred other
lawyers in this department aren't. Every one of you could
do a great job, and every one of you, I'm sure, could convict
this piece of shit. So it has to come down to public percep-
tion, and my gut." He paused. "I should sleep on this," he
continued, "because you all did make good presentations,
I'm serious; but I don't have the luxury of doing that. The
mayor and the city council and the newspapers and TV stations and every Tom, Dick, and Dumbfuck is on my case

like white on rice, so I've got to choose, and hope to God I'm doing the right thing."

He stood up. "Helena's right. The lead DA should be a woman. This is a crime against women, it's payback time, and that's how I want the public to perceive it."

The four men at the table shook their heads in disagreement and frustration.

"Sorry, guys," Pagano told them. "There's more where this came from."

That was patent bullshit and they all knew it. But that was it; he was the boss.

He turned to Helena. "It's yours. You'll have the entire resources of this office at your disposal, including everyone sitting here if that's what it takes."

"Thanks, boss." She was shaking inside. "I won't let you down."

All business now. "Who do you want to be your co-counsel?"

"Norman," she said without hesitation, looking at Norman Windsor, who was sitting across the table from her. He was the only black senior deputy at the table.

"Great choice," Pagano seconded. "Norman, will you do it? I know it's not the lead, but there's plenty of glory to go around."

Say yes, schmuck, he thought. We need a black face at our table.

"Yeah, I'll do it," Norman Windsor said. As if he had any choice. He knew the politics involved. He reached across the table and shook Helena's hand. "Let's kick ass, lady."

"That's what I do for a living," she answered him.

A few blocks away, in the Public Defender's offices, a similar process was taking place. Walcott's own office was too small, so the meeting took place in what passed for their conference room, a large storage space in the basement where decades of old files were kept.

There were no windows in this decrepit mausoleum. The lights were old flickering hanging fixtures in wire cages. The crappy, inadequate ventilation came from two overhead fans that moved the tepid air around, blowing papers onto the floor more than cooling things down. The room was hot and muggy, the walls leaked moisture. People sweated freely; after fifteen minutes you felt like you were in a Turkish bath.

Walcott hated this space. Tempers flared easily, things got personal. But there were times when he had to get everyone together in the same room. This was one of those times.

Besides Walcott, Wyatt, and Josephine, every single senior lawyer in the Public Defender's office had crammed into this space, two dozen advocates for the public welfare and their own ambitions.

Wyatt was seated near the head of the table, to Walcott's right. Josephine was squeezed in next to him, their chairs touching.

"You haven't met most of the team, have you?" Walcott asked Wyatt.

Wyatt looked around. None of the faces were familiar. "No, not yet," he answered easily. "But I'm looking forward to it."

No one smiled back. He didn't expect anyone to.

"That'll come," Walcott said. "Right now we've got a situation on our hands."

"We've got a crisis is what we've got. A disaster if we don't get our shit together muy pronto." The voice came from the other end of the table.

Wyatt didn't feel comfortable; even though his jacket was off, he was sweating. You can't think straight under physical conditions like these, he thought. More important than any physical discomfort was the resentment toward him from the lawyers in this room; he was the outsider, the invader.

Tough shit. He had come here to do a job and that's what he was going to do.

He got up from his seat and walked the length of the table to where the man who had spoken out was sitting. The man was middle-aged, rumpled, overweight but solid. He looked like a junior high football coach.

"Wyatt Matthews," he said, offering his hand.

The man, startled by Wyatt's temerity, shook his hand before he realized what was happening. "Josh Dancer," he said.

"Good to meet you, Josh." Wyatt walked back the length of the table and took his seat.

"This is not a disaster, Josh, or anything like it." Walcott took charge. "We've got a case here and we're going to win it, and when we do, we're going to be heroes."

"*If* we win this," a second voice, another middle-aged man's, said, "we sure as hell aren't gonna be heroes. More like pariahs, you ask me."

"What're you talking about?" Walcott asked testily.

"Young black kid? Got a juvie record an inch thick? You walk this kid, the public's gonna roast your ass."

Others murmured agreement.

"Even if he's innocent?" Walcott asked Dancer.

"Like O.J. was in the criminal case?" the speaker shot back. This man, like several of the lawyers in the room, was black. "How many people're happy about that?"

This was true, Wyatt thought. Moira had been outraged by the process in the Simpson criminal trial, and had felt a sense of relief when the civil verdict came down on the side of the Goldmans and the Browns. Why would anyone defend him? she and others had asked at the time. She was going to be asking him the same question about Marvin White—and taking the answer personally. He knew that, and dreaded it.

"Anyway, this case has already been tried in the press all over the damn country," a third lawyer said.

"So what?" Walcott said. "Does that mean you think he's guilty? Beyond a reasonable doubt? What do you know about this, Larry?"

"I'm just saying it's going to be an uphill struggle," Larry, the man who had spoken up, pointed out.

"All our cases are," Walcott said. "That's why the DA has a ninety percent conviction rate." He exhaled through his nostrils. "Okay." He looked around the room, avoiding Wyatt. "How are we going to divvy this up?"

"What does that mean?" Wyatt asked immediately.

Walcott turned to him. "You're not trying this case," he told Wyatt bluntly.

"What?"

"You're not a trial lawyer. You've never tried a criminal case in your life."

"I've tried dozens of cases. For millions of dollars. Billions."

"Who gives a shit about any of that crap?" Dancer was on his feet now. "I've been in this office almost twenty years, paying my dues. I'm a good lawyer—I could go into the private sector and make much more money than I do here. I'm in this job for the same reasons the rest of you are—the indigent need good lawyers, more than most defendants. And I'm an action junkie, I admit it. So if you think I'm gonna sit back and let some hot-shit silk-stocking lawyer from the outside come in and steal this from under our noses, you've got another think coming." He thumped the table for emphasis. "This belongs to one of us. Not him," he said, pointing a meaty finger at Wyatt.

Walcott made a time-out signal with his hands. "Let's calm down, everyone." He turned to Wyatt. "I can't do this. I'm sorry."

Wyatt took a deep breath before he responded. "Well, I'm sorry, too," he said. "But this man is my client. That relationship has already been established. That's protocol, that's the way the law is practiced everywhere I know. If I wanted to turn it over to someone else, that would be a different story. But right now this is my case, my client." He looked down the length of the table. "And I, for one, am not about to give up on him before I even start." He turned to Walcott. "A few days ago you were telling me what a brilliant job I was doing. Well, I'm the same lawyer I was then." He stood up. "I didn't give up a multimillion-dollar practice to push papers around down here," he said aggressively. "I came because I have skills and talents *you* need. And I'm going to use them. On this case."

"I make those decisions," Walcott answered him stiffly. The man was trembling, he was so angry. Wyatt wished he hadn't thrown down the gauntlet so nakedly; but this was a power game, at which he was a master.

"I'm going to give this serious thought," Walcott told the assemblage. "We'll meet again tomorrow and make our decisions. My decision," he added for Wyatt's benefit.

Wyatt and Josephine were in a bar a few blocks from their offices. A no-frills place where people came to drink and talk after a day's work. Hard liquor and beer—he didn't see three wineglasses.

"It's funny," Wyatt said, looking around, "in all the years I've worked downtown I've never been in here." He was drinking Johnny Black on the rocks with a water back.

"This is a cop bar," Josephine said. "Cops, prosecutors, defenders. Like goes to like." She took a sip from her margarita. "Where do you drink, hang out?"

"I'm a member of the University Club." He felt a tickle of discomfort, telling her that.

"Very uptown," she teased him. Leaning in closer, she said, "Listen, Wyatt. You are a winner and these people aren't. You know that better than me. The Public Defender's office has a loser mentality, especially with high-profile cases like this one. And especially with people at the bottom of the food chain, like Marvin White. Even the black guys in the department hate clients like him; they think of him as one more piece-of-shit nigger without a future."

He looked sharply at her.

"Hey, it's their word, not mine. I don't use words like that. You hear it all the time, all the time. Especially from the black lawyers. That's what they call people like Marvin. They hate people like him."

"You won't hear it from me," he said with genuine anger.

"Or me either again, okay?" She could feel the heat of his passion.

"Okay." He smiled at her.

"What it really is, they're scared," she confided.

"Of what?"

"Of 'there but for the grace of God.' " She finished her drink. "I'm going to have one more, for the road. Can I buy you one?" she asked.

"I'll join you, but I'm buying."

"Okay. This time." She caught the waitress's eye, pointed at their glasses, and twirled her finger. "The thing is," she said, "I know what they're talking about."

"About what?"

" 'There but for the grace of God.' That's me. That's how I feel. That's why I know how scared you can get, and how much that hurts."

Moira was late getting home (not that she was on a compelling timetable). She'd had lunch with some friends at a new French bistro out on Highway 83 and lingered with them over coffee and dessert until after three. They were old companions from college she didn't see very much anymore; their husbands, while successful, weren't in Wyatt's stratum, and over the years they'd drifted apart. But once or twice a year they got together and talked about their lives, their kids, old times and new.

After she'd finally left the restaurant she had gone by the new bookstore site. The lawyer (not Wyatt's firm—they'd be too expensive, and anyway she wanted this to be all hers, so they had hired a local attorney who was perfectly adequate) was preparing the lease. She and Cissy would be signing it next week. She'd had butterflies in her stomach, standing in the parking lot and looking at the vacant shop, visualizing what it would look like when it was full of books and CDs and people.

After that she'd dropped by her tailor's to have a pair of slacks altered, which had taken longer than she'd anticipated, and then she had stopped at a few specialty shops to pick up certain things the supermarket didn't carry—a particular type of wine she wanted to have with dinner tonight, some bagels for breakfast tomorrow. It was already dark when she drove down the road toward home.

She was actually past the Spragues' house when out of the corner of her eye she saw the For Sale sign planted in the grass next to the driveway. She hit the brakes, backed up until she was level with their driveway, and turned her car in, pulling up in front.

There were lights on inside. She walked up to the front door and rang the bell.

The door, secured by a chain, swung open a few cautious inches. Ted Sprague peered out at her.

"Oh, Moira, it's you," he exclaimed with relief. "Hold on a second." He closed the door so that he could unlatch the chain, then opened it fully.

"How's Enid?" Moira asked, feeling guilty; she hadn't been over to check on the older woman's condition since the night of the shooting.

"She's okay. She's doing fine. Come on in." He stepped aside so she could enter. "She's in the den watching the news."

"I can only stay for a minute," Moira said apologetically.

"Hi, Moira," Enid called out from inside the house. "Come look at my scars."

Enid was sitting in a wing chair, her slippered feet propped up on a brocaded ottoman. "Do you want something to drink?" she asked. Holding up a flute of champagne, "I'm into the good stuff. I'm pampering myself these days."

"As well you should," her husband asserted stoutly.

"No, thanks," Moira demurred. "I can only stay a minute. I wanted to check up, find out how you're doing." Her elderly neighbor didn't look good. She'd aged five years since she'd been shot.

"I'm still ticking." The older woman smiled. "I was lucky. Another inch and I wouldn't be here."

"Yes." Moira didn't know what else to say about that. "You're selling your house," she said instead, almost blurting it out.

"Yep," Ted confirmed. "We're flying the coop. Moving out to California. Carmel. Golf every day, and no shoveling snow."

"That'll be awful, losing you as neighbors." Moira was genuinely upset at the prospect. "But I guess you've outgrown this; or it's outgrown you, more accurately."

Enid shook her head. "I thought I'd live in this house until the day I died. Which I almost did." She shivered reflexively, poured herself some more champagne from a bottle sitting in an ice bucket at her elbow. "I don't feel safe here anymore," she said. "I'm afraid of what's going on, all around us."

"I can understand that," Moira sympathized.

"You *think* you can," Ted corrected her sternly. "But until it's actually happened to you, you don't really know."

"I guess that's true," Moira said defensively. She didn't want to be here anymore—there was a smell of decay in the air, emotional more than physical. She leaned over and kissed the older woman's cheek. "I'll try and stop in on you tomorrow."

"That would be nice." Enid looked up at Moira. "You know, there's only one thing I really regret about this horrible incident."

"What's that?" Moira asked.

"That I didn't shoot the bastards when I had the chance." She looked up at Moira from the comfort and security of her armchair. "If you ever find yourself in a similar situation," she warned the younger woman, "don't ever make that mistake."

"The Spragues are selling their house."

Wyatt nodded. "I saw the sign. I wonder what they're asking."

"They're afraid of living here anymore."

"Probably about a million two, a million three, wouldn't you say?"

"Old people shouldn't be afraid like that. Not in their own homes. Nobody should be."

"Although I heard the housing market's going up again, finally. It's a good place, they could maybe ask a million five. It doesn't matter," he went on, "a couple hundred thou one way or the other won't mean much to them. Is Michaela going to be home for dinner? I hardly ever see her anymore."

He'd gotten home later than he'd wanted—his one more with Josephine had turned out to be two more, with a lot of conversation wrapped around the drinks. The case primarily, but a few personal things, too, not only from her but from him as well; he had been surprised that he had talked about himself to someone he didn't know that well. Josephine was a good listener; they had an easy camaraderie. You either have that with somebody right off or you don't, he thought.

"She's already had dinner. She went to the library. Group study time." She looked sharply at him. "You haven't heard a word I said."

"Michaela had dinner. She's at the library. I heard that." He was uncorking the bottle of wine she had bought.

"About why the Spragues are moving."

He looked at her calmly. "I know why they're moving."

"Doesn't it concern you?" she asked, her voice rising.

"No, and it shouldn't concern you, either."

"How could it not?"

"Because what happened to them could have happened anywhere in this country. Anywhere in the world, for that matter. What do you think, this neighborhood's going to be a hot spot for robberies all of a sudden?"

"That's my whole point, Wyatt! That's what I'm afraid of."

They were in the living room, waiting for Cloris to warm

up the dinner that had been prepared to be eaten an hour ago. He pulled the cork with a loud pop. Pouring two glasses, he handed one to her. "Well, it isn't happening here, not this moment, so take it easy, okay?" He clinked glasses with her. "How was the rest of your day?"

She told him about her lunch and about going to the bookstore site, how good it felt that it was actually going to happen. "And you?" she asked, trying to keep it light. "How go the wars down there wherever it is you're fighting them these days?"

"The head of the Public Defender's office wants to take me off the case," he told her glumly.

"Finally," she said brightly. "Rationality returns."

"I'm not giving it up."

The glass from which she was about to drink stopped halfway to her lips. "Oh, Wyatt. Why?"

"Because it's what I want to do. What have I been talking about for the last month if not this? I thought you were behind me on this."

"Where did you ever get that idea?"

"Because you've always been behind me, on everything."

"And I am, but for God's sake, not this—this is going to be an absolute quagmire. This is going to be one of those awful cases where the lawyers are on TV every day, and the press is going to be snooping around our house, everything. We'll be in *The National Enquirer*!"

"Don't get hysterical, Moira. I'm defending a man who's been accused of a crime. It's what I've been doing the last twenty-five years."

"A kid from the ghetto who raped and killed seven women!" she screamed. "That is *not* what you have been doing the last twenty-five years!"

He set his glass down. "Which bugs you more? That he's accused of these crimes—and I say 'accused' deliberately; so far he hasn't been convicted of anything, in case you've forgotten—or that he's 'from the ghetto,' as you so elegantly put it?"

"Don't try to guilt-trip me. You know what I'm talking about."

"This is part and parcel of what happened next door, isn't it?"

"Yes," she answered firmly.

"And the fact that this kid is black—is that a component?"

She stared at him. "Are you saying I'm a racist? I can't believe I'm hearing this."

Cloris stuck her head into the room and coughed discreetly. "Dinner is on the table," she said. She disappeared immediately.

Moira pointed at their housekeeper's retreating back. "What about Cloris?" she asked. "Do you think I'm prejudiced against her?"

"No." He'd pushed too hard. "Look, honey, I know you're not racist, or anything remotely like that. It's—"

"I don't want you defending a rapist and a murderer," she said coldly, cutting him off. "I don't give a damn what color he is." She brushed by him, leaving the room. "You can eat dinner alone tonight. I've lost my appetite."

Helena Abramowitz sat a safe ten feet away from Dwayne Thompson, in interview room 1 at the county jail. The walls, ceiling, and floor were all white, and the overhead fluorescent lighting cast deep shadows under Helena's and Dwayne's eyes, which made both of them look older and him more sinister. The room was bare except for the chairs they were sitting on, and it was completely secure—no one could listen in to what they were saying, including members of the sheriff's office.

It was 8:15 in the morning. Helena had been up half the night going over Thompson's grand jury testimony, highlighting the most significant areas, where he had the most specific knowledge of the murders and Marvin's links to them. She had also tagged certain parts of his testimony that were of concern to her; either they were too nebulous, too general, or more troubling, were not credible—to her. She knew the police would buy what they wanted, that they would skew anything that made their case look better, but she couldn't afford to do that. Whatever she used at trial had to be as clean as it could be, because the other side would hammer at any inconsistencies.

This case would have racial overtones—it was inevitable. She assumed that at least half the members of the jury would be black, and although there was widespread outrage regarding the rape-murders, the black community's hostility toward the police ran deep, and with good reason—the same reasons there was tension between black communities and police all over the country.

Countering that antipathy would be the racial makeup of the victims. Most of them had been black women, and although they were prostitutes (except for the latest one), they were still victims whose skin color was black. She wouldn't need a jury consultant to know that the more black women, particularly young and independent, that she could pack into the jury, the better off she'd be.

Today was the first time Helena had actually laid eyes on Dwayne. She found his presence unsettling. Anyone who had been around the system could see that he was a psychopath. She hated this kind of witness because even when they were right, in the legalistic, technical sense, they were wrong. And he was her main witness, the only one who could conclusively put Marvin White in the murderer's shoes.

She had gone over Dwayne's jacket and his psychological profile. They were in the open folder she held in her lap, along with his grand jury testimony. He really did have the crack stoolie's knack for getting people to open up to him and confess their worst sins. He had sent three men up for life, not counting the case in progress he'd been brought down here for.

Marvin White would be five. They were all good cases. Solid, compelling testimony.

"I'm Helena Abramowitz," she said, introducing herself. "I'm the senior deputy district attorney who will be trying this case." She didn't offer her hand.

He nodded, his reptilian eyes scanning her top to bottom. She was not dressed flamboyantly, but she hadn't worn her most conservative outfit, either. She was wearing a knee-length wool-knit dress, dark stockings, and black pumps. She could feel his eyes on her legs.

His eyes locked onto hers. The whites were tinged with yellow, like a wolf's. "Dwayne."

"Dwayne Thompson." She tapped the thick manila folder on her lap. "I know all about you."

His eyes hadn't moved, hadn't blinked. "No one knows all about me," he told her in a low monotone.

He was wearing his infirmary whites. Legs planted on the floor, palms on thighs. His eyes moved slowly down to her breasts, brazenly checking them out, to her legs again, then back up to her face. She felt an urge to cross her legs, to flash some thigh and jerk him around with the swishing sound of rubbing nylon, but she resisted it. You don't fuck with heads like his, even when you're in the jail and he's your witness.

"What about you?" he asked her.

"What about me."

"How long you been a DA?"

"Over a dozen years."

"How many murder cases have you tried?"

"This will be my eighth."

"How many have you won?"

"All of them."

The barest of smiles edged his mouth. "Sounds like you're the right woman for the job."

"I'm the right lawyer for the job, yes."

"The right woman lawyer."

She let that run over her back—she wasn't going to get into any bantering with him. She flipped through a few pages of his testimony until she got to a highlighted section. "Let's go over some of your statement," she began.

"You married?" he asked.

She looked up. His eyes were boring into her. Curtly: "No." Pressing straight on: "The first time you and the accused, Marvin White, talked about the killings was in the jail infirmary the day after he was brought in? Or was it later? The information is unclear on that point."

"Divorced, or never were?"

"Divorced, no children, my life is my own and none of your business, please answer the questions I ask you and that's all."

"You want to win this, don't you," he asked, sizing her up. "You want to win it bad, you can taste it. You'd rather win this case than have sex with Kevin Costner and that other faggot, what's his name." His eyes were locked on her calf.

Helena smoothed her skirt down over her knees. She had

been in close contact with hundreds of hardened male criminals in her time at the DA's office, and she had handled all of them with comparative ease, but there was something about this one that set him apart. This man seemed to be totally devoid of any human feelings. She'd heard of people like this—the Jeffrey Dahmers and Ted Bundys of the world. The scariest part was that if this case went to trial, and she won, Dwayne Thompson was going to walk out of prison a free man.

"When did Marvin White first broach the issue of the Alley Slasher murders?" she asked, consulting her notes again. "Was it the first day after the night he was brought in?"

"Something like that. Yeah, that sounds right."

"It's what you said in your testimony. Do you remember precisely what the circumstances were?" This interview had started off on the wrong foot. If he couldn't remember something as basic as when he and the defendant had started talking about this case, how could he remember the more important and much more specific details?

His smile was that of the cat who had finally caught and eaten Tweety Pie. "It was the first morning I was on infirmary duty," he began. "Eleven o'clock, I had switched the television set to the news at the top of the hour. The lead story was about the latest killing and they had a shot of a reporter standing in the location where the killing had taken place. I had finished changing the dressings on his ass—excuse me, his posterior—where he'd been shot up with birdshot. We were watching together. He said, 'I know where that is,' or words to that effect, and he told me he used to work in that neighborhood. He knew the exact address of the alley." He stared at her hard, challengingly. "I've got a photographic memory, lady lawyer. Once I hear something, or read something, I know it. Cold. So don't worry about my testimony holding up, if that's what you're thinking."

I've got to be careful with this one, she thought. A photographic memory? What other surprises did he have in store for her? Aloud, she said, "The more precise you are the better it will be for us. And for you, given the deal you cut with my boss."

"I scratch your back, you scratch mine, lady prosecutor,"

he said. "I give good back-scratch. You want to check it out, you let me know."

He leaned back in his chair, arms now folded across his chest, and as she looked up from her notes she saw that his pants were rising in the crotch. He looked at her; and then slowly, deliberately, he licked his lips, his serpentine tongue traversing his mouth from one side to the other.

"I have a back-scratcher," she informed him, looking away. "In case you forget it sometime."

When pigs can fly, asshole.

Looking up again, she saw that his pants were quivering from the force of his erection. Don't come in your pants, you piece of garbage. Not while I'm alone in the room with you.

"I need to take a short break," she said. "I'll be right back. Maybe you need a break, too." She stood up. The door immediately swung open, the burly deputy on duty sticking his head in.

"We're going to take a five-minute break," she informed the deputy. "Mr. Thompson needs to use the bathroom."

She smoked a cigarette in the lawyers' lounge and reread some of his testimony. His grand jury statement about how he and Marvin White had first started discussing the murders was exactly what he had told her, almost verbatim. He really must have a photographic memory. He'd be a tough witness to break down under cross-examination.

She didn't have to like Dwayne Thompson. She didn't like plenty of the witnesses she used, especially the criminals. All she wanted from them was their help in winning the case.

When she returned to the interview room he was already there, waiting for her. The bulge in his pants was gone. She asked him questions, he answered them. The light was gone from his eyes.

The storm came down from the north overnight, bringing a hard, driving rain. It fell in heavy, cold sheets, the strong wind off the water blowing it sideways.

Wyatt and Jonnie Rae Richards sat in a coffee shop across

the street from the jail. Outside the greasy storefront window the drops punched the potholed asphalt street like BB pellets, bouncing high into the air. Already, at seven-thirty in the morning, the gutters were overflowing onto the sidewalk, sloshing muddy water on the shoes of the passersby who were running to get inside wherever they were going.

Even though she had an umbrella Jonnie Rae had been soaking wet when she pushed the door open and sat down in the corner booth across from Wyatt. She grabbed a handful of napkins from the dispenser on the table, took off her plastic rain hat, and patted down her face, neck, and hair.

"Excuse me," she apologized to Wyatt, "but I can't afford to get a cold."

Balling up another handful of napkins, she unceremoniously pulled off her shoes and stuffed the paper around in the insides of her low pumps, which were misshapen from years of conforming to her wide, flat feet. Wyatt noticed that the heels on her shoes were run-down and the soles had holes in them.

"How far away did you have to park?" he asked. He'd lucked out, finding an empty space right in front.

"I don't have no car," she said, shucking out of her raincoat and draping it over the back of the booth to dry out. "Took the E bus to Merchant Street and then the 34 trolley," she told him. "The trolley-stop roof leaks like a sieve, that's how come I got so damn wet. Damn transit company ought to fix up their trolley stops," she complained.

Wyatt hadn't been on a trolley car in decades. His mother used to take him for rides when he was little, for a treat. It had been fun, watching the driver shift the levers that activated the overhead electrical current. He rarely took public transportation anymore; the cars were crowded and dirty, and it took too long to get from one place to another.

"If the weather's like this next time I'll send a taxi for you," he volunteered. It was inconvenient having to ride the buses for however long it took to get here; an hour or more, with the transfers and the waiting. Getting soaked to the skin on top of that was ridiculous.

"Don't worry about that. I ride three buses every day to get to my work. I buy the monthly pass, so I can ride as many times as I want, don't cost me any extra."

The waitress came over to their table, pad in hand.

"Just coffee for me," Wyatt ordered.

"I'll have the same," Jonnie Rae seconded.

"Are you sure you don't want anything else?" he prompted. "We pay for it," he added, trying to make it sound like it was an everyday occurrence. It would come out of his pocket—big deal.

"Well, in that case, let me have a bowl of hot cereal and some toast. White toast," Jonnie Rae told the waitress.

"Oatmeal or Cream of Wheat?"

"Oatmeal. With brown sugar if you've got it."

The waitress went away to put in their order. "Something hot to take this chill off," she said, as if apologizing for his spending money on an order of cereal and toast.

The waitress plonked down two thick mugs of hot, tarry coffee. Jonnie Rae put three sugars and a large dollop of cream in hers.

"Let me explain what's going on," Wyatt began.

She licked her coffee spoon clean before putting it down on the table. "We're meeting with Marvin, aren't we?" she asked. "To do whatever it is you lawyers do?"

"Yes and no."

This was not going to be an easy conversation. In a few minutes he would walk her across the street to the jail, where they would meet with Walcott and Josh Dancer, who, Josephine had cued him, was the senior Public Defender in the office. Wyatt knew that Dancer had been working overtime behind his back to convince Walcott the defense had to be handled by a career staffer, not Wyatt. If Walcott and Dancer got their way, by lunchtime Dancer would be the lead attorney on the case and he would be a backup.

He would never be a backup to anyone.

Walcott had called him with the news last night Dancer was going to be given the case. He'd lost his temper and reamed Walcott's ass royally, accusing Walcott of using the good offices of Wyatt's prestigious firm when it was expedient and turning a cold shoulder when it wasn't.

Walcott had held firm. His men and women had to be taken care of.

Wyatt took a sip from his coffee. It was too hot; he scalded his lips. He put the cup down.

"I'm not an experienced lawyer in criminal trials," he told Jonnie Rae. "I'm a very good lawyer, of course, I've won hundreds of important cases"—he wasn't going to back off who he was—"but in this situation, Marvin should have someone who has been down this road before, so to speak. You see," he explained, "I don't practice this kind of law for a living. I'm working for the Public Defender as a volunteer."

"What do you mean?" she asked, confused. "You done good by him already, with that robbery charge. Why couldn't you do good on this part of it?"

Good question, he thought. "The head of the department makes these decisions," he told her. "It's out of my hands."

"Not if I have anything to do with it," she came back.

"It's not your choice."

"Why not?" She was getting angry, and building up a good head of steam behind it. "I'm the boy's mother, ain't I?"

"Yes, but he's legally of age, so the decision will be his, not yours or anyone else's. You can counsel with him, and you should, but it's a decision he has to make."

"It sounds like a bunch of bureaucratic bullshit to me," she said.

Wyatt had no answer for that, so he didn't offer one.

The waitress put Jonnie Rae's cereal and toast down in front of her. Jonnie Rae liberally sprinkled the cereal with brown sugar, buttered her toast, and went directly at her breakfast.

Wyatt took another try at his coffee. It wasn't too hot to drink now; it just tasted like shit in his mouth. He drank it anyway.

Walcott and Dancer were waiting in the front lobby. Walcott looked wary, but relatively calm. Dancer was fidgety, bouncing from the ball of one foot to the other. He avoided direct eye contact with Wyatt, who ignored him in turn.

Wyatt made the introductions. Jonnie Rae looked disdainfully at the two men, whom she'd never met. They didn't make much of an impression, compared to Wyatt. They wouldn't be sending taxicabs for her and buying her breakfast, one look at them and she knew that for a fact.

"Before we talk to your son," Walcott said to Jonnie Rae, trying to be charming and considerate, neither of which he was good at, "we should talk for a minute amongst ourselves. We can go in here," he added, pointing to a small visitors' anteroom off the main guard station.

She shook her head emphatically. "He's the one got his butt in the sling," she said. "You do your talking to him. I'll listen and counsel him, if it comes to that. That's what a mother is for when her child becomes old enough to get hisself into trouble."

Wyatt turned away so they couldn't see him smiling. She was almost parroting what he'd told her, word for word.

"Fine by me," Walcott said, taken aback. He walked over to the duty sergeant and announced their presence.

A deputy accompanied them through the secure gates and into a small visitors' room. They sat at a table, all on the same side. Wyatt sat next to Jonnie Rae, shielding her from the others.

The door from the other side, the jail side, swung open. Marvin was led in by two deputies. He was in handcuffs and leg-irons, shuffling his slippered feet along the floor. His complexion was ashen, his hair was all kinked up like it hadn't been washed or combed out in days, and his eyes and nose were runny. He looked down at his feet as he came in, unable to look up at his mother's face.

"Oh, baby," Jonnie Rae cried out. "What have they done to you in here?" Instinctively, she jumped up and tried to reach across the table to hug him.

One of the deputies immediately stepped between them, blocking her. "No physical contact," he said sternly, pointing to the instructions on the wall.

Wyatt was on his feet, and not as a courtesy to Marvin. "Why is this man shackled?" he demanded. "Who authorized this?"

"The sheriff," one of the deputies answered curtly.

"Shackling an inmate in the presence of his attorney and family is against regulations," Wyatt told the deputy. He was pissed—Marvin had been under indictment less than forty-eight hours, he still hadn't been formally arraigned, and they were already treating him like an animal. Walcott started to stand also, to add to the protest, but Wyatt waved him to sit down. "This man has been convicted of no crime," he said aggressively, "and has demonstrated no threat to anyone in this institution. So take the metal off him right now, or I'll get an order to do it, and I'll file an official complaint against your department and against the two of you personally."

The deputies exchanged a look. "You assume full responsibility for his behavior?" the lead one asked.

"Don't play games with me, pal," Wyatt warned the deputy. "Take off those handcuffs. Right now."

The deputy made a show of shrugging, as if to say "It's on your head"; then he unfastened the cuffs and leg and waist irons, gathering them up in his arms. Marvin rubbed his wrists vigorously.

"We'll be right outside the door," the deputy said ominously.

"We're shaking," Wyatt answered back. As they were leaving: "I don't need to remind you that this is a privileged conversation. If you give us one iota of suspicion that you're violating our confidentiality, you'll be in front of the grand jury. And please close the door firmly behind you on your way out."

The deputies left, making a show of shutting the door tight.

"Sit down, please," Wyatt said to Marvin.

Marvin sat. "You bad, man," he said to Wyatt.

"That's not my style, but you do what you have to do," Wyatt told him. "There are better ways to get someone's attention than to get in their face, but sometimes a two-by-four between the eyes is the only way."

Marvin laughed. "Shit, man, I know how that one goes."

Walcott and Dancer had watched the display between Wyatt and the deputies, and his easy bantering with Marvin, with interest and some apprehension.

"That was a good show," Dancer told Wyatt, breaking into their conversation, "but it can have repercussions down the line." He nodded toward Marvin as if with grave significance.

"It won't in this case," Wyatt answered.

"How can you be sure?" Dancer countered.

"Because I won't let them." Taking a deep breath, he plunged in. "Marvin, these men are with the Public Defender's office. This is Mr. Walcott"—he indicated Walcott, sitting to his left—"and his senior associate, Mr. Dancer," leaning across Walcott to point to Dancer.

"May I?" Walcott asked Wyatt.

"Yes." Wyatt turned back to Marvin. "Mr. Walcott is an experienced and highly regarded defense lawyer," he said. "So listen carefully to what he has to tell you."

Walcott leaned his elbows on the table so that he could be closer to Marvin. "You've been accused of a very, very serious crime," he said as prelude to his presentation. "You understand the seriousness of this, right?"

"Yeah, man, I understand all right, but I didn't do it!" Marvin said loudly.

"Okay, I hear you, and that's good," Walcott said, "but you are going to go to trial for murder, whether you did them or not. The grand jury has brought a bill of particulars against you—that means they've charged you with seven counts of murder. The charges will be formalized by the end of this week or earlier. Which means you have to have the best and most experienced criminal-trial lawyer you can afford."

"I do," Marvin answered. He pointed to Wyatt. "I got him."

Walcott nodded slowly. "Mr. Matthews has been your attorney up to now, that's true. And he has done an admirable job for you." He leaned forward again, steepling his fingers, talking slowly and precisely. "Mr. Matthews is one of the best lawyers in this country. One of the very best—"

"Yeah, I figured that out myself," Marvin interrupted. He flashed his mother a grin.

Jonnie Rae was gripping the edges of the table so hard her knuckles were almost white. Wyatt put a calming hand on top of hers.

"—but he is not experienced in criminal cases such as yours," Walcott went on. "He has never tried a capital case. A murder case in the first degree with extenuating circumstances, which could bring the death penalty, if you were to lose," he said, emphasizing his point.

"I didn't do it, man," Marvin said, flaring. "This is a frame-up."

"Well, the state is going to have to prove you did, beyond a reasonable doubt," Walcott said, "and they are going to have a very heavy burden of proof; and if you didn't do it, as you claim, it's going to be very hard for them to prove otherwise."

Marvin flared up immediately. "What do you mean, 'as I

claim'? I flat-out *did not do it,* man. I don't give a shit who says otherwise. Whoever says I did is a goddamn liar, and I'll tell him to his motherfucking face!"

"Marvin!" Jonnie Rae called out.

"Sorry, Mama," Marvin said, abashed. "But these guys're saying I killed those women, and I didn't!"

"No," Walcott corrected him. "You misunderstood me. The state is claiming that. They have to prove it. We don't have to prove you didn't. All we have to do is show the jury that the state hasn't proved that you did."

"Same difference," Marvin said.

"No, it's a huge difference," Wyatt cut in. "May I?" he asked Walcott.

Walcott nodded reluctantly.

"I can explain this," Dancer cut in. Coming up out of his chair and leaning toward Marvin, he said, "It doesn't matter if you're guilty or not—"

"That is not what he wants to hear," Wyatt said, stopping him. To Marvin: "You don't have to prove anything. They have to prove everything. That's the whole deal. Since they've accused you of all of those murders they have to put you at every single one of those murder sites, at the time the murders occurred. It's a long chain and every link in it has to be solid. And Marvin," he said in a calm, reassuring voice, "I don't think they can do that."

"No fucking way," Marvin said stoutly. "Sorry, Mama," he apologized again.

"It's okay, baby," she said. "You're under a lot of stress here."

"Okay, thank you," Walcott said to Wyatt. He turned his attention to Marvin again. "Let's not get sidetracked here, okay? We have a lot of work to do together. You and your lawyer are going to be working hand in hand for the next several months, preparing the best defense you can have. And a lawyer who has never walked down that road before—we can't let that happen. It would be unfair to you."

Marvin stared at him. Then he looked at Dancer, then at Wyatt, then at Walcott again. "So what're you telling me? That he ain't my lawyer anymore?" he asked, pointing at Wyatt. Then the finger swung to Dancer. "And he is?"

"Yes," Walcott said. "That is our intention."

Marvin looked at Wyatt. "Where's this coming from, man? I thought you were my lawyer."

"I was," Wyatt answered. He didn't want to go to war with Walcott—not in front of Marvin, anyway.

"And he can tell you what to do?" Meaning Walcott.

"He's the boss."

"I thought you were a private lawyer. I'm confused," Marvin said.

"I am a private lawyer, but I'm working for the Public Defender's office on this case." Even as Wyatt said the words, they sounded ridiculous. He didn't work *for* anyone, except his clients.

Marvin looked at Dancer. "How many murder cases you tried, man?"

"I've tried over a dozen cases of murder in the first degree," Dancer answered.

"And how many you won?"

"I've won more than my share. You can't win them all," Dancer said.

"I don't give a fuck about them all," Marvin said. "All's I care about is me." He shook his head. "I've seen too many of my friends go down because they got lame defenses from the Public Defenders. You guys don't have what it takes to go up against them big guys."

Wyatt winced. He shifted in his chair, away from the two lawyers to his left.

"We do as well as anyone in the private sector," Walcott interjected strongly, stung by Marvin's accusation.

Marvin glared at him. "Let me ask you a question," he said.

"All right."

Watching this bitter repartee, Wyatt felt compassion for Walcott. The man was doing the best he could under difficult circumstances. The sad reality was that there was a basic truth to Marvin's accusation. Everyone knew the Public Defender's office in the city, like public agencies all over the country that catered to the underclass, was woefully underfunded—deliberately—so that the prosecution would have a clear edge over them. An equal playing field was not what the public wanted. They wanted the Marvin Whites of this world to go down, and go down hard.

"Ain't this my decision?" Marvin asked, "I mean I am

being tried as an adult here, so I should make an adult's decision, ain't that right?"

"Yes," Walcott conceded, "it is your decision to make. And it is our obligation to help you make the best decision you can. The best decision for you."

"Well, my decision is, I want him." He pointed to Wyatt. "I want me a private lawyer who wins big cases. You still my lawyer, man?" he asked Wyatt.

"If that's what you want."

"That's what I want."

"This is not a good idea," Dancer interjected forcefully. "The state bar is going to look closely at this, not to mention our opponents in the prosecutor's office. We could stand accused of malpractice, or worse," he impressed upon Walcott.

"Hey, man, let me ask you a question," Marvin interjected.

Dancer turned to him.

"How many Rolexes you own?"

"What?" Dancer asked, confused.

"Rolex watches, man. How many do you own?"

"Watches? Oh, I get it," Dancer said, catching on. "Rolex watches."

"Yeah. How many?"

"You don't get rich in my job," Dancer said. "But you have other rewards. You get to help people who really need your help. People like you," he said pointedly.

The sarcasm, blunt as a hammer blow, was wasted on Marvin. "That's real good—for you," he said. "Me, I want the lawyer does good enough he can buy a *armful* of Rolexes. That's the lawyer I want."

Wyatt leaned back in his chair. It had come down to the watch on his wrist. But as he thought about it, he could see the logic. Winners got the rewards. And that's what Marvin White wanted, more than experience. A winner.

Wyatt sent Jonnie Rae home in a taxi. Then he cornered Walcott in the lobby before he left the jail. Dancer had already stormed off.

"I didn't want it this way," Wyatt said. "I want this case, and I'll bust my gut, but I wasn't trying to go around you."

"Well, for Marvin White's sake, I hope it works out," Walcott said. He turned and walked out.

Wyatt ran across the street in the rain to his car. He thought to ask Walcott if he wanted a ride, but he knew the answer would be no. The man's pride had been hurt; he wouldn't accept the offer.

As he got into his Jaguar he saw the small figure trudging down the street. The Public Defender's umbrella was of little use to him—as Wyatt drove away he could see that Walcott was already soaking wet.

Darryl Davis reached Wyatt on his car phone. It wasn't an unexpected call. He drove down to the firm, parked in his designated spot, and rode up to his office. After greeting the receptionist, he strode down the long corridors to his office. "Let Darryl Davis know he can come see me as soon as it's convenient," he instructed Annetta, his secretary. Then he went into his office, shut the door firmly behind him, and sat down at his desk, swiveling around to look outside at the rainy day, the wet streets far below, the river running fast and brown.

His phone buzzed. "Mr. Davis is here, Mr. Matthews," Annetta announced.

He opened the door and drew Darryl in, taking his colleague's arm and practically dragging him into the room. As he closed the door behind him: "No disturbances," he told Annetta. "I'm not even here."

"I already heard," Darryl said, cutting to the chase. They sat cattycorner at his coffee table, facing each other. "Walcott called. He ain't too happy with you, pilgrim."

"Good news travels fast. What'd he tell you?"

"That you're a hog and a prima donna and a jive ass. Nothing I didn't already know."

"Seriously, what did he say?" Wyatt shifted uncomfortably in his chair.

"That you're putting this kid's life in jeopardy because of your ego."

Wyatt exploded. "Oh, man, that is such a crock of shit! Marvin White *wants* me to be his lawyer. I offered to step aside. The kid wouldn't hear of it, nor would his mother. These guys down there"—pointing with a cocked finger at some nebulous place below him—"they're the ones with the swollen egos."

Darryl looked at him squarely. "I think everybody needs to park their egos outside the door and start looking at the big picture. Especially you," he said bluntly.

Wyatt started to respond—something hot, which was how he felt. But he thought better of it in a flash. There was truth to what Darryl was saying. His ego *was* large; he had won the right for it to be with his success over the years. No one would deny that. In this situation, however, while what he had done wasn't wrong, it wasn't exactly in key, either. "You've got something to say, go ahead and say it," he told Darryl.

Darryl crossed his long legs and eased back into the deep couch. He stroked his goatee, which he had started wearing in college, an homage to his boyhood idol, Bill Russell. Now when people looked at him they thought of Cornel West, if anyone. Facial hair had helped when he was a young man, making him look older, which for a lawyer normally meant more qualified, more trustworthy; but this particular beard, with its Vandyke upswirl around the lips, was not a standard-issue confidence-inspirer. This kind of beard had a subtle threat to it; it was a beard vaguely of the street.

Darryl knew that his beard made some people uneasy, in a subconscious way. But it also conveyed a certain power, the power of being his own man. And like all powerful men, he had a big ego. However, he had been studying Zen for years, and he knew when his ego was an encumbrance rather than an asset.

"What the PD guys said is true," Darryl began. "You're not qualified to handle this," he said bluntly. "You don't know from trial law, and you're going up against a machine that grinds out guilty verdicts by the boxcar load. And you don't know your client's world. Lots of white people do—cops, social workers, probation officers, teachers. And regular folks. But you've been isolated from all that."

Wyatt bristled but held his tongue.

Darryl continued. "The one thing in your favor is, because you haven't been exposed to that life, you don't have an attitude formed from hundreds of negative experiences. All you know about it is what you see on TV and read in the papers. And that's always a glorification of the negative, never the positive, because shootings and rapes and drug busts and all that crap sells. Getting by day by day doesn't. So maybe, in a weird way, you being a naif will be a good thing for your client." He paused. "Walcott's intentions were wrong, but his reasoning was right. This is an extremely important case—"

"You think I don't know that?" Wyatt interjected.

"—not just for justice in this city," Darryl continued, "not just for the safety and peace of mind of the people of this city, but for race relations in this city."

Wyatt whacked the sides of his skull with his knuckles. "Am I missing something? Why is this a racial issue? The victims were black, most of them. If any segment of the community should want to solve this thing, I would think it's the black community."

"It isn't that simple. Lookit here," Darryl said, leaning forward. "What we've got—your client—is a young, big, strong black man with a criminal record. A man who when he walks down a street is automatically suspect, especially in a white neighborhood. Who scares women and children."

"What does that have to do with my being his lawyer?"

Darryl took his time before answering. "Okay. This is a *racial* trial," he said, drawing out the word "racial." "Any time a black man goes on trial, it automatically is a *racial* trial. The black man may be guilty, and his victim might be another black, and the jury might be black, and the judge might be black, but it's still a *racial* trial. And this case in particular is going to be a racial trial, Wyatt, because this is about taming the black beast. This trial is going to be only partly about whether or not this kid did these killings. What it really is going to be about, deep down underneath, is putting the animal back into the cage—or worse, eliminating him."

He got up and started pacing around, the way a lawyer does when he's deep into his jury summation and is starting to pull out the stops. "Here's the thing. Young black man. Disadvantaged—in some way he is bound to be disadvantaged, it's a given in our society, kid with his background. Poor, of course, people with money don't go the public defender route. So here he is, accused of the crime of the century the way the press in this city's going to play it. And who is defending him? Why, it's none other than the great white father. The great benevolent white liberal who has given his time, free of charge, to help out this poor black youth." He stopped. "Do you see what's wrong with this picture?"

"You're telling me I can't defend him because I'm white? That's outrageous!"

"Yes, but it is the way it is. It isn't just the white part. A white public defender, some guy with gravy stains on his tie, who went to law school at night, all that stuff, he could do the job. He'd be accepted, because he has his problems, too. Or someone like William Kunstler—God rest his ornery soul—he had the history, he was cool with black folks before it was cool and after it was cool, too. But you—you don't have any problems, Wyatt. You're rich, you're talented, you do your lawyering for corporations like Microsoft and AT&T. The jury isn't going to be able to relate to you, man. They're going to be suspicious of you from the minute you walk in that courtroom until the minute you walk out of it."

"But that's racist," Wyatt protested. "That's reverse racism."

"Yes, well, it is, but it is. You think Robert Shapiro would have got O.J. off? If he had done the exact same things, word for word, that Johnnie Cochran did? I don't think so. It was a brother doing it that pulled that off."

"O.J. had white lawyers."

"A Jew from Brooklyn. One step up from a black. But putting that all aside—those men were professional criminal-defense trial lawyers. They had all done this before. Lee Bailey's probably been involved in over a hundred murder trials. You have never, not ever, tried this type of a criminal case, let alone a capital crime."

Wyatt thought about that for a moment before he answered. "Well, that's true," he admitted. "But you know what? I don't care. I'm not one to brag on myself, but I am one terrific lawyer. And there are a hundred and fifty members of this firm who know that, including you."

"You've got no argument there," Darryl agreed. He sat down next to Wyatt. "Maybe you should take this out of the Public Defender's office altogether," he said. "Run it out of my division. You'd have a lot more support that way, and you'd still be doing what you want to do."

Wyatt cracked his knuckles backward. "Believe me, I thought about that. A lot. But I can't."

"Why not?"

"Walcott's already had to eat crow, big-time. Taking the case out of his office would be a brutal insult. But that's not the real reason." Now it was his turn to get up and start pacing. "If I bring this case in here, I'll have every tool I'll need. Your guys will do the legwork, and I'll be left to run the show. Which would be fine normally—I've been on that track for twenty years now. But that's not what I want to do, in fact it's the opposite of what I want to do. I want to do the work, as much of it as I possibly can. I mean hitting the bricks, finding and interviewing the witnesses, formulating the philosophy of the case, all of it. That's as important to me as the results. That's why I left. You know what?" he continued, really seeing what it was that was troubling him about that idea. "If I leave the Public Defender's office with this case, then I've lost. They'll be right. I'll be this prima donna who's pulling rank. I don't want that. I want to win this because *I* can do it, not because of my surroundings. Because *I'm* better."

"Well, I hope you're right," his partner said. "Because in a situation like this there's no prize for second. We're talking experience in this particular field, for which there is no substitute."

"You're wrong," Wyatt responded. "All Walcott's horses and all Walcott's men have plenty of experience and they couldn't do the job for Marvin White that I'm going to do, not if they stood on their heads on the Fourth of July and spat out rubies, pearls, and diamonds. And do you know why? Because I've got something better. I've got passion." He pointed to his heart. "You can't buy my passion for this case."

Wyatt's meeting with Walcott later in the day, if not sweet, was mercifully short. "I'm going to do a great job with this," Wyatt said, "and I assume I'll have your full backing and the full backing of your department."

"We'll do whatever we can," Walcott said evenly. He had not offered his hand in greeting, nor had he risen in his chair. "It won't be like what you're used to," he cautioned Wyatt. "We have our limits, financial and manpower-wise, but we're all here for the client. Just like you."

"That's all I ask," Wyatt responded. "Obviously, I'll run everything by you."

"Yes."

"I know I won't have a lot of full-time staff helping me," Wyatt continued, "but I would like Josephine's services on an exclusive basis."

Walcott stiffened. "As much as possible, yes," he answered noncommittally.

"It's a capital case."

"If you feel you need her on a full-time basis . . ."

"Look," Wyatt said, feeling his temper rise and trying to keep it in check. "Let's quit pussyfooting around, okay? You got your feelings hurt this morning. I'm sorry about that but it's history now. I'm asking you for one lousy person to be assigned to this. I'll scrounge for the rest of it, like everyone around here has to do."

"All right." Walcott folded his arms magisterially across his bantam chest. "You can have Josephine."

"Thank you." Wyatt reached his hand across the desk. "We don't have to be friends, but it'll be deadly for Marvin White if we're enemies."

Walcott took the offered hand. "You're right."

"And I know you'll make sure the rest of this department feels the same way."

"No one here is going to be your enemy."

No one was home. Wyatt changed into his running gear. There was still enough light to get in a half-hour run. He stretched in the driveway, feeling his quads and hamstrings start to loosen. Punching the timer on his watch, he started an easy, comfortable jog, circling around the back of his house.

Normally Wyatt ran on the county road. It was little traveled because it didn't go anywhere except to the houses that were set off from it, and he could run as fast as he wanted without worrying about his footing. Occasionally, though, he would go to the end of his property line, behind his pool house, and take off into the woods that abutted his lot, running along a narrow fire road that meandered through the undeveloped area for dozens of miles. The road had been cut through the woods by a state agency to facilitate firefighters in case they ever had to get back there in an emergency. In all the time Wyatt had lived here, over a dozen years now, there had never been an occasion for a fire company to use it; but it was cleared out once a year, at the end of winter, to make sure it was usable, just in case.

The road, hard-packed dirt with a thin covering of gravel, was peaked in the center, so it drained well. Along the edges there were random pools of water from the earlier rain, but in the middle it was dry enough, easy to navigate. Here and there deep root-systems from old-growth trees would break through the road, so you had to watch your step, but he had run and walked and biked it enough that he knew where the problem areas were. The road was flat for the most part; where there were grades they were gradual, gentle slopes, so it wasn't like a normal trail through the woods, where you were constantly going up and down and you had to keep a sharp eye out for your footing.

These woods—it was more like a forest, the growth was so dense in most places—went on for miles. He ran at an easy, comfortable pace, sweating out the negative garbage through his pores, thinking about the day's events. He had pulled off some bold moves: manipulating Marvin White and his mother so that he, Wyatt, stayed on the case—an act of muscle, guts, and bravado. And pulling rank on Walcott, which he hadn't been particularly subtle about.

He was okay with that, because he was doing this for the right reason. He was going to defend Marvin White with every breath he drew, and he didn't need to apologize to anyone about it.

He'd only had one misgiving, which had come to him late in the day as he was driving home: he had to go through with this now. He had to follow it to the end—the train had left the station and there was no getting off. For a moment, sitting there in the cocoon the Jaguar provided against the world, he'd panicked, his butt literally had puckered up; but that had passed almost as fast as it had come. That was the point. He wanted to have to take this all the way. This was what he had been preparing for, for twenty-five years.

Snatches of Frost's poem "Stopping by Woods on a Snowy Evening," which he had memorized in a high school English class, flitted through his head as he ran. "The woods are lovely, dark, and deep, But I have promises to keep, And miles to go before I sleep. . . ." He gazed up at the trees alongside the pathway as he ran, thick stands of hardwoods, hickory and maple and cherry. Miles and miles of trees, thick, lush fern-growth underneath, heavy gnarly bush, berry and poison ivy, roots, mushrooms, native grasses. Everything green, lush, the smells of wet black dirt pungent in his nostrils as he pressed on, stride following stride. The humidity was high because of the rain; he sweated through his singlet and shorts and all down his arms, under his arms, between his legs, his brow, his neck. He should have worn a sweatband, he thought, rubbing his forearm against his eyes and forehead to clear the salty moisture off.

He was so free here, he could run forever, and he thought then of Marvin White, who was in a nine-by-six-foot jail cell, three paces long, confined like an animal in a cage, which was the point—that's exactly what he was.

The sun set and he ran in the soft light of dusk, emerging onto his property as it was getting too dark to see anymore. Sticking his head in the pool to cool down, he slicked his hair back and went in the house through the back door.

Moira and Michaela were in the kitchen preparing dinner: take-out lasagna, garlic bread, and Caesar salad. Cloris was off, so it would be the three of them. Wyatt realized they hardly ever ate as a family anymore; Michaela wasn't home at dinnertime usually—she either ate earlier by herself and then went out to study with friends, or she and her friends would grab a quick pizza somewhere.

"Hey," he said, giving them each a lean-over kiss so he wouldn't drip on them. "Where have you two been?"

"Here and there," Moira answered gaily. She was in a good mood, he was glad to see. Mother and daughter looked at each other and shared a smile, from which he was definitely excluded.

"What's the secret?" he asked.

"Nothing," Moira assured him. "Just girl stuff. Jump in the shower, we can eat anytime."

They ate in the kitchen. He opened a cheap bottle of Chianti, which they drank from tumblers. Michaela had a Coke and talked about her day. She was writing away to colleges with the help of her adviser; she would take her exploratory trip pretty soon. She definitely wanted to be in the East, and she was thinking about an all-women's college, Smith or Wellesley. She'd check out Bryn Mawr, too. Brown was still her first choice, but she wanted to look at other schools. Wherever it was, it had to be near where she could dance.

"And how was your day, darling?" Moira asked pleasantly, turning to Wyatt.

He washed down a mouthful of lasagna with a swig of wine. "I came close to quitting the Public Defender's today," he told them. "It's not a good situation. We're oil and water—they don't like some 'hotshot' coming in and stealing their thunder."

Moira beamed. Holding her glass high, she said, "I'll drink to that."

She didn't hear me, he thought, his heart sinking. She's pulling the wool over her own eyes.

Michaela looked at him. "Why would you do that, Daddy? I thought that's what you wanted."

He put his glass down. "It is. But I don't fit in there." He spread his hands, a gesture of resignation. "I'm on a different level professionally than they are, sweetie, and we're having a hard time finding common ground."

She nodded. "But you wouldn't get to do what you want," she said with concern. "Defend that murder suspect."

"I know," he answered her. "That's why I decided to stick it out."

Moira, who was helping herself to a little more lasagna, dropped her utensils and stared at him. "You're not going to quit?" Her voice was shaking. "Then what was the point of even bringing it up?"

"You asked me how my day went," he reminded her.

She spoke slowly, under strong control. "Why are you still doing this? Why are you working on this murder?"

"Because I want to." The room was quiet. "Because I have to."

She stood up and walked out of the room. "Moira," he called after her. He put his own knife and fork down. "Fuck"—under his breath.

Michaela watched with a sense of nervousness coupled

with excitement. Her father was defending the Alley Slasher. The kids in her school were going to freak.

"I wish I could make this right by her," he said sadly to his daughter.

She touched his hand with hers. A light touch, no heavier than the alighting of a butterfly. What a womanly gesture, he thought.

He looked at her. She was seventeen years old. She was, in fact, a woman.

"It's okay, Dad. She'll come around. She's always supported you in everything you've done." She smiled—the child parent to the father. "You'll see. It'll all be fine."

They lay in bed side by side. Not touching. Moira stared at the patterns of the curtains on the ceiling lit by the three-quarters moon that was moving in the breeze from the barely open window.

"I feel like I don't know you anymore," she told him, her eyes staring up ahead, not to the side where he lay.

"I'm the same man I always was."

"No, you're not. You've always been aggressive but I never thought you were reckless."

"I'm defending a man in a trial. What I've always done."

"No. You're trying to help a killer get loose so he can go back into society and kill again. I hate what you're doing, Wyatt. The thought that anyone would do it sets me on edge, but that it's my own husband . . . I don't know where to go with this, how I'm supposed to react."

He didn't answer her. Anything he said would only provoke further argument. He was going to have to let this take its normal course. Over time she'd understand why he was doing it, and that it was all right to do it. More than all right, the right thing. "I love you," he said instead.

"That's good," she replied, "but life is more complicated than that."

How long had they been married now? Almost twenty-three years. It had been an easy life. He had always had a good job, they never feared for anything. Everything had gone on an upward curve. Where was this anger coming from, he thought, this irrational fear? It wasn't like he'd lost a job, as was happening to so many men his age recently, including some of his college classmates, or committed a crime, or had an affair, or become an alcoholic, or . . .

"Life is change," he said. "Life is challenge."

"I like our life as it is. We have a wonderful life. I don't want it to change. We're not kids anymore, Wyatt. I like the path we're on. I don't want to start anew."

He reached over and took her hand. She was still a young woman. What was there to be afraid of? "Nothing's going to change. Nothing important."

"It already has." She withdrew her hand and rolled over onto her side, her back to him.

After he was sure she'd fallen asleep he got out of bed, quietly put on sweatpants and sweatshirt, and left the room. He went downstairs, let himself out the back door, and in the moonlight walked across the yard to the pool house.

His trombone sat where he'd left it on its stand in the corner. He opened the slide, sprayed some water in it, blew a few easy first-position F's to freshen his lip. Softly he started in on a ballad, "Yesterday," letting the vibrato resonate in the old-fashioned Tommy Dorsey swing style. The notes came out of the end of his horn like bubbles from a child's water pipe, fat and round and lush, filling the room with the sad sweetness he could feel in his heart for his wife.

Josephine was already at the office when Wyatt arrived at a quarter to eight the next morning. She handed him the *New York Times*. "I called your secretary," she explained as she handed him the paper. "She said you can't get started until you've had the *Times*. Wanted to make you feel at home."

"Don't start spoiling me," he warned her, "or I'll come to expect it." Setting his briefcase on his desk, he started to take off his raincoat.

"Another thing," she told him, "before you get too comfortable, this isn't your office anymore. The boss wants you to have a bigger space. More room, more quiet. You're doing the office's biggest case, so you need a better office." She grabbed his briefcase. "Follow me."

She led him through the maze, through a fire door, up a flight of service stairs, to a series of single cubicles that occupied a floor that seemed to be used for storage—there were rows and rows of old files stacked almost to the ceiling. Unlocking one of the doors, she spread out her arms. "It ain't what you're accustomed to, but at least you'll have privacy. Technically this floor isn't supposed to be used because of fire regulations, but . . ." She shrugged.

The room was small, about one-fifth the square footage of his own office. And there didn't seem to be anyone else up here. Still, it was a one-person office, with walls that went all the way to the ceiling and a small window that looked out onto the brick exterior of the adjoining building, ten feet away.

They've sent me to purgatory, he thought, almost breaking into laughter. Petty little shits.

"Mr. Walcott thought you'd be more . . . comfortable," she said, groping for words. "Away from the others." Smiling brightly: "I'm right next door. By this afternoon we'll have phone service, fax, copy machine, computers. Everything we need."

He hung his raincoat on a wire hanger, tossed the newspaper onto the corner of the desk. "It doesn't matter," he said.

She stood in the doorway. "What do you want me to get you first?" she asked.

"Has the grand jury indictment been sent over yet?"

"Yes."

"That."

By midafternoon he'd filled two legal pads with notes and was well into a third. This case was going to take a lot of legwork, a lot of time. Seven separate murders, seven different sets of circumstances, with just enough common threads linking them up to pin them all on one perpetrator.

The computer guy came at three-thirty, linking him and Josephine up to the system. He took the opportunity to go down to Walcott's office. Walcott kept him waiting a few minutes as he wound up a telephone conversation.

Wyatt didn't beat around the bush. "I need more space."

"I just gave you a bigger office," Walcott responded, clearly annoyed. "What you're used to, we don't have."

"My personal space is fine. I'm not talking about that," Wyatt said. "I need space for the files, the work. I'm going

to be subpoenaing police records, prison records, jail
records, medical records, I'm going to be interviewing
dozens of witnesses, potential alibi witnesses, there's going
to be a blizzard of paperwork to go through, and we need
space so we can get to whatever we need when we need it.
We're going to—"

Walcott stuck up his hand like a traffic cop. "Whoa! Rein
it in, man."

Wyatt stopped. Calmly: "You know what this is going to
take. I don't have to tell you."

"But there are things that *I* have to tell *you*." Walcott
picked up a thick stack of files on his desk. "Murder, arson,
armed robbery, rape. All these came in the last month, like
yours." He dropped the files with a thud. "We have one hundred eighteen major felony cases currently on our docket,
with more coming in every single day. They're all important, they all need attention. We have three, count 'em, investigators to handle this entire office's workload." He
stood up. "Let me ask you a rhetorical question. What do
you think this case would cost to defend if a private firm
were handling it and the defendant could afford to pay?"

"Several hundred thousand dollars."

"Think a million, or more," Walcott informed him. "You'd
have forensic experts, DNA experts, psychologists. You
would have a *team* of investigators pounding the streets,
looking for needles in haystacks. Dozens of paralegals, research staff." He paused. "None of which you're going to
get. Hell, assigning you Josephine full-time is a luxury. We
hardly ever do that, but because of the notoriety of this case,
we're bending our own rules." He shook his head. "Why do
you think the prosecution wins ninety percent of these
cases? We're outmanned, Wyatt. We're using a peashooter
against a howitzer."

"I get the picture," Wyatt said. "I'm still going to need
more space."

"You can have some of the other vacant offices up there,
as long as the fire marshal looks the other way. It's the best I
can do."

Wyatt started to press the issue, then checked his impulse.
Don't sweat the small stuff. It doesn't matter.

"Don't take this personally," Walcott said. "I'm not pun-
ishing you. Everyone here works under these constraints."

"That's comforting—I guess."

Walcott walked him to the door. "We're going to meet once a week—progress report," he reminded Wyatt. He stopped at the threshold. "I've been doing this for a long time. My door is always open."

"I'll remember that."

"Let's start with the basics. You do know Dwayne Thompson?"

"Yeah."

"How do you know him?"

"He was working in the infirmary when I was down there. He changed my bandages from where I was shot up."

"Did you and he talk at all about these murders? Any conversation at all?"

"Yeah, a little. It was on the TV."

Wyatt and Marvin were in a small, windowless room in the heart of the jail. Wyatt had wanted to bring a stenographer with him, but it wasn't in the budget.

"Did you say anything that might have implicated you in these killings? Anything, no matter how innocuous it might have been?"

"How what-cuous?"

"Ordinary. Unimportant."

Marvin bit his lip. "I might've said something like I knew where some of them took place or something like that. Shit, man, everybody in town knew that kind of stuff."

"So you did talk about them. And what you knew."

"Well . . . yeah, but it wasn't no secrets or nothing."

"Did you know that Dwayne Thompson is a convicted felon, and that he is currently doing a stretch at Durban?"

"Yeah."

"He told you?"

"Yeah."

"Did he tell you what he was doing down here in the county jail?"

"Said he was gonna be a witness in a trial."

"He didn't tell you he was a snitch?"

"Say what?"

"A stool pigeon. An inmate who works with the police in exchange for favors."

Marvin came out of his chair. "Shit, no!"

"You didn't know the reason Dwayne Thompson was down here was to be a state's witness and that he would get some benefits out of it?"

"Shit, no!" Marvin cried out again. "I didn't know nothing about that!"

"Sit down and calm down," Wyatt ordered Marvin.

Marvin slouched into the plastic chair. He started biting his nails. Wyatt noticed the cuticles were gnawed raw on most of Marvin's fingers. The kid had huge hands.

"Tell me what you told him," he said to Marvin. "Everything you can remember."

Marvin started whining. "The thing is, it was different times and I was in the middle of getting my bandages changed. . . ." He didn't want to tell his lawyer, this rich white man, that he'd been worried about Dwayne taking sexual liberties with him. It didn't seem manly somehow, like he couldn't take care of himself, or worse—that he had been thinking about that at all, like the lawyer might think he was interested in that kind of shit.

"Time out." Wyatt reached across the table and took Marvin's jaw in his hand, forcing Marvin to look him hard in the eye. "Do I have your attention?" he asked.

"Yeah, man." He tried to twist away from the hand that was holding him like a vice. Damn, this white dude was stronger than he looked.

"There's one thing, Marvin," Wyatt said in a firm tone of voice, relaxing his grip. "You don't bullshit me, okay? I'm your lawyer and my job is to get you off. And the way I do that is for you to be absolutely straight with me. No games, no con, no jive. Do I make myself clear?"

Marvin's memory was hazy about what he'd said to Dwayne, and when—they had talked about the killings more than one time; first when there was something about them on television, then later when Dwayne had brought the subject up.

"So you did tell him you knew where this latest killing took place. You knew where the location was?"

"Yeah. I knew where it was."

"How would you know that? That's not a club you frequent, you're underage."

"My delivery route. It went by there."

Wyatt leafed through his notes from the first meeting he'd had with Marvin, when the charge had been attempted armed robbery, not multiple murder.

A thought came to him. "This club. Is it close to the store you were going to rob?"

"Yeah. Pretty close."

"How far?"

"Two blocks. Three."

"That's not good."

Marvin was silent.

"Were you in that alley that night?"

"I was *by* it."

"*By* it?"

"I walked by it. On my way to the store."

"On your way." He glanced at their previous discussion again. "Which time? The first time or the second time?"

"The first or second time what?" Marvin looked confused.

"You were going to rob the store," Wyatt said, referring to his notes of their earlier meeting, "but it was too crowded, so you left and went somewhere for a smoke, and then you went back. So which one of those times was it you were by the alley, the first time or the second?"

"Umm . . . it would've been the second. Between them."

"So I've got it straight: you left the store, you walked by the alley, then you went back to the store."

"Yeah."

"Did you go *into* the alley?"

"I went through it."

"You went *through* it."

"Yeah."

"Well, if you went *through* it, that means you were *in* it."

"Yeah. I went through it."

His client was in the alley the night the killing took place. Around the same time. "What were you doing there?" he asked Marvin.

"Chillin'."

"I mean why there? That specific place?"

"It was quiet. Dark."

"So you went through the alley so you wouldn't be out on the street where you might be seen?"

"Yeah."

"Is that where you smoked your cigarette?"

Marvin shook his head. "I only took one puff off it. I don't smoke tobacco. That shit's no good. I just lit up 'cause . . ." He shrugged his shoulders.

They slogged on. Marvin had talked about the killings with Dwayne, and plenty. Everything he knew or had heard; and he'd embellished his knowledge, trying to show the experienced con that he, Marvin, was also a badass.

It was getting late, after four. They hadn't broken, not even for lunch; a couple piss calls, that was it. Wyatt needed to wrap this up—Marvin was going to be in court tomorrow morning to be formally charged, and he had more homework to do in preparation for that. Over the next few months they would be spending plenty of time together.

"One last thing." He took the female witness's statement out of his briefcase, skimmed through it rapidly. He had read it the night before. It was a damaging document. "When you were in that alley, where the latest victim was discovered. Did anyone see you? Think hard. This is important."

This witness had positively ID'd Marvin in a police lineup as the man she had seen in the parking lot shortly before Paula Briggs had gone out there. But Marvin wouldn't know that; he wouldn't know that anyone had testified to that.

Marvin cracked his knuckles backward. It sounded like rifle fire, sharp and loud. Then he bit at a cuticle that was already bleeding from his worrying it.

"Yeah," he allowed, obviously reluctant to admit to it. "There was this woman, saw me for about a second."

"White or black? Or was she Latino, or Asian?"

"She was a white bitch." He remembered her, all right. She had ranked him out, hassling him about looking in her sorry-ass car. "It was dark out there, man, she couldn't have got no good look at me."

Good enough to pick you out of a lineup, Wyatt thought glumly, and corroborate the testimony of a man you have admitted you discussed the murders with.

This witness was another element he would have to check

out. Maybe she had been there, but the police could have seized on that and pointed her in the right direction. It wouldn't be the first time.

At least the kid hadn't lied about it. That was encouraging.

He crammed the papers into his briefcase, stood up. "That's it for today. I'll see you in court tomorrow morning. Your mother is going to bring some decent clothes to the jail for you to wear at your arraignment. Make sure you clean up. Shave, shower, wash your hair. You want to make a favorable impression—there will be a lot of media present, we want them to see a clean-looking young man, not some scruffy-looking hood, okay?"

"Yeah, okay," Marvin mumbled. "I'll have my act together."

They shook hands. "We're in this together," Wyatt promised Marvin. "I'm there with you. All the way."

The formal arraignment was scheduled for eight-thirty in the morning. By seven the area in front of the courthouse was packed with reporters, camera crews, and other various and sundry media personnel. The two local papers had over a dozen representatives between them, while the city's four TV stations were on board with full crews—reporters, camera, sound. In addition, there were contingents from the *New York Times,* the *L.A. Times,* the *Washington Post, USA Today.* National television—ABC, NBC, CBS, CNN—was present in force. They jockeyed for position on the courthouse steps, spilling down into the street and along the sidewalk for a solid block in both directions. Across the wide boulevard, which was one of the central arteries for the city, vendors had already set up stalls, selling coffee, hot dogs, and T-shirts with pictures of Marvin White silk-screened across the fronts.

The police had barricaded the street for two blocks down on either side. Only officially sanctioned vehicles could get in and out. A squad of mounted cops, riding up and down, kept a semblance of order, aided by dozens of officers on bicycles who joined them in providing crowd control.

Walcott had telephoned Wyatt at home shortly after six to warn him of the scope of the situation. It was arranged that Wyatt would park in a private lot behind the courthouse and be escorted in through a back entrance, which was blocked off to everyone except those who had to be inside. The same procedure would be in place for Marvin's mother and siblings.

Even so, as Wyatt approached the area surrounding the courthouse he was astonished at the size and energy of the mob. It was a creature unto itself, live and pulsating. Wyatt wasn't sure how this kind of energy would play into the proceedings, but he knew it would have a role, not only at this hearing but all down the line. No one was immune to it—not jurors, judges, prosecutors, or defense lawyers. They would feel the heat of the public. The TV stations and newspapers would chronicle their triumphs and defeats on a daily basis, issuing scorecards of who won on a given day, and more importantly, who lost.

He showed his ID to the policeman guarding the entrance to the parking lot. "This is pretty amazing," he commented.

The cop scowled as he checked Wyatt's name against a list he had on his clipboard. "Waste of time and money," he scoffed as he realized who Wyatt was. "Ought to ice the son of a bitch right now and save us all the expense."

"And you have a pleasant day, too," Wyatt replied, rolling up his car window and driving through.

Inside, he made his way to the small room set aside for defense counsel. This would be a simple proceeding, lasting less than ten minutes. Marvin would be brought in, the charges against him would be read, and he would make his plea: not guilty. Of course, anything could happen.

Walcott showed up a few minutes later. "Quite a show," he commented.

"I've been involved in some pretty huge cases," Wyatt agreed, "and I've never seen a circus like this."

"Murder has sex appeal," Walcott observed sardonically. "Back in medieval times, when they'd hang a man in the public square, the whores would do their best business."

There was a knock on the door. A deputy ushered Jonnie Rae and her three younger children in. Two girls and a boy, dressed up in their finest and scrubbed squeaky-clean. Wyatt guessed their ages to be between sixteen and nine or ten. Cute kids. They were intimidated by the entire process, he knew; what kid wouldn't be? He could imagine Michaela having to deal with something like this.

Actually, he couldn't.

"How are you?" Wyatt asked Jonnie Rae solicitously, offering her a chair.

"Frightened to death." She looked over at Walcott.

"I'll meet you inside the courtroom," Walcott said. He went out, closing the door behind him.

"Marvin got his fresh clothing?" he asked.

"Had them at the jail six on the dot, minute they opened."

"Did you manage to get here without too much trouble?" he asked. He should have sent a car for her; having to go to the jail and then come here, with three children in tow, was unfair. If he'd been working this case out of his office, arranging her transportation would have been taken care of automatically. This was a different world. He couldn't take anything for granted.

"One of Marvin's friends carried us down," she said.

A bailiff opened the door and stuck his head in. "They're ready upstairs."

Wyatt sat at the defense table. Walcott and Josephine were in the first row directly behind him, alongside Jonnie Rae and Marvin's half-sisters and brother. Marvin hadn't been brought in yet.

Helena Abramowitz was in the lead position at the defense table. Her matching skirt and jacket were dark blue, her blouse was white, her stockings were ultrasheer black, and her black pumps had a three-inch heel. Her lipstick was dark red.

When she had entered the chamber, a few moments after he did, she took her place at the prosecution table, made eye contact with Wyatt, and nodded blandly. Then she consciously turned away from him and began conversing with other members of her team. Wyatt noticed that the other prosecuting attorney was a black man.

They were in the big courtroom, Room A, a much more commodious and formal room than the one he'd been in last week. It was a high, domed-ceilinged room, with seating for 108 spectators. All the seats were taken; there were people standing in the aisles in violation of the fire regulations. About three dozen seats, in the first three rows, had been allotted to the press and certain police and government officials.

All the way in the rear, standing with their backs to the wall, he noticed three very tough-looking young black men. Looking more closely at them, he recognized one from the earlier time they'd been in court, when the picture had been considerably rosier: the one wearing the $1,500 suit with all the accessories. That's who brought the family today, he realized, which accounted for how they'd gained entrance to this hot-ticket event. Marvin's friends, who by their appearance were drug dealers or gang leaders.

The young man caught Wyatt looking at him. He stared back, his eyes black and impassive, showing no feeling of anything.

He'd have to ask Marvin who that was. If the fellow, who looked to be Marvin's age, was close enough to Marvin to have driven the family here, and then hung around to watch the proceedings and take them home, he would be someone Wyatt would want to talk to.

There was a stirring in the audience as Alex Pagano entered the room. He came in from the doors in back, stopped briefly and dramatically to milk the moment, then slowly made his way up the crowded aisle, greeting various friends in the congregation until he reached the turnstile and pushed through.

He approached Wyatt, holding out his hand. "A fair fight," he said. "A good fight."

"Like letting me find out about it on the eleven o'clock news instead of calling me first, a professional courtesy I've always extended. You want a fight, ace, I'm your man."

Pagano's smile abruptly faded. He turned away and sat down with his people, engaging them in conversation.

A sudden collective gasp: Marvin White, dressed in white shirt, tie, and dark pants, was led in by two jail deputies and brought to the defense table. The deputies removed his handcuffs and took their places along the far wall close to the defense table, assuming an at-ease but alert position.

"Don't you have a sports coat?" Wyatt whispered in Marvin's ear, leaning in close to his client.

Marvin shook his head. "Not one I could wear in here." He rubbed his wrists where the cuffs had chapped them.

Wyatt made a mental note to get Marvin's sizes and send

Josephine out shopping. The kid would need some decent clothes when he came to trial—a couple sports coats, some white dress shirts and ties, decent slacks. He wouldn't bother going to Walcott for the money—he knew what the answer would be. He would pay for it out of his own pocket.

"How do you feel?" he asked, turning to Marvin again.

"Scared," Marvin answered with a nervous hiccup.

"This'll be over fast. When the judge asks how you plead, you stand up and say, slowly and clearly, 'Not guilty.' Don't be belligerent, or embellish it with some line of crap," he instructed Marvin. " 'Not guilty' and then sit down."

Marvin nodded.

A small door opened behind the judge's bench. "Oyez, oyez, oyez," cried out the bailiff. "All rise! This court is now in session, Judge William T. Grant presiding."

Judge Grant was the senior judge in superior court. He was going to run this one himself, to make sure it was done the right way. And if the publicity helped him get a seat on a state appeals court, or better yet, a federal judgeship, that would be okay, too.

Wyatt knew Bill Grant socially, to say hello to. Grant was a conservative, a stern jurist who didn't put up with any nonsense in his courtroom. He knew the law and expected the advocates standing in front of him to know it as well. He'd reamed plenty of lawyers out over the years for not being prepared to his standards. The stories about Grant had amused Wyatt when he'd heard them at cocktail parties. He didn't know how funny they'd be if they were directed at him.

Wyatt rose to his feet, buttoning his jacket as he did so. He touched Marvin's shoulder to make sure Marvin didn't take his time standing up. First impressions were important.

Judge Grant swung his gavel once, hard. "Be seated," he commanded. There was a shuffling of chairs as 115 people sat back down. "Call the case," Grant said to his bailiff.

"People versus Marvin White," the bailiff sang out.

Grant looked down toward the prosecution table. "Are the people ready?" he asked.

Helena rose, smoothing her skirt. "We are, Your Honor."

He swung over to the defense. "And the defendant?"

Wyatt stood in place. "Ready, Your Honor."

"Nice to see you in my court, Mr. Matthews," Grant said,

his pale gray eyes flashing a brief tight smile behind his rimless wire glasses.

"It's an honor to be here."

He remained standing for a brief moment; not so long as to be overtly obvious, but enough so that his psychological presence, his gravitas, was clearly felt. Then he sat down. In the legal world he was important, a major player nationally; not in criminal court, perhaps, but a force to be reckoned with. Grant couldn't help himself; he'd had to acknowledge that.

He glanced over at the prosecution table. Pagano had studiously turned his back, but Helena was staring at him, taking his measure. Seeing that she'd been caught looking, she turned away—a bit too quickly for the nonchalance she wanted to affect.

Grant leaned forward in his chair, his eyes on Marvin. "The accused will rise."

Wyatt nudged Marvin. Marvin stood up.

"You have been accused of the crime of murder," Grant said, looking down at Marvin with a stern visage. "How do you plead?"

Marvin took a deep breath. "Not guilty," he said, slowly and clearly, like his fancy lawyer had told him to.

Grant nodded. "I'm going to set the trial date for"—he leafed through his calendar—"July sixth."

"Isn't that fast?" Wyatt asked with concern.

"The law guarantees every defendant the right to a speedy trial," the judge answered. "I would think you would want to get at this as quickly as possible, Mr. Matthews, for your client's sake."

"For my client's sake I want to be as prepared as possible," Wyatt rejoined. "Mr. White has been arraigned on seven counts of murder. Setting up a defense for seven crimes of anything, let alone murder, could be a long process, Your Honor. I don't know that it's possible to prepare properly in that short a period of time."

Grant looked over at the prosecutor's table. "Do you have a position on this?" he asked.

"We can be fully prepared in that time," Helena said smoothly, rising to her feet. "We don't feel it would be in the interests of justice to drag this out unnecessarily."

"The court agrees," Grant said without thinking further

about it. "July sixth it is. If you run into unforeseen hardships, Mr. Matthews," he said to Wyatt, "you can come back in here and ask for a continuance. I'm not trying to tie your hands in any way, Counselor, but I agree with the state—it's in everyone's interest to move this along."

The deputies handcuffed Marvin and led him out. Wyatt spoke for a moment with Jonnie Rae, reassuring her as best he could. She left in the company of her children and Marvin's tough-looking friends.

Wyatt handed his briefcase to Josephine. "I'll be back in the office in about an hour. We'll start looking into discovery."

"I'll be there." Lugging the bulky case, she left with Walcott.

Wyatt waited until the courtroom had cleared. Then he went outside.

It was bedlam. The entire corridor was jammed with reporters. Wyatt pushed his way through the throng, assisted by some deputies who flanked him and shoved people out of his way, literally pushing them to the side.

"Mr. Matthews. Can you tell us . . . ?"

"What is your reaction to . . . ?"

"How did you get involved in . . . ?"

He pushed forward, not answering, fighting through the thicket. Then he was by them and on the elevator and the police were blocking access to everyone else, and he rode it down to the ground floor. He wanted to make a statement but he needed a few minutes to get his thoughts in order.

The major television networks and stations had set up shop on the courthouse steps. Alex Pagano stood in front of a massive bank of microphones, simultaneously answering questions and issuing his statement, putting his spin on what had happened inside. Standing behind him, his staff, with Helena Abramowitz in the foreground, hovered like a protective and adoring flock.

"Today is a giant step in the right direction for this city," Pagano was saying. "Tonight, for the first time in a long time, our citizens can sleep with the knowledge that in one way at least, they have freedom from fear. Thank you." He moved off, protected by a dozen or more policemen who cleared his path.

Wyatt, watching and listening to this, wanted to spit. What sanctimonious, pompous bullshit. There had been 796 homicides in the metropolitan area the previous year: he knew, he'd looked it up. This case comprised seven, over two years. Whoever had been doing this was a monster, he agreed with that. But to say that things were better, in any way, was a lie.

"Mr. Matthews!" a reporter's voice called out. "Do you have anything to say about this morning's proceedings?"

Wyatt nodded. He walked down the granite stairs to the same bank of microphones Pagano had just vacated and stood in the glare of the midmorning sun, feeling the lights of the camera crews beating down on his face, trying not to squint in the ten-thousand-watt glare.

"What is your reaction to the charges?" a reporter called out.

"Unlike the district attorney, who is a politician first and a lawyer in search of justice second, if at all, I'm not going to try my case in front of the media."

He paused for a moment. Speaking publicly during a trial wasn't something he was accustomed to; his work almost always took place behind closed doors.

"However—I'm not going to *not* speak out when I feel I have to set the record straight, and this is one of those times. Basically, I only have one thing to say: this whole episode is a charade, a travesty, a joke. Except it's a bad joke, and it's on all of us. This isn't about justice, about who committed these terrible crimes. This is about finding a scapegoat as soon as possible, and ramming him down the collective throats of the public. What a wonderful convenience this whole thing is," he went on, building a good head of steam, "that in such a short period of time after the latest killing the police find a young man, who—surprise, surprise—happens to be black, who has no adult criminal record whatsoever, who has been working for the past two years to help out his mother and younger sisters and brother, and who happened to be at the wrong place at the wrong time. And because some career criminal with nothing to lose concocts some wild fairy tale, this young man is going to spend the next several months in the city jail, until I can convince a jury that he had nothing to do with any of this." He stopped, looking out over the crowd, waiting to make sure his words were being felt, and transmitted.

"The case the DA is bringing is not about innocence or guilt. It is about expediency, and getting it over with. Eeny meeny miny mo . . . you know the rest." He shook his head, a broad gesture for the TV cameras to catch. "They want to put a young man, a lifetime resident of this city, on death row solely on the testimony of a hardened convict. Well, I can tell you this: we're not going to let them. Because if they can do this to Marvin White, they can do it to any one of you.

"Think about that."

Wyatt hit all three networks' nightly news shows, plus CNN. Moira didn't see him on the six o'clock nationals; she hadn't come home yet. But she did catch the local news at ten.

They sat in the den, flipping from channel to channel. Michaela, back from studying at the library, watched with them. He was on all the local stations. The actual clip that showed his face was short, less than fifteen seconds, but still, there he was.

He could feel the tension coming off Moira, particularly since much of the spin on the story, which went on for a couple of minutes, wasn't about the case per se; it was about a famous, well-entrenched corporate attorney, whose client list ran to Fortune 500 companies, abruptly shifting gears in midcareer and taking on a highly controversial criminal case.

"So who are you pretending to be now, Johnnie Cochran or F. Lee Bailey?" Moira asked acidly.

"Just me," he said, refusing to rise to the bait. If she wanted a fight she'd have to look elsewhere. He wasn't going to argue with her. As this went on she'd get used to it and realize it wasn't anything to get upset about. He hoped.

"You looked good, Dad," Michaela opined, trying to calm the waters. "I like you in that suit."

"I'm going to bed," Moira said bleakly. She got up and left the room.

An hour later, when he went upstairs, the room was empty. "Moira?" he called out.

She didn't answer. He walked down the hallway to the guest room. Moira was in bed, reading. "I'm sleeping here tonight," she announced without looking up from her book.

He went to bed alone.

Father and daughter had breakfast together in the morning. As they were finishing up, Moira came downstairs. She was in her nightgown and robe, and hadn't put on any makeup. Pouring herself a cup of black coffee, she kissed Michaela on the forehead. "Have a good day at school, sweetie," she said, pointedly ignoring Wyatt.

If she wanted to cold-shoulder him there was nothing he could do about it. "We'd better get going," he said to Michaela, carrying his dishes to the sink, where he rinsed them and placed them in the dishwasher. Michaela rinsed her own dishes, then went upstairs to get her books. "I'll call if I'm going to be late tonight," he told Moira, putting on his suit coat, "but I'll try not to be."

"I won't hold my breath."

He bent over to kiss her, but she turned away from him. He kissed the back of her neck, where the tendrils of her hair ended. "I love you," he told her.

She turned to him. "I hope you know what you're doing."

The recent rains had exploded all the plants and flowers into bloom. The air was thick with fragrance and the pungent smell of earth. Wyatt lowered his window so he could enjoy them as the Jaguar cruised down the quiet streets.

Michaela was reading a schoolbook. "I've got a first-period chemistry quiz," she explained as he glanced over.

"Didn't you study last night? I thought you were at the library."

"I like to look it over again at the last minute."

She was a hard worker. He'd never had to worry about her. As he looked at her concentrating on her textbook, he wondered if she was seeing a boy and didn't want him and Moira to know about it. Or maybe Moira knew things he didn't—it wouldn't be the first time.

"Daddy?" she said, looking up.

"Yes, honey?"

"What you're doing? This trial?"

"Uh-huh?"

"I think it's a good thing," she said with conviction.

"You do?"

She nodded. "Everybody deserves a good defense, isn't that right?"

"That's the way it's supposed to be," he agreed.

"I mean it's not his fault that he's a black kid and doesn't have any money."

"No. It isn't."

"The kids at school think what you're doing is cool."

"They do?"

"Well, not all of them," she admitted. "Some of them think they should just execute him on the spot, but that's their parents talking. Some of these kids don't have any original thoughts of their own. Not my friends," she quickly added.

"I'm glad to hear that," he said. "That your friends are independent thinkers. I know you are. I wouldn't ever want you agreeing with me just because I'm your father."

"I wouldn't. I mean I don't agree with Mom about it."

"No." He hesitated. "This has been a shock to her. She needs time to adjust."

"Maybe she won't be able to," Michaela said candidly. "I don't think she thinks you should be defending him at all."

"Even if he's innocent?" he asked.

"Yes." She looked at him. "Do you think he's innocent, Dad?"

"I don't know. I haven't thought about that yet. I've been too busy with the work. He tells me he is, so unless I find reasons not to believe him, I will. That's how I always deal with a client."

"Well, I hope he is innocent," she said. "If it turned out that you had defended the real Alley Slasher, that would be hard to take. Especially if you got him off."

There were over five dozen phone messages waiting for him when he got to work, most of them sent over from his office. Friends had called from all over the country. There were also several calls from reporters—newspapers, magazines, TV, radio—all requesting interviews. Larry King, *The New Yorker,* CNBC, Oprah. Not to mention the *New York*

Times, People, A Current Affair. All to be put on hold. That
stuff was dicey and potentially dangerous. He didn't want to
come across like some road-show Alan Dershowitz, especially since he was new to this part of the game.

Josephine stuck her head in his door. "You're a popular
guy this morning," she said, handing him the requisite
newspapers. She was dressed in a sexy outfit—shortish
skirt, heels, tight blouse. She usually dressed this way—a
little on the tight-flashy side. It was who she was. Nothing
calculated.

"It'll pass," he said.

"Don't count on that. This case has legs. You're going to
be in the limelight for as long as it lasts, whether you want
to be or not."

"I guess. It's a funny feeling."

"Funny ha-ha or funny weird?"

"Strange. But I'll get used to it. I'll have to, because
Pagano will be trying this case in the press. By the time we
get to trial everyone in the city, county, and state will have
formed an opinion. It's going to be a bitch getting a jury,
that's for sure." He sipped his coffee. It was good—she had
brewed it herself. "I want every police report on every one
of the murders we're charged with," he said. "Prepare the
necessary discovery documents and have them ready to file
as soon as possible. Every murder that's been attributed to
the Alley Slasher, back to the first one."

Two days later there were six large cardboard boxes filled
with copies of police files sitting on the floor in Wyatt's office. Each box contained all the material the department had
on each individual murder. They were numbered one
through six, in the order in which the killings had taken
place. The file was thinner on the most recent murder, number seven. It contained Dwayne Thompson's grand jury testimony, the affidavit of the woman, Violet Waleska, who
had seen Marvin at the murder site and had subsequently
picked him out of a police lineup, and the police reports pertinent to finding Paula's body. The material in that file was
in a manila envelope on a corner of his desk.

"What we're looking for are similarities," Wyatt told

Josephine as they looked at the large paper-filled boxes that had been delivered that morning, in accordance with his filing the discovery motions. "In location, time of day, method of killing. Similarities in who the victims were—age, color, where they lived, what they wore, where they worked, whether they were married or single, lived alone or not, anything."

"What are we trying to find from all of this?" Josephine asked.

"Alibis," he answered. "As far as anyone knows, there has never been an actual eyewitness to any of these killings. But maybe there's something in here"—he pointed to the huge volume of paperwork—"that belies that, stuff the cops didn't want the public to know."

"That's always been one of the reasons the police have given for not being able to solve this," she said.

He nodded. "No one's ever seen the killer—assuming it isn't Marvin. The closest so far is this friend of the latest victim's who saw Marvin in the parking lot some time around the time of the killings." He shook his head at the volume of material they had to go through. "Let's have at it. I'll start with the most recent, you go back to the beginning. Highlight everything that seems pertinent, anything that could cast suspicion on Marvin's involvement, any areas of similarity that seem strange. At the end of the day we'll compare notes."

After lunch Josephine went to the Auto Club and got the largest map of the city they had. She took that to a custom photography store and had it blown up ten times. The finished product was twelve feet square. She pinned the gargantuan map up on the wall outside their office and stuck pushpins into the locations where each of the murders had taken place, numbering them in the order they had happened.

The day was dying. Wyatt had a crick in his back from sitting hunched over at his desk reading the police material. He had also reread Dwayne's grand jury testimony and Violet Waleska's police statement and identification. After that he had worked his way backward in the police reports of the previous murders. Dwayne's testimony, in contrasting and comparing it with the police reports, was compelling and convincing. In instance after instance he had given the grand jury information that only someone with direct and in-depth knowledge about the murders could have known. Even small details—the color of a victim's shoe, the brand of cigarettes she was carrying in her purse—were in both his testimony and the police reports.

"There is so much damn detail in this stuff," he remarked to Josephine. "How in the world could Marvin have remembered all this minutiae?"

"But what if Marvin really is the killer," she countered. "I'm talking hypothetically, of course, but if he was he could be completely obsessed about them. He could remember every single detail. The killer might even have kept a journal, so he could read about it and relive it. I've read about those things happening."

"Marvin doesn't strike me as a diarist," Wyatt said with a frown. "He's functionally illiterate. But it's something we should explore," he added, not wanting to dampen her enthusiasm. "Good thinking."

"Thanks." She could feel the blush, still on her neck and jaw.

"Which reminds me—we're going to have to have him examined by a psychologist. And we should check to see if there are any outstanding IQ tests, other measures of his intelligence, especially his memory. Get hold of his school files."

"I'll do it first thing tomorrow."

They stood looking at the map. The pushpins, although not clustered, were all located in the same section of town. Wyatt ran his finger along the line of pins from top to bottom.

"Hooker alley," he said. "It's a big area, but not that big in comparison to the city as a whole. Here's another avenue to explore: check the arrest records of the women who were killed and see if there are any pimps attached to them. Or any johns, although they weren't listing the johns until recently. Maybe more than one of them had the same pimp. That would be a big break."

"Don't you think the police would have investigated the pimps pretty thoroughly?" she asked.

"I'm not thinking of them as suspects. Sources of information. Did any of the victims have regulars who might have been a customer with another one of them, that kind of thing." He stretched, massaging the small of his back. He'd love to get a run in tonight, but that wasn't going to happen. He had other things to do that took precedence.

"Tomorrow you're going to start making a list," he instructed her. "Every witness the police interviewed. Every name in those police reports. We need to find out if any of them have something to say that isn't in these records." He paused. "We also have to find out if any of them are going to come forward and testify that they saw Marvin around when this shit was happening."

"That would be awful," she said with a shudder.

"Yep, it would. But better we hear it as soon as possible than get blindsided with it in the middle of the trial." He got his briefcase and suit coat from his office. "Don't work too late. I'll see you in the morning." He started to leave. "One more thing. Have a locksmith in here tomorrow morning. I want this floor to be secure, as much as is possible. And order a couple safes, so we can lock up the critical stuff."

"A tad paranoid, are we?" she chided him.

"Damn straight." He shrugged into his coat. "Don't work too late, and have fun this evening."

He wondered if she had a boyfriend. She hadn't mentioned one, but they hadn't known each other very long. He realized that there was a tiny seed of jealousy about thinking that she might. That he was a married man—happily married, despite the recent problems—should mean he had no right to think that. But he did anyway. Human nature.

"You, too," she answered. "Are you going home now?"

"No." Earlier, he had called home to let Moira know he'd be working late. She hadn't called back. "I have something to attend to outside the office."

Wyatt knew the city—he'd grown up in it; and although he'd gone away for college, law school, the service, and a few jobs early in his career, he had lived here most of his life. But he didn't know this part of it, where he was driving now. Even as a kid and young man, when he'd gone to jazz clubs in black areas, he hadn't been in locations like this.

This was urban hell. Block after block featured boarded-up storefronts covered with spray-painted graffiti, most of it gang-related, or closed-up businesses with heavy metal grates pulled down over them to prevent vandalism and theft. The people on the streets looked like they had nowhere else in the world to go. Not even drug dealers or hookers were hanging around this part of town. You saw it on these reality TV shows, cops busting junkies and dealers and hookers, people living in rat-infested tenements, but it didn't quite seem real, it felt staged somehow, a relic from some other America. It wasn't just his city—it was every urban area. Even the great garden spots, like San Francisco. New Orleans, he knew from having recently been there, was now considered one of the most dangerous cities in the country.

He didn't see one single white face.

The street he was on, Martin Luther King Jr. Boulevard (he knew of at least three other cities with large black populations that had a King Boulevard), was the main artery of this part of the city. It ran for miles. He checked his directions to make sure he was going the right direction. He was—it was longer than he had realized it would be. It was a huge area, a city within a city.

The housing project comprised several six-story brick-and-concrete buildings. The project, Sullivan Houses, was named after the congressman who had gotten the funding. Thirty-some years old, it was built at the height of the Great Society and had been obsolete from the day it was finished.

Wyatt had done some research on the area. It had the highest incidence of violent crimes in the city, a statistic it had owned for over a decade. Less than twenty percent of the kids raised in the Sullivan Houses graduated from high school, and of that select group only a handful went to college. There was one player currently in the NBA, one in the NFL, and two playing big-league baseball from these projects. They must have had strong wills, Wyatt thought, to make it through here without succumbing to the endless temptations. He wondered if there had ever been a doctor, or an engineer. Or a lawyer.

Several blocks before Wyatt reached his destination he saw the buildings rising up out of the pink-tinted smog that was caused by smoke and chemical waste coming from the refineries across the river. Even with his car windows rolled up and the air-conditioning on, he could smell the air—acrid, tear-inducing.

Wyatt turned off King Boulevard and drove into Sullivan Houses. The interior of the project was more depressing than the outside world surrounding it. The streets were riddled with potholes, many the size of small craters. There had been no attempt to fill them in, even temporarily, the way the city customarily took care of the pothole problem. Large piles of trash lined the sidewalks, everything from discarded furniture to large plastic garbage bags that were ripped, overflowing the battered garbage cans. Rats the size of small cats darted in and out of the garbage piles. The sanitation department didn't put a high priority on a maintenance schedule, he thought as he looked at the scene with repulsion. Or maybe they simply didn't come in here until they absolutely had to.

He had been looking forward to this visit, from an outsider's abstract point of view. Now that he was actually here, he hoped he hadn't made a bad decision. There was danger on these streets—you could feel it exuding right out of the asphalt.

The streets in the project were lettered A to L, and the buildings were numbered from 100, each section a different hundred number. Jonnie Rae and her family lived on Avenue E, building 522, apartment 5G. Marvin had lived there, too, until a few weeks ago.

Jonnie Rae's two youngest children were outside their building, waiting for him. As he slowly drove down the street toward them they spotted his car (which he had described earlier, over the phone) and waved their arms, jumping up and down and pointing excitedly to a parking place right in front that they had been saving for him.

He parked and got out, locking the door with the remote alarm. A crowd started gathering. Kids, teenagers, adults. It was dinnertime or later, people were in their homes and outside, watching some white man get out of his Jaguar.

He couldn't help it—he felt nervous. He assumed that the people who lived here never saw a white face in their neighborhood, except for a cop or a welfare worker. He tried to act cool, nonchalant, but he didn't feel it. In his entire life he had never set foot in a housing project, although there were dozens of them situated all over the poor sections of the city. The closest he'd come was driving by them on a freeway, looking down, with his windows up and the doors locked.

You wanted to try something new in your life, you've got it, he thought to himself.

"Don't be using that alarm," a man's voice said behind him.

He turned. One of the young men who had been standing at the back of the courtroom during Marvin's arraignment came out of the crowd and walked toward him. *Strutted* would be a more accurate description of the way he moved, Wyatt thought. Or *swaggered*. This was his territory and he walked the walk.

Wyatt looked at the man as he approached. He wasn't the one who had worn the expensive Ralph Lauren threads. Instead of the fancy leather jacket he'd worn in the courtroom, he was now casual, in T-shirt, sagging pants, and new Air Jordans. He was wearing a hairnet over his head, and over that a bandanna signifying what Wyatt assumed were his gang colors. He looked about Marvin's age, eighteen going on forever.

"Kids'll set that off before you can turn your back," the young man explained. "I'm Louis," he said. "Friend of Marvin's." He didn't offer to shake hands.

Despite Louis's tough demeanor, Wyatt couldn't help but think of him as a kid. His daughter wasn't much younger, as he'd observed in contrasting her with Marvin, and he still thought of her as a kid—she had called him "Daddy" a few days ago. He'd have to watch that he didn't say "kid" out loud.

"Kill that sucker," Louis said, meaning the alarm. "Your wheels are safe here, man. You're Marvin's lawyer. Ain't nobody gonna mess with your car."

Wyatt did as he was told.

A beeper went off on Louis's belt. Louis looked at it, took a cell phone out of his pocket, punched in some numbers. "Yeah?" He listened for a minute, his face scrunching into an angry frown. "Hey, fuck him. Let him buy—" He realized that Wyatt was standing right next to him, but disregarded him. "—his product some other place." As he punched some new numbers into his phone he turned to Marvin. "Go with her," he said dismissively, pointing to Marvin's sister. He walked away, talking low on the cell phone.

Marvin's sister and brother led him inside her building, which had a broken lock on the front door. There was an elevator off to the side with a Not Working sign taped to the front. It was an old sign.

He followed the little girl and boy up three flights of stairs. Cooking smells, predominantly the smell of grease frying, came from behind the closed doors. They mixed with the funky stench of urine and vomit, odors that had been soaking in for decades. Most of the lightbulbs in the stairway were out. Roaches as big as his thumb scurried along the floorboards, and there were rat holes and piles of rat droppings everywhere. He was careful to watch where he stepped, especially when he saw discarded drug paraphernalia—needles and crack vials—on a landing. Halfway up the stairs there were some discarded condoms. The kids walked by them as if they didn't exist.

The small apartment was stuffed with mismatched furniture and bric-a-brac. Old copies of *Ebony* and *TV Guide* were piled in one corner. The television in front of the sofa was on to *Wheel of Fortune*. From off in the kitchen came the aroma of fried chicken.

Jonnie Rae came bustling out of the kitchen, wiping her hands on her apron. As he reached out to shake her hand, a horrible thought went through his mind: *Aunt Jemima pancake syrup.*

You prick, he thought. You ugly bastard. Underneath it all you really are a latent bigot. That he had thought that almost made him sick to his stomach. And as all those feelings and emotions roiled inside him he understood with a wonderful clarity that what he had embarked on was going to be more than a change in the way he did his job. It was going to be a sea change in how he looked at the world, and dealt with it. No matter what else happened to him, he was going to make sure of that.

At the same time, he had to laugh at himself. Judge not, etc. He'd been coming down on Moira, judging her so moralistically. Who was he to judge anyone?

Jonnie Rae had no idea what was going on inside his head. "This is an honor," she gushed, obviously nervous, "you driving all the way down here, a man with a busy schedule like you must have."

"I was happy to do it," he said, realizing that he actually was, and at the same time being washed with guilt from those spontaneous shitty thoughts he'd had. "I appreciate you inviting me into your home."

"No trouble at all. Least I can do, you driving all the way down here this time of the night. You sit down and make yourself comfortable. You want something cold to drink?"

"Yes." The apartment was hot and closed-in; he was already beginning to sweat under his arms. He sat on the center of the couch. The little boy plopped down next to him. On the screen, Vanna White was turning some letters.

"You like this show?" the boy asked.

"I've never seen it," Wyatt replied. "I don't watch much television," he explained.

"It's a bitchin' show. You can win all kinds of shit, money and shit like that. I'd like to get on that show."

The little girl brought him a green-colored drink with some ice cubes in a *Jurassic Park* glass. She sat on the other side of him. "You like this?" she asked him.

"What is it?"

"Kool-Aid. Lemon-lime, my favorite."

He took a sip. It was sweet, almost to the point of gagging. "It's good," he said.

"I put in extra sugar."

He took another sip, set the glass down.

"You gonna do good by my brother?" the girl asked.

"I'm going to try," he answered.

"That's good, 'cause he needs some smart man helping him. He's too dumb to help his own self."

The little girl, whose name was Toni (named after Toni Morrison, the famous writer, Jonnie Rae informed him proudly), turned to her mother. "Can I show him my drawings?" she asked.

"Ask him."

"Can I show you my drawings?" she asked Wyatt.

"Sure," he said, trying to sound enthusiastic.

Toni ran out of the room, coming back a moment later with a loose-leaf notebook, which she set on the sofa next to Wyatt. Slowly, she turned the pages.

The book was filled with colored-pencil drawings, all

taken from her everyday life. There were drawings of the street outside, drawings of her school (he knew it was a school because it said "school" in big block letters on top), drawings of her mother, her sister and brothers. There were several drawings of Marvin, looking like a fierce urban warrior.

"These are excellent," Wyatt exclaimed as he looked at them. He meant it; and he was surprised. "I'll bet you're the best artist in your class."

"We don't have art in my school," she said.

"They don't have art in her school 'cause people were stealing the supplies," Jonnie Rae said, her voice rich in anger. "They don't have music or sports, either. They don't have nothing for these kids. No after-school programs, either, then they complain that the kids get into trouble. They don't have nothing to do but get in trouble."

He nodded. This life was so far away from his as to be incomprehensible. "How did you learn to draw so well?" he asked the girl, changing the subject.

She shrugged and giggled. "I just did."

"You know," he said to Jonnie Rae, "there are art classes at the museum on Saturdays for children. They're free," he added. "I'm sure they would welcome Toni."

"I work Saturdays. I don't have time to cart them around."

He sat alone with Jonnie Rae in the small living room. She had sent the kids outside to play in the warm evening air. "Don't be leaving this block!" she yelled at them as they ran down the stairway. "You play where I can keep an eye on you out the window." To Wyatt, she explained: "This whole place is crawling with drug dealers and gangbangers and they all carry guns. People get shot around here for no good reason."

"Did you know Marvin carried a gun?" Wyatt asked, using her statement to get into the reason he had come down here.

"I never did see it on him, but I figured he probably might have," she admitted. "Boy round here don't think he's a man if he ain't packing."

Wyatt nodded. "I need your help," he said. This was why he had called and asked to come down and see her. He had wanted to see where Marvin came from, what his life was like. He felt, in his gut, that it would help him round out the picture.

"Whatever I can do." She seemed flattered by his request.

"Let me ask the obvious question first. Do you think he did it?"

She looked away.

"Let me put it another way. Do you think he *could* have done these killings?"

"*Could have?* I don't know, not for sure. I can't see it, not with Marvin, but I couldn't swear to that on a Bible. I used to know him, but anymore, I don't think I do. Not the way he's got into trouble like he has."

"Here's a for instance: before it happened, did you think he was capable of the robbery he tried? Holding a man up with a gun?"

"He did it, so he was capable of it," she said flatly.

"But before it happened, did you think he could have done something like that?"

She sighed, a sigh from way deep in the pit of her gut. "I don't know what to think about him anymore." She looked at him. "I don't think he could have done those things to those women, but how can I know for sure, after what he's pulled? All he cares about anymore is wanting to be a drug dealer like his friends, make a bunch of money, 'Mama, I'm gonna take you out of this place,' as if I'd want to move somewhere better if it came from drug money." Her face turned angry. "Damn that boy. He could've, I guess. He's done enough bad things, it's on his record, so maybe. Damn him to hell," she exclaimed.

"Okay. I can understand why you're angry with him. I would be, if he were my son. And you might even be ready to throw in the towel, think he's getting what he deserves. But if he didn't do these killings, then you have to help him." He looked at her, silently beseeching her. "You have to help me help him. I can't do this by myself."

She looked away for a moment. "I don't think he did," she said, turning back.

"Good."

"So what do you need from me?"

He retrieved an envelope from his inside jacket pocket, took out some folded-up sheets of paper, spread them on the couch between them. "These are the times and places when all the murders were committed, going back two years. I want you to look at this. I'm going to leave it with you because I want you to take your time."

She looked at the list. "Uh-huh."

"I'm looking for alibis," he explained. "From you or anyone who knows Marvin. Look over this list and see if there was any time when he couldn't have been where they happened, when they happened. Maybe you were away visiting relatives, or he was playing in a sports tournament, anything."

"I don't know." She shook her head dubiously. "I don't know if I can remember back any particular day very far."

"I understand. Most people can't. But there might be one time when he just couldn't have been where one of these murders happened. That's what I'm looking for—one time. If I can show he wasn't at one of these, that's all I'll need."

"All right. I'll look at it. But don't get your hopes up."

"And show it to everyone Marvin knew during that time. Maybe a friend or a teacher, anyone who might remember something."

"That's a bunch of people. But I'll do my best," she reassured him.

The word had gotten out that Marvin White's lawyer, the one who had been on the television shows, had come to see Marvin's mother. There were a hundred people, all residents of the project, waiting outside when he emerged from the building. They stood in the street and on the sidewalk, watching him. There was no threat in the air.

His mouth went dry anyway. He stopped as he saw them, frozen in place. Then he began walking to his car. No one had touched it.

"Hey, man!" A male voice called out. He jerked around toward the sound. "You gonna get Marvin off?"

"Hey, man, you do good by Marvin now, you hear?"

"I seen you on TV! You looking *good*!"

He grinned nervously, impulsively almost waving like a politician or sports celebrity might. But he caught himself; this was not his place—he was an interloper here. Darryl's lines resonated in his head: *The great white father. The benevolent white liberal.*

He was here doing a job, that was all.

As he was about to open his car and get in, a young man

stepped out of the crowd and approached him. He recognized him at once—three-piece Ralph Lauren suit, all the expensive accessories. Marvin's friend, the one who had brought Jonnie Rae and the kids to the arraignment.

Wyatt stopped, waiting expectantly.

The man walked to within a few feet of Wyatt. "Can I talk to you?" he asked. His voice was low, soft, without any street inflection or threat. He could have been a yuppie stockbroker, the way he talked and was dressed.

"All right." Wyatt leaned back against his car.

Quickly: "Not here." The young man looked around—the crowd was beginning to disperse. "Get in your car and drive on down to where you came in. Park it on King. I'll meet you there." He paused. "If that's okay with you," he added.

Wyatt drove through the project. The guy trailed him in his Jeep Grand Cherokee. This is Marvin's role model, he thought. A $1,500 suit and an expensive car. And you know he doesn't pay a dime in taxes.

He parked on the corner, using the alarm this time. The Cherokee pulled up alongside. The passenger door swung open. "We can talk while we ride around."

He got in. As they were pulling away he noticed two young men saunter over and stand nearby. "Keep an eye on it for you," the driver explained. "Like when you go to the ballpark, 'cept you don't have to pay no vig."

They cruised along King Boulevard. A police scanner under the dashboard droned out dispatcher calls. This guy's wired, Wyatt thought.

The driver stuck out his hand. "Dexter. I'm Marvin's best friend. We're like this," he said, pressing his forefinger and thumb together. "Totally."

They shook. Dexter Gordon had been one of Wyatt's favorite jazz musicians. He had five or six Dexter Gordon albums at home. He wondered if this Dexter had ever heard of his namesake.

"I've heard about you," Dexter said. "You're important." Without taking his eyes off the street he reached across Wyatt, opened the glove compartment, took out a copy of *Business Week,* and thumbed through the magazine, finding an article about Wyatt. There was a picture, taken at an extreme up-angle, standing on the steps of the Supreme Court building in Washington, D.C. The headline of the article read: "Matthews Humbles Uncle Sam. Again."

"You kicked the government's ass big-time," Dexter said admiringly.

This Dexter is a real entrepreneur, Wyatt thought. "Do you read *Business Week* frequently?" he asked.

"Got a subscription," Dexter replied. "*Forbes,* too. And the *Wall Street Journal.* You got to know what the markets are doing so you can figure out how to invest your money."

"Where do you invest your money?" Wyatt asked. This conversation was starting out rather surrealistically.

"Computers, communications, shit like that. And product." He abruptly pulled over to the side of the street, double-parked in the middle of the block. A young boy, no more than fourteen, came out of a doorway and walked around to the driver's side. Dexter hit the down button on his window. "How's biz tonight?" Dexter asked the kid.

The boy cast a wary eye in Wyatt's direction.

"Don't worry about him," Dexter told the kid. "He's cool."

"Business is all right," the kid said. "It's happening." He kept an eye on Wyatt.

"So what do you got for me?"

The kid reached into his pants pocket and pulled out a roll of bills, which he handed to Dexter. Dexter quickly riffed through them. "Good enough," he said approvingly. "You got enough product?"

"I could do with some more."

Dexter cocked his head to the rear of his Cherokee, releasing the latch under his seat. The kid walked back as the rear door swung open. He reached in and took a heavy paper bag out from under a blanket, slammed the door shut.

He walked back to Dexter's window, tucking the bag under his shirt. "This'll hold me."

"Fine. Now get your ass back to work."

They high-fived and soul-shook. With a last quick look in Wyatt's direction the kid scampered back on the sidewalk and took off down the street. Dexter rolled his window up and pulled back into traffic.

"Did I just see what I think I saw?" Wyatt asked.

"What did you see?"

"Is that kid one of your . . . what do you call them, mules?"

Dexter laughed. "A mule is something you ride, man. I don't need no mule, I got this." He patted the dashboard. "This'll take me anywhere a mule can go."

"If you're dealing drugs out of this car, I can't be here. I won't be here."

"You're cool, Mr. Matthews. I ain't gonna do nothing to get you in trouble. Anyways, the cops round here, me and them got an understanding."

Like the understanding the police had with the owner of the convenience store, Wyatt thought. All it takes is money.

A nagging idea came to him, one that had been floating in his subconscious. How corrupt were the police, anyway? He had dismissed the idea that the authorities had fed Dwayne Thompson information, if for no other reason than pure logistics, but from what he was seeing, first on that videotape and now here on the street, he'd better take a close look at that. If an eighteen-year-old kid could buy off the cops on his beat—and Wyatt knew Dexter was telling the truth; there had been no braggadocio to his statement, just statement of fact—then the police were capable of much more nefarious conduct.

"Is there a reason we're riding around together?" he questioned Dexter. "Other than you're showing me how brazenly you conduct your business?" He was uncomfortable with this; and driving these streets with a drug dealer who was plying his trade was getting him angry. If the kid wanted to show off, let him do it with one of his sycophants who would feel thrilled to be included. He wasn't.

"Yeah, there's a reason," Dexter answered, stung. "I got business I got to take care of that can't wait, but I wanted you to come ride with me because I want to talk about Marvin, and I don't want none of them dummies back there in Sullivan Houses trying to listen in, you dig?"

Wyatt nodded curtly. They stopped for a red light. Dexter surveyed the pedestrian traffic. He gave the high-sign to a couple of teenage prostitutes who were crossing in front of his car. One of them winked at him and blew him a kiss. "You want a blow job?" Dexter asked. "A freebie. On me."

"No, thanks." That's all he needed.

The light turned green. They cruised along. "Let's get

with the program, Dexter," Wyatt said sharply. "If you've got something to tell me that can help out, do it. Otherwise drive me back to my car. I've had a long day and it isn't over yet."

Dexter pulled over to the curb. He turned to face Wyatt, his dark face in shadow, only one eye glistening. "What you got to know is this: Marvin didn't do it. He didn't kill none of them bitches."

"How do you know that? Do you have some information about this that we can use?"

"Like who did it for real, or something?" Dexter shook his head. "No. But Marvin wouldn't do that kind of shit. He wouldn't need to."

"Wouldn't *need* to?"

"Marvin don't need to rape no damn scabby hooker. Who the hell would fuck a hooker nowadays anyway, with all that AIDS shit going around? Marvin got more pussy than he could handle, man. He been beating the ladies off with a stick ever since he got hair on his pecker."

"He's a ladies' man?"

Dexter laughed. "He's got a johnson on him like a fucking stallion. He's a legend in the locker room, for serious. Every goddamn woman on that delivery route of his was hitting on his ass, wanting to give that snake a try." He laughed again. "Maybe one of them big ol' women's husbands got jealous and framed Marvin. I know more than one married woman would do about anything to get in his drawers."

"You have firsthand knowledge?"

"Marvin did this group thing one time," Dexter said. "He went over to this house where this lady lived, middle-aged old bag, must've been in her forties. Real nice house, big lawn. Her and another bitch her age were waiting there. It was morning, their husbands were off at work. They was all dolled up, waiting for Marvin, and as soon as he hit the door them ladies liked to tear Marvin's clothes off. They wanted a piece of him so bad they fought over who got him first— they had to flip a coin for it. You know all that shit you hear about, how white women want black men? It's true, at least in Marvin's case. And let me tell you, he delivered the goods. He was wham-bam-thank-you-ma'aming both of them, all morning long. I guarantee you them ladies were walking bowlegged the rest of that day."

"This is something he told you?"

"He was laughing about it that afternoon."

"Maybe he was bragging. Maybe it didn't happen at all."

Dexter shook his head. "Marvin didn't have to brag about getting pussy. I seen it with my own eyes. Me and him would be cruising, some whore would jump right into my car, suck him off in the backseat while I'm driving. Trust me—when it comes to women and Marvin, there ain't no bullshit. No call for it."

"Maybe. But because he can get laid whenever he wants doesn't mean he wouldn't go out and rape. That's not how it works, Dexter. Rape isn't about sex. It's about control, and hurting someone."

"Shit, man, I know that. But the thing about Marvin is, he wouldn't ever hurt a bitch, 'less she fucked him over, and then he wouldn't rape her to hurt her, he'd just kick the shit out of her. Trust me, Mr. Matthews. Marvin White has done some stupid shit, but raping 'ho's ain't one of them."

In court he'd be laughed at if he ever advanced a theory like that. He needed to talk to a shrink about all this.

He took a flier: "Did these women pay him, that you know?"

Dexter nodded vigorously. "He wouldn't have done it otherwise. Not some middle-aged cunts." He glanced out the window, a nervous habit born out of the necessity of someone in his line of work always having to watch his ass. "What I'm thinking is, Marvin might have been with some of them customer ladies when some of these killings went down. He said something to me one time about how he was getting dressed after being with one of these bitches and some news bulletin came on about how they'd found a body. It was like the killing had happened when he was in bed with one of his customers."

"That won't hold water. He could have murdered one of those women hours before he did his studly duty."

"Normally that would be true," Dexter agreed. "But this time, the woman's old man had been out of town, so Marvin had been in her house with her all night long. Even a magician good as David Copperfield can't be in two places at the same time."

They started back toward Wyatt's car. Dexter stopped a few times to do business. Wyatt looked away—there was no fascination in what Dexter was doing. Some kids out there were buying the drugs that had bought Dexter's car and his fancy clothes. It could be Marvin's sisters and brother.

Dexter pulled up behind Wyatt's Jaguar. The two boys who had been watching it when he left with Dexter were still there. When they saw the Cherokee, they vanished into the shadows.

Dexter swiveled around to face Wyatt. "Marvin's my blood," he said. "We're brothers, even if he is a fuckup. What can I do to help him?" He reached into his pocket and pulled out a roll of bills that would have choked an elephant, let alone a horse. "I don't know who's paying for this shit, but do you need money?" He started peeling off bills, fifties and hundreds.

Wyatt put up a hand. "I don't need your money. Even if I did, I wouldn't take it, not where it comes from."

Dexter shrugged. "No big thing." He stuffed the roll back in his pocket.

"But you can help me."

"Name it."

"I'm going to talk to Marvin about what you told me regarding this woman who could be an alibi for him. But that's a long shot—he might not remember her name, or where she lived, and even if he does, she's a married woman. I doubt she's going to be eager to stand up in court and say she was having a sexual affair with a seventeen-year-old delivery boy."

"Seventeen-year-old delivery boy who's a nigger."

Wyatt winced—he hated that word, and that someone black had said it didn't make it all right to him. "I need someone who will testify under oath that Marvin was with them during the time when one or more of these murders took place," he said. "An ironclad alibi. Even if what was going down was bad or illegal, like with a married woman—or with you, for instance, when you were doing a drug deal. Anything that would have made it impossible for him to be where the crime was committed when it was done."

Dexter was listening intently.

"Talk to everyone who knows him," Wyatt continued. "His gang friends, lady friends, anyone."

Dexter nodded. "You got it, Mr. Matthews. We'll alibi him for every one of those killings."

"They have to be legitimate. Every one would be fine, but I only need one, two at the most. But they have to be legitimate," he said again for emphasis. "No bullshit, no fairy tales."

"Don't worry," Dexter reassured him. "Any alibi me or the brothers come up with, it will be for legit. You got my word. But you check out that lady with Marvin. That could be the answer."

"It's going to the top of my agenda." He took a card out of his wallet. "Call me if you have any information."

"Definitely." Dexter removed his billfold from his inside breast pocket and put the card in. Alligator, Wyatt noticed, from Gucci. Billfolds like this ran upwards of three hundred dollars. Young Dexter was doing well for himself.

Dexter shook Wyatt's hand. "Hey, can I see that Rolex watch you're wearing?" he asked as he caught a glimpse of Wyatt's watch under his left cuff.

Wyatt held his arm out so that his watch extended past his cuff. Dexter looked at it—then he shot his cuff, showing his own watch. "Same kind," he said. "Exactly." He smiled. "You are definitely the right lawyer for Marvin."

It was almost midnight by the time he got home. He was beat, but there was a rush coursing through his system. He knew he wouldn't be able to fall asleep right away, probably not for hours. Two months ago his work had taken him to New York, where he stayed in a suite at the Peninsula and had dinner at Lutece and Montrachet. Tonight his work had taken him to the Sullivan Houses project, the worst slum in the city, where he had drunk Kool-Aid in a murder defendant's apartment and driven around with a drug dealer who did his business right in Wyatt's face.

From the penthouse to the outhouse. What he was learning, almost daily, was that there were rewards to be found in both places. He was certain now that he had made the right decision in taking on this new job, and then fighting to keep

Marvin White. He was almost fifty years old, and he was getting a fresh perspective on life. It was an exhilarating feeling.

As he pulled into his driveway he saw the light on upstairs, in his bedroom. Was Moira still up, waiting for him? He took the light to be a hopeful sign. Unless she was sleeping in the guest room again.

He had a quick steadying cognac, leafed through his mail. Nothing that couldn't wait until tomorrow. Hoping that things were okay, he climbed the stairs.

Moira was awake, in their bed. When he entered the room she put her book aside—*The Recognitions,* by William Gaddis. Her book group had been working their way through it for four months.

He kissed her lightly on the lips. She accepted it. "How is that?" he asked, sitting on the edge of the bed on his side. It was a huge novel—he had always wanted to read it, but he'd never started it because he knew he'd never have the time to finish.

"Great. I'm sure I'm not getting half of it, but it's fascinating writing." She took off her reading glasses and laid them aside. "Where were you so late?" she asked.

"Interviewing people who might be able to help out on the case. I left a message; didn't you get it?"

She nodded. "I didn't know you'd be this late."

"Working people. I had to see them after dinner. It was all the way on the other side of the city." He took off his shoes, shirt, tie and walked into his closet, where he took off his pants and hung them up with his jacket. "How was your day?"

"Nothing special. Wyatt." She paused. "I don't want us to fight anymore. I can't handle it. I stayed up to tell you that."

He felt awful, hearing her say that. "I'm truly sorry for what's been happening, Moira. I didn't want to do anything that's going to upset you, you know that." He had a strong need to apologize. It would make her feel better, he hoped.

"You already have. I have to figure out how to deal with it, that's all."

He slipped into bed under the sheets, opening his arm, an invitation for her to slide over and cuddle. She didn't move toward him. Instead she asked: "On the other side of town where?"

He propped himself up, turning to her. "A place called Sullivan Houses. It's a housing project on the south side."

He could feel her stiffening, as if a key had turned inside her heart.

"Moira?"

She lay motionless for a moment. "You're kidding, aren't you?"

"No." He shouldn't have told her. He should have lied.

"That's the worst part of town," she said, still not moving. "People get killed down there all the time."

"It's where his mother lives. And all his friends."

"Couldn't you have seen them in your office? Isn't that where people normally meet with their lawyers?"

"I wanted to see how he lives. It's important for me, to get a complete picture of this. I don't know anything about people like Marvin White. I can do a better job defending him if I can learn something about him, about his family, something other than the crimes he's accused of."

"So now you're becoming a sociologist as well."

He fell back onto his pillow. In their entire life together, twenty-five years almost, he had always told her everything about what he was doing, and she had pretty much accepted everything. But starting tonight, that was going to have to change.

A sob came from her throat. She had been trying to hold it back, but she wasn't able to. "Wyatt," she said. "What you're doing . . ." She took a deep breath to compose herself. "Taking a new direction like you have, you know I'm not in favor of it. I'm a conservative person, I'm not comfortable with change, I like the tried-and-true, as you've pointed out to me. That's who I am and I don't apologize for it. And I'm trying as hard as I can to accept this. But what you did tonight, what you just told me you did, that's crossing my line. Look at me," she beseeched him.

He turned his face to hers.

"You have a wife and a child. We love you and depend on you. You're our rock, Wyatt. That's one of your roles in this family, the main one. I cannot go on with you if you're going to put yourself in danger like you did tonight. Are you listening to me?"

"Yes, Moira."

"If anything happened to you, it would destroy this family."

"Nothing's going to happen to me," he said, flashing back to the moment when he had come out of Jonnie Rae's apartment building and there were a hundred people on the street, all with skin a different color from his, and he'd had a panic attack. "I'm very careful," he said, trying to assure her.

Which, of course, was another lie, a biggie. Riding around with a crack dealer isn't being careful. Dexter could have rivals all over town, waiting for the opportunity to take him out.

"I'm going to ask something from you," Moira said. "As your wife."

"What is it?"

"I don't want you to go into the projects anymore. If you're with the police and it's absolutely a life-and-death situation, then all right. But never alone. Will you promise me that?"

He turned to her. Oh baby, he thought with anguish, what you are asking of me is impossible.

"I promise," he told her. "I won't go into that part of town again."

Her body slid next to his, her head snuggling protectively on his shoulder. "I love you," she told him. "If I didn't love you, I wouldn't care."

I love you, too, he said silently. And from this moment on I'm going to have to deceive you.

Doris Blake, redolent of sexual desire and White Shoulders, let herself into the infirmary before dawn, making doubly sure that no one spotted her. She had master keys to every cellblock and cubbyhole in the place. She and the other high-ranking officers had these keys so that they could get in anywhere in case of an emergency. In practical terms, the keys were rarely used. Mostly it was when an officer needed to be in a section he or she wasn't normally assigned to, and didn't want to go through official channels. The procedure usually involved seeing a prisoner you didn't want to be on the books as having seen. There had been occasions when a prisoner wound up in County General Hospital after one of these visits, as the result of an unfortunate accident, like tripping and falling down a long flight of concrete stairs.

Dwayne, wearing a jail-issue T-shirt and loose-fitting boxer shorts, was sleeping on one of the beds in the back. As Blake snuck toward him on tiptoes, having removed her size 12 oxfords, she could see that he was in the middle of a dream. He was twitching, his body jerking spasmodically, and under his closed eyelids the pupils were moving rapidly. What are you dreaming about, my darling? Blake thought. Are you dreaming about me, about my pussy wet with desire for you? Your hands on my ass, your mouth on my nipples? She was already wet between her legs.

Dwayne's dreams were nothing so common and unprovocative as her thumb-sized nipples and Pillsbury doughboy ass. He had indulged in several prison cocktails the night before, drinking solitarily and aggressively, the pure alcohol going straight to his brain like a heat-guided missile. When he woke up he'd be in a clammy sweat and his mouth would be dry as cotton from all that alcohol and crap, he wouldn't have clear memories of what he'd been dreaming of, but he'd know he'd been on a triple-E ride to hell and back and he would savor the unconscious rush he'd had.

When he was awake he was straight, straight as an arrow to the heart. He had to be, to control his destiny. That's why he occasionally let himself go when he slept. He needed that liberation, that freedom.

They were almost over, the dreams. Soon it would be morning and he would be back in the small world of the jail infirmary: the world he would be living in until the Marvin White trial, and his final, absolute trip out.

Before he had fallen asleep, when the rush was coming on, the euphoria mixed with energy, he had played with himself, nothing cataclysmic, just good feeling, the hardness and the feeling of ejaculation on the horizon. He didn't actually come, he backed off when he felt he was about to explode—he wanted the sensation of anticipation rather than the actual eruption, and after bringing himself to the brink two or three times with visions of Julia Roberts and Brad Pitt and Michelle Pfeiffer and Keanu Reeves all jumbled up together in one sexual cocktail the hallucinogenic sleep had grabbed him and taken hold, and he was out of the physical-sexual world.

Which is why his limp cock was lying exposed out the fly of his boxer shorts.

Doris started tingling with excitement and anticipation, seeing Dwayne's manhood perched there so innocently. His penis was of average size, neither particularly large nor small, but to her it was perfect, God's creation. This was the real snake that got Adam and Eve kicked out of heaven, she thought, not some biblical horseshit about an apple—the snake that bound men and women to each other and drove them crazy, so crazy they thought God lived between their legs. Which for all intents and purposes, he did. At least in the most important ways.

She knelt down at the altar and took the snake between her lips.

Dwayne came out of his sleep like he had been shot out of a cannon. Out of pure jailhouse instinct and paranoid psychology he lunged forward, grabbed her by the throat, and slammed her to the ground, his hand tight on her throat, ready to break it.

She screamed at the unexpected, violent reaction.

"Jesus Christ!" he exclaimed, once he realized who had been touching him. "Don't ever do that!" He backed away from her, his body shaking with fury. "I could've killed you, you dumb fucking bitch!"

"I'm sorry," she whimpered, coming up on her knees. "I didn't think . . ." She had thought he would love it, is what she had thought.

He had scared the shit out of her. He was capable of killing, of that she had no doubts. Her, or anyone.

What Dwayne had thought, felt, dreamed in the last throes of sleep, coming out of his nightmare, was that he was having sex with a man. Not that that was something he didn't do; he'd had sex with scores of men during his life in prison, pitching and catching both—sex with men was more common to him, over the past fifteen years, than sex with women. But in that last moment of sleep his dream was that he was having sex with a man he despised, a man who terrorized him, and he wasn't the one who was the dominant, the butch; he was the sissy, the fuckee.

In the real world, this dark, empty jailhouse infirmary,

where he was alone but for his corpulent, feverishly horny big-woman lover, he was being administered to as the lord of the manor; but in the nightmare world he was being fucked and fucked royally, a public tormenting and humiliation. He was taking it in the ass and everyone in the prison, hundreds of men, inmates and guards both, were watching. And laughing.

For Dwayne, his manhood, his macho, was the most important thing he had. It was everything to him, almost all the time, the only thing that kept him going. And the fear of having it taken away, of being violated, was ever at the edge of his mind, his conscious fear.

It was only Doris. She was giving him head, something she did well. He was safe.

"I'm sorry," she said again, her voice almost breaking into tears. "I thought you'd like it."

"I do. You took me by surprise, that's all. This is a jail, Doris, there's all kinds of vicious predators in here, you know that."

Like you, she thought. You're one of the worst.

He looked around. It was dark; all the lights were off, and there was no daylight coming in yet through the high-barred slits of windows. "What time is it?" he asked, swinging his feet over the edge of the bunk and sliding his pecker into his shorts.

She glanced at her watch. "Five-fifteen."

"Jesus. What're you doing here so early?"

"I wanted to see you. I mean . . . be with you. Like . . . you know." She felt girlish, stupid. She didn't know how to deal with these emotions because she never had them. She was the toughest woman she knew, tougher than most men. Except around him.

He owned her. About eighty percent of her hated that, hated the feeling of powerlessness; but the other twenty percent that liked it was overwhelming. This was what it must be like to be in thrall to a man, blinded by love. All her life she had dreamed of being a normal woman, a normal-sized female being, blinded by love. And now she was.

So why did it feel so bad, so shameful?

Because he didn't love her back. In her heart she knew that, try as hard as she could to sabotage her feelings.

"A penny for your thoughts." He was staring at her with those cold milk-blue eyes.

"I was thinking how good your cock felt in my mouth." Which wasn't exactly what she had been thinking about, but close enough.

"Feels good to me, too, babe." He leaned forward and gave her an openmouth kiss. "If we're going to fuck, we'd better get it on."

She put her uniform back on. She had taken everything off to make love to him. It felt right that way, like real lovers, not some quick fuck in the jail infirmary, which was the truth of it. "I'd better get going," she said, looking at her watch. "The shift changes in twenty minutes."

He nodded. "We don't want to get caught," he agreed.

She tied her shoelaces, sitting on the edge of his bed. "I'll try to come down tonight, after everyone's left," she said.

He moved away from where he was sitting next to her. "Maybe that's not a good idea."

"I'll be careful, don't worry. I'm not going to put you in jeopardy."

"It's you that should be worried," he said. "I've cut my deal, they can't fuck with me. But you could get busted, big-time. They'd fire you in a New York minute. Maybe even bar you from practicing law."

She stared at him. "I can handle this."

"Yeah, maybe. But if we ever did get caught, even a whiff of suspicion, that DA would have my ass up a hundred-foot pole. We've got to be careful, Doris, cool it a while."

She turned away so he wouldn't see the pain on her face; worse than pain, the shame. How did she ever get into this? How did she allow him to do this to her?

It wasn't worth thinking about. She looked in the mirror every day.

"I've got it covered," she told him. "I'll make sure that you're safe."

No one saw her leave the infirmary. She rode the elevator up to her floor and signed in, taking the keys to her unit from the night watch commander.

"How's it going, Doris?" he asked, yawning.

"Can't complain, Willie."

"Yeah." He sniffed the air. "You wearing perfume?" he asked, as if that was not possible.

"A little." Don't blush, fool. He's a jerk.

He grinned. "Smells nice." He nudged her bicep with an elbow, winked conspiratorially. "If I didn't know better . . ." He grinned again.

If you didn't know I could never have a man? Is that what that means? If you only did know, for real.

She had a man. A man in a cage. A captive. But soon, he would be let out of that cage, be free to fly away.

Would she have a man then?

This shit with Doris had to stop. He'd gotten what he needed from her and then some; he was in a dangerous space now. If they found out about Doris he'd be busted, the DA might have to drop him. More importantly, it could lead to people sticking their noses in places that could be injurious to his health, like finding out he had used her computer and played some silly games with it.

He switched his thought to that lady DA. Helena Abramowitz. Now that was fine pussy, first-class. Brittle around the edges, but her meat was close to the bone, the way he liked it. Those perky little titties, those long, lean, backbreaking legs.

She wasn't married. And she knew of his desire, she had stared right at his erection, almost taunting him to do something about it.

One thing he knew about Helena Abramowitz, with her tight Jewish-princess pussy: she wanted to win this case, wanted it bad. She would rather win this case than make five million dollars. She would do anything to get that goal. And maybe to get it she'd have to do something nice for him.

"**O**h, he was not a bad boy. He did the job okay enough, most of the time." The man sighed: a deep basso-profundo lamentation. "He was lazy, that was his problem. He wanted it all right away, without working for it. Like his friends, who sell their dirty drugs to little kids on the street. I see it, it happens right under your nose. I said to him, 'Marvin, you can make money honestly. You can be proud of yourself.

You can rise above your heritage, those crummy surroundings.' " The man spread his hands in a hopeless gesture. "He don't want to hear that. He wanted it all right now, like his friends, without having to do honest work."

The man passing judgment on Marvin was his former boss, Artis Livonius. He spoke with a pronounced accent, the English of one who had taken it up in his teens or later, long after he was at home in another language. He and Wyatt were in the back of Livonius's cleaning establishment, amid the noise of the pressing tables, industrial-sized washers and dryers, and dry-cleaning machines. Livonius had a small work area tucked away in the corner, where a Macintosh computer sat on an old beat-up wooden desk. The room was steamy from all the machines running full blast; Wyatt had taken his coat off and loosened his tie.

Livonius extracted a large jar of kosher dill pickles from a small cube refrigerator tucked in between his desk and the back door, extracted one from the brine, and bit into it, taking half the fullness in one large mouthful. He held the jar out to Wyatt, who shook his head. "No, thanks. I've already had lunch. Looks good, though."

"Salt," the owner confided. "It gets muggy in here and you're on your feet all day, you cramp up in the legs if you don't keep your salt intake up. Better than salt tablets. It's an old Lithuanian trick. Pickles and salted herring, the national dishes of Lithuania."

You learn something new every day, Wyatt thought. There were definite perks to practicing law bargain-basement style. One night you're cruising the mean streets with a teenage drug lord and another morning you're learning about the national dishes of Lithuania.

Before coming uptown to see Livonius, Wyatt had spent the morning with Josephine, hunkered down in their own private gulag, outlining his strategy—where he wanted to go, how, and when. Josephine had sat across the desk from him, taking copious notes as he talked it out in an almost stream-of-consciousness flow.

Ticking off on his fingers: "We're going to find this woman Marvin was supposedly with on the night of one of the old murders, if she actually exists. We're going to talk to everyone Marvin knows, to see if anyone has a good alibi for him for some other time. We're going to get with his employer and trace his delivery route to see how that matches up with the murderer's timetable. We're going to go to every one of those murder sites, to see if there's anything there we can use. And we are going to learn everything we can about Dwayne Thompson. He's the state's case. If we can find something to discredit him, we'll blow them out of the water."

He was enjoying being out on the street, investigating on his own, which he'd never done in his life—it had always been done for him. Making his own case, meeting the people where they worked and lived, seeing it all firsthand. It felt more real doing it this way, less removed. He was connecting more.

Livonius polished off the rest of his king-sized pickle with one bite. Wiping his massive hands on his smock, he said, "So. What do you want from me?"

"You know about Marvin, of course."

The dry cleaner shook his head sadly. "Unbelievable," he uttered.

"What's unbelievable, Mr. Livonius?"

"That the poor bastard's in jail, what else?"

"It's not unbelievable that he might have committed these crimes?"

The man snorted a short harsh laugh. "I didn't say that. I think it's unlikely, but . . ." He shrugged again. "Who knows? He was capable of robbing from me, a man who took him under his wing and tried to teach him right from wrong. But rape? Murder? I think Marvin's out of his league there."

Wyatt wanted to believe that, too; but he couldn't. He had seen the tape with his own two eyes, he'd seen Marvin White try to shoot a man. If Marvin's gun hadn't jammed he would have, and he would be facing a murder charge he couldn't possibly find a way to beat.

That tape was Alex Pagano's hole card. If Pagano felt his back was to the wall—that the case was slipping away from him at some point deep in the trial—he would use it. He would take a piece of the police department down to get his conviction, without thinking twice about it.

"I know Marvin stole from you," Wyatt said to the proprietor, "and you fired him over it, which is completely understandable. But putting that aside—if you can, which I know is asking a lot—how did you feel about Marvin? Until you caught him stealing did you like him? Tolerate him?"

The man leaned against a large dry-cleaning machine that was humming away. All around the room, women in smocks were sorting laundry, operating pressing machines, folding and bundling. Most of them looked like they were Mexican, Wyatt noticed. Probably illegal.

"I liked him okay. He's a likable kid in some ways. Oh, he's a slacker, a petty thief, and a punk, and like I said, he was lazy, which is the worst crime in the world in my book—but he was no fool. He could have amounted to something. That's what I said to him, many times. 'Marvin,' I said, 'you can have a career here. This is a good business, dry cleaning. You could learn the trade and someday you could start your own business. Own your piece of the rock.'" Another shrug. "He never listened. Long-range planning, honest work, they weren't part of his outlook. Look," he said, his voice becoming passionate, "I came here from Lithuania, when the Communists ran it. I had nothing, no language here, didn't know nobody. And here I am today, I own my own business, I pay taxes. These colored kids, they have no drive, no sense of responsibility. It's 'gimme gimme gimme.' They should live in Lithuania the way it was, they'd sing a different tune." He shook his head and spat on the floor.

Wyatt flipped through his reporter-sized notebook. "He was your delivery man."

"One of them. I got two. Too much work for one, we deliver all over the city. Private and commercial both."

"He drove a truck?"

"Sometimes. Sometimes he took the bus, or the subway. I always gave him money for the fare," he said quickly.

"Do you recall if he was ever in the particular areas where the murders took place, when they took place? Like he had a particular delivery to make at a certain address that was close to a murder, around the time it would have occurred?"

"He must have been. He was all over the west side every day."

"What about night?"

Livonius shook his head. "Not during working hours. We don't deliver at night."

"Some of the murders—most of them—took place at

night. Which stands to reason, since prostitutes work more at night."

"They work in the daytime, too," Livonius contradicted him. "Go outside and drive two blocks down the street. You'll get solicited."

Wyatt knew that was true. He had seen several hookers on his way here. "So Marvin would have had to come back to this part of the city after work, if he was going to kill a prostitute at night."

"He wouldn't come back," Livonius asserted. "A kid like him, black. He isn't comfortable hanging around somewhere that ain't his place. He was a homeboy—didn't feel comfortable outside his own area." He cracked a couple of huge knuckles. "In some of these areas a black man sticks out like a two-headed baby. These krauts and Poles and other eastern Europeans that live in these neighborhoods, they don't like black people, especially black men." He shook his head. "If Marvin had been in those places after dark, he would have stayed after work, done what he had to do, and gotten out of there."

That was a positive—a small one. "I'm trying to establish alibis for Marvin. Is there any way you could remember, or check up in your records or whatever, a time when it would have been improbable, or better yet, impossible for Marvin to have been in the area where one of the killings took place, when it did? Like he was home sick, or at school, on vacation, anything like that?"

Livonius frowned. "I don't think I could remember anything that exact," he said. "He worked after school and on the weekends until he quit school, then he worked during the regular day. People like him don't take vacations," he added.

"I don't mean a regular vacation," Wyatt said, regretting his choice of words. Of course people like Marvin didn't take vacations. People like Marvin and Jonnie Rae could barely pay the rent—which was why dealing drugs or robbing numbers drops didn't seem as wrong to them as it did to people in better economic circumstances: people like Livonius, and him. "But maybe he was out of town—visiting a relative, something like that."

"No."

This guy wasn't much help. "What about your records?

Wouldn't you have records of when deliveries were made, and to whom? Something I could use to cross-check against the times of the murders. Maybe one of the customers Marvin delivered to on those days would have some kind of alibi for Marvin. Like he went over after work and helped move furniture or something." *Or spent the night in one of the lady customers' beds.*

"I don't know," Livonius said reluctantly. "My customers aren't going to want to be disturbed with this. It's already hurt my business, my customers finding out that vicious killer was delivering their dry cleaning. Especially my female customers. That he was in their house with them, alone."

He knows about Marvin's reputed sexual escapades, Wyatt flashed. Or has a damn strong suspicion. "Did any of your female customers ever complain to you that Marvin acted inappropriately toward them. Threateningly, or sexually?"

The man looked away. I've touched a nerve, Wyatt thought. That story Dexter had told him, which he had taken with a large dose of salt, was starting to become more plausible.

"No," Livonius admitted reluctantly. "No one ever complained about that."

"Then doesn't it make sense that if he never threatened one of your women customers, physically or sexually, that he wouldn't do it elsewhere? If he wanted to rape and kill women, his job delivering for you would be perfect. He would be alone with helpless women, over and over. But you never had a complaint, not one."

Livonius went through some inner turmoil—Wyatt could see it playing on his florid face. Finally, he opened up. "Marvin wouldn't have to rape women. He had all the women he could handle. He was shtupping plenty of ladies on his route, especially the older gals who are working overtime to hang on to their looks. They call me up for delivery and they got this baby-doll little voice." His deep voice rose in falsetto: "Oh, by the way, will you make sure Marvin does the delivery? Your other driver, he doesn't know the area so good, I have to wait for him too much." Dropping back into his own speech: "Like it was an afterthought, just came into their heads. My other driver, Luis, who covered for Marvin when he was a no-show, he's a humpback greaseball with garlic on his breath, no teeth, a woman would never get twenty feet near him. But he's an honest man, he works hard. And if Marvin was out that day they'd say, 'It can wait until tomorrow.' So Marvin would take over their dry cleaning and a twenty-minute delivery would take an hour and a half. And he'd have a nice, juicy tip." His face darkened. "Which made me even madder, when I caught the lazy schwartzer ripping me off. The tips weren't enough, he had to steal my profits."

"I'd like a list of the names and addresses of the customers Marvin made deliveries to on the days of the murders," Wyatt said. "I'm sure you have records of that on your computer. We could punch them up right now, I'll bet." He started to move toward Livonius's desk.

The big man danced around him, blocking his way. "I don't think that's a good idea. My customers don't want to get involved, like I told you. Screwing the colored delivery boy, I don't think they want anyone to know that. Especially their misters."

Wyatt took a step back. "Mr. Livonius. I don't want to cause you any problems. And I appreciate your having seen me on such short notice, especially under these circumstances. But those records could be important to our case, and I need them. Now you can let me look at them with you—unofficially—or I can get a warrant for them. And if I have to do that, it will become a public spectacle. I'm sure your female customers won't welcome that." Whether or not he could obtain a warrant for this fishing expedition was dubious, but this man wouldn't know that, he guessed.

His hunch was right—Livonius glowered, then gave in. "I'll go back through my records and make up a list for you of whatever I can find. Give me your fax number."

Wyatt hadn't memorized his new fax number yet. He had to look it up on a card he had in his wallet.

"I'll get it to you tomorrow," Livonius promised him grudgingly. "I'll work on it tonight, after I close up. Right now I'm too busy."

"Sure, that's fine. I appreciate this, Mr. Livonius. And so does Marvin."

Livonius coughed derisively. "Marvin. He don't appreciate nothing. He stole from me, in case you forgot. His own boss, who treated him good. No, sir. Marvin screws up everything that comes across his path. That's why he's in this trouble."

Security was ultratight. The jail personnel knew who Wyatt was, but he nevertheless had to show his driver's license and another piece of ID, sign in, have his briefcase pawed through, clear a metal detector, then pass two sets of chambers with locked doors at either end to get to his client.

Except for when he would have to make an appearance in court, Marvin was now confined to the cellblock on his floor. He got to exercise one hour a day, watch television two hours a day, take a ten-minute shower every other day, and talk on the telephone as much as he wanted, but only to approved callers: Wyatt; Walcott and other designated members of the Public Defender's office, including Josephine; his mother and siblings; and a small group of friends whose names had been submitted to the court and cleared by Judge Grant. Wyatt, other people on the PD staff, and his mother were the only visitors he could see whenever he wanted. All others had to be approved in advance for each individual visit.

Surprisingly (to Wyatt), Dexter had been one of the friends approved to send and receive telephone calls.

"It's because he doesn't have a record as an adult—yet," Walcott had explained to Wyatt when the two of them went over the list. "And let's get real—Grant isn't going to be a prick on the small stuff. He'll save the shitty rulings for where it'll really hurt us."

Wyatt had spent a few minutes with Walcott that morning, filling him in on what he was doing. The briefing went well, considering their somewhat adversarial relationship. As Wyatt was wrapping it up he mentioned his trip to Sullivan Houses, which had led to his meeting with Dexter and pointed him in new directions. But when Walcott realized that Wyatt had actually gone down there his countenance darkened, and he became visibly upset.

"What was the point of that?" he asked, his voice and body language showing a lack of sympathy for the undertaking.

Wyatt was taken aback. "To talk to the mother on her home ground. And to get the lay of the land. This is not the kind of world I live in, not remotely. I can do a better job for my client if I know where he's coming from."

"You're a lawyer, not a social worker."

"I know that. Do you have a problem with my going down there?" *And if you do, so what? It's none of your business— I'm his lawyer, not you.*

"You need to prepare his defense. You don't need to become a part of his life. You're his lawyer, not his fairy godfather."

Wyatt looked at him. "Is there a hidden agenda I don't know about? What's your real objection to what I did?"

Walcott squared his shoulders. "We're swamped in this office. You start working this extracurricular stuff, it gets around. Then every petty criminal will want that kind of attention, and we don't have the manpower to provide it."

"This is a capital case. I'm going to turn over every rock I can," Wyatt said. "I'm building trust by going down there, and making valuable connections I couldn't make otherwise. This boy Dexter would never have come to the office, but when he saw me in his own backyard he decided he could confide in me. These people are suspicious of us; you know that. Anything I can do to alleviate that, I'm going to. It can only help."

Walcott threw up his hands. "Do it your way. You're going to whether or not I approve. But if any of this backfires on you, you'd better be ready to take the blast. Alone."

A small concrete-walled dayroom at the end of the cellblock, painted a washed-out puke green, had been requisitioned for use as a visiting room, specifically for Marvin. It was a windowless room and the door was solid steel, with only a peephole at eye level for guards to look in. There was a television camera positioned high in one corner with a fish-eye lens to capture the entire room, but sound was not recorded.

The first time Wyatt saw the camera he flashed back to the one he had discovered in the Korean market that Marvin had tried to rob. Anticipating his objection, since he was new to the criminal-justice system, one of the deputy wardens explained the reason for the camera. "We have to make sure nothing funky goes on, for your protection as much as ours. We've had family members or friends slip inmates drugs, weapons, everything you can think of. Lawyers, too.

The camera keeps everyone clean, removes temptation. There's no sound, an outside agency sweeps the place every week. The last thing we want is to get some scumbag's conviction thrown out because we violated his rights."

Wyatt and Marvin sat across from each other at the small metal table in the center of the room.

"What about this woman?" Wyatt asked his client. "Do you remember her name?"

Marvin shook his head. "Nah, man," he mumbled.

Wyatt cocked a dubious eye. "How many women on your route did you spend the night with? There couldn't have been that many."

"There wasn't. I just don't remember. It was like, what, a year ago or more? I can't remember these different women, they're just . . . you know . . . women. I fucked some of them. So what?"

"So what? We're looking for an alibi witness for you, Marvin. If you were with a woman when one of these murders took place, that gets you off that murder, don't you get it? If you're off one, you're off them all. This is important, Marvin. Crucial. Think! Now. A name, an address. Anything." He was losing his temper, but he didn't care. Something had to wake this kid up, and fast.

Marvin shook his head, his eyes on the pocked tile floor. "I can't, Mr. Matthews. They all blur into each other."

He stopped talking for a moment, his mind working; then he looked up, the first time he was making clear eye contact with Wyatt. "I never saw them, you know? I looked at their faces, but I didn't *see* them, you understand me? I didn't want to see them, because they didn't exist for me as people. Like I didn't exist for them as a person. I was something to make them feel like a woman, like they had some sex appeal left in them. They used me and I used them back. It was business. It wasn't about what their name was or what they looked like."

The case of *People v. Walter Malone* was being tried in courtroom C, one of the regular-sized courtrooms. There were forty-eight seats for spectators, but although it was a murder trial the room was only about half-full, with most of

the attendees being reporters. There wasn't much sex appeal
to this case; it was four years old, and there were no big
players involved. The accused was a lowlife petty habitual
criminal, the murder victim was a petty lowlife loan shark,
and nobody, except for the prosecutor's office and the accused himself, had any stake in the outcome.

The meat of Alex Pagano's case was the confession that
Walter Malone had made to Dwayne Thompson at Durban
prison the previous year, when both men were briefly cell-
mates. In his insinuating, inimitable fashion, Dwayne had
played on the con's need for absolution and had gotten poor
Walter to spill his guts. Walter, of course, had never dreamed
that a fellow con would turn against him. Like all men, he
had needed to tell someone about what he had done, because if no one knows, there's no acclaim, no status; and
also, it's a hard thing to keep inside you forever, that you
killed a fellow human being. In the old days the chaplain
served that purpose; except criminals rarely went to see the
chaplain, except in Pat O'Brien movies.

Dwayne had been outfitted in a decent sports jacket, white
shirt, tie, slacks. Nothing fancy or flashy—presentable, neutral. He had a fresh haircut, square-style, combed back on the
sides in a modified ducktail, held in place with Vitalis. He sat
upright in the polished oak wooden captain's chair, hands
resting lightly on the arms, one leg crossed nonchalantly
over the other. He was at ease—he'd been here before.

The assistant DA, a tough veteran named Neil Rior-
dan, began taking Dwayne through the story—how, why,
when, where. Dwayne answered the questions directly and
simply, without embellishment.

There were two spectators seated in the back of the room,
on opposite sides of the aisle as far away from each other as
they could get, who were watching these proceedings with
more than the idle interest of the press or the normal courtroom groupies. Wyatt was one of them. He sat in the last
chair in the back row, close to the window, watching and
taking notes. He wasn't paying attention to what Dwayne
was saying, the particulars—he didn't know anything about
this case and had no interest in it. His attention was on
Dwayne the man, the witness. How he presented himself,
how cogent and precise his responses were, how truthful

they seemed to be. Most importantly, how the jurors were responding to him.

It's hard to read a jury, he knew; they can be paying close attention to a witness, hanging on every word he says, taking notes, everything a jury is supposed to do, and afterward, when a verdict comes in, you discover they didn't believe a word he said. Conversely, a jury can be inattentive, collectively skywriting in their heads, their notepads under their seats, even seemingly dozing off; yet later they will report that was the most convincing witness of all those they had heard.

Dwayne Thompson, in Wyatt's opinion, was doing a slam-bang job. He had his facts down cold, and the way he talked about how Walter had spun his yarn, the two of them sitting in a lonely prison cell late at night (Walter was doing time for shylocking and pimping, and was looking at another two years maximum on this particular stretch) had the ring of truth to it. Dwayne was a storyteller, and dangerously believable.

Sitting on the other end of that aisle, in the closest seat to the door, Helena Abramowitz was also watching and taking her notes. From time to time she would glance over at Wyatt, who was studiously ignoring her. She had been wondering about him since she had come on this case. He was an unknown. He had a great reputation in the corporate law world, but he had no experience in this side of the law, none.

Why he was doing this she had no idea, but his *being* disturbed her. Her gut instinct told her she should try to psyche this guy out. Push him hard from the get-go, try to keep him on the defensive.

She turned her attention back to Dwayne. He was a great prosecution witness. To watch him, to listen to him, you wouldn't know he was a savage, a mad dog sociopath. He came across as a criminal, yes; but also as a man with human values, a conscience.

If anything was disturbing to Helena it wasn't Dwayne's demeanor or anything about his performance on the stand. It was his actual testimony that was causing her discomfort, in a vague, undefinable, but very real way. Her concern was how Dwayne had gotten Walter Malone to confess his crime—to a total stranger. She knew that jailhouse informants had been around forever. Her problem was the way

that Dwayne presented his story. It was too polished. Too
many specifics, too many facts that were exactly on the
money. It didn't smell clean, totally clean. Dwayne didn't
know his story well enough; he knew it *too* well.

When Dwayne had finished testifying for the day she was
going to get a transcript from the court reporter and go back
to her office and compare it with the original facts—the police reports and depositions and so forth—in the Walter
Malone case, and then compare both to Dwayne's prior testimony to the grand jury in that case. She wanted to see how
good the fit was. If it was perfect, that would be a problem
for her. Like the almost too perfect fit between the confidential police reports and Dwayne's incriminating testimony in
her case, the case of the decade.

Dwayne's keepers escorted him, in handcuffs, waist chain,
and leg-irons, back to the jail, where he changed into his
prison-issue and returned to work in the infirmary. He had
done well; he always did well. This one was a no-brainer—
he'd be on the stand with this prosecutor another day, two
max, then the defense lawyer would take a whack at him,
which would take a day, maybe spill over a little. The defense attorney wouldn't lay a glove on him. He'd seen the
fear in the man's eyes from up on the witness stand. The
poor bastard looked like a deer caught in the headlights. By
the end of the week this would be over and done with.

He was glad he was doing this trial. It was like a tune-up
for the main event. He could feel the juices flowing, the
blood rushing. You could get a hard-on doing this shit—
there was a strong sexual component to it.

Having Helena the DA sitting in the back of the room
catching his act didn't hurt with the sexual energy-flow. Her
eyes had been riveted on him all day long.

The infirmary closed down for the day. The male nurse
locked all the cabinets and signed out. What that mincing
little shit didn't know was that Dwayne had found the duplicate keys, taped to the bottom of a desk drawer. Anybody
stupid enough to hide a key that poorly deserved to get his
goodies ripped off.

He wouldn't take drugs; not yet. The drugs were counted

carefully, and if his keepers found anything missing that would be the end of his ride on this gravy train. For now the grain alcohol would do the trick nicely. He'd make himself a couple of potent highballs and take a trip inside his head.

The captain of the guard, whose name tag ID'd him as Walt Michaelson, opened the door. Michaelson was a certified no-neck, a former NFL offensive guard. It was common knowledge that beating the shit out of recalcitrant inmates was his idea of a good time. There weren't many like him in the system anymore, but one or two were tolerated, even encouraged. He looked behind him, to someone who was standing in the corridor outside. "He's in here, all right," Michaelson said.

Alex Pagano walked into the infirmary. "Thank you, Captain," he said politely. "Now if you'd leave us, please. I have things to discuss with Mr. Thompson that are private."

"I'll be outside the door if you need me, sir."

"Good. Thank you."

Captain Michaelson left, shutting the door behind him. Dwayne, who had been surprised and slightly unnerved by the sudden and unexpected intrusion—no one ever came down here after hours unless there was an emergency, and he would be forewarned in that case—eyeballed the DA carefully.

Pagano walked to Dwayne. "That's good work you've done in the courtroom," he said, offering his hand. "Congratulations."

They shook. "Thanks," Dwayne responded. He didn't go any further; Pagano hadn't come down here to tell him he'd done okay. DAs don't jawbone with prisoners. This one was here for some other reason.

"This is your duty station?" Pagano asked, looking around. "I've never been in the jail infirmary. Nice setup," he continued, strolling about.

Dwayne nodded. You know fucking aye well it's where I work. You think you know everything about me; but you don't.

"I understand you're bunking here, too?" Pagano sat on the edge of a counter.

"Yes sir."

"How did that come about? Allowing a prisoner to inhabit an unsupervised area?"

"It was the sheriff's decision, sir."

"Oh?"

He should have thought before he spoke. The DA might check that. On the other hand, what else could he have said? That a certain female deputy, whom he happened to be fucking, had set it up for him?

"Putting me in the general population . . . that could cause problems for me. Word gets around. I'm a marked man in certain quarters in here. There are people who don't like what I do."

Pagano looked puzzled. "I can understand that. But we have facilities for isolating inmates who need protection." He looked around the room some more. "Leaving an inmate unsupervised in an area that has large amounts of medicines and so forth could be construed as letting the fox guard the henhouse, don't you think?"

Dwayne threw up his hands. "I don't mess with that stuff. I'm not going to do something stupid and jeopardize my future."

Pagano nodded his agreement. "Yes, that would be stupid, and you're not stupid. Still, it makes for a bad appearance. And appearances are important."

"Absolutely, sir." He didn't know where this was leading exactly, but his cocktail hours were definitely about to end.

Pagano stood up. "Let me talk to the sheriff about arranging more suitable sleeping arrangements for you, Thompson. I'd hate for this Marvin White case to get befuddled in some public relations snafu. If the press or his lawyers knew about this, it could be ticklish."

"Sure," Dwayne said. "I understand you have to keep up appearances."

Pagano opened the infirmary door. "It's too late to do anything tonight. I'll post a guard outside the door, to prevent anyone coming in here and finding you. We'll set up a permanent solution tomorrow."

He left, closing the door behind him. Dwayne heard the key turn in the lock. Through the small safety-glass window he saw the captain and Pagano holding a conversation. Then they were gone.

A minute later, a jail deputy took up his post in the hallway outside the infirmary. No one was coming in or out of this place without the officials knowing it.

Dwayne wasn't all that pissed off; he'd known this would happen sooner or later. He wondered who'd ratted him out. That dipshit nurse, most likely. The little prick thought the infirmary was his own private domain.

Well, there was going to be one positive thing to come out of this. Doris Blake wouldn't be paying him any more nocturnal visits. Her cock-scoring days were over.

Josephine found the woman Marvin had spent the night with. It hadn't taken her very long. She took Livonius's list—which, to Wyatt's surprise, had come through their fax machine the following morning—and started knocking on doors. She knew that trying to accomplish this delicate task over the phone would be a waste of time, and counterproductive—you had to get in your object's face, up close and personal. Part of her training, which she had initiated herself because she wanted to do a better job, had been to ride around with some of the detectives who worked cases for the department. Face-to-face, she learned from them, worked about a hundred times better than anything else. It's a lot harder for somebody to close a door on your face than to hang up the phone.

She called Wyatt at home, at night again. Dinner was over. Moira wasn't in a chatty mood and his head had been somewhere else. Casual in T-shirt and sweatpants, he was sitting in his study, reading over his notes.

Moira stood in the doorway to the study, the cordless phone from the kitchen in her hand. "It's for you," she said curtly. As he got up to take it, she asked, "What is it with you and this woman you're working with? Is there something going on?"

He took the phone from her. "You know better than that, Moira."

"She seems eager to call you at all hours. Maybe she's hoping I won't be here." She paused a moment as if to say something more, then turned and left the room, pointedly shutting the door behind her.

He sighed. "Hi," he said into the phone.

"Bad time to call?" Josephine sounded concerned.

"No, we're just . . . never mind. What's up?"

She told him.

"Where are you now?" he asked.

"In her house. We're drinking sherry."

She gave him instructions. "It'll take you awhile to get here from where you live. I don't want to be pushy, but don't take your time, okay? This lady likes her sherry, if you get my drift."

He threw on a sports shirt, khakis, an old blazer—he had to look presentable. Moira was reading in bed, propped up with pillows, the bulk of *The Recognitions* opened to the middle. She watched him change clothes without comment.

"I have to go out," he told her. "There's a potential witness I have to see."

"Who doesn't keep nine-to-five hours."

"Give me a break, okay? This may take some time," he added, to his ears sounding apologetic and not wanting to.

"Please make sure all the doors are locked," she requested. On his nod she added, "Michaela and I will have gone to sleep, I'm sure. I'll have the alarm on, so don't forget to check it when you come back."

Ever since the robbery next door, she had been religious about using the alarm, something they'd been lax about before. He wasn't crazy about always having to turn it on and off; it bred insecurity, anxiety. But it made her feel protected, so he did it.

"Will do." He leaned across the wide expanse of mattress to her side and kissed her lightly on the lips. Her lips were cool to the touch.

He double-checked that all the doors were locked before he left. All he needed was for Moira to come downstairs and find one unlocked.

The Jaguar hummed along the freeway. Traffic had thinned, and he kicked back and enjoyed the drive, his windows open to the night. Frank Morgan sang a ballad through his alto sax on the car's CD, and he played along with it in his head.

Josephine was waiting for him outside the house, fidgeting by the bottom of the front steps, a small cut-crystal glass of sherry in her hand. He parked at the curb and walked over to her, the remote chirping as he locked the car.

"Dry Sack," she informed him, sticking her tongue out. "Want a taste?"

He shook his head. She dumped the contents into a bush. "This stuff gives me a headache, I drink more than a glass," she said. "Bad mojo." She cocked her head toward the house. Lights were burning in all the downstairs windows. "I told her I wanted to wait outside so you wouldn't miss the address, but I really needed to get out of there for a while. She's got an elbow problem and I didn't want to play keep-up."

This was no proletarian neighborhood. The homes were substantial dwellings on half an acre or more, with two-car garages in the back. An older neighborhood, but you needed to have good money to afford to live here. The residents were prosperous small-business owners and professionals. There was also a concentration, two blocks over, of mob-connected families who lived quietly behind curtains that were always drawn. It was considered one of the safest neighborhoods in the city because of those families.

"Her name is Agnes Carpenter," Josephine said. "Her husband's a doctor, ob-gyn. Has a private practice and privileges at St. Johnny's." St. John the Baptist was one of the better hospitals in the city. "He isn't home tonight, she was glad for the company. I've got the feeling he isn't home a lot of nights."

She rang the doorbell, which played the first two bars of "The Sound of Music." The door opened almost immediately, as if the woman was waiting there for them, perhaps trying to eavesdrop.

"Agnes, this is my boss, Wyatt Matthews," Josephine said by way of introduction.

The woman extended a plump hand that had rings on three of the fingers. The other hand held her glass, which had been refreshed moments before, judging from its fullness. The diamond engagement ring on that hand was at least three carats. It looked like the sort of ring Elizabeth Taylor would wear. "How do you do?" she said pleasantly. "Please come in."

They followed her through the foyer into the living room, which was jam-packed with furniture, a potpourri of old-fashioned overstuffed styles, mostly Queen Anne and Chippendale. "Please," she said. "Sit down."

He sat next to Josephine on a couch that sagged under his weight, shifting forward slightly so as not to be trapped in its mushiness. There was a feeling of decadence to the room, as if it were a well-preserved museum rather than a place in which people lived a daily life. Or a funeral home, he thought.

"Would you care for a libation?" she asked him. She had crossed to a small mahogany-colored side table that was set up as a bar, with four or five bottles on it, and several glasses on a shelf underneath. There was an ice bucket and tongs alongside the bottles. She picked up the bottle of Dry Sack. It was three-quarters empty.

"No, thanks," he declined.

She sipped down half of her own small glass and refilled it. Then she sat in an overstuffed chair that was set at a close angle to his end of the sofa.

He did a quick sizing-up. Early to mid-fifties, with a puffiness around her eyes that was the inevitable residue of decades of steady, unremitting drinking. The rest of her face was tight; she'd had a facelift, maybe more than one. It was a decent job—her husband was a doctor, she would have had someone good do it. And she knew how to put on makeup; she wore a lot of it, skillfully applied. Carefully coiffed hair, dark blond with light blond highlights. Her dark green knee-length wool jersey dress clung snugly to her body, which was firm for a woman her age. She'd had work there, too, he assumed. Her crossed legs, sheathed in dark Donna Karan hose, were sleek, free of cellulite. In soft light, with the right clothes and accessories, she was a reasonably attractive, albeit flashy, woman—a woman who spent a lot of time and money to look as good as she could. She reminded him of one of the Gabor sisters, the one from *Green Acres*.

Marvin had fucked her. More than once, Wyatt assumed. He speculated on how much she had paid him.

"Thank you for seeing me at this late hour," he began.

"I feel I have no choice," she replied. "Not that I want to get involved in this sordid mess. But ..." she hesitated. "I'm not going to let some innocent boy die because it might put me in scandal. *Will* put me in scandal," she amended.

"I don't know how to put this delicately. . . ."

"Don't," she interrupted. "Frank talk will be cleaner, and healthier."

"Yes, I agree. All right, then. Tell me about your . . . situation with Marvin White, Mrs. Carpenter. Particularly on the night of . . ."

"Last August eighteenth," Josephine prompted. "That was the night of the fourth murder," she told Wyatt, reading from her notepad.

"Please call me Agnes."

"Agnes."

"It's such an old-fashioned name." Her voice had a built-in world-weary complaint, as if she was shouldering an exceptionally heavy burden. "It was my grandmother's name, my paternal grandmother. My friends call me Aggie." She giggled, a quick burp-laugh. "But you'd better call me Agnes. We aren't friends; yet." She waited a moment, as if inviting objection. Hearing none, she held up her glass, which had somehow gotten empty. "Do you mind? This is going to be difficult. I need all the support I can get."

"Not at all."

She got up and walked over to the little bar in the corner, her hips swaying rhythmically.

"If she starts calling you Marvin, I'm out of here," Josephine whispered behind their hostess's back.

"I'll be right behind you," he whispered back.

She sat back down, crossing her legs again. "You've met Marvin," she said.

"Of course. He's my client."

"He's handsome, isn't he? A young black Adonis. Don't you agree?" she asked Josephine.

Josephine bit her tongue. "Absolutely." She snuck a glance at Wyatt, who was maintaining a poker face. "A real good-looking kid. Man."

"I wanted him immediately. Don't be shocked. I'm very open about sexual matters."

Wyatt knew that called for a response. "Uh-huh."

"So I propositioned him," Agnes said matter-of-factly. "Not in any vulgar way, of course. I'm not vulgar. But I am a normal woman, with normal sexual desires, and he appealed to me. He appealed to me strongly."

"How long did you and he . . ." He was having trouble with this. He was no prude, far from it, but this woman's blatant, almost triumphant eagerness to talk about her sex life to a complete stranger was unnerving.

"Fifteen months. Usually twice a week. Whenever he made a pickup or delivery. I never wear a garment more than once without having it cleaned, so I have a considerable amount of cleaning that has to be picked up and delivered. Usually Mondays for pickup and Thursdays for delivery. In the morning, around eleven."

"I see." Wyatt thought for a moment. "If your . . . sexual encounters . . . were in the morning, how was it that he was in your home that night?"

"I asked him to," she said. "I knew my husband wouldn't be coming home that night, so I told Marvin that I wanted him to spend the night here. He was happy to do so," she added. "There was never any coercion. I did pay him, I admit that. He was a poor boy, he needed money. But there was never any pressure. He wanted me as much as I wanted him." Another glass of sherry went down the hatch. "I'm an exceptional lover."

Wyatt tacked in another direction. "How could you be sure your husband wouldn't come home that night? Was he out of town?"

"No," the woman answered in a voice heavy with suppressed anger. "He was in town. He was staying at the Carlton Hotel. Room 1422."

"How did you know that?" Josephine asked bluntly.

Agnes laughed without mirth. "I knew because the detective I hired told me. Leonard was there with his mistress. A twenty-nine-year-old X-ray technician," she said derisively. "They've been having an affair for at least three years that I know of." She waved her empty glass in the air like a conductor's baton. "He wasn't coming home, for love or money. Especially love. So I used some of his money to buy my own love."

Wyatt looked at her. "Where's your husband tonight?"

"Where do you think? If he was here, or if I thought he was going to be here, would I be talking to you?"

Josephine had a portable tape recorder in her purse. She set it on the coffee table and turned it on. Agnes Carpenter began giving her statement.

"She wants to fuck her husband. Fuck him over." Josephine was so disgusted she felt like spitting.

They were outside the Carpenter house, by his car. The

moon was three-quarters full, low in the sky under a soft cloud-blanket.

Josephine looked back at the house. One by one, the lights were going off downstairs. A moment later a single one went on upstairs.

"Lonely women make good lovers," Josephine cackled. "Ha!"

"Have some compassion."

"Ahhh." Her shoulders sagged. "I do." She glanced up at him. "That really is true, you know. About lonely women making good lovers."

"How would you know?"

"You'd be surprised."

"If you're alone it's by your choice, and you know it."

"If you say so."

He didn't want this conversation to play out any further. He needed to get home. "It's late. Time to go."

He walked her down the block to her car. "Mañana," he said.

She gave him a peck on the cheek. "Don't let the bedbugs bite."

He waited at the curb until she drove away, then walked back to his car. As he was getting in, he looked up at the lit second-floor window in Agnes Carpenter's house. A figure was silhouetted in it, staring out at him. He wasn't sure, but it looked to him like she was naked.

He glanced at the clock in his dashboard as he drove up his driveway: 11:35, later than he would have liked. The outside floodlights, on a movement sensor, lit up as the Jaguar drove into the front yard. The garage doors, activated by the remote on his visor, rose with a grinding of chains. He parked his car next to Moira's and pushed the button inside the door to close it.

Moira had left the porch lights on, and one lamp in the foyer; otherwise the house was dark, and still.

Slipping out of his shoes and turning off the porch lights and hallway lamp, he was halfway up the stairs to the second floor when he remembered that he hadn't killed the alarm, which was located in a hide-a-box inside the coat closet near the front door. The timing mechanism was set for forty-five seconds; he'd been in the house almost that long.

Racing back down the stairs, he yanked open the alarm door. The lights were red and blinking, a process that didn't start until there were ten seconds left: nine, eight, seven . . . five, four, three. Rapidly, he punched in their five-number code.

The blinking stopped—the lights switched from hot red to benign green. He let out a sigh of relief—if he hadn't caught it, not only would an alarm have gone off in the security company's control center, which would have called forth an immediate armed response, in three minutes or less, guaranteed—their cars were constantly patrolling the neighborhood, particularly since the robbery at the Spragues' house next door; but the system would also have triggered a second alarm in the township's police station, and they, too, would have radioed the nearest squad car to check it out.

It was a silent system. There was no Klaxon to warn off an intruder. Silent, and deadly.

Wyatt hated having the alarm on, particularly when they were in the house. Once, a few months ago, waking before dawn and groggy from too much entertaining the night before, he'd gone outside to get the newspaper and had forgotten to disarm the damn thing. Standing on the wet green grass of his large front lawn in his boxer shorts and thongs, looking at the scores at the back of the sports section, he'd been startled and nearly scared shitless to see a security company sedan barreling up his driveway, brakes squealing as the car got within fifteen feet of him, a burly guard jumping out with a .357 magnum in his hand.

It had been okay; the driver knew him and people did forget to turn their alarms off. The cops, who arrived moments later, were okay with it, too, because he was Wyatt Matthews, solid citizen. But after that incident, he hadn't set it when they were in the house, only when they were out and there was no one home.

Until the Spragues were robbed, and Moira insisted on using it at night as well.

He reset the system to on. God forbid she should wake up before him and find out it was off. Tiptoeing up the stairs, he undressed in his bathroom, brushed his teeth, and climbed into bed.

Moira was sleeping on her side, turned away from him. He lay on his back under the cool sheets, thinking about his interview with Agnes Carpenter. She was full of shit in a lot of ways, but her story had the ring of truth to it.

Still, it was only her word. Who could tell how she would hold up under cross-examination? But it was an alibi, and hopefully there would be more. One such alibi as this might not sway a jury; two or three would be irrefutable. Chalk one up for their side.

Moira's breathing was deep and regular, but for some reason he thought she was faking it, that she wasn't really asleep. It would be nice if she would roll over and meld into his arms.

Frank Sinatra's voice drifted into his head. *When you're worried, and you can't sleep, just count your blessings instead of sheep, and you'll fall asleep, counting your blessings. . . .*

He had much to be thankful for. A wonderful home, wife and daughter, more money than he'd ever imagined he would make, good friends, a great career. And he was doing work that moved him in his gut. Which might, when it was all over and done, actually make a difference in the world.

Doris Blake freaked when she rounded the corridor leading to the infirmary and found a deputy sitting in front of the door. She had worn a pair of silk underpants, bought at a special boutique that catered to large, full-bodied women— a fat girl's store, with bra sizes up to 56DDDD. It was comforting to know there were women much larger than she.

The deputy jumped to his feet. "Good morning, Lieutenant. How can I help you?"

"Why are you here?" she asked, trying to keep the panic from her voice.

"Guarding the prisoner, ma'am," he said. He was young, a year out of the academy, and scared of this large woman. Her temper was legendary, and he didn't want to do anything to provoke it. "District Attorney Pagano's express orders. And the sheriff."

"Oh, I see." She affected a satisfied air. "I thought perhaps there had been a situation."

"No, ma'am. No problem."

"Good," she said to the guard, asserting her authority.

She signed in upstairs, exchanging gossip with Walt Michaelson, bantering with the crew that was finishing their shift. They were okay people, most of the time. There was some joking from the men about her personal life, but it never got vicious. They knew better; also there was some feeling of protective sympathy toward her. The other jailers knew her to be a hardworking, dedicated peace officer who had gone to law school at night and was out to better herself. You had to admire someone who did that.

Dwayne's reassignment was one order she couldn't finesse. She'd taken a big risk having him transferred down there in the first place, but this was beyond her. Dwayne would still be working in the infirmary during the day, and she could see him there, but they couldn't have sex, not there, not with other people around.

Maybe she could figure out a way to get him into the law library occasionally. It would be risky, having sex there, but it was doable. It would be fast, though, a fuck and nothing else—no languid foreplay, no lying in his arms afterward.

That was a dream. It had been a good ride while it lasted, but it was over.

In a few weeks she would be leaving this institution, starting a new career, trying to hook on with a law firm. She'd made some preliminary overtures, but so far there hadn't been any definite job offers. It was a tight field, and law firms weren't looking for forty-something neophyte lawyers who were just starting out. She still had more interviewing to do; there were some all-women firms that might not care what she looked like.

That wasn't her concern; not now. Her concern was sustaining a relationship with Dwayne. Her whole life, every thought, feeling, and emotion, was tied up in him. If she couldn't see him anymore, she didn't know what she would do.

Michaela had two weeks off from school—spring break. Moira was taking her on a college tour. Come fall she would have to decide what schools she would apply to.

They were going to be gone for ten days. Wyatt would be alone.

He was sorry to see them go, especially Moira, because there was unsettled business between them. They needed to find a way to get back on an even keel, right their marriage again.

It was still dark out when he drove them to the airport. Their plane left at seven-thirty. They checked their bags with a porter at the curb and walked into the terminal.

"Have fun," he told them, kissing Michaela first, on the cheek, giving her a hug for good measure, then embracing Moira with a hard kiss on the mouth, with some desperation behind it.

"I'll call you tonight; or tomorrow, depending," she told him.

"Don't worry about me," he said. "I'm going to use the time to work. Maybe I'll stay in town tonight."

"I never worry about you, Wyatt," she said wistfully. "That's part of the problem."

"I need you, babe."

"I want to believe that."

He spent the day on the telephone. At seven Josephine stuck her head into his cubicle. "I'm taking off," she said, as if reluctant to leave. "Don't work too late."

"Don't worry. Just a little longer."

She lingered in the doorway a moment before leaving. She had been angling for an invitation to stay, that was obvious. Maybe have dinner—he'd told her he was batching it for the week.

Don't worry. She was the second woman he had said that to today. In both cases he hadn't thought about what that had meant to them.

He worked until eight-thirty. Then he closed up shop for the night, got into his car, and drove a mile to the downtown Four Seasons Hotel. The firm maintained an account there; if a partner needed to spend the night, he called and they had a room for him. In Wyatt's case, as with the other seniors, a suite. There was no point in going home—he could stay here and avoid the traffic, productively use the time that would have gone into travel. He'd brought his toilet articles and a change of clothes with him, figuring this might happen.

He ordered a cheeseburger and a couple Heinekens from room service, eating off a tray while watching a baseball game on ESPN. He'd thought he would get more work done—he'd brought his bulging briefcase with him—but he was too antsy. He needed to get out, move, be in the company of people having a good time.

Exchanging his suit for a more comfortable outfit of khakis, polo shirt, sport coat, and Top-Siders, he rode the elevator down to the lobby, ambling around. He wasn't sure what exactly he wanted to do. A quick look into the crowded bar showed a bunch of solitary male drinkers, professionals like himself; a few small groupings, men and women there on business together, talking animatedly and laughing at their own jokes; and a smattering of single women, business types, plus a few ladies who appeared to be expensive-looking prostitutes. One, sitting alone at the bar, caught his eye and smiled encouragingly, but he quickly looked away. That type of woman didn't interest him, not even for a drink and casual conversation.

There was a small newsstand set off the reception area. He leafed through a magazine that featured the entertainment the city was offering that month. Under the section CLUBS he saw a listing for a place called the Jazz Table, which he'd never heard of or been to. They were featuring a quintet tonight—tenor sax, trombone, plus the usual piano-bass-drums rhythm section. The address was in a mixed-neighborhood area of the city, heading down toward the general direction of Sullivan Houses.

The jazz scene in the city had gradually evaporated in the last two decades. All the old, established clubs had died out. Lack of patronage, uneasiness about crime in the areas where most of the clubs had been located, the paucity of a core group of younger fans—the market wasn't there anymore, certainly not for the nationally known players. Wyatt couldn't remember the last time he'd been to a straight-up local jazz joint.

Trombone and tenor, his two favorite instruments. Sit back, have a few drinks, listen to some good music. This was a hopeful sign, that there was a new club in town. It wouldn't hurt to throw it his business, help keep it open.

It had been several years since he'd been in the area where the club was located, and it wasn't as he'd remembered it. No longer mixed (meaning a smattering of white families), it was solidly black, the only exceptions being a few stores with Asian lettering on the fronts. Vietnamese or Thai, it looked like. The stores were closed, protected from break-ins by heavy steel-chain awnings pulled down and locked into the concrete sidewalk. This city is so balkanized now, he thought as he drove down the avenue, looking for the address he'd scribbled on a Post-it. During the day—walking the downtown streets, at work, in stores and restaurants—you saw whites, blacks, Latinos, Asians, all bumping up against each other, asshole to elbow; but once the sun went down they all went back to their own little enclaves, and the drawbridges were pulled up.

He turned left off the avenue onto a narrower side street that was part apartment buildings, part stores. It took some concentration finding the right street—he had to take several left turns and a few rights, doubling back on his tracks a couple of times, before he found his place. The club was halfway down the block, a converted shop of some kind. A large plate-glass display-type window, protected by wrought-iron bars, fronted the sidewalk, covered with an ersatz black-velvet curtain with a likeness of Miles Davis in the center. Above the door the maroon awning proclaimed *The Jazz Table* in white stenciled-on script.

There was a space big enough for his car across the street, a few doors down. He parked and locked the car and crossed over toward the club. Half a dozen black men, middle-aged and nattily dressed, were standing around outside the entrance, talking and smoking cigarettes. They looked like the kind of men who had been hanging around jazz clubs for as long as he could remember.

He pushed open the heavy wooden door and went inside. To his left as he entered was a long bar, with high stools in front of it. The rest of the room was taken up with tables for four, covered with white tablecloths. Each table had a candle in a hurricane-style holder and a single rose in a glass flute in the center. The bandstand was set up to his right, behind the window with the velvet curtain. A small upright white piano, a drum kit, and a stand-up bass laid down on its side were at the back, and the trombone and tenor were on stands down front. A Sonny Rollins chart he recognized but couldn't name came out of the jukebox.

He checked out the trombone. A Yamaha, the same kind
J. J. Johnson played.

He looked around to get his bearings. The place was
about threequarters full, more men than women, but enough
women to make it feel smooth, cozy. There were a few
younger customers, men who looked like they would be
devotees of Joshua Redman and Wynton Marsalis, but most
of the patrons were his age or older. Old-time jazz fans, like
himself.

There were only three other white people in the place, in a
group. They looked like regulars. For a moment he felt uncomfortable, as if he were an intruder, but that passed—he
had been in jazz bars before where there hadn't been many
white faces. That's how it was. He loved jazz and they loved
jazz, that's all that counted.

A young woman sitting behind a table by the door, reading a college chemistry textbook, hit him up for a five-dollar
cover charge. He handed her a ten. As she gave him his
change she stared at him, a puzzled look on her face. "Have
you been in here before?" she asked.

"No."

"You look familiar somehow," she said. "I thought you
might have been."

"No, I've never been here."

He walked down the length of the bar. As he was making
his way through the room a few people, as the covercharge
girl had done, took a closer look at him. He could have told
them that they had seen him on television. That he was the
lawyer for the man accused of those murders. A young man
from their own community. Over time, as this trial became a
big celebrity shindig, with the lawyers trying the case in the
media, his face would be familiar to everyone, including the
denizens of this establishment. For now he was happy with
his anonymity. He found an empty barstool near the back
and parked his behind.

"What'll you have?" The bartender, a barrel-shaped
man with an unlit cigarillo tucked behind his ear, sidled up
to him.

He was tempted to say "Scotch and milk"—legend had it
that's what Coltrane drank—but he thought that would be
an affectation, and he didn't know if he'd like it. "Johnnie
Black with a splash. Club soda back."

"Ice?"

"A couple."

The bartender set his drinks in front of him. The man poured a generous shot—the thick old-fashioned glass was almost full. He made change from Wyatt's twenty, which Wyatt let ride on the bar, pushing a dollar forward for the tip. Hoisting his glass to the bartender in salute, he took a sip.

Mother's milk. He'd have to watch himself—two drinks tonight would be his limit. He had to drive back to the hotel through unfamiliar streets, and he had a ton of work to do tomorrow.

The quintet reassembled on the bandstand. The tenor man was the leader—he made a few remarks, thanking everyone for coming out tonight, made a couple of jokes, then put his horn to his mouth and counted out four beats with his foot. The group started playing an old classic, "Stella by Starlight."

Wyatt sat at the bar, eyes closed, his foot tapping against the railing in time. Grooving with the rhythm. He'd forgotten how much he loved this life, these sounds.

He stayed throughout the hour-long set. When they broke, and the musicians ambled over to the bar to chat up the customers and order their drinks, he struck up a conversation with the trombonist. The man was a few years older than he, and had played with the Basie band for a brief time in the sixties. They compared axes—his Bach, the trombonist's Yamaha ("It's the easiest horn in the world to pick up cold and play, which is important when your gigs are as infrequent as mine are now"), vintage Kings and Conns. Clubs on both coasts they'd been to, some of which the professional had played in. They sat there at the bar, talking like old chums, until it was time for the trombonist to go back to work.

Wyatt had planned to leave after one set, but now that he'd made the connection with the 'bone player he decided to stick around for a few more tunes. He nursed a drink, listening to the music, occasionally looking over the other patrons.

The group was good. They had been playing together a long time, he figured. The way they moved in and out of each other's solos, the piano comping on the breaks, the drum and bass keeping everything level, driving. No one was paying him any attention—he had faded into the scenery. If someone was heading to the bathroom, which was located at the rear, they glanced over as they passed by him. He smiled pleasantly, and most of the time they would acknowledge him. No one frowned or gave him the impression that he was trespassing.

The music, the Scotch going down easy, the dark smoky low-ceilinged ambience, it all made for a warm, comfortable, seductive experience. He was feeling horny; for his wife, and for other women, too. He hadn't been horny like this for some time. Maybe it was because he and Moira were on the outs and were having sex hardly at all the past couple of months. He thought about her, then about Josephine, and about women sitting here with their men. Women.

This was another aspect of the changes he was going through. Switching the kind of work he did was the tip of the iceberg; a symptom, not a cause. He was going to have to be careful about how he handled some of these changed feelings, especially on the sexual front.

"Last call."

He came out of his thoughts. The bartender was leaning on the bar. He looked at his watch: 1:15. He had completely lost track of the time. The band was starting on their final song; less than a dozen people were still in the club.

How many drinks had he had? Only a couple, he thought, yet when he looked at his change lying on the bar from his twenty there were only a few bills left. He must have had more than a couple, without thinking about it.

He felt fine. His head was clear, he wasn't at all tired. He had been carried away by the music, and time had literally flown.

"Any chance of getting an Irish coffee?" The caffeine wouldn't be enough to keep him awake, but it would help him stay alert on the drive back to the hotel.

"No problem." There was a half-filled pot of coffee warming on a hot plate on the backbar. "Don't see too many of your type in here," the barman said, placing the hot drink on a coaster in front of Wyatt. They were the first words he had spoken to Wyatt all evening, except to ask if he wanted another Scotch. "That'll be four dollars."

Wyatt slid him a five and held up his hand to signify that he didn't need change. The bartender rang his drink up on the register, poured himself a shot glass of cognac.

"I don't get down this way often." Wyatt looked around. "It's a nice room. And I like the group. They cook." When was the last time he had used the expression "They cook"? College, maybe.

"Yeah, they're good," the bartender agreed.

Wyatt finished his drink. "It's been a pleasure."

"Come on back, then."

"Thanks. I will."

The band finished their last song and played a sixteen-bar coda tag. The houselights came on.

"Thank you one and all," the tenor player said into the microphone, which went dead in midsentence. "And take it cool getting home."

Standing up, Wyatt felt a momentary dizziness from sitting for hours without moving. He thought about going to the bathroom before driving back, but he'd gone once, during the break. As he walked out the door the trombone player gave him a raised finger in salute, and he nodded back and smiled.

The cool night air hit him with a rush. He stood on the sidewalk, swaying, taking in a healthy gulp. Around him people were leaving, saying their good-nights to each other, making their way down the street. Wyatt walked to his car. The street was empty now, not a soul in sight. Long shadows cast by the overhead streetlights gave the scene an Edward Hopper feeling.

He got in the Jag, maneuvered a U-turn, and headed back toward the center of the city. Tomorrow night, when he went home, he'd spend a couple of hours with his trombone. Listening to the sounds tonight and talking to his fellow trombonist had gotten him energized about making his own music.

A couple rights, a couple lefts—this didn't look familiar. After fumbling around to get here he thought he knew his way back from the club, but this definitely was not a street he had been on before.

He was feeling the effects of the alcohol. Two Heinekens,

three Scotches in the bar (maybe four, he'd lost track?), the Irish coffee. Plus he had been up almost twenty hours. He wasn't drunk, not even high; a light buzz. Just enough that he was disoriented as to his directions.

Lombard Avenue, the main thoroughfare he had taken to get down here, had to be to his left, which would be west—he knew he was heading in a vaguely northward path, because the tall high-rises of the center-city area could be seen glowing that way, some miles off. Swinging the car around in another U-turn, he took off back down the street, then turned right.

He didn't know this street, either. But he knew enough to sense that he didn't want to be on it. It was completely dark—all the streetlights were out. Shot out or burned out, he didn't know. It felt like a shot-out kind of street.

This wasn't good. He needed to get out of this area. He checked his doors to make sure they were locked.

At the end of the block he hesitated, looking out the windshield in both directions. North didn't look promising; he'd already been there. South, then west. That had to lead him to where he wanted to go. He turned right.

Before he had gone a block he knew that he'd made another mistake. This street was a dead-end, a cul-de-sac. He could see where it terminated a block away, ending at a high cinder-block wall covered with spray-painted gang graffiti.

This is like being in an English box-garden, he thought, the kind that is cut like a maze. That trapped, claustrophobic feeling. *Alice in Wonderland.*

Turning around and heading the opposite way, he saw some lights on at the end of the street to his right—an all-night 7-Eleven. They'd be able to give him directions out.

He parked directly in front, locked the car, and went inside. For a moment he thought it was empty; there were no customers at this late hour, and there didn't seem to be a clerk, either. It was well after midnight and he was lost in a section of town he had no business being in.

The clerk was in the back, restocking the refrigerated section. A young, tall, thin mocha-colored man with a headful of dreadlocks and a pair of John Lennon-style granny glasses. He did a literal double take when he saw Wyatt standing at his front counter.

"You want something?" the clerk asked suspiciously.

"I'm lost," Wyatt explained. "I need to get back to center city. Lombard Avenue would be the way I know."

"How'd you get down here?" There was an edge to the question.

"I drove."

"Yeah, of course. I mean . . ."

"The reason? To hear some music. A place called the Jazz Table. It's not far from here." *What difference does it make? Just tell me how to get the hell out of here.*

"Shit, man. How'd you get here from there?"

"If I knew that I wouldn't be here."

The clerk nodded as if Wyatt had imparted a heavy truth. "Yeah, okay. Okay . . . pull out of here, hang a right, then another right, then go two blocks to Dover Street, you got that?"

"Two rights, two blocks to Dover Street."

"Left on Dover, that'll take you right smack into Lombard."

Wyatt's inner compass would have told him to take a right on Dover. No wonder he was lost.

They were leaning against his car, four of them. Boys. Black, of course. They were young—none of them looked older than fourteen. One was so small he probably wasn't yet in his teens. They didn't look like they wanted to be friends.

"Nice wheels." One of them, the oldest, the putative leader, took a step toward him.

"Thank you." *Stay cool, man, they want to play head games with you, get Whitey all flustered and frightened.*

He could handle this—be polite, get in the car, drive away. Right to Dover, left to Lombard.

"Never driven a Jaguar," the boy stated. "They ride good?"

"Very nice."

"I'd like to check it out. The handling."

He smiled at the thought of this kid driving anything. "Let me see your driver's license first," he said, trying to keep it light. He wrapped his hand around the keys in his pocket, just to be safe.

"I can drive. I've driven cars before. Lots of them."

That you've stolen?

Enough of this. "I'm running late." He started to push his way past the boy.

"I can drive," the kid said again. His voice was harsh.

They were surrounding him, a loose circle. Behind him, the lights went out inside the 7-Eleven.

The white man's urban nightmare was right in his face. He knew these things happened—he saw the television shows: the drive-by shootings, the random murders over a handful of credit cards. Over nothing.

This is not real, he thought. These things don't really happen.

He looked at the leader. These were young boys—but they were deadly serious.

"Fuck this shit." One of them was pulling a gun out of his jacket pocket.

For a second he froze in disbelief. Then instinctively, without any premeditated thought, he rushed at the boy with the gun and knocked him off balance to the ground, running through the hole he had created in their ranks. He was off, running out of the parking lot.

"Hey!" He heard the yell behind him. Without consciously thinking about it he took a ninety-degree turn, like a tailback running for daylight, and the first bullet exploded behind him a fraction, missing him and ricocheting off a parked car across the street. A half second's hesitation in that turn and the bullet would have caught him right between the shoulder blades. And then he was out into the street and there was another shot, which missed him, and he was heading for darkness, and they were running behind him, all four of them. Catching them by surprise had enabled him to pick up half a block's head start, but they were coming fast, and they were young and motivated.

He came to the end of the block and rounded the corner at full speed. He could feel the drinks cutting into his wind. But if he could stay ahead of them for three or four blocks he might find refuge somewhere. Or they might run out of steam.

For a fleeting moment he thought about running up to one of the dark houses and pounding on the door, for shelter and safety. But who would take a strange white man in at two in the morning?

These fucking Top-Siders. Running in them was almost

as bad as trying to run in bedroom slippers. He thought about shedding them, but the streets were dark and pot-holed, and if he stepped on a piece of glass and cut his foot he'd be finished.

Another corner loomed in front of him. Glancing behind him, he saw that he was maintaining his distance—not gaining ground, but not losing any either.

As he reached the corner he looked to his left. Up ahead in the distance, three or four long blocks away, he could see lights. Lombard Avenue, right where the clerk had said it would be.

He started running that way, feeling the bile rising in his throat. He wanted to throw up, he knew if he did he would feel better, but he couldn't take the time to stop. Three blocks and he would be safe. Three long blocks.

Another fast glance back. There were only three chasing him now. One had dropped out.

His lungs were starting to burn. His training was for distance, not speed. He felt like he was running under water, in quicksand. But he was almost at the end of the first block, and they weren't gaining. He was coming closer to safety.

Then the fourth boy, who he'd thought he'd dropped, came tearing down the cross street in front of him, a gun in his little hand. They knew the neighborhood and they had cut him off.

He was trapped.

He stopped and threw up his hands. His breath came out in painful gulps and he bent over double, trying to force air back into his lungs. Seeing that he was cornered, his pursuers slowed down. They were sucking wind, too.

"Whatever you want," he gasped. He threw his car keys onto the ground. "It's worth fifty thousand dollars," he said. "Take it."

The lead kid, who was also holding a gun, advanced on him, shaking his head. There was blood in his eye, in all their eyes. Wyatt stripped the watch from his wrist and held it out. "Here, take this, too. Take everything. Whatever you want."

"You lost that chance," the boy said. "Back there." He spoke with the cold authority of a man. He came closer to Wyatt, his gun held at waist level.

"Don't shoot me! For God's sake, you don't have to do that!"

The boy raised his pistol, the business end pointing at Wyatt's gut.

"No. God's sake, no!" Wyatt reflexively fell to his knees in supplication. If he had to beg for his life, he would do it. Whatever they wanted.

"Get up, sucker. I ain't gonna shoot you while you're down."

"No." The word came out choked.

"Get up, you fucking pussy! Don't make me shoot you while you're on your knees."

A sudden flash of light shone up the night. A car turned the corner down the block and headed for them. The driver blinked his bright lights.

"Fuck!" The boy reached down and grabbed Wyatt by the collar, jerking him to his feet. "Get the fuck up, you punk!" He started to pull Wyatt out of the way.

The car, a Jeep Grand Cherokee, came to a stop in the middle of the street, its bright lights still shining, illuminating them like a searchlight. Wyatt saw Dexter get out. Two other men got out with him. Big, solid men. Both held guns in their hands, bigger guns than the one the man holding Wyatt had. He had seen these two before, in the courtroom and Sullivan Houses. One was the fellow who had warned him about using the alarm on his car.

Dexter walked over. Coolly, like nothing out of the ordinary was going on, he looked at Wyatt, nodding in recognition. "What's happening, little bloods?" he asked.

"He knocked Ricky over," the leader said. "Bruised him all to shit."

"Yeah? What was Ricky doing in front of him?" He glanced at Ricky, who didn't seem to be the worse for wear.

"Trying to get him not to go nowhere." The boy smirked for the benefit of his friends.

Dexter pondered this. "If Ricky tried to make me not go nowhere, Thomas, I likely would do the same thing. Especially if I disagreed with Ricky's intention."

The smirk turned ugly. "Ricky's intention ain't none of your business, Dexter. This is 44th Street territory. This punk is ours. You're encroaching on our turf. So chill."

Dexter looked at the boy named Thomas. Then he walked

over and slapped the boy as hard as he could across the face. The boy screamed and Dexter grabbed him by the neck. "You know who you're fucking with here, fool?" he said, pointing to Wyatt.

"Fuck no. And I don't give one shit, neither," Thomas said defiantly.

"Well, you ought to, you ignorant little shit. 'Cause if you waste this dude you're going to go down as the dickhead who shot Marvin White's lawyer."

The boy gaped; then he took a step back. The others with him gawked at Wyatt. "No," he said. "You're trying to run a number on me."

"No, I ain't. This is the only man standing between Marvin and the hangman."

"Well, shit." The boy turned to Wyatt accusingly. "Why didn't you say so, man?"

Wyatt would have laughed if the situation hadn't been so perilous and ludicrous simultaneously. "I don't recall the opportunity arising," he managed to say.

"Go home, Thomas, you dumb little bastard punk," Dexter told the kid harshly. "And take these pieces of street shit with you," he added, indicating the other three.

"Hey, man, it was a mistake." Thomas was saving face as fast as he could. "People make mistakes."

"See to it you don't make this mistake again," Dexter told him sternly.

"Don't worry 'bout that." Thomas turned to Wyatt. "Sorry, man. How were we to know?" He stuck his gun in his belt. They started to leave.

Dexter stopped them. "Give," he ordered.

Thomas stopped. Then he reached into his pocket and handed Wyatt his watch and car keys, which he had picked up earlier.

"Anything else?" Dexter asked.

Wyatt shook his head. "This is everything."

Dexter made a dismissive sweeping motion with his hand: "Get the fuck out of here."

Thomas didn't need to be told twice. He and the others in his set vanished into the night.

The street had become preternaturally still, as if all the air had been sucked out of the area for blocks around.

"Your car back at the 7-Eleven?" Dexter asked. Wyatt nodded. "Hop in," Dexter said. "We'll take you back."

They climbed into the Jeep. Wyatt sat next to Dexter. The other two climbed into the back. "This here's Mr. Matthews," Dexter told his friends. To Wyatt: "This is Louis and Richard. Friends of mine, and Marvin's."

"Glad to meet you." Very glad.

They drove down the street. "You get lost?" Dexter asked.

"Yes."

"It's easy to do around here, if you don't know where you're at."

"I know that now."

"You drive all the way down here from where you live?"

"No. I'm staying at the Four Seasons. My family's out of town." He didn't need to tell Dexter where he was staying, or why, but he wanted to—he wanted to fill the void, and he felt that the connection they had established justified it. He turned to Dexter. "How in the world did you happen to be around here? Not that I'm complaining, but it sure was a lucky coincidence for me."

"Nuh-uh. Luck had nothing to do with it," Dexter answered emphatically. "We been keeping tabs on you, man."

"What?" He was floored. "You're *spying* on me?"

"Not spying, nothing like that," Dexter corrected Wyatt. "Not around your work or home or nothing. But like, when you're down in our 'hood, we like to know that. Your life is your own, man, but this part of the city? Shit happens, you know?"

Of course he knew—a ton of it had just fallen on him.

"Here's the thing, man," Dexter went on. "Something happens to you, you can't stay on the case working for Marvin, he's gonna be screwed, you know? 'Cause these other suckers, them lawyers with the Public Defenders, they're burned out. See, brothers go down all the time for shit, and they get these Public Defender lawyers, or else the court assigns some lawyer to them, which is usually worse, 'cause to them it's a lost cause and they can't make any money and so it's like another nigger gets thrown on the scrap pile, no big thing. But you, you give a damn, and you're good, too. So the thing is, we need you, man. Not just Marvin—everybody that knows Marvin. His family, us, whoever.

'Cause that blood is gonna get railroaded right into death row, somebody don't get in the way of it. And you are that somebody, Mr. Matthews. So it's up to people like me to make sure you stay healthy."

This was blowing his mind. Dexter and his friends might be young in years, but in handling their lives they were veterans. "So how did you 'keep tabs on me,' as you put it, tonight?"

"A friend of mine—the cover-charge girl at the Jazz Table? She made you. And she knew you and me were working together, I mean that I'm trying to help you out. She called me up and told me you were hanging there, so I thought I'd cruise by and check it out, but I got tied up on business." He looked behind him in the rearview mirror at his friends, who giggled. "By the time I got that piece of nonsense straightened out and swung by the club, you'd left, so I started driving around, me and these guys. Then we heard the police call come over the scanner—the brother back at the 7-Eleven called it in." He pointed to the police radio under his dash. "I figured maybe we should check that out, just in case."

"It was awfully lucky for me that you did."

"For you—and Marvin."

They pulled up in front of the convenience store. Wyatt got out. Dexter looked over his shoulder. "I'll ride back with him to his hotel. You follow us."

The cross streets whipped by, a blur of lights. There was no activity on the pavements, almost no traffic. The Jeep tailed close behind, its lights a beacon in his rearview mirror.

He pulled up in front of the hotel. A valet came out and handed him his claim check. He and Dexter got out. The Jeep was parked at the curb, waiting.

"Again, thanks for everything," Wyatt said.

Dexter looked at him. "Do you know why I'm doing all this shit for Marvin?"

"You're his friend."

"It goes deeper than that." He took out a pack of cigarettes and a Dunhill lighter, fired up without offering one to Wyatt. "Here's the good things about Marvin," he said. "He's big, strong, handsome, great with the ladies. Now here's the bad things about Marvin: he's big, strong, handsome, great with the ladies, and dumb. He's so dumb he thinks all you need to succeed is the desire. He don't know from the work, and even if he did, he couldn't do it. Not at the level he wants to—like me."

Wyatt nodded. He knew that. Standing outside his hotel with the young drug dealer who had saved his life, he felt a swirl of conflict going on inside of him. Despite his revulsion for Dexter's illegal business, his admiration for the young dealer was growing. With the right guidance and some gentle nudging, Dexter could be a positive force instead of a negative one.

"I've got to protect Marvin," Dexter said.

"I understand. You're his friend, and he needs someone like you."

Dexter shook his head. "That's petty shit. There's a deeper reason." He took a deep drag from his Camel 100. "I'm a couple weeks older than Marvin, but he was always the one protected me, when we were little. Let's face it, I ain't no Hercules. And when you're growing up where we did, little guys get their ass kicked, regular. But I never did—because Marvin never let it happen. Now the shoe's on the other foot, like they say. So it's my turn to do the protecting, whatever I can."

Wyatt nodded.

Now that Dexter had bared his soul, he was embarrassed— he covered it by making a show of checking the time on his Rolex. "I've got to go. See you around," he said. "And from now on, if you want to go down to my part of town, call me up first? So's I can give you an escort. Make everybody's life a whole lot easier."

"I will. And thanks for saving my life."

"You'll make it up to us."

The lobby was deserted, except for the cleaning crew. In the elevator, riding up to his floor, he started shaking. He thought he might collapse, he was shaking so hard. He had almost been killed tonight; another minute and he would have been dead. *Dead.*

He knew this would be part of him for a long time— probably forever. *You wanted a change in your life. You wanted some excitement. Well, you got enough excitement tonight to last you a lifetime.*

There were three miniature bottles of Scotch in the room

minibar, two Chivas Regals and a White Horse. He emptied them all into a water glass and drank the mixture down in one swallow. Then he lay down on the bed in his clothes, trying to will the shivering to stop.

He was never going to tell anyone about this. Especially Moira. If she heard about what had happened it would break their marriage—he'd promised her he'd never go back down there. This was a secret he would take to his grave; thank God he hadn't taken it there tonight.

"**W**hat truck did you step in front of?" Josephine wisecracked.

It was almost eleven the following morning. Wyatt had drifted off to sleep at dawn, and didn't wake up until the room maid came in and found him sleeping on top of the bed, still fully clothed. He'd showered, shaved, and put on a fresh change of clothes, but he had black circles around his eyes as big as a raccoon's and his face felt raw, like it had been scrubbed with a wire brush. And although he had brushed his teeth and gargled with Listerine and brushed his teeth again, his mouth tasted like a herd of elephants had taken a collective dump inside of it.

"A big one." He didn't elaborate, and she was wise enough not to pursue it.

He thought about going over to the courthouse and watching Dwayne Thompson testify some more, but Dwayne's testimony was going to drag into next week; he'd go back when Dwayne was being cross-examined, to see how he held up. So after lunch (lunchtime—he didn't feel like eating anything, his stomach was still emotionally churning from the events of the night before) he went to the jail to see Marvin.

He and Marvin sat across from each other. His notes were spread out in front of him on the table.

"Agnes Carpenter. She lives on Westmont Street. Pickup on Mondays, delivery on Thursdays. Do you remember her now?"

Marvin stared at him dully. "Yeah, I know Mrs. Carpenter."

"You slept with her? On a regular basis?"

"That what she say?" He squirmed in his chair, fidgeting,

his eyes roaming around the room, looking at everything but his lawyer.

"She's given me a sworn statement that on the night of one of the murders you've been charged with you spent the night at her house. The entire night. Do you remember that?"

Marvin's shoulders lifted and dropped. "If that's what she say . . ."

"No, Marvin. Not what *she* says." He was losing patience. "I want to hear what *you* have to say about that. Were you fucking this woman and did you ever spend a night at her house? Neither of those things should be hard to remember." Dealing with Marvin was like slogging through hot tar. The kid was his own worst enemy.

"Yeah," Marvin finally copped. "I screwed the old bitch, here and there. She paid me," he added forcefully, "good money. I wasn't fucking her 'cause . . ."

"Because why?"

". . . because I wanted to. I didn't find her sexy or nothing. She paid me, man. Hell, she's old enough to be my granny. It was for money. Good money, too," he repeated.

"What about spending the night? Do you remember that?"

Marvin picked at his nose. "I might've," he said grudgingly. "I don't think about shit like that, I put it out of my mind as soon as it's over."

Wyatt leaned forward, his weight on his forearms. "Listen to me, Marvin. You're not helping yourself here. Mrs. Carpenter is willing to take the chance of blowing off her marriage by going on the stand and swearing under oath that on the night of one of those murders you were with her. All night long. In her bed. Now if she's willing to put herself in that kind of jeopardy for you, the least you can do is remember it, and admit it straightforwardly. And act sure about it—'Yes, I did.' We'll research the dates, we'll find ways to refresh your memory for you. But you've got to change your mind about how you're dealing with this. You have to be positive and aggressive."

Marvin looked away. "Yeah. If you say so," he mumbled. "You're the lawyer."

Wyatt ran his fingers through his hair. He was feeling shitty anyway, from the trauma of the night before. Coddling someone accused of seven counts of first-degree murder with special circumstances wasn't a condition he felt like putting up with—not today.

"Marvin," he asked in an impatient voice that he didn't try to conceal, "what is your problem with this? Would you mind filling me in? I am your lawyer, in case you've forgotten."

"Mrs. Carpenter?"

"Yes?"

"She's gonna stand up at my trial and say this?"

"If we need her to."

"That I was fucking her?"

"She'll say 'make love' or words like that, but yes."

"And spent a whole night there? In the same bed with her?"

It suddenly hit him—so *that's* what this is all about. "Are you going to be embarrassed that this older woman is going to tell the world that you were her lover?"

Marvin rolled his eyes. "What the fuck you think, man?" There was a fear in his voice, almost a pleading. "People are gonna think I'm pathetic, screwing some old woman like that."

Wyatt exploded. "For God's sake, Marvin! The state wants to *execute* you! Is worrying about what some of your friends might think about you more important than your life?"

Marvin looked at the wall.

Wyatt took a calming breath. Then he stuffed his notes in his briefcase, stood up, and punched the button by the door to signify that he wanted out. "The next time I come down here, you'd better have had an attitude adjustment, Marvin. You hear me?"

No reply.

"Did . . . you . . . hear . . . me?"

"Yeah," Marvin barked. "I hear you."

"About the way you deal with me, about the way you face what's in store for you if you don't change. Because if you bring this kind of attitude into the courtroom the jury will *hang* you, and I won't be able to do a thing about it."

Marvin nodded. "Yeah. Okay. I hear what you're saying."

"Good. So to tie this up for today: you were having a sexual relationship with Agnes Carpenter."

In a low voice, as if the world were eavesdropping: "Yeah."

"And you did spend at least one night with her in her house? One entire night, until morning-time or later."

Marvin nodded. "But it was for the money. That's all."

"That's fine," Wyatt agreed. "We're not saying you were in love with her. You were performing a service that she requested."

"Yeah." Marvin's face lightened up a little bit. "That's what I was doing."

The door on Wyatt's side swung open. He was going back to the free world, unlike his client. Marvin would go through another door to get to where he was going.

"If I tell you something you promise you won't spread it around?"

He turned back to Marvin. "What?"

"Mrs. Carpenter? She isn't all that bad a person. I kind of like her, you know? As a person. The way her old man treats her and all. But you can't tell anybody I said that, right?" he said quickly.

"What we talk about is strictly between us, unless you say otherwise."

"Yeah. Good." Marvin exhaled in relief. "But the sex part—that was for the money, strictly," he said adamantly. "It wasn't like I did it . . . because I wanted to or anything."

"For the money," Wyatt agreed. "Strictly business."

Wyatt went back to his own office near the close of day, casually bantering with the secretaries and some of his colleagues. Alerted to Wyatt's presence, Ben Turner came out of his office to greet him. Wyatt looked better than he had that morning, but his face was still showing the previous evening's wear and tear.

"How are you?" Ben asked, showing concern beyond the normal salutation.

"Good. Frazzled some. This is no Sunday picnic in the park, I'm finding that out more every day."

"Are you making progress?"

"I am. We're doing well, better than I thought we might be at this point."

"Do you think you have a chance of winning?"

"Oh, yeah. A decent chance, maybe better."

Putting a fatherly arm around Wyatt's shoulder, Ben pulled him into his office. "Wyatt, I have to ask you this directly. Is there any chance this boy is actually innocent?"

Wyatt stiffened under the paternal gesture. "Why are you asking me that?"

"Because I want to know, that's why." Ben let go of Wyatt's arm. "I expect you to give him a crackerjack defense, a Wyatt Matthews job, whether he's innocent or not—whether you even know it or not. That's not the point."

"What is the point, Ben?"

"You may be working this case off the books, Wyatt, but you're a senior partner here, vital to the health and welfare of this office. We have very important clients to think about. About how they perceive us."

"Defending a mass murderer could hurt the firm." This conversation was getting ugly.

Ben threw it back in his face. "Of which you are a major shareholder."

"I don't know if he's guilty or not," Wyatt answered, keeping his cool. "He says he isn't. I'm going to fashion a strong defense, more than strong enough to raise reasonable doubt in any fair-minded person's mind. That's my job. Nothing more, or less."

Ben stiffened. "Then do it well. I know you will."

They walked out into the corridor. It was quitting time for those who didn't have to stay late. The secretaries were shutting their computers down for the night, some of them slipping out of their heels and putting on the running shoes that they wore to come and leave in.

"It's good seeing you, Ben."

"It's good seeing you, too, Wyatt," the old man replied. "Don't be a stranger."

"Not to worry."

Ben reached out and touched Wyatt's shirt—a light touch, barely connecting, but affecting in a way Wyatt rarely felt from Ben. "I'm not going to be around much longer, Wyatt. I'm looking to retiring toward the end of the year. This work is too rugged for a man my age. And I don't want to die in my office, passed out over a brief. You're my logical replacement; you know that and so do all the others. I want to make sure you're standing tall and unbloodied when that day comes."

Wyatt was touched. "I will, Ben. That's a promise."

"Good." Ben pumped Wyatt's hand vigorously. "Wyatt?"

"Yes, Ben?"

"Between us—is he innocent? Or guilty? What's your lawyer's gut reaction? You have a nose for these things."

"I hope he is. But honestly, I don't know. I wish I could give you more."

"I wish you could, too. I wish you could."

The reason Wyatt had come to the office was to see Darryl Davis. He had called Darryl and asked to have dinner with him, tonight—he needed to pick the brain of the head of Waskie, Turner's criminal-defense division.

He made reservations at the Steak Joint. There are times when a man needs a couple of stiff drinks, a great New York strip, charred medium-rare, with a baked potato on the side and a good bottle of California cabernet. This was one of those times.

The restaurant was one of the oldest in the city, a favorite watering hole of the politicians, lobbyists, high-priced lawyers, and all-around wheeler-dealers—men (and women) like them, along with the ubiquitous gaggle of Japanese businessmen (several parties of them were on the premises tonight, tucking into the biggest porterhouses the joint offered). There was a throwback element to the Steak Joint— it was, in the last decade of the twentieth century, still a man's restaurant, in the classic sense of the term—women were outnumbered three to one. Decorated like a private club, it featured red leather banquettes, thick plush carpeting, English hunting prints on the walls. And it was arrogantly expensive—most patrons came here on their expense accounts. Darryl would bill this dinner to the firm, since Wyatt was technically on leave.

Wyatt knew more than half the people in the place. Several passed by their booth to meet and greet and offer their encouragement. "Give Alex Pagano a good ass-kicking" was the general tenor of their remarks.

After they were left alone, he told Darryl of the events of

the night before. Darryl listened silently, shaking his head a few times in stunned disbelief. "Sounds like you had a guardian angel on your shoulder," was his first comment when Wyatt had finished.

"I could as easily not have."

"What are you going to do about it?"

"Not go down there alone at night, for one thing."

The waiter placed their two-inch-thick steaks in front of them. The plates were sizzling. He freshened their wineglasses and left discreetly.

"Let me ask you a straight-up question," Darryl said.

"Shoot."

"Are you looking for a way out?"

"No," Wyatt answered firmly. "I'm not quitting this. But I am worried."

"You should be. If you weren't I'd think you'd gone brain-dead."

"Not about my safety. I've learned my lesson there—I hope." He cut into his steak—perfect. "About my ability to try this case."

"Because you haven't done criminal work before?"

Wyatt shook his head. "Because my client comes from a world that is completely alien to me."

"Ah." Darryl held his wineglass up to the light. "Do you know what are some of the greatest things in the world about making it?" he asked Wyatt.

"You tell me."

"This kind of stuff." He waved his arm around the room. "The great wine, the food, the atmosphere. Vacations in Vail, suits by Armani, a Mercedes car. The material benefits, the so-called shallow, narcissistic pleasures of life." He took a sip of wine and rinsed it in his mouth before swallowing. "Yes, there are oceans between you and that housing project Marvin White lives in. But you can get on a Concorde airplane today and fly across the Atlantic Ocean in less than four hours. It isn't that big a gulf between any two people in this world anymore. Didn't you tell me his friend that pulled your ass out of the fire drives a tricked-out Jeep that goes out the door at thirty thou plus?"

"Yes, but look how he makes his money."

"Everything is relative, Wyatt." Darryl held up his wineglass for inspection. "Look around you. People in this room ruin and otherwise fuck up people's lives every day. That's the world. You live in it, you benefit from it."

"I try not to." The statement sounded lame before it was even out of his mouth.

Darryl cackled. "Sure you do. You own stock, don't you?"

"Okay, I get the point. I know where this is going."

Darryl cut him off. "No, let me ramble a little. I'm in a philosophical frame of mind tonight. You got me going here. Okay. We have the head of AT&T. Cuts forty thousand jobs from the payroll, fucks up *forty thousand* lives, the economy applauds it and AT&T gives him a million-dollar bonus. Some kid from the ghetto sells crack cocaine, fucks up what—*dozens* of lives?—we put him in jail. But isn't he also contributing to the economy? You think the bozo that sold him his Jeep or his suit or his fancy watch cared where his money came from? Or where Baby Doc's money comes from? Alcohol used to be illegal and cocaine was legal, so who's to say? More important, who's to judge?"

"I don't equate drug dealing with anything."

Darryl scowled. "I don't think Jonathan Swift wanted people to eat babies, either. I don't advocate drug dealing, that's not my point. This is the world, Wyatt. And it's a tiny, tiny, *tiny* little world. The difference between you and the Marvin Whites of this world is getting smaller every day. Which is a good thing, I'm sure you'd agree. Whether or not you like the means."

"What's the moral of this story?"

"You're a lawyer, Wyatt, not a social worker. If you're defending the CEO of a major corporation do you go to his house for dinner and ride around with his teenage kids?" Answering his own rhetorical question: "Of course not. You'd consider it a waste of your time and irrelevant to the issue, unless his home life was a factor, which isn't really the case here. This is about whether or not Marvin did it— not his family history, poverty in America, the corruption of the welfare system, or anything else that social thinkers like to chew the fat over. Look at the *small* picture—he couldn't have done it because a, b, c, etc."

Wyatt took a mouthful of steak, chewed, and swallowed before continuing. "But it's hard for me to separate these things out. That corporate executive you mentioned? I don't have to look at his life, because I already know it. See," he continued, feeling some kind of juice stirring, "what I think is screwing me up here is the *why* of my doing this work. Do I want to defend people who need it, or do I . . ."

"Want to change the world? Is this about some kind of rich white man's guilt trip? I thought you had resolved that issue already."

"I'm still fighting with it."

Darryl nodded sagely. "Wyatt, you didn't invite me to have dinner with you tonight because I'm some fount of wisdom. You wanted to talk to me because I'm black and you don't know how you're supposed to act." He lifted an eyebrow. "True?"

Wyatt's tension broke. "Yes. That's exactly why. Is that. . . ?" He didn't know how to put what he wanted to say without offending his partner and friend.

"Patronizing?" Darryl finished his thought. "One could say so, if one wanted to look at it that way. But so what? Sometimes it can't be helped, there's no other way."

Wyatt felt truly grateful. "Thank you."

"It's okay." As Darryl finished his glass the waiter was miraculously at his shoulder, filling it up again to the exact proper amount.

"These waiters here are good at what they do, aren't they? Came a time, not so long ago, the only black faces you'd see in here would be waiters and busboys; but that's for another long night. So okay—here's my suggestion, as a lawyer and a black man, which in this case dovetails almost completely. Either you're in . . . or you're out. If you're out, get out, right now. Tomorrow morning. But if you're in, put all this extraneous bullshit aside and prepare your case. Your soul might belong to Jesus, Wyatt, but Marvin White's ass is going to belong to the state, unless you stop that from happening."

"I just found this." Josephine dumped a thin file on Wyatt's desk. She looked unhappy.

"This is . . . ?"

"An addendum to your client's juvenile records. Somehow it got left out of what you've already seen."

"I take it you've read this." He didn't like the unhappy tone of her voice.

She patted the top of the file gingerly, as if it could be a package bomb. "The best you can say about this is that the other side won't be able to use it, since juvie records are inadmissible. Although I'll bet they'll try like hell."

He opened the file. Josephine walked out of his cubicle. A moment later, she stuck her head back in. "I almost forgot. The woman who identified Marvin in the police lineup has agreed to come in and meet with you—the one who claims she saw him outside the bar. I ran it through the DA's office. They have to comply, but they weren't overjoyed about it."

"When is this?"

"This evening. She said she could come by around seven-thirty. It was the earliest she could make it. I hope it doesn't mess up your plans, having her come in late."

"I don't have any plans for tonight," he said. "Actually, I was going to ask you if you wanted to have dinner, since I'm staying in town for the next few days. After the interview?"

She hesitated. "I'd love to. But I can't tonight. My aunt's birthday party. I have to go," she added.

"No problem."

"Can I have a rain check?" she asked.

"Any time."

"I'll hold you to that," she said with a quick smile before taking off. He heard the tapping echo of her heels growing fainter as she walked to the elevator. The elevator doors opened and closed with a whoosh. Then it was quiet, the only sounds a barely perceptible buzzing coming from a malfunctioning fluorescent light somewhere out in the hallway and the hum of traffic from the street, six floors below.

He turned to the new documents Josephine had brought in. The charge that hadn't been in what he had read was an allegation of aggravated rape, when Marvin was fifteen. The girl, who was Marvin's age and who knew him, told the police that Marvin had enticed her into going alone with him to the roof of her apartment, another building in Sullivan Houses. She thought they were merely going somewhere private to make out—she had an admitted crush on him, as did many of her friends. There he had raped her at knife-point, and after he raped her he forced her to commit fella-tio. Again with a knife at her throat, threatening mutilation or worse if she didn't comply.

The girl had not gone to the police willingly. Her mother had noticed bleeding in the girl's underpants, although it wasn't her time of the month. The girl had finally broken down and told her mother of the assault, although she didn't give a name then. The mother took the girl to the hospital, where a sympathetic female doctor examined her and said that indeed there had been penetration, which certainly could have been of a forceful nature. The doctor had re-ported her findings to the police, as is required under law. That's when the cops took over, bringing the girl and her mother in for questioning. It took some hemming and haw-ing, but the girl finally gave up her assailant's name: Marvin White. According to the girl's mother, whose statement was included, the girl had been a virgin.

Wyatt rocked back in his chair, cursing. Fucking civil-service bookkeeping. Helena Abramowitz surely would know about this. It might not be admissible in court, and there would be strenuous arguing back and forth, but it was a compelling piece of corroborating evidence against Mar-vin. He was an accused rapist and he had threatened to kill his victim if she didn't comply.

Maybe he had learned his lesson—don't let them live so they can go to the police.

Wyatt read on. Marvin had been arrested. Unable to post bail, he had been detained in juvenile custody for two months, until shortly before his trial.

At that point, everything started to get murky. Two of Marvin's friends (Dexter was one of them) swore that Mar-vin had been across town with them at the time of the alleged rape, at a Martin Lawrence movie. Also, it came to light that the girl had a record of her own, including shop-lifting and using a stolen credit card. And she had dropped out of school, which Marvin, at that point, had not yet done. All of which made her a less-than-sterling candidate to hang a successful prosecution on.

Two days before the trial was to begin the girl got cold feet and told the prosecutor's office she wasn't going to tes-tify. There was nothing she could get out of it, and she had already been humiliated enough. She flat-out was not going to get on the stand.

In a finding that accompanied the case file, there was a memorandum from the assistant DA handling the case to the head of the juvenile prosecution division, offering the strongly held opinion that there had been intense pressure put on the girl and her mother to walk away from the case. It was assumed that Marvin and/or friends of his, gang members, had threatened the girl and the mother, scaring them off.

The upshot was that the district attorney's office had no alternative—they had to drop the case. Marvin walked. But the authorities believed that he was guilty, as he had originally been charged.

One more crack in the system.

Three months later Marvin was arrested for robbing an appliance store of a video camera. This time there was no backing off by his accuser, the store owner. He was convicted and sent to six months at the county juvenile farm.

Wyatt got out the comprehensive file he'd read earlier and went through Marvin's sorry history again. There wasn't much redeeming material: no affidavits from sympathetic teachers, no letters asking for clemency from the minister of the church Jonnie Rae attended. No one seemed to give much of a damn for Marvin White except his friends, and most of them had records as bad as Marvin's, or worse. He was a gangbanger (possibly not an official member of a gang, maybe only a hanger-on), a school drop-out, a thief. And a rapist who had managed to beat the charge.

After he had reread as much of Marvin White's encounters with the law as he felt like stomaching in one sitting, Wyatt went back through the accounts given by the woman who had ID'd Marvin as being outside the club in the same time frame the murder and robbery took place. Her testimony seemed to be very straightforward, convincing material.

The elevator doors opened with their particular pneumatic sound. Then the sounds, much like those made by Josephine earlier, of a woman's heels on linoleum. He glanced at his watch—7:30 on the button.

"Excuse me," a woman's throaty voice called out, "is there anyone here?"

"Back here," he answered. He stood and came around toward the doorway as she approached.

She was wearing a rayon-cotton summer dress that clung to her body. The cavernous hallway was poorly lit, and what light there was came from behind her, so that for the moment her face was in shadow, but there was no hiding the shape of her body. The backlight had the seductive effect of illuminating her figure, which was full and womanly, attractively so, her hips flaring out from her waist under the skirt.

Generous of size without being heavy, there was a ripeness about her that comes to certain women when they've reached their thirties and beyond. An ample, tight behind. High breasts. Strong legs.

"I'm sorry I'm late," she apologized as she came toward him, "I took a wrong turn in traffic and had to circle all the way around. The streets are all one-way."

He knew all about wrong turns. "Not at all," he answered cordially, stepping out into the hallway so she could see him more easily. "Please, come in." He gestured with his arm toward his open door. "I appreciate your coming down here and meeting with me."

As she reached him, the light caught her face. It had something compelling about it. Not beauty, or prettiness—there was no conventional beauty in it, she was too much of peasant-type stock to be considered beautiful—yet it drew him in. It exuded openness, genuine warmth.

She extended her hand. He shook it. Her grip was strong, but the hand was soft. She puts cream on her hands every day, he knew. A strong woman who wants to be feminine.

"I'm Violet Waleska," she announced herself.

"Wyatt Matthews." He gestured to his office. "Come in, please. Have a seat."

She sat in the only visitor's chair in the small room, across from his desk. Crossing her bare legs, she rested her purse on her lap. The skirt of her dress rose up her thigh about six inches; nothing risqué or provocative, but he took a good look over her shoulder before he sat down in his own chair. He noticed that she didn't wear a wedding ring.

He opened her file. It contained her initial interview with Detective Pulaski at Marcus Meat Packing, her place of employment, where the murder victim had also worked. She doesn't look like someone who works in a processing plant, he thought, although she does have strong hands.

The interview with Detective Pulaski covered her seeing a young African American male, estimated height and weight and age, etc. The time it occurred, as best she knew. And what had transpired between her and the young man. Right down the line, no bullshit, no "I thinks" or "maybes."

The second report was that of her lineup identification. Again, a no-nonsense statement. He was the man who was in the parking lot. She knew it beyond the shadow of a doubt; certainly beyond any reasonable doubt, the criterion by which Marvin would be judged.

He asked her some basic questions, keeping his voice calm, deliberate. Tonight his objective was to make her feel comfortable with him. They could go on the record next time, with Josephine and a stenographer present.

"I'm looking at the time frame here," he said, the initial police interview in front of him. "You stated that you went out to your car after the band had taken a break."

"Yes." Her voice was throaty, low. It sounded like wild honey, still on the comb. "I believe that's right."

"Right after?"

"Yes, I believe so."

He thought for a moment. "Let's look at this together," he said, rotating the report around so it faced her and she could see it. He rose from behind his desk and crossed to her side, standing at her hip, leaning down to place his finger on the document where he had quoted it. Her perfume, night-blooming jasmine mixed with a delicate scent of perspiration, permeated his nostrils with a fragrant sexual aroma.

Cool it, Jack. This is an adversarial witness who must not be fucked with under any circumstances whatsoever, and you are a married man.

"Was it the first break of the evening that the band took, or a later one?" he asked.

"I'm sure it was the first," she replied, turning to look at him. "We arrived right after they started. So it had to have been the first break."

He made a mental note to check with the manager of the nightclub. Maybe they could pinpoint the time. He knew when Marvin had entered the store to rob it—the videotape was time-coded. Perhaps there would be a time discrepancy. It needed looking into.

They briefly discussed the rest of the information on her documents. Leafing through his calender, he made an appointment for her to come back late the following week, where her statement would be taken officially. He gave her his card, and scribbled his home telephone number on the back. "Call me if you have anything further to tell me before next week," he said. "You can call me at home. If anything comes up."

She placed the card in her purse.

"I have your number at work," he remembered, "but I don't know if we have your home phone. Would you mind giving it to me, just in case."

"No, I don't mind."

He handed her another one of his cards. She wrote her name and number on it in a clear, adult script. He slipped it into his wallet rather than her folder, which he shut and filed in a cabinet. "I'll walk you out."

"I can find my way." Her protest was not forceful.

"Time to call it a day for me," he said. "It's been a long day."

"I'm bushed myself," she said with a confiding smile. "I get up early."

They started walking out together. He locked his door behind him. "Where do you live?" he asked in a neutral tone as they crossed the floor to the elevator.

"Over on Randolph. Three twenty-nine, apartment twenty-four. Let me have that card, I'll write it down for you."

He retrieved the card from his wallet. She wrote her address on it. "You can call me also, if you have any more questions. It's easier to reach me at home than at work. As long as it isn't too late. I live alone, so it isn't a disturbance."

So she wasn't married, as he had guessed.

Randolph was an older neighborhood down by the waterfront that had been gentrified over the past two decades. Advertising types and upwardly mobile yuppies lived there for the most part. She wasn't either.

They exited the building. The sky was dark amber crossfading to black, glowing with a thousand lights of the city. "I'll walk you to your car," he offered.

"That won't be necessary."

"A woman who's taken the time to come down and meet with me shouldn't walk alone at night, not around here. It's an old-fashioned habit, I guess."

"A nice one. Thank you." They walked to the corner and waited for the light to turn. "At least I don't have to worry about the Alley Slasher anymore," she commented as they crossed the street.

"If Marvin White is the real thing," he said. "He's still only a suspect," he reminded her.

She frowned. "For a moment there I'd forgotten he was your client. That we're on opposite sides."

"All I want is the truth."

"The police think he did it. They say he made a confession."

"To a jailhouse stool pigeon. Not the most sterling category of witness."

"The district attorney says they are good witnesses," she said in defense of her position.

"Anybody that puts their eggs in the basket of a scumbag like Dwayne Thompson is asking for—" He stopped. It wasn't appropriate to mention the name of the state's key witness to someone outside the system, a civilian who had no reason to have that information, not that it was a secret.

She turned to him. "What was that name again?"

"Nothing." The light turned green. He placed a hand lightly on her back to turn her attention to it. She was flustered, he could feel it. The conversation had gotten too close to the bone. It was her friend who had been murdered. He must not forget that.

They crossed the street. He withdrew his hand when they stepped up onto the curb. "Sometimes the police are wrong, you know," he said.

"I hope not." They had reached her car, a decade-old Honda Accord that needed a good waxing. She turned to him as she took her keys from her purse. "You're a nice man," she said, "and he's your client. But if he isn't the one who did it, then the real murderer is still out there. And that scares the hell out of me." She got into her car.

"Thank you again for taking the time," he said. He closed the door. She started the engine, put her car in gear, and drove off.

He hoped he would see her again, he thought as he watched her leave.

Walter Malone's lawyers, two well-meaning hacks who got the cases no substantial lawyer would take, didn't lay a glove on Dwayne. They grilled him for two days solid and came up with nothing but dry holes. If anything, they hurt their client by keeping Dwayne on the stand that long.

Wyatt watched part of the cross-examination from the back of the courtroom. Helena Abramowitz wasn't present, he noticed. She didn't need to see any more of the carnage—her future witness was rock solid. And the credibility he would gain from this trial would, Wyatt knew, carry over.

After an early dinner, Wyatt picked Moira and Michaela up at the airport. They gave him big sloppy kisses and suffocating hugs. "I missed you," Moira whispered.

"Me, too," he answered; and although he hadn't been thinking that much about them, seeing them now, feeling them, felt wonderfully good.

They waited at the carousel for their luggage. "How was your trip?" he asked Michaela. "Any revelations, good or bad? You didn't say much on the phone." He hadn't talked to them every day, and when he did it was hurried and perfunctory—from him more than them.

"Everything was great. I loved New York," she gushed. "All that music, and theater, and art."

"So are you thinking about Columbia? Or NYU?" Michaela had always been artistically inclined. She was a particularly gifted dancer, one of the best young ballerinas in the city—she had performed in dozens of productions since the age of six. For the past two summers she had apprenticed with the city's premier professional company, and they had promised that this coming summer they were going to make her a member of the troupe, with pay.

It would be great, his kid at school in New York.

She shook her head. "It's really tempting, Daddy, but I'd

never go to class. The city would be too tempting." She exchanged a conspiratorial smile with Moira.

"What?"

"I've decided on Princeton, Daddy. It's perfect for me."

That was a surprise. "It's a great school."

"I'm going to apply for early admission." She was flushed with excitement about her prospects. "They told me I have a real good chance, with my grades and the SATs I had this winter. They have a great dance program, and it's only an hour on the train to New York. I met with the dance director and she was really encouraging." The words came tumbling out so fast he could hardly keep up.

"I think you've got your life all worked out."

"I do, Dad. I can hardly wait."

By the time they got home it was past ten. With the time difference and the emotional roller-coaster nature of the trip, Michaela was exhausted, and she had school the next day. She gave them good-night kisses and went to her room. In five minutes her lights were out.

"Sounds like you had a great time." They were in bed together.

"It was fabulous. It's so joyful to be part of her excitement." Moira nestled up against his shoulder.

"One more year and then she's gone."

Her body moved closer to his, as if she was trying to meld them into one body. "I'm having a hard time facing up to it."

"We can't let her see that. She's still our kid," he assured her. "She'll always be there."

"I know. I try not to. But it'll free us up and maybe"—she traced her fingernails along his chest, toying with the short, curly hairs—"that'll be a good thing."

"It will be."

As her hand took his penis he slid a finger into her, gently massaging her from the inside while she stroked him, getting him hard. They rolled over facing each other, bodies pressed up against each other, his free hand cradling her head and steadying it as they kissed openmouthed.

They made out for a long time, his finger inside her, her soft, small hand sliding up and down his shaft. Her first climax came in a sudden rush, her free hand grabbing his hair and pulling his mouth tighter against hers, hips rising off the bed, moaning into his mouth. She rolled over onto her back and he eased himself on top of her and she put him inside.

He pumped slowly, not wanting to come quickly. As he felt his ejaculation rising he reached down and touched her clitoris and she came again, right away, grabbing his ass with both hands, and as her thin hips came off the mattress grinding into his he thought of Violet Waleska, that lush body, all big hipped and big breasted and large of ass, the opposite of Moira, and he didn't know what she smelled or tasted like but it would be stronger, her female essence more pungent than Moira's.

He opened his eyes for a moment and looked at his wife, her eyes closed, moving in rhythm, rapturous in her own ecstasy that he was bringing forth, and he focused on her so that he was with her and only her, and he had an orgasm like he hadn't had for a long, long time.

The judge in *People v. Walter Malone* finished his charge to the jury at 9:55 the following Tuesday morning, after closing arguments the day before. Shortly before lunch they informed the bailiff that they had reached a verdict. The judge ordered the verdict sealed until after lunch, two o'clock.

Wyatt hustled over to the courthouse as soon as he heard the news. The hallways were crowded with media, officials, and other courthouse hangers-on, including several lawyers. He hung back from mingling with anyone—a fly on the wall was his self-assigned role.

Walter Malone was found guilty of murder by seven women and five men. They would begin deliberations on the penalty phase on Thursday. The sheriffs cuffed and manacled the ashen-faced convict and led him out of the courtroom.

Wyatt watched the self-congratulatory hugs and pats on the back from his seat in the back of the room. Alex Pagano had shown up in person to hear the verdict read. He was resplendent in a double-breasted charcoal gray Hugo Boss pinstripe, and looked well pleased. Wyatt slipped out of the courtroom unobtrusively, making sure not to catch the eye of anyone on the prosecution team.

As expected, Alex Pagano was holding an "impromptu" news conference on the courthouse steps. After praising the men and women who had tried the case on his department's behalf, he disclosed what he considered to be the defining moment in the case.

"Dwayne Thompson may be a convicted felon," he said, "but his testimony in this case was convincing and riveting. Contrary to popular belief, informants often can be the most reliable of witnesses, because they are able, through the similarities of their own situations, to gain the confidence of other criminals, in ways those of us in law enforcement can never muster."

"Are you saying that Dwayne Thompson is going to be the cornerstone of the Alley Slasher trial?" called out a veteran reporter.

"He's a part of that case," Pagano stated. "But we have much more going than one person's testimony."

I'd like to know what that is, Wyatt thought as he watched from the fringe of the crowd. And if there's any way I can do it, I'm going to find out.

One thing he had to admit, though—Dwayne Thompson had been a killer witness.

"**T**hompson. You've got a visitor." The deputy stood in the doorway.

The lunch break had ended a short time before. There were over a dozen inmates in the infirmary waiting to be treated.

Dwayne looked up. "He picked a great time to come." He had no idea who his visitor was; as far as he knew, no one from this city would come to see him. Maybe it was a former mate from Durban who had finished his sentence and was here on a busman's holiday.

"It's a she, not a he."

A *she*? There was no woman in the world who would visit him; in his entire life, in all the prisons and jails in which he'd done time, he had never had a woman visitor.

The only woman who would want to see him now would be Abramowitz, and she didn't "visit," she made "appointments."

The deputy led him out of the infirmary, up the elevator, and into the visiting area, opening the door that led into the row of cubicles that were separated by head-high partitions on the prisoner's side. A wall of safety glass bisected the room-long table, each cubicle having a telephone for the inmate and visitor to talk through. "Number seven," the deputy instructed him.

He walked down the row to the seventh stall, took his seat, and looked through the window to the other side.

"Jesus Christ." His jaw went slack. Then he picked up the phone.

"Hello, Dwayne." The voice was tinny through the connection, but it was her.

"What are you doing here?" he asked the woman, who sat still and straight on her side, the visitor's telephone held to her ear.

"Good question." Her breathing was high in her chest, shallow and rapid. She took a deep cleansing inhale and exhale to try to calm herself. Under the table, where he couldn't see it, her other hand was clenched in a fist, holding a handkerchief that she was twisting into a knot.

"It's been a long time. Ten years?"

"Longer. Almost twelve."

"You look . . ." How did she look? She'd been a young woman, in her twenties, the last time he'd laid eyes on her. Now she was—what? Let's see, he was thirty-eight. So that would put her right at forty.

He could only see her from the waist up. From waist to neck she looked the same. Same big tits, probably not as firm. Waistline not bulging, she had kept her figure, looked like. Was she married now, did she have any kids? Probably—she was the marrying, mothering type.

Her face. That was the big change. What had made her attractive when she was younger was the absolute honesty in her face, the way her eyes would look at you with total sincerity and conviction.

The honesty was still there, but now there were doubts in that face, and lines on it. Lines around her eyes, from worrying about everything, him especially. Her cheeks sagged some and her neck wasn't as firm.

She was a forty-year-old woman. Who had led a hard life, in great part because of him. Which was her problem, not his.

"You look pretty good," he said. "Ol' Man Time ain't been so cruel to you." He smiled tightly, without his lips parting.

"You look the same," she replied. "You haven't changed at all, it looks like."

"Nope. I don't figure I have."

It's true, she thought. He hasn't changed. All the years in jail haven't touched him. He still looks like the devil. When you have no conscience you never have anything to worry about.

"This is a surprise," he said. "How did you know I was here?"

"Your name was mentioned in the newspapers."

"So you decided to come down and visit me, for old-timey sake."

She shook her head. "I hoped to never see you again," she stated as matter-of-factly as her voice would allow. "I've always assumed that would be the case." All the pain, anger, and sorrow had long since drained from her, leaving a feeling—when she had one, which was almost never—of emptiness and regret that they had even been connected, in any way. "No. I came down, first to make sure it was you— I couldn't believe it when I heard it and I had to know for sure—and second, because I've got a stake in this."

"What stake could you have?"

"The last woman this boy was arrested for killing was one of my closest friends." She looked away for a moment before turning back to him. "I was the last person to see her alive." She paused. "And I was the only person who saw him where she was killed, only a few minutes before . . . before he did it."

Son of a bitch! "What goes around comes around," he said blandly.

She felt like breaking down and crying, so she took another deep breath to make sure she didn't. Crying in front of him was unacceptable to her. She would rather walk away from the whole mess before she did that; and she couldn't, she had to hang in with this. "Yes," she said. "In a macabre way it must."

"Well," he crowed. "Well, well, well. Your girlfriend got killed and I'm the boy got the confession out of her killer. I'm the one's going to pull the switch on him. That's why you came down here. Isn't it?"

"Yes. I had to know."

"That I was the one?"

"That. And that it really happened. He really did tell you he killed her. And the other women."

Dwayne pointed above his head. "They got his chocolate ass in maximum, maximum security upstairs, so I guess he did tell me. Otherwise, how would they have known? He doesn't talk in his sleep—not that I'd have any firsthand knowledge of that."

"What I want to know . . . what I need to know," she said, "is that he did it."

"He did it."

She nodded. "You've done this before. Gotten men to confess to crimes." She knew his history.

"That's why I'm down here for now—I just finished testifying in a trial of a man who committed murder and confessed the crime to me. I'm the state's key witness. They love my ass down here."

Nobody loves your ass, Dwayne, she thought bitterly. Nobody loves any part of you. There's nothing there to love.

He looked around, checking to make sure nobody was listening in. "Does anybody know about you and me?" he asked.

"No." She cut him off. "No one knows."

"That's good. 'Cause that could complicate things."

She knew that. She'd known that coming in. It was a bizarre twist, the connection between them, possibly a disastrous one. "I've thought about that."

He leaned forward on his elbows, his face almost touching the scratched-up chicken-wire-supported double-thick glass. "It would be best if we keep this between us," he said softly. "Our secret."

"I agree," she answered hastily. God! how she hated this man, and how utterly petrified she was of him.

"If it got out, it could screw things up."

"I know."

"Nobody has to know."

"Yes. Nobody has to know."

A buzzer went off. "Thirty seconds," from a guard's voice that came over a speaker.

"I have to go," she said.

He stared at her. "I'm glad you came."

She stared back. "I don't think I am." Thinking about that, she added, "I'm not."

He smiled his cobra smile. "Yeah, I can feature that, given everything that's gone down between us." The smile widened. "But that's in the past now. I can't hurt you from in here—I can only help you." Pointing his left index finger at the center of her forehead, he said, "You're coming back again—aren't you. Now that you know that I know you're out there, you're not going to be able to stay away."

He leaned back in his chair, arms folded against his chest, staring at her as if to say, "You want me to make this good for you, you're going to have to do something for me." Aloud, the words were, "I want to see you again, Violet. I don't have much else going for me in this world."

She closed her eyes. Seeing him again was impossible, but avenging her friend's murder was imperative.

She did the only thing she could. "Yes, Dwayne," she lied. It was all right to lie—he always did. "I'll be back again."

The twelve-passenger turboprop touched down at the Springfield, Missouri, airport. Wyatt picked up the keys to his rental Chevy Cavalier at the Avis counter and drove east on U.S. 60, heading into the Missouri section of the Ozarks.

It was a picture-perfect spring day. Everything was in riotous bloom—the smells of dogwood, peach blossom, apple blossom hung heavy in the thick, humid air. The weather was normal for the time of year—humongously sticky—but he rolled the windows open and turned the air-conditioning off, to better savor the scenery with all of his senses.

The instructions were spread out on the passenger seat. According to the lawyer, with whom he'd had a long conversation over the phone two nights earlier, the drive time from the airport to the farm entrance was a leisurely hour.

Past Winona he turned south, heading into the hills. The stands of trees grew thicker, the vegetation denser, the road narrowed, twisting and turning through the low pine-covered range. Then it was a right turn at a red, white, and blue mailbox with the name *Bollinger* stenciled on one side and a Zig Zag pirate's face on the other. Prominent No Hunting, No Trespassing, Keep Off signs were posted on either side of the hard-packed gravel road that led up a twisting mile through the lawyer's property, until his house was seen around a bend, sitting pretty in a sunny clearing. Wyatt noticed a satellite dish tucked around the corner of the house.

Three mangy, snarling dogs came tear-assing around the side of the house as Wyatt's car announced his entrance. They jumped up on the driver's-side door, barking loudly enough to wake the dead (should there be any dead within earshot). Two of them, Australian collie mixes, looked more bark than bite, but the third, who had some shepherd and some Doberman and probably some pit bull in him as well, was a serious-business kind of dog who would eagerly take a piece out of your ass or ankle. That dog didn't bark as much as he snarled and growled, leaping up against the side of the car as if to knock it over and pluck out the morsel that was inside.

Wyatt stayed put. He should take this mutt home with him—Moira was so obsessed with protection these days. Except this one's pedigree wouldn't fit with their neighborhood.

A moment later their owner shambled out the front door. He was wearing Levi's cutoffs, scuffed-up hiking boots that had years of wear and tear on them, and an orange tie-dyed sleeveless T-shirt with a picture of Jimi Hendrix on the front. His dark hair was long, hanging lank over his shoulders, and he had a Harley-Davidson skull-and-bones earring dangling from his left ear. A can of Pearl beer was grasped in one hand and a double corona cigar, dark maduro wrapper, in the other. Knowing some of his history, Wyatt figured he was around forty.

Transferring the cigar to the beer hand, the man put two fingers into his mouth and whistled. The dogs stopped barking and sat down on their haunches, their pink sweaty tongues lolling out the sides of their mouths.

"They aren't going to bother you, long as I'm around," Bollinger called out to Wyatt. "You can come on out, it's safe."

Gingerly, Wyatt opened the door, ready to slam it shut if any of the mutts made a move. They sat there, panting like they'd run a marathon, dog-grinning up at him as he cautiously made his way past them and approached their owner.

"Wyatt Matthews." He offered his hand.

"Brent Bollinger." The lawyer's hand was hard, callused, dirty.

"I appreciate your inviting me down here."

Bollinger smiled. "Happy to have you. The name Dwayne Thompson makes my ears perk up real fast. You want to know about Dwayne Thompson, I can tell you a thing or three."

The house was vaguely Southern Colonial in style, on a smallish scale. "Nice house," Wyatt commented, a break-the-ice compliment.

"I brought it to the site in pieces, assembling it over a period of several years. Now I live in it full-time," Bollinger explained.

Wyatt nodded his appreciation of the task.

"My wife teaches elementary school, and both my kids go there," he informed Wyatt. "Third and fifth grades." They were sitting on the back porch, which ran the length of the rear of the house and was roofed against the sun. "It's five miles the other direction from which you came." He pointed south. "Ten miles after that you're in Arkansas. It's a long ten miles." He smiled. "We think of them as poor white trash. We, on the other hand, are rural aristocrats."

Wyatt had passed up the offer of a beer for a Coke. In a glass, with ice. He sucked on an ice cube. "How did you wind up here?" he asked. It was an obvious question, but he wanted to know. He was curious, and he was also on guard. Bollinger had information about Dwayne Thompson—Wyatt knew that for a fact—and why a former prosecuting attorney was now living like a country hippie twenty miles from the end of nowhere could color what he told Wyatt about Thompson.

"I was at loose ends when I stopped working for the state," Bollinger began, "and I didn't know if I wanted to practice law anymore. I knew I didn't want to be a prosecutor. Mostly, what I wanted was some space. And time. I needed to think, figure my life out. We had this property— it's been in my wife's family five generations—so I figured this was as good a place as any to drop out and sort things out. And it was a good change for the kids, growing up in semiurban surroundings all their lives."

This could be me, Wyatt thought, if the angst had hit me a decade earlier. Although Moira wouldn't be part of this equation. Their house was as far from a center of population as she would ever want to live.

"It's turned out okay," Bollinger went on. "I'm practicing law again, for the other side, like you. Two or three cases a year, in and around Springfield. Enough to keep me busy, pay for the groceries, put a little aside for a rainy day. When I go into court I throw on my old Ivy League charcoal gray, trim up the locks, take this out"—he fingered his earring— "and I'm a respectable citizen. Respectable enough to pass muster round here. The rest of the time"—he spread his arms wide—"I'm a happy farmer. And father."

"Criminal defense?" Wyatt asked.

Bollinger nodded. "Drug cases. Beaucoup marijuana grown in this part of the country, friend. One of your major cash crops."

The word Wyatt had on Bollinger was that the man was a renegade, a former straitlaced, hard-nosed prosecuting attorney who had gone native. Passed over to the other side, now more antiestablishment than his clients in both lifestyle and behavior. From what Wyatt had seen so far, that assessment seemed accurate.

"What was it that made you leave the prosecutor's office?" Wyatt asked.

"Hypocrisy. And other, more nefarious sins." Bollinger stood up. "Let's take a walk."

From the edge of Bollinger's cleared property a couple of footpaths had been broken over the years into the thick woods. Wyatt followed Bollinger through stands of oak, birch, ash, pine. Mostly pine. He was dressed in light clothes, khakis and a cotton polo shirt, but the humidity was fierce, and he was sweating like a bandit. Rivulets of water ran down his armpits and torso. The only saving grace was that the trees were so thick they formed a canopy overhead that protected them from direct sunlight.

"A little bit farther," Bollinger called out over his shoulder. "Watch out for the poison ivy," he cautioned, pointing at some shiny leaves at the side of the path.

Wyatt felt like he was in a tropical rain forest in some exotic locale like Belize or Ecuador. Birds of bright plumage flew overhead, screaming and chattering in a cacophonous din. Insects assaulted him—he swatted at mosquitoes, flying ants, gnats.

"Bear scat." Bollinger pointed to a pile of dung at the side of the trail. "They've been out of hibernation about a month now, so it's safe to walk through here. The first couple of weeks they come out, you don't want to be around. They'll eat anything that moves or grows, from tree bark to ants to you or me."

They had been walking about forty minutes, a steady low-grade uphill climb that led them farther and farther away from civilization. Rounding one more corner, they came to a semicleared area that was hidden from the sky by tall pines. Four-foot-high stalks, spaced closely and evenly, filled the space, about half an acre square.

"Holy shit!" Wyatt exclaimed.

"It's holy, and it is great shit," Bollinger agreed.

A man came from under a protective stand of birchs at the far end of the clearing. He was young, in his twenties, wearing a battered John Deere hat and Sears overalls. Long hair and a rock 'n' roll goatee wreathed his face, so that the only thing showing was his black, wary eyes. A 12-gauge shotgun was draped over his forearm.

"Hey, Brent," the shotgun wielder called out in a deep Southern accent, relaxing his vigilance.

"Hey your own self," Bollinger sang out in return. "Say hello to a friend of mine, who shall be nameless to you as you shall be to him." He plucked a bud from the top of one of the plants and ground it up between his palms. Inhaling deeply, he held his palms under Wyatt's nose.

Wyatt sniffed. "I remember that smell."

Dusting his hands on his cutoffs, Bollinger squatted down. He scooped up a handful of thick, red-brown dirt.

"Lot of clay in this ground," he said. "Not too good for some crops, but damn good for marijuana."

"How much are you growing?" Wyatt asked without thinking.

"Who says I'm growing this?" Bollinger asked quickly. Bollinger was a lawyer. He had his alibi planned. "This isn't my property," he said, grinning slyly. "This piece of heaven belongs to Uncle Sam, all seventy-five thousand acres, God bless his law-abiding heart. Federally mandated national wilderness." He indicated the young guard, who had retreated to his place in the shade. "He works for one of our local cottage-industry syndicates. Pays better than carving Ozark-style trinkets for tourists. Most of that stuff comes from Taiwan now, anyways. I lawyer for these boys. That's as close as I care to get to the operation. I wouldn't want to lose my license over this stuff." He gave Wyatt a conspiratorial wink. "You aren't going to bust us, are you?"

"I haven't seen anything. Aren't you . . . aren't your clients . . . afraid of flyovers by the DEA or ATF?"

"This is too out of the way, and you can't see the ground from the air. The growers checked that out up front. Some of these hillbillies do have brains in their heads, L'il Abner notwithstanding." He dug a bag of sunflower seeds out of his back pocket, tossed a handful in his mouth. "I was talking about hypocrisy." He clapped a dirty, callused hand on Wyatt's shoulder, leaving a smudge mark. "You asked me why I quit the prosecutor's office, where I was the star, the one-hundred-percent-conviction poster boy. Simple reason, although not everyone thinks so. It's because I had to use people like Dwayne Thompson. Dwayne Thompson helped me put a man away for twenty-five years." He paused. "Not that the man wasn't guilty; he was. But if I have to make a right out of two wrongs, what kind of man does that make me in the eyes of my Creator?"

Wyatt didn't answer. He didn't know. Instead, he asked, "What did Dwayne get out of it?"

"We let him out. He had six more years to go, minimum, on an armed robbery charge. He walked out that prison door a totally free man. No probation, no halfway house, nothing. Free as a bird."

"How long ago was that?" Wyatt asked.

"Almost six years ago."

Wyatt whistled. "He's been in Durban almost that long," he exclaimed in surprise.

"That's 'cause he's an old dog. New tricks aren't in his repertoire. He moves to your state, he sees an opportunity, some place he thinks is a bird's nest on the ground, he knocks it off. Being a career criminal, he gets caught, he's doing six to ten. Then this Malone guy comes along, confesses to him quote unquote, they cut him way down. But then they make him for an old unsolved manslaughter deal, he's going up for that when he's done with this stretch. You have a three-strikes law in your state. That's his third strike, he's out. So Dwayne Thompson can look forward to spending the rest of his life in prison, unless he can get someone else in whatever jail he happens to be to confess to him."

They walked back to the house. A girl about ten and a boy, eight, were riding their bicycles in the yard, chasing each other in a big circle. They called out to their dad without slowing down. He called back to them by name and led Wyatt into the house.

"My wife, Annabelle. This is Wyatt Matthews, the famous lawyer who's working on that big murder case I told you about."

The woman, a pretty blonde, was fixing dinner, dredging pounded steak in flour for frying. She wiped her hands on her apron and shook with Wyatt.

"I've been showing Wyatt the north forty," Bollinger joked. "Local commerce."

"How's it looking?" she asked.

"Somebody's going to have a real good cash crop." He turned to Wyatt. "You'll stay to dinner."

They sat on the porch again. The boy and girl were playing catch with a Frisbee. This time Wyatt had a beer to match Bollinger.

"You were there," Wyatt said. "Was Dwayne Thompson fed information? By the police or . . ." He didn't finish—the implication was obvious.

"My office?" The former prosecutor shook his head. "It isn't that simple, and the bottom line is no, not exactly." He took a pull from his beer. "The man confessed to Dwayne. Sort of. Like yeah, well, he did it, but there wasn't much in the details, and maybe it wasn't an absolute, rock-solid confession, guys in jail like to brag, be the big man, you know that. So ol' Dwayneso comes to us and tells us this and it's a start, but it isn't a case. Not a lock. Prosecutors like sure things."

"So the other prisoner was set up?"

"Not exactly." He laughed. "I'm starting to sound like that Hertz commercial, aren't I? The guy was guilty, of that there was no question, none. But our case was weak, until Dwayne came along."

"How did you bridge it?" Wyatt asked. Now he was getting down to the nitty-gritty of what he needed. "From a start to a lock."

"Okay," Bollinger said. "It works like this. We say to Dwayne, 'This guy could be bullshitting us. We've got to test him, find out if he's really the one.' This was a series of rapes, so it ties into your deal. 'Ask him if the victim was wearing stockings or panty hose,' we say for example. 'Tell him that you heard she was wearing panty hose, but no underpants. See what he says. If he gets suspicious, like how come you know this shit, tell him it's a jailhouse rumor.' There's always a million jailhouse rumors, so that always works. You start with some sex stuff, kinky if possible. Their sexual fantasies are about the best things some of these habitual old cons have going for them. So Dwayne pops the question, and sure and behold, the guy goes for that bait like a starving trout goes for your best fly. 'It wasn't panty hose, it was stockings, and they had a black seam down the back, with clocks at the ankles.' Etc., etc. And of course, that's what the victim was in fact wearing, and we can put Dwayne on the stand and ask, 'Did the accused tell you what kind of legwear the victim was wearing, in detail?' and Dwayne can honestly say, 'Yes, stockings, seams,' the whole shebang. And that's how it works. At least in our situation it did. We knew Dwayne, we knew what he was capable of. It took us a month to set up, and it paid off. We got our conviction."

"And that's why you quit?"

"Actually, no. I could live with that, because the guy really was guilty, and his crime was truly awful. What did it for me was, I sent another guy up, on a stoolie's testimony— not Dwayne in this particular case. It was a murder case and we pulled the switch on the fellow and a year later found out

the stoolie had been lying from the ground up. It wasn't like
the man confessed and we helped fill in the details, like we
did with Dwayne and some others. This man actually was
innocent. Which to my mind made me an accomplice." He
spat out a mouthful of sunflower husks. "Stoolies are the
lowest. You make your bed with them, you're going to be
scratching the fleas off your back. So I quit."

He finished his beer, set it down gently on the wooden
porch floor. "I'm switching to tequila," he said. "Want a
margarita?"

Dinner was early and delicious. Chicken-fried steak and
vegetables from Annabelle's garden. Wyatt limited his alcohol intake to one tequila sunrise.

The sun was edge-painting the western sky as the former
prosecutor walked Wyatt to his car. The dogs scampered
around them, the growler nipping at Wyatt's heels. Bollinger
gave him a swift kick to discourage his antisocial behavior.

"I hope I helped you some," Bollinger said. They were
standing at the car.

"You did." Wyatt paused. "Although in my particular
case, I don't think the same situation applies."

"No?"

"Dwayne had just gotten down to our city jail from Durban, to testify in this Malone case. His first day working in
the infirmary they bring in Marvin White, who'd been shot
up. Three days later Marvin has confessed in detail to seven
different murders, Dwayne has gone to the DA with his information, and the DA gets his indictment. It happened too
fast, there's too much information, and Dwayne just got
there, he hasn't networked with any jail personnel who
could set him up. Unless there's someone there who was
working with him at Durban, which seems far-fetched, since
he's been at Durban over four years this stretch."

Bollinger thought for a moment, nodding in agreement.
"Yes, I'd say you're right. But that doesn't necessarily mean
that Dwayne did it all on his own," he pointed out.

"No," Wyatt agreed. "Anyway, I did get something out of
this trip, besides meeting you, which I'm glad I did." He
wouldn't be moving in this world if he was still practicing
corporate law, he thought with satisfaction. This world was
way more interesting. Dangerous and alive. He had never

seen a large patch of marijuana before, only plants in a friend's basement, under a Gro-Lite.

"So am I," Bollinger agreed. They shook hands for the last time. "What do you think you've learned?"

"I know that Dwayne was dirty in the past, and that his miraculous jailhouse confessions weren't solely his own doing. If he was dirty with you he's probably dirty this time, too. How he did it, or who did it with him—that's my dilemma."

Wyatt stood at the site where the first murder had been committed, two years earlier. He had flown home the night before—Moira had long been asleep by the time he finally got to the house, so he crashed in the guest room. When he woke in the morning she was already gone, leaving him a note that she had early business with her bookstore location, and to think good thoughts for her. She'd check in with him later.

There should be a plaque here, he thought, as midmorning pedestrian traffic flowed around him. A bouquet of flowers, like they bring to roadside graves in Mexico. A person was murdered here. There should be some recognition of that.

The neighborhood was working-class commercial/residential, apartments over stores. The victim, a teenage prostitute, had been found in a narrow alley between two stores, jammed in behind some large trash cans and covered with sheets of cardboard. Care had been taken to hide the body well enough so that it couldn't be seen casually. The distance from one brick wall to the other, bordering the alley, was barely wide enough to drive a car through; it was mostly used as a walkway, a shortcut to get to the next block without having to go all the way around. The trash cans that were kept there were lugged out to the sidewalk for pickup twice a week. There had been a pickup the day before, so the cans wouldn't be moved for two more days. Had the killer known that? It seemed reasonable to assume so.

The street that ran perpendicular to the alley, a medium-sized thoroughfare, had been part of Marvin's route. Livonius's laundry had two regular customers on this block, both commercial: a Chinese restaurant and a photo lab. Marvin was at both stores twice a week, one delivery, one return. The killing had occurred the night of his return day. The coroner had determined the time of death to have been between nine and midnight. He had good evidence to go by; the last person to see the victim alive had been another hooker, who'd had a cup of coffee and a slice of pizza with her at a take-out place around the corner. She had last seen her friend at eight-thirty. The decomposed pizza in the murdered woman's stomach had helped the coroner pinpoint his findings.

The victim had mentioned something to her friend about an appointment later that night with a regular, but the police had discounted that, unless the regular was someone who drove through the neighborhood and had sex with her in his car. There were no hotels to go to nearby, and this prostitute wasn't of that caliber. She was in the five-minute drive-by category.

Wyatt had the police report of the murder with him. He looked through it again. The body had been found the following day by a homeless transient who had gone into the alley in the wee hours of the morning to get out of the cold and had fallen asleep in an alcoholic stupor. When he had come to and was leaving the alley he picked through the trash cans, looking for bottles and cans he could recycle for money for another bottle. He saw the body buried under the cardboard and ran screaming to the nearest policeman.

The transient had been held briefly and questioned, then released. He was never a serious suspect. He had been seen long after midnight, the coroner's outside time for the killing, and the blood-alcohol level in his system, even several hours later, was too high for someone who had committed this kind of murder. Besides, with that much alcohol in his system, he wouldn't have been able to get and maintain an erection. The rape had been vicious. The killer had used his penis like a club.

The people on the street knew Marvin. He came through regularly on his route, although at that time he'd only been on the job about a month. Some of the hookers interviewed by the police knew who he was by sight, but he had never propositioned any of them, and they didn't know if he and the victim knew each other.

Marvin had finished work that day at 6:45. Livonius still had his old time cards. He kept them for two years, in case he was audited by the INS. Livonius still remembered Lithuania—he did everything by the rules.

Marvin usually went home right after work, but occasionally he would linger in town. Jonnie Rae was sure he had come home that night, but she didn't remember when—the usual time, about eight, or later. He had to take two buses, with a transfer. It was a long trip if he missed his connection.

No one seemed to know what he did when he didn't come home straightaway. Just hanging around, seeing what the rest of the world looked like, was what his mother thought. He had been born and raised in the same depressed section of the city, and had never gotten very far from that neighborhood until he got the job with Livonius. It was logical to think that the attractions of the city would appeal to him.

And it was also logical, Wyatt thought, that after a month on the job some of the women he wound up sleeping with had already started him on that routine. That by this time on the job he was spending evenings in the beds of some of his female customers.

One thing Wyatt couldn't see: Marvin sleeping with a customer and then raping and killing another woman that same night—or worse, killing and then going to a sexual liaison. He wasn't nearly cold-blooded enough for that. He was too immature, too emotional. These killings had been methodical and brutal. A sociopath's killings.

If Marvin had done it, he would have committed the crime and then gone home. He couldn't have taken a cab—somewhere out there a taxi driver would have seen his picture on television or in the newspaper and gone to the police. None had.

That night Marvin went home on the bus. In Wyatt's mind, that had become a given.

Normally, when Marvin was going straight home, he caught his first bus a block down the street from Livonius's establishment. This murder had taken place two miles away. Marvin wouldn't have walked two miles to catch the bus. He would have gone to the nearest stop, six blocks from the alley.

Wyatt stood in the alley. You're the killer. Marvin White. You accost this hooker on the street. Twenty to nine, a quarter to. You go into the alley for your ten-dollar blow job, but instead of that you overpower her, tear her clothes off, and rape her. She struggles—her clothes had been torn, she had scratches and bruises on her face and upper body. You're strong enough and big enough that you can overpower her, tear her clothes off, rape her, and still keep her from screaming loud enough for someone to hear.

No one had heard anything, according to the police report. They had talked to everyone for two blocks around. No yells, no cries for help.

Of course, you could have pulled the knife on her right away. Raped her with the knife at her throat. She wouldn't have resisted then, she would have taken her medicine. Chalk it up to occupational hazard.

She had started fighting you when she realized that you weren't going to merely rape her, as bad as that was, even for a prostitute. You were going to kill her. So she fought, but you were bigger and stronger, and you had a knife.

You killed her. Several stab wounds—there was considerable bleeding. You dragged her body deeper into the alley, buried her under the cardboard that you scrounged, then put the trash cans in front of her, to hide her.

Okay, it's nine o'clock, the earliest time the murder could have taken place. Wyatt was wearing the digital sports watch he used for running, which had a stopwatch built in. He punched up the stopwatch mode and started the clock.

You couldn't run to the bus stop. Running would attract attention, someone might take notice and recognize you later. You walk. Fast.

Wyatt walked to the bus stop at a good clip. When he got there, he punched the timer. Eleven minutes. Marvin wouldn't have done it any faster.

Josephine had gotten him a city bus timetable. He took it out of his pocket, scanned it until he found the listings for this route, the one Marvin would take that would hook him up with the second bus that would transport him home, to Sullivan Houses.

The last bus that Marvin could catch that would allow him to make his connection left this stop at 9:23. If the murder had occurred at the stroke of nine, the earliest possible time according to the coroner, there was less than a ten-minute window to have done it, hidden the body, and walked six blocks to catch the bus.

Ten after nine. That was the latest Marvin could have done it. It was technically possible. But what were the odds that the murder had taken place that close to the edge of the coroner's estimate? A hundred to one or more? A statistician could give him that information.

Yes, Marvin could have done it. But the odds, Wyatt was sure, were overwhelmingly against it.

Moira had had a wonderful day. She and Cissy Dugan finally signed the lease papers for the bookstore. Next week the contractor would start construction. In two months Lucy & Ethel's would be a reality.

She popped the cork on a bottle of Dom Pérignon as soon as Wyatt walked through the door.

"Congratulations," he said, kissing her robustly. She had left him a message at work, so he already knew. "I'm proud of you. And happy."

"How was your trip?" she asked. "Was it pretty out there?"

"Gorgeous. I'll take you some time. Be a great family vacation."

He filled her and Michaela in over dinner, leaving out a few parts, like the dope patch. "This stool-pigeon witness of Pagano's is dirty," he exclaimed with passion. "The more I know about him, the more I know that."

"That doesn't mean this kid—your client—isn't guilty," Moira pointed out. "That lawyer said the man in his case was guilty."

"But the one in the other case, the one they railroaded, wasn't." Michaela interjected. "Isn't that right, Dad?"

"Michaela," Moira said sharply.

"That's exactly right," Wyatt said in response to his daughter, ignoring his wife's pissed-off look at both of them. "And I've got to make sure that doesn't happen to Marvin."

"So now you're convinced he's innocent," Moira said dourly.

"I don't have to be convinced," he answered. "That's not the way it works, Moira." Softening his tone: "But I'm definitely leaning in that direction."

He told them of his day's work, reconstructing the timetable of the initial murder, how difficult it would have been for Marvin to have done it and still gotten home. "I have an alibi witness now, a timetable on one of the murders that's almost impossible, and a former district attorney who admitted he and others fed Dwayne Thompson information. If I can find one more good alibi witness, or figure out one more murder that he couldn't have done, given the times and places, I will be convinced." He looked over at Moira, who had drunk most of the bottle of champagne herself. "Would that make you feel better?"

"It would make all the difference in the world."

He poured himself the last half glass of champagne. "Oh," he said, laughing. "I almost forgot. I got you a dog."

"You *what*?"

"You said you wanted a watchdog. I found the greatest watchdog in the world. It belongs to that lawyer, Bollinger. I'm going to have him ship the dog to us."

Moira looked at him askance. "What kind of dog is it?"

"Every kind. Pit bull, shepherd, rottweiller. Probably some wolf or coyote. He's really mean, and ugly as sin. He'd scare a burglar off just with his looks. The only bad thing is, his drool will mess up your good clothes."

"That sounds awful. That's not the kind of dog I want. I don't even want a dog."

"You don't?" His grin was spreading from ear to ear.

She finally caught on. "You're pulling my leg," she exclaimed, relieved. "You're not having any dog shipped up here."

"No. But if you ever change your mind, it'll be okay."

Glancing at Michaela, Moira shook her head. "I don't want a dog," she reiterated. "We'll be fine without one."

The doorbell rang.

Moira looked over at him with a questioning expression.

He shook his head. "I'm not expecting anyone. Are you?"

"No."

"Maybe it's for Michaela." Michaela was upstairs in her room, hitting the books. It was almost ten o'clock. They were both in the study. She was knitting a sweater; he was reading police reports from some of the other murders and occasionally glancing at the television, which hummed in the corner, the sound turned low.

She put her knitting aside. "I'll get it."

He jotted notes on a legal pad. There was so much information, much of it overlapping and conflicting. The experience of the officer or detective who wrote up the initial report had a lot to do with the cogency of the material. One thing was crystal clear, however: all seven murders were the work of one man, acting alone. The class of woman (except for the accidental mistyping of the last victim), the times and locations where the killings took place, the way they were executed—all the same. The victims were raped, partially strangled by hand, then finished off by knife stabbings.

"Who . . . who are you?" He heard Moira's agitated voice filtering down the hallway, into the room. Putting his work aside, he got up and walked to the front door.

"Hello, Mr. Matthews."

"Hello." He glanced at Moira, who was obviously freaked out. "What are you doing here, Dexter?"

"It's my fault, Dad." Michaela came trotting down the stairs at a fast clip. "I forgot to tell you." She came up next to him, looking at Dexter, who was standing on the other side of the threshold. Louis and Richard were with him. And a girl. "Are you the one who called for my dad?" she asked.

Dexter looked at her, then at Wyatt. "Yes. That was me."

Michaela turned to Wyatt. "He called earlier, before either of you got home. He said he needed to see you tonight, Dad. That he'd been helping you out and it was urgent. So I gave him our address." She looked at Moira, who was watching from a conscious remove. "I hope that was okay."

"It was," he assured her fast, before Moira could say something to the contrary.

"I wouldn't have bothered you in your house if I didn't

think it was important, Mr. Matthews," Dexter said apologetically, looking from him to Moira, who was openly showing her dismay and displeasure.

"It's okay. Come in."

The four of them trooped inside, huddled together in the foyer, surreptitiously checking out the house, what they could see of it. "My daughter, Michaela, and my wife, Moira," Wyatt said in introduction. "Mrs. Matthews. Dexter, Richard, Louis," indicating the boys.

"This is Leticia," Richard said, pushing the girl forward. "Last name Pope."

"How are you?" Wyatt asked. The girl was Michaela's age, maybe even younger.

"I'm okay." She was plainly scared, speaking in a tiny voice that was barely audible.

Wyatt looked at Moira. "Would you rather we talk in the living room or the study?"

"I don't care."

"We'll go in the study. I've got my paperwork in there already."

"Dad."

He turned to Michaela. "What, honey?"

"I'm finished with my homework. Could I . . . sit in there with you? I won't get in your way."

He looked across the hallway at his wife. She was staring at Dexter and the others like they were from another world. "Sure," he told his daughter. "Why don't you grab a tray of Cokes and meet us there?"

The kids from the project ogled the house as he led them down the hallway to the study, peering into the large living room, checking the Craftsman-style stairway that led to the second floor, looking at the lamps, chairs and sofas, paintings on the walls. Soft light from sconces spread like little sunsets across the walls and up to the corners of the ceiling, warming the rooms with their glow and giving visitors the feeling they were in a safe haven.

"This is a great place, Mr. Matthews," Dexter said, awestruck.

"Thanks. My wife did the decorating. She has a touch for it."

"Someday I'd like to have me a house like this."

Wyatt studied the compact drug dealer. "Anything's possible if you work hard enough. Although I don't endorse the way you make your living," he added firmly.

"That's going to change," Dexter asserted. "I swear to God. Soon as I get me enough put away, I'm going into the straight world. Doing what I'm doing is too precarious, you know what I mean? Sometimes you don't live very long."

The others didn't say anything. They just gawked. Wyatt led them into the study. "Sit anywhere," he offered. Turning to the girl, "I take it you're the reason for this emergency meeting."

Her eyes were cast down to the floor. Dexter answered for her. "Yes sir. She's why we're here."

They sat down gingerly, Dexter next to Leticia, who barely touched the edge of her behind to the sofa, as if ready to spring up and run out at any provocation. Dexter hovered over her protectively, taking her shaking hand in his two and pressing it to reassure her. The other two boys sat stiffly side by side, across the room. Wyatt knew they were here as bodyguards—Dexter's comfort zone. This was Dexter's show.

Michaela came in with Cokes and glasses. Each guest took one, carefully pouring from the can into the glass, as if staining the carpet would be grounds for arrest. Then she took a chair at the side of her dad's desk.

Wyatt perched himself on the edge of the desk, one leg informally crossed over the other. He picked up his master file and a legal pad and balanced them on his thigh, the pad on top so he could write on it. "Why don't you tell me why you drove all the way out here this late at night."

The girl turned to Dexter, who nodded. She said something that was so low and inaudible that Wyatt couldn't hear it.

"Could you speak up?" he asked.

"She was with Marvin," Dexter answered for her.

"When one of the murders took place?" He leaned forward.

The girl nodded.

"Which one?"

"Last April eleventh or twelfth."

He leafed rapidly through the file. "The second one. That one took place near the Little Bangkok area." The area he was referring to was heavily populated by Thai refugees.

The murdered prostitute had been half black, half Thai. A beautiful girl, judging by her picture. The prettiest of the killer's victims.

"How long were you with Marvin on the night of April eleventh?" he asked her.

"All night long." Her voice was barely above a whisper, but he could hear her.

He looked at her hard. "What proof do you have? That I can use?"

"We was at a party," she began hesitantly.

Dexter nudged her in the ribs with his elbow. "Go on, girl. The man don't have all night to fool with you."

"It's okay," Wyatt reassured her, not wanting her to get scared and clam up. "You were at a party," he prompted. "From when to when—approximately."

"From about eighty-thirty to about eleven."

"Where was the party?" he asked. "Was it in Sullivan Houses?"

She nodded. "My cousin's apartment. Her old man wasn't around."

"He got busted that night for possession," Dexter volunteered. "He was in the slammer."

"When the cat's away, the mice shall *play*!" Richard boomed from out of nowhere.

Wyatt flipped to the information sheet on that murder. It had taken place late at night, between midnight and dawn of the morning of the twelfth. Marvin's being at a party with her until eleven the night before wasn't a credible alibi. It was a beginning, however. There was no public transportation from Sullivan Houses to where the killing had taken place at that time of night—the last public bus left at ten o'clock. If Marvin was the killer he would have had to drive there in a private car, or take a taxi. Both unlikely scenarios. He's going to make a twenty-five-mile round-trip after midnight on the chance there will be a hooker on the streets that he can kill?

He could have borrowed a car. Or stolen one.

"What happened after you left the party?" he asked the girl.

"We hung around. It was a hot night. We went over to Marvin's place for a while, till his mama fell asleep. Then we went out again."

Okay, getting better. "So that was when?"

"Till about midnight."

"And then?"

"We went to my place."

"Were either of your parents there?"

"My mama," Leticia said. " 'Cept she wasn't there."

"Her natural father did a Carl Lewis 'fore she was ever born," Dexter said, filling in the blanks. "Her mama done raised her, her mama and her grandmama. Raised her and two sisters and two brothers. 'Cept her grandmama's been dead three years now."

"Your mother was there but she wasn't?" he asked. "I don't understand that."

"Her mama's a crackhead," Dexter explained. "She was over to a crack house that night. She hangs around there, hoping they'll throw her a taste. Sometimes they do. Make her work for it, though."

Sex? Wyatt wondered. Something more debasing?

With a start he remembered that Michaela was sitting right next to him, taking all this in. In his tunnel-vision search for the pieces of the puzzle he had completely forgotten about her. He turned to her. "Do you want to say good night?" he asked, his tone implying the reply.

"I want to stay," she said adamantly. To Dexter, she asked, "Is that all right? With Leticia?"

Dexter looked at her, then at Wyatt. "It's all right with us. But maybe you should check with your father."

She turned to Wyatt. "I want to stay," she said again.

He thought about it for a moment. "Okay. But nothing that's said here leaves the room. This is a privileged conversation. Including your mother," he added with emphasis.

"I won't say anything to anyone," she promised.

He turned back to the girl. "Were you and Marvin there alone, or were your brothers and sisters there, too?"

"They was there, but they was sleeping in the bedroom. Me and Marvin was alone in the living room."

"What did the two of you do there?" he asked.

Before she could answer, Dexter cut her off. "You know what they did, Mr. Matthews," he said, looking at Michaela.

Michaela took the inference in stride. "I wasn't born yesterday," she said, looking straight at Dexter.

"Sorry 'bout that," he answered with a smile.

Wyatt watched this brief repartee. In another world, another time, this boy and his daughter could be friends.

"Did you do anything besides that?" he asked her.

"Watched a movie on TV. HBO. Drank some wine."

"Do you remember the name of the movie?"

"Twelve Monkeys."

"That's a bitchin' movie," Louis interjected from across the room. "I've seen it three times."

He'd look that up in an old *TV Guide*. Dexter couldn't have prepped her on that. And he'd cross-check it with Marvin.

So far so good. Getting better. Not as buttoned-down as Agnes Carpenter, but pretty good. "Is there anything else you did that could bolster this alibi?" he asked her.

"We went to the drugstore to get ice cream. All-night drugstore, on King Boulevard. Rocky road. Marvin, he got a sweet tooth on him," the girl said.

"And they got their picture took," Dexter added, almost jumping out of his seat. "Show him," he ordered her.

She dug a wrinkled picture-strip out of her purse and handed it to Wyatt. It was a three-photo strip, the kind where you sit in a cramped booth, drop in your quarters, and get three one-inch-square Polaroids.

Marvin and Leticia. Smiling at the camera. In one of the pictures, he had his hand inside her blouse, firmly on her breast.

"These pictures show that you and Marvin were together," Wyatt agreed. "But they don't establish when."

Dexter smiled. "Look on the back."

Wyatt turned the strip over. On each individual photo there was a time stamp. Time and date. The time stamped on the pictures was 2:45 A.M. The date was April 12.

Dexter and the others from Sullivan Houses sat in the Jeep Cherokee. Wyatt leaned in the driver's-side window. The girl was riding shotgun. "Thanks for coming," he said to her, talking across Dexter.

She mumbled something inaudible.

"She says she had to do it," Dexter translated. "Even though Marvin never did pay her no mind after that one time. Least he didn't knock her up."

"You know you're going to have to testify in court," Wyatt reminded her.

She nodded.

"I'll be working with you before that," he assured her. "I'll take care of you, don't worry."

"Yes sir," she whispered.

"If anyone from the district attorney's office calls you," he continued, "you notify me right away."

She nodded.

"She ain't talking to no one unless you say to," Dexter promised him.

"Okay, then. You've got a long drive back, so you'd better be going. I'll keep the pictures, for safekeeping." He reached in the window and shook Dexter's hand. "You've been a big help."

"Whatever I can do."

He stood in the driveway until their car was gone.

Moira was in bed, waiting for him. "You've gone too far," she said as soon as he walked in the door.

He undressed sitting on his side of the bed. "That happened to be a very important meeting," he told her over his shoulder. "And you told me you don't want me to go down to where they live, remember?" He couldn't resist throwing that back in her face.

"Have these important meetings at your office. And you should not have allowed Michaela to be in there with you—and them." The words were practically spat out, venom from a viper's tongue.

"Michaela learned a good lesson tonight," he countered.

"She's not old enough yet to learn these lessons."

"She's the age of those kids. She is old enough."

She shook her head in anger. "Why don't we move back into the city so she can have firsthand experience of that kind of life every day?"

He ignored her. "It's late, babe. Let's go to bed. You had a great day, signing your lease. Take that thought to sleep with you." He walked into the bathroom.

"I had a great day," she called after him, "until you screwed it up."

He sat in the kitchen, nursing a cognac. Hearing footsteps, he looked up. Michaela poked her head in.

"I forgot to bring water upstairs," she explained.

He nodded.

She drew a glass from the purifier. "Dad?"

"What, honey?"

"I'm glad you let me stay in there with you."

"Me, too."

"They seemed okay," she said.

"They are."

"They're not that much different from me, really."

He put a fatherly arm around her shoulder. "No, they're not."

"I'm lucky, Dad."

"Well . . ." She was lucky. That was true. They all were, including Moira. "Take advantage of it," he reminded her.

"I do. I will. Seeing those guys reminds of that." She kissed him on the cheek. "I'm glad you're doing what you're doing."

He smiled. Giving her a kiss on the forehead, he said, "And I'm glad you feel that way."

The call came from out of the blue, like so many of them do.

"Some guy wants to talk to you," Josephine said, leaning into his doorway.

"Who is it?" he asked, his head buried in a transcript.

"He won't tell me. Only you."

"About the case?" He looked up.

She nodded.

"What about it?"

"He wants to talk about the case. He won't give me his name, he won't tell me what he wants to talk about regarding the case. Only you. You want me to shine him on?"

Distracted: "No, I'll take it."

"Line three." She paused. "Do you want me to tape it? I've got it set up."

"Without telling him?" He frowned.

"For reference," she said defensively.

He shook his head. "If he's sophisticated he might figure it out, and then we'd be in trouble. If I decide I need you to listen in, I'll let you know." He started to pick the phone up, then hesitated. "When was the last time we were swept?"

"The day before yesterday. Monday and Thursday mornings, as you requested."

"The lines should be safe then." Tapping into someone's phone was illegal, but people did it anyway. He punched up line three, picked up the receiver. "Wyatt Matthews," he announced as Josephine flounced out of sight, not too discreetly.

"You're the lawyer on this multiple-murder charge." A man's voice, with a pronounced upper-Midwestern accent. Working-class, Wyatt would bet lunch on it. "For that nigger."

Wyatt held his tongue. "Yes, I am Marvin White's attorney. Who am I talking to, please?" He pulled pad and ballpoint toward him.

"Don't worry about that. Not yet." Wyatt heard the man's heavy breathing come across the line. He sounded like he had emphysema, or heavy asthma. Then harsh, barking coughing, a phlegmy rattle. This is a sick man, Wyatt thought. He wondered if the man was calling from a hospital.

"Dwayne Thompson." The caller's sandpaper voice cut through the line. "That name mean anything to you?"

"Yes."

"Just checking. Making sure you're not some lame can't find his ass with both hands kind of lawyer."

"I know where my behind is," Wyatt told the caller.

A rheumy chortle. "What about Doris Blake?" the voice asked. "The name ring a bell?"

Wyatt thought for a moment. "No, it doesn't."

"You're not taking care of business, pal."

"Is that what you called to tell me?" He wished now he'd had Josephine tape this call. "Long-distance, I presume."

"Don't presume nothing. Just do your fucking homework. You and I might could do with a personal face-to-face confab. I gotta think on that. See where it gets me. I'll call you back tomorrow," the voice promised. "Same time, same station." He hung up.

Wyatt leaned back in his chair, the receiver dangling from his fingertips. Doris Blake? Was that the name of one of the murder victims? He thought he knew all their names.

He buzzed Josephine. She was there immediately. "Were you listening in?" he asked.

"Only your side. Anything tasty?"

"Does the name Doris Blake resonate? One of the victims, a witness?"

She shook her head. "I don't recall it."

"Well, maybe it's nothing. But see if you can get a line on someone named Doris Blake who might have some connection to this."

"Any particular area?"

"The way the caller put it, I think she's referenced to Dwayne Thompson, but I'm not sure."

"Okay."

"And while you're at it, cross-reference any connections Thompson might have had between the jail and Durban. Any inmates he knew up there who are down here now, anyone who's presently working at the jail who might have been working at Durban."

"What are you looking for?"

"The same thing I've been looking for from day one. Thompson couldn't have mined Marvin's brain for all that information. Somebody put him in the pipeline. I'm looking for who could have done it, and how."

"**I**t's him again."

One day later. Wyatt had been waiting for the call.

"You know who Doris Blake is now?" rasped the unknown caller.

"She's a lieutenant with the sheriff's department. Jail detail."

"Good work, Lawyer. Although I had to practically stick it down your throat for you."

"I appreciate your help."

"There's more ... if you want it," the voice coyly promised.

"I want it."

The mysterious caller lived in a trailer park on the outskirts of Rawleysville, about fifteen miles from where Durban State Penitentiary was located. It was an old, established park—the neon sign that rose above the entrance dated back to the fifties. Some of the residents had lived there that long, judging by the permanence of their structures, Wyatt thought as he drove his Jaguar through rows of spiffy double-wides that looked like they had grown out of the ground, the gleaming trailers sporting manicured lawns and small, carefully attended-to flower beds, with Weber barbecues and lawn chairs tastefully set in front of the screen-door entrances.

Lamar Brown's trailer—that was the man's name—was set at the far end of the complex, like it was an afterthought plunked down. It was an old Airstream, the kind people used to tow behind Ford Country Squire station wagons as advertised in *Life* magazine, circa 1955. In contrast to most of Brown's neighbors', his front yard was crabgrass and chicken dirt that hadn't seen a sprinkler for years. There was no car in front.

Wyatt parked near the entrance and got out, taking care not to step in a large pile of dogshit that had been left a short time before his arrival, judging from its moist freshness. He rapped on the screen-door frame. "Mr. Brown," he called out. "Are you in there? It's Wyatt Matthews."

He heard some shuffling around, then a series of harsh, throat-grinding coughs. "It's open," Brown called out hoarsely.

It was hot inside the trailer, and dark. What light there was came from shafts of sunlight slicing through the louvered windows that were open on both sides, but there was no breeze drafting through them. The small main compartment—living area/kitchenette—was spartan and clean. A Formica fold-down table, Naugahyde benches on either side, a dish rack with a few washed plastic dishes that were drying, a recliner in a corner, a television set bolted to the wall.

Wyatt stood just inside the doorway for a moment, letting his pupils adjust to the low light.

Brown was sitting in the recliner. A portable oxygen tank was set up next to it. Brown took the mask off his face. "Any trouble finding me?" he asked in his raspy hoarse voice.

"No." His eyes better accustomed to the dim light, Wyatt took a look at the man. It was hard to tell how old he was— he could have been forty-five, or just as easily, sixty-five. His sparse hair, matted down over his mottled scalp, was gray and lank, in need of cutting. Broken capillaries spread like little firecracker explosions all across his cheeks and nose. He was heavy; but worse, he was flabby, his white doughboy arms flopping out of his Hawaiian shirt, which was unbuttoned across his white whalelike chest and stomach. His outfit was rounded out with billowing shorts and flip-flops. If this were an old detective movie, and Wyatt was Humphrey Bogart, Brown would be Sidney Greenstreet.

Brown took a suck of oxygen from his mask. Then he reached into his shirt pocket and took out a pack of cigarettes, the generic brand you buy in the supermarket. He flicked his Bic and lit up, inhaling deeply. After he exhaled, he took another hit of oxygen.

Wyatt watched in disgust. The man was deliberately killing himself.

"I've got terminal emphysema," Brown said as if reading Wyatt's thoughts. "No point in stopping now, it would only prolong the agony."

"Isn't it dangerous, lighting up around oxygen?" Wyatt asked.

"Not if you're careful." He took another drag from his cigarette, then another from the oxygen. "Don't worry, I didn't ask you to drive all the way up here so I could blow you up, not to mention my neighbors. That Jaguar you drove up in isn't a rental, is it? Sure is a pretty vehicle."

"It's mine," Wyatt confirmed.

There was a folding chair leaning up against the far wall. Wyatt picked it up. "Do you mind?"

"No, I got it out for you." Another cigarette drag, another oxygen drag. "I don't have much company, so I don't keep it out."

Wyatt unfolded the chair. He sat facing the fat emphysemic. "What prompted you to call me?" he asked. He'd been pondering that question since five minutes after he'd hung up after his first cryptic conversation with Brown.

"A little birdie sang in my ear," the large man said.

"Who was he?" Wyatt persisted.

"Could've been a she."

"Someone who has it in for Dwayne Thompson?"

"That would be three-quarters of the English-speaking

population, but yes, that would be true. And don't chase that
anymore," Brown went on, "it doesn't matter and I'm not
going to tell you."

Wyatt let that pass. If later on he felt it was important,
he'd try to get the information some other way. "What can
you tell me about Doris Blake?" he asked. "And Dwayne
Thompson."

"I was a guard at Durban for twenty-six years before they
cut me loose, on account I couldn't walk one length of a
cellblock without stopping for breath," Brown said. "A
sergeant. Bastards retired me on only thirty-five percent dis-
ability. Said I brought it on myself by smoking." He
coughed: a deep, rattling gasp, sounding like his lungs were
on fire. "It was job-related stress," he complained. "That's
why I started smoking in the first place, 'cause of the stress
of working in that shithole. Everybody who works there
comes out of it sick, if they don't die first."

"So you were at Durban while Dwayne Thompson was an
inmate there? Part of this stretch he's doing?"

Brown nodded. Cigarette puff, oxygen puff. It was
painful to watch, but the man did it with aggressive defiance. "Three years." A moment's pause for another deep intake of oxygen. "Two years while Blake was there," he
added.

"Doris Blake was a guard at Durban?" *Son of a bitch!*

"Yep. We served together."

"And she knew Dwayne. He knew her."

"Yeah, they knew each other." He paused. Then, with relish: "In the biblical sense, so the rumors go."

Wyatt reeled. "Dwayne Thompson had a sexual relationship with a corrections officer? Who's now working at the
same jail he's in?"

Brown shrugged, took a last hit off his cigarette, dropped
the butt into a coffee-can ashtray that had an inch of water
inside. After another breath of oxygen, he said, "I don't
have firsthand knowledge, of course. I doubt anyone does.
But it was a known thing."

"By the administration?"

"Some of them. Not the top tier; they don't know what
they don't want to know, deliberately. But it was talked
about."

"What about the inmates?" Wyatt asked. "Did they know?"

"Some, I imagine. No one ever talked about it openly."

"Jesus." Wyatt thought for a moment. "Who else besides you could I talk to about this?"

Brown stared blankly at him. After another cigarette and cigarette-oxygen combo, he intoned, "Nobody."

"You said others knew."

"Knowing and saying are two different things, Counselor. That's a felony, what Blake and Dwayne were doing. Anybody that knows about it and doesn't report it is aiding and abetting."

"What about other inmates? Do you know any of them who might talk about this?"

"Sure, there are some that might. But they're cons. People have a hard time believing a con, especially with a story like that. Besides, when this trial's over down there, Dwayne's coming back up here. He'd kill anybody ratted him out about that."

"Why?" Wyatt asked. "She's the one who would get into trouble, not him. I'd think it would be a point of pride, a convict having an affair with an authority figure."

Brown's laugh was a wheeze that turned into full-on hacking. "You've never had the pleasure of making Doris Blake's acquaintance," he managed to cough out.

"Not yet. I'm going to call on her when I get back."

"After you meet her," Brown said, "you come back and tell me if you think Dwayne would want it known that he was fucking her."

"She isn't lovely?"

Brown's laugh-coughing almost got out of hand. He had to grab for his oxygen to steady himself.

"How unattractive could she be?" Wyatt asked. "For a man stuck inside without any women, for years?"

"You be the judge of that. I wouldn't have, and I'm no God's gift."

It was becoming increasingly hot in the little trailer. "Maybe you can answer this question," Wyatt said, leaning forward and pulling the damp shirt off his back where it was sticking. "If sleeping with her was that big a burden, what did Dwayne get out of it?"

"Everything."

"Everything?"

"Everything you can do inside the walls. Blake did everything she could to make Dwayne Thompson's life as comfortable—and as profitable—as it could be."

"**I** appreciate your seeing me on such short notice."

"You'd driven all this way anyway." The warden, a man named Bill Jonas, sat at his desk. Wyatt sat across the desk in the supplicant's chair. "I'm a public servant," the warden continued. "Your taxes pay my salary, pay the bills at Durban. And I'm not going to tell you any secrets, so why not meet with you? Besides, if I didn't, you'd find a way to use it against me in the media. I know how you guys think." There was no humor backing up these opening remarks.

Who are "you guys" and how do "we" think? Wyatt thought. He kept the thought to himself.

"You're here regarding one of our inmates, Dwayne Thompson, who is going to be testifying against your client," the warden said as statement, not question. "There's nothing I can tell you that isn't part of the public record."

"Still, for the record, there are some questions I want to ask you."

"Fire away." The man had the demeanor of an ex–Marine Corps officer, and the brush haircut and stiff posture to match. He had retired after twenty years as a light colonel and after getting his Ph.D. in criminology at Indiana University had found his true calling in the administrative side of the penal system.

"There was an officer working here during part of Thompson's current incarceration who is now a deputy sheriff in the county jail where Marvin White is presently housed. Did Doris Blake know Dwayne Thompson during her tour of duty here?"

Jonas's eyes narrowed for a moment. "I'm sure she knew who he was."

"How well did they know each other?" Wyatt continued, pressing easily.

"How well?" Jonas shrugged. "Why don't you ask her? You know where to find her. You didn't have to drive all the way up here to ask me that."

"Actually, I didn't drive up here to see you," Wyatt corrected him. "I was here already, talking to another former employee of yours. Lamar Brown."

Jonas shook his head in disgust. "Don't believe anything Brown tells you," he said. "He's a liar and a malcontent. He's committing suicide and claiming we drove him to it. It's pure fantasy. If you met him you know you saw a man with no respect at all for his body, for keeping himself in shape. He's brought every calamity he has on himself, with his own negative behavior."

"He told me that Doris Blake and Dwayne Thompson were lovers while Blake was a guard here, and that the administration knew and turned their face away from it."

The only sign that Jonas was agitated was the knuckles of his hands gripping the front of his desk. They were drained of blood. His response was cool, flat to a monotone. "I don't know anything about that. And I would have a very hard time believing it."

"You'd swear to that?" Wyatt asked.

"I said I don't know anything about that. I don't have to swear to anything, Mr. Matthews, I'm not in a court of law."

"But if and when you are, you'll swear to that?" Wyatt pressed. "That no one in this prison had any knowledge of a tryst between Blake and Thompson. No rumors, innuendo, gossip?"

"Are you going to subpoena me?" the warden asked, unable to not show alarm. He looked at his watch, made a performance of standing. "I'm busy, Counselor. I think I've given you enough time."

Wyatt remained seated. "If I feel I have to subpoena you, Warden, I will," he told the man calmly. "And other members of your staff, if I feel it's necessary."

Jonas exhaled. He sat back down. "It was alluded to, rumors went around."

"Did you do anything about it? Try to check it out?"

"No." He was back in military mode again, staring Wyatt square in the face without blinking. "You have Lieutenant Blake right there, where you are," he said. "Why don't you ask her?"

"I'm going to." He stared back at Jonas. He had almost been killed by a mob of teenage gangbangers. Facing this man's stare was no threat to him.

Jonas smiled, breaking the Mexican-standoff ice. "That'll be an interesting conversation," he said.

"Everyone talks about this Blake like she's . . . I don't know what. She must be some piece of work."

Jonas massaged his temples. "Look, Matthews. I have no love lost for Dwayne Thompson. He's a reprehensible human being. Using him as a state's witness isn't my idea of good jurisprudence. That's off the record," he said hastily.

"Fine by me," Wyatt answered him. "I'm not after you. I want to find out whatever I can about Dwayne Thompson, and where he might be dirty."

Jonas leaned back, eyes ceiling-bound. He has something to tell me, Wyatt thought, looking at the man's body language, and he's trying to decide whether or not he should.

The warden made up his mind. "Has Dwayne Thompson had access to a computer since he's been down there?" he asked Wyatt.

The question caught Wyatt completely by surprise. "A computer? In the jail?"

Jonas nodded. "Dwayne Thompson is a computer virtuoso. He got a college degree in computer science while in prison, and he was the residential computer pro here for years. He used to run our law library's computer program; he even wrote his own programs. He was the most valuable inmate in the prison system."

"Dwayne Thompson? A computer whiz?"

"Don't let his looks deceive you," Jonas warned. "He has a near-genius IQ. If he had any social or emotional skills, he'd be a force to reckon with in the real world. But he doesn't, so he's only a force to be reckoned with in this constricted world."

Wyatt took a shot. "Is he a hacker?"

"The best," Jonas said grimly. "Which is why he is denied any access to computers in here anymore. We found him manipulating the system in a major, major way."

"How bad?"

"Getting into inmates' files and rewriting them. Changing sentences, release dates. We let two hard-core cons out early because of Dwayne's hacking."

"You're kidding!" Wyatt couldn't contain himself. "I can't believe what you're telling me."

"This is a huge institution, Mr. Matthews. There's no way

we can keep on top of everything. So we did the next best thing—we cut off Dwayne's access, like I said. For the past two years he hasn't been allowed anywhere near a computer. No law library, nothing."

"Isn't that illegal?" Wyatt asked. "To deny an inmate access to the legal system?"

"The law doesn't say we have to give him computer access. We bring him books." He smiled grimly. "He took us to court on it. Fortunately, we prevailed."

"This woman Blake. Is it possible she could have given Thompson confidential information?" Wyatt asked. "That would have helped him?"

The warden shook his head emphatically. "No. We had to check that possibility out, so we looked into that—thoroughly. She had no access to the files. It would have been completely impossible."

"Had to ask."

"I understand."

He escorted Wyatt to the front entrance. "Thanks for your help," Wyatt said, shaking the warden's hand. "You were more helpful than you had to be. And don't worry," he added, "I'm not interested in subpoenaing you."

"Thompson's a piece of shit," Jonas said contemptuously. "That he can help convict another piece of shit doesn't mitigate his worthlessness."

"About Doris Blake," Wyatt began. "I'd appreciate it if—"

"I'm not going to call her and warn her off," Jonas said, anticipating the question. "She's made her bed, so to speak, and she can take . . . whatever comes. It's a shame," he continued. "When you meet her, you'll understand."

"So you're saying they were lovers," Wyatt pressed.

The warden paused. "I don't know what was really going on between Thompson and Blake. Maybe nothing more than a wily con being friendly to a woman who has no male friends. Looking back, I should have done something, gotten her some counseling. But by then she was gone, and the problem didn't exist anymore, since they were physically separated." He shrugged. "This is a maximum-security prison. Every prisoner in here is hard-core, a threat to society who has to be closely watched around the clock. In other words, we're up to our ass in alligators. We have enough trouble here without manufacturing more."

Wyatt was in a state of quiet ecstasy as he cruised down the interstate toward home. What a day this had been! He kept asking himself, over and over again: How could Dwayne Thompson have gotten access to a computer in the county jail, and more importantly, what could he have done with it if he had?

Doris Blake, former Durban prison guard, now a ranking officer in the sheriff's department, was the key. *If* she was in a relationship with Thompson, *and* had fed Thompson information, *and* he, Marvin White's lawyer, could figure out how—it would be adios Alex Pagano, hasta la vista Helena Abramowitz, sayonara Dwayne Thompson. Say good night to your case against my client, Marvin White.

If he could put the pieces together. The big *if*.

Friday-night traffic approaching the city, normal heavy load, plus a major fender bender fifteen miles from his exit that slowed everything to a crawl. By the time he got home it was past midnight. Moira had gone to sleep, leaving him a note:

> *Please don't wake me, I'm getting up early to meet the construction foreman at the store. Michaela went to a dance workshop with her troupe and will be out of town until Sunday P.M. Don't forget to lock up. M.*

Undressing and performing his nighttime ablutions in the guest-room bathroom, he silently maneuvered into their bedroom and slipped under the sheets. Moira lay on her side, her back to him, breathing in deep-sleep rhythm. Lying awake, staring at the ceiling, he began a mental inventory of his forthcoming agenda, in loose sequential order.

He needed to know more about Thompson—he'd been desultory in that regard. Everything he could know about the man. Did he have any family, did they maintain contact with him? There might be good leads in that direction. Get into the specifics of this computer stuff. How good a hacker was Thompson? And how could he have gotten access to a computer in the county jail, and then plugged into . . . what? Did his jailers know about his computer expertise, and had they taken steps to keep his hands off their equipment?

Monday morning he would put Josephine to bird-dogging that trail. Blake he would handle himself. He debated whether he should confront her without warning, a sneak attack to catch her unawares and hopefully rattle her into giving up information she would instinctively want to protect, or go the more official route, formally request an interview as part of the discovery process.

Both methods of confronting her had positives and negatives. If he confronted her and she didn't crack it would be harder to squeeze anything out of her down the line. Conversely, if he went through official channels she would be forewarned, and would have time to dig in her heels and prepare a defense.

He had the weekend to decide. Maybe he'd get together tomorrow with Darryl, brainstorm it with him. Bring Walcott in, too. He didn't want to cut his titular boss out of the loop unless he had to.

He awakened with a jolt. He had been dead to the world. Deep, deep sleep, sleep below the subconsciousness of dreams. It took him a moment to realize where he was—in his own bed. He rolled over and looked at his bedside clock: 3:15. Everything was black, the moon obscured by clouds.

Moira was out of bed, in her robe, fumbling around for something in the drawer of her night table.

"What is it?" he managed to mumble, his voice thick with sleep.

"There's someone in the house," she whispered. Even as a whisper her voice came across angry, hostile, full of recrimination.

"What?" He was disoriented; his body felt heavy, like it was filled with cement.

"There's someone in our house," she hissed again, pointing to the wall near their bedroom door, on which was mounted a keypad similar to the one downstairs. The lights on the keypad blinked green.

"You forgot to turn the alarm on, didn't you?" she said accusingly.

"I . . ." He thought he had. He was sure he had. He had let himself in the front door with his key, locked it behind him, checked the alarm (she had left it off, thinking he would be home sooner than he was), gone into the kitchen to pour himself a small cognac, drunk it standing in the middle of the kitchen, come back out, activated the alarm, gone upstairs.

"You forgot, didn't you?" she asked again in her angry, frightened whisper.

"I . . . I thought I did. Set it," he stammered.

"There's someone in the house. Listen. Downstairs."

He rubbed his head to try to clear the cobwebs. She was right. He could hear noises downstairs. Footsteps, a door opening and closing.

"Someone's broken into our house," Moira said. "We're being robbed."

"Why do you . . ."

"Think that?" she finished for him. "Cloris went to her sister's for the weekend; I gave her tomorrow off. And Michaela is with her dance troupe in East Holbrook, a hundred miles from here. No one else has a key. No one else should be in here. We're being robbed, Wyatt. Just like the Spragues." She started for the bedroom door, her right hand tucked into the pocket of her thick terry robe.

Now he was awake. She was right—what other explanation could there be? He kicked himself mentally for having forgotten to set the alarm, for having taken her fears too lightly. "I'll call the police," he said quietly, reaching for the phone.

"No!" A firm whispering command.

"But we have to," he urgently whispered back.

"By the time the police get here we could be dead."

He listened again. There was definitely someone down there. His heart was pounding.

"Those kids," she muttered.

"What kids?"

"Those kids you brought here. Your killer's friends. They were here, they could look around and see how vulnerable we are."

"They wouldn't break into our house," he protested.

"They're criminals, aren't they? One of them is a big-time drug dealer, you told me that."

"They're working with me," he said, his voice hard with suppressed anger. "They aren't going to rob me."

"Well, someone down there is," she said. "And I'm not going to let them."

She walked out the door, heading for the stairs.

"Moira!" he whisper-called after her.

She didn't respond. He got out of bed, put on his robe, and went after her.

By the time he reached the top of the stairs she was at the bottom. She glanced behind her, hearing him, then pressed forward. He tiptoed down the stairs after her, as fast as he could without making noise.

He had to stop her. She could be in danger.

The noises were coming from the family room at the far side of the downstairs. All of their stereo and video equipment was there, their cameras. Thousands of dollars' worth of top-of-the-line stuff. Silently, resolutely, she moved toward the room until she had reached the door.

He crept across the floor. "Don't go in there," he whispered, but not loud enough for her to hear.

Her hand came out of the pocket of her robe. There was a gun in it.

He was blown away. Where had she gotten that? And when?

Turning her body away and pressing the weapon against her abdomen to muffle the sound, she thumbed the safety off and slid the barrel back, locking and loading.

He lunged forward to try to snatch the gun out of her hand, but she was too fast—she swiveled away from him, pushing him off her with her free hand, the left hand, the hand with the ring finger that had the wedding band and engagement ring on it he'd given her so many years ago.

And then her hand was on the doorknob, turning it, the door was swinging open, and there was a shadowy figure in the family room, standing in the middle of the floor. The curtains were drawn, blackout curtains for television watching, so it was even darker in here than their bedroom had been, all he could see in the dim light coming from the French doors was the outline of someone standing there, someone turning to them in surprise.

The figure lifted a hand. The hand was holding something. It looked like a weapon.

Moira fired.

They heard their daughter scream.

PART THREE

MICHAELA would live. The bullet had exploded in her right thigh, shattering the femur. But she would live.

"There's going to be major reconstruction," the orthopedic surgeon told them. The doctor's name was Lew Levi; he was the best man in the city. He had gotten out of bed in the middle of the night to work on Wyatt Matthews's daughter. They'd sat in the hospital corridor, outside the operating room. Levi was in his scrubs. "We'll know in a few days, once the trauma's subsided and we actually repair the leg. What we did now was to take the bullet out and clear fragments, set things up. We may have to insert a rod—it's called an intramedullary rod—down her femur canal, and there will be pins and screws above and below the fracture, for stabilization. It's going to be a substantial rehabilitation, six months or more," he continued, anticipating their questions. "We have to guard against infection, rejection of the foreign matter, shriveling of the leg. The leg could wind up shorter than the other, a fraction of an inch or so. It's fairly common. But she should be able to walk again, and in general have full range of motion."

"How long will this rod be in her leg, Lew?" Wyatt asked. The shooting had happened hours earlier and he was still shaking inside.

"Forever," the doctor replied. "It will be taking the place of her thighbone, which is the longest bone in the human body." He explained what they were doing presently. "A pin has been drilled through her tibia, and clamps with bows were hooked to weights, so that she's in what's called balanced-skeletal traction. It's to keep the leg to length, so the muscles won't go into spasm and the leg won't shrivel up before the operation."

Moira, who had been in hysterics for hours and then had shut down almost going comatose, stood beside her husband. They had wanted to give her a sedative, but the police still had to question her, and she had to be straight for that.

"I'll go to the station with you," Wyatt said to her after Levi had left.

She shook her head. "Stay with her."

"We'll drive her down and bring her back here, Mr. Matthews," the detective in charge of the investigation told Wyatt. "It won't take long."

Wyatt looked at his wife. She had shrunken into herself, looking like a wraith, her face completely drained of color. "Are you sure?" he asked gently.

She nodded. "She needs one of us here," she said flatly, "and it can't be me." She got to her feet, standing unsteadily. One of the officers put his arm around her waist to make sure she didn't collapse.

He was allowed into the recovery room an hour later. Michaela was propped up on pillows with an IV in her arm. Still groggy from the anesthetic, she mouthed the word "Why?"

Moira was at the police station for three hours. Darryl met her there, stayed with her through the process, held her hand. Charges weren't going to be filed, for now at least—the police and DA's office accepted her explanation. But they would have to go to the house and access the situation before making a final, formal finding.

The press got wind of it. Reporters converged on the hospital, waiting for a statement from Wyatt Matthews, one of the country's most prominent lawyers, who was currently defending the most notorious killer in the state.

He knew they'd be there. He couldn't duck them even if he wanted to, which he didn't. They had their job to do, but they'd have to wait until he was ready. He sat by Michaela's bed, holding her hand until she drifted into sleep from the morphine and sleep-inducing drugs dripping into her system.

Darryl brought Moira back to the hospital from the police station. He took her in through a side entrance to avoid the press. Wyatt was waiting for them outside the recovery room. He and Darryl embraced.

"If you need anything," Darryl told him.

"I'll call you. Thanks for everything."

Darryl shook his head in sorrow. "It's a tragedy for everyone."

Wyatt nodded.

"I'll check on you later," Darryl said. He gave Moira a strong hug and left.

Moira stood near the door to the recovery area. "Can I see her?" she asked in a little, grief-stricken voice.

"Yes," he answered. "She might be sleeping now; we'll see."

"Will she see me?" Moira asked.

"What kind of question is that? You're her mother."

"I was almost her executioner."

"You're going through hell," he told her. "We all are. Don't make things any harder on yourself than they already are."

They sat by Michaela's bed until she came awake again. Michaela looked at her mother. "I should have called and told you I was coming home early," she whispered, her mouth dry from the painkillers.

"Oh, baby!" Moira broke down crying, her head on the covers.

Michaela reached out and stroked Moira's head. "It's not your fault, Mom."

Wyatt stood at the foot of the bed, watching. She's right, he thought. It's no one's fault. Don't ascribe blame. Although it was hard not to.

Earlier, he had talked to the leader of Michaela's dance company, who had called when she heard of the shooting on the radio. One of the girls had taken sick en route, the woman explained, and since they were working as an ensemble they wouldn't be able to perform, so they had turned back and come home, to save the cost of the motel room.

My daughter was shot to save fifteen dollars, Wyatt had thought. Her share of the motel. But he knew that was a lie, a self-deceit. Michaela had been shot because her mother had bought the gun lobby's line.

Don't ascribe blame. He didn't know if he'd be able not to.

Michaela was going to have to stay in the hospital for two weeks, at least. The operation to reconstruct the leg and set the rod and screws was tentatively scheduled for the following week, but Dr. Levi cautioned it could be delayed until they were sure infection hadn't set in. Moira would stay with her during that time, sleeping in her room. Wyatt would commute, coming every day before and after work.

"Dad?"

He looked at his daughter. She was groggy from the painkillers. "What, darling?"

"Am I going to be able to dance again?"

Dancing was the most important thing in Michaela's life. For her not to be able to dance would be an enormous emotional and psychological tragedy.

He glanced over at Moira. She looked away, unable to face either him or Michaela. "I'm sure you will," he told her. "The doctor said he expected you to have a full recovery. But it will take time," he added.

"As long as I can dance when I'm healed."

He made a mental note to make sure Levi didn't say anything to the contrary about that when he saw Michaela. For now he wanted to help her keep her spirits up as much as he could. She had already suffered enough; anything more could wait.

He left mother and daughter and went to the main reception area of the hospital, where the press had been waiting for hours. A small contingent: one crew each from the local TV stations, some radio reporters, a reporter and photographer from the newspaper.

"How is your daughter?" a reporter called out.

"She's doing well," he replied. "She's out of danger."

"What about your wife?" called out another reporter, jockeying for position.

"She's coping. This has been a terrible experience for all of us."

"Why did your wife shoot your daughter?" a third reporter asked.

Wyatt winced at the question. "Our neighborhood has been suffering burglaries recently," he began, launching into what would forevermore be his official explanation.

"Our next-door neighbors were robbed, and one of them was shot and almost killed. My wife was understandably frightened under the circumstances, and bought a gun for self-protection."

He paused for a moment. He was lying—not this part, but the whole tone of what he was saying and doing. Moira had done the worst thing he could think of—she had almost killed their child—and he was standing here protecting her.

He continued. "We thought our daughter was a burglar. It was a tragic, senseless accident." That their neighbor was shot with her own gun wasn't a piece of information he wanted to divulge. He and Moira were grieving. They didn't need to look like idiots as well. "That's all I have to say," he finished. He started to go.

The question, shouted at his retreating back, stopped him. "Will this affect your participation in the Marvin White murder trial?"

He turned. They were all looking at him in anticipation. "Absolutely not. I have a family that needs me, and I'm going to be there for them. And I have a client who also needs me, and I'm going to be there for him as well."

It was almost dark when he got home, but he went for a run anyway. He needed to sweat, to cleanse himself. He ran longer than normal, a hard hour, at the end of the run bent over, spent, gasping for oxygen.

He showered and had a drink, a straight-up Stoli chased with a Heineken. He didn't want anything to eat, he had no appetite. His child, his precious daughter, could be dead. And then, alone, the physical part settling, it hit him: his wife had shot her daughter, the fruit of her own womb. You don't bring life into the world and then turn around and try to destroy it; that goes against all laws of man and God.

It had been an accident. Growing out of honest fear. Don't ascribe blame. It wasn't anyone's fault.

He was fighting something, and he knew what it was: his role in this drama. If he hadn't left the firm; if he hadn't taken on Marvin White as a client; if he hadn't gotten involved in the lives of Marvin White's family and friends, to the point of letting them know it was all right for them to come to his house, which he had to know would scare his wife—if all those things hadn't happened, would Moira have bought that gun, and would she have used it? If only one of those links in the chain hadn't happened, would she have been more cautious?

Don't ascribe blame. Including to yourself.

He walked across the lawn to the pool house, let himself in, and picked up his trombone. His mind started drifting, back to when Michaela was born, when they brought her home from the hospital, a tiny bundle in a pink blanket. Their only child, the first and as it turned out the last time they would come together in that most basic and binding of souls.

He started out playing "Yesterday," then "If I Loved You," and then one of his all-time favorites, "It Never Entered My Mind," hearing the round, warm tones filling the room, filling his heart, bringing solace. He played late into the night, and only stopped because he had to go on with the rest of his life.

The incident was broadcast on the Saturday night local news and appeared on page one of the metropolitan section of the Sunday paper. Wyatt called Walcott at home in advance, so the man wouldn't feel blindsided.

"Where are you with all this?" the head of the Public Defender's office asked with concern.

"Shook up," Wyatt replied. "But she's going to recover, and so will I."

"You're sure?" Walcott asked.

"Absolutely. I'm onto some very serious stuff with the case," he added, "and I'm looking forward to developing it."

"You'll be keeping me abreast, of course." The question came across veiled, as Walcott meant it to be. Don't go out soloing was what he was saying between the lines.

"I'm on your team," Wyatt assured him.

He spent most of the day formulating his theories and figuring out how he wanted to work them. Later in the afternoon he went back to the hospital. Michaela was alert, recovered from the anesthesia-induced grogginess. Moira, her face puffy and tense, was seated at her side. She had a hard time looking her husband in the eye.

"Dr. Levi was by," Moira told him. "He said things were looking good, better than he might have anticipated. He wants to operate on Wednesday."

"Good. I'll make sure I'm free all day Wednesday."

They went out into the hallway to talk. Full of remorse and shame, she told him how she'd come to have the gun. "I bought it at a gun store. It was all legitimate."

"When?"

"After the Spragues were robbed."

"What made you think you would know how to use a gun?"

"I took lessons."

Stunned: "You did?"

"I've been to the police academy four times. They tell me I'm a very good shot." She paused. "Thank God I wasn't."

He was livid. He wanted to scream at her—he could punch her in the face, he was that enraged. "What if Michaela had accidentally gotten her hands on that gun, or one of her friends?"

Shamefaced, she said, "Michaela has . . . practiced with it."

His legs were turning to jelly. Michaela knew about this? His baby? "She has?" he croaked.

"She's been to the range with me. She's a better shot than me. She's a natural."

"Didn't you stop to think of what happened to the Spragues?"

"I was thinking of the Spragues," she told him. "I was thinking of what Enid told me." She stared at the floor. "She told me the one thing she regretted was that she didn't shoot the bastards when she had the chance. Those were her exact words. If you ever find yourself in a similar situation," she warned me, "don't make that mistake." She looked up at him. "I didn't intend to. And so I almost killed our daughter."

He stayed with them until dinnertime. On the way home he stopped at the police station where Moira had been questioned. They had been holding the gun, a .32 automatic, as evidence, but since she wasn't going to be charged they didn't need it anymore. He signed for it and they returned it to him.

Driving home, he felt the weight of the weapon in his pocket. It felt hot, like a hand grenade with the pin pulled out, ready to explode. Navigating the bridge over the Sisquyouc River that was the city-county line, he stopped the car midway and pulled off to the side. He got out, walked to the railing, took the gun out of his pocket, and flung it as far as he could into the water below.

"I met your friend Leticia Pope."

Marvin squinted at him. "Where was that?" he asked suspiciously.

"Dexter brought her to see me." He didn't mention where Dexter had brought her; that was too raw, given Michaela's shooting and all that had provoked it, and where they had met didn't matter anyway.

"She's a 'ho," Marvin said contemptuously.

They were together in one of the small lawyer-client rooms. Wyatt leaned back in his chair, his arms folded across his chest, eyeballing his mindless client. "You don't have much good to say about almost anybody, do you?" he asked.

"Not them dumb bitches," Marvin said.

"What is it, Marvin, if a woman sleeps with you she's automatically crap?"

"No." Marvin squirmed uncomfortably under Wyatt's intense scrutiny.

"Then what?" He leaned forward. "You know, Marvin, there's two women, Leticia and Mrs. Carpenter, who are going to testify at your trial that you were with them on the nights of two of these murders. If you get off, it's going to be because of that, in large part. So maybe you should think about changing your attitude toward them, at least until the trial's over, okay? Alienating either one of them would not be in your interest, pal. Think about that."

"Yeah, okay." Marvin fidgeted in his chair.

"Okay is right." Wyatt pulled a folder out of his briefcase. "The night you were with Leticia. Did you go out to get something to eat, late?"

"Yeah."

"What did you get?"

"Went got some ice cream."

"You remember that?"

"Yeah. Leticia got a sweet tooth."

"She says the same about you. Sounds to me like you two are a good match," Wyatt, said, tweaking Marvin.

Marvin's face scrunched up. "No way."

Wyatt let that go. "Do you remember the flavor of the ice cream?" he continued.

"Rocky road, I think."

"And before that, you saw a movie on television? At her apartment?"

Marvin thought for a moment. His face brightened. "Yeah, it was that Bruce Willis flick. Not *Die Hard*. What do you call it? The monkey movie."

"Twelve Monkeys."

"Yeah, that's it. Bitchin' movie."

Good, good, good. The girl wasn't lying, about the little stuff or the big. He should go by the drugstore, verify that the photo machine had been in proper working order that night—if he could—so that the date on the backs of them would be firm evidence.

He stood up. "Things are going along well," he said. "Your friend Dexter has been a tremendous help."

"Dexter's good people. When I get out of here him and me's gonna be partners."

"I hope not," Wyatt said. "Not in the business Dexter's in now. Because when you get busted for dealing, I won't be around to defend you." This conversation was pissing him off, royally. "Are you ever going to learn a lesson from what's happened, Marvin? Crime doesn't pay, man. Get that through that damn thick skull, will you?"

"I didn't do them killings, damn it!"

"But you did do the botched robbery that got you put in here in the first place, so don't give me any more bullshit, Marvin!" Wyatt shot back. "Just shut the hell up and be a good citizen, even if you have to fake it." He stuck the file into his briefcase. "And another thing. No more talk about the life of crime you're going to lead *when*—let's make that *if,* there's no guarantees you are going to get off, you're not a sympathetic defendant, not the way you've been acting—*if* and *when* you get out of here."

"Yeah, okay," the boy mumbled.

"I'll see you tomorrow." He rang the buzzer to be let out. "Oh. One more thing. Was there anyone else in the infirmary when you and Dwayne Thompson were chatting things up?"

"Guy that runs it," Marvin said.

"The male nurse?" Another potential source of information. He'd try to see him today, along with Blake.

"Yeah." Marvin's face screwed up with distaste.

"He was around when you and Dwayne were together?"

"He was hovering."

"Hovering?"

"Yeah, lurking around. Like . . ."

"Like what?"

"Like every time he'd be checking me he'd be trying to get a look at my pecker, it seemed like. Trying to get his hands on me. Gave me the creeps." Marvin shuddered at the thought of it.

"What about deputies?" he asked. "Were there deputies around?"

"Deputies around all the time. It's a jail, man, what do you think?"

"Is it possible any of them overheard your conversations with Thompson?"

Marvin thought for a moment. "Don't remember that happening," he said. "Stuff like that, you don't talk about it when guards're around. You don't say jack shit when guards are around, they like to use that shit against you."

"But there were deputies inside the infirmary."

"I just said that. It's a jail, the fuckers are everywhere."

"Were there any female deputies in the infirmary when the two of you were together? You and Thompson?"

Marvin nodded. "Yeah, there be one."

"What was she doing? Escorting a prisoner?"

Marvin shook his head. "No, she's a boss. I seen her talking to Thompson."

"A big woman?" Wyatt asked. "Large in frame?"

Marvin guffawed. "Large? Shit yes! That woman is one great big woman! She's practically tall as me."

The guards opened the doors. "I'll see you tomorrow." Wyatt paused. "And work on that attitude adjustment," he reminded his client.

*   *   *

The male nurse first. He'd more likely be a cooperative witness than Blake. If Blake was in any way involved with Dwayne Thompson, she'd be smart not to talk at all.

He presented himself to the duty officer at the central desk, who called Captain Michaelson, the officer in charge. A few minutes went by. Wyatt cooled his heels. He could have simply made an appointment, but he wanted to get at this, and he wanted there to be some surprise to it, if possible.

The elevator doors opened and Michaelson stepped out, a big, burly man with a perpetually suspicious attitude. "How can I help you, Counselor?" he asked politely. The word had come down from the sheriff that Wyatt Matthews was to be treated with kid gloves, no impediments put in his way as long as he was pursuing legal channels.

"I want to interview anyone that's come in contact with my client from the moment he was brought in here," he stated. "Starting with whoever runs your infirmary."

"That'll be up to the parties involved, of course," Michaelson said, "but I can set you up with whoever you want to speak to. If they want to talk to you, fine. If not, you understand they don't have to."

"I know the law, but thanks for reminding me," Wyatt said genially; the unspoken point—I'm the lawyer, you're not—was clearly made.

Michaelson flared crimson. "Anything else?" he asked, his voice neutral.

"Who assigned Dwayne Thompson to infirmary duty?"

"I don't know."

"Can you find out? Someone must have."

"I can try. Who did what and when can get fuzzy, with all the comings and goings in here."

"I would appreciate anything you can do."

"Yes sir. In the meantime, I'll have a guard escort you down to the infirmary." Michaelson picked up the desk phone, spoke briefly. "Your escort will be right up," he said. "I'll be in my office if you need me."

"Thanks. One more thing. Do you have a current roster of your higher-ranking deputies? Captains and lieutenants, people like yourself?"

"Sure," Michaelson said. "For security reasons—which

you can appreciate—we don't release them, but if you'll stop in my office before you leave you can look it over."

The male nurse in charge of the infirmary was a geek, as Wyatt had imagined him. They sat off to the side where the nurse, Hopkins, had his desk. The facility was in a slack period; only a few inmates were awaiting treatment. Wyatt looked for Dwayne Thompson, but didn't see him. He wondered if Thompson was still working the infirmary detail.

"You were here during my client's stay?" Wyatt began. Hopkins had expressed no unwillingness to talk.

"During the day. I don't work nights unless there's an emergency, a lockdown, riot, whatever."

"And Dwayne Thompson? Was he working here as an inmate nurse while my client was in your care?"

"Uh-huh." The nurse worried a fever blister on the side of his mouth.

"Where is Thompson now? Did they transfer him out of here, once he became their witness?"

Hopkins shook his head. "He's still working here, even though I told them he shouldn't be. You shouldn't let an inmate work this kind of job, it's too tempting," the man simpered.

"So why isn't he here?" Wyatt asked. "I don't see him."

"They came down and took him out," Hopkins said. "A few minutes before you showed up."

That made sense, Wyatt thought. They weren't going to allow him to have any contact with Thompson. Even under the discovery statutes he knew Thompson wouldn't be cooperative.

"Thompson isn't bunking here anymore," Hopkins went on. "They moved him out a couple of days ago."

Wyatt had always been disturbed that a prisoner had been allowed to sleep overnight in an unguarded infirmary. "Wasn't that highly irregular?" he asked. "Have they ever allowed a prisoner to sleep here before, since you've been working here? How long have you been working here, anyway?"

"Nine years," Hopkins said. "Bunking in—never. But this place is too overcrowded. They bunk 'em everywhere now. They let guys go before they do their minimum sentence because it's too overcrowded. And they treated Thompson with kid gloves."

"Is the infirmary guarded at night?" Wyatt asked.

"Half-assed—at best. Inmates don't hardly ever spend the night in here. If they're bad enough off that they need that kind of attention they go to the jail wing at Memorial Hospital. Your guy White was an exception."

"So Thompson would have been alone in here at night."

"He'd be here. I don't know if alone. Like I said, I don't work nights. Generally."

Dwayne Thompson had been given virtual free run of the county jail, so it seemed. What else were the authorities doing for him? He'd have to nose around, check that out.

"Who assigned Thompson to work in here?" he asked, the same question he'd put to Michaelson. Maybe this guy would be more forthcoming.

"I don't know for sure." Hopkins's tone said that he had strong suspicions.

"Was it Lieutenant Doris Blake, by any chance?"

The nurse's face flowered. "What do you know about Blake and Thompson?" he asked nervously.

"What do *you* know?"

He looked quickly over his shoulder, a reflex action, suspicious that he might be overheard. "They're cozy, I know that much. Her being a corrections officer and him being a prisoner . . . pretty weird. That's only speculation," he added. "I've never seen them doing more than talking."

"You're afraid of Thompson, aren't you?"

Hopkins's mouth flopped open and shut like a guppy in a mudhole, gulping for air. "You would be, too, if you knew him."

"He's a prisoner. You aren't. What could he do to you?"

"You'd be surprised what cons like Thompson can do. Inside or outside of jail."

"Look." Wyatt leaned in close to the man, who was starting to tremble. "Anything you tell me in confidence is between us. As long as I think you're being straight with me. But if I think you're bullshitting me, friend, I'll subpoena you at trial as a hostile witness, and you'll have to testify under oath, out in the open." He gave the frightened man a reassuring smile. "Make it easy on both of us. Tell me what you know and I'll carry the ball from there."

Hopkins nodded. He understood, but he wasn't happy.

"Are Thompson and Blake having a sexual relationship?" Wyatt asked.

"Yes," the nurse answered in a whisper.

"Have you actually seen them having sex?"

The nurse shook his head vigorously. "No way. I wouldn't watch something that putrid."

"Then how do you know? Intuition doesn't cut it, Mr. Hopkins."

"I heard them."

"When?"

Hopkins leaned forward. "I usually come in a few minutes before seven, that's when we open for business. This one morning, I came in early, I was behind in my paperwork. The door to the infirmary wasn't locked, which I didn't like. I'm very careful about locking up at night." He cracked his knuckles, another nervous tic.

"Go on," Wyatt said impatiently.

"I opened it. It was dark, so I started to turn on the lights. Thompson would have been the only one in there at that time, and I didn't care about waking him up. But before I could flick the switches, I heard them."

"Blake and Thompson."

Hopkins shook his head affirmatively. "They were . . ."

"Having sex," Wyatt finished for him.

"She was wailing like an animal in heat. Really loud."

"It was a woman's voice. You're positive."

"I know the difference between a woman's voice and a man's," Hopkins replied with petulance.

"No offense meant. I have to be certain, you can appreciate that. But you didn't actually see Blake, you said that. It could have been another woman, maybe even a prostitute. The way the system here has been coddling Thompson, I wouldn't be surprised."

"I didn't see them actually fucking, that's true," the nurse agreed. "But I did see Lieutenant Blake."

He paused; Wyatt nodded for him to continue.

"They hadn't heard me," Hopkins went on. "The way she was moaning and shrieking, I could've shot off a cannon and they wouldn't have heard me. So, quiet like a church mouse, I crept out of there."

"So when did you actually see Blake?"

"I snuck around the corner," Hopkins said, "where I could see whoever came out, but they couldn't see me. And sure enough, about fifteen minutes later, out she came."

Wyatt asked a few more perfunctory questions. He had what he needed.

"Thompson isn't going to know what I told you, right?" the nurse asked nervously as Wyatt prepared to leave.

Wyatt shook his head. "Not about this or anything else."

Hopkins couldn't help being fretful. "Guys like Thompson, it's amazing what they can find out. And what they can do, once they do find out."

Wyatt had expected a big woman, but not this big. This was a *grande mama suprema,* John Madden in a bra.

"Lieutenant Doris Blake?" he said, tentatively approaching her. He was almost six feet tall, and she hovered over him. He checked out her hands, her feet, her arms filling out the sleeves of her khaki uniform shirt. Everything about this woman was Bunyanesque. If they were outside in the sunshine, he thought, he could stand in her shadow and his would be invisible.

How difficult, on a daily basis, could life be for a woman who looked like this?

She turned to him. "Yes?" She didn't know who he was.

"My name is Wyatt Matthews." He handed her his card, not the one from his firm, which was embossed, but the one he'd been issued by the Public Defender's office, which was on plain flat paper.

She glanced at it. "Yes?" she said again. It was a yes that implied "Who the fuck are you and why are you bothering me?"

"I'm defending an inmate presently incarcerated in this facility. I've been getting information from some of the deputies here. I spoke with Captain Michaelson earlier, and he gave me a roster that included your name, and suggested that I speak with you." If she checked with Michaelson the captain would say that was a lie, but he didn't think she would do that—it would open up a door, the one to her relationship with Dwayne Thompson, that she wanted to keep closed. Needed to keep closed.

She eyeballed him warily. "What's the name of this prisoner?"

"Marvin White."

It was like he'd poked her with a cattle prod. She flinched—her body language cried out as plain as day. "I don't know why you would want to talk to me about him," she managed to say. "I don't know why Captain Michaelson would think I would know anything that you should know."

They were in the officers' lunchroom, adjacent to the kitchen. Wyatt had waited in the lunchroom for her to show up—the daily duty-roster had informed him of her schedule, and a clerk in Michaelson's office had told him this was where she usually came on her breaks. He didn't come forward until he could see that she was going to be sitting alone. She manifested a lonely, pugnacious expression on her face, as if saying to the world, "You're going to reject me? No. I'll reject you first, before you get the chance to hurt me."

"If you'll allow me to explain," he told her calmly as he slid into a chair next to hers, "you'll understand why." He looked around. About twenty deputies were in the room, having coffee and snacks and gossiping with each other. "Perhaps there's someplace we can go where we'll have more privacy."

"I'm busy," she said, glancing around to see if anyone was watching or listening. "I don't have time to talk now."

"When would you have time?" he asked her, maintaining his pleasant demeanor.

"I wouldn't," she said brusquely. "I don't have anything to do with your client, so I don't have time to talk to you."

He cocked his head and looked at her as if surprised. "You know Dwayne Thompson, don't you?"

Her look turned to one of poorly disguised panic. "What does that have to do with Marvin White?"

"Thompson's a witness for the state against Marvin White, and you know him. You knew him at Durban State Prison when you were a guard there and he was a prisoner, and you got reacquainted with him here. You're not arguing that, are you?"

"No," she answered belligerently. She glared at him.

I'm in good shape, he thought, and this woman could beat the shit out of me. Which is exactly what she'd like to do right now, I'll bet.

She shook her massive head, like a Saint Bernard shaking off rain. "I don't want to talk to you, and I don't have to. Now leave me alone, okay?" She turned her back on him.

"No, it's not okay," he said.

Her body stiffened.

"You do have to talk to me," he informed her, "as part of the discovery process. If you don't believe me, check with a lawyer, or your superiors. So if you don't want to talk to me informally," he went on, boring in on her, "I'll go to court, get an order that will *force* you to talk, and we'll go on the record." He paused to let the seriousness of his intent filter down deep. "But if you make me do that, Lieutenant," he continued, "I'll play a harder brand of ball than I'm playing now." He grabbed his briefcase off the table and stood up. "Screw this. I don't have time to mess around. You'll get your notice by registered mail."

"Wait." Blake turned back to him. She was scared, which had been his intent—her face was an open window to her emotions. She looked around again. A few people had glanced their way, but no one was paying them serious attention. "Not here," she said quietly. "Let's go someplace where we can talk in private."

They sat across Blake's desk from each other. She had locked the door. "What do you want?" she asked him bluntly. "I don't know anything about Marvin White, except what I've read in the papers. I'm not sure I've even seen him. It's a big jail, you know. We have hundreds of men coming and going every day. I don't keep track of them."

"But you do know Dwayne Thompson," Wyatt said.

"Yes, but what does my knowing him have to do with anything?"

He ignored her question. He decided to sidestep the issue for a moment. "You're a lieutenant?" he asked, benignly changing the subject. He wanted to find out about her, to put her at ease with him and help in this interrogation. "Is that what those bars signify?" he said, pointing to her shirt collar.

Her hand went unthinkingly to the bars, fingered them. "Yes," she answered.

"That's a high rank, isn't it?"

"It's okay," she said modestly. "No big deal."

"It seems like a big deal to me," he said, "but I don't know that much about jail hierarchy. Although I didn't see any women's names of your rank or above," he added.

The flattery brought forth a smile. "I am the highest-ranking woman here," she admitted, a touch of pride coming through.

"You must be well thought of."

"I do my job. I haven't had any complaints."

"So your plan is to move up in the system? Do you want to be the warden here someday?" he asked.

She scowled. "No way. I'm already out the door here. I'm just biding my time."

"For what?"

"I'm a lawyer," she said proudly. She couldn't resist adding, "Like you."

He stared at her. "Really?"

She nodded vigorously. "I graduated from law school. Fairfax. Last winter's semester."

Fairfax was the local night law school. It was for people who already had careers and wanted new ones. What he envisioned for Josephine.

"That's great," he said, meaning it. "When do you take the bar exam?" he asked.

"I did," she said. "This spring. And I passed," she added proudly. "With a seventy-six."

"That's a good score. Do you have a job lined up?"

It was as if she were a balloon and he had stuck a pin in her. "No. Not yet."

"Have you sent out résumés?"

She nodded.

Poor woman, he thought, scoping out her situation. Older and unattractive. A bad combination in an oversaturated market. "What about the public sector?" he asked.

She shook her head. "The district attorney's office is full up, and there's a waiting list. I already checked."

"What about the Public Defender's office?"

"I'm a cop," she said. "I don't think I'd feel comfortable working the other side of the aisle."

"You'd be surprised," he told her. "Some of the best defense lawyers I know are former cops and prosecutors. You
guys, better than most people, know what that's like, the
convict's life—what makes a man become a criminal. Like
Dwayne Thompson, for instance," he threw in smoothly. "A
smart man like him, who knows how he might have turned
out if a good lawyer had gotten hold of him at the beginning, before he went hardcore bad."

"Maybe," she said, hoping she wasn't flushing. "I hadn't
thought about it that way."

"I could arrange a meeting with you and my boss," he
offered.

Her entire countenance changed. It was as if a light had
been turned on inside her head, where previously it had
been a dark, empty shell. She smiled, the shy smile of the
wallflower no one is ever nice to. "I'd appreciate that."

He made a show of checking the time on his watch. "I'd
better move this along," he said. "I know you're busy."

"It's okay." She was enjoying the unexpected attention.

"Let's get back to Dwayne Thompson. You knew him at
Durban State Penitentiary?"

Blake blinked her eyes rapidly. "He was a prisoner there
during some of the time when I was a guard, yes."

This was attention she didn't want. She was going to ration
her responses regarding Dwayne Thompson—grudgingly
and warily. He knew that—he was counting on it. He was
deceiving her, so that by the time she understood his true
motive—to get to the core of her personal relationship with
Thompson—she'd be in too deep to get out.

"How well did you know him?" he asked.

She flushed. "What do you mean?"

"You knew who he was. You knew his name, what he
looked like?"

"Yes."

"You knew him better than you knew some of the other
inmates." He was humming along, throwing out innocuous
little facts.

"I didn't say that," she protested.

"You just told me you didn't know anything about Marvin White, that you hadn't even seen him."

She didn't answer.

"Yes?" he pressed.

"Yes," she agreed.

"Durban is bigger than this jail. But you knew Dwayne Thompson, you talked with him on occasion, who knows what else," he threw out elliptically. "So you must have known him pretty well, better than many of the other prisoners."

"Well, yes, I did know him better than some of the other prisoners," she admitted reluctantly. "He was there a long time. Guards get to know prisoners when they're exposed to them over a period of time. Not like in here, where it's a revolving door."

"Makes sense," he conceded. "But you and Thompson were friends, right? Are friends?"

"I know who he is," she flared. "That doesn't make us friends."

"You visited him in the infirmary, where he's working."

Her exhale was caught in her throat—she had to push from her diaphragm to get it out. "Where did you get that idea?" she challenged him.

"Several people told me," he lied smoothly. "Surely you aren't disputing that. I would think it's logical, since you knew each other up at Durban."

She took the bait. "Yes, that's true," she admitted. "I did say hello to him a couple of times down there."

He had a flash of intuition. "Thompson's job in the infirmary. He'd done that kind of work before at Durban, hadn't he?"

"Yes."

"Which was why you thought that would be good duty to assign him to while he was here awaiting the trial he was testifying in."

She recognized the trap he was setting, and sidestepped it. "I don't assign jobs," she said. "That's done by the booking officer when a prisoner enters the system."

This would be easy to check. He'd bet that her fingerprints would be all over this. And if his hunch was right, he could come back and confront her with her lie, and blow her out of the water.

"Okay," he said. "I guess that's about it. Thanks a lot." He picked his briefcase up from the floor. "Oh, one more thing. I almost forgot. Dwayne Thompson knows his way around computers, right? Warden Jonas up at Durban said he was a computer genius—that he even got a college degree in computer science. You wouldn't know if Thompson had any access to a computer here, would you?"

Blake looked him squarely in the eye. "Not that I'd know of," she said.

It was after six by the time Wyatt pointed his car toward the hospital, where his daughter lay recovering. Moira was sitting by the side of the bed.

The television was on to a game show, *Wheel of Fortune*. They never watched shows like that at home. The two women were staring soundlessly at the screen, as if using the distraction to avoid interacting with each other.

"Dr. Levi was by earlier," Moira told him with a forced-bright attitude. "Things look good for Wednesday. And we're going to have a session with a psychologist tomorrow," she added.

"That's a good idea," he said neutrally. Her friend and partner, Cissy, had broached that idea, and to his surprise, Moira had responded positively. She and Michaela needed counseling, together and individually. A wide, strong bridge needed to be built to bring them back together.

He sat down next to Michaela. Her leg was extended in the pulleys and balances of the traction bar. She reached out for his hand. He squeezed back, gently. "How are you, sweetie?" he asked. She has to be so uncomfortable, he thought, lying in this position twenty-four hours a day, unable to move. Why did this have to happen to her?

"I'll be glad when it's over," she confessed.

"Me, too."

"I need to walk," Moira said diplomatically. "I'll leave you two to yourselves."

After she left Michaela clicked the television off. "How's your case going, Dad?" she asked, her face animated, eager to take a break from her own situation.

"Good," he told her. "Making progress."

She nodded. "I'm glad. For your client, and for you. You need a win, Dad."

"I've had lots of wins, honey. You getting well will be my best win."

"I'm going to get well," she said with forced assurance. "Although . . ." She didn't finish her thought.

"Although?"

"I have a premonition that it's going to be a long time before I dance again."

"You'll dance again," he said quickly. "You'll do everything."

"The bone in my leg is shattered, Dad," she said, stating fact.

"You have to keep telling yourself you'll do everything you did before. And you will. Dr. Levi's very confident."

She looked at him. "I've been wanting to say that I'm worried about recovering completely; but I can't to Mom. She feels so guilty."

"I know. I haven't been as supportive of her as I should be," he admitted.

His daughter squeezed down hard on his hand. "Sometimes I get really angry at her," she said, tears beginning to form in the corners of her eyes. "I don't want to, but I can't help it. What if I can't walk again, Daddy?" Her voice was quivering with fear.

"You will, sweetheart. I promise you," he said, bringing as much conviction to his voice as he could muster.

"That gun was like an obsession with her. She even made me go to the shooting range with her." The tears were free-flowing now; he reached over for a towel that was draped over the foot of the bed and held it to her face. "I didn't even know you and she were in the room," she cried. "Why couldn't you have said something, like 'Stop'? I would have said it was me, right away."

She was sobbing uncontrollably. He reached out and drew her to him, cradling her in his arms. She needed to get this out. It wouldn't be the only time.

And what about his own anger toward Moira? How was he going to deal with that? He would need therapy, too, he knew. To get his rage out, deal with it, put it behind him.

Michaela cried for a good five minutes, until the emotion had run its course—this time. She wiped her cheek on her sleeve. "Will you wet a washcloth for me?" she asked him. "I don't want Mom to see me looking like this."

She scrubbed her face and held ice cubes from her water pitcher to her swollen eyes. "I don't want frog eyes," she said to him, grinning through the residue of tears. "Mom's already freaked enough."

When Moira returned, Michaela was looking almost normal again. If her mother noticed anything she didn't comment on it.

He stayed with them until nine, when the night nurse came in with Michaela's sleeping pill. He kissed her good night and held her hand until she drifted off.

Moira walked him to the elevator. A few people passed them, preop patients in wheelchairs, and some postops, all bandaged and wrapped in various patterns. The overhead lighting was turned low; everything was hushed.

"How are you doing?" Moira asked. This ordeal was taking a heavy toll on her; she looked more haggard and wan every day.

"Okay."

"Your work's okay?"

"It's going okay. Seeing her makes me feel better."

"She looks forward to seeing you. It's the high point of her day." She hesitated. "It's awkward between us. I'll feel guilty all of a sudden, the guilt will come like a wave washing over me, and I wonder how she feels. She hasn't said anything to me about it, at all. Nothing." She took his hand, looking at him, searching his face. "You haven't, either."

"This isn't the time," he said.

"I hope you won't shut me out forever," she replied.

The elevator doors opened. Her lips were receptive to his light kiss, more than they had been.

"I won't," he promised, as the doors closed and the elevator took him away.

It was dark by the time Wyatt reached his house, but he went for a run anyway. The night was vibrant with sound. Bullfrogs called to each other across the lake, crickets by the thousands buzzed with a whirrlike rattle, an owl hooted. He knew this road so well he could run it with his eyes closed, and sometimes he did for short stretches, listening to the sounds around him and to his own inner sounds as well, his heartbeat, his breathing, deep inhale-exhale five steps to a breath, feet slapping pavement. He ran on the blacktop road from his house to the main intersection, a three-mile loop. Enough to clear his head, for the moment. Except instead of his head getting clearer, it filled up with thoughts he couldn't avoid thinking about anymore.

His marriage was falling apart. He and Moira had been drifting ever since he took leave from the firm and went to work at the Public Defender's office. Taking Marvin White's defense had exacerbated the situation. And now the shooting. On his way to the hospital this evening he had thought of how much he wanted to be with Michaela, how much he needed her—not her needing him, the strong father, but him needing her, the daughter who needed a strong father. And still, he hadn't wanted to go, because Moira would be there.

As he was approaching his driveway on the final leg of his run he saw Ted Sprague. His elderly neighbor was wrestling a garbage can out to the curb for pickup. Wyatt stopped and helped Ted with the heavy load.

"You need to get a trash can on wheels," Wyatt said.

"The gardener usually does this," Ted wheezed. "He forgot today." He wiped the sweat off his brow with a handkerchief. "How's Michaela?" Ted asked solicitously.

"As well as can be expected. The doctor operates day after tomorrow."

"Enid and I are praying for her."

"Thanks. I'll tell her." He was getting cool, standing there in his sheen of sweat. "I'll see you around."

Before he could finish his jog home, Ted stopped him. "They caught the . . . burglars who did our house," he said. "I thought you'd want to know."

Wyatt was surprised. That almost never happened. You collected your insurance and forgot about it. "That's good. How did they catch them?"

"Trying to sell our video equipment. To an undercover cop. The cops were running a sting, and they flushed them."

"Great. So were they a couple of black kids, like you thought? From a gang?"

Ted looked away, embarrassment spreading across his face. "They weren't kids." He paused. "And they weren't black."

Wyatt took a step back. "Oh?"

The old man shook his head unhappily. "They were white men. Who used to work for the security agency, like you said."

Wyatt stared at his neighbor's miserable face. You bastard, he thought. You and Enid scared my wife so badly that she went out and bought a gun and shot my daughter with it. Which wouldn't have happened if you hadn't been a latent bigot and a coward.

Ted didn't want to hear that; couldn't. So Wyatt merely shrugged.

The old man turned away. "Better be getting back inside. See you."

All the murders had taken place within the city limits, so the files were kept at the city's Department of Records at the old Police Annex, down by the old warehouse district. The sheriff's office ran the jail, that was county jurisdiction, but the detective work was done by city cops.

Wyatt handed the Request for Information form to the police officer in charge of records, an old albino cop named Whitey who was counting the days until his retirement at eighty-five percent pay.

Whitey looked the request over. "You want a list of everyone who accessed the Alley Slasher files? That's a lot of names."

"You do keep track of everyone who removes a file or reads one, don't you?" Wyatt asked.

"Oh, yeah. That's one regulation we don't mess around with, looking at confidential files. You want every name, starting with the first murder?"

Wyatt considered. "I don't need to go back that far." Dwayne had given testimony about every one of the murders, including the last one. "I only need to see the names of anyone who had any access to the files from the time the last murder was committed until now. Make that second to last." Dwayne could have gotten enough about the last murder from the television news to make his claim plausible; earlier than that, he had to have another source.

Whitey smiled gratefully. "That's going to make this a hell of a lot easier. Come back in about an hour. I have to cross-check a bunch of different sources."

Wyatt spent the time in a doughnut shop across the street

going over some notes. An hour later he presented himself again. "Do you have what I need?"

Whitey handed him a computer printout of several pages. "There's a lot of redundancy there," he pointed out. "Some of the detectives working these murders have taken them out dozens of times."

Wyatt leafed through the list page by page, speed-reading the names. City police detectives mostly, some sheriff's deputies from their homicide division, with a few state detectives as well. He came to the last page, read the names thoroughly. "This is it?" he asked, looking up.

"That's everyone."

"There's no way someone could have looked at these records and not got their name on this?"

"Shit no! Like I said, the protocol for taking out confidential files is strict and unyielding. They have to be formally requested, and the request is logged in, whether they do it in person or over the phone."

"No exceptions?"

"None."

"What about people who work here? They couldn't just walk in and take a look?"

"No sir. Not even the chief of police or the sheriff could do that. If you've seen these, your name is on that list. If it isn't, you haven't seen them."

Doris Blake's name was not on the list.

"Thompson, you got a cigarette?"

"You got five dollars?"

"I got something's worth a lot more than one Abe Lincoln. To you."

Night on D-block, the tier where Dwayne was now housed. A crowded, noisy, pestilent hole, like every other cellblock in the old facility. Three men in every space where there were supposed to be two. Televisions hung from the ceiling, broadcasting garbage in English and Spanish. Inmates lounged in the common corridor, playing cards and dominoes, watching the tube, gossiping, passing time. Nothing else to do and forever to do it in. In most of the cellblocks in the jail, like this one, where the inmates were deemed manageable, not in need of constant lock-down, they were allowed out of their cells from wake-up to lights-out (which was a figure of speech, because the lights were never turned out completely). Some of the men on this tier had been in the place long enough that they had gradu-ated to trustee status. They worked day jobs, manning food trays and working in the kitchen and laundry. Trustee status gave them a range of movement within the huge complex, considerably more than that of the normal inmate.

Smoking wasn't allowed but the men did it anyway, under the noses of the guards, who were powerless to stop it—there were too many convicts and not enough jailers. Cigarettes were contraband, valuable. So were whiskey and drugs. All found their way into the system. Prisoners weren't supposed to engage in sex, either, but at this moment several acts of fornication, not all of them consensual, were taking place in various cells, and other locations.

Dwayne was bunking alone—one of the perks of his situation. He had three cartons of Marlboros stashed under the mattress in his cell that had been brought in by various men entering the system and passed on to him, courtesy of his friends at Durban. The deputies knew he had this shit and could have busted him easily, anytime—he wasn't hiding it very stealthily. But the word had come down from the top on the day he was moved into this block from his cushy accommodations in the infirmary: Leave this man alone. He's important to the district attorney, thus important to the sheriff. Getting along with Alex Pagano was smart politics, and Sheriff Lowenthal was one of the smartest men in city/county government, which was why he kept getting reelected.

"Tell me what you want to tell me," Dwayne told his fel-low inmate, a weasely Latino junkie named Raul who was awaiting trial on selling a small quantity of drugs to an undercover cop, "and I'll decide what your information's worth." Raul was a compliant, laid-back guy who never gave anyone shit. He'd been a short-order cook on the out-side, and recently had made trustee, cooking meals in the huge kitchen.

Raul trusted Dwayne, in the oblique fashion of one con trusting another. Dwayne was doing his current stretch at Durban, which meant he was a lifer in the system, which meant, in the particular fashion of the world of these men, that he was a stand-up guy.

"They had me cooking lunch in the deputy's mess this afternoon," Raul said, "and this guy comes in, this civilian. Nice suit, good haircut, sharp shoes. Lawyer type. He sits down next to one of the officers, they start talking. Then after a while they leave there, and go someplace else. Together, just the two of them. The way this deputy is looking around, it's like being seen talking to this lawyer wasn't something she wanted people picking up on."

Dwayne's antennae shot up. *"She?"*

"So Lester, this other cook working alongside me," Raul went on, ignoring Dwayne's interjection, "he says to me, 'You know who that was with that deputy? It's that hot-shit society lawyer who's defending that kid they got upstairs in maximum security, Marvin White.' "

It was hot as hell on the tier, but Dwayne felt a chill all of a sudden.

Raul picked his nose with his pinkie, regarded the booger with a critical eye, wiped it off on his orange jail-issue sweatpants. The trustees wore orange to differentiate them from the regular population, who were clad in puke green. "You're part of the case against this kid White, ain't you?" he asked Dwayne. "I figured it's worth a couple cigarettes to know White's lawyer was in here, nosing around."

Dwayne disregarded Raul's previous question about his participation in the trial. He forced himself to breathe deeply, normally. "The deputy he was talking to. You said it was a she. Who was she?" He was able to keep his voice from going frantic; he couldn't let this piece of shit see him losing it.

"Can I have my cigarette first?" Raul asked coyly.

Dwayne leaned over and hooked his index finger under the other man's chin, pulling Raul close to him, inches from his face. "The name of the deputy," he intoned.

Raul choked out the answer. "It was Man-mountain Blake. You know who she is," he gasped.

That's why he had been pulled out of the infirmary this afternoon, for no discernible reason. That lawyer must have been down there, talking to that pussy-lipped nurse. And that simpering little shit definitely had stories he could tell. The infirmary nurse was nothing, though, compared to

Blake, to what she could do if she cracked. She could destroy him.

Dwayne let go his hold on Raul, who slumped back, massaging his throbbing chin. That Thompson is one strong fucker, Raul thought, it felt like his jaw was almost broken from one fingerhold.

Dwayne maneuvered his way through the cluster of rancid bodies and slipped into his cell. A moment later he came out with something cupped in his hand. He and Raul shook. Dwayne withdrew his hand and moved away, to a place of darkness and solitude.

Raul glanced down. "Thanks, man," he called out softly.

Snake-eyes had given him a half pack of cigarettes, fresh out of the carton.

Wyatt awoke before dawn. He hadn't slept well. He felt alienated in his own house. It was empty—no wife, no child. Since the shooting, and Moira's staying at the hospital with Michaela, Cloris had been coming in a couple hours a day, but she puttered around because she had nothing to do. She had waited for him last night, in case he wanted her to cook him some dinner, but he had sent her home, instructing her to come in every third day, that he wouldn't need her on a daily basis.

The first shafts of morning sunlight broke through the tops of the trees to the east. The kitchen glowed from it, the pale yellow light moving perceptibly across the floor. Normally this transformation from darkness to light would have elevated his spirits, but today it didn't. It was just light on a floor. He was not tuned in to seeing or feeling beauty this morning.

He didn't want to be here. He especially didn't want to be here alone.

He called his office at the firm. As it wasn't even seven, no one was in yet, not even the hard-charging young associates. The answering service connected him with his secretary's voice mail. "Annetta, I'm going to be staying in town this week, while Michaela's in the hospital. Book me a suite at the Four Seasons, starting tonight."

The firm was still family, his real home other than this

one. Over a hundred lawyers and secretaries had called or sent cards of condolence. He had spoken to all the senior partners personally. They were all there for him and his family, whatever they needed. Talking to Ben Turner, he had thought about what this all meant—leaving the security and prestige of his job, alienating his wife, putting his own life on the line. Was he really getting what he wanted out of this?

He packed enough clothes to get him to the weekend. He'd come home then and do laundry, look at the week ahead. He also brought a few changes for Moira, casual, comfortable stuff. He knew she wasn't going to come home, either, until she could bring Michaela with her. The sounds of her gun firing and Michaela screaming were playing over and over inside her head, he was sure of that.

Nothing left to do but leave. He set the alarm and drove away.

At the hospital he told Moira about his temporary move to the hotel for the week; to be closer to the hospital and his office was the reason he gave her. The unspoken reason, that the house was haunted by demons, was best left alone for now. Later, when their lives were back on a more even keel—*if* they were, an open question—they could talk about those demons and figure out how to exorcise them.

She accepted his explanation without question—he knew she wouldn't have been able to stay there alone, either, if their roles in this tragedy were reversed. He remained for forty-five minutes, talking mostly to Michaela. Moira used his presence as an excuse to get some exercise walking the hallways. The vibe she was throwing, under the husband-wife togetherness veneer, was "I can't be in the same space with you." Or "I'm afraid to be." Same difference, it felt like.

The operation was scheduled for tomorrow, seven in the morning. Michaela was getting scared about it, about what the outcome might be. Again he reassured her, as best he could, that everything was going to be fine.

Moira returned from her short exile. They talked inconsequentially for a few minutes, avoiding anything personal or substantive; then he left and went to work. As soon as he was out of her presence he felt relieved, and hated that he felt that way.

He spent the first part of the morning with Walcott, who climbed the stairs to his office, noting with amusement and admiration the jerry-built game-plan apparatus he and Josephine had built. Stacks of cardboard file boxes crammed with copies of all the detective reports from all the rape-murders, dozens of them, hugged the walls outside their offices. Photos of the various crime scenes were taped to the walls above the cartons, and photos of the victims were taped on one of his interior office walls, as was the huge crime-scene aerial map, with pushpins stuck in where each assault had occurred.

And there were seven sets of photos, two or three per victim, side by side: in one, the victim as she had appeared in life, taken from various sources—high school yearbooks, family-album-type pictures, pictures taken on the run by friends. Some smiling, some serious, some looking straight into the camera lens, others taken when the subject was unaware. Those were the best ones—there was real life to those pictures, and to the people in them.

Then there were the police photos, one per victim. What they looked like in death. Features distorted—bulging eyes, black-and-blue eyes, lacerated jaws, fractured necks. Sad, brutal photos.

The pictures were arranged in sequential order, from the first murder to the most recent one. Walcott studied them.

"This feels more like a prosecutor's wall than a defense lawyer's," he commented. "What's the point?"

"They're part of the package. I want them to be my allies. Allies from the grave, as it were. We've already alibied Marvin for two of these killings," he added, tapping the pictures of the two women who had been murdered on nights when Marvin was with Mrs. Carpenter and Leticia, "and I'm hoping we can find more." He walked over to the set of pictures of the most recent victim, Paula Briggs. "The videotape of the robbery," he said, tapping his knuckle on Paula's face, in the picture taken of her when she was alive, "that's our alibi for this one, if it comes to that."

Walcott frowned. "How do you figure that?"

"The time frame. It's too tight. I know it's doable, but it isn't reasonable. Maybe it would be by a cold-blooded killer who murders by a stopwatch, timing his movements to the minute. But not a kid. Don't forget, Marvin was sixteen when half of these murders occurred."

"Don't compute that into the program," Walcott cautioned him quickly, his tone fearful. "It's pouring gasoline on a fire."

"I'm not going to—unless there's no choice."

"Abramowitz may use that tape herself," Walcott mused out loud. "It's strong evidence that Marvin set out to do a crime that night. Did one, in fact. That he botched it doesn't mean he didn't attempt it. Still, I see your point about the timetable; but I don't think a jury would. I think it would backfire on you, reminding them that Marvin was all set up to murder someone else that night, and actually tried to."

Wyatt changed the subject. "I've started to get some real dope on this Dwayne Thompson character." He filled Walcott in on his trip to Missouri, his discussions with the ex-Durban prison guard, his conversation with Warden Jonas. When he got to the stuff about Blake, her connections to Dwayne, the diminutive defender became excited.

"This is strong stuff," Walcott enthused. "Do you think she could have fed Thompson information about the murders?"

"I don't know. She isn't listed as having accessed the police files, but I'll bet there's ways that could be gotten around without having your name on the list. And that we can use."

Walcott clapped Wyatt on the shoulder. "Good going."

Wyatt smiled. "She wants to be a lawyer," he said. "Actually, she already is."

"Who?"

"Doris Blake. The female deputy sheriff in the jail. She graduated Fairfax Law last semester and just passed her bar exam. Did well, too—she scored a seventy-six, which has to put her in the top ten percent.

Walcott gave him a funny look.

"She hasn't had any luck hooking up with a job, which explains her still being a deputy," Wyatt continued. "So far she's only been trying the private firms. If you saw what she looked like, you'd understand why she's been shit out of luck. She did try the DA's office," he remembered, correcting himself, "but they're way over budget on staffing, and they've got a three-year waiting list."

"If she graduated last semester," Walcott said, pursuing his own chain of thought, "that means she would have taken the spring bar, in March."

"That's what she told me."

"The spring bar results haven't been released yet," Walcott informed him. "It takes four months—they won't be out until July. We have two recent applicants on tap that we want to bring in. They both took the spring bar exam, and we haven't been able to officially hire them yet."

"Maybe I got the dates mixed up. Because she definitely knew her score."

"You had to." Walcott checked his watch. "I've got appointments piling up. We should mock-trial in about three weeks. Can you be ready?"

"I'll do my best."

Walcott turned to go, then turned back. "I forgot to ask—how's your daughter?" His concern seemed genuine.

"As good as can be expected. The operation's tomorrow."

"I'll light a candle for you."

Wyatt watched him go. He's not a bad guy, he thought. I've been selling him short. Then he thought, Who else have I been selling short?

The early-morning infirmary rush had come and gone. About a dozen inmates sat in various areas, awaiting examination, treatment, release to their tiers or jobs. The doctor moved from one to the next with his practiced bored efficiency. He handled the more serious cases. Dwayne worked alongside him, dispensing medicines, bandaging minor wounds, taking notes that the nurse would follow up on.

The nurse himself took care of the prisoners whose problems were minor. Throat swabs, bandage changing, eye care—easy stuff that was a waste of the doctor's time. He had successfully avoided direct contact with Dwayne all morning long, although Dwayne had let him know, when he'd come down to start his workday, that they had business to discuss.

"I have done all I can for these poor unfortunate souls,"

the doctor announced in a stentorian W. C. Fields voice to Dwayne and the air as he rolled his stethoscope and tucked it into his bag. "And now, kind sirs, with your permission, I shall take my leave."

Out of here in fifteen minutes, in the bag in forty-five, Dwayne thought. "Have a good day, Doc," he said. "Hoist a couple for me."

The doctor belly-chuckled. "I shall, my friend," he said with hearty bonhomie. "I shall, indeed."

As soon as the doctor was gone the nurse began busying himself with paperwork, studiously avoiding Dwayne. The tattooed wonder finished his treatments of the last of the patients the doctor had left for him and walked down the buffed linoleum floor to the nurse's workstation, positioning himself over the nurse's right shoulder. The way the light fell from the ceiling cast his shadow over the nurse's pages—a foreboding presence.

Hopkins ignored Dwayne as long as he could. "What do you want?" he asked finally, studiously not looking up from his work.

"You had company down here yesterday afternoon. They pulled me out of here for no good reason. Which meant you were meeting with someone they didn't want me to know about, is how I figure it."

Hopkins sat dead still, not moving a muscle.

"Marvin White's lawyer?" Dwayne stated. "Was that who was down here? He was here a while back, before Marvin's shit hit the fan. Then he was down here again yesterday, jawboning you." He paused. "Wasn't he."

The nurse's voice rose high, in fear. "I don't know what you're talking about. I've got work to do," he said with as much conviction as he could muster, "and so do you, so I suggest you get to it."

Dwayne put a hand on the man's shoulder, the tips of his fingers touching the collarbone, a light but firm touch.

Hopkins froze. "Take your hands off me," he managed to say. His heart started going a mile a minute.

Dwayne increased the pressure slightly, his fingers pressing on the man's thin clavicle. "What did you tell him?" The fingers stayed where they were.

He could snap my neck like a twig, the nurse thought. "He wasn't down here," the man lied. He had to lie—he couldn't tell what had happened, or he would be a dead man for sure.

"Don't fuck me around, pussyface. What did you tell him? Did you tell him anything about me?"

"What would I tell him about you?" Realizing he'd almost given his lie away, Hopkins continued hastily, "If he had been here, which he wasn't."

"What I do." Dwayne paused. "Who comes to see me."

The nurse turned as best he could, considering the pressure on his throat, and looked at Dwayne. He was scared completely shitless now. "Who comes to see you? What's that supposed to mean?"

He couldn't mention Blake by name. As far as he knew, no one had ever seen them down here together, not in a compromising way. "Anyone. Anything."

Hopkins pulled himself together enough to turn and face Dwayne. "Who comes to see you is none of my concern," he said, "and I want to keep it that way." He turned further in his chair and looked up at the pale face staring down at him, the dead milky blue eyes that were locked into his own. "If you're doing anything in here that's illegal I don't want to know about it, okay? Just don't involve me in your crap. Now for the last time—take your hands off me. Or this will be your last day working down here," he threatened: an empty threat; there was no weight to his actions.

"Where I work is not up to you, ace," Dwayne reminded him softly. "And if you ever do talk to anyone about me— anything about me—you'll regret it later. Are we in synch here?" He hovered over the nurse a moment longer, slowly increasing the pressure on the man's clavicle.

The pain was almost unbearable. The nurse wanted to scream, but his throat was paralyzed.

Dwayne leaned down, his lips touching the nurse's right ear. "I can kill you anytime I want," he whispered. "Which no one will do a thing about, because your life isn't worth shit compared to what they need from me."

And then he pressed down, one sharp pressure-point jab.

The pain was excruciating. The nurse couldn't even scream; he was unable to breathe—it was as if all the air had been sucked from his lungs. He fell to the floor in a ball, writhing in agony.

Dwayne knelt down next to the injured man, a hand at the

nurse's mouth to shut him up in case he caught enough wind to cry out. "That's a calling card, ace," he whispered. "A reminder of how we understand each other."

Leaving the nurse in a fetus ball on the floor, Dwayne walked to the door and called out to the hallway for the guard. "You'd better call the ambulance, man. Hopkins fell off his desk trying to change a lightbulb. I think his neck's broke or something."

Blake was the one Dwayne was worried about.

She came down midmorning—he'd gotten word to her through the prison grapevine, once Hopkins had been taken away. The nurse hadn't said word one to rebut Dwayne's account of how he'd almost killed himself.

"I need to speak to this inmate," Blake informed the deputy who was guarding the facility. "It'll only be for a few minutes."

"Yes, Lieutenant," the deputy said deferentially.

"I'll take him to my office," she said.

As soon as they were alone in her cubicle and she had closed and locked the door (another infraction, but getting caught flagrante delicto would be much worse), she came to him, trying to engulf him in her embrace, but he sidestepped her and moved away.

"Not now," he said sharply. "We've got to talk." He nodded toward the door. "You'd better unlock that. We get caught behind locked doors, we'll be in more trouble than we already are."

She walked over and undid the lock. "What kind of trouble are we in?" she asked, panic smothering her. "Did something happen down in the infirmary?" The word of the nurse's accident had circulated throughout the place.

"That was a real accident," Dwayne lied. He looked hard at her. "What did you and that hot-shit lawyer talk about yesterday?"

He had confirmed her unacknowledged fear. She had been waiting for this shoe to drop since Matthews had braced her in the lunchroom.

"I . . ."

"I know you talked to him, so don't lie to me, Doris." He crossed to her and held her hand. "I'm not mad. You couldn't not do it. But I need to know what you told him."

"He knew I'd worked up at Durban and asked if I knew you there."

"What did you tell him?"

"That I did. I'm not going to lie about that, that's stupid. He already knew that, he was testing me to see if I was lying to him."

"Okay," he conceded. "What else?"

"He asked about your work here, in the infirmary. Whether or not I got you the job."

"And what did you say?"

"That I didn't. Which is the truth, luckily."

"But if he finds out you wired it so I could bunk here, that wouldn't be so lucky. That would be a lie."

"Don't worry about that," she said. "That's not a big deal. I knew you at Durban, I knew you were working in the infirmary there, the jail's overcrowded. It's not a big deal, Dwayne. Don't worry, he isn't interested in that," she added, trying to convince herself that was so.

"The hell he isn't! Lawyers like him don't ask questions about things they're not interested in. Every question he asked you had a purpose, Doris." He exhaled a loud whistle, jittered on the balls of his feet.

"I can cover that," she said. "Believe me, it is no big deal."

"Yeah? We'll see. What else?"

"He wanted to know if you'd had any access to a computer since you'd been brought down here. Warden Jonas up at Durban told him about your computer expertise."

"Son of a bitch!" he uttered under his breath. "Did he say anything about hacking, anything like that?" How much had Jonas told this lawyer about him?

"No," she answered. "He just wanted to know if you'd been on a computer at all."

"What'd you tell him?"

"That to my knowledge, you hadn't." She paused. "And he believed me."

"How the fuck do you know that, you dumb bitch? Since when did you become a licensed mind reader?" he said viciously.

Her neck flushed red from the force of the insult. "Because he didn't ask me about it, except that one question," she answered, holding on to her composure. "That's not what he was driving at; but he couldn't ask me what he really wanted to ask me, because he's not allowed to, it's outside his legal boundaries. I may not have passed the exam, but I actually do know the law."

"Really?" He looked at her with arched brow. "So this big question he wanted to ask you but couldn't—what was it?"

"Did I feed you information, of course."

The telephone rang. She picked it up. "Blake," she spoke. She listened a moment. "Yes, I have him here." She looked over at Dwayne. "Yes, I'll be returning him directly." Another pause. "Not a problem." She hung up.

"Who was that?" he asked suspiciously.

"The duty officer for the infirmary. They're changing shifts. Just wanting to make sure you're still on the reservation." She looked at him and sighed. "I can't wait to leave this hole," she said.

"Me, too," he echoed for sentiment.

"That was what he was leading up to—Matthews," she said, getting back on track while reassuring him and herself. "Whether or not I'd helped you shape your case."

"Well, you don't have to lie about that," he said, relieved. "Because you didn't."

"No."

"All right." He started mollifying her. "I'm sorry I came down on you like I did, but this is heavy shit for me, baby. This is my only ticket out of here. Otherwise, I'm buried forever."

"I know," she said softly, her heart going out to him.

"About your computer. That's one thing they can never know. Never." He engaged her, eye to eye. "For both our sakes."

"I know that, Dwayne. Believe me, I've had my sleepless nights over that."

"It's okay, Doris," he reassured her—she was worried about the bar exam. "No one's ever going to know." He wasn't going to explain otherwise.

Wyatt went to the jail at lunchtime. "Lieutenant Blake? Got a second?" he asked, plopping down next to her in the deputy's cafeteria again.

She jumped. He had snuck up on her. "Yes?" she answered. She hoped he didn't notice that she was shaking.

"I spoke to my boss about your coming to work at the Public Defender's office," he said cheerfully. "Do you recall our conversation about that yesterday?"

"Of course I remember," she answered, relieved.

"He thought it might be a good match. He wants to meet you."

"He does?" She felt faint. "When?"

"Well, not for a few weeks," he apologized. "We're swamped with other things right at the moment." He lifted his gaze to the ceiling, in the direction of the maximum-security unit where Marvin was housed. "But I thought I'd get the ball rolling by getting hold of your transcripts, so we can look them over. Do you have a copy of your law school grades, with any favorable comments on them from your professors?"

"Yes, I have a copy at home. I could mail them to you, or fax."

"I'm here almost every day, seeing my client," he reminded her. "I'll catch you some time when I'm around."

"All right," she said. "Thank you. I really appreciate this."

"We can always use another good lawyer. Let's see, that was the winter quarter you graduated?"

"Yes."

"And that was the spring bar exam you took?"

"That's right."

"Good, good." He stood up. "When you bring those grades in," he said offhandedly, "don't forget to include a copy of your bar exam score." He reached out and shook her hand. "See you around."

"The bar exam score," she repeated dumbly, the enormity of her gaffe hitting her in the forehead like an anvil. She'd stuck her tit in the wringer; hopefully he wouldn't squeeze the handle.

"We need it for the record. To make sure you're legal," he winked, to let her know he was teasing her.

"I . . . uh . . . I don't know exactly where that is."

"Oh?" He looked puzzled.

"I'm in the process of redecorating," she ad-libbed frantically. "My stuff's all over the place."

He nodded understandingly. "No big deal. As I said, we can't take any action on an application for a month or so anyway. Whenever it's convenient."

She nodded.

"In the meantime, we'll send you out an application. Do you want me to send it here . . . since you're moving?"

She searched his face for any sign of skepticism. She didn't find any.

"Yes. Send it here." She had a month. By then the bar exam scores would surely have been published, and she could finesse her screwup.

Before leaving the jail Wyatt made one other unscheduled stop.

"Thanks for seeing me without an appointment," he said, leaning across the desk and shaking Sheriff Lowenthal's hand. "I know how busy you are."

"You're lucky you caught me," the sheriff answered. "I'm on my way out of town, for a conference. This is not a social visit, I presume."

Wyatt and Lowenthal were superficial friends, as Wyatt was with everyone in the local political/legal establishment, as he was (had been) with Alex Pagano. He got along fine with the sheriff, but they had never been in an adversarial situation before. As the county's head cop Lowenthal was a main player in the prosecution and incarceration of criminals. He and Pagano were a smooth team. Wyatt Matthews was on the other side now, therefore an enemy. Nothing personal. When this was over, and Wyatt returned to the corporate world, they'd be superficial friends again.

"No," Wyatt answered. "This isn't a social visit."

"I hope your client isn't complaining about the way he's being treated. We're bending over backward to make him as comfortable as possible, under the circumstances."

"No," Wyatt said, "he's not complaining about that. His beef is about being here at all. What I wanted to ask you is how is it that a key prosecution witness, a convicted felon, is working in your infirmary and has the run of the place?"

"Do you mean Dwayne Thompson?"

"Yes."

Lowenthal shrugged. "He was qualified to work there and we needed the help. That's not unusual. It sounds like you're sore that he was in a position to hear your guy's confession, not about whether his job is suitable or not."

"That's part of it, I admit that. But it still seems unusual to me."

"It is what it is—was. We weren't violating any regulations." He checked his watch. "Listen, I've got to go. When this is over we'll have lunch."

Wyatt got up. "One other thing."

"What's that?"

"I can understand Thompson working in the infirmary. I don't like the circumstances, but I see the rationale. But why was he sleeping there? What possible benefit could there be to your organization in that?"

Lowenthal shot him a look. "Who says he was sleeping there?"

"You didn't know?"

"Where did you get this information?" the sheriff asked. He was clearly upset.

"It's common knowledge."

"Not to me." He gave a snort of exasperation. "I'm always the last one to know about these things. Which doesn't make me happy, I'll admit that." He escorted Wyatt to the door. "I'll look into it when I get back from this conference. It's not a big deal, Wyatt," he added hastily, "don't get thinking you've got something here, because you don't. But I'll see what's going on and take the proper steps to remedy it." The sheriff stood up. "I'll get this straightened out." He opened his office door. "Your client is guilty, Wyatt. We're not going to screw this up on any technicality."

Wyatt stopped at the hotel to check in and drop off his gear, then drove over to the hospital. It was a few minutes before four. Dr. Levi was in Michaela's room when he arrived, with a retinue of orthopedic-surgery residents, interns, and nurses.

"Ah, the paterfamilias is here," Levi called out when Wyatt entered the crowded room. Moira was standing off to the side, observing everything with a worried eye. "We just finished explaining the schedule to your daughter, Wyatt." He was holding Michaela's hand. The doctors made room for

Wyatt to slide by them so he could take her other hand. She squeezed it tightly.

"How are you doing, sweetheart?" he asked, his voice reassuring. He glanced over his shoulder at Moira. Her face was blank.

"Okay, Dad. I'm nervous, but not too much."

"You're going to come through like a champ," Levi told her, his demeanor sunny and bright. "Everything looks good."

Thank God for this man, Wyatt thought, looking at his daughter. Being with Moira all day couldn't be good for Michaela's spirits; her mother was walking around with a perpetual black cloud over her head. He needed to spend more time here.

Levi led his entourage out. Father, mother, and daughter were left alone with each other.

"Anything I need to know?" he asked. He felt awkward; he knew Moira did, also.

"We saw the psychologist," Moira said.

"How did it go?" he asked guardedly.

"Okay. I mean . . . Rome wasn't built in a day. She wants to meet you. You should be participating, at least some of the time."

"I know. I'll try." He hadn't thought about the need to see a therapist.

"My adviser came by earlier," Michaela volunteered, feeling the tension and changing the subject to deflect it. "She brought me some books and a schedule. They're going to send a tutor to the house when I get home, so I can keep up. And Ramona came by, too." Ramona was Michaela's dance instructor. Michaela had been six, not even in first grade, when she had started ballet lessons. That seemed like another lifetime ago.

Michaela looked over at her mother, who was staring out the window. "She brought me that, from all the girls." She pointed to a table by the bathroom door. A huge teddy bear sat on the table. The bear was dressed in a pink tutu and toe shoes.

He smiled. "Very cute."

The afternoon slid by slowly. All three of them were in a torpor, awaiting tomorrow's unknown. No one said much; Michaela was tired, while Wyatt and Moira were locked in their own thoughts. Wyatt had instructed Josephine not to put any calls through. Nothing couldn't wait until midday tomorrow, after the operation.

Michaela was served dinner shortly after five. She picked at her food; she had no appetite. None of them did. A couple hours later the nurses began prepping Michaela for the operation. They added a tranquilizer to the painkiller dripping into her vein through the IV and in minutes she was asleep.

Wyatt and Moira stood outside Michaela's darkened room. The corridor was quiet; patients were sleeping. Visitors, except those, like Moira, who were spending the night, had gone home. Moira sagged against the dusty-peach walls that had been painted with an eye to cheeriness, although now the place felt sterile, like an exhibit under glass of preserved life, not life itself.

She needs you, he thought. And you should need her, too.

He didn't feel need, so he manufactured it. He pulled her to him and held her in a hug, feeling her weight sag against him. It felt like dead weight. "She's going to be all right," he whispered through her hair.

Moira was crying, sobbing soundlessly. He held her tighter, not saying anything, letting her cry. He held her after she finished crying, waiting for her breathing to come back to a semblance of normality.

"I'm going to go now," he said. "I'll be back by six tomorrow morning."

She nodded. They walked back to Michaela's room, his arm around her shoulder. "Take care," he said.

She stared at him. "Don't leave," she asked.

"There isn't room for both of us here. I'll spend the night with her if you want to go home and take a break from this."

She shook her head. "I didn't mean that."

He looked at her.

"Don't leave me."

He pulled her close again. Her heart was fluttering under her skin like a hummingbird's. "I'm your husband, Moira. I'm not leaving you." He held her for a minute, rubbing her back. "I'll be here first thing in the morning."

He kissed her again. She went into their daughter's room, which was dark except for a low-wattage night-light near the floor. It reminded him of Michaela's bedroom, when she was small and slept with a Mickey Mouse night-light.

The night-light was burning, so she should feel safe. Or at least have the illusion.

Sheriff Lowenthal called Doris Blake into his office. "Close the door."

She shut it and stood in front of his desk, trembling like a leaf.

"Why did you authorize the prisoner Dwayne Thompson to have the run of our infirmary?" he asked. Lowenthal was a decent guy and liberal by law-enforcement standards, but he could be brutally tough.

"I didn't do that," she stammered. "The assignment officer did. When Thompson was transferred to our facility from Durban."

"That was a *work* assignment. Not sleeping there overnight, with no supervision. I've been informed you made that transfer."

She squared her shoulders. "Yes sir. I did do that."

"On whose authority, may I ask?"

Go for it. It's your only chance to escape this alive. "I thought yours, Sheriff."

He was on his feet like she'd lit a fire under his ass. "What gave you that notion, Lieutenant?"

"I knew he had been assigned to work in the infirmary, and I also knew he was to be . . . protected. Because of his importance to the district attorney's office." She was thinking on her feet amazingly well, which was unusual for her. "There had been some unpleasantness on his tier. Someone had found out he was a stool pigeon, and his life was threatened. I thought you had requested he be moved to a location where he would be safe. Since he was already working in the infirmary I thought that would be a safe place. I did make that decision, sir, but I thought it was following your and the district attorney's guidelines, if not explicit orders."

He stared at her. She stood stock-still in front of him. Sweat was pouring from every orifice.

"You were wrong," he said finally. "I never gave any such orders, direct or implied."

"I'm sorry, sir. I apologize."

He calmed down some. "All right. It was an honest

mistake—I hope. That you knew this man at Durban doesn't help you, Blake."

"I only knew him as a guard knows a prisoner, sir."

He looked at her but didn't say anything. "I'm going to let you off with a reprimand," he said. "This time. But if you have any more contact with this prisoner—any—you will be suspended, and you may be fired. Your conduct is certainly cause for either of those actions. Am I clear?"

"Yes sir."

The sun had come up early and clean, breaking through the morning clouds. Wyatt watched it enter the horizon line as he drove from his house to the hospital. It was going to be a beautiful day. Hopefully, an optimistic day.

He and Moira sat in the operating section visitors' lounge. Wyatt tried to go over some notes but he was too antsy, so he worked on the daily crossword puzzle. Moira had *The Recognitions* with her and was slowly reading, from time to time looking at the clock on the wall, then at her watch, as if by doing that the time would pass faster.

Levi's prognosis had been three hours. At nine Wyatt went down to the cafeteria and brought back two cappuccinos and croissants—neither'd had breakfast; they had stuck like glue to this room, to be as close to Michaela as possible.

At a quarter to ten Moira got up and started pacing. To the elevators, to the nurses' station, down the length of the hallway and back. She tried to sit, but she couldn't. He watched her, and felt his own anxiety rising.

The clock struck ten. Their eyes swung to the double doors that led to the operating area. Willing Levi to come out, with a smile on his face.

Ten-ten. Ten-twenty. The doors remained closed, no one entering or exiting.

"Something's wrong," Moira fretted. Her voice was on the verge of breaking.

"Nothing's wrong," he said, almost furiously, trying to be reassuring, to her and to himself as well. "If there was something wrong, they'd tell us about it."

"If there was something wrong they'd all be working as hard as they could to make it right," she countered.

"They wouldn't have time to come out here and schmooze with us."

"Nothing's wrong," he said again. He spoke to her back; she was up and pacing again. He walked over to the nurses' station. The nurse, a middle-aged Jamaican who had an air of authority about her, looked up at him. "Everything is fine," she reassured him in a lilting voice before he could ask the question. "We've been monitoring the situation. There's no cause for concern."

"Okay," he said. "Thanks."

Moira saw him talking to the nurse and hurried over. "It's under control," he told her. "They're monitoring the situation."

Moira turned to the nurse. "What does that mean?" she asked. "Why are you monitoring the situation?"

"Because you might be worried, and I want to be able to tell you not to," the nurse answered her.

"Whether I should be or not?"

"We wouldn't tell you she was all right if she wasn't," the nurse answered calmly. She was used to families being on edge; soothing them was the most important part of her job.

They sat down again. Wyatt didn't want to look at the clock, but he couldn't help himself. He watched the second hand sweep across the face, number by number. Five seconds, ten, twenty, thirty, another minute gone. Five seconds again, ten, thirty.

Moira was slumped over in her chair. "I don't like this," she muttered to herself. "I don't like this."

She got up and paced again, marching like a soldier. Wyatt tilted his chair back until he hit the wall behind him. He closed his eyes and started deep-breathing.

Wham! The double doors burst open. Wyatt jumped out of his chair. Levi came striding through.

Wyatt looked up at the clock. It was 11:15 in the morning. The operation had gone on almost fifty percent longer than had been anticipated.

Levi looked at them. Then he smiled. "That one was a bitch," Levi admitted. "But she's going to be fine," he added, reading the concern and fear on their faces. "She is a strong, strong trooper. You two should be proud of her."

"It took so much longer than you said it would," Moira said. "Is she going to be all right?"

"Yes, Moira. She should recover completely—full range of motion and feeling."

Wyatt grabbed Levi's hand and shook it vigorously. "Thank you, Lew. I can't tell you how much your help and support means to us."

"Yes, Lew," Moira added, remembering her manners. "Thank you," She kissed him on the cheek. "When can we see her?"

"She'll be out of it for a couple of hours. Why don't you two take a walk? It's a beautiful day outside. Michaela isn't going anywhere."

They found a small, quiet park on the hospital grounds and sat on a wooden bench that had a commemorative plaque attached to it and took in the sunlight and the smells of the grass, which had been freshly cut. Moira slipped off her canvas shoes and stretched her bare feet out on the grass, leaning back on the bench for support, her arms splayed out to either side, eyes closed to the almost high noon sun. Wyatt looked at her. Her face was beginning to relax, the first glimmer of a smile he'd seen on her lips in days, from the moment the gun had fired and Michaela had screamed.

"Do you feel better?" he asked.

She nodded, her eyes still closed. "I'm ready to go on now," she said. "I haven't been for days."

"We need to thrash all this out, so we can put it behind us."

She nodded again. "But not this minute. Right now, I just want to feel alive again."

Michaela came to three hours later. They visited with her in the postop room. There were dozens of stitches along the side of her leg where it had been opened up, and she was wearing a heavy knee brace. Screws had been put in the bone above and below the fracture to hold the rod in place. The leg was in a traction device attached to the bed.

Relieved that she was in no immediate danger, Wyatt headed over to the jail. He wanted to begin tracking Dwayne Thompson's comings and goings, from the moment he had entered the facility to be a witness in another trial until when he had gone to the grand jury and testified against Marvin White. He tried to put himself in Thompson's shoes. You've come down here from Durban to testify in a trial whose origin goes back several years. The DA working the case is going to sit with you, prep you. A ton of paperwork to review, documents to refamiliarize yourself with, including your previous testimony. Where do you do that inside these walls?

"Afternoon, Mr. Matthews." The duty officer greeted Wyatt professionally. "How can I help you?"

"I'd like to get a look at your law library. You do have one, I assume?"

"Yes sir." The officer, a sergeant, paused. "May I ask for what purpose?"

"To see what you've got there." He didn't elaborate. "Is there a problem?" he asked, putting an edge on his question.

The duty officer knew the drill—treat this important lawyer with respectful deference as long as he didn't ask for anything improper. Checking out the jail law library didn't seem like an improper request. After all, the man was a lawyer.

"No, no problem. I'll have one of the deputies walk you down."

It was a decent-sized library. He had never been in a jail law library so he had no frame of reference to judge it against, but it seemed to be adequate for the needs of the inmates here, who weren't doing long stretches and researching intricate, lengthy appeals. He looked around the facility, gazing at the various books and legal journals. Most of the code was there, along with a random sampling of other material. Fairly comprehensive, but half a decade or more out-of-date. Criminal law had gone through a lot of changes recently, he knew, although until now it hadn't been his field. It would be a bitch trying to do anything on your own out of this place.

Along one wall there was a row of computers on a long table, bolted down. Old 386s, good enough for word processing but nothing more sophisticated. A couple of inmates were hunched over the machines, typing into them. Wyatt noticed that none of the computers were connected to outside telephone lines. The only telephones in the room were public pay phones, which were all occupied.

He approached the deputy who was monitoring the room and introduced himself. "Can I ask you a couple of questions?" he inquired pleasantly.

The deputy in charge looked at the other deputy, Wyatt's escort. The escort deputy nodded approval. "What do you want to know?" the library custodian asked.

"Who has access to this library?"

"Inmates who need to."

"What determines that?"

"The sheriff."

"What is his criterion?"

"There's different ones. Usually an inmate's lawyer will file a petition asking permission for a specific reason. We don't like them hanging around. Some guys would stay in here all day if we let 'em."

"What percentage of inmates use the facility?"

"Not many. Ten percent or less. Most of the doofuses in here, they're not sophisticated enough to put what we have to use. And since we're a jail, by the time they'd work something up that could do anything for them they're out of here, either sprung or sent to a regular prison facility. Mostly it's men who have a long wait before their trial's coming up, because of delays, postponements, continuances."

Wyatt thought about that for a moment. "Does every prisoner have to sign in and out every time he uses the place?"

"Absolutely."

"One more question. Do these computers have modems? Can anyone connect to the outside through them?"

"The answer is no and no," the deputy said. "That would be like handing a pyromaniac a can of gasoline and a book of matches."

Wyatt nodded, thinking. "Can I use your phone to make a call? It's local."

The deputy shook his head. "Sorry. Only authorized personnel can use this. I have to keep it free, in case of an emergency. You can use a pay phone." He pointed to the bank of pay telephones on the far wall.

"I thought inmates had use of the telephone free of charge."

"They do, up in their cellblocks. In here they have to pay. The county hasn't put in free phones here yet. Funding's held up," he explained. He opened his desk drawer and took out a spare quarter. "On me," he said, handing it to Wyatt.

Wyatt waited until a telephone was free, then called his office. Josephine answered on the second ring. "Where are you?" she asked.

"In the law library at the county jail."

"Don't tell me they finally caught up with you," she teased.

"Shhh." He smiled. "Look something up for me. I don't have my calendar, I had to check my briefcase with the front desk."

"What do you need?"

"Look up the dates from when Marvin was arrested and booked into the jail until the date Dwayne Thompson went to the grand jury. I'll hold on." He took out a ballpoint and a small reporter's notebook from his inside breast jacket pocket.

He leaned against the wall, gazing around. A few inmates looked him over. They don't know who I am, he thought. He didn't want them to.

Josephine came back on the line. "Okay, I've got it. April third to April eleventh. Anything else?"

"That's it for now." He jotted the dates down in his notebook. "See you later." He hung up and walked back to the deputy on duty, who was chewing the fat with his escort. "How far back does your sign-in book go?" he asked.

"First of the year."

"Can I see the sign-ins for the dates of April third to April eleventh?"

The deputy shook his head. "That's against regulations." He nodded toward the inmates. "To protect confidentiality. You could get a court order," the deputy said helpfully.

"Maybe I will." He turned to his escort. "I'm done here."

The hospital wasn't far from the jail. Wyatt swung by on his way back to the office. Michaela was back in her room, propped up on pillows, watching television, an old Katherine Hepburn movie on HBO. She quickly clicked it off as Wyatt came in. He had a bouquet of roses with him.

"A rose by any other name . . . ," he quoted. Moira wasn't there, he noticed.

"Thanks, Daddy. You're always so thoughtful."

"What were you watching?" He arranged the roses in a plastic water jug, filled it from the tap, and set it up on the windowsill. The afternoon sunlight caught the facets of the flowers, glimmers of light playing among them.

"An old movie. My favorite kind. I'm not supposed to be watching," she said guiltily. "I'm supposed to be studying." She pointed to the pile of books arranged alongside her bed. "Keeping up. I don't want to fall behind, more than I already have."

"Don't get crazy over schoolwork. There's plenty of time for that. Where is Mom, by the way?"

"She went to her store. She wanted to get a look at how things were going."

He cocked an eyebrow.

"I told her to," Michaela said. "We're starting to get on each other's nerves."

"She's going stir-crazy," he agreed. "I could stay here some evenings, give her a night off."

Michaela looked at him. "I'd rather neither of you stayed."

"Oh?"

"I'm only going to be here a few more days. Dr. Levi told me they're discharging me on Monday."

"That's good—coming home, seeing your friends."

She nodded. "Sally, Claudia, and Jasmine came by earlier. It was really good seeing them. I miss my friends, Dad. I miss my life."

"I'll bet."

She worried the hem of her top sheet. "You and Mom aren't getting along well, are you." Her statement was declaratory, not a question or an accusation.

He wouldn't lie to her. "No. We're not."

"Are you thinking of separating?" There was a vibration to her voice.

"No." He paused. "But I think we need time off from each other," he admitted.

"I hate her sometimes." There was a concealed venomousness to her statement, which took him by surprise—not that she felt it, but that she'd express it so baldly.

"That's natural." Now it was coming out. "That's why you're seeing someone professional."

She pushed up on her pillows, adjusting her position. "Do you want to know one thing that really bugs me about Mom? It's like *she's* mad at *me*. For being there to be shot. Like it was my fault she did it." The words came pouring out as fast as she could spit them out. "It's like she can't take the responsibility on herself, you know? Like we're all supposed to share in this guilt trip, so she doesn't have to feel so bad."

"That's a natural reaction. She has terrible feelings of guilt. That's how people deal with it sometimes."

Even as he said that he thought, *Why are you explaining Moira's actions away? You feel the same way Michaela does. Moira committed the deed. She should take the responsibility.*

"Let her deal with it somewhere else than around me. It's like she's guilt-tripping me. I don't deserve it." She rapped her knuckles on her brace. "I've got enough shit to carry around right now without her shit, too."

He had never known Michaela to be so angry. "I know how you feel."

"Doesn't it bug you, Daddy, the way she's been? With me, with your work, with everything?"

"Yes, but there are things I do that bug her, too. We all bug each other, that's how it works in families."

She got in the last word. "Shooting someone and almost killing them is different than bugging them."

He stayed with her for over an hour. They turned the television back on and watched the end of the movie. As the orderly was wheeling Michaela's dinner in, Moira telephoned. Michaela answered it. "Hi, Mom." Her voice wasn't enthusiastic. "Okay. Yeah, he's here." She passed the phone over to Wyatt.

"How's the store?" he asked. He listened for a minute. "That always happens in construction, you have to deal with it." He listened some more, at one point pulling the phone away from his ear and smiling at Michaela, who smiled back. He felt a pang of guilt about doing that—conspiring against Moira, particularly at this unsettling time in their lives, wasn't helpful. Even if it was a minor conspiracy.

"I'll talk to you later." He hung up. He hadn't said "I love you" or "I miss you." Neither had she.

"Mom'll be here soon, hon," he told Michaela. "Tell her how you feel. Without getting angry, if that's possible," he advised.

"Why should I have to worry about her feelings?" Michaela demanded. "I'm the one lying here with a steel rod in my leg. She's out with her friends, pretending like she's a serious businesswoman."

"That's harsh."

"That bookstore is just so she won't get bored. Mom doesn't want to run a business."

"Maybe she will. Maybe this'll be a change for her." He wasn't going to admit to his daughter that he agreed with her. Those were issues for him and Moira to work out on their own—if they cared enough to try to work them out.

He kissed her on the cheek. "See you tomorrow."

"Bye, Daddy. Love you. Thanks for the pretty flowers."

"Love you, too."

The following morning he arrived at the office shortly after eight. Josephine was already there, waiting. "You want to see something really bizarre?" she asked.

"Will it make my day?"

"Or break it," she said portentously, handing him a sheet of paper with the sheriff's official logo stamped on the top. "Everyone who was seeing Dwayne Thompson in the jail. It wasn't easy to get this, because it's confidential material. Actually, your seeing it is probably a violation of jail regulations."

"My conscience is clear—clear enough for government work, anyway—and you're not going to tattle on me, so let's not worry about it." He glanced at the single page. It looked like some kind of roster. There were only a few names on it.

She watched him attentively as he read the list.

The name jumped out at him like it was etched in neon lights ten feet high. "Holy shit!"

"My exact words," she said.

"Are you sure?"

"Positive. I've used my source before. He's totally reliable."

"What could this mean?" The name was burning a hole in his brain.

"I don't know. But it's heavy."

"Heavy?" he repeated. "This could change everything."

Wyatt stood across the street, watching the gate where she would come out. He checked his watch—five more minutes. He had been standing there over half an hour, checking his watch every couple of minutes. It didn't make the time go any faster.

The shift ended. Hundreds of workers came out of the plant. They all exited the same main gate, heading for the block-square parking lot across the street. She would have to pass by him.

He waited a long time. People went by him to their cars, singly and in small groups, talking or not. In the wind the residue of their occupation drifted to him. It burned his nostrils, a dark pungent tang. What a way to make a living, he thought.

Finally, after twenty minutes, she emerged from the front door, came out the main gate, and headed for the parking lot. She was alone, and her hair, uncovered, was damp, glistening in the late-afternoon sun. She wore a simple T-shirt, baggy shorts to the knees, thongs. Seeing her again, in this unadorned outfit, her full figure unself-consciously presented to the world, reminded him of how she had turned him on when they'd first met.

She's showered, he realized, watching her approach him. So she wouldn't carry the smell into her car and home.

She was coming closer, but she hadn't recognized him. He was hiding in plain sight, a man on the street. When she was three paces from him, about to pass by, he stepped out and approached her.

"Excuse me. Miss Waleska?"

She turned to him, squinting for a moment, her hand in a salute over her eyes to shield herself from the sun, which was shining in her face. Then she brightened in recognition. "Mr. Matthews?"

"Yes."

"I have to ask you some important questions," he said without preamble.

She knew there was something wrong—she saw it in his face. "My place isn't far from here."

Her apartment was on the second floor, up a flight of stairs. He followed her, his eyes drawn to her behind and her calves. He had the feeling she knew he was watching her in this way. If that either annoyed her or made her self-conscious, she didn't show it.

"Can I get you something to drink?" she asked, dumping her day pack, which was what she used for a purse, on the pine table in the small dining alcove. She had stopped downstairs to take her mail out of the box; she flipped through the stack, set a couple of pieces aside. The rest got tossed into the trash. "I'm going to have a glass of white wine, if you don't mind." She stepped into the small kitchen, temporarily out of his line of sight.

"Not right now, thanks." He felt like a cop about to confront a suspect. A cop wouldn't have a drink with a suspect, would he? Especially while he was on duty.

"Anything else? I've got beer, soft drinks. I think there's a bottle of Scotch around somewhere." He heard the popping of a cork, the pouring of a glass of wine.

He drifted into the living room and sat on a white canvas-covered couch. A nice couch, the kind you buy from an Eddie Bauer mail-order catalog. The apartment was small, clean—when he had looked into the kitchen he'd seen that she'd done the dishes before she went to work. Made her bed, too, he'd bet, and neatly folded the towels in the bathroom. The apartment was specifically furnished, meaning everything had been picked out with a purpose—a special vase, with fresh flowers in it, detailed picture frames with photos in them of friends, mostly women. She was in some of the pictures. He noticed the murder victim in one of them, along with this woman, Violet Waleska, and another woman. There weren't any children in any of the pictures, and no older people who might be parents. No brothers, and the women weren't sisters—there was no resemblance. She had no family, none she was close to. Her life was her friends.

"On second thought, if you can find that bottle of Scotch, I'll have a taste. A small one." What the hell—he wasn't a cop, and this visit wasn't official. Pagano would have a hemorrhage if found out about it. That didn't matter now. It was something he had to do; as soon as he'd seen her name on that visitation list he knew he had to confront her directly.

"I found the Scotch," she called out. "Why don't you come in here and pour the amount you want."

She handed him the bottle—Cutty Sark—and a glass. He poured a conservative two fingers. "Do you want ice?" she asked.

"One, thanks."

She opened the freezer, took out a single ice cube between thumb and forefinger, and daintily dropped it into his glass. Then she led him back into the living room. He sat down on the couch again, in the same indentation he'd made earlier. She sat across from him in an easy chair that was covered in the same white canvas material. Slipping her feet out of her thongs, she curled her legs under her. He noticed she was wearing blue toenail polish—an offbeat touch that, for reasons he didn't understand, pleased him. Except that who she was—her aura, her vibe—pleased him.

"Cheers." She lifted her glass in salute, took a sip. He nodded and raised his own, but didn't drink. First he'd ask her why; then he'd drink.

He set his glass down on the coffee table in front of him. She leaned forward and moved it onto a coaster. Then she leaned back in her chair again, staring at him over the rim of her glass.

"Why did you visit Dwayne Thompson in the jail?"

She stared at him, her mouth open in a silent O.

"Unless this is all a setup."

She shook her head.

"Dwayne Thompson is the state's case against my client. Without him, they have nothing. Your testimony, about seeing Marvin White outside the club that night, is incidental. They think it can help them, buttress their client. I don't know, you can look at it both ways, helpful or hurtful, I plan to try and use it against them, but who knows? That's not the point. Why were two witnesses brought together, Miss Waleska? What did Alex Pagano tell you the reason was for bringing you and Dwayne together? He's not supposed to do that; it could screw him up, pardon my French. Unless," he said, leaning forward, elbows on knees, "he wanted to make sure your stories checked out, that you don't contradict each other."

"No," she said, shaking her head.

"Or is it all a plant? Your testimony, Dwayne's. A story made up in the back room of the DA's office and given to two people who have their own reasons to see my client put away. You, because your friend was murdered and you want someone to pay for it; Dwayne, because he's going to spend the rest of his life in prison unless he gives them something so juicy, so important, that letting him out is the lesser of two evils."

She looked up at him. "There is no evil greater than Dwayne Thompson. I know that better than anyone." She nodded at his glass. "I think you'd better have that drink. There's more where that came from. Which you may want, after you hear what I'm going to tell you."

She went back into the kitchen, came back with her wine bottle and his of Scotch, and set them on the coffee table, side by side. She didn't bother putting coasters under them. "This will take a while."

"Take your time. I'm not going anywhere."

She squirmed in her chair, trying to get comfortable. Unable to do so, she sat back, collapsing into herself. She took a deep, preparatory breath.

"I wasn't always a butcher in a slaughterhouse," she began. "I was a professional, a college graduate. I was a nurse, a good one." She paused momentarily. "I was the first member of my family to graduate from college," she said with pride in her voice. "I was looking forward to marriage, children, the life I'd always dreamed of."

In her previous career as a nurse, many years before, when she had started working in the hospital, especially when she had passed her exams and become an operating-room nurse, and then the head of her section, a prestigious, high-paying job, she had thought she would marry a doctor, one of the surgeons she worked with. Other nurses had. It was a reasonable expectation.

It hadn't happened. She wasn't what they wanted, those

stars of the operating theater. She was attractive—she had a full, voluptuous figure and a pretty (if unrefined, she had admitted to herself long ago) face; she was smart, funny, nice. What man—a doctor particularly, doctors always went for lookers—wouldn't be interested?

The answer, as it turned out, was that few were. Not seriously, as in getting married, having their babies. Oh, they would sleep with her; happily, eagerly, with great hunger and desire. She had done that for years before she wised up and realized that sleeping with men you worked with was a bad idea, a dead end. You lost stature, became a topic for seedy gossip.

But that was bullshit, a lame excuse. There was a major reason none of these doctors had ever gotten serious about her. She had a past—a man in her life, a sick, violent bastard who thought he owned her. He had been part of her life forever, and she had never been able to shake him. An upwardly mobile doctor doesn't bring a woman with that kind of man in her background home to mother, even if she is smart, pretty, and charming, and has excellent manners and a master's in clinical/surgical nursing.

Many years earlier she'd had her one big romance. A resident, a surgeon, of course, a nice man, quiet, very shy, even a little dull—an atypical surgeon—but sweet, and he cared for her like she'd hung the moon.

Despite all her efforts to keep that part of her life a secret, the man from her past found out about her relationship with the sweet doctor. He stalked them for weeks, without them ever knowing it. Then he made his move. Out of sheer evil and possessive sickness he waited outside her apartment building one evening while her shy doctor lover kissed her good night and came outside, heading for his car. She lived in a decent, quiet neighborhood; her lover had no reason to expect trouble.

The first blows hit the doctor like a pallet of bricks falling off a roof. The sick bastard had jumped him—blindsiding him—and for ten minutes solid he proceeded to beat the poor man, who'd never raised a hand in anger, within an inch of his life. .

"You're fucking Violet? I'll fuck you up, shithead, I'll fuck you up so you'll never fuck anyone again." Fists rain-

*ing down, long after her lover had collapsed into uncon-
sciousness in a flood-pool of his own blood.*

*The damage had been extensive. Recovery was slow—it
took months. The doctor's hands had been broken so badly,
especially his thumbs (the son of a bitch knew exactly where
to cause the greatest damage), that he couldn't use them
in his work, and had to quit practicing surgery. He moved
all the way across the country, as far away from her as
possible, and became a teacher of doctors. And from
that same night, when she'd gone rushing into his intensive-
care room, out of her mind with fear and grief, and had
been told in a firm voice by the nurse on duty that he'd given
instructions that she was not to see him, she had never laid
eyes on or heard from him again.*

Not once.

*More than a decade later she still thought about him some-
times; mostly when she was lonely, but occasionally out of
the blue, for no conscious reason.*

She would have made him a great wife.

That was life.

*The word about her spread like an out-of-control brush-
fire. For months afterward, people passing her in the hospital's corridors would look at her the way you look at a train
wreck. No one blamed her—not to her face, anyway—and
her lover's assailant went to prison. But that was it for the
possibility of snagging one of the hospital's doctors for a
husband.*

*She never saw the attacker again, except to testify against
him at his trial. The few letters he sent her from prison, early
into his sentence, she threw unopened into the trash, and she
obtained a permanent restraining order against him.*

*After a while he figured it out and stopped writing. She
hadn't heard from him in years. If she never heard from him
for the rest of her life, she'd be happy.*

*But she'd had to give up nursing. The burden was too
much to carry. All those years of studying at night, the giving up of having fun to stay in and hit the books, because
she was going to rise above her station—gone.*

*She went to trade school and learned how to be a butcher.
The work was bone-tiringly hard in the huge slaughterhouse
where she'd been employed the last seven years, but it paid
well. It was a union job, she made over twenty dollars an*

hour, plus good health benefits and a pension plan. A single woman needed to plan for her medical and retirement.

Now and again she dated men she met at parties, at church, social functions. Nothing serious came of any of these encounters; the men weren't up to the standards she'd worked so hard to set.

She never dated men from work. The image of the smell from the floor, on them and her both, had no romance to it. And besides, she had a college degree.

Wyatt poured himself some more Scotch. A generous amount this time. He freshened up Violet's drink, too.

"The man who attacked your doctor . . . friend—that was Dwayne Thompson."

She nodded her head.

"Dwayne Thompson had been your lover, before you and the doctor met up," Wyatt continued. "Dwayne couldn't stand the thought of losing you to another man. So he made sure he didn't." He felt sick to his stomach as he thought of the ramifications of such a vile action; even worse was knowing that she had been romantically involved, regardless of the circumstances, with Thompson.

She looked up at him. "Not my lover," she said. She drank down her glass, poured herself another, drank it. Then she started crying: loud, gut-wrenching sobs.

If I'm being set up, he thought, it's a masterpiece. Setting his drink down, he went around the table and put a consoling hand on her shoulder.

She rose up and fell against him, wrapping her arms tight against him, pressing her body against his, head to toe. She was shaking, her fingers digging into his back, holding on as hard as she could. He could feel her tears on his neck.

He shouldn't be holding her. He shouldn't be here at all. He could get thrown off the case, disbarred, his career ruined, his marriage as well.

He held her tight to him, his hand on the back of her head, caressing the still-damp hair.

They stood there like that for minutes, until she stopped shaking. Then she looked up at him, her eyes raw.

"Not my lover," she said again. She buried her head in his chest. "My brother."

*   *   *

They talked for hours. About everything, no pattern, no order. Who they were, where they had come from. He talked mostly about his work. She talked about her work, her friends, the things she liked to do. It was all easy and comfortable, as if they'd known each other for a long time.

The conversation (as it had to) got around to the upcoming trial. "I have no ax to grind," she said, "except I want to see whoever killed Paula and the others put away forever."

"Why are you so sure Marvin is the killer?" he asked, feeling anxious. They had built up a reservoir of good feelings, and he didn't want to burst the bubble. But he had to know.

"I never said he was. They asked me to come down and see if the man I'd seen in the parking lot that night was in their lineup. And he was."

"You're sure."

"Absolutely."

He wasn't about to contradict her—Marvin had already told him he'd been in the parking lot and had been accosted by a white woman. She was the woman, that was certain. "What can you tell me about Dwayne?" he asked her, moving the conversation toward his primary target.

"He's evil." She shuddered. "He always was, since I can remember. No one in our family could ever understand how he was that way. It was genetic, right from conception. Like he came from somewhere else and got dropped in on us."

"He's a liar."

"To the marrow. Dwayne never told the truth if there was a lie he could think of, even when telling the truth would have been easier for him. He's a liar, a user. He's hateful. Pure hate."

"Could he be . . ." He wanted to say "making this up," but that wasn't the fit he was after. He couldn't have made his story up; he had the facts.

"If someone fed him the information he'd run with it," she said, anticipating his line of thinking. She paused. "Do you think someone did?"

"I don't have any other explanation."

"Unless your client really is the killer, and really did tell Dwayne. Isn't that a possibility?"

That was the state's entire case, so of course it was. "It's a possibility," he said, "but I don't believe that's what happened." He could tell her about his belief regarding Marvin's inability to retain all those specific facts, years after they had occurred, but there was no reason to. She wasn't the jury.

He was at a dead end here.

He excused himself and went into her bedroom to call the hospital. He couldn't come tonight, he had to work late, interviewing a witness. He'd stop by in the morning.

Michaela was fine with that. Her father was in pursuit of justice. Moira could care less about justice. All she knew was that her husband wasn't going to be with her again tonight, that she was stuck in this crummy hospital room with no relief. She had major cabin fever: she was sick of the hospital food, sick of take-out Chinese and pizza. She'd call Cissy. Cissy could come by and take her out for a few hours.

It was painful to listen to her, even though he knew her complaints were legitimate. In a few days Michaela would be discharged and they could go home, be a semblance of a family again—her description.

If Moira knew what was really going on, she wouldn't be thinking of them in family terms, even lousy ones. She'd be hiring her own lawyer, or blowing his brains out with a new gun.

He disengaged from the call as rapidly as was judicious; he didn't want to hear it. The guilt of lying and deceit was too painful. He wanted to hear about this other woman, Violet Waleska.

"You changed your name," he said to Violet, coming back and sitting next to her.

"Waleska was my mother's maiden name. I changed it during Dwayne's trial. I didn't want to have anything to do with him anymore. I especially didn't want to have the same name."

"If you didn't want to have anything to do with him, why did you go see him now, after all these years?" This was the question that had been nagging at him: why had she gone?

"Because I couldn't believe it was him. After you let slip his name that time I came to your office I called the district attorney's office. They confirmed it. I almost had a heart attack; but I was drawn to go down there, I had no choice. I know that sounds stupid, even crazy, but I don't have any other explanation. Why does the moth fly to the flame, when he knows it will kill him?" She leaned toward him. "How do you think I feel? That the person I hate the most in this world turned out to be the same person who was going to be the one to convict my best friend's murderer. It was too surreal. I had to see him in the flesh to know it was true."

He sat back, looking up at the ceiling.

"You don't believe me," she said.

"Would you? A man you hate so much you changed your name so you wouldn't have any connection with him? Who you completely lost touch with over the years, by your choice? Who almost killed the only man you say you ever loved?"

"I can't help what it sounds like," she answered. "It's true."

"And it was," he said. "The same man."

Bitterly: "Yes. You don't know how horrible I feel about that. You have no idea."

He got up and paced around the room. "You're a hell of a woman," he told her, "but I have to think this could be a setup, even an unintentional one. Let's face it, I'm out on a limb here the way we've been with each other. This has gone way past professional propriety."

She nodded in understanding. "If I was setting you up why would I admit that Dwayne was my brother? No one knows that, I've taken great care to make sure of that. The District Attorney's office certainly doesn't know it," she said emphatically. "Look, Wyatt . . ."—it was the first time she had called him by his first name—"I would never have told you this stuff if I wanted to mess things up."

If that was true—and he believed her, he realized that he did believe her, because he truly believed her or because he wanted to, it didn't matter—Pagano would shit his pants. And where did this information put him? He was defending Marvin White, whom she was going to be testifying against.

"You can't say that with certainty," he responded to her declaration. "You don't know me. I'm the lawyer for the man accused of raping and murdering your friend. I'm going to have to cross-examine you, and that's going to be a bitch now—for both of us."

A colossal understatement. That she was the sister of the state's star witness, which by every canon of his profession he should divulge, was a major ethical and professional dilemma.

She took a goodly amount of time to answer. When she spoke, the words came slowly, gravely. "You held me when I needed to be held. You helped me say something I've been holding in, that I needed to get out." The tears were coming once more, silently this time.

They were on the couch. He took her in his arms again. She pressed herself against him and he held her tight, comforting her, knowing it was all passion behind this, that it wasn't about helping someone through a crisis. Passion—how a man wants a woman, how she wants him, how this passion is insane, dangerous, destructive, ruinous. Inevitable, unstoppable, impossible.

"I will never hurt you," she said, looking up at him and reading his thoughts. "I will never betray you. No one will ever know of this. I'd kill myself first."

"There's been enough killing already," he said, "so don't talk like that."

"I know. You're right. But I mean what I say about protecting you."

He wanted to believe her. He knew she was telling the truth, as it felt in her heart, this moment. But things could change, and somewhere down the line she might have to hurt him, even betray him. As he might her. Although he didn't want to, and would try as hard as he could not to.

That was in the future, and the future was unknown.

Their lovemaking went on for a long, long time. While they were in it, it felt like it was going to go on forever, and if it did, that would be all right. Everything—her touch, her taste, her smell, the way she felt when he entered her—it was right. All of it.

He showered and put his clothes back on. It was two-thirty in the morning. She watched him, sitting on the edge of her bed, naked. He stood over her, buttoning his shirt, tucking it into his pants. "We can't do this again. At least not until everything's over."

She nodded. She understood. She would want to—she would want to the moment he left—but she understood. And she had this. They had each other, for this.

"We can't be seen together."

"I know."

"You know I'm married." He didn't wear a ring, but he knew that she knew.

"I know that, too. Let's not talk about that. That's for later. Everything else is for later."

They said good night at her front door. "Thank you," she said.

"And you."

"Good night."

"Good night."

One final kiss, and he was gone.

He didn't remember the drive back to the hotel. He was in his room, lying in bed, looking at the clock, when it hit him. What had he done? My God, what had he done?

She would never hurt him. She would never betray him. He knew that she meant that to the depths of her heart. But he was defending the man who was accused of murdering her best friend. How would she feel when she saw him in the courtroom with that man, standing shoulder to shoulder?

By all rights, he should bust her. Tomorrow morning he should tell Judge Grant that the state's two most important witnesses were brother and sister. The judge, after recovering from the shock of this incredible news, would declare a mistrial. Most likely the DA's office would be censured as well, even though they hadn't known. In the short run that wouldn't matter, because they should have.

But in the long run, what difference would the information make? Worst case scenario, Violet wouldn't be allowed to testify—they'd drop her from their witness list. It would be a hit against them, but one they could survive. They would still have Dwayne, and Dwayne was their case.

Wyatt had another reason for why he wasn't going to discredit Violet, a much bigger and more personal one. A mistrial—that was a given—would push this case back at least a year. And when that happened it wouldn't be his case any longer. He'd be long gone, and there would be issues with the ethical side of it even if he did somehow figure a way to stick around that long.

He knew the argument—he was jeopardizing his client's defense. Well, maybe he was; it didn't matter. He couldn't give this case up. He had too much invested in it, on all sorts of levels.

Someone else would be trying his case. And after all that had gone down, he wasn't going to let that happen.

They brought Michaela home, stretched out on the backseat so that her leg could be propped up. School would be out in a week, and she couldn't wait to go for that one week. She would be on crutches and she wouldn't be up to the work but she was out of the hospital, finally, on the road to recovery.

Moira was down on him. It was his fault she had shot Michaela—she was blunt about that. Bringing gangbangers into their home, street hoods, crack dealers—who wouldn't have armed themselves, having to live with that? The fact that the instigation of it all was the falsity of the robbery next door, and what had really happened—that didn't matter to her in the least. She was adamant that she would have bought the gun even if nothing had happened next door.

He didn't argue with her. He slept in the guest room. Neither of them said anything; it was an unspoken feeling that they wouldn't sleep together, occupy the same intimate space. That he had been with another woman the night before was a reason, but not the important one. The connective tissue between them had been ruptured before that.

He would keep their relationship at arm's length, which was the only way he could deal with it. He was about to go to trial for a man's life. Their problems would have to wait. When it was all over they would go into therapy and see if it—they—could be fixed. More and more, he was beginning to doubt that it could, and at the moment he didn't know if he cared, one way or the other.

"We can't have anything to do with each other anymore. Sheriff Lowenthal chewed me out but good. I thought he might suspend me." Blake started shaking as she recounted the incident, still scared about it.

"Because you associated with me?"

She nodded.

"This is a fucking crock of shit!" Dwayne exploded. "I'm their fucking case, and they damn well know it. What's he so pissed about, that you let me sleep in the infirmary instead of on the tiers with the scumbags?"

"Yes. And that I helped you."

It was early evening. They were in her office, the door closed and locked, which was against regulations, but she couldn't take the chance of someone coming in on them. Everything they did was against regulations. Time and again she had put herself out for him, and now she was skating on ice so thin it looked like it would crack if she took one more misstep.

All for love, which she couldn't do without. Except this wasn't love, this was sickness. But it didn't matter, she couldn't do without him, although for now she was going to have to. Make that *try* to. Her life was so pathetic it didn't matter if she lost everything else. Everything else had made her miserable—if she stayed away from him her life would be shit, and if she kept on seeing him her life would be shit. There was no way out. She was the frog crossing the river, and he was the scorpion on her back.

She had intercepted him on his way upstairs from the infirmary, after it closed. That in itself had been risky: after being warned by the sheriff in no uncertain terms that she was to have nothing to do with Dwayne Thompson, zero, getting caught with him here would be automatic dismissal, and possibly criminal charges brought against her.

One last time. She had to chance it.

"Well, fuck it, then," Dwayne ranted. "You're useless. I should've known better than to think you would stand up with me when the chips were down."

She was stung. "I did stand up with you," she lamented. "I got you the infirmary. I let you use my computer, which was completely against the rules, especially with your jacket from up at Durban. I let you use me," she said defiantly.

"I used you?" He laughed in her face. "Give me a break, Doris. You're going to be a lawyer because of me, you stupid bitch. If it wasn't for me you'd be pounding a beat in this shithole till you died or your legs collapsed. We both used each other, baby, remember? From day one. So don't come on high and mighty with me now."

She had meant "use me" in the sexual sense, but she wasn't going to tell him that. He might say something that would hurt more than she could stand.

"Well," he said, calming down—he always knew how and when to throw that switch—"you did what you could. You'd better let me out of here. I don't want to get you into any more trouble." He headed for the door.

She stepped in front of him. "I'll be okay," she said with false bravado. "I can handle this. Those deputies out there are scared to death of me," she boasted truthfully. "None of them would bust me. No one knows you're in here, anyway," she added cautiously. "I made sure of that." With utter, insane, reckless abandon she moved toward him with carnal intent. This would be the last time they'd ever be together. She had to take one last chance. Fuck the sheriff and the horse he rode in on. Fuck them all.

He sidestepped her adroitly, his eyes bulging in alarm. "What're you, crazy! In here? After just getting your ass reamed out?" He stared at her. She was round the bend, truly gone. "It isn't worth it, Doris," he said, forcing himself to be calm. "You've got your law career to think about. We have time."

She stopped, deflated like a flat tire. "I suppose you're right," she said dully.

"They're watching you, Doris. We have to be supercool."

"As long as . . ." She didn't dare voice her thought.

"We have time," he said again, smooth as molasses. The room reeked from his insincerity. "The rest of our lives, once this is over. So let's not jeopardize it now."

She unlocked the door and sent him on his way. Then she sat down at her desk and cried.

Less than six months earlier Wyatt Matthews had been one of the most successful and prominent lawyers in the country. His income was seven figures, his picture was on the cover of mass-circulation magazines, he was the bright shining star of his nationally recognized firm, he was lionized by his peers, he had a comfortable, secure marriage, his child was fine. There wasn't a cloud on the horizon.

Now he was working out of a makeshift office that

couldn't pass a building inspection, he was defending a mass murderer who had already been convicted in the press and the public eye, he had almost been killed, his daughter had been shot and almost killed, he and his wife were estranged, and he was an adulterer. Not just the common, garden-variety type, either. He had slept with a major witness for the opposition, who by some miraculous negative force was the estranged sister of the state's key witness.

How had this happened? What death wish did he unconsciously harbor to have allowed his life to get to this point? And could he get out alive, his marriage, career, and honor unscathed?

Not his honor. That was already compromised. For the rest of his life, no matter what happened, he couldn't look at himself in the mirror and say, "you are an honorable man." He had burned that bridge the night before last.

It was early morning, the crack of dawn. No sun yet in the sky, only a thin yellow-gray line stenciling the eastern sky. He stood in the guest-room shower, the needles scalding him, ferociously scrubbing his body with a rough loofah. He had already had a forty-minute run in the dark. Now he was washing off the sweat and as much guilt as he could.

The sweat went down the drain with the shower water. The guilt had been absorbed into his system.

He had to come into their bedroom to dress. Moira was awake, propped up on her pillows, watching the morning news on TV.

"How was your run?" she asked formally.

"Good. I needed it." He pulled some changes from his drawers—underwear, socks, shirts. "I'm going to be spending some weeknights in the city," he explained as matter-of-factly as he could. "I'm gearing up for eighteen-hour days. I might even sleep in the office sometimes." He was turned away from her as he pulled out what he would need.

To his back, she coolly asked, "Are you sleeping with another woman?"

He paused before turning to her, wondering what emotions his face was revealing.

"That hot little paralegal of yours? The one who calls here whenever she feels like it?"

"Her name is Josephine, and I'm not sleeping with her."

He looked at her, trying to maintain his composure. He hadn't lied—not specifically.

"You wouldn't tell me if you were anyway, would you?"

"I'm not sleeping with her. I'm married to you."

"For what that's worth."

Bull's-eye. "Maybe I should move out for a while, until this trial's over and we can take a deep breath."

"That's up to you." Her tone was unquivering, blunt.

"Although I don't want to burden you with Michaela," he said, feeling lame as the words came off his tongue, which felt like it was forked.

"She's not a burden. And I should be her nurse, I'm the one who did it to her."

"It isn't just you. There's enough blame for all of us to spread around."

"You're saying that, but you don't believe it."

They looked at each other across the room. "I want to." The first honest statement he'd made this morning.

Emotional shadows played across her face. "Where did our life go, Wyatt?" she asked.

He didn't say anything; he didn't know what to say.

"That's a good idea," she said, alluding to his offer of moving out. "We do need to put some space between us."

"I'll come home some nights, and weekends," he offered. "It's a case, like any other." He started throwing stuff into a soft suitcase.

She watched as he hurriedly finished dressing. "Be quiet when you leave. Don't wake Michaela."

He picked up the bag and grabbed a handful of hangers with suits on them from his closet. "I'll be staying at the Four Seasons as usual, in case you want to call."

She stared at him blankly, as if he were speaking a foreign language she didn't understand.

Joe Ginsberg and Wyatt were old acquaintances. Both were lawyers, roughly the same age. Joe was a partner in a nice, medium-sized firm, similar to Wyatt's but on a smaller, less-stressful scale. Joe's practice was eclectic, casting its net among the shoals of criminal defense, personal injury, and class action, among other areas. Over the years the combination of work, family, and different lifestyles precluded them seeing much of each other, but there was mutual respect and easiness between them.

It was the end of the workday. Wyatt and Joe were comfortably ensconced in a back booth at McGulligan's, the oldest pub in the city, dating back over one hundred and fifty years. Schooners of draft Guinness and shots of Johnnie Walker Black sat puddled on the scarred wooden table. Joe lit up a cigar, a big Fonseca 10-10, the smoke drifting lazily up to the twenty-foot-high stamped-tin ceiling.

"You didn't know I've been teaching at Fairfax?" Joe asked.

Wyatt shook his head. "Not until Darryl Davis told me the other day. Although I'm not surprised. How long?"

"Six years. I teach one course a semester. That's all I can manage—it's a load, but it keeps me on my toes."

"I'll bet. I'd like to try doing that someday. Seeing's how I'm into the new and different."

Most of the faculty of Fairfax Law School were men and women like Joe, working professionals with a love for teaching who brought real-life experience into the classroom, along with the academic side. Teaching for them was an avocation, a chance to merge their love for the law and the legal system with the practical workaday world. Wyatt had phoned Joe as soon as he discovered he had a personal relationship with someone on the faculty.

"I can imagine," Joe replied. "That was a gutsy move, doing what you're doing. A lot of guys're envious of what you've done."

"Sometimes I wonder if I did the right thing. I've had my sleepless nights."

"Sure, that's to be expected. How's it going? The case?"

"We're making progress. It's going to be a struggle," Wyatt admitted honestly. "But I'm holding some cards." Bringing the conversation around to his purpose: "So do you remember a student named Doris Blake? Did you ever teach her?"

"Doris Blake." Joe scrunched his brow, trying to put the name with a face.

Wyatt described her.

"Oh, yeah. Her, I remember. You don't forget someone who looks like her." He took a sip of Scotch, a swallow of stout. "What about her?"

"How was she as a student?" Wyatt replicated Joe's pattern of drinking.

"Okay. Nothing special. I had her in procedures one semester and then another time I had her in environment law, I think it was. I could go back and check if you're interested in the specifics."

"No, that won't be necessary. I'm interested in your overall impression of her. As a student, a scholar."

Joe blew a smoke ring skyward. "She's not a scholar. I'd describe her as a plodder, not much of an original thinker. Hard worker, I'll give her that. She got by by working her tush off. I'd be in the law library sometimes late, she'd be there until the place closed and they kicked her out. Usually worked alone." He took another hit of Scotch. "Why, you guys thinking of hiring her?" he asked, his tone expressing surprise.

Wyatt shook his head. "Not at the firm, no."

"She wouldn't fit in." He meant, Wyatt knew, her appearance. "If she was a Larry Tribe, somebody particularly bright like that, you could justify her, but she's going to be a ham-and-egger, the kind that's always scrambling to make a living. Her best bet'll be hooking on with some government agency."

"I agree. I mentioned that she should look into applying to the Public Defender's—not that I'd give her a recommendation. They're way too classy for her."

Joe polished off his Guinness, held his glass aloft to signal the barmaid for another round. "Why're you asking about her?"

"She's peripherally involved in my case." He could talk freely with Joe. "Maybe more than peripherally."

The barmaid took Joe's empty glass. Wyatt finished his and handed it to her. "She's got a history with this informant who's the backbone of Pagano's case against my guy."

Joe whistled. "A *history*? That's got a sinister ring to it, Wyatt." He grabbed a handful of bar nuts from the bowl in the center of the table, threw them down.

"I know. Which is why I'm pursuing it."

The barmaid set their fresh drafts in front of them, gave the table a cursory wipe with her dirty cloth to sop up some of the spillage. "I love the atmosphere in here," Joe commented, loud so she could hear. "Surly and surlier."

The barmaid kissed her fingers and shot him the bird. He smiled pleasantly at her as she lumbered away.

"She told me she got a seventy-six on her bar exam."

"No way." Joe sucked the collar off his fresh glass. "That's too high. I'd be surprised if she passed the first time, a woman with her intellectual limitations. But a seventy-six? That's ... she'd have to be the luckiest lady alive. Which you and I know she isn't."

"That's my impression, too."

"Anyway," Joe continued, "how the hell does she know what score she got? The earliest she could've taken the bar exam was this spring, and they haven't been posted yet."

"That's a good question, isn't it?"

"If she knows what she's got, that's illegal," Joe said. "Not to mention immoral. Your first move out of the box from law school you do something illegal? Now that would really be dumb. You sure she told you her score?"

"Positively."

"Well, I guess it's possible to get your score without technically breaking any laws. But I guarantee you that woman didn't get a seventy-six. She couldn't."

Wyatt nodded. "There's all kinds of wrong things going on with her. This is only one of them."

Joe thought for a moment. "I've got someone on the testing board I could put you in touch with," he offered. "Off the record. He could find out if what she told you is accurate."

"Thanks, Joe. That would be helpful. I'll owe you one for that."

"You're buying the drinks, didn't I tell you? Don't sweat it, it's no big thing. The more important thing, I'd think, is who got those results for her? If she's telling the truth, that is."

"She was pretty steadfast."

"I don't know." Joe's head was enveloped in a nimbus of cigar smoke. "I think she's blowing smoke at you," he deadpanned. "I'll bet she doesn't know her score," he added, "and I'll bet that when she does find out, it won't be seventy-six. Ten points lower would be my guess."

"Why would she do that?"

"To impress you, for God's sake. Big-shot lawyer, condescending to talk to a small fry. She wants to make a good impression, so she says the first thing that pops into her head. She lies to try to build herself up. Of course it's stupid, and people do stuff like that all the time. It's human nature—I mean look at the poor woman, Wyatt. Doesn't your heart go out to her?"

"Normally it would," Wyatt agreed, thinking of Marvin, of how he would have inflated his importance to Dwayne Thompson to impress the seasoned con. "But if she's part of a scam to put my man away? I'll tear her heart out and feed it to the jackals."

Elvis Burnside, a thin, rapacious-looking man, had been tossing down a few after work. He was gainfully employed in a tool-and-die plant over on the west side, a journeyman grinder with a union card, $21.50 an hour plus guaranteed overtime. While nursing his third 7&7 he made the acquaintance of a woman who was hanging around the bar by herself. She was friendly, they worked out their arrangement, and they headed over to a nearby motel she knew about to consummate the deal. He bought a pint of Absolut from the bartender to make the encounter more convivial, and was driving a Toyota 4-Runner with a split flip-down backseat, which he'd bought off a friend who ran a chop shop; it came with legal papers and everything.

On the way to the motel Elvis decided he didn't want to pay for a room, seeing as how he had plenty of space right here in his vehicle. He turned off the street they were on, pulling into a small commercial side street that was quiet now that business hours were over.

"I don't feature throwing thirty dollars at some crater-faced motel clerk," he explained of his sudden change of plans. "I'd rather pay you the extra money," he said, leaning over and lowering the backseat.

"What do I have to do to earn it?"

"Fuck my brains out. Long and slow."

"I guess I can do that." She was a couple sheets to the wind herself.

"I've been known to last an hour."

"Jesus. I might even have an orgasm of my own, you ride

me that long. Although that's gonna run you—time is money, honey."

"I got the money, honey."

"Then I got the time."

"After which a journey down the chocolate highway has always pleasured me," he said with a smile. "With a rubber, of course. I wouldn't want to spread infection. From you to me."

"Thanks for the safety concern," she said, "except that's not my style." She threw open the door, which she had pulled the lock up from, and started to jump out.

This maneuver did not go down well with Elvis. He was out of the truck in a flash and had her wrapped up before she took ten steps, throwing her to the ground and ripping off her underpants with one hand while covering her mouth with the other.

He managed to penetrate her—the straight way—but she fought him like a wildcat, which gave him added satisfaction; hurting a woman while fucking her was particularly pleasurable.

He was about to climax when down the street came a police car.

Elvis's getting caught was just dumb bad luck. Somebody had been breaking into one of the closed stores down the block, and the police had responded to the silent alarm. There had been a spate of burglaries in the neighborhood recently, and the cops were on extra alert. Finding a rape in progress wasn't what they were looking for, but the bust was free for the taking, so they took it.

Which was why Elvis Burnside found himself in the county jail, going through the booking process, and about to enter the general population.

Elvis knew the charge against him was bullshit. The woman was a known prostitute, she had solicited him in the bar and he had witnesses—the bartender and a couple guys he knew from work—and they had been fucking. So they were doing it on the ground instead of inside his car or in a motel room. He had bought her and had every intention of paying her.

The deputy escorted him and sixty-eight other men into D block, which was going to be his home for the next few weeks until he was arraigned and went to trial. On the way to his cell, carrying his bedroll and toilet articles, he spotted a friend from his prison days. The friend was hanging by himself in a corner, reading a book by the dim light. No one was bothering him. He was the kind of guy people didn't bother, unless they were ignorant, and when that happened they learned their lesson, usually fast.

But Elvis could bother him. They were asshole buddies.

He dumped his roll on the bunk he'd been assigned to—the top of a double, with another single sandwiched in. If a man had to pee at night he had to straddle the third man's bunk while pissing, and sometimes the man in the third bunk would get piss drippings all over him.

Leaving his cell, Elvis sauntered down the hall and flopped next to Dwayne. "Hey, pard. Long time no see."

Dwayne looked up, startled. "Elvis Burnside," he exclaimed in ill-concealed distaste. This was the last thing he needed, someone from Durban who knew him.

"In the flesh, good buddy." Elvis flashed a depraved smile.

Dwayne glanced around to see if anyone was paying them special attention. No one was—in this crowded cesspool they were just two more bodies, taking up space.

"How long you been in here?" Dwayne asked, shifting his position to get more comfortable and to have a better look at Elvis.

" 'Bout an hour."

"What'd they bust you for this time?"

"Fuckin' a whore."

"Since when's that illegal?"

"Hey, you tell me. I asked the cop the same damn question."

They both laughed.

"What about you?" Elvis asked. "I thought you were still pulling time at Durban."

"I'm here temporarily. Testifying in a case."

Elvis knew Dwayne was a snitch, one of the most notorious in the entire prison system. A lot of men would hate Dwayne for that and would tear his heart out if they could, but Elvis was cool with it. You do what you do and leave me the fuck alone. "Hey, it's good to see you again," he said.

Dwayne looked at him. He smiled warily. "It's good to see you, too, Elvis."

"This case you're into," Elvis said, "big deal?" Meaning, what are you getting out of it?

Dwayne's snake smile creased his eyes into slits. "You been following this Alley Slasher story?"

Elvis's double-take was classic. "You're the snitch? Hot damn!" He knew all about this story. Every ex-con on the street knew this story—especially the ones, like him, who had a documented history of rape. He had been pulled in for questioning after the fourth rape-murder, when the authorities had started taking this shit seriously, but he'd had a rock-solid alibi: he'd been in jail at the time. The only time in his life he'd been glad he was in jail instead of outside in the free world.

Dwayne nodded yes to Elvis's question.

"Well, shit, I reckon." He looked his old friend up and down. "So what's in it for you, ace?"

"The whole enchilada," Dwayne told him. He couldn't help bragging a little on himself. "Easy women, fast cars, lots of money. Especially the money." In the joint, you kept what you knew and was happening to you to yourself, or you could find yourself in a world of pain. Witness Marvin White. But Elvis was different—they knew each other in ways that would preclude either from fucking the other up. "They'll cut me loose, brother. Now and forever."

Elvis cocked his head, regarding Dwayne with a peculiar look. "You got them authorities jumping through hoops, don't you, bubba? You got them by the fuckin' balls, man."

"They don't see it that way. They think it's a righteous deal for all concerned."

"Well, fuck, they should, man. You're the man, Dwayne." He paused. "Everywhere you go, that's what people are saying."

"They are?" Dwayne was skeptical, and also edgy. Talk among the people they knew was never complimentary without some jive contradictory appendix.

"They're saying this key witness for the state—meaning you, now that I know it's you—and the powers to be are going to run some poor motherfucker right into the gas chamber. Except it's lethal injection now, ain't it? Pussy way to die, if you ask me."

"Run him in?" Dwayne was instantly on guard. "I'm not

running anyone in. This boogie did what he said he did. All I'm doing is repeating his words back."

"Yeah, and my mother's Oprah Winfrey," Elvis said derisively.

"What's that supposed to mean?" This fucking Elvis. This fucker could demoralize God.

"The word on the street," Elvis said, "which I hear now and again, being as I am someone who lives and works thereon, is that this young black person is not the man the police want him to be."

"Meaning?" Be cautious here. Be very cautious.

"Meaning that the one who did it ain't even a nigger, Jack."

"How the hell would anybody know what color he was?" Dwayne exploded. "There's never been any witnesses." He exhaled hard in exasperation. "The fucker *confessed* to me. He sat there and told me he did it. He provided details." He dismissed Elvis with a wave of the hand. "You don't know what the fuck you're talking about, man. That's bullshit."

Elvis leaned in to Dwayne, so that their heads were inches apart. "Maybe it is, Dwayne, and maybe it isn't." He paused. "My instinct tells me the real killer is still out there."

The air hung over and isolated them like a shroud for two.

Dwayne shook his head strongly. "Your instinct's gone wrong this time, Elvis. He did it, believe me."

Elvis nodded sagely. "I don't have to believe you, Dwayne. I ain't gonna be sitting on that jury, unless Heaven and Hell change places, which ain't likely." He got up. "See you around, Dwayne. Hang 'em low."

He walked away. Dwayne watched him disappear into the throng. His stomach was flipping. Elvis knew too much; nothing more than a con's intuition, but it was unsettling, more than enough to put Dwayne on guard.

Tomorrow he'd transfer out of here, or get Blake to transfer Elvis. He had enough shit to worry about without someone from his past looming in front of him, fucking with his mind.

The psychologist's office was in the suburbs, one township closer to the city than theirs. Her building was part of a small medical-therapeutic complex shaped like a horseshoe, low two-story cedar-shingled buildings with outside walkways leading past the various offices. Lots of shrubbery, a central rock pond. Spring through fall the pond was stocked with koi, but they were transplanted to an indoor pond in the winter, when this one would freeze over.

Wyatt parked his car and checked the office number on a piece of scratch paper. Moira's Audi station wagon was already tucked into a space in the shade. He couldn't find a shady spot, so he left his sunroof open a crack. He was only a couple minutes late—he rationalized that he'd had a longer drive than Moira and Michaela.

Moira and Michaela had seen the therapist half a dozen times, individually and together. Now it was his turn to join them. He knew it was important, vital; and he wasn't looking forward to it.

In truth, he was dreading this meeting. He wanted them to come together and heal, whatever that meant—but the timing was lousy. He was about to go into the most important trial of his career. Never before, in all his years of practice, had a man's life been in his hands. To be ready for that and at the same time have to bare his soul and deal with the heavy emotions going on in his family, especially regarding his marriage, was too much on one plate.

He had to do this. He owed it to Moira. Somehow he'd get through it.

"Mr. Matthews." The therapist stood and shook his hand. "It's good to meet you, finally."

"You, too," he answered formulaically. He shook her hand. She had a firm handshake.

"Please, sit down. May I call you Wyatt?"

"Sure."

Moira and Michaela were seated side by side on a small couch. He sat in a cushioned rocking chair next to Michaela. She reached out and took his hand and squeezed. He squeezed back, looked past her to Moira. Moira had a look of apprehension on her face. *I feel like she looks*, he thought.

"Hi," he said to her past Michaela.

"Hi," she answered back.

The therapist, whose name was Roberta Kell, sat in her

leather desk chair. The desk faced the wall, so she could swivel in her chair and face into the room. She was a short, slender woman with curly red hair. Dark red, auburn. Freckles. She was probably fun outside the office, Wyatt thought. This—in here—wasn't going to be fun.

She broke the ice. "How are you feeling?"

"In general or specifically?"

"Whichever you'd prefer to talk about." She paused, her gaze shifting to Moira and Michaela for a moment, then back to him. "How do you feel about the way things are right now between you and Moira?"

"They're not very good."

"Could you talk about that?"

He shrugged. "Our communication's lousy. I don't think we trust each other very much. Basically, I don't think we're on the same page, Ms. Kell. I don't know that we're even in the same book."

"Roberta, if you don't mind, Wyatt." She smiled, then turned to Moira. "How do you feel about what Wyatt just said?"

"It's the truth—as far as it goes." She looked at Wyatt, then turned away.

"Where doesn't it go?" Roberta asked.

"He hates me."

"Mom!" Michaela looked at Moira with alarm, then at her father to see his reaction.

Wyatt was maintaining his cool on the outside, but inside he was churning. He hadn't expected this—not so strong, and not so fast. He started taking deep, slow breaths, like he did after a hard run.

Everyone was looking at him. When he felt under control enough to respond, he said, "I don't hate you, Moira." He said it looking straight forward, into a middle distance, not focusing on anyone or anything.

"You hate what I did."

"Yes, I do. But what you did and who you are are two different things."

"I don't think you've been separating the two," Moira said, pressing him.

He sighed. "There's a lot of stuff going on. I haven't been analyzing all my feelings—as you obviously have," he said, his voice taking on a tense, defensive posture.

Roberta intervened. "Let's take a step back. You're not being judged here, Wyatt. Nobody's accusing you of anything."

"That's not how it sounds to me."

"I can understand that." She looked at Michaela. "Where are you with all this?"

Michaela looked down. "I feel guilty."

"No!" Wyatt said quickly. He reached out and took her hand again.

"No, how?" Roberta prompted.

"You aren't guilty of anything," Wyatt told Michaela, leaning over to look her in the eye. "You didn't do anything wrong. You know you didn't."

"I feel it," she said.

"But you didn't," he persisted.

"Wyatt." Roberta spoke his name.

He looked up.

"Putting aside what Michaela did or didn't do— physically—what about the *feeling* she expressed? What about her *feeling* that she's guilty? Not whether she is or isn't in some real-world context."

"I . . ." He felt overwhelmed. "I don't know how to separate the two. Not about this."

"Are you trying to tell her how she should feel?" Roberta asked.

"Like you tell all of us?" Moira kicked in.

He looked at her, hurt and angry. "I don't do that."

"You don't?" Moira countered.

"I . . . no." Which wasn't exactly true. "But so do you," he responded.

"I never said I didn't," she answered. "I said *you do*. There's a big difference."

He nodded. Turning to Michaela, he said, "I shouldn't tell you how you should feel. You should feel however you feel. It's not right for me to even try to make it that. I'm your father, that's all, I mean, I want you, I want you to be happy. I mean, what's wrong with that?"

Michaela smiled at him. "Nothing, Daddy. I like that. That you want that."

"Good. At least we agree on something." He felt like he'd been punched hard in the stomach, several times. He was having a hard time with the simple, natural act of breathing.

"What about what Moira said, Wyatt?" Roberta asked. "Is there any truth to that? For you?"

"That I tell everyone how they should feel?"

"Yes."

He nodded, several times. "I guess . . . there is."

Roberta also nodded. "Can we talk about your feelings?" she asked.

"That's why we're here, isn't it? To talk about my feelings?" His voice took on a defensiveness again.

"We're not in court, Wyatt," Moira said. "No one's being cross-examined or put on the spot, except if you do it."

"Come on," he said, pissed off. "You're doing it right now with that kind of remark."

She shook her head in disgust.

Roberta put her hands up. "Space, guys. Give yourselves some air. Here . . ." She got up from her chair. "Wyatt, would you stand up for a moment? And you also, Michaela?"

They both stood.

Roberta pulled his rocker next to her leather chair. "Michaela, you sit here next to me, all right? So you're not in the direct line of fire. Wyatt, would you mind sitting next to your wife?"

"No, I don't mind." He and Michaela took their assigned seats. Moira shifted slightly, so that their bodies weren't touching anywhere.

"Okay." Roberta stroked Michaela's hand. "Your mom and dad. How do they look?"

"Miserable," Michaela laughed. "Like that Grant Wood painting. You know, the old farmer and his wife."

"Thank you very much," Moira said.

"It's true, Mom. You look like you just sucked up a whole lemon. You too, Daddy."

He felt like he'd swallowed a bushel of lemons.

Roberta looked at Wyatt. "I'd like to ask you some questions."

"Fire away."

Moira's laugh was cynical.

"You're not helping here, Moira," Roberta said seriously. "You've already started your processing. This is Wyatt's first time. He needs space and he needs support."

"So do I," Moira answered.

"Then let's give the process a chance, okay?" She turned back to Wyatt. "First question. Your wife shot your daughter. How do you feel about that?"

"Angry, of course. I'm very angry about it."

"Have you told her that?"

"I . . ." He paused. "No, not directly."

"Tell her now."

He turned to Moira. "I'm angry at you for shooting Michaela. I'm enraged."

"I know you are." She sat there calmly, taking his shot.

"What else are you angry about?" Roberta asked. "In connection with this?"

"She knows I hate guns but she bought one anyway. And didn't tell me. We had a gun in our house. Something you use to shoot people with. And she didn't even tell me."

"What if Moira had told you she was going to buy a gun?"

"I would have said no, of course."

"Ahhhh!" Moira shivered in anger.

" 'Ahhhh' what?" he asked, also angry.

"What we've been talking about is what," she answered hotly. She moved farther away from him, pushing up against the arm of the couch.

"But what if Moira had insisted?" Roberta asked. "She wants a gun in the house for protection. She's adamant about that."

He shook his head stubbornly. "You saw what happened, didn't you?"

They all looked at the large brace on Michaela's leg.

"Yes," Roberta said. "We see that. But getting back to my question. Moira wants a gun. She insists on having one. What then?"

"No guns. I'm sorry."

"But doesn't she have as much of a right to what she wants as you do?"

"Yes, she has a right to what she wants," he began. "But . . ." He stopped.

"But what?"

"She has a right," he said. "She has . . . rights."

"Thank you," Moira said acidly.

"But not *absolute* rights," he said with force. "No one has absolute rights."

Roberta put up a quick hand of warning to Moira, to restrain her from coming back with a zinger. Moira slumped in her place, shaking her head negatively but holding her tongue.

"Can we continue along this line?" Roberta asked Wyatt.

"Do I have a choice?" This was slipping away—he felt like he was on an ice floe that had broken off and was drifting out to sea.

"You always have a choice. In here at least."

He reluctantly acquiesced. "Go ahead."

"Owning guns is an extreme example. Yes? Do we all agree on that?"

"I do," he said.

Roberta looked at Moira.

"Yes," Moira acknowledged. "An extreme example."

"I don't ever want a gun in my house again," Michaela piped up. "I did before but I didn't understand what it really meant."

They all sat silently for a moment, digesting that.

"Moira's about to open up a bookstore," Roberta said, navigating the session back to less-tense waters. "How do you feel about that, Wyatt?"

"I think it's a great idea."

"You approve."

"Absolutely."

"What if she wanted to open a whorehouse?" She turned to Michaela. "Excuse me."

"I'm okay." Michaela was composed, attentive to both her parents.

Wyatt stared at Roberta. "Come on," he said curtly.

"Or a strip joint? A porno shop."

"That's ridiculous."

"Why?"

"Because those are scuzzy, awful things. Moira's not . . ."

"Scuzzy? Awful?"

"She isn't those things."

"But still—you are making judgments on her behalf, aren't you? Judging what Moira should or shouldn't do?"

"Yes," he admitted grudgingly. "In those cases I would."

"Because you're her husband."

"Yes."

"And what she does impacts on you. Affects you."

"Yes."

"Not only that people would say, 'Oh, isn't Moira Matthews awful, opening a whorehouse,' but that it isn't good for her. As a moral, ethical person. Which makes it not good for you two as a couple, among other issues."

"Yes," he agreed. "That's right."

"But if she really, really, really wanted to open up a whorehouse—assuming it was legal and there wasn't any chance of spreading disease or whatever, like they have in Nevada—you wouldn't support her, would you?"

"No. I wouldn't."

"So husbands and wives shouldn't unilaterally support each other in everything?" Roberta continued. "There are certain things that are wrong, and it's your obligation to not support her. By *not* supporting her operating a whorehouse, you'd really be *supporting* her, wouldn't you?"

"I think I would be," he answered. "Yes."

"Okay," she said. "I agree with you. Does that surprise you?"

He looked at her. "I don't know."

"Because I'm Moira and Michaela's therapist and we're in cahoots against you?"

He nodded. "I've thought about that."

She smiled. "I wouldn't have believed you if you'd said otherwise. But I'm not in cahoots with them against you. I am in cahoots—with all of you, for you."

"You should hear how Roberta defends you when you aren't here, Daddy," Michaela chimed in.

"She's boxed my ears severely many times about my attitude toward you," Moira added acidly.

Roberta kept her focus on Wyatt, "You're my patient," she told him. "The *collective* you—you three sitting here."

He nodded, but his body language belied that acceptance.

"You don't have to believe me," Roberta said. "You don't know me yet. Hopefully, trust will come."

"Hopefully." At this point he was dubious about that—about everything that was going on in here.

"Good." She smiled at him. "Let's keep on this train of thought—about how sometimes *not* supporting your partner is really support." She paused. "You changed careers recently, didn't you?"

"I didn't change my career. I'm still a lawyer."

"Excuse me. I meant *focus*. You're practicing a different kind of law now than you were for the bulk of your career, isn't that right?"

"For a while. I've changed to a different aspect of the law. It isn't permanent—I don't think." He stole a look at Moira. She was looking right at him. He turned his attention back to Roberta.

"It was a big change, wasn't it?" Roberta asked. "From the kind of law you were practicing to the kind you're practicing now?"

"Very big," he agreed. "About as different as two disciplines can be and still be under the same umbrella."

"It's affected your family, hasn't it."

"Big-time."

"That change was one of the reasons Moira bought the gun, isn't it."

"Yes. I'm sure it is. One of them."

Roberta paused. "When you decided to change careers—let's not argue semantics—what was Moira's reaction?"

"She was against it. She still is."

"He's right," Moira stuck in her two cents' worth. "I am against what my husband is doing. Firmly."

"Which you knew from the beginning," Roberta asked.

"Yes," he said.

"But you did it anyway."

"Yes. I had to."

"Even though your wife—your partner in life—was dead set against it."

"Yes. I had to. I would've burned out otherwise. I came really close. And I don't feel there was anything wrong with what I did. I still don't."

"So there are times when one has to operate unilaterally, regardless of the consequences to anyone else."

"Yes." He admitted it. "That's true."

"Following that logic, your partner should support that decision."

"I wanted her to."

"But even if she didn't, you did what you had to do."

"Yes. I did what I had to do."

"And when Moira bought the gun, knowing you couldn't, wouldn't, support it, she did what she had to do."

"Ahhh." He closed his eyes.

"She did what she had to do," Roberta repeated. "The same as you did."

He opened his eyes. "Abstractly, you could say it's the same."

"But it was wrong."

"I think it was wrong. I'm not going to back off that."

"And what you did was right."

"Yes. I'm not backing off that, either."

"So it's all right for you to operate unilaterally, but not Moira. You should be able to call the shots, and she should fall in line."

"That's pretty harsh coming from someone who isn't in cahoots against me."

"I'm only parroting what you've been telling me."

He shrugged.

"By the way, you're doing great, Wyatt."

He didn't feel like he was doing great. He felt like he was barely surviving.

"Do you know that basic law of physics?" she asked. "For every action there is a counteraction of equal strength and force?"

"It's been a long time since high school physics," he said. "But okay, I'll buy that."

"Do you see how that applies here? To your family?"

He stared at her.

"You took an action. You changed—if not careers, a large shift within your career—which caused some severe but inevitable counteractions. When you changed jobs you turned your family dynamic upside down. That was inevitable. Wasn't it?"

"I didn't know it had to be," he said.

"Oh, it had to be," she assured him. "What you didn't know was that it would bring about *negative* consequences. Which it didn't have to," she added. "More often than not these kinds of changes are positive counter-actions, for everyone. In this case, that didn't happen. But *something* had to happen. A decision of this size has to send ripples out that go on and on, way past where you can see them."

He nodded. "I can see that now."

Roberta glanced at the clock on her desk. "I'm really glad you came in, Wyatt. This has been a very productive session. When can you come again?" She reached for her appointment book.

"I don't know. I'm in the middle of a trial that's consuming me." He stood up. "I've got to say something." He moved away from the couch so that he could look at all three of them at the same time. "Philosophically, or . . . what's the word—therapeutically?—I can understand that my trying to control Moira's life is as wrong as her trying to control mine. I have no quarrel with that—as a concept. But you're talking about process, and I'm looking at the real world, and there's a difference. For me, anyway. I know that changing the kind of law I practice was traumatic for Moira, and I should have been more in tune with her. But I'm not doing anything wrong. That's an important distinction. I'm defending a disadvantaged kid on a murder charge who I've come to believe is innocent. Right now I'm not blowing my own horn when I say I'm all that's standing between him and the abyss."

He focused on Moira. "I'm sorry that anything I've done has caused you pain. I can't tell you how sorry I am about that. Causing pain for someone is wrong, especially for your family. But the rest of what I did isn't wrong and nothing that will be done or said in here will make me change my mind about that. And nothing that will be done or said in here will make me change my mind that buying a gun and shooting and almost killing my child—our daughter—can be justified. Or that my defending a black kid and bringing his world into ours can be equated with shooting someone. What you did and what I did are not equal. There is right and wrong in the world—my world, anyway, maybe that's why I became a lawyer—and nothing anyone can say or do will make me change my mind about that." He turned to Roberta. "So if the point of my coming here is to find some justification for that, then there's no reason for me to come back."

"Daddy . . ." Michaela started to break in.

"I hope someday we can work through this," he pressed on, overriding his daughter's interruption, "but I will never accept that there was anything right about it."

Moira was rigid, her expression cast in stone as she listened to him.

"Daddy . . ." Michaela began again.

He turned to her. "What is it, darling?" He was suddenly spent, completely drained of all feeling, emotionally and physically.

"Do you think you can ever forgive Mom? Completely forgive her?"

He stared at her, then looked at Moira, then back to her.

"I don't know," he said honestly.

"Will it help if you know that I have?" she asked.

He took a deep breath. He could feel Moira's and the therapist's eyes on him, but all his attention was with Michaela. His daughter, this young font of wisdom and forgiveness.

"Yes," he said after some reflection. "It would." He knelt down to her. "You're a wonderful young woman," he said. "You're a far better person than I am."

She shook her head. "That's not true."

"If you can forgive this quickly, you are."

"I have to, Dad. She's my mother."

Behind his back he could hear Moira sobbing.

He put a hand on his daughter's forehead, and she leaned down and hugged him fiercely.

Joe Ginsberg's bar examiner friend called Wyatt at the office.

"I snuck a look at that score you're interested in," he said over the phone. "Which you don't know I did."

"I appreciate that."

"It was a seventy-six, like you thought."

Wyatt cursed to himself.

"It puts her in the eighty-five percentile," the examiner said.

"That's hard to believe." He had met Doris Blake, spoken with her. She had given no indication of being that smart, or even close.

"It is awfully high," the examiner agreed. "One of the highest we've ever had from a part-time law student. Usually it's the cream of the Harvards and Yales who get those high scores."

Wyatt had been in the top ten percent of his class at Yale, twenty-five years earlier. He'd scored a seventy-four, which was considered very respectable for someone of his exalted position. This convict-fucking shlub had outscored him. He couldn't believe it.

"Is there any chance the score was misrecorded?" he asked, throwing himself a lifeline.

"One in a million."

"Bad odds."

"If you want, I could cross-check it against her test book, to be sure. It is an elevated score, and her class standing doesn't merit her doing that well. But stranger things have happened, as we all know."

"I'd appreciate it." He was grasping at straws but he had to be one hundred percent sure.

"It'll take me a few weeks. Right now we're rereading the sixty-nines and sixty-eights."

A score of seventy percent was passing. About half of those who took the twice-yearly exams passed each time, scoring seventy percent or better—mostly in the seventy to seventy-two percentile. Test scores that had just missed the mark were reexamined to see if another point or point and a half could be squeezed out of them. The trauma of taking the bar exam was extreme—your entire career hung in the balance. To fail by a point or less could make someone suicidal. Wyatt had heard of people who'd taken the test a dozen times and never passed. He would have figured Blake for that category before he put her in the upper echelon.

"What about her knowing her score before it was officially posted?" he asked the examiner.

"That's serious," the man said, "and we will look into that. Leaking scores could ruin the credibility of these tests."

"If you find anything out I'd appreciate knowing that, too," Wyatt said.

"I'll be getting back to you."

So Blake had found out about her bar exam score before she was supposed to. It wasn't kosher, but as Josephine had pointed out, people were always finding things out they weren't supposed to. The important thing was that she'd passed with flying colors; and that meant he had one less piece of ammunition to use against her.

S̲chool was over. Summer was officially less than two weeks away. Already the mercury was climbing into the high eighties and nineties, with the humidity correspondingly brutal. And the trial of the *People v. Marvin White* was coming like a runaway freight train. Wyatt was going to have a long, hot summer.

He was going to be spending it alone. Moira and Michaela weren't going to be home for the summer.

"I've rented a house on Martha's Vineyard," Moira told him. "Michaela and I are going to spend the summer there. It's too hot in the city." Stating the obvious: "And she can't work."

"When did you decide that?"

"Last week. After the session with Roberta."

He nodded. "I wish you'd told me."

"Would it have mattered?"

"I don't know."

"I don't feel we needed permission, if that's what you're insinuating."

That stung. "I don't own your life, Moira."

"No," she said, more aggressively than he would have liked. "You don't."

That stung, too.

"We'd be a drag on you."

He shrugged.

"It's true."

"What about your bookstore? It's opening soon."

"Cissy can handle it while I'm gone. This is more important. Michaela and I being together."

"Maybe it's for the best."

"Michaela and I have to work our stuff out," Moira said. "And you can think about what you want to do."

"I want to work. On us."

"Maybe you do and maybe you don't," she answered with

brutal honesty. "But that kind of work is full-time, and you don't have that kind of time. I understand that. But that is the truth."

"When the trial's over . . ."

"We'll see."

Their flight was called. He hugged them both, hard. They hugged him back. Michaela had tears in her eyes; Moira was resolutely dry-eyed. "I'll call you tonight," she said briskly.

"Good-bye, Daddy," Michaela said. "Take care of yourself."

"I will, sweetheart. You, too."

One last dry kiss from Moira. Then they were handing their boarding passes to the flight attendant and walking down the ramp, disappearing into the fuselage.

He stood at the window, watching the plane taxi out onto the runway. It took off, picking up power, the flaps lowering—then it began climbing, up above him, banking away from the terminal and heading into the sun.

He watched until the plane was out of his line of sight. Then he walked out of the airport, got into his car, and drove home to an empty house.

PART
FOUR

WYATT woke up in his hotel-room bed at three-thirty in the morning and knew he wouldn't be able to fall back asleep, so he threw on shorts, a T-shirt, and his Nikes, and went for a run. The streets were deserted except for delivery trucks, street-cleaning vehicles, and an occasional cop car cruising by. This section of town was considered safe—it was the hub of both commerce and tourism, so the police patrolled it stringently: hookers, purse snatchers, drug dealers, and other criminal types were roughly removed and relocated to scuzzier environs.

Even though it was the apex of the night, the heat and humidity, so viscid it felt like he was moving through a film of oil, hung over the city, giving him the feeling of being inside an immense Turkish bath. The air was dead still. Discarded dog-pissed-on newspapers lay limp in the gutters, and the faint perpetual smells of garbage and sewage rose up through the street vents and manhole covers like the aromas of a devil's stew cooking far underground.

The city at rest, he thought, with all its age and imperfections exposed, an old dame way past her glamour years who somehow, before the break of every day, manages to get up and get dressed and put on her makeup so that she can display a presentable face to the world.

Wyatt loved his aging city. He knew her smells and wrinkles and curves and secrets. His forays into the huge uncharted sections inhabited by the African American population had clearly shown him some of the things he didn't know—but he was learning. What the city was; and what it wasn't.

He was keyed up and at the same time he was calm, much calmer than he'd expected he would be. So much had gone

down in these last few months, personally and professionally (the two pretty much intertwined), that all the anxiety
had been driven from his system and replaced with clarity,
self-belief, and power. He had been preparing for this day
all his life, from the day he graduated law school. He was
going into a courtroom to fight for another man's life.

He was at the courthouse by a quarter to seven, the first
party from either side to arrive, driving in unnoticed via the
back subterranean entrance to the underground parking lot.
The proceedings would commence at nine, but he wanted to
be there early. For the next several weeks this was going to
be where he lived, and he wanted to become as comfortable
here as possible.

On the street in front of the courthouse, as well as in the
central downstairs rotunda, the media circus was beginning
to set up its tent, camera crews already jockeying for the
most advantageous positions.

He thought about how slow the first few weeks would be.
Judge Grant's opening remarks and the selection of the jury
would take at least two weeks. For the principals, however,
jury selection would be crucial. By the time the jury was selected, the case would be well on its way to being won or
lost. Trying to find twenty men and women (twelve jurors
plus an ample alternate pool) who had not formed an opinion about Marvin's innocence or guilt was going to be close
to impossible because it was a given that everyone in the
city had heard or read or seen something about Marvin
White and these killings. Something bad. Wyatt and his
team had to ferret out the few people from the jury pool who
had any kind of open mind, because there was no residue of
goodwill built up around Marvin, whose profile was that of
men, particularly black men, who in situations like this were
convicted ninety-eight percent of the time.

Because of the notoriety and the sheer numbers of the
murders, Wyatt had made a pretrial motion to separate the
cases, a normal procedure, especially since some of the prosecution's evidence was based only on the circumstances of
the final murder. Grant had denied it—he felt the connec-

tions were strong enough to warrant one trial for all seven. That it would be prohibitively expensive to conduct seven separate murder trials went unspoken, but everyone knew that was a big factor.

Josephine arrived at 7:15. She had a sheaf of telegrams from friends and supporters, almost all of them other criminal-defense lawyers. *"Illegitimi Non Carborundum"* was the general sentiment. The Missouri renegade prosecutor Brent Bollinger's was more specific: "Break that son of a bitch Dwayne Thompson down. He's the key."

Innocence or guilt was not their concern—most of those who sent telegrams figured Marvin White was guilty as charged. They were supporting Wyatt because they were part of a small, beleaguered fraternity, fighting a rising tide that proclaimed the credo "Innocent until proven guilty beyond a reasonable doubt" was only words on paper, no longer to be taken seriously in the real world.

By 7:30 the other members of his team had drifted in. Walcott, Darryl (in an unofficial, cheerleading capacity), and Freida Berman, his jury consultant.

Berman was a jury specialist, a sociology professor from the University of Chicago. Wyatt had brought her on a month ago, when the questionnaires from the jury pool had been returned and needed to be analyzed by an expert. Freida's fee was $250 an hour, a low price for someone well qualified in the field. Wyatt had petitioned the court for money to pay her. The prosecution had their own team of consultants; their bill would run close to $10,000, more if they needed it. He should have equal access to expert advice, he argued.

Judge Grant awarded the Public Defender's office $2,500, a ludicrously low amount. On his big billion-dollar corporate case Wyatt and his team had spent $150,000 on jury consultants alone. Wyatt had complained about the paltry award but Walcott had given him the facts of life, lesson 97, the same lesson as numbers 1 through 96: the courts are not about to help you out. You fly on a wing and a prayer.

He couldn't operate that way, not with a life and his reputation at stake, so he paid Berman an additional $5,000 out of his pocket—out of the firm's pocket. Ben Turner wasn't about to let his star go into combat without some ammunition. "We're not a bottomless pit on this," he told Wyatt, "like we would be if we were defending a deep-pockets client, but we're not going to let a member of the family drown, either."

Berman had reviewed the questionnaires, marking the candidates who appeared to be the most promising. There weren't many. Most of those available were middle-aged and older, and more than half of them were not African American. A large percentage were people who formed their opinions through a narrow prism and held strong, uncompromising attitudes about right and wrong. These prospective jurors would be highly predisposed to believe what the police and prosecutors told them.

Wyatt and Freida separated the candidates into three broad categories: pretty good, barely possibly, and NFW (No Fucking Way). This would change when they saw and questioned the individuals face-to-face, but it was a start. There were twice as many NFWs as the other two categories combined.

Their big concern was black men, especially younger black men. Of the fourteen black men (out of two hundred jury candidates) on the list under the age of forty-five, six had been arrested, and three others had had some kind of trouble with the criminal justice system. Being arrested wasn't in itself grounds for disqualification, but Wyatt was afraid the prosecution would try to make it one, and he was concerned that Judge Grant would let them.

Wyatt's bottom line was one young black man on this jury. It was paramount. He would prefer someone from the streets, a true peer to Marvin, but any black man would be better than none, even a college graduate who might want to put the ghetto shit behind him, or pretend it didn't exist.

"Ready?" Walcott asked.

Wyatt smiled. "I've been waiting for this day for a long time," he said.

"Good luck. I'm not going to be here much," Walcott told him, "but I'll always be reachable. So give 'em hell." The head of the office gave him a firm punch on the shoulder as he left.

Wyatt sipped from his coffee mug. "Finger-lickin' good, as usual," he complimented Josephine. "You'll be close behind me?"

"Every inch of the way."

He could go to the bank on that. She would be doing most of the legwork during the proceedings.

"Thanks for coming," he told Darryl.

"I wouldn't miss this for the world." Darryl smiled his devilish smile.

He'd thought about bringing Darryl in to sit second chair: having an experienced defense lawyer by his side, who happened to be black, like the defendant, was a tempting notion. In the end, though, he'd decided not to. He had left the security of workplace and home to do this, and it was his to do alone.

A marshal stuck his head in the door. "The courtroom's open. You can come up anytime now," he said.

Except for a couple of deputies checking to see that everything was in order, the large, classically styled courtroom was empty. Wyatt stood in the aisle between the defense and prosecution tables, soaking up atmosphere.

The trial had been playing in his head for weeks. Sometimes he would close his eyes and watch it unfold, as if viewing a movie. Witnesses, exhibits, examinations, cross-examinations, a swirl of images alternately coalescing and diverging, in constant flux. Sometimes these daydreams would take on a surreal quality, faces interchanging, his witnesses becoming adversarial, prosecution witnesses becoming his allies. He would hear his opening argument filling every inch of space in the room, the sound of his voice spreading to the ceiling and out the windows. There were times when he was so focused, so in the zone, that it was as if a shaft of light from above came down and shone upon him, spotlighting him in an almost spiritual, protective sheath.

As if in a time-release moment, the courtroom suddenly came to life. Marvin hadn't been brought in yet, and Judge Grant had not taken the bench. But there, not ten feet away, sat Helena Abramowitz, looking over some notes, talking to her cocounsel, Norman Windsor. Sitting alongside them was their team of jury consultants, a man and a woman.

Freida Berman sat next to him, Josephine next to her. On his other arm there was an empty chair for Marvin. Sitting behind him in the gallery were Darryl and Marvin's family and a few friends: Jonnie Rae, his sisters and brother, Dexter, Richard, and Louis. Other than them, the room was empty.

He walked over to the railing and leaned in close to Jonnie Rae. "How are you doing?" he asked.

She shrugged and gave a half smile. "Okay, I guess."

"Jury selection is going to take days, weeks. It'll be boring. You don't have to be here for this part."

"I need to be here for him," she said, nodding toward the empty chair.

She had kicked her son out of the house for slacking, lying, and thieving. Now she was standing foursquare behind him. This is a good woman, he thought. This kid is lucky to have her.

"Okay," he said. "That's good. It'll make a good impression." He glanced over at Dexter, nodded a greeting. Dexter, looking grim, nodded back.

Marvin was brought in. He was dressed nicely, in sports coat, white shirt, and tie, and he had a fresh haircut. A handsome young man, Wyatt thought, as Marvin stood compliantly while his handcuffs were removed. In appearance, at least, he posed no threat to the prospective jurors.

Marvin leaned over the rail and hugged his mother. The deputy in charge gave them a few seconds before tapping Marvin on the shoulder and shaking his head.

"You okay?" Wyatt asked.

Marvin nodded.

"Stay calm and look people in the eye, but not threateningly. Don't make any unnecessary gestures, and for sure don't make signs of disapproval, even if you don't like what's being said or done. Some of these people will wind up sitting on the jury, and the first impression they get of you will be an important one. If you need to tell me something whisper in my ear, as quietly and unobtrusively as possible. Okay?"

Again, a nod.

He patted Marvin on the thigh. "We're going to get through this. Trust me."

Marvin turned to him. "I do."

They all rose as Judge Grant entered the chambers, then

sat down again. Grant opened his jury portfolio. "Is the prosecution ready to proceed?"

Abramowitz rose, nervously smoothing her skirt. "We are, Your Honor."

Grant to Wyatt: "Is the defense ready?"

Wyatt stood up. With one hand on Marvin's shoulder, he said, "Yes, Your Honor."

"Bring them in," the judge directed his bailiff.

Two hundred members of the jury pool filed in and were seated in the courtroom. Judge Grant made a brief speech, explaining the selection process, how important serving on this jury would be, and thanking them in advance for their cooperation and participation. That someone was willing to serve, or even strongly wanted to, was not cause for selection. Many critical criteria had to be met. If they were disqualified they shouldn't take it personally—most of them would be, for all kinds of reasons that they might not understand but that were legitimate.

Each prospective juror had been assigned a number. All the numbers were put into a glass bowl. The bailiff blindly drew the first twelve and called them out. Those twelve people whose numbers had been selected got up from their seats and entered the jury box. A few of them glanced over at Marvin as they passed through the swinging gate.

After they completed the initial voir dire the individual selections were done privately in the jury room, adjacent to the courtroom. Joining Judge Grant were Wyatt, Marvin, and Freida for the defense, and Helena, Windsor, and their jury experts for the prosecution. Both sides had requested that their jury experts be allowed in the room as each prospective juror was individually questioned, and Grant had allowed it. The experts' active participation would make the process go slower than normal, but he wanted to guard against either side later bitching that they hadn't been able to present their case to the best of their ability. William Grant had almost never been reversed at the appellate level; he definitely wasn't going to be this time.

Each prospective juror was brought into the chamber in the order in which his or her number had been drawn. Grant did the questioning; if either Wyatt or Helena wanted to ask a question they would tell him. Most of the time they didn't have to, because before they got to a particular situation the juror had already been disqualified for cause by Grant.

His first question eliminated twenty-five percent of the prospects. "This is a capital case in which the death penalty is an option if the defendant is found guilty. Do you have any problems—morally, religiously, philosophically, whatever—in handing down a death sentence if the findings in the trial warrant it?"

One in four people couldn't hand down a penalty of death. They were automatically dismissed.

Marvin gulped hard the first time Grant made that statement. Wyatt put a calming hand on his shoulder and kept it there. After it had been repeated half a dozen times, each time with the same neutral inflection, Marvin was able to bear it without openly flinching.

Wyatt had thought about arguing against this blanket dismissal policy, even filing a formal brief. To only qualify people who could vote for a death penalty was prejudicial against a defendant, in his opinion. But at the end of the day, he backed off. He'd researched the case law, talked with Walcott, Darryl, and other criminal-defense lawyers, and concluded that he wouldn't have a prayer of winning and could prejudice Grant against him, so he let it slide.

Out of the first group of twelve, two were accepted, both women. Wyatt and Berman conferred at length before agreeing to the inclusion of one of them, a middle-aged white female postal worker who was a regular churchgoer from a Pentecostal sect. After a lengthy, careful discussion they decided not to fight her. A lot of Pentecostal churches were integrated, and as a postal worker she was in daily contact with hundreds of black people, fellow members of the civil service and customers. She shouldn't have a knee-jerk antiblack attitude. And she'd never been raped, nor did she personally know any woman who had.

The proceedings moved glacially, each prospective juror taking up to an hour to be questioned. There was considerable consulting with experts on both sides. Anyone Wyatt liked Helena opposed, and vice versa. By the time the lunch break was called they'd only gotten through the initial group of twelve.

The first indication there was going to be trouble came

midway through the afternoon session. The first black male jury prospect, number seventeen, a twenty-eight-year-old construction worker, ambled into the room. He laser-beamed Marvin with a badass stare while folding himself into the oak captain's chair, facing Judge Grant.

Definitely copping an attitude, Wyatt thought, quickly sizing him up. He looked at the man's questionnaire. Frieda had put him in the top twenty percent. This one was someone to fight for.

In answer to Grant's death-penalty question, the prospect answered in a streetwise voice: "Absolutely. You do the deed, you pay the price." Looking again at Marvin: "Not saying the brother here did it. I don't know one way or the other."

Grant turned to his list of questions, the same basic questions he asked every prospect, but before he could get the first question out of his mouth Helena, having been whispered to by one of her jury specialists, raised an objection. "Request dismissal for cause," she said forcefully.

Wyatt's head whipped around.

"On what grounds?" the judge asked.

"This man has a criminal record," she stated. "He did six months in the Iowa reformatory for breaking and entering."

On his feet immediately, Wyatt responded, "So what? That was in a youth-detention center, when he was a juvenile. He didn't try to conceal it, he admitted it on his questionnaire. That isn't grounds for dismissal, Your Honor. If counsel wants this man disqualified she'll have to use a challenge."

"In this case there are grounds, Your Honor," Helena shot back. "There is ample case law backing up our position."

"There's as much case law opposing it," Wyatt retaliated. He knew; he'd researched this issue carefully. "Having been arrested is not automatic grounds for dismissal from serving on a jury, Your Honor. If that were the case almost half the black men under forty in this country would be disqualified from sitting on a jury. If my client is denied this segment of the jury pool he won't have anyone resembling a peer sitting in judgment on him. That's blatantly unfair."

Grant thought for a moment. " 'Peer' is a broad term, Counselor."

"You know what I'm talking about, Your Honor."

Grant turned to juror number seventeen. "Wait outside for a moment, please."

The man cast a baleful eye upon them all and exited.

"This would be letting the fox into the henhouse," Helena stated vehemently, as soon as the door was closed. "This man has absolute contempt for the criminal-justice system."

"Who endowed you with mind-reading powers?" Wyatt shot back. He turned to Grant. "He fulfills all the criteria for serving on a jury. He wouldn't be in here if he didn't—unless being young, masculine in gender, and black is ipso facto disqualification."

He looked over at Marvin. His client was sitting rock still. So, he noticed, was Deputy Prosecutor Windsor.

Grant leaned back in his chair and looked up at the ceiling as if asking for divine guidance. "I'm inclined to go with Ms. Abramowitz's motion," he said finally.

"What is the basis for this ruling, Your Honor?" Wyatt asked. If this was the beginning of a trend, it was very disturbing.

"Because his record indicates he will be prejudicial." Grant sat up straight. "This is not to be taken as a blanket endorsement," he said to Helena.

"So he's out?" Wyatt asked, his voice rising in indignation.

"He's out," Grant answered gruffly. To his bailiff: "Call the next in line." He turned to Wyatt again. "This is my courtroom, Mr. Matthews. I make the decisions. Don't question them."

At the end of the day they had three jurors: the two women from the morning session and a man, a retired accountant. Two whites—the postal worker and the accountant—and one black woman, who was elderly and (at least on paper) fit the profile of a law-and-order type. She had a son in the air force, a major, and liked how he looked in his uniform. On the other hand, she did volunteer work in inner-city school remedial programs. Wyatt thought hard about excluding both her and the retired accountant, but he had already used four of his preemptory challenges and didn't want to run out before some totally unacceptable candidates came up.

Grant adjourned the proceedings at the stroke of four. They'd start in tomorrow at nine o'clock.

While none of the three selections had been in his top one-third group of desirables, they hadn't been at the bottom of the list, either. Not a great beginning, but not a disaster. None of the other young black men in the jury pool had come up for consideration, so that issue was still in the air.

But not for long. It came up again the following morning. The third prospect brought in was a black man in his thirties. Neat and tidy in appearance, he was a parts manager for a local Buick dealership. A high school graduate, two years of college, had never been arrested. He glanced passively at Marvin as he sat down, looked with curiosity at Assistant DA Windsor, and turned his attention to Judge Grant.

In response to Grant's initial query regarding the death penalty the man replied that it should be used very carefully, because it was the ultimate price someone paid, and if later on it turned out a mistake had been made it couldn't be fixed; but he wasn't against it in any absolute way. There could be situations that would warrant it.

Wyatt really wanted this man. He had him rated in the top ten of his preferences. Abramowitz could try to find some excuse other than race to use one of her preemptories on him, but there was no substantial reason to, and she would risk alienating her black cocounsel. And he knew she was far too smart to overtly risk a constitutional violation regarding race.

Grant asked a few questions. The man answered them precisely and carefully.

"Have you ever been stopped or otherwise detained by the police for a reason you felt was wrong or unfair?" Grant asked. He was about to wrap the questioning up and add a fourth juror to the list.

"One time I was," the man answered after a moment's deliberation.

Helena had been taking notes. She looked up; simultaneously, her male jury expert whispered in her ear.

"Could you tell us what that was about?" Grant asked.

"My cousin is Michael Towles."

There was no reaction from Grant.

"He used to play linebacker for the Denver Broncos," the man explained.

Wyatt remembered Michael Towles. He'd played in the late eighties. Not a star, but a good, heady team player.

"A football player," Grant said. "Not my sport. Go ahead."

"He got a signing bonus, so he went out and got himself a new car. A Mercedes. Real nice car. He bought it in Oakland and was driving it to Denver and asked me to come along with him, so I did."

The prospective juror hesitated for a moment, then continued. "We were driving along Highway 80, just cruising along, and we got into Salt Lake City."

Wyatt was listening with half an ear to the conversation while looking through the questionnaires of the next batch of candidates.

"Out of the blue, this Salt Lake City policeman pulls us over."

Wyatt looked up fast. He caught Helena's stare, turned to look at the man.

"And?" Grant asked, prodding.

"He made us get out of the car, spread us on the hood, frisked us and searched us. Searched our car."

"What was his reason?" Grant asked. On the prosecution side of the room Helena and her jury consultants were whispering energetically.

"Said we looked suspicious."

"That was all?" Grant asked.

"That was all the reason they gave us. DWB."

"DWB?" Grant repeated, befuddled.

"Driving while black," the man said. "Two black guys driving an expensive Mercedes, some places call that reasonable cause."

Abramowitz's hand shot up like she was a third-grader bursting to please the teacher.

"What is it?" Grant asked.

"Request for dismissal for cause, Your Honor."

Wyatt stood up. "These are clearly insufficient grounds, Your Honor," he said vigorously, managing to restrain himself although he wanted to scream. "There is absolutely no reason in the world that incident is grounds for dismissal."

"Indication of prejudice, Your Honor," Helena responded with equal force. She glared at Wyatt.

"That is pure ... fantasy," Wyatt said, since he knew "bullshit" wouldn't go down well with Grant. "Use one of your preemptories," he challenged her.

Grant turned to the prospect. "Did anything else happen?"

"The cop called for backup. He was going to find some excuse to arrest us. Except the other cop who responded knew who my cousin was, 'cause he was a sports fan. So they let us go. We got out of Utah as fast as we could."

Smart move, Wyatt thought.

"We still request dismissal for cause, Your Honor."

Wyatt looked up again, this time in amazement. The request had come from Norman Windsor. Windsor was bent over, listening intently to the prosecution's female jury specialist. As she spoke quietly to him he frowned, listened again, then nodded.

"This man has a deep suspicion of police motives," Windsor said, standing erect, "no matter how innocuous or well founded. He would not be able render an impartial verdict. We request dismissal for cause," he said again.

"I repeat, this doesn't amount to cause, Your Honor," Wyatt answered. What bullshit. Grant would stuff this crap right down their throats.

"State's request to strike the juror is granted," Grant said. "This candidate is dismissed for cause." He turned before Wyatt could express his outrage. "And please don't ask me why again, Mr. Matthews. I have more than ample grounds to take this action."

Wyatt looked at Marvin. He was sagging in his chair, his eyes dull. He knows, Wyatt thought. Any way they can screw him, they will.

It took a full two weeks but a jury was finally sworn in, along with eight alternates. Wyatt went through his preemptory challenges halfway through the proceedings. Abramowitz had some left; Grant did yeoman work for her.

Eight women, four men. Four black jurors, three of them

women. The only black man was a retired public school custodian who had grown up in the rural South. Hardly a jury of Marvin's peers.

Friday afternoon. Court was in open session again. Jonnie Rae, Marvin's sisters and brother, and Dexter and his other friends sat in the rows behind the defendant's table. As Marvin was led to the defendant's table Dexter saluted him with a clenched fist. Marvin, his back to judge and jury, returned the salute, his fist held up against his chest to hide it from view.

The twelve newly selected jurors were seated in the jury box, in the order in which they had been chosen. Judge Grant took the bench. "We will reconvene Tuesday morning," he said, "at which time we will hear opening statements. Will the people be ready to proceed?"

"We will, Your Honor," Helena said, rising in place.

"The defense?"

Wyatt stood. "We'll be ready."

Grant slammed his gavel down. "This court stands adjourned until Tuesday morning."

"Ladies and gentlemen of the jury . . ."

The trial of the *People v. Marvin White* had officially commenced. Helena Abramowitz stood at the lectern, ready to begin her opening statement to the jury.

The courtroom was packed, every seat taken. Wyatt had provided Jonnie Rae and the family with a set of bodyguards who had muscled them through the crowd of people, especially the vultures of the press. They sat in the first row behind the defendant's table, dressed in their Sunday best. Dexter and a few other supporters flanked them.

At the defendant's table, Wyatt, wearing one of his A suits, sat with Marvin. Marvin was dressed up in one of the new ensembles of sports coat, shirt, tie, pants, and shoes that Wyatt had bought for him. Marvin sat up straight, looking at the jury, per Wyatt's instructions. Wyatt had a legal pad and some sharp pencils laid out in front of him, to take notes of the prosecution's presentation.

The train was leaving the station. Everyone that had to be on board was.

"You may think this is a complicated case," Helena said. She was wearing a conservative dark gray dress, pearls, low heels. "But it's really very simple. You are going to be asked to judge the guilt or innocence of a man charged with the murders and rapes of seven members of this community. Brutal, senseless murders." She turned to look at Marvin. Pointing a finger at him, she intoned, "This man, Marvin White."

She held her look, the hand pointing the accusatory finger rigid, fixed. Time froze. Everyone was looking at where she was pointing.

Wyatt stared back at her without blinking. Marvin tried to, but he was unable to keep his eyes fixed on her. He looked down at the table.

"Look up," Wyatt whispered fiercely without moving. "Keep your eyes up."

Marvin forced himself to raise his eyes and stare back at Abramowitz. He took deep, steady breaths, trying to stay calm.

After ten seconds that felt like a small eternity Abramowitz lowered her hand and turned back to the jury. "It is our job—the prosecution's—to convince you beyond a reasonable doubt that Marvin White is the perpetrator of these heinous, despicable acts. And ladies and gentlemen," she said, forcefully gripping the sides of the lectern, "we are going to do exactly that. By the time we have finished presenting our case there will be no doubt in anyone's mind that Marvin White is the man who committed these crimes. We will not convince you beyond a reasonable doubt. We will convince you far beyond that. We will convince you completely and absolutely. So that when you go into that jury room to deliberate you will have no problems whatsoever—no doubts—that Marvin White is guilty as charged."

She paused for a moment, taking a sip of water. Then she continued, her voice becoming almost evangelical in its sincerity. "We have a mountain of evidence that will place Marvin White at the scenes of these murders. And more importantly, ladies and gentlemen, we have a confession. Marvin White has already confessed to these crimes." She opened a portfolio that was lying flat on top of the lectern. "Marvin White confessed to a fellow inmate in the county jail while he was waiting to go on trial for another charge. He confessed, ladies and gentlemen. That is irrefutable."

A few jurors picked up their pads and starting taking notes.

Abramowitz went on. "I will grant you the man Marvin White confessed to is no angel. He is presently serving a term at Durban State Penitentiary, the toughest prison in this state. But he is also a man who has the quality of getting other criminals to tell him their deepest, darkest secrets, which he has done in several other cases, including one that is currently pending."

Wyatt immediately rose to his feet. "Objection, Your Honor. Any other case is not part of this trial."

Grant thought for a moment. "Objection denied," he decided. "Opening statements are presentations of intent and premise, not previously verified facts." He turned to Helena. "Proceed."

"Thank you, Your Honor," she said, glaring at Wyatt. Turning back to the jury, she pressed on. "But that's not all the evidence we have," she said. "Not by a long shot. We will lay out a timetable for you, showing that these murders, which all fit the same identical pattern and point to one man, one perpetrator, started less than a month after Marvin White began working at Livonius's Commercial Laundry & Dry Cleaning on West Sixteenth Street. That all the murders took place in neighborhoods he serviced in his job as delivery boy."

Wyatt could feel Marvin wince at the appellation "delivery boy." Not the same social status in his circle as "high-class drug dealer," "drive-by gunman," or "pimp." Be glad that's what you were, he thought. If you really had been a dealer, you'd be even farther up shit's creek than you are now.

Abramowitz had used that description as a deliberate put-down, signaling to the jury that Marvin White was a worthless piece of garbage for whom there should be no sympathy. Having dropped that little stink bomb, she moved on. "We have witnesses who will place Marvin White in the specific crime areas on the specific days of the individual murders. And we have evidence, physical evidence, that was found on Marvin White's person that directly links him to the scene of the most recent crime."

Abramowitz, pausing momentarily for a drink of water, moved on. "The murders began shortly after Marvin White began working in those neighborhoods. The last one occurred the same night he was arrested for attempted armed robbery. In addition," she continued, "we have an eyewitness who was at the scene of the last murder, literally within minutes of the time the murder and rape took place. This witness saw Marvin White there; and he saw her. They were standing less than twenty feet from each other. This witness picked Marvin White out of a police lineup without hesitation and without any doubt whatsoever. He was there, this witness saw him there, and she will testify to that. So we will prove to you, without question, that Marvin White was at the murder site when the murder took place."

The room was quiet, a faint buzz of traffic from the street outside the only conscious noise. Everyone's attention was on the trim woman standing at the speaker's lectern.

She took another sip of water. "And we will also introduce evidence," she said, "that will show this man has a pattern of rape and a pattern of violence. A few years ago, just before Marvin White began working as a delivery boy at Livonius's Dry Cleaning, he raped a girl at knifepoint. And that girl will come in here and testify about that to you."

"Objection!" Wyatt was on his feet. This time he was truly livid. "That accusation, which was dropped and for which my client never went to trial, is part of his juvenile record, inadmissible in these proceedings. Move this part of the prosecution statement be stricken and the jury instructed to disregard it."

They had fought over this part of her opening in a hearing with Judge Grant before the trial had started. Wyatt had fought vigorously against allowing this information in but Grant had deferred his ruling, preferring to decide when it actually came up, if in fact it did. Now here it was, for all the world, especially the twelve jurors, to hear.

Before Grant could begin to think about his decision Abramowitz had picked up a lawbook. "Normally that would be true, Your Honor," she stated, "but recently, in *Maine v. Loudermilk,* the courts ruled that a juvenile record could be introduced into an adult trial if the portion of the record helps establish a pattern that carries over from the juvenile phase to the adult. The appropriate appellate courts upheld that ruling. Marvin White is accused of rape and murder, the instrument of murder in most of these crimes being a knife. So bringing in an earlier accusation of rape at knifepoint is completely within our limits."

"That applies to a *conviction,* Your Honor," Wyatt said. He was prepared for this. He had prepared an "issue memo," which he handed to the clerk of the court, who passed it up to the judge. Grant gave it a perfunctory look, then laid it aside.

"Marvin White was never convicted," Wyatt continued. "He never even went to trial. *Loudermilk* doesn't apply here, and I repeat my request that this section be stricken and the jury instructed to disregard it and counsel for the prosecution be admonished."

Judge Grant motioned with crooked forefinger for the lawbook. A deputy took it from Abramowitz and brought it to the bench. He opened the page she'd bookmarked and began reading.

Wyatt watched Grant closely. If that girl was allowed to come in here and testify it could be major bad news.

Grant was taking his time. Wyatt leaned in to Marvin. "How're you doing?"

Marvin nodded "Okay. What's she mean about evidence on me that puts me at the murder?" he whispered.

"I don't know," Wyatt whispered back, "but there is none, so when she brings that up we'll blow it out of the water."

Marvin smiled grimly upon hearing that, but Wyatt knew he was still scared about whatever it might be.

Grant closed the book and looked up. "This witness will come in here and testify under oath that she was raped at knifepoint?" he asked Abramowitz. "Which will mean contradicting herself regarding her earlier testimony," he added significantly. "That could leave her open to charges of perjury, in either case, or both."

"Yes, Your Honor," Abramowitz answered. "Regardless of the consequences of perjury, which she's aware of, she wants to come and tell her story."

"Then I'm overruling the objection," Grant said, blowing Wyatt off. "The prosecution's remarks will stand." To Abramowitz: "Go ahead."

Thanks, you son of a bitch.

Abramowitz sneered in Wyatt's direction. Turning to the

jury, she said, "The state will prove to you that the defendant, Marvin White, was in the very places these murders took place, when they took place. An eyewitness will place him at the location of the final murder within minutes of when it happened. And you will hear his own confession, backed up by copious police reports. If any case was ever open-and-shut, this is that case. Ladies and gentlemen," she concluded, "convicting a man of a capital offense is a difficult and painful decision to make, individually and collectively. But making those decisions is what the heart of our jury system is about. Twelve men and women, hearing the evidence presented, and making an informed judgment based on it. It is why we are a nation of laws and why we are a great country. Ladies and gentlemen of the jury, you are the eyes and ears and hearts and brains of this community. This city is looking to you for justice. And when all the evidence has been presented, and all the facts are known, there will be only one conclusion you will be able to reach, one decision you will be compelled to render. That Marvin White, the defendant sitting before you, is guilty of seven rapes and seven murders. And that he must be punished for those terrible crimes to the fullest extent of the law."

Court was recessed for lunch. When they came back at one-thirty it was Wyatt's turn. He strode to the edge of the lectern, rested one hand on the mantel, and stuck the other casually in his pocket. He had no portfolio in front of him, no notes. He knew what he wanted to say—he had rehearsed this speech several times—and he was going to say it. Comfortably, personably, without a trace of threat or malice.

"Good afternoon," he began. "First of all I want to thank you for being here. For taking the time out of your lives to do your civic duty. It's no small thing, sitting on a jury, especially when the case is as important as this one." He paused, glancing from one juror to the next, establishing eye contact with each in turn.

"My opponent here for the prosecution"—he waved his hand behind him in the vague direction of the prosecutor's table without turning to look at them—"made a nice speech to you. Fiery, passionate. She has this killer everybody's been thirsting after in her sights and all you've got to do is pull the trigger for her and we'll all go home happy." He shrugged. "Pretty uncomplicated. Slam dunk." He nodded, as if accepting the wisdom of Helena's theses. "Except there are a couple problems with her argument.

"First off, there've been seven killings, spaced out over close to two years, in a large area of the city. But no one's ever been a witness to any of them, and no murder weapon's ever been found. No witnesses, no weapon. Now I grant you, circumstantial evidence can be a powerful tool, but that's all it is—circumstantial. In case you don't know exactly what the term 'circumstantial evidence' means in this setting, I took the trouble to look it up, because I wasn't exactly sure myself, and I knew the state was going to base their case on it."

He plucked a three-by-five index card from his inside jacket pocket and read from it. " 'Circumstantial evidence. Evidence not bearing directly on the fact or facts in dispute but on various attendant circumstances from which the judge or jury might infer the occurrence of the fact or facts in dispute.' *Webster's Unabridged Dictionary* said that."

He put the card back in his pocket. "To me that means they don't have any direct evidence. It's all coming in from the sides. But no *facts*—no witnesses, no weapon, and a big one—no motive. In over ninety percent of all murders committed in this country, probably in the world, the person doing the killing knew the person they were killing. If only for a little while. But Marvin White didn't know any of these victims. Had never met them, talked to them, had any relationship with them. Most of the victims, as you may know, were prostitutes. Streetwalkers, not the high-priced kind. Which is not to in any way denigrate or otherwise demean them. They were God's children, as we all are. Their lives were as valuable and important as any of ours, yours or mine. But the point is, they were women that needy men paid money to for cheap, quick sex. And we will show you—I believe conclusively—that Marvin White never paid a woman to have sex with him. Never.

"So—no motive. No prior knowledge with any of the victims. No witnesses, and no weapon." He paused for a moment to let that sink in. Several of the jurors were taking notes, he noticed.

"But they do have one thing," he continued. "A confession, all wrapped up in a pretty package with a big blue ribbon tied around it. Not a *legal* confession, of course," he added quickly, emphasizing the word "legal." "Not a confession on the record, to a policeman or a prosecutor or anyone in a position of *legal* authority. No—they don't have that. They have what is commonly known as a quote 'jailhouse confession,' unquote. You know what a jailhouse confession is? A jailhouse confession is where one bad guy bares his soul to another bad guy because he's so overcome with remorse at the terrible things he's done that he has to tell someone, so he tells that first bad guy, 'cause if you can't trust another criminal, who can you trust?" He stopped for a moment. "Especially some other criminal you've never laid eyes on before in your life, who you don't know from Adam. But my worthy opponent would have you believe that these so-called jailhouse confessions are carved in stone, from God's mouth to your ears." He shook his head. "Uh-uh. Wrong! Snitches—in the old days they were called stool pigeons—because that's what these jailhouse informants are; informant is just a fancy name for snitch, folks, you've seen the old Jimmy Cagney and Humphrey Bogart movies on your cable channels—these snitches and their testimony have been discredited from coast to coast. Sometimes they're just flat-out lying—they know one or two things and make up the rest—and other times they've been fed their information. By policemen, prosecutors"—this time he didn't merely wave behind his back at the prosecution table, he turned and stared at them for a moment before turning back—"who want to get a conviction, *have* to get a conviction, for lots of reasons; but none of them are the right reason, the only reason—which is that justice should prevail."

He could feel Abramowitz's eyes shooting daggers at his back. Good. He wanted her to take this personally—it would help him control the flow of the trial.

"Now I'm not saying the police collaborated with the state's key witness. Or the prosecution or anyone else. But I am telling you it has happened. And you have to know it and be on guard for it."

He paused for a sip of water. He wasn't thirsty, but he wanted to take a dramatic moment. Then he continued.

"But that's their case, which we don't have to disprove. They have to *prove* it, beyond a reasonable doubt, as my opponent told you. They have to prove their case. And while they're trying—futilely, I suspect—we'll be presenting our own case. You will hear witnesses who will tell you Marvin White was with them on the dates and times when those crimes were committed. And not just one date, ladies and gentlemen. We have solid, credible, honest witnesses for two of the days when these women were killed. People who will swear, and will offer real, physical proof, that Marvin White was with them on the days or nights in question, and couldn't have—could *not* have—committed those murders, because he wasn't there to commit them. And since the prosecution firmly maintains that one man committed all seven crimes, then if Marvin White didn't commit two of them, we know he couldn't have committed any of them."

Now he leaned forward on the lectern. "They don't have any eyewitnesses. But we do."

He took a step back, assuming his more relaxed, user-friendly position again. "These seven murders have been horrible. We all agree with that. And we all agree that whoever committed them should stand before the bar of justice and face a severe penalty. But you can't scapegoat someone because collectively we need catharsis. You can't throw an innocent young man to the lions because you want blood."

He walked around the front of the lectern and stood in front of the jury box.

"The only reason Marvin White was bound over for trial, ladies and gentlemen, was not because some snitch who's spent his life behind bars got some unbelievable confession out of him. No. He's here as a sacrifice. One Marvin White, served up on a plate, so a million people can rest easy in their beds. One for a million. Good trade-off. The ancient Egyptians and Mayans and other civilizations that practiced human sacrifice would have loved those odds. They wouldn't have thought twice. But we're not barbarians anymore, ladies and gentlemen; thank God. We don't sacrifice one for the good of many, just because it's easy or convenient. One of the great beauties of our legal system is that we respect each and every one of us as unique and special. Which is why we don't find innocent men guilty of crimes they didn't commit."

He walked back to the lectern and stood in front of it so all twelve jurors and eight alternates could see him easily.

"My client isn't the easiest person in the world to defend. He has a juvenile record, he comes from a class of people who are nowadays too often automatically under suspicion. But that's one of the great things about our criminal justice system, ladies and gentlemen of the jury. Someone's background, or what they did in the past, doesn't count in a trial. All that matters are the facts in this case. That's what innocent until proven guilty is all about, and it's one of the main reasons we're considered the greatest country in the world."

He was cloaking Marvin in the flag, apple pie, and motherhood because he had to. His client was everything juries looked for in justifying a guilty verdict. So you had to massage them, guilt-trip them. And remind them of their sworn duty.

"You have a sworn obligation to judge the evidence in this case carefully, soberly, and with great attention," he said. "Only the evidence—*not* what my client looks like, *not* where he comes from, *not* what he'd done in the past. And I know that is exactly how you're going to conduct yourself.

"Marvin White didn't kill these women," he told them. "You'll see. And when you do, you'll return the only verdict possible. A verdict of *not guilty* of these crimes. And you'll free this young man who never should have been here in the first place, and let him walk out of this courtroom a free man."

He and Josephine had a working dinner in the office. Walcott stuck his head in. "Heard it went well today," he commented.

"Pretty good," Wyatt agreed.

"Considering it's your first criminal-defense opening, I'd say it went better than 'pretty good,' " the head of the office told him.

"He kicked serious ass," Josephine chimed in.

"This one's a tough critic," Walcott said. "She doesn't pull her punches."

Wyatt gave a mock shit-kicker shrug. "The jury was paying attention. The stuff about building a case on nothing but circumstantial evidence and a jailhouse confession—they definitely heard that. And if I can work in any evidence of collusion with the police or the DA's office—*anything,* even if it's off the point—that'll hit home hard. These people want to trust the cops on this one but I think it'll be easy to turn them around if we can find something discrediting." He looked at Josephine. "Review every instance we've got of police, sheriff's, and district attorney's office malfeasance or other kinds of fuckups over the past five years. Let's see if we can find any kind of pattern we can use."

She jotted the request down in her always-ready notebook.

"See you mañana," Walcott said, leaving them.

Josephine leafed through her notes. "I checked into the stuff from this morning," she said. "Physical evidence on the last body linking her to Marvin—I don't know what that means. They do have sperm samples from her and the two previous victims but they never did DNA comparisons with Marvin's."

"They have a confession and an eyewitness placing him where it happened. Why take the chance of muddying the waters with a complicated DNA result?" He took a bite from a slice of mushroom pizza. It was cold, but he scarfed it down anyway. "Let's spring for a microwave tomorrow. The least we should be able to do is eat a slice of hot pizza." He stuffed his papers into his briefcase. "See you tomorrow."

The message light was blinking. He called in. There were two messages.

The first one was from Moira and Michaela. *"Hi."* (Moira.) *"We're doing fine here. The weather's starting to clear, we were able to go to the beach today and get in some swimming. Michaela's amazingly active, considering she's lugging ten pounds on her leg. We went to Boston yesterday and had it checked—she's doing great, ahead of schedule,*

she does her exercises religiously. We found a nice psy-
chologist here and we're going to start seeing him twice a
week. The good thing is we're talking to each other, really
talking. I hope you and I can do the same some day."

Michaela kicked in. *"I hope your first day at the trial*
went really well, Daddy. We're having lots of fun here. I
miss you a lot." (There was a pause—he could hear talking
in the background.) *"Mom does, too. I wish you were here,*
so finish your trial off as fast as you can and come."

Moira came back on. *"We've been going to bed early, so*
if you're going to call us it's better to do it in the morning or
early afternoon. We're always home by eight—we've been
watching videos every night. Talk to you soon."

The message ended. He checked his watch—it was after
ten. If he had the time he'd call tomorrow during the lunch
recess, or right after court finished for the day.

His daughter missed him. His wife did, too, after some
prompting.

The second call was more recent, logged in at 9:30.

"I'm glad I'm talking to a machine. I don't know if I
would have had the guts to stay on if you had answered. I
know I shouldn't be calling you. I wanted to be in the court-
room today but Mrs. Abramowitz said since I'm a witness I
can't come until after I've finished testifying.

"My friends who were there told me you were very good.
My stomach was churning as I talked to them—I have such
strong emotions about the boy you're defending and think-
ing that my friend was murdered and the police are so sure
he did it. I want whoever did it to pay but I don't want you to
get hurt. It's hard. If you did get hurt, I'm sure I'd feel bad,
too. I hope it's proved he's guilty or not guilty conclusively,
one way or the other.

"I know I shouldn't have called you—I said that, didn't
I—but I guess I couldn't help myself. You take care of your-
self. Maybe when this is all over ..." There was a long
pause, as if she was going to say more; then the phone
went dead.

He lay on top of the covers in his clothes, nursing a
Scotch and watching CNN. There was a brief blip about the
opening of the trial, less than thirty seconds. A quick shot of

him entering the courthouse after lunch, a longer one of Helena Abramowitz. Nothing of Marvin or the family.

As much as he could he wanted to shield the family from this. They had no media savvy—they could come across as bumpkins, victims, cheap fodder. Their lives had already been devastated; anything he could do to protect what shreds of privacy and pride they had left, he was going to.

That was all background for what he was thinking about. Violet had called. He'd felt his breath stop, listening to her voice. He would have loved to have heard it in person, spoken to her, but at the same time it would have been a load to handle.

He stripped down, brushed the whiskey off his teeth, had a good piss. He fondled his cock, thinking of her, thinking of their night together. When he got hard he stopped playing with himself.

He had to put her out of his mind. An impossibility; but he had to try. He had a life to defend, a family to worry about.

Sleep came hard. His family, the trial, Violet—they all swirled around in his head. His last physical sensation before he fell into a troubled sleep, so strong that it could have been happening in the very moment, was remembering how Violet's body fit so naturally and effortlessly with his.

"**Y**ou're one of the lead detectives on what have been referred to in the press as the Alley Slasher murders?"

"I am."

"How long have you been a detective on the force?"

"Nineteen years."

"You're one of the senior detectives on the force?"

"Yes, ma'am."

"You have been cited numerous times for being one of the best detectives in the city, haven't you?"

"I don't know about that," the man answered modestly. "There's plenty of good detectives on the force. They don't assign you to the homicide division unless they think you can do the job."

"Have you been assigned to these cases from the beginning?"

"Yes, although it wasn't until the fourth body turned up that we realized we had a definite pattern—a serial-type series of killing, almost definitely by one perpetrator. I had investigated the first one, and then that fourth one, and when we realized there was a pattern, like I said, then I backtracked and checked out the second and third ones, and they matched the MO of the ones I'd been working on, numbers one and four, so from then on I was one of the lead detectives. And still am," he added.

Abramowitz was questioning her first witness, Detective Dudley Marlow from the police department's homicide division. Homicide detectives weren't limited to any particular precinct or area; they covered the entire city. Like most large-city homicide units, they were considered the elite detective division in the force, as Abramowitz was making sure the jury understood and appreciated. They had one of the highest percentages of solved murders of any police force in the country, a fact they were proud of. And over ninety-five percent of the murder cases they brought to the district attorney's office for prosecution resulted in convictions. In general, if they arrested someone for murder, he or she was guilty. At least found guilty in a trial.

Wyatt listened. He had Marlow's police reports from the seven murders opened in front of him on the table. Some of the reports were computer printouts, others were copies of reports that were handwritten. From the way the reports were entered it looked to him like the detective had taken notes by hand at the scene and later on, when he was in his office and had the time, had typed them up and entered them into the computer, which was sent to the Department of Records, the agency he had visited when he was trying to find out if Lieutenant Blake had accessed the files.

All the detectives who had worked on the murders had done their reports in this fashion—making notes at the crime scene while it was still fresh, then typing up their reports later.

The typed, computer-stored reports were the public record as such. They were similar to the handwritten ones, but the syntax, grammar, and accounts of the event had been cleaned up and made more readable and coherent; also, some of the material in the handwritten reports didn't get into the computer. Either the detective didn't think it was important, or he was too busy (or lazy) to put in every detail.

Wyatt had subpoenaed all the reports, computer and handwritten, and had gone over them carefully. They corresponded in great detail to the information Dwayne Thompson had given the grand jury. Which to him meant that unless Marvin had sold him a bill of goods, which he didn't accept—not because Marvin wasn't capable of lying, but that he wasn't good at it; he could never have carried off a deception this elaborate for this long—then someone in a position to get his hands on this stuff had given it to Dwayne.

The problem with that theory was that Doris Blake was the obvious candidate, and she hadn't done that. He hadn't figured out where to go from there.

Abramowitz's voice brought him back to the present. "Would you describe for the jury, Detective Marlow, the way in which the victims were murdered? Not only murdered, but everything that was done to them physically." She walked to the prosecution table and picked up a packet of photographs that been blown up to eight-by-eleven. "The state would like to introduce these into evidence."

Wyatt had seen the pictures. They were full-color photographs taken of Paula Briggs, the latest victim. Ugly, gut-wrenching pictures.

"So ordered," Grant said.

During the pretrial hearing Wyatt had tried to exclude the photographs as being prejudicial, but Grant had denied his motion. He knew he'd be shot down again, but he had to go on the record.

"Objection," Wyatt called out.

"Overruled," Grant answered immediately.

The clerk assigned them a number—exhibit #1—and Abramowitz carried them to the witness stand. One of the courtroom deputies set up an easel next to the stand, angled so that both Detective Marlow and the jury could see what was on it. Abramowitz set the stacked pictures on the easel. "Can you identify the body in this photograph, Detective Marlow?" she asked him.

"Yes," he said. "That is the body of Paula Briggs."

It was a particularly grisly picture. She was lying on the

ground, the scant remains of her mangled clothes twisted around her body. Her private parts were exposed. There were several wounds that looked like knife wounds, particularly around her neck and upper torso. One of her breasts had been sliced open, and lay askew against her rib cage.

The effect on the jury was powerful. There were gasps, hands to mouths. One of the women covered her eyes almost immediately, then looked down at the floor.

Abramowitz turned to them. "I'm sorry to have to subject you to this," she apologized, "but it's important that you understand the viciousness of these murders and their similarities. The killer didn't merely kill his victims—he tortured and mutilated them."

She turned back to Marlow. "Please describe to us what you saw when you arrived on the crime scene." She handed Marlow a pointer. "You may use this to point out certain details if you want to."

Marlow took the pointer from her and turned to the easel. "We went there as soon as the call came in. We knew—my partner and I—there was a good possibility this was another one like the ones we'd been tracking. She was still in the truck then—the garbage guys hadn't moved her."

Abramowitz moved the first picture to the side of the easel, revealing a shot of Paula in the garbage truck, as the garbage collectors had found her. "This is how you found her?"

"Yes."

"Do you know how she got into that truck? The body?"

"She had been stuffed into a garbage can. When they emptied it into the truck, that's when they discovered her."

"So there was some attempt at concealment. So that the body wouldn't be found immediately after it—excuse me, she—was murdered."

"That would be the logical assumption, yes."

"All right. Go ahead."

"We took the body out of the truck as carefully as we could—we were wearing latex gloves, of course—and laid her on the ground, like you see in this first picture."

"Let me interrupt you for a second, Detective. Who took these pictures?"

"A police photographer. Jack Russett. He was called when we were—he met us at the scene. We didn't move the body until he took that picture and some others of the victim where she was found."

"Okay. Continue, please."

"We looked her over. We didn't want to disturb the body too much, we wanted it to be as close to the way it was found as it could be for the coroner to look at. We checked it over enough to satisfy ourselves that it was done by the . . . whoever had done the other ones."

"And what was your conclusion?"

"That it was."

"That the victim had been murdered by the same man who had done the previous six that resembled it."

"Yes."

"Would you describe what you saw for the jury, please." She took a third photo from the stack and set it next to the other two. It was a tighter shot of Paula, waist to head.

Marlow nodded. He touched the photo with his pointer. "As you can see, her clothes had been ripped off her, almost completely. Which had happened, to different degrees, with the other six. Since she had been in the garbage truck we couldn't tell for sure if the killer had done it or the truck had done it—torn the clothes off her. To my eye it looked like the killer had done most of it and the action of the truck mechanism had taken what was ripped and made it worse; but I wouldn't swear to that."

Abramowitz nodded. She looked over at the jury to make sure they were all watching—they were. "All right. Continue, please."

"There were several knife wounds to her head, neck, and chest areas." He touched the photo with the pointer at some of the visible wounds. "I knew right away that's what killed her, which the coroner later confirmed. Probably this one." He pointed to a large knife wound at the right side of her neck.

"What about some of these other wounds?" Abramowitz asked. She took the pointer from him and pointed to the dismembered breast. "What about this one?"

"My guess is that happened before the ones to the neck."

"So not only was she raped, but she was tortured before she was killed. Murdered." That to the jury. She turned to Marlow again. "In your capacity as a detective, not a medical examiner, you could tell the following: the victim had been murdered."

"Yes."

"By knife wound."

"Yes."

"That she had been mutilated." She touched the pointer to the area on the tight photo of the butchered breast.

"Yes."

"Could you tell whether or not she was raped?"

"No. That's the coroner's job. We could see that her underpants had been ripped off and there was blood between her legs. There was a knife wound down there, too."

"She had been cut with a knife in the region of her vagina?"

"That's what it looked like."

Wyatt looked at the jury. They were completely caught up in the Abramowitz-Marlow colloquy. This was awful, what had been done to these women. Separating the revulsion over the crimes from an attachment to Marvin was going to be one of the most important parts of his defense.

Abramowitz put a fourth picture on the easel. It was a close-up of the abdominal and vaginal areas of Paula's body. "Is this what you saw?" she asked. She pointed to a dark gash alongside the vagina, the pubic hair clotted with blood. "This is the wound?"

"Yes."

She stepped back from the easel. "Question: You were called to the murder scene where you found a body in a dump truck."

"Yes."

"It had been discovered by two workers from the trash company who had dumped it in from a trash can in the alley."

"Yes."

"The victim's clothing had been torn, her body mutilated, possibly before she was murdered, and the cause of death, as you could best ascertain it, having the experience of thirteen years as a detective on the police force, was by knife. And that since the other victims had been raped it was logical for you to assume that this one had been, too."

"Yes. I thought it would turn out she'd been raped, and she was. Also sodomized," he added.

"Was sodomy a feature of the other killings?"

"Some of them. Four of the other six."

There was no point in Wyatt's objecting to any of this. The coroner would establish it later; to raise the issue further would more deeply embed it in the jury's minds—the last thing he wanted to do.

"Okay," she said. She took him through the similarities with the other murders, a long, painstaking procedure.

"Given all that information," she said in finishing, "which you could see with the naked eye, and knowing what you knew about the previous murders that were similar to this one—was there any doubt in your mind that this was another one of those murders?"

He shook his head firmly. "None whatsoever. The man who murdered this woman murdered the other six. There's no question about it, as far as I'm concerned."

Wyatt stood at the lawyer's lectern looking at the witness, Detective Marlow. He had Marlow's official reports for all seven of the murders in a folder on top of the lectern. "Who called you to the murder scene, Detective Marlow?"

"The homicide division dispatcher."

"What time was that?"

"About eight o'clock in the morning."

"Where were you?"

"I was at home."

"You were asleep?"

Marlow nodded. "Yes. I'd been out late the night before." He smiled at the jury. "One of the detectives in our division was getting married, so we had a bachelor party for him. It went pretty late."

"So you went right over? What time did you arrive at the crime scene, Detective?"

"About nine-thirty, quarter to ten. I showered first and grabbed a cup of coffee on the way."

"You don't record when you arrive on a crime scene? The exact time?" He looked at Marlow's report. "It says here you got there at nine-fifty-five a.m."

Marlow pursed his lips. "That sounds right."

"Okay. So you went over there and you met your partner"—he looked at his notes—"Detective Conners. At five to ten. Was he already there?"

"I picked him up. We'd both been to the same party."

"So you took a shower. Got dressed. Shaved?"

Marlow nodded. "Yes."

"Stopped on the way for coffee. Picked up Detective Conners—is my chronology right? Did you get the coffee before you picked up Conners?"

"Yes."

"You figured if you needed an eye-opener, he would, too?"

"Objection," sang out Abramowitz from behind him. "Irrelevant and trivial."

"Detective Marlow made several acute observations when he got to that crime scene, Your Honor," Wyatt explained. "I'm trying to establish his mental acuity at the time."

Grant nodded. "I see your point. Overruled. You may answer the question," he said to Marlow.

"I wanted a cup of coffee and I knew Conners would, too. I wasn't hungover, if that's what you're implying," Marlow said testily.

"I'm not implying anything," Wyatt returned. "Now when the dispatcher from homicide called you, Detective, did he—"

"She," Marlow interrupted. "The dispatcher is a woman."

"Sorry. She. Did she give any indication that this murder victim you were going to look at was an Alley Slasher victim?"

"No," Marlow answered quickly. "It was a murder victim. I'm a homicide detective, sir. I investigate murders."

"So why did she call you?"

Marlow looked at him quizzically. "Because that's what I do. I just said that."

"I meant you specifically. How many detectives are there in the homicide division, Detective Marlow?"

Slowly, Marlow answered, "Forty."

"Forty detectives. So out of those forty detectives why were you called, if it wasn't pertaining to one of your active files? Are you saying you just happened to be the one that was called? What do they do, pick the names out of a hat?"

Marlow glowered. "No. We go by roster."

"So you and Conners were next up."

Marlow started to answer, then hesitated. "No, we weren't."

"Then that leads me back to my initial question. Why were *you* called? You in particular?"

Marlow's eyes darted to the prosecution table for a moment. He looked at Wyatt again. "I guess because maybe they thought . . . maybe they thought it was connected with the Alley Slasher murders," he admitted. "*Might* be connected," he amended.

"*They?*"

"The lieutenant who was commander of the watch at that time."

"So it wasn't an accident you were called. A roll of the dice."

"I guess not, no."

"It was another one like the ones you'd been investigating for almost two years."

"Yes."

"I'm glad we cleared that up. Finally." He shuffled through some notes. "This was the biggest case you were working on at the time. The most important one."

"Definitely."

"You wanted to apprehend whoever did this really badly, didn't you?"

"Yes sir."

"You wanted to catch him so badly that upon hearing the news that another Alley Slasher victim had been found, you got up out of bed, took a shower, shaved, got dressed . . . did you take time to polish your shoes?"

"Objection!" Abramowitz called out. "Mr. Matthews is badgering the witness."

"Sorry, Your Honor," Wyatt apologized before Grant could sustain her. "I withdraw that last part."

"Stay on track," Grant admonished him.

"Yes, Your Honor." He returned to his questioning of Marlow. "You got out of bed, you took a shower, you shaved, got dressed, drove to pick up your partner, on the way stopping for coffee—two coffees, one for each of you . . . did you pick up something to eat, too?"

"A couple of bagels," Marlow said.

"Stopped for coffee and bagels, picked up Detective Conners, and drove to the murder location. Where the body was waiting for you two hours after you got the call. Is my chronology correct, Detective?"

"The body wasn't going anywhere," Marlow answered curtly.

Wyatt couldn't hear it, but he knew Abramowitz was groaning to herself.

"Not on its own," he shot back. "But isn't it important—imperative—to get to a murder site as quickly and expeditiously as possible? Isn't that what you just told us? How important it is to get there fast?"

"Yes," Marlow admitted.

"Because every minute that goes by—every minute that is lost—is precious, isn't it? The trail grows colder, vital evidence gets lost, gets tampered with, compromised, tainted, there's more of a possibility of contamination of the crime scene. Isn't that true?"

"Yes," Marlow said again.

Tacking away, Wyatt asked, "Who calls the medical examiner to the scene?"

"The detective in charge, usually," Marlow answered.

"In this case, that would have been you?"

"Yes. I called the examiner. The coroner."

"Does the coroner's office come to every crime scene where it's suspected a murder took place?"

"Yes. They have to, legally. Also it's in the police code of regulations."

"But the coroner himself doesn't usually come, does he? Usually it's one of his minions, isn't it?"

Marlow nodded his head in agreement. "It's usually an assistant, or sometimes paramedics with special training for it, yeah."

"But this time Coroner Ayala himself came, didn't he? Because of the prominence of these cases."

"Yes."

"But he couldn't come until you called him, right? He lost valuable time, didn't he."

"Objection, Your Honor," Abramowitz spoke up. "Calls for conjecture by the witness."

"Sustained."

Wyatt looked at his notes. "You canvassed the area pretty thoroughly, didn't you?" he asked. " 'You' meaning several policemen by this time? Once you got there?" he added.

"Extremely thoroughly," Marlow answered, not rising to Wyatt's gibe.

"Did you find the murder weapon?"

"No."

"You looked for it."

"We fine-tooth-combed that neighborhood, looking for any evidence. The murder weapon, of course, but anything that might give us a lead. We handpicked through the contents of that entire garbage truck, looked into every trash can in a two-block radius, swept the streets clean. We also talked to anyone we could find who had been in the club at the time, might have seen her with the victim, and so forth. We were damn thorough, believe me."

"I do." He riffled through his notes again. "Did you come up with anything?" he asked. "Any concrete leads?"

"No, I'm sorry to say. The killer had been very good at covering his tracks. He didn't leave anything we could find."

Wyatt made a note regarding that. Then he looked up. "You've given a very good and complete recitation here, Detective Marlow. I guess a policeman gets trained to remember his facts."

"It's an important part of the job," Marlow stated blandly. "A good memory is one of the most important things a good detective has."

"And you're a good detective."

Marlow shrugged modestly.

"You have a good memory."

"It's pretty good."

"But it isn't that good that you wouldn't refer back to your notes and reports when you're investigating a case, is it?" Wyatt asked.

"I'm not going to trust my memory for things that are important," Marlow said. "I go back over them, especially in a scenario like this one, where you have one murder following another in a particular pattern."

"You want to see what the consistencies are. Or inconsistencies."

"That's right."

"And when you come to testify in a trial—as you're doing now—you'd go back over your notes, to refresh your memory, wouldn't you?"

"Yes."

"You went over your notes before coming in here to testify this morning, didn't you."

"Yes," Marlow admitted. "I looked them over."

"How did you go about doing that?" Wyatt asked. "What was the process?"

"Well, I have my own handwritten originals," Marlow explained. "I looked them over. And I went down to the Police Department of Records and pulled the computer data that I'd entered on the different murders, including the most recent one."

"All the computer records are kept there? In one central location?"

Marlow nodded. "So everyone knows where they are, so that they can access them easily."

"How does someone access a file?" Wyatt asked. "Can anyone do it?"

"Not anyone can do it," Marlow said. "They're privileged. You have to have the authority to get into the files. If you're a policeman, like me, you have to give your name, badge number, and so forth."

"So it would be difficult for someone who wasn't authorized to look at a police file to do so, is that right?"

"Almost impossible," Marlow answered firmly.

"You go down there and what? You fill out a form, give it to the clerk, he goes back and gets the file. Like that?"

"Exactly like that."

"You've done that several times, haven't you? Gone down to the records department and pulled files on these cases?"

"I've pulled some files from time to time, yes."

"And each time you went down to the records department and filled out a form? There's no other way?"

Marlow thought for a moment. "Well, there is another way."

Wyatt paused before asking his next question. "What's that?"

"You can do it through a computer. More and more, officers do that, especially the younger ones. You access it through the modem. It saves a lot of time."

"But you still need authorization. You have to be in the loop, so to speak."

"Absolutely. It's still the same procedure."

Wyatt walked back over to the defense table. He picked up a handful of papers, brought them back to the lectern. "I have your handwritten reports here," he said, "and I'm comparing them to the reports you filed into the police computer. There seem to be some discrepancies. Some items have been left out. Could you explain why that is?"

Marlow nodded. "Sure. I can't put everything in. It's not always relevant, sometimes there are redundancies, you could call them, I just don't have the time. It's like any other organization—the paperwork can kill you; if that's all you're doing, you're not doing the job."

"I sympathize with you there," Wyatt said. "But doesn't using your computer make the job easier rather than harder?"

"I guess if you're good on computers it could," Marlow told him. "I'm not much on computers, to tell you the truth. I've never quite gotten the hang of them. I'm an old-fashioned handwriting kind of cop, I guess. But like I said, I've always got my handwritten originals to back me up."

"Okay," Wyatt said. "I think that's it." He started to leave the lectern, then turned back. "One more thing. Have you ever met Dwayne Thompson? One of the state's witnesses in this case?"

Marlow shook his head. "No."

"Never spoke with him, never been in contact with him in any way?"

"No."

"Did you read his grand jury testimony, by any chance?"

"No. I never had contact with him. Directly, indirectly. No way at all."

Wyatt stared at the detective for a good, long beat. Then he turned away. "That'll be all, Your Honor."

D r. Robert Ayala had been the county coroner for seven years. He was a trim, dapper, middle-aged man who sported an out-of-style pencil mustache, the kind Clark Gable wore. He was a competent-enough pathologist; there hadn't been any major scandals involving his office since he'd come aboard.

What he was particularly good at was dealing with the politics of his job, an indispensable quality given the politically charged atmosphere of the county's labyrinthine, backbiting system. He was comfortable in the courtroom—he testified in over a dozen trials every year, and occasionally journeyed out of state in the capacity of "expert witness." He sat now in the witness chair, one leg crossed casually over the other. He was wearing a dark, conservatively cut suit, white starched shirt, and dark tie. His oxblood shell cordovans were shined to a high gloss.

Abramowitz walked him through his bona fides, which were solid. Then she got down to the job at hand.

"You have been the coroner during the time period that all these murders known as the Alley Slasher killings have taken place, is that true?" she led off.

"Yes."

"Were autopsies done on all seven victims?"

"Yes, that's SOP in any murder case. But at that time we hadn't formed a nexus linking them up; those initial ones seemed like random killings, particularly since the victims' lives exposed them to more than a normal share of violence. It wasn't until the third victim turned up that we realized we had a serial killer on our hands."

"And what brought about that realization?" she asked.

"The method of killing," he stated unequivocally. "The types of wounds inflicted, the ways in which the victims had been assaulted. And the fact that they were all prostitutes showed a consistent pattern."

"So at the time the third murder occurred you came to the conclusion that they were all the work of one man."

"That is correct," he stated. "The knife wounds in particular, and some of the ways in which the victims had been sexually abused, caused me to conclude that it was the same person who had done them all."

"And that followed through for the rest of the killings?" she asked. "Up to and including the last one?"

"Yes. They were all done by the same man. I have no doubts about that."

"They were all raped, and then mutilated, and then murdered."

"Yes."

"Was the same weapon used in all of the murders?"

"I couldn't guarantee that it was the same weapon, since we don't have it to test, but I'd bet on it. If not the same knife, then knives that are very similar in design and size. But my guess is," he repeated himself, "they were all done by one knife."

"Could you infer from the wounds as to the type of knife?"

"Something with a long, thin, very sharp blade. The kind of knife that would be used to fillet meat or gut a fish. It would cut very sharp, very clean, and wouldn't have to be forced. Whoever used it knows his way around knives."

She noted that, then moved forward with her interrogation. "Was there anything else about the murders that stands out?" she asked. "Anything distinctive, out of the ordinary?"

"All but two were sodomized," the coroner answered.

Several members of the jury shook their heads or showed other signs of disgust.

"And was there anything else?" Abramowitz said.

"In two of the cases a foreign object had been shoved into their rectums."

"A foreign object?" she asked. "What kind of foreign object?"

"A cigarette."

"A cigarette?"

He nodded. "A cigarette butt. Most of it had been smoked."

"Were you able to ascertain the brand?" she asked.

"It was a Marlboro."

"A Marlboro cigarette. That he forced up her rectum."

Another affirmative nod. "We also detected what appeared to be a burn mark along the rectum wall," he said.

"A burn mark? The cigarette was still lit when he inserted it? Forced it in?"

"Yes," he said. "My conclusion was that the killer had used the victim's anus as an . . ." He paused.

"As?" she prompted.

"As an ashtray."

"Good morning, Dr. Ayala." Wyatt greeted the pathologist respectfully.

"Good morning."

Again, Wyatt stood at the lectern, a sheaf of notes spread out in front of him. He looked at a couple of them, set them back down.

"I want to question you about one of the answers you gave Ms. Abramowitz. You stated that all seven of these crimes are linked, and that they were all done by the same man. Is that correct?"

"Yes. That's what I said."

"And you're absolutely sure about that."

"Absolutely."

"You have no doubts whatsoever."

"None at all. I'd bet my professional reputation on it."

"You don't have to bet anything, Doctor," Wyatt said smilingly, "I'll take your word for it. Seven killings, one man. I have no argument with that. So," he continued on this line, "you'd bet your professional opinion that if someone didn't commit one of the murders, he couldn't have committed any of them. Is that correct?"

Faced with this blanket statement, Ayala seemed rattled, but he had no choice in his answer.

"Yes," he said. "I would."

Wyatt shuffled through his papers again. "I'm looking at the autopsy reports here on the various victims." He made a show of shuffling through the papers as if he was looking for one specific item. Looking up, he continued, "But I don't see sperm samples taken for all of the victims. Comparing sperm from one to the other. Did you take sperm samples from all of them, Doctor?"

Ayala hesitated for a moment before answering. "Not for all of them, no."

"Isn't that SOP?"

"Not necessarily," Ayala said. "We ascertain that there is sperm present, but as for typing and comparing them, that's not done as a matter of basic procedure in our jurisdiction."

"Wouldn't that help you in determining that all the killings were done by the same man, as you have so strongly stated?"

"Maybe. And maybe not."

"Oh? Why wouldn't they? If they all corresponded, I mean."

"Because of the lifestyle that all these ladies lived," was the response.

"You mean that they were prostitutes?"

"Yes."

"Why would the fact that they were prostitutes make a difference?" Wyatt asked.

"Contamination," the coroner explained. "These women might have—most likely did have—vaginal, oral, or anal sex with a number of men, over an extremely short period of time. Or a combination of those . . . options. It would be extremely difficult to sort out the various combinations."

"But if one particular sperm configuration showed up in all of them," Wyatt continued, "wouldn't that be a good confirmation of your 'one-man' theory?"

"Possibly," Ayala admitted. "But tests are expensive. In this case there were other factors involved in typing the killer, such as the specialized method by which the victims were killed, so I didn't feel it was necessary." He shifted his weight in the chair. "We have a budget we have to live with, and we can't do every test that's known to man."

"Was there any genetic testing done at all?"

"No."

"What about comparing sperm samples to a blood sample from my client? Was that done?"

He knew there had been no tests. He might not have allowed one to be done if it had been requested, but the request had never been made.

"No. There weren't," the coroner said grudgingly.

"Have you had any training in the practical use of DNA as it relates to cases like this?" Wyatt asked.

Ayala wriggled defensively. "Some. Not much," he admitted.

"I see." He'd established his point; the coroner's office hadn't done the most cutting-edge, sophisticated tests.

"All the victims were prostitutes," Wyatt said. "Is that your understanding?"

"Yes," Ayala answered. "From my examinations I discovered various sexual diseases, evidence of needle use relating to drug abuse, and other physical signs that would indicate the lifestyle commonly associated with prostitutes of their position."

"All female prostitutes," Wyatt repeated, seemingly adding the gender as an afterthought.

"Not all females," Ayala corrected him.

Wyatt stared at him. "One was a male prostitute?"

"One of them was a man, yes."

"Interesting," Wyatt observed. He looked at the jury to make sure they were hearing this. They were all attentive. "Isn't that unusual?" he asked. "A man killing six women and one man? In your opinion, as an expert, isn't rape almost always gender-specific? You rape one sex or the other, but not both, because rape is an act not of sex but of violence in which the rapist is acting out his anger and rage at a particular sex?"

"Objection!" Abramowitz called out. "Dr. Ayala is testifying as a coroner. He is not certified as an expert on the philosophy of rape."

"On the contrary," Wyatt rebutted her. "Coroners are often considered authoritative on matters of rape, Your Honor. There are reams of case law regarding that issue." He started to go to his table to get a lawbook.

Grant stopped him. "That won't be necessary," he said. "Objection overruled." He turned to Ayala. "You may answer the question."

Ayala sat up in his chair. "I would say your statement is correct, regarding rapists and gender orientation. But this instance was different."

"Different? How?"

"The victim was a transvestite."

A buzz went through the courtroom. The jury members began scribbling furiously in their notebooks.

"A man who dresses as a woman?" Wyatt said.

Ayala nodded in agreement. "There are many transvestite prostitutes," he added.

"They can actually pass as women?" Wyatt asked. He knew all this—it had been in the police reports as well as in Dwayne Thompson's grand jury testimony. But since Abramowitz had in essence finessed it, he wanted to make sure it got on the record, and that the jury heard it.

"Sure. Many of them are taking hormone treatments to enhance the size of their breasts and decrease their masculine indicators—heaviness of beard, body hair, things like that."

"So a man out on the street trolling for a prostitute could be easily fooled?"

"I guarantee it's done dozens of times out there every night," Ayala said, pointing out the window. "It's dark outside, the john and the prostitute have their liaison in a dark car or alley, and the sexual act in these situations is normally oral. Most men would never know."

Wyatt looked over the autopsy report. "In this instance there was anal penetration." He showed Ayala the report.

Ayala glanced at the report, handed it back. "Yes, I know," he said. "I remember it well. It was a particularly vicious rape, even for this rapist-killer."

"Why do you think that was?"

"We know that anyone who rapes is angry, full of rage and hostility. In this case, when the rapist discovered his victim was a man instead of a woman, the rage would have been intensified, due to his being deceived in such an unmanly fashion. He was not only raping, he was having sex with a homosexual. He's almost certainly a latent homosexual himself, in heavy denial. So to have one of his most deeply rooted fears shoved in his face would trigger unbelievable rage."

"So you would categorize the man who is doing these killings as a repressed homosexual who's heavily into denial about it," Wyatt said, repeating and rephrasing Ayala's answer.

"It's textbook."

Wyatt switched gears. "Let's talk about time of death," he said. "In each of your reports you list approximate times of death. Each one has a window, so to speak. They died between hour X and hour Y. Can you tell us how you arrive at these time-of-death figures?"

Ayala sat back, permitting himself a faint smile. "There are a variety of ways to do that. I use whatever evidence I have, or can reasonably deduce."

"You're considered an expert on time of death, aren't you?" Wyatt interjected. "You've been an expert witness in trials outside this jurisdiction on that issue, haven't you?"

"Yes."

"All right, then. Tell us some of the things you look for; some of the details that tell you, as a pathologist and expert in forensic medicine, when somebody died."

"The amount of rigor mortis that's set in is a primary indicator. Samples of the contents of the victim's stomach. There are many indications, and they all speak to you if you know how to read them and what to look for."

Wyatt leafed through some pages. "Take a look at this one, Dr. Ayala, and tell me how you arrived at the conclusion you did. You gave this one a very narrow window of death, less than one hour. How did you pinpoint it so finely?"

This was an easy one—the girl who'd been killed right after she ate a slice of pizza.

Ayala looked over the document. "That was cut-and-dried," he said. "We could tell from the amount of digestion of the food in her stomach how long it had been between the time she ate and the time she was murdered. We knew when she ate, so we were able to make that deduction easily."

"What if you hadn't known when she had eaten?"

"It still wouldn't have been hard. You take her body weight, the amount of rigor mortis that had set in, sometimes the clotting of the blood around her wounds, the state of decomposition of food in the stomach, and the picture is quite clear." He spoke with easy, if self-congratulatory, authority.

"This really is a science, isn't it, Doctor."

"Yes. It is all scientific. The body doesn't lie—it can't. If you're properly trained in knowing what to look for, the body will tell its story."

Wyatt walked back to the lectern, grabbed another autopsy report, and brought it to Ayala. "What about this one?" he asked.

Ayala studied the paper. "This is the most recent one," he observed.

"Yes. How did you estimate the time of death in this case?" Wyatt asked.

Ayala looked at the paper some more. "A number of factors. The blood had settled in the lower portion of her body. May I explain that point?" he asked.

"By all means."

"The blood in a corpse descends to the lower portion of however the body is positioned when killing takes place. In other words, if the dead person is lying on her back, as was the case here, the blood will collect on the bottom portion of her body, the bottoms of her arms and legs, buttocks, back, and so forth. If she was lying on her side, it would be to that side. Depending on how much she weighed, what the temperature was between the time she died and the time she was found and examined, the density of collected blood, and other such details, you can make a fairly accurate finding. Within hours, of course."

Wyatt looked at the report again. "This particular victim didn't have her autopsy done until one-thirty in the afternoon. The body was found at six-thirty in the morning. Wouldn't it have made your job easier and more accurate if you had been able to do the autopsy sooner?"

"Yes," Ayala admitted, "but that's usually the case. The way it happened here. Police work is tedious because it has to be thorough. Our detectives are among the most thorough in the country," he declared. "I know that, having visited other jurisdictions. They take their time, and do the job right."

Touché, Wyatt thought. Aloud, he said, "You estimated the time of death between ten o'clock at night and one in the morning. Is that accurate?"

"Yes, it is."

"It couldn't have been earlier, or later?"

"No. I was pushing the envelope on both ends, to be safe. My real thinking is that the killing occurred between ten-thirty and twelve-thirty."

"So you can state, as an expert in the field, without any fear of making a mistake, that the murder of Paula Briggs could not have happened any earlier than ten o'clock on the night in question."

"Yes. I will stand by those times."

"What about your other autopsy reports?" Wyatt asked. "For the earlier killings. Numbers three through six. Do you stand behind the times of death for them with equal certainty?"

"Yes," Ayala answered. "Each one of those women died within the hours I described."

To rebut the seed Wyatt had planted during his cross-examination of Detective Marlow about police records being sloppily taken out and dispersed, Abramowitz called in the head of the records department to the stand. He was a uniformed police lieutenant with twenty-five years on the force, named Quinn.

Abramowitz: "Describe in detail how police files are accessed, Lieutenant Quinn, and what security measures are taken to ensure they don't fall into the wrong hands."

Quinn: "Only police officers, sheriff's deputies, highway patrolmen have access. And a handful of civilian officials, members of the police board mostly. No politicians—if the mayor himself walked in and asked for a record we'd tell him no. There's no exceptions to that."

Abramowitz: "How is a file given out?"

Quinn: "Officer comes in, fills out a form, gives his badge number. We check to make sure he's who he says he is. He signs out for his document, and when he brings it back, he signs it back in."

Abramowitz: "So there's no way an unauthorized party can get a file?"

Quinn: "That is correct."

Abramowitz: "Thank you." She turned to Wyatt. "Your witness."

Before she had taken her seat Wyatt was up. "No way?" he repeated.

"That is correct," Quinn said. He had a big, red, bulbous drunk's nose. He stared at Wyatt.

"They sign in, they sign out, they show ID."

"Correct again."

"Authorized policemen only?"

"Yep?"

"What about members of the district attorney's office? They can't take out files?"

Quinn reddened around the jowls. "Them, too. Of course they can. They're officers of the court."

"So am I. I took some out."

"You had a court order permitting you to do that, didn't you?" Quinn looked at him suspiciously.

"Yes—but the point is, I got the files."

"Okay," Quinn conceded. "With a court order, you got them."

"A reporter could, too, right? With a court order?"

"Anybody with a court order could," Quinn snapped. "But you'd have to have authorization. When I was talking about it before I meant without court authorization."

"What about computers?" Wyatt asked, moving in the direction he really wanted to go. "Detective Marlow testified earlier you can access files through your computer if you have the authority to do so."

Quinn shifted his ass on the stand. "Well, yes, that's done. This is the computer age, you know."

"So how does that work?"

"Same way. They have to ID themselves, declare their badge number, get the case file number, and so forth."

"But there's no visual, as there would be over the counter."

"No," Quinn conceded. "But there's enough checks and balances for protection."

Wyatt jumped on that. "Isn't it possible for someone to impersonate an officer via computer? Get the officer's information and call in and access a file?"

Quinn thought about that. "I guess it's possible," he conceded. "But whoever did it would have to have a lot of information. It's never been done," he added.

"It's never been done? You've never heard of these hackers who get into top secret files in the Pentagon?"

"I mean it's never been done to us," Quinn retreated, his bulbous nose lighting up.

"How would you know?" Wyatt asked. "Are you a computer expert?"

"No, I'm not a computer expert, but we have guys that are. And they check this stuff out, and they tell me it's never been done. They'd know if it was."

"After the fact," Wyatt said. "They'd know after someone had hacked in."

"I guess so," Quinn admitted. "All I know is, our people say it's never been done. And that's good enough for me."

Wyatt looked over at the jury. Their faces were blank; not one of them was taking notes—his line of questioning had gone right over their heads. They weren't interested in hardware, or software, or anything about computers; or DNA, PCR, or any other esoteric matters. They wanted to know who did it, when, and why. People matched up to situations.

They wanted to find the killer. And burn him.

The duty officer at the time Marvin had been brought into the jail recited the inventory of Marvin's personal effects that had been on him when he was admitted. "One five-dollar bill. Two singles. Thirty-eight cents in change. A driver's license, current until his twenty-first birthday. A Swiss Army knife. One pack of Marlboro cigarettes. One book of matches." He looked up from the list he was reading. "That's it."

Abramowitz was making a note as he talked. "Was the Swiss Army knife sent to the lab for examination?" she asked.

The deputy looked at his own notes. "Yes," he said. "They checked it out and sent it back to us the next day. It's locked up with his other stuff."

The knife was not the murder weapon. That was the first thing they'd checked out. It was the wrong size and shape, the blades weren't nearly sharp enough to have made the kinds of cuts the coroner had described, and there was no blood on it. The killer had used a different knife.

She looked up. "Wasn't there also a gun on the accused's person at the time of his arrest?" she asked.

"Objection," Wyatt called from his seat. "That is not on the list of the effects that were inventoried when Mr. White was admitted to the jail."

"Sustained," Grant agreed. "The jury will disregard that last question."

Abramowitz frowned, made a note, then moved on. "This pack of cigarettes. Marlboro cigarettes, you said."

"There was a pack of Marlboro cigarettes in his possession, that's right," the deputy responded.

"Was it a full pack?"

"No."

"Some were missing."

"One," he said. "It was one shy."

She turned to the jury. "One cigarette was missing from the pack of Marlboros that the accused had on him at the time he was brought into the jail," she said.

Wyatt looked at the jury. Most of them were taking notes. He knew what they were writing: One missing cigarette from the pack of Marlboros Marvin had on him when he was admitted to the jail. One Marlboro cigarette found in the anal canal of the latest murder victim, Paula Briggs.

"Yes," the deputy reconfirmed. "One was missing."

Abramowitz walked away from the witness. "No further questions."

Wyatt stood up at the defense table. "You recited the

list of items found on Marvin White when he was booked into the jail. There was nothing else you might have overlooked?"

"No," the deputy said. "That was everything."

"The coroner has testified that the same weapon—a knife—was the murder weapon used on all seven victims, including the last one. Was a knife fitting that description found on Mr. White?"

"No, it was not."

"There's no possibility it might have been overlooked in your inventory?"

"No."

"Thank you. No further questions."

Over the lunch break Wyatt and Josephine reviewed the list of people who had taken out files between the time Marvin had been arrested and sent to jail to the day when Dwayne Thompson talked to the district attorney and subsequently testified before the grand jury. Everyone who had signed out any pertinent files were police officers—over a dozen, men and women who were working on the Alley Slasher murders. They were all city policemen—no members of the sheriff's department or district attorney's office. Josephine cross-checked the names against lists they had drawn up of anyone who might have had contact with Thompson, no matter how slim the odds were.

They came up empty—none of the cops who had accessed those files had made contact with Thompson, none they could make any kind of plausible case for.

"Let's face it, Wyatt," Josephine said. "The police didn't give him those files."

"None of these did," he reluctantly agreed. "The obvious suspect would be Blake, but she didn't take them out. Her name's nowhere on this," he said, tapping it with his finger. "So how in hell did he get the information?"

She looked at him. "There's always the possibility . . ."

He shook his head. "It wasn't Marvin. He's too damn stupid. And he didn't do it," he added angrily.

"Could the DA's office have done it?" she asked. "Marvin did tell Thompson some details, he's admitted to that."

"And Thompson went to them with whatever information he had and they filled in the blanks?"

She nodded.

"It's possible, I guess," he admitted. "Good thinking." He remembered the situation Bollinger had told him about. "It would be an unbelievable scandal, but stranger things have happened."

"What other possibility is there?" she pointed out.

"None I can think of off the top of my head." He slumped in his chair. "Shit. That would tear this city up. Alex Pagano is an ambitious man, but I can't see him going that far. He's too smart for that. He's dying for a conviction, but taking a chance like that? If it blew up on him he'd go to jail until he was ninety-nine years old. No—it wasn't Pagano. He's the recipient, but not the instigator."

"Someone else in his office?"

He shook his head. "And kept him in the dark? And Abramowitz, and the other senior prosecutors? That would be a conspiracy of epic proportions."

"What else do we have?" she asked, as exasperated as he was.

"I don't know," he admitted.

"Wyatt," she said. "You're a fast learner, but the semester isn't over yet. Police departments and DA's offices are full of shit! How many cops a year get busted? How many prosecuting attorneys get reprimanded for crossing the line? And for every one that gets caught—planting evidence, suppressing evidence, manufacturing evidence, you name it—twenty don't. Our office sees it all the time. It makes Walcott and every other career lawyer down there crazy." She pulled her blouse away from her chest, fanning herself. "You're insisting that someone told Dwayne Thompson. If we don't come up with who that someone is, it becomes Marvin by default."

"And we die." He looked at this watch—time to go back. "If you have time, see what you can find out. But be very circumspect. If Pagano finds out we're checking up on his office for leaks . . ." He didn't finish his thought—it was too grim.

Wyatt, Abramowitz, and Norman Windsor met with Judge Grant in his chambers. Wyatt was livid.

"She can't testify," he practically screamed.

"Her name's on the list," Abramowitz shot back.

"That doesn't matter. That girl never testified and the case never went to trial. She backed off, Your Honor. The case was dropped. It doesn't exist. Anything she would testify to is inadmissible. That's not the case we're trying," he argued as strenuously as he could.

The potential witness in question was the girl who had accused Marvin of raping her two years earlier but had gotten cold feet at the last minute (or was pressured by Marvin's friends) and refused to testify, resulting in the case against Marvin being dropped.

Grant nodded, seemingly in agreement. He turned to Abramowitz. "What's your precedent for this? If the accused had been tried and found guilty of that crime, I'd have no problem admitting the conviction; but as Mr. Matthews has pointed out, it's not part of his record, and it's prejudicial."

"Marvin White was bound over. The girl made a statement to the police that resulted in White being arrested. That is part of the record," Abramowitz said passionately. "There is clear precedent for a witness to come forward upon hearing of a crime that has been committed, to state that the same kind of crime was committed against her, but she didn't press charges at the time for any number of reasons. Fear of retaliation is a big one, and that's what we're looking at in this instance, Your Honor. This girl will testify that Marvin White raped her at knifepoint. And that she backed off at the last minute because he threatened her. His friends threatened her."

"It's easy to get religion after the fact, Your Honor," Wyatt spoke up, "but that's over. It's highly prejudicial, and the prejudicial effect outweighs its probative value. It's going to be inflammatory to the jury, and that's not allowable."

Grant closed his eyes in thought. "I'm going to have to do some research on this," he decided. "We'll adjourn for the rest of the day. I'll announce my decision when court reconvenes tomorrow morning."

"He's gonna let it in," Darryl said.

"It's automatic grounds for appeal," Wyatt replied.

It was after work hours. They were having a drink in their favorite watering hole.

"It doesn't matter," Darryl said. "Grant's gung ho law-and-order on stuff like this. He can rationalize letting this testimony in; I guarantee you he won't lose one minute of sleep over it. And if you lose and use that as grounds for appeal, the appellate court'll shine you on. Besides, he's gotta let it in, for political reasons. If he excludes it, Pagano goes to the press and makes him look like he's coddling a monster." He tapped his finger on Wyatt's forearm. "Deal with it—and then leave it behind. If you start to get enmeshed in paranoid fantasies, even if they're real, you'll lose your focus. And then you'll lose your case."

Judge Grant called Wyatt that night, at the hotel. Wyatt was in the shower, having passed on dinner and gone for a late run. He shut the water off, hastily dried himself, and slipped into the hotel courtesy bathrobe as he picked up the phone.

"I'm letting you know in advance that I'm going to allow this witness to testify," the jurist told him. "There are arguments for and against it; but because of the similarities, I've made this decision."

Wyatt groaned silently. He was dripping a puddle onto the floor; he dabbed at his wet legs. Even though Darryl had predicted this, he had been hoping against hope Grant wouldn't let the girl testify.

"What are these extreme similarities?" he asked wearily. It was considerate of the judge to call him and warn him, but it was going to cost him any chance of sleep now.

"The knife," Grant said. "If it was merely allegation of rape, I wouldn't admit it. But the knife makes the cases too similar to ignore. There is a pattern here," he went on, "and the jury needs to know it."

"It's only a pattern if he's guilty, Your Honor," Wyatt pointed out.

"I've made my decision," Grant said frostily. "I'll see you in my courtroom in the morning."

The phone went dead in Wyatt's hand. He resisted the temptation to tear the plug out of the wall.

The girl's name was Mavis Jones. She was eighteen now, the same age as Marvin. By law she was an adult, although she had been living a hard, grown-up life for years, starting with the night Marvin supposedly stuck a knife at her throat and ordered her to spread her legs or he'd gut her.

Wyatt looked at her. She was cute—he could see boys, Marvin included, being attracted to her, despite his claim of nonattraction. She still had some baby fat on her. But her expression was closed-off and suspicious: the world was going to fuck her over, from the day she was born until the day she died; but once or twice in her lifetime she was going to have payback.

Today was going to be one of those times.

She was dressed almost in a parody of a parochial school uniform: starched white blouse, dark plain jumper over it, thin white socks, and Doc Martens. Her hair was pulled back into a twist. A small gold cross hung from her neck, small crosses were her earrings. Her makeup was minimal. She looked like a good student getting ready to go to college. The kind of girl Michaela, his daughter, would be friendly with.

She swore to tell the truth and sat down, legs primly crossed at the ankles. This girl had been coached, he knew that. The prosecutors had been working on her for days; not only her testimony, but how she handled herself. Spoke, sat, moved.

Abramowitz smiled at her from the lectern. "How are you this morning, Mavis?" she asked.

"Okay." The girl's voice was low. She reminded Wyatt a little of his witness, Leticia.

"Are you frightened?"

"A little." She looked over at Marvin. Marvin was staring at the notepad in front of him.

Abramowitz looked at the defense table also. Then she turned back to her witness. "You don't have to be," she assured the girl. "No one is going to hurt you. No one in this courtroom," she added pointedly, glancing in Marvin's direction again.

The jury followed her look. Wyatt shifted his body in an attempt to block their view of his client, but it didn't help.

"You know the defendant, don't you, Mavis?" Abramowitz asked her.

"Yeah." The girl nodded her head.

"How long have you known him?"

" 'Bout three and a half years. Since my fam'ly moved into Sullivan Houses. We got thrown out of our apartment on account of my daddy got sick and couldn't work no more so we had to move into the project."

"This was a few months before the . . . incident?"

The girl nodded again. "Yeah."

"And shortly after you moved there, you met Marvin White?"

"Yeah."

"Were you friendly with Marvin?"

Mavis looked down. Even though she was dark complexioned, it was clear that she was blushing. "Kind of," she said softly.

"Did you have a crush on him?"

She nodded. "Yeah."

"Many of the girls in your neighborhood had crushes on Marvin, didn't they?"

The girl gave an "I don't know" shrug.

"He's big, handsome. I can understand a girl your age having a crush on a boy that looks like that," Abramowitz said empathetically. "When I was a girl your age I had crushes on boys that didn't know I existed."

The girl looked up at her. A kindred spirit.

Wyatt wanted to puke, watching this bullshit. He wasn't going to tolerate much of this crap; he was in a lousy mood to begin with, this faux-girlie-girlie sympathy shtick was annoying in the extreme.

"A lot of the girls liked him," Mavis admitted.

"Including you," Abramowitz prompted.

The girl looked down again. "Yeah. I liked him."

"So when he finally paid you attention you were excited, weren't you?"

Softly: "Yeah."

"Would you tell the jury what happened the night . . . that night?" Abramowitz asked. "Take your time," she said protectively.

The girl squirmed in her chair to get a comfortable position, then sat up straight. Her hands were folded in her lap. "He said he'd been checking me out," she began. She looked in Marvin's direction. Startled, he looked away.

Abramowitz watched the byplay between the two. "All right. Marvin White said he'd been checking you out."

The girl nodded. "He told me he thought I was really bitchin'."

"Bitchin'? Does that mean pretty?"

The girl tittered. "Yeah," she said. "Kind of."

"Go ahead."

"So he said, 'You want to go up on the roof?' And I said, 'Well, all right, but don't be tellin' no one, I don't want my mama to know.' 'Cause my mama, she's real strict, she don't want me truckin' with no boys from the projects where we live at, she been wanting me to finish high school and stuff. To better myself. She thought the boys in Sullivan Houses was trash. Trash. She was hoping my daddy'd get better so he could get another job and we could move out of there."

"So did you? Go up on the roof?"

"Yeah."

"What did you expect was going to happen up there on the roof, Mavis?" Abramowitz asked. "Didn't Marvin have a reputation in Sullivan Houses as being a ladies' man?"

"I guess," the girl said. "I hadn't been livin' there all that long. I just knew he was real cute."

Sitting next to Wyatt, Marvin put his head down and groaned. Wyatt poked him in the ribs, under the table. "Sit up," he hissed. "Keep your eyes up. The jury's watching you."

Marvin sat up. "Keep yourself steady," Wyatt whispered at him. "The jury's watching how you react to this."

Marvin nodded glumly, but sat up straight.

"See, the thing was," Mavis continued, "I hadn't never been with no boy before."

Abramowitz folded her arms across her breast. "Are you telling us you were a virgin on the night you went up on the roof with Marvin White?"

The girl looked down. "Yeah," she muttered.

Wyatt didn't have to look at the jury to know they were taking notes.

Abramowitz handed the girl a cup of water. Mavis drank it in one gulp. She set it down.

"All right," Abramowitz said. "Go ahead."

"There was this beat-up old couch up there that people used when they went up there, and we sat down on it and started kissing and stuff."

"What kind of stuff?"

"He put his hand on my titty, that kind of thing. On top of my dress," she added hastily, "and I had a bra on."

They'd told her to say "titty" when they'd prepped her, Wyatt knew. Don't say "breast." You're from the street, talk like it. People will believe you more.

"And then what?" Abramowitz asked.

"He said he was gonna . . ." She stopped.

"Gonna what? Going to what, Mavis?"

"He said he was gonna fuck me."

Wyatt couldn't help but look at the jury now. Most of the women were looking grim.

The women were going to decide this, he knew. The men were along for the ride.

"What did you do?"

"I told him no. That I didn't go all the way. That I never had, and I wasn't going to then, not the first time I'd been with him."

"Then what happened?"

The girl looked over at Marvin. "He pulled out a knife," she said. "He tol' me if I didn't let him fuck me he'd jam it down my throat."

Abramowitz crossed to the prosecution table and removed a pair of latex gloves from a package. Windsor helped her slip them on. She then picked up a manila envelope and brought it forward with her, opening it and removing the contents.

A Swiss Army knife slid out of the envelope. With some difficulty Abramowitz tried to open the largest blade. Smiling up at Judge Grant, she said, "I have to apologize for my clumsiness, Your Honor. I don't handle knives like this very often, and these gloves are slippery."

"Take your time," Grant allowed.

She got the blade open. Holding it up, she walked to within a few feet of Mavis sitting in the witness chair. "Did the knife he pulled out that night look like this knife?" she asked.

The girl looked at the knife for but a second before she answered, "Yes."

"I'd like to introduce this into the record," Abramowitz said. "This is the knife that was on Marvin White's person on the night he was arrested."

"Without objection, so ordered," Grant said.

"Wait a minute, Your Honor," Wyatt stood up. "I have an objection."

"What is it?" Grant asked.

"The inference being made here is that this knife is the same knife that the witness claims was used. Aside from the fact that we haven't established that any knife was used on her, there's no way that this one could in any way be assumed to be a knife Marvin White might have carried on him three years ago."

"We're not saying this is the same knife," Abramowitz retorted. "All we're saying is that it is similar to the one this witness claims was used against her by the defendant."

"But there is absolutely no proof that any kind of knife was ever used against this witness," Wyatt answered hotly. "That's my point. By coming in here and making an unproven allegation and then using evidence that has no connection to that allegation you're casting improper aspersions on my client. The only 'fact' not in dispute here is that on the night my client was arrested—not on these charges, I should point out, but on a completely different case that was resolved prior to trial—he had a knife. Which was not the knife used in any of the murders that this case is supposed to be about. Dr. Ayala has already gone over that issue to everyone's satisfaction."

Grant pondered the question for a moment. "I'm going to allow this knife to be admitted as an exhibit," he decided, "but only as a piece of evidence that the defendant was holding on the night he was admitted into custody in the jail." He turned to the jury. "You are to draw no inference that this knife was used in any way against this witness," he instructed them. "Please continue," he told Abramowitz.

"After he pulled the knife, did he rape you?"

"Objection. Leading the witness."

"Sustained."

"After he pulled the knife, what did he do?"

In a whisper, the girl said, "He raped me."

Abramowitz led her through the rest of her story. How he had raped her and forced her to give him a blow job. How her mother had discovered her bleeding, taken her to the hospital, wrung her confession from her.

"Just before Marvin White was set to go on trial for raping you and threatening to kill you, you withdrew from the case," Abramowitz said, picking up the thread. "You wouldn't testify, so the case had to be dropped. Why didn't you testify, Mavis?"

"Because they tol' me they'd kill me if I did."

"Who is 'they'?"

"Friends of Marvin."

"Objection!" Wyatt couldn't keep his cool. "This is absolutely improper, Your Honor. There is no foundation whatsoever for this testimony."

"Sustained," Grant said immediately. He looked sternly at Abramowitz. "You're not going anywhere with this. Do we understand each other."

"Yes, Your Honor," she said. "I understand you."

Grant turned to the jury. "You will disregard any references to why this defendant did not testify in that case," he instructed them.

"No further questions," Abramowitz said.

Josephine had been sleuthing. Wyatt looked over the information she'd discovered during the break.

"Good work," he complimented her.

"I hope it's strong enough," she fretted.

"It's what we have, so we'll go with it."

"So, Mavis." Wyatt smiled at the girl. "Is Mavis all right, or would you prefer I call you Ms. Jones?"

"Mavis is fine," the girl muttered.

"Mavis. Good." He squared up his notes. "Let's talk about this alleged rape you say happened three years ago, shall we?" He leaned on his elbows, affecting casualness. "You had been living in Sullivan Houses for only a few months when you went up on the roof with Marvin White. Is that right?"

"Yeah, that's right," the girl said.

"You didn't know anybody there very well, did you?"

The girl shook her head. "No."

"You hadn't been going to school with them, hanging out with them, anything like that."

"No," again.

"And you had never spent any time with Marvin, had you? Maybe saying hello in passing, but no time alone, just the two of you. Is that right?"

She nodded.

"You'll have to answer for the record," Judge Grant instructed her. "You can't shake your head or use body language. Was the answer to that last question yes?"

"Yeah," she said, nodding again. "Tha's right."

"So you only knew him by sight."

"Yeah."

"And reputation."

The girl looked at him quizzically.

"You heard things about him."

"Yeah."

"From other girls."

"Yeah."

"What did the girls you talked to say about Marvin?"

"That he was . . ." She stopped.

"That he was what?"

"Stud."

"A stud? What does that mean?"

"That he liked girls."

"He liked girls." He smiled. "That sounds like most fifteen-year-old boys I know. Did the girls like him back?"

"Most of 'em." She was talking very quietly, almost in a whisper.

"You'll have to speak up," Grant admonished her gently. "Everyone has to be able to hear you."

She looked at him with fright in her eyes.

"Did the other girls in Sullivan Houses like Marvin?" Wyatt asked again.

"Yeah. They liked him."

"Had some of them gone up to the roof with him? That you knew of?"

"Yeah," she answered.

"Did they tell you what they did up there?"

She looked over at Abramowitz, her eyes widening with apprehension.

A deer caught in the headlights, he thought. They're using you, you poor thing. Don't you know that?

"Answer the question, please," Grant instructed her.

She licked her lips. "Yeah."

"They told you," Wyatt said. "What did they tell you?"

"They did stuff."

"Stuff? Does that mean they had sex with him?"

She looked down at her shoes. "Yeah," she answered.

"The girls that went up on the roof with Marvin had sex with him. They told you that."

"Yeah."

"So when he asked you to go up on the roof with him, what did you think was going to happen?"

She answered plaintively. "I didn't know."

"You knew that when the other girls, the girls you'd talked to about it, when they went up on the roof with Marvin it was to have sex. Isn't that right?"

"Yeah."

"If Marvin asked a girl to go up on the roof with him, and she said yes, he expected her to have sex with him. He knew that she knew that was the reason, and he expected it."

"I guess so," she said, her words slurring together.

"So when he asked you to go on the roof with him, he could reasonably expect that you would have sex with him. That you were willing to."

"I don't know," she answered. "It wasn't why I was going up there."

"It wasn't?" he asked dubiously. "What were you going up there for, then?"

"To . . ."

"To what?" he pressed her.

"Make out."

"To make out? You mean kiss?"

"Yeah."

"What else? Was it okay in your mind if he felt you up?" The girl looked away.

"Had you decided, when you went up there with him, that if he put his hand on your breast that would be all right with you?"

She sighed. "Yeah. That would have been okay."

"In fact, you wanted him to kiss you, didn't you. You wanted him to put his hand on your breast."

"I didn't mind."

"You didn't care one way or the other?"

"If he did it, that was okay."

"So if he put his hand on your breast that was okay, and if he didn't put his hand on your breast that was okay, too? Either way, it was okay with you?"

"Yeah," she mumbled. "It was okay."

"What if he had put his hand under your dress. Would that have been okay?"

She didn't answer.

"In your mind, thinking about what might happen up there on the roof, if Marvin had started kissing you, and put his hand on your breast, and then put his hand on your leg under your dress, or whatever you were wearing, would that have been all right with you?"

She hesitated.

"Please answer the question," Grant admonished her again, this time less gently.

She paused before answering. "I guess so."

"Okay," Wyatt said. "Now what if he had put his hand on your vagina. On your underpants."

The girl looked down.

"Yes or no," Wyatt pressed. "His hand on your underpants, feeling your vagina underneath. Was that all right with you?"

"I don't know," she answered.

"You don't know meaning you hadn't thought about that, or you don't know meaning you weren't sure."

"Yeah."

"Both reasons?" he asked.

"Yeah."

"So maybe you hadn't thought about it, and maybe when he did it, it was all right. You didn't care one way or the other if he put his hand on your breast, and you didn't care if he put his hand on your vagina. Is that right? If he did, that was all right, and if he didn't that was all right, too?"

"Objection," Abramowitz spoke up. "That's not what she's saying."

"Overruled," Grant decided immediately. "Please answer the question, Ms. Jones."

"I guess." It was as if the words had been forcefully yanked out of her mouth.

"It sounds to me, Mavis, that Marvin could do anything he wanted with you, except actually have sex. Is that right?"

"Objection!"

"Sustained. Restate your question," Grant told Wyatt.

"Was there anything short of actual sexual intercourse with Marvin that you were prepared to say no to?" he asked.

She moistened her lips again. "Blow job," she got out.

"You were not willing to have oral sex with him? Is that what you mean by 'blow job'?"

"Objection," Abramowitz shouted. "Everyone knows what the term she referred to means."

"Overruled."

"You weren't willing to go down on Marvin, is that what you're telling us? Give him head?"

"Yeah," she said.

"Did you tell him that?"

"Huh?"

"Did you say to Marvin, 'I'm not willing to go down on you,' or words to that effect?"

More lip licking. "No."

"You knew that when he went up on the roof with other girls it was for the purpose of having sex, didn't you? Consensual sex?"

"Say what?"

"That the other girls were willing to have sex with him."

"Yeah."

"He didn't have to force them. It was okay with them. Better than okay."

"Yeah," she said again. "It was okay with them, I guess."

"None of the girls who had gone up on the roof with Marvin and had sex with him told you he had forced them to, did they? That he forced them to do it against their will?"

She nodded. "Nobody ever told me he made 'em, if tha's what you mean."

"That's exactly what I mean," he said. "But you weren't going to," he went on. "You weren't going to go all the way."

She shook her head. "No," she said.

"Because you were afraid?"

She nodded.

"Does that nod mean yes?" he asked.

"Yeah," she said. "I was afraid."

"Because you'd never done it before?"

"Yeah. That's why," she agreed.

"What I'm hearing," Wyatt said, "is that you wanted to have sex with Marvin White, but you were afraid to. Is that correct?"

"Objection, Your Honor! That is not what the witness said. Counselor is putting words in her mouth."

"Sustained."

"Mavis." He looked her in the eye. "Did you want to have sex with Marvin, but you were afraid to?"

She fidgeted in her chair.

"Answer the question, please," Wyatt pressed her.

"I don't know," she answered finally.

"You don't know if you wanted to, or you don't remember if you wanted to?"

"Both," she admitted.

"So maybe you did, but you don't remember."

"Objection!"

"Overruled." Grant turned to Mavis. "Did you want to, or you don't remember whether you wanted to or not?" he asked her.

"I don't remember," she answered meekly.

Wyatt stared at her, taking his time before asking his next question, then raising his voice a notch. "At the time you were allegedly raped you had a juvenile record of your own, didn't you, Mavis."

"Objection," came from the prosecution table. "Ms. Jones's record, if there is one, is not germane to this questioning."

"It absolutely is, Your Honor," Wyatt answered quickly. "This witness is testifying to something that is considered hearsay under most circumstances. Her credibility is important in judging whether or not she's telling the truth."

Grant nodded. "Overruled," he said.

Wyatt picked up her rap sheet. He showed it to her. "Had you ever been arrested at the time you accused Marvin White of raping you?" Wyatt asked.

"Yeah," she said grudgingly.

"You had been arrested for shoplifting?"

"Yeah."

"Using a stolen credit card," he continued.

"That wasn't me stole it," she said. "That was . . ."

"A friend?" he finished for her.

"Yeah."

"But you used it."

"Yeah."

"So you weren't such an innocent little girl after all, were you? You'd done a lot of bad things. You just hadn't gotten around to having sex yet."

"Objection!"

"Sustained. Save the editorializing for your summation, Mr. Matthews."

"Yes sir." He paused to take a sip of water. Then he picked up another document and skimmed it. He walked over to the witness stand and showed it to her. "Do you recognize this?" he asked her.

She looked at it, then turned away. "Yeah. I seen it."

"Would you tell the court what it is."

"Arrest sheet."

"Your arrest sheet?"

"Yeah," she said. "It's mine."

He looked at it again. "This is dated . . . let's see . . . about six weeks ago. You were arrested six weeks ago?"

"Yeah."

He looked at the rap sheet again. "For prostitution? And possession of crack cocaine." Reading on, he said, "You solicited an undercover policeman for the purpose of having sex for money? And when you were arrested and booked they found three vials of crack in your purse?"

"They wasn't mine," she protested. "They was my girl-frien's. I was holdin' 'em for her."

He nodded. "What's the situation with this arrest?" he asked. "Have you gone up for trial yet?"

She looked at Abramowitz.

"Or have the charges been dropped," he continued without waiting for her to answer.

"Yeah," she said under her breath again.

"Why were these charges dropped, Mavis? Did you do something for the police, so they would drop the charges?"

"Objection!"

"Overruled," Grant shot back before Abramowitz could explain why she was objecting.

"Did you make a deal with the district attorney's office?" Wyatt asked her. "That if you came in here and testified against Marvin White they would drop all charges against you?"

The girl looked down.

"Did you?" he demanded.

"Yeah," she said. "They cut me a deal."

Wyatt paused to allow the jury, all of whom were writing in their notebooks as fast as they could, to catch up to him. Then he proceeded.

"It says here you have a child. A two-year-old girl named Abyssinia. Is that true?"

She nodded.

"But you're not married."

She shook her head. "No, I ain't married."

"Do you know who the father of your child is?" he asked.

She glared at him under hooded eyelids. "I ain't sure."

"So around the time you became pregnant with her you'd had sex with more than one man. That's true, isn't it."

"Yeah."

"Not too long after you claimed Marvin took your virginity."

"I guess. I don't know."

"Six months after Marvin White allegedly raped you at knifepoint, when you had never had sex before, you were sleeping with so many men that you don't know who got you pregnant. Isn't that right?"

"It wasn't all that many," she said.

Wyatt stepped back and checked the jury for their reaction to that. Some of them were shaking their heads in disbelief.

Looking at her again, he asked, "Is Marvin the father?"

Her mouth flew open. "Hell, no!" she said emphatically.

"You and Marvin never had sex again, consensual or not, after that one time, did you?"

"No. We never did."

"He didn't want to be bothered with you, did he? Especially after you trumped up that phony rape charge on him, right?"

"Objection!" Abramowitz screamed.

"Sustained!" Grant swung his gavel on that one. "That

kind of questioning is inflammatory and unacceptable," he admonished Wyatt sternly.

Wyatt nodded. Glancing at her rap sheet again, he asked, "Did the police threaten to put Abyssinia in social services if you didn't cooperate with them on this case?" he asked.

She mumbled something unintelligible.

"They said they were going to take her away from you if you didn't cooperate, isn't that right?"

"Yeah. They said they might."

"That scared you, didn't it?"

"Yeah. I don't want nobody takin' my baby."

"I can understand that," he said sympathetically. "I have a child myself, and I wouldn't want anyone taking her away from me."

He leafed through some pages in front of him again until he found the one he was looking for.

"After Marvin allegedly raped you, you didn't tell your mother, did you?"

She stared at him. "No."

"You were afraid to."

She nodded. "Yeah."

"You knew your mother would go ballistic if she found out you were having sex. Especially with someone from Sullivan Houses, a place your mother felt was beneath her and that she was being forced to live in by dire circumstances. Isn't that right?"

"Objection, Your Honor. She was raped, she wasn't 'having sex,' as opposing counsel so delicately puts it."

"If your mother found out you were having sex with a boy from Sullivan Houses, she would have been angry with you, wouldn't she?" Wyatt asked. "Enraged?"

"Real angry," the girl agreed.

"So if you were having sex with a boy, you wouldn't tell her, would you?"

"Objection!"

"Overruled."

"So if she ever found out you were, you would have to lie about it, wouldn't you?"

"Objection!" Abramowitz was on her feet.

"Overruled!"

"So when you went up on the roof with Marvin White, a boy all the girls liked, and had sex with him up there, you couldn't tell your mother, could you?" he said, his voice rising.

"Objection!"

"Overruled!" The gavel came down hard.

"So that when your mother found your bloody underpants, you couldn't tell her the truth, could you? That you'd had sex with Marvin of your own free will!" Racing on: "So you told her you'd been raped—because you couldn't tell her the truth. You lied to her and to the police because you were afraid of telling the truth, which is that you had sex with Marvin White of your own free will! That you went up to the roof with him knowing that was what was going to happen, and you wanted it to happen! You wanted to have sex with this big, good-looking boy all the girls talked about, and when you did lose your virginity to Marvin you lied to your mother and said he raped you, because it was the only thing you could think of to say that would keep her from killing you!" His voice dropped, almost to a whisper. "And that's the truth, isn't it, Mavis!"

Again, prosecution and defense met with Judge Grant in his chambers. Alex Pagano joined his team to take part in this argument. Earlier, Wyatt had privately apologized to Grant for his aggressive conduct, but not for attacking Mavis Jones as he had. Grant accepted the apology and the incident was behind them.

"This is a thorny one," Grant said, considering the prosecution's latest request. Pagano and Abramowitz wanted to introduce Marvin's botched armed-robbery attempt, since both crimes had occurred on the same night. To that end they had subpoenaed the Korean shop owner as a witness. In addition, they wanted to bolster their case by using the portion of the videotape showing the attempted robbery, which would clearly reveal Marvin's use of deadly force on the same night he murdered Paula Briggs—a pattern of ongoing, habitual criminal intent.

"Hasn't that case already been settled?" the judge asked Abramowitz and Wyatt.

"Yes, Your Honor," Wyatt answered. "We have a binding agreement."

"Wait a minute," Pagano protested. "That was before this

indictment came down. I don't consider any settlement made then to be binding now, Your Honor."

Wyatt took the agreement out of his briefcase and handed it to the judge. "Signed by all parties concerned," he said.

"That agreement is worthless," Pagano protested again. "It was done without subsequent knowledge of these crimes."

"So what?" Wyatt countered. "Once it's over, it's over. It doesn't matter if new information comes up afterward, prosecution can't appeal after the fact—any first-year law student knows that."

Grant put his hand up for them to quit bickering while he read the settlement agreement. He looked up, taking off his reading glasses and folding them into his shirt pocket.

"The defense's position regarding the legality of that plea bargain is the right one," he said. "That case has been settled. It's on the record." He looked at Wyatt. "Your client has pleaded guilty to a violent crime. And under the rules of evidence that record can be used against him if it helps establish a pattern, which this clearly does."

"Bringing in the witness is permissible, I agree with that, Your Honor," Wyatt said. "But to use videotape of it as evidence is of great concern to us. It's inflammatory and will color the jury's attitude toward my client."

"I understand your concern," Grant acknowledged. "But if I'm allowing prosecution's witness to testify I don't know what grounds would be for denial of admission of those videotapes. How do you plan to argue it?" he asked.

He was giving Wyatt the chance to help him deny admitting the tapes into evidence; he was still smarting from the Mavis Jones fiasco of the day before, Wyatt figured.

Pagano jumped in with both feet. "There are no grounds, Your Honor," he argued vigorously. "The witness and the tapes are of a piece. And allowing someone as sharp as defense counsel to find a way is improper."

"Thanks for the kudo," Wyatt said, smiling at his opponent. "I'll use it in my memoirs." He looked at Grant. "I don't know how to help you, Your Honor. I can't find any precedent that will allow me to, since you're going to allow the witness to testify."

"You're not going to contest this?" Grant asked in surprise.

"I can't find a reason to back me up, Your Honor. I wish I could," he added ruefully. "It's going to hurt."

Grant gave him back the document. "In that case, I have no option but to let this videotape be admitted into evidence."

"Thank you, Your Honor." Abramowitz turned to Wyatt. "Sorry, Charlie," she said, dripping sarcasm onto Grant's threadbare carpet.

He gave a little shrug and smiled. "Can't win 'em all."

Darryl grabbed a couple of Rolling Rocks from his fridge, twisted the tops off, and handed one across the desk to Wyatt. "Man, you're walking a tightrope across the Grand Canyon without a safety net," he said, his voice etching concern. "Are you sure this is a workable angle of attack?"

"No," Wyatt answered candidly. "I'm not sure at all. It could blow up in my face—in Marvin's face. But I have to be aggressive in the way I try this case, take some chances. He's sixty to seventy present convicted already, so playing it book-safe isn't going to cut it. As long as it's my case I've got to go with a strategy I think might work. I know it's high-risk, but sitting on my ass will kill his."

Darryl nodded. "I know where you're going. It's a risky tactic. I don't know if I'd have the guts to try it."

"Maybe I'm too damn dumb and inexperienced to know any better."

"No way, José. You can't pull that neophyte shit anymore. You're doing as good a job as anybody could." He raised his bottle in salute.

"Thanks." Wyatt sucked down some brew. "Coming from you that means a lot. You know," he mused, "prosecutors are used to rolling over people like Marvin White. A couple days picking a jury, two or three days prosecution testimony, a day or two for the defense, it goes to the jury and out rolls another guilty verdict. Assembly-line justice—it's what they're used to, and it's what works for them. The poor outgunned defendant's down for the count before he ever saw the punch coming. And I don't mean to cast aspersions on Walcott's office when I say that. They do as good a job as they can, but the more I'm around there the more I realize how stacked the odds are against them."

He took another swallow of beer. "My feeling is you

throw them some unexpected moves, change up on your fastball, and they don't know what to do—they spin their wheels and crash into a wall." He paused. Soberly, he added, "At least I hope that's what I can force them to do."

Over one more pro-forma objection from Wyatt the Korean shop owner was on the stand, as impassive as a stone Buddha. Abramowitz was questioning him about the happenings of that night.

"Had you ever seen the defendant, Marvin White, before that night, Mr. Kwon?" she asked. She looked over to the defense table and pointed at Marvin.

The shopkeeper looked over. "I see him."

"He had been in your store before?"

"Yes, he come in before."

"There's no doubt in your mind? You couldn't be mistaking him for someone else?"

The man shook his head. "I see him in my store before. He always sulking around like he's gonna shoplift something. So I keep eye on him. I know him," he said forcefully.

"Had he been in the store before on the night he tried to rob you?"

The man bobbed his head. "He come in earlier."

"What did he do?"

"Buy cigarettes."

"He bought a pack of cigarettes. Do you remember what kind?"

"Marlboro cigarette. Regular box."

"He bought a pack of Marlboros." She looked over at the jury. "Then what did he do?"

"Leave store."

"All right." She glanced at her notes, looked up. "He came back later?" she asked.

Another nod. "He walk in when no one in store. Like he wait until it empty."

"Than what did he do?"

He told the story; how Marvin had put a gun to his face, made him take the money out of the cash register, tried to shoot him. The gun had jammed, giving the shop owner the chance to get his own shotgun out from underneath the counter. That as he had raised it in self-defense Marvin had tried to shoot him again. That upon seeing him about to fire, Marvin had turned tail and run, and he had tried not to shoot, but he had no control over his emotions and his finger pulled the trigger involuntarily.

"We have collaborating evidence of this witness's account, Your Honor," Abramowitz said, "which we would like to present now."

Grant nodded. "Go ahead."

A large television set connected to a VCR was wheeled into the room and set up at an angle that allowed the jury to easily see the screen. Abramowitz inserted the tape. "Would you lower the lights, please."

The room lights were dimmed. Abramowitz hit the play button on the VCR remote. The tape started.

The jury had been properly attentive before, listening to the prosecution witnesses' testimony. Actually seeing the commission of this crime, however, ratcheted their attention span up. As there was no sound on the recording, the dialogue between Marvin and the shop owner could not be known conclusively. In addition, since the clicks from the misfiring of Marvin's gun weren't heard, his intention could not be satisfactorily judged. The camera was too far away and the lens angle was too wide for anyone who hadn't actually been there—anyone other than Marvin and the shop owner—to be able to tell whether he was pulling the trigger, and that only because the gun jammed was the store owner not killed; or conversely, that he was not pulling the trigger at all. It could be argued either way.

The tape stopped after the shop owner fired his shotgun and ran out of frame toward the door in the direction in which he had fired. Marvin was not shown being shot—the camera didn't cover that action.

Abramowitz turned off the VCR. "Lights, please," she asked.

The lights came back on. She looked with intensity across the room toward the defense table, where Marvin was sitting, staring straight ahead, seeing nothing.

"Look at her," Wyatt whispered. "Now!"

Marvin turned and faced Abramowitz. She was standing

in front of the jury, so that looking at her meant he was also looking at them. The jury was staring at him intently.

"Keep looking at her," Wyatt ordered him.

It took everything he had, but Marvin kept his eyes focused on Abramowitz.

She broke eye contact, turning back to her witness. "You clearly heard the defendant's gun misfire, is that correct? That he tried to pull the trigger. His intention was to shoot you so he could take the money, but the gun didn't go off—which is the only reason you are able to be here in court today, isn't that right?"

"Yes," the man hissed. "He try to kill me. Gun no good. Otherwise I dead man."

Abramowitz looked toward the jury. "This man had a gun to his head," she said, pointing to Kwon, the store owner. "If it hadn't misfired, the defendant would be on trial for that murder as well. We are pointing out the venality of this man," she forcefully told the twelve men and women who had watched the videotape. "This man that raped, sodomized, and murdered a woman, then calmly walked a few blocks away and tried to rob and kill an innocent store owner."

"Objection," Wyatt said. "Prosecution is giving her summation, not eliciting testimony. The defendant has not been convicted of anything, Your Honor, and there is no proof he was trying to kill this man here. The pictures are highly ambiguous."

"Maybe to you," Abramowitz fired at him. "But not to anyone who can see. Or has compassion for these seven innocent victims."

Grant hammered his gavel. "Objection sustained. Please restrain from this type of editorializing," he admonished her.

Abramowitz gathered her paperwork. "No further questions, Your Honor."

Wyatt waited until she was seated, then walked over to the prosecution table and leaned down over his knuckles, so that he was right in her face. "Can I have the control gizmo for that tape player of yours?" he asked her.

Startled, she drew back in her chair, pushing the remote across the table in his direction. "Thanks," he smiled at her. Walking to the lectern, he turned to the deputies guarding the door. "Would you fellows please douse the lights again for me?"

The room went dark again. Wyatt hit the rewind button, playing the tape backward until Marvin was first seen, approaching the counter where the store owner stood with his back to him. As soon as Marvin entered the frame, Wyatt hit the pause button.

The picture froze on the television screen. A high black-and-white shot from above, the figures small in the frame. "Could I have the pointer, please?" Wyatt asked.

A deputy brought it to him. He walked to the television set, making sure he wasn't blocking the view of any of the jurors. He pointed to a small bar code imprint in the right-hand bottom of the screen.

"Could you tell us what that bar code is for?" he asked the witness.

Mr. Kwon stared at the screen. "Identification," he said in a flat, inflectionless voice.

"Identification," Wyatt repeated. "The tape is bar-coded to identify it, is that correct?" he asked.

"Yes."

"So you can tell it from other tapes?"

"Yes."

Wyatt pushed the play button again. As the picture came to life, the bar code changed. He let the tape play a few seconds, then froze it again.

"If the tape is merely for identification," he asked, "why is the bar code changing?"

"Objection," Abramowitz called out immediately. "The bar code is irrelevant, Your Honor."

"Overruled," Grant said immediately. "Answer the question," he told the shop owner.

Wyatt put a restraining hand up. "Let me get back to that in a minute, okay, Your Honor? There's another line I should clarify first, if I can." He turned to the shop owner again. "Why do you think the defendant picked your store to rob?" he asked. "Little mom-and-pop convenience store, you couldn't have too much in the register. It looked like less than five hundred dollars. There must be other stores around with more cash at hand."

"Objection," Abramowitz called out. "Calls for conjecture by the witness regarding a motive he couldn't possibly know."

"This bears directly on this bar code thing," Wyatt said quickly before Grant could sustain her. He went over to his table, got some papers, and brought them up to Grant for inspection. The judge looked them over. "If you want to enter this into evidence it should come during the presentation of your case in chief," Grant pointed out.

"That's fine," Wyatt said. "I wanted to authenticate the accuracy of prosecution's evidence, that's all. I'm not fighting what's on that screen, Your Honor. I'm agreeing with it. I want that to go on the record."

He walked over to the television set and pointed at the bar code on the bottom of the screen again. "Isn't this bar code really a time code?" he asked. "Each different bar represents a different time, doesn't it?"

"Objection!" Abramowitz yelled.

"Overruled," Grant said sharply. "Answer the question," he told the witness.

The shop owner stared at Wyatt. "Means time code," he agreed.

Wyatt glanced over at the prosecutor's table. Abramowitz looked like she had swallowed a ten-pound lemon. "Did the prosecution . . . did Ms. Abramowitz ask you what the bar code was for?" he asked.

The witness nodded. "Yes," he answered after hesitating.

"Did you tell her?"

"Yes," again.

"And she was shown how to decode it? So she could read the times that bar code represented?"

"Uh," the man grunted.

"That's a yes, I take it." Without pausing, Wyatt punched up rewind on the tape machine, again pausing it when Marvin was first seen entering the picture. Walking over to the defense table, he picked up a computer printout with similar bar code symbols on it, each one followed by a specific, sequential number. "Let me show you a matching bar code to the one on the TV." He handed the printout to the witness and pointed to the top set of numbers. "Would you read those numbers for the jury?" he asked the witness.

The man squinted at the sheet. "Twenty-two-twenty-five thirty-eight," he read in his fractured English singsong.

"Twenty-two-twenty-five thirty-eight," Wyatt repeated. "Would that mean that the time represented on the screen right there is exactly ten-twenty-five and thirty-eight seconds in the evening?" he asked. "This is set up on military time, is that correct?"

The man bobbed his head. "That what it mean."

"So Marvin White walked into your store at ten-twenty-five at night. These tapes confirm that. Now let me ask you another question about these tapes, Mr. Kwon. You have a camera in your store that recorded these tapes, is that correct?"

The man stared at him. "Yes."

"The camera is in operation whenever your store is open, is that also correct?"

"Yes."

"Your store hours are six in the morning until midnight, seven days a week?"

"Yes," again.

"So eighteen hours a day, seven days a week, this camera is operating and recording tapes, right?"

"Yes."

"Is that in case a crime is committed? So you would have a record?"

"Yes."

Wyatt walked back to the defense table, looked at whatever lay on top without reading it, then walked back to the defendant, standing between him and the television set. "If the point of having this camera and recording on these tapes is to document a crime in your store, why do you keep the tapes? You don't recycle the same tape," he said, "you store them. Two weeks at a time. Why do you keep those tapes, if there's nothing on them?"

The shop owner stared at him without answering.

"And the camera," Wyatt continued, not waiting for an answer. "It's hidden from the public's view, isn't that correct?"

"Yes."

"Isn't the point of having a camera recording the activities in the store to *deter* a crime? It's standard procedure when you go into a store, or a bank, or whatever, to see signs posted saying 'This store is under video surveillance.'

The point is to deter crime, not to have a record after the fact, isn't it?"

Another reluctant "Yes."

"But your camera is hidden, and there are no signs stating that your premises are under surveillance." He turned to the jury. "That's because you don't want people to know there's a camera there. Isn't that right, Mr. Kwon?"

The shop owner sat motionless.

"Which brings me back to the question of why someone who had just raped and murdered a woman, who was already the subject of a massive manhunt because he had already raped, sodomized, and murdered six times, would risk robbing your store. If he had done what he is alleged to have done, wouldn't he get away from there as quickly as possible?" He paused. "Unless there was a lot more cash in that store than your normal little corner grocery should have."

"Objection!" Abramowitz yelled. "This is irrelevant and immaterial."

"Isn't the real reason Marvin tried to rob your store because it's a numbers drop for the Thai Mafia?" Wyatt shot at the witness, his face inches from the Korean's. "That he'd been scoping it out and knew that you were holding over twenty thousand dollars? Isn't that the reason he tried to rob you?" he thundered.

The storekeeper seemed to be trying to shrink into the back of the chair.

"And isn't that the real reason your store's activities are recorded and the tapes kept? So that your bosses can make sure *you* aren't skimming their profits? The tapes aren't to catch criminals, are they! They're an eye on *you,* to make sure you don't rob them of their illegal gains. Why don't we play the tapes of you handing off twenty thousand dollars to your bagman, to keep all this in proper perspective?"

"Objection!" Abramowitz was screaming, running around the front of her table and rushing up to the bench.

"Sustained!" Judge Grant's gavel resounded in the vaulted chamber. "The jury will disregard that last line of questioning! Whatever business is transpiring in that store, legal or not, is not germane to our purpose." He stared down at Wyatt. "You are crossing the line of propriety," he admonished Wyatt. "If you don't moderate your behavior you may not be trying your case much longer."

Wyatt stared back at him. "Sorry," he bit off. He pushed the power button on the tape player. The television set went blank. "No further questions."

He went home for the weekend, taking his files with him in five large boxes. They were spread out all over his dining-room table. It felt good to be home, in his own space. The lawn, front and back, was lush and green, and all the trees and bushes were in full summer bloom. He ran both Saturday and Sunday mornings, long, slow, cleansing runs. And he played his trombone. He brought it into the house and set it on its stand in the corner of the dining room. Whenever he felt like taking a break from reviewing the work in front of him he picked it up and blew a few tunes, or just notes.

The house felt empty. He missed his family life, Michaela especially. She was going to be out of their lives soon, away to college. Every minute he could have with her between now and then, he wanted.

But he couldn't have that. Not now. Coming up were the prosecutor's biggest guns. Violet Waleska, the woman who saw Marvin in the parking lot where the murder had been committed; and Dwayne Thompson, the state's key witness, the master informant who had heard the confession of a mass murderer.

And there was that secret between Violet and Dwayne. It would have blown a hole in the state's case an 18-wheeler could drive through, maybe even gotten the case thrown out. Violet and Dwayne, sister and brother. Only they knew, and they would never tell. The prosecution didn't know; they would have had to disclose the information. How sweet it would have been to throw that one in Abramowitz's and Pagano's faces.

But he couldn't; not now. He had compromised his professionalism and worse, much worse—he had compromised his ability to successfully defend his client.

He had tried to rationalize to himself that it didn't matter—that they hadn't collaborated, exchanged information. Violet had only seen him the one time, long after she and Dwayne both had told their stories. And he wanted to use her testimony to bolster his own case, to debunk the prosecution's timetable.

All that was true, and it was all bullshit.

Anyway, that they had made love to each other was secondary. What mattered was that she had told him of the relationship voluntarily—a woman pouring her heart out to a man she didn't even know and yet seemed to care about in some deep, unfathomable way. He could no more have exposed her after that confession than he could quit the case.

He prided himself on being a tough hombre, and he was—you don't get to the position he was in without making hard choices and leaving some bodies in your wake. But everyone has to draw his line in the sand somewhere, and he drew his with Violet Waleska.

Dwayne was a different story, in its particular way even more complicated than his convoluted relationship with Violet. How was he going to break this bastard down and catch him up in a lie, something that would unravel the state's entire case?

These thoughts recurred in his mind all weekend. He ran, he played the trombone, and he studied. He also talked to his wife and child. Michaela's leg was steadily getting stronger, Moira informed him, and so was the bond between them. The shooting had been an accident. Moira didn't secretly hate her, nor was she subconsciously acting out some dark revenge fantasy against him. Sometimes there aren't ulterior motives—sometimes there are only accidents.

"I'll call you whenever," he said as they signed off with each other. "It's hectic."

"We'll be here. We aren't going anywhere."

Violet sat up straight in the witness chair, one leg demurely crossed over the other, hands folded in her lap. She was wearing a dark blue cotton dress that broke over her knees. Her stockings were sheer, her shoes low-heeled bone pumps. No jewelry, no makeup save for a slight touch of pale lip gloss. Her thick brown hair was pulled back into a loose bun.

He could sense from where he sat, twenty-five feet away, that she was tense. He had watched her walk up and take the stand, swear to tell the truth, arrange herself in the chair. She hadn't wanted to look at him—he could feel that vibration humming across the distance between them. When she finally had, and their eyes locked for a split second, it was as if an electrical impulse passed between them. She had quickly looked away, and hadn't looked in his direction since.

He was glad he wasn't cross-examining her yet. He needed a few minutes after seeing her for the first time since that night to get his equilibrium rebalanced to a more even, manageable keel.

"The man you identified as being in the parking lot outside the nightclub on the night Paula Briggs was raped and murdered," Abramowitz said. "Is that man in the courtroom today?"

"Yes," Violet answered.

"Would you point him out for the jury, please?"

Violet looked to the defense table. "He is sitting at the defense table."

Everyone was looking at Marvin.

"Deep breaths," Wyatt counseled him. "Stay calm."

Abramowitz milked the moment. Then she took up her questioning again. "Describe for the court, please, the circumstances under which you saw the defendant."

Violet nodded. "I had to go out to my car," she began. "My time of the month had started unexpectedly and I didn't have any Tampax in my purse. There was a box in my trunk, so I went out to get it."

She told the story as it had happened, simply, without embellishment or histrionics. That upon approaching the car she had seen a young black man looking in the rear window, as if trying to see whether the car was unlocked. Her first thought had been that he was preparing to rob her, so she had called out to him to move away from the car.

"Did you think that was dangerous?" Abramowitz asked. "Challenging someone at night, alone, who you thought might rob you?"

"No. I didn't think of that. I wanted him to move away from my car."

Abramowitz frowned—that wasn't the answer she had wanted. "You didn't feel any fear?" she asked.

"Not when I yelled at him. Not at first," she added.

"What about when you approached him? Were you at all afraid then?"

Violet thought for a moment, recalling the event. "As I ran toward him I did for a brief moment, I guess," she said. "But I was more concerned about him breaking in than I was afraid. It was a public parking lot," she added, "there were people out there. I wasn't alone."

Wyatt made a note. That had been a mistake on Abramowitz's part—he could see the chagrin in her body language. He could, and would, use that.

Violet went on, explaining how she had gone right up to the car, so that she and the defendant were close to each other, staring at each other.

"How close were you to each other?" Abramowitz asked.

"Ten to fifteen feet. No more."

"And you looked at him? You got a good look at him?"

"He turned and looked right at me. He stared right at me for a good five seconds."

"Were you at all afraid then?" Abramowitz asked.

"A little," Violet admitted.

"But you stared back at him for at least five seconds."

"Yes."

"What were you thinking, looking at him?"

"His eyes looked like they were blank; devoid of feeling. So that scared me. He looked like he wasn't feeling anything."

"He had a frightening look?"

"Yes. Not like he was crazy, or out of control. More the opposite, that he operated without feeling."

"Objection," Wyatt had to speak up.

Involuntarily, she looked over at him. He turned away, looking at Judge Grant.

"Prosecutor is asking the witness to draw conclusions rather than state facts, Your Honor," he said, explaining the objection.

"Sustained," Grant agreed. "Let's stick to verifiable and observed facts, please."

Abramowitz nodded. "How much time elapsed between the time you went out to your car and saw the defendant, and the time that Paula Briggs went out to the parking lot?"

"Less than five minutes."

"And how much more time passed before you and Peggy Knox realized Ms. Briggs hadn't come back inside?"

"Between twenty and thirty minutes."

"Where were you during that time?"

"On the dance floor. We both were. We dance with each other—the fast ones," she added with some embarrassment. "We dance with men, too, of course, but we don't go out looking to get picked up."

"When you noticed she wasn't there, what was your reaction?" Abramowitz asked her next.

"We were . . . I don't know if worried is the right word. Concerned would be better."

"Why were you concerned?"

"Because she wasn't there, of course. I did flash on that kid . . . man . . . I had seen by my car."

"The defendant."

"Yes."

"You thought he might have done something to her?"

"It wasn't that rational. I just remembered him."

"What did you do?"

"We went out to look for her."

"Did you find her?"

"No." Violet looked down. "We didn't find her."

The court recessed for fifteen minutes. When they came back, it was Wyatt's turn. He wasn't looking forward to it—he'd had butterflies in his stomach the entire break.

Violet looked pale. He wanted to protect her—but he had a client to defend.

He questioned her from the lectern—he wasn't going to get any closer to her than he had to. "Ms. Waleska," he started off. "You identified my client from a police lineup, is that right?"

"Yes."

"They called you and told you they had a suspect and would you come down and see if you could identify him?"

She thought for a minute. "Not in so many words," she answered, trying to recall the exact conversation she'd had with Detective Pulaski, "but that was the gist of it, yes."

"Okay." He glanced at his notes. "You had previously told the detective who interviewed you"—he looked at his notes again—"Detective Pulaski. You told him that the man you saw outside the club that night by your car was African American, is that correct?"

"Yes."

"Did the police present a lineup of black men?" he asked. "Only black men?"

"Yes," she said, remembering. "There were three groups. He was in the third group."

This was going nowhere. The lineup had been conducted legitimately. He changed tactics. "Let's get back to the night you were at the club. You went out to your car right after the band took a break?"

"Yes. They were just leaving the stand."

He shuffled through his notes until he found the one he wanted. "That was following their first set?"

"Yes."

"According to the club's performance schedule that would have been at nine-forty, give or take five minutes. Does that time sound right to you?"

"I wasn't looking at my watch, but that sounds right."

"So at approximately nine-forty you went out to your car and saw a man who you have identified as the defendant."

"Yes."

"You saw him for about how long, a minute? From the time you first spotted him by your car until the time he walked away and was out of your sight?"

She thought back. "That sounds about the right amount of time."

"And of that minute, you saw his face clearly for about ten seconds?"

Thinking of the moment again, she said, "Yes. Maybe a little longer."

"And then you saw him leave. He walked away, turned the corner, and was gone. He didn't linger on the edge. He was out of sight, off the premises."

"I saw him leave."

"Completely."

"Completely."

"By the way, did you see any weapon in his hand? Like a knife?"

She shook her head. "I wouldn't have approached him if I'd seen him holding a knife."

"After this man left, how long were you out there by your car?"

"Thirty seconds, tops. I opened my trunk, grabbed a handful of Tampax, locked up, and went back inside."

"So you got back inside around nine-forty-five."

"I guess so."

"You went to the ladies' room, applied a Tampax? Did you freshen up? Fix your lipstick, wash your face?"

"I took two minutes," she told him.

"You're one in a million," he said, the light bantering of a lawyer wanting the other side's witness to be comfortable with him. "Continuing on our timetable. At about ten to ten you returned to your table, all freshened up, and Paula Briggs promptly got up and left. Is that right?"

"Yes."

"She left right away? It wasn't five or ten minutes later?"

"No. As I was sitting down, she stood up."

"Did you think to tell her about the man you had seen by your car?" he asked.

"After she left, I did."

"How long after she left?"

"I don't remember."

"But you didn't follow her out to warn her."

"No."

"Because you didn't think there was any real danger there, did you?"

She looked down. Somehow her hands had come together in her lap, clinched tightly. "No," she said in a small voice. "I didn't." She looked up. "I've been tortured about that ever since."

He stepped away to let some air blow that one away. That was a strong emotional hit against Marvin.

Continuing on: "So then the band came back on"—he checked his notes again—"at ten. And you and Ms. Knox danced several dances."

"Yes."

"Continuously. You didn't take any breaks to go back to your table?"

"No. We stayed on the dance floor."

"You didn't glance over, see if she was there at all during that time?"

"No, but it wouldn't have mattered. You couldn't see our table from where we were dancing."

"So it would have been about ten-ten or ten-fifteen before you noticed that Paula Briggs was missing?"

"Maybe longer."

"But maybe less time?"

"Yes," she agreed. "It could have been a little less time."

"You noticed she was missing and you went out to look for her, but you couldn't find her. Did you call the police?"

"No."

"Why not, if you were concerned?"

She looked away for a minute. When she looked back, she answered, "Because we weren't that concerned."

"You weren't, were you," he said, supplementing her statement. "That man you had seen out there by your car—you really weren't worried about him, were you?"

"No."

"What did you think had really happened to your friend, Paula, Ms. Waleska?" he asked. Before she could answer, he continued, "Wasn't what you thought, you and Ms. Knox, was that Paula Briggs had met a man? Either inside, earlier in the evening, and she didn't tell you, because she knew you would disapprove; or outside, when she went to catch some air. And that she had left with him. Isn't that what you thought had happened?"

She nodded. "Yes, that's what we thought." Her eyes started to tear up. She dabbed at them with a Kleenex. "We were angry with her. I admit it. Not that she'd stood us up, although that was part of it. The real reason we were angry was that she'd gone off with someone she didn't know. But that's how she was. She was impulsive. And she was lonely." She bowed her head, the tears flowing freely. "And now she's neither."

Already, at 6:45, the thermometer was well above 70, going up like a hot rocket. The humidity was brutal, too; you couldn't dry your hair with a blowtorch; shirts and blouses stuck to clammy skin straight out of the shower. Half the fire hydrants in the city would be illegally open by midmorning—the kids who were stuck in the furnace of the streets, whose families couldn't take them on vacation or send them to camp, would be dancing in the festive, heat-beating spray.

Even at this early hour the block around the courthouse was crowded with press, spectators, security. Today was the main attraction, what everyone had been waiting for—the state's key witness was going to take the stand.

Wyatt slowly drove down the street and into the underground parking garage. He'd been up well past midnight, reviewing everything he knew about Thompson. He had the material down cold, backward, forward, and sideways. In and of themselves the informant's story and presentation were rock solid.

Marvin was brought over from the jail at eight o'clock. The two sat in the small meeting room off the courtroom.

"You have to be on your toes for this," he cautioned Marvin.

The defendant listened carefully. He's done some growing up, Wyatt thought as they talked. Events like the ones that had happened over the past few months had to mature you in some way.

"You have to listen to everything Thompson says—without flinching, no matter how ugly or full of shit you think it is. And you're going to have to be real alert, because I'm going to need your help."

"I hear you, Mr. Matthews," Marvin said solemnly.

They would have the grand jury testimony in front of them, and he would be taking notes as Thompson testified, checking it for discrepancies against the previously given testimony. "What I need from you, Marvin, is to try to remember what you told Dwayne, and more importantly, what you didn't, in every instance. I'll be writing down, as best I can, everything Dwayne professes to have been told by you, and you have to let me know whether or not Thompson's telling the truth."

Marvin nodded nervously, trying to take it all in.

"Don't bullshit me," Wyatt warned Marvin sternly. "If he says you told him something and you did, admit it—to me. Put a check mark next to the things you told him, and an X next to whatever you didn't. You've got to pay attention. No daydreaming, no nodding off. Do you understand?"

"Yeah."

"Good."

Wyatt left Marvin in the care of his deputy-keepers and went into the courtroom. Josephine, Walcott, Darryl, Marvin's family, and Dexter were already in place in the first rows on the defense side of the aisle. Wyatt chatted briefly with his people, then went over and talked to Jonnie Rae. On the other side of the room, Abramowitz, Windsor, and their minions were huddled, heads together, going over last-minute details.

"How are you holding up?" Wyatt asked Jonnie Rae solicitously.

She shook her head. "Not too good. I lost my job 'cause of all the time I've been taking off."

How much more was this poor woman going to have to endure? "We'll take care of you until the trial's over," he assured her, "and then I'll find you another job. A better one."

Better was relative—she had no marketable skills. He'd talk to the firm's office manager about putting her on their nighttime cleaning crew. It would mean her kids would be alone all night, but it was the best employment he could think of.

The courtroom doors were flung open and the spectators, those lucky enough to have entry, pressed in. Most were press—they took up two-thirds of the available seats. The rest were people who had specific reasons for being there, relatives and friends of the seven murder victims.

Violet wasn't among the spectators. She'd told him she wouldn't come while her brother was on the stand, but he looked to make sure. Better she wasn't there, he decided. If she took only one percent of his attention, that would be too much.

Marvin was brought in under guard. He sat down at the defense table. Wyatt excused himself from his client's mother and sat down next to him, patting him on the shoulder, one last buck-up. A moment later the jurors filed in and took their assigned seats. Most of them looked across the room at Marvin, as if checking to make sure he was still there.

"All rise!"

Judge Grant strode into the courtroom. He took his seat, asked everyone to take theirs, looked toward the prosecutors. "Call your next witness," he instructed them.

"Call Dwayne Thompson," the bailiff sang out.

Thompson was led in through a side door by a sheriff's deputy. His albino blond hair had been freshly cut, short. It lay lightly on his skull, an inch of white neck showing above the slightly darker but still pale skin that was normally exposed. He was dressed like an off-duty cop would be—they bought his wardrobe at the store where they buy their own, Wyatt guessed: generic gray lightweight wool sports jacket, button-down white shirt, a red-and-green striped tie. Polyester-blend dark blue slacks, dark socks, black loafers. But if you looked carefully you could still see the signs of the sociopath, Wyatt thought—Thompson couldn't hide the emptiness behind his eyes.

As Dwayne took the stand his eyes flickered rattlerlike over to where Marvin was sitting. Looking at his fellow inmate for a second, he flashed a light smile, as if to say, "Shit happens, man. Too bad for your sorry ass you had to get in my way."

"Do you swear to tell the truth? The whole truth? And nothing but the truth?" the bailiff recited for the millionth time, pausing between each phrase.

Kabuki, Wyatt thought. Meaningless ritual. Truth to a man like Dwayne Thompson? A word, nothing more.

"So help you God?"

"I do," Dwayne drawled. He eased down in the witness chair and made himself comfortable.

Abramowitz got up from the prosecution table and walked toward him. "Good morning, Mr. Thompson," she greeted him impersonally. She was going to maintain her distance from him.

"Good morning," he answered her. He could feel himself coming alive between the legs.

She knew exactly what was going on in his mind. She looked away from him, taking a moment to compose herself. "Before I begin questioning you about the events relating directly to this trial, I want to establish certain things for the jury about who you are—and who you are not. You are currently incarcerated in the state's prison system, is that true?"

"Yes," he said. "I am an inmate at Durban State Penitentiary."

"How long have you been in custody there?"

"A little less than five years."

"And how much more time do you have to do?"

"Three more years, assuming I meet the conditions of my sentencing."

"What does that mean?"

"That I don't get into trouble. Keep my nose clean. Which I'm doing."

"What are you in prison for?"

"Second-degree murder."

The jury gawked at him.

"Was that your first offense?"

"No, ma'am."

"How many other times have you been convicted of a crime?" she asked, reading from her notes.

"Two others. But one was nonviolent."

"I take it, then, that you've spent a considerable amount of your adult life in the prison system?"

"Over half of it."

"While you've been locked up in prison," came her next question, "has anything out of the ordinary happened to you? That you brought about? I'm not referring to prison-related activities, such as what you're going to be doing here today. I mean on a more personal level."

He nodded vigorously. "I got my college degree."

"Really," she said enthusiastically, as if she'd never heard of that until this very moment. "You got your college degree while you were in prison? Isn't that unusual?"

"Yes, ma'am," he said. "About one-half of one percent of prison inmates have done it, nationwide. But the government's cut off the grant, so there won't be any more of us."

"That's a shame," she threw away. In truth, the Pell Grant program, which was the program under which Dwayne had gotten his degree, was a waste of time and taxpayer money, in Helena Abramowitz's staunch law-and-order opinion.

She kept her opinion to herself. "What is your degree in?" she asked.

"I have a bachelor of science degree from the University of Maryland. They run a worldwide extension university, mostly for the armed forces. I graduated cum laude," he added.

"So people can change," she commented. "Even people who have spent much of their lives in jail, for doing bad things." She didn't believe a word of that, of course; but she was going to do anything that could help ingratiate him with the jury.

Opening her file, she got to the matter of hand. "Would you tell the jury in your own words how Marvin White confessed to you that he committed seven rape-murders?"

The informant sat up straight in his chair, closed his eyes for a moment, then opened them and began talking.

"I'd been brought down to your local jail here to testify in another criminal matter. While I was waiting to give my testimony and be returned to Durban, I was assigned to work in the jail infirmary, because I had done that kind of work before and they were shorthanded. The defendant, Marvin White, was brought in with a shotgun wound. It was pretty nasty—he had to have his dressings changed several times a day, to prevent infection. It's not the most fun part of the job, so the guy in charge of the infirmary assigned it to me."

"In other words," Abramowitz interrupted him, "you and the defendant were in close contact together."

"Yep. We were."

"Please continue."

"I'm changing him in the afternoon. The TV's on to the local news. They're going on about the latest murder in this Alley Slasher thing, and he pipes up and tells me where that is. Where it happened. And not only that, he says, he was there that night."

"The defendant voluntarily told you he was at the murder site on the same night the murder took place?" she asked with mock incredulity.

"Uh-huh. He told me the name of the club and the address."

"Had that information been spoken about on this newscast the two of you were watching?"

"No, it wasn't. It looked to me, watching, that they were making sure they didn't give out exactly where it had been."

"And it had happened the night before?"

"The night before, that's right."

"So he had to be telling you the truth."

"That's what I thought. I couldn't figure out any other

way he could've known, since he'd been arrested that same night and brought in."

"Before the body of the latest victim was found?"

"Hours before," Dwayne said.

"What did you do when he told you that?" she asked.

"Right then, nothing. He changed the subject and started telling me why he was in jail and why he was shot. Bragging on himself."

"What did he tell you?"

"That he'd tried to rob this store and his gun jammed and the owner got the jump on him."

"He confessed to an armed robbery? With intent to commit murder?"

"Yes, he did."

"Why do you think Marvin White confessed to having committed a serious crime to a man he didn't know?" Abramowitz asked.

"For the same reason every other guy in the joint does it," Dwayne answered smoothly. "To puff himself up, look good."

"That's all?" she asked. This time her curiosity, although foreknown, appeared to be genuine.

Dwayne nodded his head enthusiastically. "People in jail are not smart people," he explained to the jury. "If they were they wouldn't be there. The most important thing to your common jailbird, generally speaking, is his status. They want to come off tough—usually tougher than they really are."

"He told you he'd committed this serious crime to *impress* you?"

"What other reason could there be?" Dwayne asked reasonably.

Wyatt didn't have to make a note about that remark. He knew how pathetically true it was.

"Was it because he knew that you were 'big-time,' so to speak?" Abramowitz continued.

"Absolutely. If I was some petty credit card scammer or dope smoker he wouldn't have done it, because his status as opposed to mine wouldn't be threatened."

"He knew you were in jail for a serious crime?" she asked, nailing down the point.

"He knew I was in transit from Durban. Everyone knows

you don't pull your time at Durban unless you're doing serious time for heavy sh—" He caught himself. "Stuff. Heavy stuff."

Wyatt didn't have to check this out with Marvin, either. He knew his client had shot himself in the foot.

"When the defendant gave you this unsolicited information about the latest Alley Slasher murder, as well as the crime he'd been arrested for, what did you do?"

"I told him to cool it."

"You asked him not to tell you about it?"

"Uh-uh," he said, shaking his head. "I told him he should be careful about who he was talking to."

"How did he respond to your advice?"

"He made a few more remarks, and then he let it go."

"He didn't say anything else?"

"Not that time."

She flipped to the next page in her file. The room was quiet; the hum of the air conditioners fighting to keep pace with the scalding temperature beating in on the windows was the loudest perceptible sound. "Did you have occasion to speak to the defendant about these crimes another time?" she asked.

"Oh, yeah," Dwayne answered expansively. "We talked about them on many occasions. We were together in there three days; not only during the day, but at night, too, 'cause they had me bunking down there. Three nights is a long time. He could've told me his life story starting from the day he was born in three nights."

"Describe the next occasion you talked about the murders."

"It was the next day," Dwayne said. "I'd finished changing his behind again . . ." He smiled over that; a few of the male jurors did, also. "The TV was on and they were talking about those murders. You couldn't get away from it. So we're watching, him and me, and he starts telling me stuff about them."

"What kind of stuff?"

"All kinds of stuff. How this delivery route of his took him by where all the crimes had been committed, how he'd seen all those sorry hookers out on the streets, how he laughed at them when they hit on him because he could get as much . . . can I say the word?" he asked modestly.

"Use the words the defendant used when he talked to you, as accurately as you can remember," Abramowitz told him.

"He said he could get as much pussy as he wanted. He was beating the ladies off with a stick. He had no need for whores . . . he said ho's, the way black guys do on the street. He was contemptuous of them. Very contemptuous."

"Go on," she prodded Dwayne. Not that he needed it.

"He said he'd been where all them 'bitches'—his term— had been murdered. The specific streets and alleys. Then he started bragging about his status—that the delivery route was a cover for his real business, which was dealing drugs. He was making thousands of dollars a week dealing drugs, and he had a Jeep Cherokee on order, and all kinds of crap."

"Did you believe him?"

"Not about the big-time dealer stuff. A big-time dealer doesn't pull a holdup, no matter how much money's at stake."

Wyatt caught Dexter's stare from the second row. Marvin's best friend was shaking his head in sad agreement.

"What about the other things he told you? About his delivery route, his prowess with women, things like that."

"That sounded real to me," Dwayne said. "He was on sure ground when he said those things. And like, I was changing his bandages, down there by his private parts. I got a look at his package—I couldn't avoid seeing him. He has the goods, for sure. He'd be real popular in prison, I can tell you that."

Marvin groaned, sitting next to Wyatt.

"What about his connections to the murders?" Abramowitz asked. "Did you think he was truthful talking about them? About his connections, what he knew?"

"I was skeptical at first," the informant admitted. "Guys are all the time copping to crimes they haven't done. Status, like I said. In prison, status is all."

"What changed your mind?"

"When he started telling me things that no one who wasn't close to those murders would know. Either he'd been there, seen them when they were committed, or he had heard about them from someone who was."

"You're saying he either had committed the murders himself or knew who did."

"From all the things he told me, I couldn't see any other explanation."

"Go on."

"So then I got to probing. Let's face it, I'm an informant. I've done this before. I know how to get guys to open up."

"How do you do that?" she asked. "Get men to confess their crimes to you?"

"It's easy," he told her. "Anyone can do it. All you need is to show them that you care. And you give them the impression you're sharing your secrets with them. That's how you get them to trust you, even though anyone with a brain in his head would know not to, that there's spies everywhere."

Marvin had spilled his guts out all over the floor of that infirmary. Wyatt knew that for a fact—he didn't dispute that. It was *what* he'd told Thompson, and what he *didn't* know, that he *couldn't* tell—that was the crux of all this.

"So he said to you, 'I'm the Alley Slasher, I committed all those murders they're talking about'?"

Dwayne shook his head like she was a schoolgirl asking a dumb question. "No. It doesn't work like that."

"Describe to us how it does work."

"You lead him into it. Nice, easy talk. You talk about the crime you know he did—the armed robbery—and you move on from there. 'You're shitting me, man,' you josh him. 'Give me a real piece of information that you know about that hasn't been all over the newspapers.' "

"And he did."

Dwayne nodded in the affirmative.

"What was the first piece of information he gave you that hadn't been publicized."

"The name of the club and the street location where the last victim was found."

"Which was not public knowledge at the time."

"I didn't know it. And he'd been in there with me all that time, so if I didn't know it, he couldn't, either."

"But he saw that location on television, so he could have known where it was from prior knowledge."

"That's true," Dwayne admitted.

"What was the first thing he told you that he couldn't have known from prior knowledge, couldn't have seen," she asked. "That only someone who was there at one of the murders, or knew someone who was there, could know?"

"He told me that victim number three was a transvestite."

A low murmur rippled through the room.

"He told you that?" she asked.

"Yes. And he described some articles of clothing the transvestite was wearing."

Marvin grabbed Wyatt's pad and scribbled ferociously on it. Wyatt read the note: "I never tell him nothing about no clos."

Wyatt knew that already. He irritably pushed the pad away, keeping his attention on Dwayne.

"What was the piece of information the defendant told you," Abramowitz asked, "that made you believe he could be the murderer? What convinced you?"

"He was telling me different things about different ones," Dwayne said, "all of which were 'insider' type information, but things a street-smart person might have heard—although he knew an awful lot about all the crimes. You wouldn't expect someone to pick up that much secret information about so many of them unless he was close to them."

"But the specific piece that convinced you," she pressed. "Was there one specific piece of information that pushed you from thinking he *might* know who did it to your thinking it was him?"

"Yes."

"And what was that?"

"He told me something about the last victim, which nobody could have known about, except the actual killer."

"And what *exactly* was it he told you about the last victim, Paula Briggs, that only the real killer could have known?"

"He said he had raped and killed her deep in the alley, in a hidden doorway, where nobody could see them. Then after he'd killed her, he was all hyped up, excited. From doing it, you know, and also because he wanted to go out and rob that store he'd been waiting on. So he had a smoke, to calm his nerves. And when he finished he wiped the butt off on the hem of her dress, to get rid of his fingerprints, and shoved the cigarette butt up her . . . up her behind. Kind of like a calling card, you might say. Before he dumped her body in the trash can."

"He told you that?" she asked, her voice almost choking with shock.

Dwayne nodded. "That he did."

"What did you do? What did you think?"

"I looked at him, kind of bad guy to bad guy, you know, like we're both down for the count, we share all our secrets, and I said to him, kind of sly and casual, like it wasn't no big thing, 'Fess up, man. You're bullshittin' me, ain't you.' Because at the time, nobody knew about that. And it sounded so weird and preposterous. I figured it had to be a shuck. And he looked at me and said, 'You'll see, Dwayne. It's true. I did it.' "

In the pandemonium that ensued Grant hammered his gavel for quiet and called for a half-hour recess.

Abramowitz spent the rest of the day and all of the next walking Dwayne through the seven murders. Like an idiot savant who has memorized verbatim the entire unabridged *Oxford English Dictionary,* he recited, chapter and verse, everything he said Marvin had told him. The most minute details were remembered—how many hair barrettes victim number five wore, and what color they were. That victim number two's bra was a front-fastener, rather than one that hooked in the back. The peach-colored rayon underpants victim number three, the transvestite, was wearing (size large). On and on, an encyclopedic catalog of the rapes and murders.

Wyatt listened intently, cross-checking Dwayne's statements against those he had given to the grand jury. He wrote Marvin a volume of questions: Did you tell him this? This? This?

"No," Marvin answered. "I didn't tell him none of that."

Wyatt believed Marvin. Not only because he thought his client was innocent, which he did, but because of the incredibly specific and often arcane nature of the information. It wasn't just that Marvin wouldn't have remembered such details; he wouldn't have noticed them in the first place, particularly at night, in dark, unlighted places. To observe and analyze and recall such details took time and an analytical mind, and Marvin possessed neither of those qualities. He was pure immature impulsive, acting before thinking out the consequences of his actions.

The botched robbery was a prime example. A smart, analytically inclined man would have test-fired his weapon prior to using it, to make sure it worked properly. Marvin White couldn't remember what he'd had for breakfast three days ago, let alone the color of a skirt worn by a woman he had allegedly raped and killed eighteen months before.

He watched the jury's faces. They weren't thinking what he was thinking. They were thinking this was a great witness; a convict, to be sure, but not such a bad person—he had gotten his college degree with honors, hadn't he? He—Dwayne—was trying to reclaim his life, do the right thing. Dwayne Thompson was giving them dozens, hundreds, of good, logical, convincing reasons to lay their doubt aside and do the right thing themselves.

At 5:15 on the second full day that Dwayne had been on the stand, Helena Abramowitz turned to Judge Grant. "We have no further questions for this witness, Your Honor."

Grant didn't have to look at the clock on the wall to know that enough was enough. He gaveled the session closed. "Cross-examination will begin tomorrow morning at nine o'clock," he informed Wyatt.

The computer printout of Dwayne's second-day testimony was delivered to Wyatt's hotel by seven-thirty that evening. He paid a premium for it, as he had for the previous day's—out of his own pocket, of course—but it was essential that he study it tonight, as completely and thoroughly as possible.

Josephine ordered club sandwiches and Cokes from room service. They sprawled out on the floor across from each other, the testimony spread out on one side in front of them, Dwayne's grand jury testimony on the other.

Wyatt had formulated a plan of attack, and having the full documentation at his fingertips was essential. It was, in fact, the key to everything he hoped to accomplish. Attacking Dwayne on the specifics—trying to refute or discredit them—was a nonissue. It would be counterproductive and a dangerous waste of time.

He was going to go the other way: acknowledge fully everything Dwayne said, but attack how he'd gotten it. This was where the testimony came in. Last night he and Josephine had taken the first day's transcript and compared what

Dwayne had said at trial to his grand jury testimony. Each case that was talked about, each specific phrase, detail, even sentences and choices of words within a sentence. It was amazing how they matched up. Entire phrases that had been spoken in trial were exactly, in some cases word for word, as they had been uttered to the grand jury, months before. Dwayne not only had an incredible memory; the information spewed out as if it had been typed into a computer and then brought up on demand.

After comparing the trial transcript with that from the grand jury, and noting the hundreds of similarities, Wyatt and Josephine compared both of them to the police reports that had been filed on the seven murders. Again, the similarities about what the police had written concerning a particular rape-murder, and Dwayne's testimony, both to the grand jury and at trial, were eerily similar. Sentences, particular turns of phrases—they matched up too well. Way too well for comfort. There was no other explanation for it: someone had given him the information.

But he'd run into a brick wall trying to find out who'd done it, and the brick wall was still intact. He hadn't made a dent in it.

They wrapped at one-thirty. At his insistence Josephine had brought a change of clothing and her toiletries, and he'd booked a room for her. She'd be too tired to drive home, and they could last-minute strategize in the morning, during the short ride to the courthouse. They rode down together on the elevator between his floor and hers, and he walked her to her room.

"Good night, kiddo," he said wearily, pulling her to him in a hug. Her body, sweaty though her blouse from the combination of being up more than nineteen hours and nervous energy, pressed heavily against his.

"Good night," she whispered into his neck.

He disengaged gently, rubbed her shoulders for a few seconds. "I'll meet you in the lobby at seven sharp."

"You got it, boss," she said, giving him a weary salute; then she turned and shut the door behind her.

He'd told the hotel operator not to send calls up to his room unless it was an absolute emergency. There were two messages on the machine.

The first was from Moira and Michaela. "We know

you're busy, but we wanted to say hello, and tell you we miss you, and wish you luck. Call us when you have a free moment."

The second was from Violet. "Glad you're not in, since I promised I wouldn't call. But I had to." There was a pause, the voice lowering. "Good luck tomorrow."

One quick cognac from the minibar, then showering the day's gunk off, brushing his teeth, climbing in bed naked under the sheet; his thoughts drifted to Moira to Violet, to Marvin, to Dwayne Thompson, to the hundreds of pages of testimony and police reports he had to master. And when sleep finally came they all were still there, all part of his life, and all as unresolved as they had been when he was awake.

"Good morning, Mr. Thompson." Wyatt stood at the lectern, facing Dwayne.

Dwayne nodded his greeting. He was more alert than he had been during his interrogation by Abramowitz. This lawyer facing him was going to skin him if he could.

"You've been in prison a long time, haven't you?" Wyatt asked his first question.

Another nod. "A fair amount."

"More in than out," Wyatt said. "Most of your life."

This time Dwayne's answer was a shrug.

"You've been a witness for the state in other trials before this one?"

"Yes."

"And every time you testified for the state the prosecution cut you a deal, didn't they?"

"Cut me a deal?" Dwayne affected being offended.

"They gave you something in return for your testimony, isn't that right?"

Dwayne looked at him. "That's how it works."

"Two of those times," Wyatt said, reading his notes, "your reward was not being prosecuted on a felony charge that was outstanding, isn't that right?"

Dwayne stared balefully at Wyatt. "In those instances it was decided it wouldn't be in the interest of justice to try me," he said.

"The decision was made after they found out what you could do for them, wasn't it," Wyatt stated. "Rather than it being an objective reading of the merits of each case."

Another shake of the head. "After I went to them, yeah."

"So instead of two violent convictions on your record, you could have four, couldn't you?"

"I could've been acquitted for both of them," Dwayne answered.

"That's true—anything can happen," Wyatt agreed. After a quick glance at his notes again, he said, "But isn't it true that every time you have gone to trial you have been convicted and sent to prison?"

Dwayne spit out some air. "Yeah."

Wyatt leaned forward. "Have you made a deal with the district attorney's office for giving testimony in this case?" he asked.

A slow nod. "Yes."

"What kind of deal did you make?"

"Reduction in time. That's the normal deal in these things."

"Reduction in time. How much reduction in time?"

Dwayne shrugged. "Time," he said.

"Is that it?" Wyatt asked.

"Yeah," Dwayne lied with a sociopath's glibness. "They'll cut some time off my sentence."

Wyatt looked at another note. "They're going to commute the rest of your sentence, aren't they? You won't serve any more time on it, even though you've got, what, three years left to go?"

Dwayne fidgeted in his chair. He hadn't squirmed once in the two days he'd been under questioning by the prosecution. "Yes," he finally admitted. "They're going to cut it to time already served."

Wyatt walked over to the defense table and selected a file from the several that were stacked there. Walking back to the lectern, he flipped through it until he got to the information he was seeking. "According to public records," he stated, "you have another trial pending, on a charge wholly unrelated to this current one." He walked around to the front of the lectern so that he was close to both Dwayne and the jury. "Did you and the DA's office cut any kind of deal on that charge, as well as on the one you just told us about?"

Dwayne's eyes flickered toward the prosecution table. Abramowitz gave him an almost imperceptible nod. Wyatt, his eyes following Dwayne's look, caught the nod.

"Any deal on that charge?" Wyatt repeated. "Some nice little bone, like they'll forget all about it?" He looked at the file in his hand again. "That's a heavy charge," he said. "Manslaughter in the commission of a felony. You're found guilty on that one, they throw away the key, man. So let me ask the question again: Have you cut a deal, with this district attorney's office, on this charge?"

Dwayne took a deep breath, let it out. "Yes."

"What're they going to give you? Reduction in sentence?" he sneered. "Only one lifetime instead of two?" He walked closer to Dwayne, only a few feet away from the informant. "Or did they promise they'd drop that charge as well if your testimony helped them convict my client?"

"They're dropping that case," Dwayne said. "It isn't that good a case anyway," he said, trying to soften the blow.

Wyatt laughed in his face. "Yes, I'm sure. A real loser." Staring at Dwayne, he said, "You've got a lot at stake here, don't you? Your freedom or a lifetime in prison. If I was facing that choice, I'd do anything to fix it. I'd tell anyone any damn thing they wanted to hear," he said, pausing dramatically. "Even if it's true or not."

"Objection!" Abramowitz was practically out of her shoes she jumped up so fast. "This is—"

"Sustained," Grant said before she could tell him why he should. "I'm warning you once again, Mr. Matthews. Save your opinions for your summation."

Wyatt walked back to the witness. Picking up another file folder, he opened it and laid it down in front of him. "You received a college degree in computer science, with honors. Is that correct?"

"Yes. I was one of the best students they had," Dwayne bragged.

"So I've heard. Warden Jonas up at Durban told me how good you were."

Dwayne's eyes narrowed.

"They had to bar you from using their computers because you could hack your way into anything, and you were causing all kinds of mischief. Isn't that true?"

"The prison officials decided inmates shouldn't have the kind of free access I had," Dwayne parried.

"You used to brag about how you could hack your way into Fort Knox, didn't you?"

Dwayne shrugged.

"Of course, you can't hack your way into anything if you don't have a computer and a modem, can you?" Wyatt said. "And a phone line out."

"Those are the essentials," Dwayne agreed.

"While you've been down here in our county jail," Wyatt asked, "how many times have you had access to a computer?"

Dwayne stared at him. "Good trick question, lawyer. The answer is none."

"You did research in the law library there. They have computers. Didn't you ever use one?"

Dwayne shook his head. "They wouldn't let me. Anyway, none of those computers have modems, so you couldn't hack with them."

Wyatt frowned. "If they didn't let you use them, how come you know none of them have modems?" he asked.

Dwayne caught himself quickly. "I looked at them. They were right there."

"Some modems are internal. How can you tell by just looking at them?"

"They'd be plugged into a phone line. Otherwise, they'd be useless."

"Couldn't they have modems that weren't connected?"

Dwayne shrugged. "I guess."

"Your Honor," Helena said, standing up, "I fail to see the purpose of this line of questioning. Cross-examination is not supposed to be a fishing expedition."

"Agreed. Narrow your examination of the witness to the issues before us," Grant told Wyatt.

"Fine. I just want to be certain. During the time that you have been incarcerated in the county jail, you have never used or had any access to a computer or a modem. True or false?"

"I've never had access to a computer, period."

"Glad we put that one to bed," Wyatt said. "Because there's something funny about your testimony, Mr. Thompson. Do you know what that is?"

Dwayne eyeballed him warily. "No, I don't."

"It's too good."

He looked at the jury as he spoke to Dwayne. "You know everything there is to know about these murders. You know as much as the police. A cynic would say you had a pipeline into their files; but since I'm not a cynic, I won't make that claim. I might *think* it," he added, "but I won't come straight out and *say* it."

"Objection!" Abramowitz almost hit her head on the ceiling, she was so forceful coming out of her chair.

"Sustained!" The gavel came down.

"Okay," Wyatt said. "I got carried away, Your Honor. I'm sorry."

He waited a moment for passions to settle, then took Dwayne through a timetable: what Marvin said, to the best of Dwayne's recollection, when he said it. Dwayne was better at *what* Marvin told him about a particular murder than he was about *when* he told him about the same murder.

They would talk mostly at night, when it was only the two of them in the infirmary. "Once he got to talking, and opening up to me," Dwayne said, "I couldn't get him to shut up. He'd go on and on for hours."

"Did you ever ask him to stop?" Wyatt asked. "Or remind him that it was dangerous to talk about these terrible things?"

"Are you crazy?" Dwayne answered. "I'm not naive, man, he was my ticket out and I knew it. I encouraged him every chance I could."

During the break, Wyatt and Marvin reviewed the morning's testimony.

"I never tol' him none of that crap," Marvin whined. "I didn't do none of them murders, Mr. Matthews. You know that. And my memory ain't nearly good enough to remember all that shit he says I tol' him."

"I know," Wyatt told him. "We're going to get into that issue this afternoon."

At one-thirty, when court was back in session, Wyatt strode from the defense table to the lectern, his arms laden with files, which he stacked in front of him. He opened the top file. "I'm going to read some of the statements you've made," he told Dwayne. "Either here or to the grand jury. When I read each statement to you, I'd like you to tell me whether it was in here you said that particular remark, or whether it was back in the grand jury room. If you don't remember which place it was, say so. And if you made a statement to the grand jury, and then repeated it here, tell us that, also. Okay?"

Dwayne nodded.

Wyatt read: " 'When I realized it was a man, I went crazy. I was ashamed at myself for being with a man, and I was angry at him for tricking me into thinking he was a woman. That's when I stabbed him in the balls.' "

"That was to the grand jury," Dwayne said. "Ms. Abramowitz didn't ask me about that part of that murder."

"Okay. What about this? 'She was sitting at the bar of this ratty hotel I went into to get change for the bus. I'd never been in there before, so nobody knew who I was. She came over to me and looked me up and down and said if I rented a room she'd show me the best time I'd ever had. I told her I didn't have money for no room but we could go back outside and do it. So we went in the back there and she started to want to give me head, but I told her I wanted the real thing, and she said she didn't do that lying on her back on some dirty street, and that's when I said you are this time, and then I raped her and stabbed her. It felt good, feeling that knife go in. I stabbed her seventeen times.' "

Wyatt looked up. "Did you also tell that to the grand jury?"

Dwayne thought for a moment. "Part of it. I don't think I mentioned the part about her telling him she wanted to get a room and him saying he wouldn't."

Wyatt picked up another file, flipped it open, turned to a previously marked page. "There was seventeen stab wounds. Three in the left breast, four in the right breast, nine in the neck, one across the vagina." He looked up, chagrined. "Sorry. We just covered that material, didn't we?"

"Yes," Dwayne answered disdainfully, "and I told you where I'd said it."

Wyatt looked at the page again. "Actually, you didn't say that."

"What?" Dwayne said, caught off balance.

"That's part of the official police report I was reading from." He walked over to the prosecution table and set both files down in front of Abramowitz, side by side, pointing to the sections in question. Leaving them with her for the moment, he walked back toward the witness. "Doesn't it strike you odd," he asked Dwayne, "how uncannily similar your testimony is to confidential police reports?"

"That's got nothing to do with me," Dwayne answered, his anger showing. "I'm telling you what he told me. I'm not the one on trial here." He pointed an accusatory finger at Marvin. "He is." He forced a grimacing smile, his lips tight against his teeth.

Wyatt knew what the smile was supposed to be telling him: "Fuck you, Jack. You're not going to break me down."

But he was. He picked up another file. "Let's try this one. 'Her head was lying faceup in a pool of her blood, which had stained her hair and the back of her blouse.' " He looked up. "That's a simple one, isn't it? Which victim was that again?"

Dwayne thought for a minute. "I think that was number five. I don't know why, but my memory's a little hazy on the number."

"He's human after all!" Wyatt observed caustically, looking at the jury. Flipping a page, he read again: " 'She was wearing a knee brace on her left knee. Under the brace, there was a fresh scar, as if she had been operated on recently.' " He looked questioningly at the witness.

Dwayne sat stone-faced. "Grand jury. It wasn't mentioned here."

Wyatt nodded. Snapping his fingers, he said, "I meant to ask you something at the beginning of this session and I completely forgot—you were shown your grand jury testimony before you came in here to testify, isn't that true?"

"Yes."

"So those last two statements I read to you, for instance— the blood on the victim's head, and the knee brace and scar. That was grand jury testimony, not trial testimony. Agreed?"

"Yes," Dwayne answered.

Wyatt frowned. "I've got a problem here. Maybe you can help me out. I can't find those statements in your grand jury testimony." He flipped through a bunch of pages. "Nope. Not here."

Abramowitz was on her feet immediately. "If we can take a short recess, Your Honor, I'm sure we can assist defense counsel in finding the references in question."

Before Grant could respond, Wyatt said, "Don't bother. They aren't there."

"You made them up?" Grant asked.

"No, I didn't make them up," Wyatt responded. "But they aren't in this witness's grand jury testimony. And they aren't in the official police reports that have been entered into the computer, either," he added.

"Then if you didn't make them up, where are they?" Judge Grant demanded.

"Here," Wyatt said, holding up a sheaf of papers. "In Detective Marlow's *handwritten* notes. Remember how Marlow testified, Your Honor, about how he didn't transfer everything from his notes to the official computer reports because it took too long, or the material wasn't relevant to the investigation? Here are two examples of that."

He walked to the bench and handed the notes up to Grant. Abramowitz scurried over to join them. "I've researched that matter thoroughly, Your Honor," Wyatt said. "There's something very interesting about this witness's testimony, both in here and earlier, at the grand jury proceedings. Everything he has said corresponds to data that has been entered into the police department's computer files. Conversely, he has not given one instance, not one single fact or allegation, that wasn't in those files but is in the handwritten notes of the various detectives who have worked on these murders. That's over fifteen detectives, by the way."

Abramowitz was livid. "This is unconscionable, Your Honor. He's still trying to ride that dead horse of the witness having access to the police files. It's been proven conclusively that he could not have. This is not allowed under cross. It's a smoke screen, a desperate diversion from a lawyer who doesn't have a shred of a case and is trying it with smoke and mirrors."

"This isn't smoke and mirrors, Your Honor," Wyatt rebutted. "This is strong evidence of collusion."

Grant pondered the situation for a moment. "This is serious," he told Abramowitz. "Don't think it isn't. But I agree with you that cross-examination is not the proper forum for this. Introduce this in your case in chief," he told Wyatt. He handed the pages back. "I'll be happy to hear it then."

Wyatt walked back to the lectern. Whether he'd use it in his own presentation wasn't the point, he thought with satisfaction. He had introduced a major element of doubt into the credibility of the state's key witness.

He faced Dwayne again. "How long have you known Deputy Sheriff Doris Blake?" he asked.

Dwayne started to say "I don't . . . ," realized he would be caught in another lie, recovered nicely. "About six years," he said evenly.

"You met her at Durban, while you were a prisoner there and she was a guard?"

"That's right."

"And then you renewed your relationship when you were temporarily transferred down here and you discovered she was a deputy sheriff in the jail division?"

"We don't have a relationship," Dwayne said flatly. "I know her. She knows me. End of discussion."

"That's all?"

"That's all."

"Then why, out of over a hundred deputies who work in the jail, was she the one who arranged for you to sleep in the infirmary, when you had been assigned elsewhere?"

Dwayne thought for a moment. "She knew I was down here to help out the district attorney on this other case. I think maybe the sheriff gave her that order."

"Think again," Wyatt said. "The sheriff didn't know anything about it, did he? In fact, when he found out about it, he blew up, didn't he? And even before that, District Attorney Pagano changed your situation, didn't he?"

Dwayne blinked, but didn't answer.

"The fact is, you and Lieutenant Blake had a relationship . . . call it a friendship if you want, but it was more than just knowing who the other one was, years ago. And when you came down here you renewed your friendship, and she did you some favors, isn't that right?"

Dwayne looked down at the floor, looked up at the ceiling, twisted his neck to get a kink out, then answered. "Okay, so she did me a favor? What's the big deal?"

"You tell me."

"There was none."

"She didn't happen to feed you any information about the Alley Slasher murders, did she? Being a corrections officer, she could have gotten her hands on that information pretty easily, I'll bet."

"Objection!" Abramowitz called out. "That issue has already been resolved."

"Not to my satisfaction it hasn't," Wyatt returned.

"Sustained," Grant called out. "There is no factual evidence that has been shown to this court that the officer in question had access to the files relating to the Alley Slasher murders."

Wyatt bore in on Dwayne. "The fact that you, a prisoner who is currently serving time in the toughest penitentiary in the state, and a female corrections officer who worked up there and is working down here now, the fact that the two of you are sexual partners, that isn't a big deal?"

The courtroom exploded. Abramowitz leaped to her feet as if a mortar shell had been detonated under her. "This is truly outrageous, Your Honor," she protested vehemently. "This is an outrageous, horrendous accusation which has absolutely nothing to do with this case. It is a pathetic smear tactic designed to throw tar all over the facts. You're despicable!" she screamed at Wyatt. "I object to this scurrilous reviling of the witness, Your Honor, and I object to this entire line of questioning!"

Grant was hammering his gavel like it was a jackhammer. "Both of you stop this behavior this minute," he warned them. "Or I'll hold you both in contempt."

Dwayne stared at Wyatt, his pale snake eyes hooded almost to closure. "I'll answer his question. If you ever saw Doris Blake," he said coldly, "you'd know what a stupid question that is. I have never had any kind of sex with her."

Abramowitz's redirect was short. It dealt with only one issue.

"Has anyone from any law-enforcement agency, or any other outside agent, given you any information files or otherwise, about the murders the defendant is on trial for?"

"No. Absolutely not."

"Everything you know about this case you learned from conversation with the defendant."

"Yes."

"Marvin White confessed to you that he is the Alley Slasher murderer."

"Yes."

She turned to Judge Grant. "We have no more questions for this witness, Your Honor." She gathered up her material from the podium. "And pending rebuttal, the prosecution rests."

The trial ran on a four-day week, Friday being the court's dark day. Wyatt spent all of Friday prepping his two key witnesses, Agnes Carpenter in the morning, Leticia Pope after lunch. Josephine sat in on the sessions, taking notes. From time to time Walcott popped in and observed for a while, occasionally scribbling a note on a piece of scratch paper and handing it to Josephine, for Wyatt to look at when he had the time. Other than that he remained in the background, nodding occasionally in approval at a question asked or clarification made.

Mrs. Carpenter, dressed as if she were going to a reception for the Queen Mother, was quite calm and composed, given the circumstances. Weeks before, she had given Wyatt her own detective's report about her husband's whereabouts on the night she claimed Marvin had stayed over, to bolster her story that she'd been alone, rather than with Dr. Carpenter. Now, sitting in the run-down offices, they went over her statement incident by incident, line by line. Her answers matched up to the letter—she was a strong, credible witness who was going to provide a rock-solid alibi for Marvin.

"Does your husband know you're going to be testifying?" Wyatt asked with concern.

"No," she answered firmly, "and he isn't going to until after the fact. He'll be served the divorce papers on the very morning I testify," she told Wyatt with relish. "My only regret is that I won't be there to see the look on his two-timing face."

Dexter, appropriately attired for the weather in a Shaquille O'Neal tank top, baggy shorts, and hundred-dollar high-top Reeboks, brought Leticia in after lunch. He frowned as he checked out Wyatt's work digs. "I've been in shooting galleries looked better than this, Mr. Matthews," he said with obvious disappointment. "What's an ace like you doing working in some crap-hole like this? Don't you have some fancy uptown office?"

Wyatt laughed out loud. Status and symbols of status were all important to these kids. "My uptown office is for the clients who can pay the big bucks, no offense meant to your friend Marvin. And don't worry—I'm as good a lawyer working out of this office as I am working out of that one."

Dexter nodded. "Well, if I ever get into trouble and I hire you to get me off, we're meeting in that fancy uptown office, you hear?"

"Our office doesn't do drug cases. I've given you my advice before, Dexter. Get out of the trade. You're going to take a fall sooner or later, and you've got too much going for that."

"I'm going to, I promise, Mr. Matthews," Dexter swore earnestly. "By the end of the summer." He squared his shoulders. "I'm going to college in the fall," he told Wyatt with pride.

"Well, good for you," Wyatt congratulated him, although he knew the assertion was either bullshit or a pipe dream.

Wyatt went all afternoon and into the evening with Leticia. Going over her story dozens of times, from every angle he could think of. Grilling her hard, bucking her up, not letting her stray off the point. He cross-examined her as he guessed Abramowitz would, yelling at her, belittling her, jumping on every minute discrepancy in her testimony.

"I'll be protecting you," he told her, trying to reassure her as they sat in the gloomy, cheerless space. "All you have to do is tell the truth and not let her scare you."

"She ain't gonna scare you, is she?" Dexter, who was there the entire time, butted in. "You gonna get right *in* her face, she disrespects you, ain't you, girl?" he browbeat her.

"Back off, Dexter," Wyatt told him. "She has to do this herself."

"Nobody gonna scare me," Leticia told him in her quiet, high voice. She wasn't at all assertive saying it.

Walcott joined them for the last hour of their session, nodding in silent agreement at Wyatt's handling of his witness. "This is my boss," Wyatt said magnanimously, introducing him to Dexter and Leticia.

"I'm not his boss," Walcott told him, disclaiming proprietorship. "I feel very lucky to have him working on this case," he told the two young people. "And so should your friend Marvin."

"He is," Dexter sang out. "Marvin knows."

Finally, after seven hours of working with Leticia, Wyatt couldn't think of anything more for them to do. They were the last ones left in the building—everyone else was long gone for the day. "We'll talk again the night before you testify," he told the girl. "Get plenty of rest, and stay out of trouble."

"Me and my guys, we're sticking to her like Super-glue," Dexter promised him.

"Good. See you in a few days."

He bought Josephine dinner at a nearby red-checkered-tablecloth Italian restaurant. They ate Caesar salads and lasagna and split a bottle of Chianti, polishing off the meal with made-on-the-premises cheesecake and espresso. "What're you doing this weekend?" he asked her as he walked her to her car.

"I'm at your beck and call."

"Don't be. Go out and do something. Have fun, put your brain on hold. It needs the rest. We all do."

"Is that what you're going to do?"

"I'm going to do some running, play my trombone, read magazines, watch television, talk to my family, and sleep. I'm not going to worry this case to death. I'm as prepared as I can be, so that's it. The rest is in the hands of the gods."

Abramowitz and Windsor had grilled Dwayne intensely after he left the stand, going over what had transpired, Abramowitz asking him over and over again if he'd had access to a computer. As many times as she asked him he swore up and down to her that he didn't, and she finally quit beating him up about it. But he could see the suspicion in her eyes.

"I don't want a bomb dropped on me," she warned him strongly. "If there's something I don't know about, you'd better tell me. I can protect you if I know everything, but not if I'm caught unawares."

Dwayne Thompson made her skin crawl, almost literally. Every time she had to come down to see him it would take her an hour to psychologically gird herself for the encounter. She never wore a dress cut above the knees when she came to see him, preferring slacks whenever possible. She would strip her face of almost all makeup, and would wear her hair pinned back as severely and matronly as she could. She knew he regarded her with pure lasciviousness, mentally fucking her every single moment they were together. She refused to look at him anywhere below the belt, although he tried various guises to pull her look downward, to his scrotum.

Despite these defensive measures, she could feel his sexual agitation building over the course of each interview, to the point that by the time she left—as soon as possible—his pale skin would be flushed. Sometimes he would brazenly rub his hand against his crotch as he stared at her with fierce intent.

Fleetingly she would regret that she'd campaigned so hard for this assignment. Helena knew of women who had succumbed to the dark charms of inmates. Some had even gone so far as to have sex with them, smuggled in drugs, money, tried to help them escape. She knew of women who gave up their lives for men who were worthless and were only using them.

She had to keep the prize in focus. The end would justify the means. When this trial was over, and Marvin White was on his way to death row, she would be set up professionally for the rest of her life.

But she felt sick to her stomach when the persistent memory of her last private session with this snake insinuated itself into her consciousness, despite her struggles to forget it. It was a nightmare that loomed when she least expected it, and was emotionally and psychologically vulnerable.

He had asked for some expensive clothes to wear while he was on the stand, so he'd look good for the cameras. She had refused him—it wasn't in the budget, and wearing an expensive suit would look suspicious. He had stared at her with hooded eyes, his tongue a sliver out the side of his thin lips, for all the world looking like a cunning cobra. "In case you've forgotten," he reminded her, "I am your case."

"And without me," she countered, "you're going to spend the rest of your life behind bars." She wanted to add "so screw you," but she couldn't. He was their witness, their linchpin, and no matter how much she hated him personally, she had to maintain their relationship.

At his request they moved him before he testified. To prevent contamination, and to protect him. Now that he was actually going to testify, he could be the target of any number of crazy cons who didn't like snitches. He was being held in a single cell on a high-intensity floor, similar to the one they had Marvin on. Him, a few other prisoners, and beaucoup guards. Here were housed men who, for one reason or another, couldn't be placed in the general population—men with threats on their lives, psychotics, men who were unpredictably violent. There were two hermaphrodites who had no other place to be. And then there were men like Dwayne.

In addition, Dwayne's work detail in the infirmary had been curtailed. The political fallout was too risky. Letting an inmate, particularly one with his background, have that kind of free run was no longer an acceptable risk, regardless of his desires or demands.

Dwayne told Abramowitz why he wanted to move. "There's a guy they brought in recently. An old-timer like myself, I knew him up at Durban. We were in some group-therapy sessions together. It can get pretty heavy in those sessions. He knows some of my dark side," he added cryptically.

"What does he know about you?" she asked suspiciously.

"How I get men to confess their sins to me."

"And how is that?" she parried.

"With a little help from my friends," he sang-sung.

She stared at him across the table. I didn't hear you say that. "Are you insinuating . . ." Where was this going?

"My friends help me, I help my friends," he answered. "I'm helping you, so you must be my friend. So if you're my friend, then I must be your friend." He smiled his snakeskin smile. "Are you my friend, Ms. Abramowitz?" He drawled out the "Ms."

Her nostrils winged. "Our relationship is not about friendship. It's about—"

"Mutual advantage?" he finished for her.

"*If I get a conviction of a guilty man and in doing that you get a benefit, then we would both come out ahead, yes.*" Her leg was vibrating under the table. She pushed down on her knee to still it.

He stared at her. "*'A guilty man'? You want the conviction, lady. The jury will do the guilty bit. Your job is to get a conviction.*"

She stared at him. "*I wouldn't want to be a party to convicting an innocent man,*" she said carefully. "*If I knew for sure he was innocent.*"

"*You wouldn't, huh? Who anointed you Diogenes?*"

"*No. I wouldn't.*"

"*If all of a sudden some angel came down from on high and whispered in your ear,*" he persisted, "*which happens to be very lovely and sexy, lady prosecutor . . .*"

She felt herself flushing. A wave of hatred for him washed over her. *Don't let him get to you,* she berated herself. *That's what he does.*

"*. . . that little ol' Marvin White was being railroaded, that he was actually an innocent babe, you'd tell the world that and walk away from this case?*"

Helena began to answer him; then she checked himself. *He's trying to suck you in. Don't let him.*

He shook his head. "*No way in hell. You've got to have this conviction. Your boss has to have this conviction. A million people in this city have to have this conviction. And I want my freedom. And they're all wrapped together in a tight, tight knot that can't be cut, not with a sword, not with a pang of conscience.*"

He leaned in close. His breath was sour gossamer. "*I am Satan walking the earth,*" he announced melodramatically. "*And you, Helena—I'm going to call you by your first name from now on, because you and I are soulmates—you are Faust. And we both have to uphold our end of the bargain.*" He paused, enjoying his hegemony over her. And then his hand was on hers and he was guiding it to his erect penis, which was protruding from the open fly of his pants.

She tried to scream. but she was paralyzed. Then she felt him shudder, the thick slime-wetness spurting onto her hand and up along the inside of her wrist.

She managed to pull away from him, her legs rubbery with fear and rage, her entire being aflame with humiliation

*and intense hatred toward Dwayne. She felt she might choke
on the bile rising in her throat as he grabbed her hand
again and rubbed his jism across her blouse. "Remember
me when you go home tonight," he whispered.*

*Before she managed to ring for the guard to release her
from this hell, he taunted her one last time. "You don't have
to know how I know what I know. All you have to know
is that it's the truth. The truth, Helena, that will get your
conviction.*

"And the truth will set me free."

She hadn't told anyone about that incident, not even Alex
Pagano. Particularly not Alex. He didn't want to hear any
excuses, doubts, or human anguish. He wanted a conviction.

Wyatt presented his first witness, Dr. Joseph Stroud, who
was an old hand at expert-testifying. A specialist in intelligence testing and memory retention, he had spent eight
hours with Marvin in the weeks before the trial, administer-
ing the standard IQ-type tests—Stanford-Binet and Wechs-
ler Adult Intelligence Scale (WAIS), revised. Dr. Stroud told
the jury that Marvin fell in the low-normal range of intelligence, but his skills were poorly developed—his reasoning
and deductive abilities were far below average, and his
reading level was terrible. He was functionally literate, but
barely.

His memory retention was similarly weak. He had been
given a WRAML: Wide Range Assessment of Memory and
Learning, as well as the Detroit Test of Learning Aptitude.
There, also, he did poorly, well below average.

"Is there a scientific or clinical definition for this condition?" Wyatt asked.

"It's basic ADD," Stroud answered. "Attention deficit dis-
order. The subject typically is unable to focus on any one
topic for an extended period of time."

"Given the results of these tests you had Marvin White
take," Wyatt continued, "could he have remembered the details of these murders as the state's witness has described
them?"

Stroud shook his head emphatically. "Not a chance. He

had a hard time remembering numbers or words in sequence, let alone common phone numbers, street addresses, things that were part of his daily life. He couldn't remember what he had eaten for dinner the night before one of our interviews. To remember the complex details of something that had happened a year or more after the event, particularly in the heat of passion and nervousness that would accompany such a violent episode, is not within his capability."

"In other words, it was psychologically and physiologically impossible for Marvin to remember and recall what the state's witness testified Marvin told him."

"Yes."

Wyatt glanced over at the jury box. A few jurors were noting this; most of them sat with their hands in their laps, listening impassively.

"What other tests did you give Marvin White?" he asked Stroud.

"I tested him to see how prone he would be to committing repeated acts of violence, of any kind. I also profiled him regarding how he fit the profile of a rapist."

"And what conclusions did you draw, Dr. Stroud?"

"He's capable of random acts of violence. His record as a juvenile offender clearly shows that. Because of his intellectual deficiencies he tends to solve problems by physical and emotional mechanisms, rather than working them out more logically and intellectually."

"So he is violence-prone?" Wyatt asked, conceding the point.

"In an impulsive, spur-of-the-moment mode. Not in a preplanned, calculated way."

"How would you relate his personality tendencies to these series of rape-murders?"

"They don't. Those crimes are a series of similar events, thought out and executed in careful, deliberate, repetitive fashion. Which is not the way he thinks."

"What else can you tell us?"

"The rapes would be the most incongruous part of this overall picture. Rapists have severe sexual-identity problems. Rape, as is commonly known, is not a sexual act. It is an act of physical violence and extreme hostility toward the opposite sex. Marvin White is not hostile toward women, in the sexual sense. If he's hostile toward women at all, it's as authority figures, which for him would apply equally to men. He's comfortable with his sexuality, much more so than the typical male, particularly of his age—he's had a substantially higher number than average of willing sexual partners, even given the sexually active milieu in which he lives. The profile of a rapist is usually the opposite—someone who is not fulfilled sexually or emotionally and carries out the act of rape to avenge and compensate for that, as well as for other arrested psychological and emotional needs."

"In other words, Marvin White is not a rapist."

"None of the psychological parameters that are commonly applied would classify him as one."

Norman Windsor, Helena Abramowitz's associate, conducted the cross-examination for the prosecution. "Isn't it true," he led off, "that these intelligence tests you gave the defendant are skewed against African Americans? Particularly the Stanford-Binet, which discriminates against young impoverished black men who come from the kind of background the defendant comes from?"

"There is some disagreement regarding the accuracy and objectivity of these tests as regards certain minorities," Stroud conceded.

"So he could be smarter than he tested. He might be a bad test taker, and the tests might not reflect his true intelligence and reasoning capability, because of his race and other factors, isn't that true?"

"It is within the realm of possibility, but it's improbable. Highly improbable."

"So the same could be true about his memory, couldn't it? He could remember some things better than the tests say he could."

"All tests are subjective," Stroud said. "But the indicators are constant, and in Marvin White's situation the indicators are clear. He has a bad memory," he stated firmly.

"Do you know who Charles Murray is, Dr. Stroud?" Windsor asked, going off on a sudden tangent.

"Yes, of course," Stroud answered. "Everyone in the field is aware of Charles Murray."

"*The Bell Curve* is his most recent book that's widely known, isn't it?"

"It is a well-known book in its field."

"One of the assertions of *The Bell Curve* is that blacks as a race—African Americans—are intellectually inferior to Caucasians, isn't that true?" Windsor asked.

"That's an oversimplification," Stroud said cautiously.

"It's a conclusion almost everyone who has read the book has drawn, isn't it?"

Reluctantly, Stroud answered, "Many people have."

Windsor held up a printed program. "Did you serve on a panel with Dr. Murray at Johns Hopkins University in 1994, Dr. Stroud?" he asked.

"Yes," Stroud answered.

Wyatt was watching and listening with concern. He didn't know anything about this, but he knew that invoking Charles Murray's name was not a good thing for his side.

"Was the subject of intelligence and race discussed at this panel?"

"Many topics were discussed at that panel. Intelligence and race was touched on briefly. It was not the theme of the event."

Windsor stared at Stroud. "Do you subscribe to Charles Murray's theories on racial differences regarding intelligence?"

"No, I do not."

"Race has nothing to do with intelligence."

"Not in my opinion. I'm not an expert in that aspect of intelligence testing," he added, carefully clarifying his position.

Wyatt winced. Don't tread water, man. Be assertive, aggressive.

"You don't think I'm any less intelligent than any other lawyer in this room?" Windsor challenged Stroud.

Wyatt looked at the jury. The black jurors in particular were listening to this with great interest.

"I don't . . . no. I have no way of knowing without testing all of the lawyers present, but I wouldn't think you were less intelligent." He looked as defensive as he sounded.

"If it is true," Windsor continued, "that you disagree with Dr. Charles Murray, then why didn't you call him on these findings of his? If you don't believe them."

"That forum was not the appropriate time or place."

"Have you ever told Charles Murray you disagree with those findings? Publicly or privately?"

"No. It would not be my place to. That's not my field."

"You don't have any moral concerns about it?"

"Objection!" Wyatt said quickly. "Dr. Stroud's private morality is not relevant here."

"Sustained."

The damage had been done. Wyatt could see that on the faces of the black jurors.

Windsor looked at his scribbled notes. "You said that the defendant was violence-prone, but not in a calculated way. Only in a spontaneous way. Is that right?"

"I didn't say it that way, but that's the gist of it," Stroud agreed.

"Then how do you account for the defendant's attempted armed robbery of that convenience store?" Windsor asked. "Wasn't that carefully planned and premeditated?"

"Yes, but it was a onetime incident, not a series of them."

"But it wasn't spur of the moment," Windsor persisted. "It was planned in advance and carried out as he had planned it. It only failed, in fact, because of an unforeseen mischance, not because the planning wasn't thorough."

"In that case, yes," Stroud acknowledged.

"So Marvin White is capable of violence, he is capable of planning things and executing them, and he might be smarter and have a better memory than these tests that are designed for white middle-class kids showed. He might have committed these crimes and remembered them later, is that right?"

"All those things are possible, but in my opinion, taking all the factors into consideration, the answer is emphatically no. He couldn't have committed these crimes and remembered them in the kind of detail that has been ascribed to him."

Windsor glared at Stroud. "In your opinion," he finally said belittlingly. "No further questions, Your Honor."

Grant called for a half-hour intermission before the next defense witness. Wyatt went ballistic during the break. Josephine watched wide-eyed as he tore into his psychiatric expert—she had never seen him lose his temper like this before.

"Why didn't you tell me about this Charles Murray connection?" he demanded of Stroud. "Christ Almighty, man, I paid you thirty-five hundred dollars, plus expenses."

"You didn't ask me," the psychiatrist answered calmly. He was used to clients venting their frustrations on him—it came with the territory. Not that he liked it, especially when it cost them points. "And I don't feel my knowing Charles Murray counts as a *connection*. Everyone in academia knows or has met Dr. Murray. You wouldn't be able to find any expert to give testimony for you if that was the criterion."

"I asked you if you had any skeletons in the closet!" Wyatt ranted. "You said nothing."

"Being on a panel with two dozen other people, one of whom happens to be Charles Murray doesn't qualify as a skeleton in my book," Stroud said. "But I'm sorry if my testimony disappointed you. I don't feel good about that, either."

"You don't agree with Murray, do you?" Wyatt asked, still bent out of shape.

"No, not in that regard. Although there are plenty of other things he says I do agree with. The man is preeminent in his field, and he enjoys controversy."

Josephine put a placating hand on her boss's forearm. "Dr. Stroud did fine, Wyatt," she said, casting a wary eye in Stroud's direction. "He testified unequivocally that Marvin couldn't have committed those murders and then remembered the details the way Thompson said he did. That's the important thing, and that's what you'll remind the jury of during your summation."

"You're right," Wyatt agreed, forcing himself to calm down. Antagonizing his own witness was not a Phi Beta Kappa idea. "Sorry 'bout that, Doc," he said, offering his hand. "I blew it out of proportion. They tried to rattle me and they succeeded."

"No harm done," Stroud assured him. "For what it's worth, I was sincere about what I said in there. Your guy couldn't have done it."

"Thanks."

Wyatt slumped into a chair after Stroud left. "I shouldn't have come down on him like that," he said.

"You sure shouldn't have," Josephine agreed.

"I should be coming down on myself," he groused. "I'm where the buck stops—I can't take my frustrations out on anyone else." He looked at his watch. "We're back in five minutes." Then he smiled. "Our next witness will make up for Stroud," he told her. "And then some."

The second defense witness looked like the keyboardist for a grunge band. Tall, lanky, scraggly bearded, he was resplendent in a two-decade-old Grateful Dead tie-dyed T-shirt. His hair, dyed jet-black, was short and ragged. Although he was straight today, he looked like his normal condition was one of being perpetually stoned, part of his essence.

Garrett Green was his name. Twenty-two years old, he was a legendary computer hacker genius in the worldwide hacker underground. Among his most notable accomplishments was breaking into the confidential accounts of three of the world's largest stock brokerages and transferring $1.5 billion into a series of Cayman Islands banks. The money was never touched—he just did it to prove to his hacker buddies that he could. A week later he transferred the money back, but by then an investigation of one of the brokerages had been started by the SEC (which ultimately resulted in a seven-figure fine), and several high-level managing partners had been canned.

The feds didn't think his little prank was funny. As he had already caused a ton of mischief by setting viruses into the ATF's top-secret Unabomber files, the library at the University of Chicago, and Bob Dole's presidential campaign, they set up housekeeping for him in the federal penitentiary at Lewisburg, Pennsylvania.

He did his eighteen months, came out, and went to work for a small Internet start-up company. On the side he did private consulting. Wyatt had hired him for his expertise in the areas in which he no longer practiced his clandestine arts, since going to jail again was not in his game plan.

"Nice T-shirt," Wyatt commented admiringly from the lectern after Green had recited his idiosyncratic résumé to the amusement and/or horror of those present in the courtroom.

"Bill Walton gave it to me after I set up a computer system for one of his sons," Green said proudly. "He's a major Deadhead, you know."

Wyatt walked to the defense table, picked up a laptop computer, and brought it to the stand. At the same time, Josephine and Willa, another public defender paralegal Wyatt had borrowed for the day, wheeled in a thirty-two-inch monitor receiver and situated it between Green and the jury, where the witness and all twelve jurors and eight alternates could view it easily.

"What's this all about?" Abramowitz groused. She knew Wyatt was going to have a computer expert testify as part of his defense strategy that Dwayne might have been fed information, and that he might have accessed it through a computer and modem. She wasn't prepared, however, for so elaborate a presentation.

"Accessing supposedly confidential information is part of my defense, Your Honor," Wyatt explained as he handed the computer to Green. "We're going to show everyone, in open court, how easily it's done."

Grant was looking on with interest. He turned to Abramowitz. "Were you thinking of objecting?" he asked her.

She read the tea leaves in his question. "No, Your Honor."

Green turned the computer on. It hummed to life. Then he hooked up the TV screen to the computer so that the image on the computer screen was transmitted to the larger screen. Finally, he connected a telephone line to his modem port, and handed the other end of the line to Wyatt.

"With your permission, Your Honor," Wyatt asked.

Grant nodded. Wyatt walked the phone line to the court reporter's table in front of the bench, on which three telephones had been installed, the outlets situated on the floor underneath the table. Unhooking one of the telephone jacks from its outlet, he plugged in the computer phone line.

"That should do it," Green told him.

"You are now connected to the world via this phone line, right?" he asked Green. "World Wide Web, Netscape, Microsoft Explorer, E-mail, whatever."

"That's right."

"The same connections that I or any other computer user with an on-line service can access, correct?"

"Correctamundo," Green told him.

"What about information I'm not supposed to be connected to?" Wyatt asked. "How easy is it to access that kind of information?"

"No *problema*." The reformed hacker turned to Judge Grant. "Would you give me your Social Security number?" he asked. "I could do this demonstration with your address and phone number, but this will save me some steps and condense the time."

"I'm not going to get into any trouble, am I?" Grant asked lightly.

"Not unless you're running some kind of illegal scam, Judge," Green said with a grin.

"I think I'm clean," Grant said. "I hope I am," he added, as the courtroom broke into laughter. He recited his nine-digit number.

Typing fast, Green brought up a program and entered Grant's Social Security number into his machine. A few seconds elapsed; then the computer started spewing out numbers that simultaneously came up onto the big screen.

Wyatt was watching with interest. So were Abramowitz, the other prosecution lawyers and staff, and the jury.

Green paused in his typing and looked at the television screen. "You have a Citibank Visa Gold Card, an American Express Gold Card, a MasterCard with First National Bank of Wilmington, Delaware, a Sears credit card, some gasoline credit cards, and some others too mundane to mention. Also an ATM account at Richardson Savings and Loan here in town, that can be accessed through Star and Cirrus."

Grant gaped at the screen. "Jesus," he muttered under his breath.

"Do you have your wallet on you?" Green asked the judge.

Grant reached into his hip pocket and pulled out his billfold.

"Check your Amex card against the screen," Green told him.

The judge extracted his credit card. Green read the account number off the screen. "A match?" he asked.

"Yes."

"Last month you charged six hundred thirty-eight dollars and forty-seven cents on that account." He read off the various purchases and services from the account.

"I thought these accounts were confidential," Grant said, both upset and intrigued.

"They're supposed to be. But they leak like a sieve. Any ninth-grader who's computer-wise can do this stuff. And they do, all the time. Privacy's a thing of the past." The whiz typed some more data into the computer. "Let's get up close and personal." Looking at the screen, he told Judge Grant, "As of this morning you have fourteen hundred twenty-five dollars in your basic checking account and thirty-two hundred thirty-five dollars in your savings account. I assume you only keep small amounts in those accounts because they don't pay interest, yes? Those are the correct amounts, aren't they?"

"Yes," Grant answered. "I'm sure they are."

Green typed in some more directions. "All righty now!" he crowed. "Now we are getting somewhere. Your PIN number, Judge, is five-four-three-three-three, and I have figured out your code on the magnetic tape on your bank card. So now, your money"—typing in some more data—"is my money."

On the screen the numbers in Grant's bank accounts went to $0.00.

The courtroom erupted with a tumultuous hubbub.

"What the hell! Where's my money? How did you do that? Quiet in here!" he yelled, gaveling for silence.

"Your money's in a safe place, Judge," Green promised him. "In fact"—he typed in some more commands—"it's in your account. Now you see it, now you don't."

And there on the screen the money was miraculously back in Judge Grant's accounts.

"Now I've seen it all," Grant marveled.

"You ain't seen nothing yet, Judge," Green forewarned him. He typed in yet more commands. "I just canceled your PIN number, in case some wise guy listening in decided to rip you off. We'll give you a new one later in private, when I'm done here."

Abramowitz stood up. "This is fascinating, Your Honor, but I fail to see the relevance of any of it. This is a murder trial, not a computer magic show. I must object to any further displays of this kind."

"Sit down, Ms. Abramowitz," Grant told her. "I know exactly where this is going, and I'm going to grant Mr.

Matthews wide latitude in presenting this portion of his case. Please proceed, Mr. Green," he told Wyatt's colorful witness.

Wyatt stood at the lectern and watched with enjoyment and building excitement. He didn't have to do a thing—Garrett Green the slacker hacker was doing all the work for him.

Green looked over at him. "Could I have that information sheet you showed me the other day?" he asked Wyatt.

Wyatt handed him a single sheet of paper with the city police emblem on the top. Green glanced at it and began typing a series of letters and numbers into the computer.

"This paper has badge and case numbers of the detectives who have worked on these cases, is that true?" Wyatt asked his witness. He handed the sheet to the jury for their perusal. "You are using their IDs and case numbers to access information?"

Green nodded without a break in his typing.

"What are you doing now?" Grant asked, unable to control his curiosity.

"Watch and learn," Green said. "This will only take a few moments and it won't hurt at all."

Judge Grant, Wyatt, the prosecution team, Green, and the jury watched the television screen as a document came up.

"Very interesting," Wyatt commented dryly. He walked to the bench and gave Judge Grant a file. "If you'll notice, judge, the material on that screen matches the material I'm handing you."

"Which is what?" Grant asked, peering intently at the television set.

"The official police files from the Alley Slasher murders, of course." Turning to his witness, he requested of him, "Go to page one thousand and seventeen, please."

Green moved his cursor. Page 1017 came up on the screen.

The courtroom was deathly silent.

Wyatt turned to the jury. "We have just accessed the entire computer record of the Alley Slasher murders," he told them. "The very files the state's police witness told you couldn't be accessed. That were secure." He pointed to the screen. "Here's your proof that they aren't." He waited until the severity of the information and what it meant had sunk in deep. Then he turned away from the jury and back to Green. "I think we've seen enough."

Green closed the file and exited the program. The screen went blank.

Wyatt looked at the dark screen. "Was that hard to do?" he asked Green.

"Piece of cake."

"You've reviewed Dwayne Thompson's computer abilities? His degree from college, his work in the state penitentiary system, and so forth?"

The hacker nodded. "You gave me that information and I checked it out."

"In your opinion, could someone of Dwayne Thompson's capabilities as a computer hacker have gotten into these files as easily as you just did?"

"Absolutamundo. It's not brain surgery. With your handy-dandy computer, modem, and phone hookup, you're on your way. If you know how, of course," he added immodestly.

"So if Dwayne Thompson had been able to get his hands on a computer with that setup, he could have hacked in easily to these so-called confidential police files?"

"I just did, didn't I?"

"That you did, Mr. Green. That you did."

They were the lead story on all the local television stations that night (and the front page of the next morning's newspaper). Wyatt was featured in his courthouse-steps mode, decrying the lack of security in the police department and emphasizing how easy it was to transport information that had a direct bearing on this case. Pagano and the chief of police, grim-faced and determined, vowed to plug any leaks in the system, but were vehement in their assertions that no one had given any files to Dwayne Thompson, and that he had never had access to a computer. Wyatt's work was a clever smoke screen sent up by an accomplished lawyer. Pagano was gushing in his tribute to Wyatt, calling him "the preeminent corporate attorney in America." But when the smoke clears, Pagano continued, one basic fact remains: Dwayne Thompson had no way to get his hands on a computer. The evidence clearly shows that, and Marvin

White did confess his crimes, and all the rest is a desperate attempt—stunning and brilliant, but still desperate—to derail the facts:

1) Marvin White raped and murdered seven women.
2) Marvin White confessed to Dwayne Thompson, a cagey jailhouse informant whose credibility was just enhanced in another trial in this very city.
3) Marvin White has to pay the price.

The spin by the local political observers who were analyzing the case on a daily basis was that although Wyatt had blasted a hole in the prosecution's case, he hadn't driven his truck through it—yet. Unless the defense could prove that Dwayne Thompson had access to a computer while he was in the county jail during the tiny, crucial window between when Marvin was arrested and when Dwayne went to the district attorney with his information—only a few days—their demonstration was meaningless. Innocent until proven guilty was a nice abstraction, but the burden of proof was still on the defense.

Despite that yet-unsolved problem, Wyatt felt as good and strong as at any time since the day the case had taken its monstrous, unexpected turn. For the first time since the curtain had lifted he'd raised real doubts in the jury members' minds about the prosecution's case. Now he needed to keep building his momentum; the more he could discredit Dwayne Thompson, the better Marvin's chances were. That's what was happening—Garrett Green had been a giant step forward. And he still had his two aces, the alibi witnesses.

He resisted partaking in a minicelebratory dinner with Josephine and Walcott. Instead, he talked to his wife and daughter, filling them in on the day's good news (which they took more casually than he'd hoped for—they had their own lives going, and being physically distant insulated them from his excitement), went for a run though the city's canyons in the early evening heat, ate dinner in his room, and worked.

He slept the night through, awakening at the crack of dawn, standing at the window as the sunrise, pale rose-yellow, come up over the river into his twenty-first-story room. He couldn't wait to get to court, couldn't wait for the new day's work to begin.

Nurse Hopkins, the jail-infirmary guardian, one arm taped to his side, fidgeted on the stand, twisting and turning, crossing one leg over the other, then recrossing them. He was awash with nervous tics: a hand going to his nostril with a vigorous scratch; a finger harshly rotor-rooting into an ear, the residue, wax or otherwise, wiped across his trousers; a constant blinking of the eyes and wrinkling of the forehead.

He broke his collarbone falling off a table? Wyatt thought cynically. With Dwayne Thompson as the only witness? What a likely story.

That wasn't the issue here, however. Hopkins's condition, and how he'd been injured, wasn't the concern. All he cared about were the facts the nurse could provide.

Hopkins recounted his story of coming in early, hearing the sounds of male/female lovemaking, retreating out of the infirmary but with a clear view of the entrance, and seeing Blake coming out.

"What did she look like?" Wyatt asked her.

"Objection. Calls for conjecture," Abramowitz protested.

"Overruled," Grant said summarily. A prison guard having a relationship with a prisoner, although not unique, was nevertheless shocking.

Wyatt had checked Abramowitz out when she stood up to make her objection—she had lines etched in her face that hadn't been there when the trial had started. It was getting to her, to everyone on her team. She wasn't sleeping—she had developed raccoon rings around her eyes and her well-cut dresses now hung loosely on her slim frame—she had lost weight from worrying. The horse they were riding, Dwayne Thompson, was a runaway mustang, not easily controlled.

"What did Deputy Sheriff Blake look like when she came out of the infirmary that morning?" Wyatt repeated.

"She was flushed," Hopkins said. "She was smiling, like a grinning kid. I've seen that woman almost daily for four years, and I'd never seen her smile like that before. She almost never smiles."

"So to sum it up," Wyatt said, "there is absolutely no question that Lieutenant Doris Blake of the county sheriff's office, and Dwayne Thompson, a prisoner in custody in the jail, were meeting secretly and having a sexual relationship."

"I heard it, I saw her come out," Hopkins replied, pulling on his earlobe and scratching his oily, flaking scalp. "There was no one else there. What other conclusion could anyone draw?"

Abramowitz shied away from whether or not Blake had physically been in the infirmary. "You claim you *heard* a man and a woman laughing?" she aggressively questioned Hopkins.

"I *did* hear it," he said with conviction.

"You *heard* them having sexual intercourse?"

"Yes."

"How can someone *hear* the sound of sexual intercourse?" she demanded, as if he was a fool.

"I'm an adult," he said with prim hauteur. "I know what sexual foreplay sounds like."

"What does it sound like?" she asked maliciously.

"I'm not going to make the kinds of noises she was making." He literally recoiled at such a thought.

"Was Lieutenant Blake laughing? Was that one of the sounds?"

"Yes."

"Well, couldn't he have been telling her a joke? Couldn't that have been the cause of her laughter?"

"It wasn't that kind of laughter," he said with disgust.

Wyatt looked at the jury to see how they were taking this. They seemed to be repelled, both by what Hopkins was saying and by his personal tics and unhygienic behavior. He prayed the nurse would last through the cross-examination without falling apart and damaging his credibility.

"You didn't see them together, you hear some laughter, and from that you infer they were having sexual intercourse? As a corrections officer, Lieutenant Blake has the right, the duty, to be anywhere in the jail, doesn't she? For all we know she was merely checking to make sure things were all right down there with the prisoner, who we concede knew her from an earlier posting. So what? He told her a joke, and she laughed at it. Prisoners and guards banter all the time. They have to get along with each other, or the system would be chaos."

"Objection! This is editorializing, not cross-examining," Wyatt complained.

"Agreed," Grant said. "The jury will disregard Ms. Abramowitz's extemporaneous remarks. Save your subjectivity for your summation," he cautioned her.

"Yes sir." She turned to Hopkins again. "Besides hearing what may well have been innocent laughter, what other sounds did you hear?"

"Moaning and such."

"Oh, come on, sir. You heard *moaning*? Give us an example of this *moaning*."

He stared hatefully at her. "I'm not going to stoop to their animal level," he said prissily.

Judge Grant admonished Abramowitz to move on; but suddenly, unexpectedly responding to her hectoring, Hopkins lunged up in his chair. " 'Oh, Dwayne,' " he mimicked in a hoarse falsetto, " 'Oh, Dwayne! Yes! Yes! More! Yes, yes, yes!' " He sat back down, flushed and out of breath. "Is that what you wanted to hear?" he asked her with delicious salaciousness.

The courtroom dropped its collective jaw. For the umpteenth time Judge Grant was forced to use his gavel to silence the discord. Abramowitz, standing at the lectern, looked like she'd been poleaxed.

Grant looked at her. "Are you finished with this witness?" he asked sympathetically, although his hand went to his face to cover the smile he couldn't suppress.

She shook her head gamely. Trying to salvage this disaster, she asked Hopkins, "When Lieutenant Blake came out of the infirmary, did she have a computer with her?"

He thought back for a moment. "I didn't see one."

"Later on, when you did enter, was there any evidence of a computer there, in the infirmary?"

"Just the one I use, and that's locked up when I'm not there."

"So Dwayne Thompson did not have use of a computer during the morning in question."

"No."

*   *   *

Warden Jonas was not a man Abramowitz could fuck with. Not only was he on her side, a peace officer; he was one of the most highly respected law-enforcement officials in the state, who was known to be incorruptible. She wouldn't dream of baiting him as she had done so disastrously with Hopkins.

Wyatt went first. "Is it true that Dwayne Thompson is barred from using a computer in your prison because of illegal hacking?"

Jonas framed his answers in terse institutionese. "He was using our computers for other than legitimate purposes, yes."

"Is he considered by people in the know up there to be a genius at computers and hacking?"

"Yes."

"Was it common knowledge that Dwayne Thompson and Doris Blake were having a sexual relationship during the time both were at Durban Penitentiary, he as a prisoner and she as a guard?"

"It was rumored," Jonas answered cautiously. "There was never any proof, to my knowledge."

"But it was commonly accepted that they were lovers. By the staff."

"That's what people thought. I don't make judgments based on innuendo."

"Did the rumors concern you?"

Jonas nodded gravely. "They concerned me a great deal."

"Enough to warrant your requesting Ms. Blake to seek employment elsewhere?"

"I was going to," Jonas admitted, "but she beat me to the punch. She resigned."

"Did she give a reason?"

"She said she wanted to go to law school, and had to be where there was a law school she could go to when she wasn't working."

"And you approved of that?"

"Very much."

"Because she was going to law school, or because she was saving you an unpleasant confrontation?"

"Both. I was pleased for her, and relieved for myself."

"When Ms. Blake applied for her job in the sheriff's department here, did she give you as a reference? Did she ask for a recommendation?"

"Yes."

"And you gave her one?"

"Yes. She was a good corrections officer. I assume she still is, since she's achieved the rank of lieutenant."

"Did you mention these rumors of her relationship, sexual or otherwise, with Dwayne Thompson in your recommendation?"

"No. If I had, she wouldn't have gotten the post."

"Why didn't you, if it bothered you enough that you were going to ask her to quit working as a guard at Durban?"

Jonas steepled his fingertips. "She was leaving an unhealthy situation. I assumed it was a onetime thing. I didn't want to ruin her life because of one possible indiscretion."

"If Lieutenant Blake has, in fact, resumed her close personal relationship with Dwayne Thompson down here, would that give you cause for concern?"

Jonas looked at him with dismay. "Very much so."

"Would you consider that sufficient grounds for dismissal of Lieutenant Blake?"

"Unquestionably."

"If it turned out they had had a relationship, would that, in your opinion, be grounds for bringing charges against her?"

The room was still, waiting for Jonas's answer. "Yes," he said. "I would recommend dismissal and an investigation if such allegations were substantiated." He looked toward the jurors. "The public has to trust their officials. That's essential for the system to work. I'm proud of the work I do, and of the men and women who work with me. When a trust is violated, it rubs off on every man and woman working in law enforcement. And when that trust is eroded, the system breaks down. Which is why we try to keep our guard up to see to it that doesn't happen."

Windsor cross-examined Jonas. Abramowitz barely kept track of the questions and answers. Her associate was circumspect in his interrogation.

"These stories about Lieutenant Blake and Dwayne Thompson. They were only rumors, that is correct? There was never any physical proof."

"No."

."So it could have been malicious gossip. Factions who didn't like Lieutenant Blake trying to make her look bad."

"No." Jonas was firm. "No one wished Doris Blake ill. She was sometimes the object of pity or jokes, but no one wanted to hurt her."

"Were there ever any rumors that Lieutenant Blake had assisted Dwayne Thompson in obtaining a computer?"

"No, none."

"She never was around when he was using one?"

"I don't know. She could have been in a room when he was using one. But as far as helping him obtain a computer for illegal reasons, the answer is no. Once Dwayne Thompson was pulled off the computers at Durban, he never got his hands on one again."

"**C**all Doris Blake to the stand."

Blake was wearing an off-white linen suit that stretched snugly over her large frame; given her size and girth, it was relatively flattering. In defiance of her height she wore heels, her legs sheathed in pale white tights. Her hair was pulled back in a tight bun, and she had an ample amount of makeup on.

Someone with taste had taken her shopping, Wyatt thought as he walked from the defense table to the lectern. And a professional had done her makeup. He had called her as a witness, but the prosecution was going to do whatever it could to make her look as presentable as she could be.

"This witness is here under subpoena, Your Honor," he told the court for the record. "She resisted all entreaties to appear voluntarily, so I wish to have her declared a hostile witness."

"So ordered," Grant said.

Wyatt smiled at her. "Good afternoon, Ms. Blake. It's nice to see you again."

She stared daggers at him.

"Or would you prefer Lieutenant?" he asked cheerfully.

"I would prefer Lieutenant."

"Lieutenant it is, then." He arranged his papers in front of him. Looking up again, he asked his first question. "Do you know Dwayne Thompson, inmate #3694, serving a sentence at Durban State Penitentiary, the state's maximum-security penitentiary, who is temporarily incarcerated in the county jail of which you are a deputy?"

"Yes." Her eyes bore in on him.

"Did you know him at Durban, while you were a guard there?"

"Yes."

"And you renewed your relationship when he was brought down here."

"I have no relationship with Dwayne Thompson," she stated firmly. "Or any other prisoner."

"You have seen him in the county jail."

"Yes."

"On several occasions."

"I have not seen him on several occasions."

"More than one."

"Yes."

"More than three?"

She hesitated. "Yes. I can't help seeing him. He's an inmate, I'm a guard. That's my job, watching them."

"Let me rephrase my earlier question," he said calmly. "Do you have a personal relationship with Dwayne Thompson, Durban State Penitentiary inmate #3694?"

"No."

"None whatsoever. It's strictly business."

"Strictly."

"Then why did you *personally* arrange for Dwayne Thompson to sleep in the jail infirmary? Which is not only uncommon, it's unheard of."

She rearranged the folds of her skirt. "I thought I was acting on Sheriff Lowenthal's orders."

"Sheriff Lowenthal told you to transfer Dwayne Thompson, a man serving a lengthy sentence in the state's toughest prison, where only hard-core, repeat offenders are sent, into a section of the jail that is unguarded at night? Is that what you're telling this court?"

A second rearrangement, then a smoothing of folds. "Not directly, no," she admitted.

"You arranged for that transfer on your own, without receiving orders from higher authority. Didn't you?"

"Yes." Sitting erect, she continued, "It was a mistake. I thought that was what Sheriff Lowenthal wanted. When I found out it wasn't, Thompson was transferred into the general population, and subsequently into protective housing."

"But *you* didn't transfer him out of the infirmary. In fact, you didn't know it had happened until you went down there to see him one morning and were told by another deputy that Thompson was no longer there at night. In an unguarded part of the jail," he added emphatically.

"No. I did not arrange for the transfer." She spat the words at him like BBs.

"In fact, you were upset when you found out about it, weren't you?"

"Of course not. Why would I be upset?"

"Because you couldn't see him clandestinely anymore."

"Objection!" Abramowitz sang out. "The witness has already stated under oath that she was not seeing Thompson, clandestinely or any other way."

Grant pondered for a moment. "Sustained," he said with some reluctance.

"Witnesses have said she did, Your Honor," Wyatt protested. Putting up a hand like a traffic cop, he went on, "But that's okay. I'll pursue another line of questioning." Turning back to Blake, he asked her, "Did you ever see Dwayne Thompson in the infirmary at night? After lights out?"

"No, never."

"We have had a witness on the stand who swore you did."

"He's lying."

"That he heard the sounds commonly associated with a man and woman making love, and shortly after saw you emerge from the infirmary."

Her large face went blotchy florid. "That's a lie!"

"How many times have you and Dwayne Thompson had sexual intercourse, Ms. Blake?" he asked forcefully. "Half a dozen? A dozen? A hundred?"

"Objection!" from Abramowitz.

"Sustained. The witness has stated she has not had sex with Dwayne Thompson, Mr. Matthews. That's enough of this."

"Well, if that's true, Your Honor, then someone is lying. Either Ms. Blake or Nurse Hopkins."

"That's a decision the jury has to make, isn't it?"

"Yes, Your Honor. It absolutely is." He rummaged through

his papers on the lectern until he found what looked to be a receipt. "Do you own a computer, Lieutenant Blake?"

"Yes," she nodded.

He looked at the receipt. "You spent a lot of money on your computer, Lieutenant. You must be good on it."

"Not really. I know how to work the programs I need."

"Do you ever bring it to work, to the jail?"

She took a moment to reply. "Yes."

"You use it in your office?"

"Yes."

"Anywhere else?"

"No, not that I remember."

"You didn't use it in the jail's law library? While you were going to law school at night?"

"Yes," she admitted. "I did use it there."

"On several occasions?"

"Some."

"But until I jogged your memory you'd forgotten you had used it there even once."

"I forgot. Those were the two places I used it—my office and the law library."

"When was the last time you brought your personal computer to the jail, Ms. Blake?"

"I . . ." She thought for a moment. "I can't remember."

"Did you bring it to the jail after Dwayne Thompson had been transferred there?"

Again: "I don't remember."

"*Don't*, Ms. Blake?" he asked. "Or don't *want* to."

"I don't remember," she told him, her anger starting to show.

"But you might have."

"I don't think I did. I didn't have any reason to bring it by that time."

"Because you were using it to study for your bar examination, and by the time Thompson was sent down to the jail you had already taken the bar?"

"Yes," she answered. "That's the reason I didn't bring it to work."

"That's the bar exam you took in the spring? The one you told me you passed on your first try? With a seventy-six, which is a very high score." He looked at the jury. "Passing your bar examine with a score of seventy-six puts you in the top twenty-five percent of those taking the test. It's a real accomplishment."

Pridefully, she answered, "Yes." Then the implications of his question hit her. "I mean no," she said, quickly revising her answer.

"You said yes."

"I meant no." She was getting flustered; her body language was giving her away.

"Yes or no. Which is it?"

"No. I said no."

"You didn't take the bar exam this past spring?"

"Yes, I did take it. . . ."

"You just said no."

"The no is, I never told you I passed it."

Wyatt threw up his hands in astonishment. "Then how did I know your score, if you didn't tell me?"

"I don't know my score," she said.

"Excuse me?" He gave the jury a "Can you believe this?" look. "You told me your score on several occasions, Lieutenant, and I told my boss. And other people as well, including some of your former law professors."

She shook her head vigorously. "The bar exam scores won't be posted for some weeks," she said. "There's no way I could have known my score, or even if I passed."

He cocked his head, eyeballing her across ten feet. "So now I'm lying, too?"

"I'm not saying you're lying, Mr. Matthews," she said cautiously. "I think you misunderstood me."

"How so, Ms. Blake?" he asked, his voice dripping sarcasm.

"I told you I *thought* I did well on the exams, and *might* have done as high as seventy-six," she offered guilelessly.

"Gee. That sure wasn't the way I heard it."

"I'm sorry if I somehow misled you."

"Yeah, I'm sure you are," he barked at her. "Like you've been misleading me and everyone in the world about your sexual relationship with Dwayne Thompson, and how you helped him fabricate evidence against Marvin White!"

"Objection!"

"Sustained!"

*   *   *

Abramowitz watched Wyatt's examination of Blake with loathing. Of course this bitch fucked Thompson. Her lies about that oozed right out of her pores. But who gives a shit about who fucks who? Passing information, that's all Abramowitz gave a damn about.

She replaced Wyatt at the lectern. "We'll keep this short," she told Blake, forcing a smile. *But not sweet.* "Did you ever give any records of any kind, directly or indirectly, to Dwayne Thompson?"

"Absolutely not."

"Did you give records of any kind to any prisoner, or to anyone who wasn't allowed access to them?"

"No, I didn't," Blake swore, the look on her face that of a kid caught with her hand in the cookie jar, the mother calling from another room—she hadn't actually taken the cookie out, but her chubby fingers, closed around the prize, reluctantly open and withdraw, empty. "I never took any records out. I swear it." Her lower lip began to tremble. "I'm a dedicated officer," she said, looking like she was actually going to break down right there on the stand. "I'd kill myself before I'd do something like that."

Wyatt, listening to this predictable, self-pitying exchange with half an ear, passed a note to Josephine. "Issue a subpoena to seize her computer." She read it, nodded, and quietly left the courtroom.

Abramowitz gathered up her slim set of notes. "No more questions for this witness, Your Honor."

The daily end-of-the-day summing-up and plotting out the next day's work took place in Wyatt's cramped, gothic-feeling office. The Hunchback of Notre Dame would feel at home here, he thought—but he had come to like it here. He wasn't so romantic about the situation to want to work out of these kinds of digs for the rest of his life; but for now, with this case, this was the right place to be. These were underdog offices. You didn't entertain here, you didn't impress, you didn't schmooze. You brought your lunch pail to work and you did your job.

The meeting was him and Walcott. Darryl had stopped by as well; he came to the trial a couple times a week, whenever his busy schedule permitted, to lend weight to Wyatt, silently cheer him on. Once in a while he would pass a note along about some aspect of how Wyatt was conducting himself, but pretty much he was there to be a body for the cause.

The three men—in shirtsleeves, ties askew—sucked longnecked Buds. The ancient window air conditioner was fighting a losing battle with the brutal heat and humidity. Wyatt pressed the cold, beaded bottle to the back of his neck.

Josephine would be here in a minute. She was tripleverifying last-minute details about tomorrow's witness, Agnes Carpenter, and taking care of tonight's creature comforts for her. Up until now, the defense had been serving up appetizers. With Agnes Carpenter, however, Wyatt was beginning the main course, shifting into high gear. Attacking the opposition's credibility and punching holes in their witnesses was good, and important. But showing how ridiculous they were was not the same as offering proof—concrete, physical proof the jury could see, touch, take a bite out of—that what Pagano and his gang had accused Marvin of doing was physically impossible. No matter how anyone framed it, he could not have been in two places at the same time. When he presented these two women, Agnes and Leticia Pope, that would be the match that lit the dynamite.

"You could see Blake's nose getting longer every time she opened her mouth," Walcott said derisively.

"Do you think the jury saw it as clearly as we do?" Wyatt asked. He knew things the jury didn't, which meant his feelings about her were colored by that knowledge. All of theirs were.

"If they didn't, they're blind." This from Darryl. "The nurse, as nervous as he was, nailed her cold. Trying to lie her way out of that—and it was ugly to watch, she was so transparently lying to them—discredited everything else she said."

"And that stuff about the law boards," Walcott chimed in. "She screwed up royally there, too."

"Speaking of which, I need to find out what's going on with that," Wyatt said for his own benefit, making a note to call his pal Ginsberg first thing in the morning and see if he'd got anything about Blake's score. "What's with the request for her computer?" he asked Walcott.

"It'll be ready tomorrow. We're gonna serve her and she's gonna turn us down," he cautioned Wyatt. "Pagano's gonna tell her not to, in case she doesn't get it. Then we'll see if we can get an order from a judge, preferably Grant."

Josephine breezed in as Darryl and Walcott polished off their beers and reached for their jackets. Wrinkling her nose, she lifted her arm and sniffed at her blouse. "I showered this morning, honest to God. I even shaved," she said joshingly.

"Our departing is mere coincidence," Walcott said, smiling.

"I can't help it if the humidity's Fahrenheit 451," she complained. She slumped into a chair as the two men took their leave, indecorously shedding her high heels and wiggling her stockinged toes.

"Are we all set for tomorrow?" Wyatt asked, trying to sound at ease. In fact, he was nervous. People like Agnes Carpenter, who lived in a world that was part dream-fantasy, part revenge, and much preening and showing off, gave him the jitters when they were his witnesses. But thus far, in every encounter, every mock trial and tough question-and-answer, she had come through like a champ. She had her story, she stuck to it, she was rock solid.

"I'm going right back to the hotel as soon as you and I powwow over whatever we have to do," she assured him. They had put Agnes Carpenter up at the downtown Hilton, registered under a pseudonym. As usual, Wyatt was paying out of his pocket. Josephine would be in a room next door, with access from her side only. Everyone, including room service, would come through her room to get to Agnes.

"Good. Anything new I need to know?"

"Yes," she said, eyes alight with excitement.

"What, have you been holding something out on me?" he asked. He didn't need any surprises from her, not with the meat of his case starting tomorrow.

"Relax, boss, I just got here," she chided him gently. "Take a look at this." She handed him a file folder with some pages clipped together inside. "I've been looking at these things for months, and I finally figured out what was bugging me."

He opened the folder and glanced at the contents. "A record of withdrawal of police files," he noted quickly. "What's the point?"

"Check out who checked them out."

He turned to the last page. "Detective Dudley Marlow," he read aloud. "So?" he asked, a bit annoyed. "We knew he took out the files. He told us in court he did."

"Open your eyes, Wyatt. Look at the code."

He turned the last page over, the one with Marlow's name on it. Then he did a double take. "This says it was accessed by computer."

"Give that man a teddy bear!" she crowed.

"But he never did that. So he claimed."

"No shit, Sherlock."

"Which means he was lying."

"Looks like it, doesn't it? Now look at the date."

He stared at the date on which the files had been electronically withdrawn, silently counting to himself on his fingers. "Less than a week before Dwayne Thompson took his dog and pony show to the grand jury."

"Two days before he went to Pagano with it. We may have found our leak," she said, unable to restrain her excitement.

"Slow down," he cautioned her. "Don't jump to any conclusions. He would have taken the files out, given that a fresh murder had just been committed; he's already testified to that. And maybe he did do it through his computer, and forgot, or maybe one of the other detectives working with him did, and his name wound up on the request because Marlow's the lead detective. It's interesting, Josephine, but it could be nothing."

"Or it could be something," she came back, defending her find.

"It definitely could be," he agreed. "Let's bring him back for redirect, after Agnes."

"You've got it."

"And enjoy your evening," he said straight-faced.

"Up yours," she rejoined.

Agnes Carpenter, poised, calm, and composed—remarkably, almost eerily so—sat in the witness chair. She was wearing an expensive silk dress, and was accessorized to the max.

"You are a married woman, Mrs. Carpenter?" Wyatt led off after the swearing-in and initial introductions.

"Yes," she answered. Her voice was low and well modulated, the essence of an old-fashioned culture that seemed more appropriate to a woman of seventy-five than one a generation younger.

"For how long?"

"Thirty-one years."

"Your husband is a physician here in the city?"

"Yes."

"Do you work, Mrs. Carpenter?"

"I do volunteer work," she said with a patrician air. "I don't have a profession."

He took a deep mental breath. Then he plunged forward. "Within the past two years, Mrs. Carpenter, have you had a relationship with the defendant, Marvin White?"

"Yes, I have," she answered clearly.

"Would you describe that relationship to the court, please."

Without hesitation, she said, "It was a sexual relationship."

Wyatt looked over at the jury. Several of them looked like they were in shock. They gaped at her, then altered their looks to stare at Marvin, who sat impassively at the defense table, stalwartly staring at the wall behind Judge Grant's head.

"Approximately how long were you and Marvin White in this sexual relationship, Mrs. Carpenter?"

"From shortly after he became the deliveryman for my laundry service until he was let go."

"So that would be about a year and a half?"

"Yes."

She gave the details of their biweekly sexual encounters as she had done at her house, during their first interview. At one point in her description Wyatt looked at Jonnie Rae, who was in her customary seat in the first row of spectators behind the defense table, directly to the rear of her son. Marvin's mother was rocking silently, eyes closed shut, teeth biting the knuckles of a hand.

Wyatt extracted a slip of paper from his notes. "Did Marvin White spend the night of August eighteenth of last year at your home, is that correct?" he read from the paper.

"Yes, it is," she answered.

"When did he arrive," he asked her, "and when did he leave?"

"He arrived after he was finished work, about a quarter

to seven, and left the following morning shortly after seven-thirty—he had to be at work by eight and he didn't want to be late. I made him breakfast," she added. "Pancakes, from scratch."

"How is it that Marvin was able to spend that entire night at your house, Mrs. Carpenter, if you are married? Did he sleep in your bed with you?"

"Of course he did. That was the point."

He looked at her inquiringly.

"My husband was not home that night," she answered in reference to the earlier part of the question.

"You knew that with certainty?" he asked.

"Oh, yes." Her jaw was jutted in front of her like a centurion's shield.

"And how did you know that?"

"The private detective I hired to follow my husband had phoned to tell me he had booked a hotel room for that night, and had checked in by four-thirty. So I knew the good doctor wasn't coming home." She paused. "He did that frequently—stayed out all night. This time I was prepared to make my own arrangements."

Wyatt walked briskly to the defense table, picked up a two-page report, and walked back to the witness stand. He handed it to her. "Does this report from the Floss Detective Agency confirm what you have just told us?"

She glanced at it. "Yes, it does."

"I offer this report in exhibit," Wyatt said to Judge Grant.

"So ordered. This will be defense number . . . seven," he instructed the clerk, looking at his sheet.

Wyatt handed the detective report to Grant, walked across the narrow aisle, and gave a copy to the prosecution. Windsor snatched it from Wyatt's hand and passed it to a subordinate without looking at it.

"If you'll notice, Your Honor," Wyatt said, "this is dated August twentieth. It refers to August eighteenth as the night Dr. Carpenter was not going to be home, because he had booked a hotel room at the Carlton Hotel, and had checked in earlier in the afternoon." He paused. "As I'm sure you recall, the fourth Alley Slasher murder was committed on the night of August eighteenth, between the hours of ten that night and three the next morning, according to Dr. Ayala's official report."

"Objection," Abramowitz called from her seat. "Dr. Ayala's conclusions and reports are not the subject of this examination."

"Sustained," Grant gave her. "Save these linkages for your summation, Mr. Matthews."

"Certainly, Your Honor." The jury had heard the connection; that's all that mattered. He'd hammer it home during his final summation. "No further questions," he said, gathering his notes and returning to his chair.

"How many delivery boys or other men you aren't married to have you had sex with since you've been married, Mrs. Carpenter?" Abramowitz asked, going straight for the jugular.

"I had one other affair, many years ago," Agnes answered with an equanimity that was amazing, under the circumstances. "The man was a colleague of my husband's who knew of Leonard's philandering. It lasted only a brief time. I had no other sexual partners after that until Marvin."

"No one-night stands?" Abramowitz bore in. "No quickies with the pizza boy, the plumber, the UPS man?"

"Objection," Wyatt sang out. "This is not only irrelevant, it's offensive in the extreme. Mrs. Carpenter has put her reputation at great risk by appearing here, and she doesn't need to be treated shabbily."

"I agree," Judge Grant said. "You're risking a contempt citation with this kind of badgering," he warned Abramowitz.

She nodded curtly, but didn't apologize.

Agnes answered anyway. "I have had no 'one-night stands' or 'quickies,' as you crudely put it, Miss Abramowitz, or whatever your married status is. Perhaps you are ascribing your own standards to me; I don't appreciate it," she said firmly.

Oooooh, Wyatt thought. Talk about being hoisted on your own.

Abramowitz, frozen in place by the vicious barb, flushed crimson. She started to retort, but bit her tongue. A thousand-dollar contempt fine was a healthy chunk out of her paycheck; much more importantly, she didn't want to alienate the jury. "Did you pay Marvin White to sleep with you?" she asked instead.

"Yes," Agnes answered without hesitation.

Wyatt had gone over that issue thoroughly with her in their practice sessions. "Don't lie about stuff like that," he'd cautioned her. "They'll catch you up, and it'll tarnish all your other testimony."

"How much?"

"It varied."

"What is the most money you ever paid Marvin White to sleep with you, for one encounter?" Abramowitz asked.

"Objection. The witness has already testified she paid the defendant to have sex with her. The amount is irrelevant."

"Sustained."

Abramowitz tried to compose herself. This was going nowhere. "Does your husband know you're testifying here?" she asked.

Agnes scowled. "Yes. He knows."

"When did you tell him about this?"

"Three days ago."

"What was his reaction?"

"He's enraged," Agnes answered. "He's filing for divorce. As far as he's concerned, I've ruined him." She stared at Abramowitz with hurt and pain—the first signs of suffering Wyatt had ever seen in her. "He can sleep with every chippie nurse in the hospital, flaunt it to my face, and then accuse me of ruining him because I'm standing up for a boy whose life is at stake? I'm ruining my own reputation," she cried out.

"Thank you," Abramowitz said hurriedly. "That will be all."

Agnes wasn't finished. "Don't you think my life is going to be a disaster because I'm testifying about this?" she wailed. "I could have kept quiet and protected myself. I'm the one who's ruined," she lamented loudly. "But I had to, I couldn't stand quietly and watch an innocent boy die." She looked up at Judge Grant. "Doesn't that count for something?"

*T*op *that,* Wyatt thought. And he would, with Leticia. Agnes Carpenter, although a compelling witness for Marvin, had no backup witnesses to buttress her story that she and Marvin had been together on the night of August 18, only her

own naked, public humiliation (which situation Abramowitz, who by the time she got to her summation and had recovered from today's horrifics, would hammer home).
Agnes Carpenter was a spurned woman who could be accused of lying to protect a young stud who had given her
something no man had given her in years—a good fucking
on a regular basis. Plus the fact that she obviously hated her
husband for his philandering, and knew her humiliation
would be his as well.

Leticia Pope, on the other hand, had no axes to grind,
complicated or simple. She and Marvin had spent a night together. End of story. Except the night was the night of another Alley Slasher murder, and she did have witnesses, lots
of them. And there were the photographs—hard, incontro-
vertible, physical evidence.

Some housekeeping first. "Recall Detective Dudley Marlow to the stand," the bailiff sang out.

Abandoning the lectern, Wyatt stood as close to Marlow
as he could, the police report Josephine had discovered in
hand. "Do you recognize this?" he asked the veteran detective, handing him the sheaf of pages.

Marlow leafed through the report. "Yeah, of course. It's
some of my reports from the murders."

"All of them," Wyatt corrected him. "Everything that's on
file at county records."

"If you say so," Marlow answered affably. "Didn't we go
over this already?"

"Yes, we did, but there's a discrepancy here I've discovered. My staff discovered," he added, wanting to give
Josephine her due. "Do you see the date these files were removed?" He flipped to the proper page and pointed it out
for Marlow.

"Yeah."

"This is what, about five days after the last murder took
place?"

"Five days, that's about right, yeah."

"You were back on the case and you wanted to review the
earlier killings, is that why you took them out?"

"Sure."

"That's SOP?"

"Yeah," Marlow answered laconically, shooting his cuffs.

"So what's the problem?" he asked with the peevish voice of a busy man who's wasting his time here.

"I'm trying to find out if there is a problem," Wyatt told him, "because the particular time you took these files out you did it via your computer. They were transmitted to you through the modem in your computer, Detective. Here." He turned to another page and showed Marlow where the access status was listed. "It says it right here: 'accessed via computer.'" He turned to face Marlow directly. "You testified under oath that you had never accessed these files by your computer, didn't you?"

"Yes," the detective answered grumpily.

"That you always did it by going down to the records department and taking them out in person. You said that?"

"Yes," came the world-weary response.

Wyatt shook his head. "This says otherwise, Detective. And the fact that it was done three days before Dwayne Thompson went to the grand jury makes me suspicious, you know what I mean?"

Marlow reared up in his seat. "What, are you accusing me of passing information on? You gotta be crazy. I never even met this guy."

"Then how do you account for this?" Wyatt demanded, shaking the report in Marlow's beefy face.

"I don't know. But I never took any files out over my computer. I don't know how to do it," he said plaintively. "Ask anyone in the department. They'll tell you."

"You're certain you didn't take this set of records out through your computer," Abramowitz asked, now that it was her turn.

"I just said that, Ms. Abramowitz," he told her, clearly showing signs of stress and anger.

"But you might have taken them out," she went on. "By going down to the records department. You were taking records of the murders out around this time, correct?"

"Of course. Especially after this last one, with all the heat that was coming down."

"Let me show you something, Detective." She walked to her table, picked up a bound stack of papers, and carried them back to the witness stand. "Would you look at these, please?"

While he shuffled through the set she'd handed him one of her flunkies tossed a duplicate set onto the defense table. Wyatt glanced at them quickly and put them aside.

"Do you recognize these reports?" she asked.

"Sure," Marlow replied. "They're the files from a series of armed robberies I worked on about three years ago."

"Your files."

"Yes."

"Turn to page seventeen, please," she asked him, "and read the sentence I've highlighted."

He turned to page 17, which was the second-to-last page. " 'Report accessed via phone line to requestor's computer,' " he read.

"Did you request this report to be transmitted to your computer three years ago?" she asked him.

"Hell, no." He turned to the jury. "Sorry." He looked at Abramowitz again. "I didn't even own a computer three years ago."

"Then how do you account for . . . ? Ah, one moment, please." She turned the last page over. "Here we are." She read, "Transmitted over counter. Correction to previous listing." She showed the last page to Marlow. "Is that what this says?"

He glanced at where her manicured finger was pointing. "Yeah," he agreed, "that's what it says."

Wyatt looked at the last page of the report. The mistake had been fixed, in living black and white. He dropped the report on his table like it was a steaming dog turd.

"In other words," Abramowitz continued, "the previous accounting for how this was given to you was in error."

"That's what it looks like," he agreed again.

"Clerical error."

"Yeah."

"Does that happen occasionally," she asked him. "Clerical errors in the police department? Or are you guys normally perfect, and this was a onetime mistake?"

"Perfect we're not," he said. "We're way out-of-date, Ms. Abramowitz. These kinds of mistakes happen all the time."

Putting that report down, she referred to the one Wyatt had brought in. "So it's possible that the way you got hold of this report was also erroneously recorded?"

"Very possible."

She walked back to her side of the room, shooting Wyatt a smug "Don't fuck with me" expression. "No further questions, Your Honor. I hope we've finally put this red herring to bed," she added pointedly.

Win some, lose some. Abramowitz had made a point with the jury with that clerical-error bullshit, but that didn't mean the transmission of the Alley Slasher files had been screwed up the same way. There was no correction on the current report. As far as he was concerned, until he was shown conclusively that it hadn't been sent via phone line to someone's computer, he was going to go on the supposition that it had.

No biggie. Agnes Carpenter had come through great, and his ace was still in the on-deck circle. Tomorrow, when she testified, he was going to nail this fucker shut.

From the rear of the large chamber, hunched down in her seat so she wouldn't be spotted, Violet Waleska had watched Wyatt's virtuoso handling of Agnes Carpenter. He's convincing me, she thought; and although she wanted only the best for him, her paramount concern was seeing her friend's murderer brought to justice. But the deeper they got into it, the more doubts she had about whether or not Marvin was guilty. The woman could have been lying, to make her husband look bad. Any woman knew that feeling and could empathize with her, but it also meant that any woman could understand her less-than-pure motives; more than a man could, even a man as smart as Wyatt Matthews, her once and pray-to-God future lover.

She went to lunch, and by the time she got back it was too late to get inside for the Marlow reexamination. She would do so after the next break; if that wasn't possible, she'd be here bright and early tomorrow morning to make sure she got the seat she wanted. Now she sat on one of the hard, worn, epithet-carved wooden benches outside the courtroom, watching the astonishing variety of human experience pass before her eyes.

A group of male prisoners, shackled, handcuffed, and bound together by waist chains, shuffled by her. They were led fore and aft by deputies, who ushered them into the courtroom across the hall from the one in which the murder case was taking place. As they passed her, something about one of them made her look at him more closely.

For a moment, the prisoner's eyes met hers. Then he turned away and followed the man in front of him into the courtroom.

Who is that man? she thought. I've seen him somewhere. Where could it have been? She burrowed into her mind, but couldn't place his face with a location. Having nothing better to do, and feeling a nagging urge to satisfy her curiosity, she got up and pushed open the double doors, entering the courtroom where the prisoner had been taken.

The room was almost empty; only a few spectators were scattered about in isolated pockets. The prisoners, now unshackled and uncuffed, sat shoulder to shoulder in the front row on the other side of the barrier. Violet, taking a seat near the rear exit, found her man easily; she could identify him by the back of his head—the hairdo looked familiar.

The men were being arraigned. As each name was called the prisoner stepped forward, to be joined by one of the lawyers who were congregated in the first few rows up front. The charges against them were read, they made their pleas in turn, the judge set bail, and the next prisoner was called.

"Elvis Burnside," the bailiff read off from the list on his clipboard.

The man she'd been watching stood up. As he did, he glanced lazily around the room, as if to convey his extreme boredom with the proceedings. Again, for a fleeting moment, his eyes met Violet's.

She remembered where she had seen him.

Staggering to her feet, her legs suddenly gelatinous, she walked as fast as she could to the doors and out, barely hearing, as they swung shut behind her, the charge against him, aggravated rape with deadly force, and his plea—"not guilty."

She fidgeted nervously, shifting her weight from foot to foot, praying for a recess in Wyatt's courtroom before the proceedings in the one she'd just left were over, so she wouldn't have to see the man again when he came out.

Mercifully, the doors to courtroom 1 swung open. Spectators came out, stretching their limbs from the confinement of sitting still. She pushed past them into Judge Grant's courtroom.

Wyatt was standing at the defense table, talking with his client and a black woman who was there every day and must be the client's mother. As she walked down the aisle toward them he looked up and saw her. His eyes narrowed as he recognized her; he immediately gave an imperceptible shake of his head.

She knew better than to approach him. Instead, she walked to the woman who was working with him, his paralegal assistant she had talked with over the phone.

"Could I have a word with you?" she asked Josephine, bending her head in close so she could keep her voice low.

Josephine, startled by this sudden, unexpected approach, looked to Wyatt, who nodded, his eyes engaging Violet's for the briefest of moments. "Okay," she said warily. She led Violet to the rear of the courtroom.

Violet told Josephine about what she had seen in the adjacent courtroom. "Are you sure?" Josephine asked, feeling a rush of blood to her head.

"I'm positive."

The two women stood in the doorway, looking out into the corridor. From the front of the courtroom, Wyatt watched them with intense curiosity. In a short while, the doors to the other courtroom swung open, and the prisoners, again cuffed and shackled, were led out by their deputy guards, heading for the elevators that would take them to the basement and then back to the jail.

As Elvis emerged into the hallway, Violet shrank back so that he wouldn't see her. "That's him," she whispered to Josephine. "That's the man I saw in Teddy's bar the night Paula was murdered."

By the time Wyatt had gotten back to the office at the end of the day, Josephine had culled through their messages and told him everything Violet had told her. That was awesome, shocking news. A man who was right now being arraigned for aggravated rape had been in the nightclub on the very night the last murder was committed?

Leafing through the message slips, he saw one that sparked his interest more than normal. Another chink in the armor, he hoped. Settling down at his scarred, paint-chipped desk, tie loosened, beer in hand, he dialed the law-bar examiner Joe Ginsberg had turned him onto.

"What have you got?" he asked. He listened for a moment. "You're shitting me. Son of a bitch!" Some more dialogue from the other end, confirming his suspicions. "I can't tell you how much I appreciate your doing this for me," he thanked the man. Hanging up the phone, he called out to Josephine, "Hey! Come on in here!"

She scurried in, her own beer in one hand, a passel of paperwork in the other. Always with her hands full from the day I met her, he thought fondly. What would he have done without her? Whatever happened after the conclusion of this trial, no matter his status at the firm, he had to bring her along with him.

"What now?" she asked.

"Blake's bar-exam score?" He smiled, leaning back in his chair and sucking at his beer bottle.

"What about it?"

"She got a sixty-six, not a seventy-six. I just got off the phone with my inside man."

"So she was lying. Poor sad woman."

"Uh-uh." He waggled his head. "Not that simple. Her test book had sixty-six; but the recorded score on the computer was seventy-six." He cocked his head at her, as if expecting her to figure out the rest.

Which she did. "The score on the computer was wrong."

He nodded. "And . . . ?"

"It was altered. Someone had changed it."

His grin was wide and deep. "You betchum, little lady. Somebody hacked into their computer and changed her score. They're compiling the information and messengering it over. I'll have it before the end of the day tomorrow."

She shook her head in amazement. "I wonder who."

"Yes, it's a mystery to me, too," he said sarcastically. "Could the mystery hacker's intials be D.T.? We need her computer, right now. What's the deal with the court order for it?"

"Grant turned us down; the nexus isn't strong enough, given that there's no record of her taking out those files."

"I'm going to go back to him again. He needs to hear about this latest development. There's enough circumstantial evidence around Blake's computer that we should be able to see what's inside it."

"If that doesn't work, maybe it could get lost and some friend of ours could find it," she offered. "People lose things. Stealing computers is a major industry nowadays."

"I think not," he said, reining in her enthusiasm. "It's considered against the law to steal someone's property."

"I meant . . ."

"Let's keep trying through legal channels. One more go-around, at least."

"Okay." She dropped into the chair opposite his. "This guy the Waleska woman saw. That's major."

"Maybe. Let's not get our hopes up. Who's baby-sitting Leticia Pope?" he asked, changing the subject to his main concern of the moment.

"Dexter and his posse. They've got her surrounded. Do you need her in here tonight, last-minute go-around? I could call Dexter on his pager."

Wyatt shook his head. "That's not necessary. I'll spend an hour with her tomorrow morning before we go into session. She's ready; she's going to do fine." He reached for his suit coat. "Let's wrap for the day."

They walked to the elevator together. "They've got Dwayne Thompson, we've got Leticia Pope," Josephine commented as they rode down to the garage. "It doesn't seem like an even match."

"It isn't," he agreed. "He's experienced, he's persuasive, he's done it before. She's none of that." They reached her car. He waited while she unlocked it and got in. "She only has one thing going for her that he doesn't have. She's telling the truth, and he isn't."

Wyatt had Leticia Pope's bio in front of him. Seventeen-year-old high school dropout. Family three generations on welfare. Barely literate. No dreams, no prospects, no knowledge of the world outside the cramped parameters of where she lived, hung out, saw friends. Her visit to Wyatt's house had been the first time she'd been to that part of the metropolitan area; her only visits outside her tiny circumscribed circle were trips down to Texas, where her people came from before they moved north, and where some of her relatives—older grandparents and great-aunts and uncles, mostly—still lived.

She had never been pregnant, and was not on drugs. Two big plusses. The rest of her life, societally speaking, was a minus—she had never had a job; she had no idea of what work was, or even how to go about looking for it. Like most everyone around her, she lived off food stamps and welfare checks.

Now she sat in the hard wooden chair on the witness stand, back straight, hands folded in her lap. She looked nice. Josephine had taken her shopping, bought her a couple of simple outfits from the Gap—pleated skirts and complementary tops, and a pair of small, classy imitation-pearl earrings.

Wyatt had spent two full days working with her. The majority of their time together, during which they were joined, at various junctures, by Josephine, Walcott, and other lawyers from the office, particularly women lawyers who became surrogate Abramowitzes, had been spent instructing her how to stand up to the prosecution's cross-examination. Wyatt knew Abramowitz's attack would be withering, ruthless.

Leticia was ready. As ready as she would ever be.

Slowly, carefully, brick by brick, Wyatt walked her through her testimony. He had interviewed everyone he could find who had seen her and Marvin that night; he had their statements, which he wove into his questions.

His examination of her was brisk and succinct. He wanted her on and off the stand as quickly as possible—the more she was on the stand, the greater the possibility she could inadvertently say something that could be damaging. From time to time he looked over at the prosecution table, where Abramowitz, Windsor, and their assistants were listening carefully, taking notes, passing notes back and forth, getting up and rushing out of the room to come back moments later with law books, microfiche flimsies, old newspapers.

They were going to come at her tomorrow, but that was okay. She was solid, she was handling this beautifully.

He introduced the Polaroids into evidence near the end of his question period. After Leticia had identified them, and he had pointed out the date that was time-coded on the backs of each one, he passed them to the juror sitting in seat number 1. The juror, a middle-aged black woman who worked for state government, looked at the photos carefully, front and back, writing the information down in her notepad. Each juror in turn, as the photos were passed down the line, looked at them carefully, thoughtfully, writing notes about the small, crumpled photographs in their notepads.

Gold, Wyatt thought, watching them handle the pictures like they were rare jewels. The mother vein.

Retrieving the pictures after all the jurors had seen them, he placed them as exhibits and looked at Grant. "No further questions at this time, Your Honor."

Grant made a few notes of his own. Looking up, he said, "Court will stand in recess until tomorrow morning at nine." He gave his daily end-of-the-day warning to the jurors to refrain from talking to each other or anyone else about the case, not to read any newspaper articles or watch any television shows that discussed the case, and to keep an open mind until all the evidence was presented and the final summations had been given. Having said that, he wished them a pleasant evening, whacked his gavel once, and ended the session for the day.

As he left the bench, he looked down at Wyatt and Abramowitz. "I'll see you in my chambers in five minutes. One from each side."

"Thank you, Your Honor," Wyatt said.

Abramowitz didn't say anything, but her scowl was a powerful statement.

Judge Grant's small, dark-paneled office was cooler than the courtroom. The air conditioner in the window was going full blast, and he had an east-facing view, so there wasn't the direct late-afternoon sunlight that baked the courtroom windows and caused them to conduct the heat throughout the large, still space. Grant hung his robes on a corner coatrack, doffed his tie, unbuttoned his white dress shirt, which was wet with perspiration, and took a large pitcher of ice water out of his small refrigerator.

"Anyone want some?" he asked. In the room with him were Wyatt, Abramowitz, and his secretary. Without waiting for a reply, he poured out four large glasses. Even Helena, whose appearance had been spartan thoughout the entire day's testimony, eagerly picked up the proffered glass and drank several large, fast gulps. Wyatt could see the outline of her bra under her moist cotton shirtdress. Her hair, impeccably in place when she came in every morning, was askew now, tendrils breaking off from the coif in random, wild directions.

Grant looked over the bar examination documents that Wyatt's contact had sent over. "This is serious stuff," he stated. Turning to Helena, he asked her, "What do you think?"

"It's serious and it has nothing to do with this case," she said belligerently. "It's a wild-goose chase like the rest of the defense's presentation."

"Oh, come on!" Wyatt responded. "There's a pattern here, which anyone with half a brain can see. Thompson was laying Blake, Judge. You think if she's going to take a risk that huge she wouldn't let him use her computer?"

"This is not germane to anything," Abramowitz started arguing, but Grant put his hand up to stop her.

"It's too late to do anything today," he informed them, "but I'm going to issue a court order to have her computer brought in here. We'll see what the contents are, if anything's there that could have a bearing on this trial."

"Thank you, Judge Grant," Wyatt smiled.

"But Judge—"

Again, Grant cut Helena off with a brusque flip of the wrist. "You'd better hope this computer comes up clean," he told her sternly, "or you could be looking at a mistrial, possible charges of perjury, theft of government property, collusion, and God knows what else." He turned his back on them. "You're dismissed," he said curtly.

Josephine was waiting for him in the hotel bar, sitting at a small table in the corner—fidgeting would more accurately describe her posture—one shoe nervously jigging off the end of her foot. The two were going to join Walcott and Darryl for dinner in the hotel dining room.

After leaving Judge Grant's chambers, Wyatt had spent a half hour with Leticia. There wasn't much for them to do—they'd done it all already. All she had to do was tell the truth. He'd be there to protect her.

Dexter and his main men, Richard and Louis, had taken her away with them. Wyatt had offered a hotel room, but she hadn't wanted it; she was intimidated by it. "It's under control, Mr. Matthews," Dexter promised him. "She's in good hands. I'll have her in court tomorrow, bright and early," he said as they drove away in his tricked-out Jeep.

He dropped a file folder on the table in front of them. "I've been out checking on this Burnside character," he said, explaining his tardiness. "He's a repeat rapist, he's violent, he fits the profile perfectly. And he was in Teddy's that night," he reminded her. "It all fits."

"What do you want to do?" she asked, her excitement building to match his.

"We need to put him at the scene of one of the other murders. Besides this last one."

"I've got Angelo on alert. He's waiting to hear from you."

Angelo Pasquelli was a private investigator Wyatt often used in his own practice. If there was something to be found, Angelo was your man.

"Call him. Tell him to get like a bloodhound, tout suite."

While she was dialing the PI and making the arrangements, Wyatt reexamined Elvis's file more closely. If you were going to compile a dossier on the perfect suspect in this case, it would be this man. Of course, the odds of him being the actual killer had to be . . . what? Ten to one? A thousand to one?

Immediately, he thought of Violet—in his brain, his heart. She did this, and not because she had doubts about Marvin. She had done this for him.

"Penny for your thoughts, big fella." Darryl had come up behind him, unawares.

Not these thoughts. They private. "I'm famished," Wyatt said. "Let's chow down."

Wyatt's cell phone rang in the middle of their meal. He answered it with his mouth full of food. "Hello?" he said, his voice garbled. "Wait a minute." He swallowed, spoke again. "Hello?" He listened for a moment. "What?" he said again, his voice louder, agitated.

No one was eating—they were all staring at him.

"When?" He listened. "Where?" Another moment. "Hang tight. I'll be there as soon as I can."

By the time they arrived there were already two ambulances and half a dozen black and whites on the scene, all with lights flashing, pulsating arhythmically. The police had cordoned off the area, flares ringing the crime scene for a square-block radius, police tape strung up around the perimeter to keep everyone at a safe distance. Sawhorse barricades were set up in the middle of the street to prevent traffic from coming through.

It had been drizzling for an hour, a light, steady downpour that made the already brutal humidity even worse. An oil slick had formed along one side of the street, its rainbow droplets glistening under the halogen-lit streets. Dozens of people, all black (they were less than a mile away from Sullivan Houses), had come out onto the street from the apartment houses and other gathering places in the vicinity to check out the disaster. They stood behind the barricades, for the most part watching quietly, talking and watching as the paramedics worked quickly and efficiently and the police shuffled around, trying to keep order.

The Jaguar skidded to a stop in front of the barricades. Wyatt jumped out ahead of the others, racing toward the smashed-up Jeep Grand Cherokee that was inside the secured area, the vehicle tilted at an angle against the curb, two tires blown, bullet holes in the windshield and all the driver's-side windows, a plume of water spouting into the air from the hydrant it had crashed into.

A burly city policeman tried to block Wyatt's entrance as he came barreling through. "Hey, nobody's allowed in here! This is a crime scene, can't you see?" The cop's hand went to his holster.

"I'm their lawyer!" Wyatt screamed.

As the officer reached out to physically impede Wyatt, a

plainclothes detective, recognizing Wyatt, hustled over and intervened. "He's okay," the detective told the cop. "Let him through."

Josephine, Darryl, and Walcott waited and watched from outside the police line. Wyatt ran to where he saw a body lying on the ground, outside the Jeep on the driver's side.

Richard and Louis, dazed but seemingly unharmed, were leaning against the side of a police cruiser. "What happened?" Wyatt yelled as he rushed to them.

"We were ambushed, man," Louis mumbled. He had a bloody handkerchief to his forehead.

A nearby cop, overhearing, put in his two-cents worth. "Drive-by shooting," he said with resignation. "We get 'em every week."

Dexter was laid out on a blanket on top of the wet asphalt. A team of paramedics was cutting off his bloody clothes and applying temporary compresses to the wounds. He had been shot in the left side twice, and once in the left arm. He looked up, his eyes wet with tears, as Wyatt hunched down next to him.

"I'm sorry, Mr. Matthews," he gasped as an IV was inserted into the biceps that hadn't been shot. "I fucked up, man."

"Don't say that," Wyatt said, trying to stay calm. "Tell me what happened." He knelt down, disregarding the oil and filth that caked his suit pants, putting his face close to Dexter's so the boy wouldn't have to strain to talk to him.

"I took my business into another gang's territory," Dexter said, shamefaced. "This is their style of telling me to stay the fuck out."

Wyatt's head was reeling. "Oh, shit," he said to Dexter, feeling an acrid bile rising in his stomach. "I'm sorry, Dexter." He didn't know what else to say.

The boy tried to smile through the pain. "You better check out Leticia, man."

Wyatt looked around with a start. He hadn't noticed the second body, obscured by a phalanx of paramedics and cops, lying on the sidewalk on the other side of the Jeep. He ran to where the girl lay on the wet grass, the skirt of her dress—the dress she had worn in court all day long— bunched up around her thighs. An oxygen mask was clamped over her mouth and nose, while a team of paramedics was working feverishly to stem the slow, steady flow of thick dark-purplish blood that was pumping out of a large hole in the center of her upper body, near her heart. They weren't making an impact stanching the wound, even with the aid of the oxygen being pumped into her system.

Abruptly, one of the paramedics felt Leticia's pulse, lifted an eyelid and shined a penlight into her eye, waited a second, then gently rolled the lid down. They all stopped working on her, sagging in frustration and despair.

"What?" Wyatt screamed.

The paramedic who had checked one last time for Leticia's vital signs, a young woman who had her hair in a French braid, turned and looked at him.

"She's dead, that's what," the woman said, her voice inflectionless.

They covered Leticia with a blanket. Then they lifted her onto a gurney and placed her inside the ambulance. The doors slammed and the wagon, lights flashing and siren wailing, took off into the wet night.

Wyatt stood at the side of the other paramedics' van as Dexter was placed in it for his trip to the hospital. "I'm sorry, Mr. Matthews," Dexter told him again. "It was my job to protect her for you, and I fucked up!" he cried out in despair.

"Don't talk about that stuff now, Dexter," Wyatt counseled him. "Right now all that matters is making sure you're taken care of, and you're going to be all right!" The words came bitter out of his mouth—he didn't believe them, not for a second.

"He's going to be okay," one of the paramedics who had been working on Dexter reassured Wyatt.

They closed the doors to the second ambulance. It, too, drove off into the wet, desolate night; Wyatt stood in the middle of the street, watching it go, the rain beating down on him like a funereal drumroll.

You dumb motherfucker, he thought, watching the lights disappear down the long dark street. He was thinking that about Dexter, but it applied more to himself. This was what he got for letting the end justify the means. He had needed Dexter's help, his ability to open the doors of Marvin's community to him, so he had turned a blind eye to Dexter's basic amorality—selling drugs, any way you cut it, was evil. And now his key witness lay dead because he, the hot-shit lawyer, had sacrificed principle for expediency.

But Dexter was also the one who had saved his life—so maybe there was a balance to all this. Right now, he was too distraught and anguished to know his feelings.

The bile rose in his stomach again, up his throat into his mouth, and he stood at the curb and puked his guts out.

There were no fireworks or outbursts of emotion in Judge Grant's chambers this time. The mood was somber, depressed. Helena Abramowitz picked some imaginary lint off her skirt. Finally, she spoke up.

"This is a tragedy, Your Honor, and I feel sorry for everyone concerned, particularly this young girl and her family. But the law is crystal clear on the subject: if a witness is not subjected to cross-examination, for whatever reason, their testimony does not stand. I'm sorry," she repeated herself.

She and Alex Pagano hadn't celebrated when they'd heard the news last night, but they hadn't shed any tears, either. That girl had been the rock of the defense's case. Now it would be as if she had never existed.

Grant cast a questioning eye in Wyatt's direction.

"I don't know if there's any precedent for this, Your Honor," Wyatt admitted. He, Walcott, and Darryl had stayed up almost all night trying to find a loophole in the argument Abramowitz had just presented. They hadn't found one.

Grant looked at Abramowitz. "Are you thinking about asking for a mistrial?"

Wyatt cringed. He had been waiting for this shoe to drop. Abramowitz had every right to ask for a mistrial, and the judge could easily grant it.

Abramowitz and Pagano exchanged looks; clearly, Wyatt thought, they had discussed this at length. Any decent lawyers would have, and they were several cuts above decent.

"No, Your Honor," she declared. "We have already expended an enormous amount of time and energy, not to mention hundreds of thousands of dollars of the people's money to bring this case to a speedy trial. It wouldn't be in the public interest to delay several months and start all over. All we ask is that her testimony be stricken from the record, and the jury instructed properly as to their obligations."

A small alarm went off in the back of Wyatt's head. They should be asking for a mistrial. Judge Grant could tell the jury in the strongest terms possible to forget Leticia's testimony—but they couldn't. Her testimony, given the horrific circumstances of the situation, would now be even more sharply etched in their memories.

Grant nodded gravely. "Ms. Abramowitz's appeal is going to be upheld. Do you have your next witness on tap?" he asked Wyatt.

Wyatt shook his head. "I was planning on resting my case after redirect of this witness. I don't know where I'm going from here," he admitted. "If the court would indulge me, I'd like a couple days to regroup."

"Do you have a problem with that?" Grant asked Abramowitz.

"It's highly irregular, Your Honor. These things happen, and everyone has to be prepared for it."

Grant looked at her in disbelief. "A drive-by murder can hardly be trivialized as 'these things happen,' " he said with ill-disguised contempt.

She flushed. "All right," she agreed. "Since this is such an extraordinary circumstance."

"Thank you," Grant thanked her sarcastically.

"I thank you, too," Wyatt added. *You shameless bitch.*

"As long as we're going to be down for a few days, however, in the interest of doing something so we can move this along, I'd like to bring in a rebuttal witness in advance of defense resting their case," she asked.

Grant pondered the request for a moment. "I don't have a problem with that," he decided. "Do you?" he asked Wyatt.

Wyatt's mind was already elsewhere—he needed to get his hands on Blake's computer, and he needed to find out from Angelo about this Elvis character. "I guess not," he said distractedly.

"Good. When can you bring your witness on?" Grant asked Abramowitz.

"I can have him here after lunch, Your Honor."

*   *   *

"The witness who testified yesterday, Miss Pope, was murdered last night," Grant informed the jury. The courtroom was empty, cleared of spectators. Only participants were present.

Although the jury was not sequestered, they were barred from reading, seeing, or hearing any news pertinent to the case; so this announcement blindsided them. There were gasps, outcries of disbelief. Some of the women dabbed at the tears that formed in the corners of their eyes.

"The law clearly says that every witness must be examined by the opponents to that witness," Grant instructed them. "In this situation the district attorney's office has the fundamental right to question every defense witness, and vice versa. If the opponent is denied the right to cross-examine, that witness's testimony *must* be stricken from the record; there is no discretion in the matter. Thus, this morning it is my sad duty to inform you, the men and women of this jury, that the testimony of Leticia Pope, which you heard yesterday, will be stricken from the record. It cannot be used by either side in this trial, and you are to completely disregard it. For the purpose of this trial, it never happened."

Court stood in recess until two o'clock. Wyatt knocked on the door to Grant's private office.

"Come on in," the judge called.

Wyatt closed the door behind him. "Thanks for seeing me," he said. "I know seeing me without the prosecution present is irregular, but I have good cause, as I can explain."

"You got reamed," Grant said sympathetically. He laid aside the *Sports Illustrated* he had been reading. "Tell me the purpose of this meeting."

"Judge, I'm seeing you alone because I want to seize Blake's computer, and if the other side knows about it, and it leaks, she may get rid of it."

Grant arched his eyebrows.

"There's too much smoke for there not to be a fire somewhere," Wyatt continued. "Her relationship with Thompson, their liaisons in the jail infirmary. This snafu with her law exams. It's dirty. It needs to be brought out into the light of day. If we draw a blank, so be it, but if there's something in there, we deserve the right to find out." He leaned on

Grant's desk, palms supporting him. "I need help," he confessed, opening himself up. "You can justify this."

Grant thought about it. "Do you have the papers drawn up?"

Wyatt reached into his inside coat pocket and took out the papers. "Right here. All you have to do is sign it."

Grant scanned the request. Then he reached for a pen, signed it, and handed it back to Wyatt. "Give this to the marshal's office. They'll serve it." He picked up his magazine. "Pagano's going to have a conniption fit, but that's life. For your sake, I hope there's something in this."

Angelo the gumshoe, who could be Jimmy Breslin if Jimmy Breslin were Italian, was waiting for Wyatt back at his office. "I got a good fix on this Burnside character," he informed Wyatt. "The guy's done umpteen gazillion rapes and other heavy shit as well. And I was able to place him in the vicinity of three of the murders, so far."

"Great!"

Angelo frowned. "Not so great. He fits the profile perfectly, except for one small detail." He handed Wyatt a two-page booking sheet. "He was in the slammer when the fourth murder was committed. You're using the one-size-fits-all theory to exonerate your guy, so the same criterion applies here. If he couldn't have done that one, he couldn't have done any of them."

Wyatt looked at the document. Burnside had been in lock-up during that single murder—the fact was undeniable. "Motherfucker!" he spat out.

"Yep. He wasn't in for long, either, more's the pity. His probation officer paid him a surprise visit, found a six-pack of Coors in his fridge. No biggie, but it was a parole violation. He had free room and board courtesy of the county for the next forty-five days—not much time, but enough to knock him out of the box for you."

Wyatt flipped the sheet into the air. It parachuted slowly down to his desk. "Back to the drawing board," he groused. God fucking damn it!

"Sorry to be the bearer of bad news," Angelo said, hoisting his bulky frame out of his chair. "If there's anything else I can do for you, don't hesitate to call."

It was pitch-black save for one needle-sliver of moonlight piercing the edge of the drawn venetian blinds where they abutted the window frame. Dwayne and Doris Blake had just enough light so that they could see each other's outlines, but not the expressions on each other's faces. That's how Dwayne wanted it—he didn't want her to see the look of contempt, betrayal, and primal disgust on his face, and he sure as hell didn't want to see the dismay and anguish that she'd exhibit when he delivered his news, which was going to crush her.

It didn't matter that they shouldn't, couldn't, dare not see each other, that the sheriff would be incensed and would ream her to shreds. Dwayne had gotten word to her through the grapevine that she had to see him, it was a matter of life and death—literally. So now here they were, in her office, way past midnight.

"I heard your testimony went good," he started out, wanting to ease into what it was he had to tell her.

"I held my ground," she said. "That lawyer tried to break me down, but I held my ground."

She wanted to move closer to him, so that they would be touching. She needed his touch so badly.

It was not going to be. The vibe coming off him had a jolt stronger than an electric fence.

"You didn't tell them about the computer." The jail guards, prosecution allies, fed him information illicitly, so he knew; but he hadn't been there, and he needed to hear it from her mouth, directly.

"And bury my chances of ever practicing law? I may be stupid sometimes—I'm definitely stupid when it comes to you—but I'm not crazy." *Like you, she thought—you're certifiable, I can't not look at that any longer.*

"Not that time," he said impatiently. God, he wanted to kill this bitch, beat her fucking head into the floor. Grab her by the neck and choke her until her tongue turned black. He was quivering, he wanted so badly to stomp her into a puddle of nothingness.

"What time?" she asked. She could feel that energy flow he'd get. That's why he'd spent his life in prison, and always would—that insane, uncheckable impulse to inflict pain.

"The time I borrowed it overnight." His voice a viper's hiss.

She had forgotten about that other time. Whether intentionally or unconsciously, it didn't matter. "Oh," she breathed.

"You didn't." Hard, insistent.

"No."

Not only did she hear his exhalation, she felt it. It filled the dark room like a cloud of poison gas.

"You never can, Doris. Never. No one can ever know I used it."

She had known what he had done, known it in her gut, but she had fought it, managed to convince herself that he hadn't lied to her. But now she couldn't; the betrayal was there, in front of her. "You did what they said you did, didn't you?" She knew it but had to ask anyway. "You broke into the police files and got the information about the murders, and used it against that boy."

Dwayne actually laughed. "*You* did it."

"*I* did . . . I didn't do . . ."

"You volunteered to get me some information that could help me," he said, laying out his scenario. God, how he relished doing this to her. "I knew it was wrong, but I was weak. I was in a vulnerable place. It was my only chance to be free. So I let you talk me into doing it. It's all there, in your computer." He paused, feeling her slowly collapse, as if he had reached inside of her body, her bag of skin, and pulled out everything alive. "I couldn't do it," he said; "you know they won't give me access to computers."

She was going to faint, vomit, explode. Disappear, vanish from the face of the earth—that was what she wanted to do. "How could you . . . *why*?!" she cried out in anguish.

"It's who I am, Doris. Don't you know that by now?"

Not all detectives look alike, but there is a similarity to the breed, especially among the older guys who have done their thirty on the force before retiring to private practice. One of them, Abramowitz's rebuttal witness, took the stand after lunch. In his tight shirt and tight dress pants, with his tie pulled tight around his bull neck, he looked like ten pounds of Jimmy Dean sausage squeezed into a nine-pound casing. He had a big, pumpkinlike head, and a Wimpy mustache that made him look like Oliver Hardy.

"Detective Petty, have you been employed from time to time by Dr. Leonard Carpenter?"

"Yes, I have," the side of beef answered.

"In what capacity?"

"Surveillance."

"Who were you watching?"

"Mrs. Carpenter. Dr. Carpenter's wife."

"Who resides with her husband at 1973 Lecroix Avenue?"

"Yes."

Where the fuck is this going? Wyatt thought. This guy hadn't been on the prosecution's witness list.

"How long have you been doing this surveillance work for Dr. Carpenter, Detective Petty?"

"About two years."

"Why did he hire you?"

"He suspected his wife was sleeping around with the colored delivery boy, and he wanted proof."

"And did you get the proof Dr. Carpenter was hoping you would get?"

"Yep. They were a couple of lovebirds. Five or six times a month, sometimes more."

"When you presented your evidence to Dr. Carpenter, what did he do?"

"He laughed."

"Objection, Your Honor," Wyatt called out. This was terrible.

"Sustained. Confine your questions to answers that are objectively verifiable, Ms. Abramowitz," Grant said.

"Certainly, Your Honor." She was angry with the judge. He had granted that order to seize Lieutenant Blake's computer out of sheer sympathy for Wyatt Matthews, a friend from the fancy-lawyer's club. When you scratched the surface, all these male lawyers were the same. Well, the hell with them. She was going to toss their little red wagons right into the fire, alongside Rosebud.

She glanced at her notes. "On August eighteenth of last year, were you keeping tabs on Agnes Carpenter?"

"Yes, I was."

"That was the night—or a night, there may have been more than one, I presume—when the defendant, Marvin White, spent the night in Mrs. Carpenter's house? The entire night?"

"No, he didn't spend the night at her house. Not that night. He wasn't there at all that day," Petty said. "Or night."

What the fuck? Wyatt's head swiveled to look at Marvin. Marvin looked back at him, shrugging as if to say, "I don't know what's going on."

"There were some nights he slept over?" Abramowitz asked. "With Mrs. Carpenter?"

"Yeah, there were a few nights, but that wasn't one of them."

"You're certain of that night? August eighteenth?" she asked.

"This White kid couldn't have spent that night at her house," Petty said.

"Why not?"

"Because she wasn't home that night."

Wyatt felt the blood rushing to his head. He looked over at the jury box. All twelve jurors were sitting on the edge of their seats, listening.

"Agnes Carpenter wasn't home that night?" Abramowitz repeated, trying to sound disbelieving. "Where was she?"

"New York."

"New York?"

"Yes, New York. I saw her get on the plane with my own two eyes." He reached into his hip pocket and pulled out a small notebook. Reading from it, he said, "She took USAir flight number three-sixteen to New York, nonstop. It departed locally at ten-thirty-five in the morning, arriving at La Guardia at two-seventeen. She took a taxi to the St. Regis Hotel, where she had reserved a room. She went to the Metropolitan Opera that night, to see *La Boheme*. Prior to going to the opera she shopped at Bloomingdale's and Bendel's, and had an early supper at the Cafe Des Artistes restaurant. (He Americanized the pronunciation.) The next day she did more shopping, ate dinner at the Meridian Hotel dining room, and went to a concert at Carnegie Hall, featuring a person named Yo-Yo Ma on the cello. She flew home the following day on USAir flight number sixty-six, arriving here at four-thirty-five in the afternoon."

"Did she travel alone, or in company?" Abramowitz asked.

"She went alone. She met a friend there, a Mrs. Gloria Epstein, of 935 Park Avenue, in Manhattan. They did some shopping together, and also went to the opera."

"Thank you, Detective Petty."

"You're welcome." He folded the notebook and stuck it back in his pocket.

"I have tried to contact Mrs. Epstein, Your Honor," Abramowitz said to Grant, "but she is out of the country for the summer and has not returned my calls. I do have these receipts to place into evidence, however, to support Mr. Petty's testimony."

As she reached for a file Wyatt got to his feet. "This is totally improper, Your Honor," he said, his face thick with anger. "Under the rules of discovery we must be notified of any evidence presented here—*before* the fact, not during or after."

"We were going to, Your Honor," Abramowitz immediately responded, "but when you allowed the defense a postponement in presenting the rest of their case—over the prosecution's opposition, I must point out—there was no time to do so. I tried to get to Mr. Matthews earlier this morning, but he was unavailable. He was in conference with you—to which I was not invited—and then with his own detective, a meeting which I was also not privileged to attend. We tried to get this material to defense counsel, Your Honor, but he simply was not available."

Grant ran a hand through his thinning hair. "I'm afraid I'm going to have to overrule your objection," he said. "Under these special circumstances, I do believe that prosecution should be allowed to present their case."

Wyatt sunk into his chair.

Abramowitz opened her file. "I would like to introduce the following items into evidence," she stated. "One Visa receipt for an airplane ticket, round-trip to New York City. One copy of the tickets, which we obtained from USAir." As she handed each item to the clerk a second copy was passed across the aisle to Wyatt by one of her gloating aides. "An itemized receipt from the St. Regis Hotel, room

number twenty-eight twelve, for the nights of August eighteenth and nineteenth."

She droned on, listing the restaurants, stores, Lincoln
Center, Carnegie Hall. As each duplicate was passed across
the aisle Wyatt sat ramrod straight in his chair; his world
was collapsing, but he wasn't going to let the jury see that.

A woman scorned. The oldest syndrome in the book, and
he'd let it happen to him. Agnes Carpenter had wanted to
help Marvin, all right; but more importantly, she'd wanted
to fuck her husband over, for the fucking-over he'd been
giving her for years.

He'd had two alibi witnesses. Now one was dead, the
other totally destroyed. And the slim hope Violet had presented him with the guy she'd seen in the bar had been nothing more—a hope, not a reality.

Yesterday, he'd been riding high, the summit in sight. At
the end of the day he had felt—known—that he was going
to win this case.

Now he was dead. And so was Marvin.

The signs had been there, but he'd been too blinded by
his own light to see them. When Pagano and Abramowitz so
casually and easily let the mistrial opportunity go by he
should have smelled the rottenness of his own case. But he
was so fucking sure of himself.

Hadn't he always been a winner? Why should this case
have been any different?

Hubris—if he looked in a dictionary his photograph
would accompany the definition. He had been soaring,
handling difficulties left and right (so he thought) with the
blithe assurance of an Olympian god. Now the reality had
come home with a thunderous crash.

Darryl had been right after all. He wasn't equipped to do
this, no matter how talented and smart he was in his own
field. Talent could only take you so far; then experience
took over. This was a seasoned, battle-scarred criminal-
defense lawyer's job, someone who had been there before
and could see three moves ahead, who wouldn't have taken
the word of a spurned woman without checking her out in-
dependently. The knowing defense lawyer would operate

like a great chess master, seeing the entire match unfolding
from the opening move and planning accordingly; or in a
more popular analogy, doing his job the way a Magic Johnson operated on the basketball court or a Wayne Gretzky did
the same on the ice.

He hadn't done that. And now he would pay the price.

Blake's computer. That was all he had left. He had to get
his hands on it, and hope for a miracle.

Grant had given them the rest of the week to put some
kind of alternate case together. A decent thing to do, but
would it make any difference?

Doris Blake had not shown up for work, calling in sick.
There was no answer at the door to her rented condo when
the marshal, armed with Judge Grant's court order, knocked.
It was late afternoon, a few minutes before five, and the
scorching midday heat was still lingering. The small patch
of front lawn was withering brown; it didn't look like it had
been watered for some time.

Her door fronted the walkway. It faced west, in a direct
line with the afternoon sun. There was no shade. The front
blinds were drawn shut; the marshal couldn't see inside.
The sun beat down on his back, raising sweat through his
white dress shirt. After waiting impatiently for five minutes,
and knocking at regular intervals, he left. Whether her car
was in the underground garage or not, he didn't know; he
didn't look, and he wouldn't have known which car was
hers, anyway.

Wyatt went home. He wanted to run, really blow it out, and
the hot tarry streets of the city weren't the place to do that.
And he was sick, all of a sudden, of living in a rented room.
He wanted to be in his own space, sleep in his own bed.

It was late in the day and it was still hot as hell out
and humid; everything was wilting. He ran along the road
from his house to the highway and back, his road run, seeing again the For Sale sign posted in front of the Spragues'
house. That house was empty—they had gone to Maine to

escape the heat. The timer to their sprinkler system was set to a solenoid that activated when the sun went down—water spiraled in graceful pirouettes from rainbirds situated on the corners of the front lawn, a light moist blanket on the dark green hybrid bluegrass.

Turning into his own driveway, he skirted his house, running around the back and taking off onto the trail that led into the woods. Normally he didn't do this run if he'd done the other, but he hadn't had a run on his own territory for some time, and he wanted to feel as much of it as he could. And he wasn't tired enough yet; he needed to run himself into exhaustion, he realized. Run until it hurt and then push past that. For punishment, for some kind of earthbound penance. Which wouldn't solve any of his problems, but might, in some dim, immature way, make him feel like he was paying his dues. A small down payment.

He didn't know where he was going with his case. The marshal had reported his inability to serve the order; Blake must have been tipped off that it was coming, and had vamoosed from work. Maybe from the city entirely, even the state. If she was gone and had taken her computer with her, he'd be screwed. By the time they found her and brought her back it would be too late.

He ran for an hour and forty-five minutes. His longest run in months. He skinny-dipped half a dozen laps in the pool to cool down, went inside, threw on a pair of shorts and a T-shirt, and made himself a margarita in the blender.

He hadn't talked to Moira and Michaela for several days—he felt guilty about that, too. He felt guilty about everything, all the guilt in the world was on his shoulders, he wanted it there. He wanted to crumble under the weight of guilt. To be buried under it.

"Hi there," he said to Moira, who had picked up on the first ring. They were in; that was good.

"Hi, Daddy!" Michaela sang. She was on the extension. "How are you? I miss you, Dad, when are you going to be finished so you can come be with us?"

"I don't know. Not much longer, I don't think. Let me talk to Mom for a minute, sweetheart, then I'll talk with you."

"Okay." She hung up.

"I didn't know if I'd catch you in," he said to Moira. "You've been out a lot. I never know when to call."

"I'm expecting a call from Cissy," she said. "There's a problem with the store."

"Oh. Nothing terrible, I hope." Instant deflation. She wasn't waiting by the phone in case *he* called, or hoping he would. She didn't care one way or the other.

"Who knows? I'm not there. How was your day?" she asked dutifully, with the same inflection she would use to remind him to have the gardener cut back the ivy before it burned.

He told her. Leticia Pope, Agnes Carpenter, the suspect who hadn't panned out, Blake's disappearance.

"That's too bad," she said.

Too bad? Leticia Pope was dead and Marvin White was going to be sent to the executioner and her reaction was that it was "too bad"?

"But you've done your best," she went on. "Look at it this way—maybe he didn't do what they've accused him of here—"

"He didn't," he answered sharply.

"Whatever. But he did try to kill another man. So it balances out in the end, doesn't it?"

He didn't answer. He didn't know how to.

"Have you been by the store lately?" she asked him, shifting gears as if they hadn't been talking about his case at all.

The question threw him for a loop. "No," he said.

There was a pause from her end. "Have you been by at all, even once?" She was clearly angry.

"I've been busy, Moira," he reminded her.

"Not even on a Sunday, not once? This is important to me, Wyatt. It's as important as your work is to you."

Then why aren't you here, taking care of it, if it's that important?

"I want you to do me a favor, Wyatt. I want you to go down there. You can wait until Sunday if that's the only time you can go"—her tone clearly implying that she didn't believe he couldn't go earlier—"and have Cissy explain to you what the problem is, so you can relay it to me. Will you do that?" She paused. "Or is even that too much to ask?"

He didn't know why he said it, but he did. "I'll try."

"Try hard, okay? Now do you want to talk to Michaela? Don't take long, please; Cissy should be calling any minute and I don't want to miss it."

Michaela came on. He told her about the drive-by shooting.

"Oh, Dad!" He could feel her sagging. "Oh, that's so horrible. That poor girl. And your friend. Dexter, was that his name? And she was so important to your case."

Which of them was the girl and which the mature woman?

"How are you doing, sweetheart?" he asked her.

"Better, much better." She lowered her voice. "I wish you were here, Dad. Mom's really difficult these days."

"Like how?" He could imagine.

"Everything. Guilt, blame, mad at me because I can't run around with her like she wants me to, angry at you for still being in this case. Just angry."

Shit. He felt so impotent. "Hang in there, kiddo. It won't be too much longer."

"I'm sorry, Daddy," she told him. "I don't want to guilt-trip you. You have so many problems already. I'll be fine, don't worry about me."

"I do; I can't help it."

"I love you, Dad. I wish I was there."

"I love you, too."

He sat on the back deck, nursing a second margarita. It was dark now; crickets and bullfrogs sang their calls and responses, vibrating and booming out of the night.

A girl had been murdered, Dexter almost. Marvin was facing the gallows. Lives by the dozen were being brutalized, and Moira was angry at him because he hadn't been out to her little vanity shop.

Had they once been closer in how they saw the world, and over the years suffered an erosion, a slow, imperceptibly widening chasm? Or had the differences always been there, papered over by the comfort of their circumstances?

That cover wasn't there anymore.

He sat in his study, going over his paperwork yet again. Was there anything in this mountain of print he could use, or were his entire case and Marvin White's life going to come down to whether or not Lieutenant Doris Blake had helped Dwayne Thompson invent the goods on Marvin?

The odds seemed astronomically long, especially since the good lieutenant seemed to have flown the coop; but it was the only play he had left. Those two incidents involving computer misuse stood out like neon signs in Vegas: the records showing that Marlow had downloaded the Alley Slasher files onto his computer, which Marlow had flatly denied, which meant that unless it was a clerical mistake, someone else had, under his name; and Blake's bar exam score being altered, almost certainly via phone-line computer contact.

That Burnside character, the one Violet had spotted. He would have been perfect, except for that one indispensable detail of being in jail during one of the murders. Maybe they had gotten the dates confused, or something. Anything.

He scrounged through his files until he found Burnside's jail record of when he'd been in. The dates were there, in irrefutable black and white—booked in on date X, released on date Y. Forty-five days, like Angelo had said. Murder number four had occurred on day twenty-eight after Burnside entered the facility.

He mulled over Burnside's sheet again. This man, this serial rapist, would have been a perfect fit, except for that jail time.

Was there something missing?

The notation, written in ballpoint and smudged from handling so it was almost illegible, was under the section headed "Work Detail: See attached."

There was nothing attached.

The deputy sheriff clerking at the jail's record desk knew Wyatt so well by now he didn't even have him go through the formal process of showing ID. "This is a copy," he told Wyatt. "Let me go find the original."

He came back five minutes later, a three-by-five card in his hand. There was both typing and handwriting on the card, some signatures. "You want me to make you a copy?"

"I'd appreciate it."

The wrecking yard was an entire city block square, bounded on one side by the river. Thousands of old cars, flattened like metal pancakes, were stacked on top of each other, a dozen or more in a pile. Trucks rumbled in with old scrap, barges tied up alongside the long dock, buttressed up against the pilings, unloading and loading cargo.

Wyatt stood in the small, cramped manager's shack, talking to the foreman, their heads huddled together. He had the copy of the three-by-five card in his hand. The foreman pointed to something on the card and nodded. Wyatt pumped his hand vigorously, ran out of the shack, jumped into his Jaguar, and left rubber leaving the yard.

Richard and Louis parked Richard's dilapidated old Honda Accord down the block from the Four Deuces. They got out and stood on the sidewalk, surveying the scene. Although it was night, almost eleven, the street was teeming with pedestrian traffic: people getting out of their hot, stuffy apartments, people going to bars where it was air-conditioned. Standing there next to Richard's banged-up wheels, they felt a keen sense of estrangement, danger, excitement, and pure fear-energy. This was 44th St. Gang territory, and they were most definitely persona non grata.

"You sure this is the only way to do it?" Louis asked, eyes darting about apprehensively, dragging heavily on a cigarette.

"Ain't the best idea in the world," Richard agreed, "but it is a sure thing."

"Sure thing gettin' the shit kicked outa us."

"We got to get arrested, man. A split lip ain't no big thing."

Striding down the block, they pushed through the swinging doors into the Four Deuces, and were spotted before they reached the bar, which wasn't far from the door. "What the fuck you doin' in here?" called out an angry voice from somewhere back in the room. "This 44th Street territory, mo'fuckers. Get the fuck outa here."

They ignored the voice and leaned into the bartender, a tough-looking older woman. "Couple of Miller Lites," Louis growled.

"I ain't serving you," the woman answered him in an ugly

voice. "Get your black asses outa here. I don't need the kind of trouble you're bringing."

"Give us our beers and we won't be no trouble," Louis answered. He was talking to the woman, but he was keeping an eye on his back through the full-length back-bar mirror. Richard was standing with his own back to the bar, checking things out.

Louis took a deep breath, "Who in here can give me a good ass-rimming?" He asked the bartender in a voice loud enough to carry the length of the room. "I heard all these 44th Street dudes like it that way."

It happened immediately—fists, knives, chairs. Richard and Louis were ready; they stood shoulder to shoulder and stoically took the enemy on. The woman bartender was dialing 911 before the first bottle broke, and the cops were there in less than two minutes.

The damage wasn't that bad, considering the hatred between the warring parties and Louis's bow-shot. Dexter's men were beat up, and some of the 44th St. guys were, too. No serious injuries—no guns had been drawn. A few chairs broken, glass bottles smashed behind the bar, the usual dust-up residue.

The two were arrested for disorderly conduct. After spending the night in a holding cell, they were brought before a magistrate in the morning. Although their bail was set low, since it was a relatively minor offense, they chose not to post. They were remanded to the custody of the sheriff to await trial. By one-thirty in the afternoon they had gone through the formal bookkeeping process and were assigned to a cellblock.

It was hot inside the jail—every inmate who wasn't considered a threat to the population was allowed out. Marvin White and Dwayne Thompson weren't among those afforded this privilege, of course (for very different reasons), but almost all the other prisoners were.

How the fight got started, no one knew. Most likely an argument over hogging time in the weight area. All of a sudden Richard and another prisoner, a white guy, got into it big-time. Richard was banged up pretty good, but the white dude got the worst of it. By the time some of the trustees and guards were able to pull them off each other he had several teeth knocked out, possibly some broken ribs, and numerous bruises and contusions.

They were both brought to the infirmary for treatment. Samples of blood were drawn from each man, a precaution to make sure neither man was HIV-positive. The blood samples were labeled and sent to a certified lab for testing.

Since no one knew (or was willing to come forward to tell) who had instigated the fight, neither man was charged with the assault. It was noted on their records, and could be used against them if the authorities decided they wanted to, although generally, if a prisoner kept his nose clean for the rest of his stay, they let things go. The jail was badly over-crowded, and keeping a man in for fighting was a waste of time, resources, and space.

Richard's punishment was confinement to his cellblock; Elvis Burnside was kept in the infirmary overnight for ob-servation, although he insisted he was fine.

Doris Blake hadn't shown up for work again and she hadn't called in, either. Calls to her condominium were taken by her answering machine.

The marshal went back three days in a row. The same response—nothing. Newspapers were piled up in front of the door, and her mail slot was overflowing. There was no record of her traveling on any scheduled airline, train, or bus.

They finally located her Toyota Camry late Saturday after-noon. It was parked in the far corner of the lot, away from her assigned space. It had a thin coating of dust on it, as if it had been parked there for some time.

Complying with a court order, the manager of the com-plex unlocked her door with his master key. The marshal and two members of the sheriff's IAD team, wearing latex gloves to prevent contamination, opened the door and went inside.

The apartment had been closed up tight, and the air-conditioning was off. It was like being in an oven, close to 130 degrees, and the stench was overpowering. All three men involuntarily gagged, their hands going to their mouths and noses. They staggered outside. Then they called for backup.

Doris Blake's huge body—naked, immensely bloated, the top two-thirds paler than marble, the bottom portion purple-black with settled blood—was sprawled out in her bathtub. The barrel of her .357 automatic was still stuck into the corner of her mouth, the hand that pulled the trigger frozen onto the gun butt. The back of her head and most of her brains were splattered against the back tile wall, over the faucets.

Her suicide note, found propped up on her bedside table, was a plaintive, pathetic cry for understanding and forgiveness:

> *Dwayne Thompson was my lover. Because of my blind love for him, the only man who ever returned my love, I compromised my position as a guardian of the people's trust. I do not deserve to be a lawyer; nor do I deserve to be a police officer, because I have broken the law. That I did it out of love makes no difference. The one thing I never did, however, was let Dwayne use my computer to get evidence against Marvin White or any other prisoner. Please forgive Dwayne for helping me, and please forgive me. Unless you have never known love, you cannot understand why I acted as I did.*
>
> *(Signed) Doris Blake.*

They searched the place high and low, but her computer was not to be found.

Judge Grant, reached at a restaurant where he was having dinner, immediately ordered the letter to be sealed. It would not be made public or admitted into evidence unless the contents of her computer, when and if it was found, revealed that it had been used to obtain information directly related to the trial.

Wyatt was at home when he got the call from Josephine informing him of the suicide.

He was struck dumb. "That's horrible."

"I know," she said softly.

"That poor, sad woman." He pressed the cradle of the phone to his forehead. "I'm responsible for this."

"Don't be ridiculous," she answered sharply. "She was an adult, she knew what she was getting into when she took up with Thompson."

He sighed. "I suppose."

"It's true," Josephine insisted. "You can't beat yourself up over something like this. He used her, she let him, and she couldn't face the consequences."

"You're right. Still, I feel . . . something."

"The computer. We have to find it," she reminded him. "That's the important thing."

"It wasn't in her apartment? They tossed it?"

"Thoroughly—her car, too."

"Maybe she threw it away," he half joked.

"You think she'd do that?"

"I was skywriting, but when you think about it, it makes sense, doesn't it? She knows she's not going to have any more use for it, and she doesn't want to leave a piece of incriminating evidence behind."

"Which means it could be in any trash can in the city. Good luck finding that."

"Or it could be right under our noses." He was getting excited. "She testified that she hadn't brought it to work since she'd taken her bar exam. Okay, let's say she lied and brought it in for Thompson, hacker extraordinaire, to use. He uses it for what he needs—"

She cut in, finishing his thought: "—accessing the files and using Marlow's name and ID—"

"—and she takes it back home!" he finished up. "And it sits there, in her house, until she rushes home from work, barricades the place, and eats her gun."

"But gets rid of her computer first," Josephine thought out loud.

"Someplace close," he prompted her. "Very close. She was tipped off the marshal was coming to serve her and she wanted everything done before he got there."

She was on his wavelength, as always. "I've wondered what it would be like, being one of those bag ladies who live out of trash cans."

"Be careful," he cautioned her.

"Of what? I'm looking for a ring my feeble old mother

threw away by mistake. A family heirloom." She laughed over the phone. "Don't worry. I won't embarrass you."

There was a torrential downpour all Sunday morning and well into the afternoon, and when evening came and it was over and had moved on, the weather broke. While it was still humid, the temperature was cooler, and the misery index wasn't nearly as oppressive as it had been. People felt optimistic again.

The workweek had begun. Monday morning, nine o'clock. What remained of the cast of characters was in place. Wyatt sat at the defense table, Marvin stiff and upright next to him, Jonnie Rae and her brood in the first row behind. Dexter was still in the hospital and Louis and Richard were in jail. Across the aisle, Abramowitz and her team sat smugly in their places, waiting to see if Wyatt had one last gasp, one final, implausible straw to grasp at before he went down. Judge Grant was moments away from making his entrance.

The heavy rain had kept Josephine from going through the trash cans and Dumpsters in Blake's condo complex. Since she had to be in the courtroom to help Wyatt, Angelo had been enlisted to do the dirty work.

Wyatt leaned over to Josephine. "Any news yet from Angelo?"

She shook her head, pointed to the beeper on her belt. "He'll call me if he finds anything."

Grant entered the courtroom, strode purposefully to the dais, and took his seat. "Bring the jury in, please," he instructed the bailiff.

The jurors filed in. Their expressions were blank—they didn't know anything about Blake's suicide or the missing computer.

"Call your witness," Grant instructed Wyatt.

Wyatt nodded to the clerk, who read aloud from her witness sheet. "Call Dr. Gloria Lynch."

Abramowitz stood up. "This witness was not identified to us as part of discovery, Your Honor."

Before Grant could say anything, Wyatt gave his reason. "We weren't planning on using this witness, Your Honor," he said. "But new evidence has just come to us that compels her testifying. I think that when you hear what she has to say you'll agree with me."

Grant nodded. "I think we should be generous in interpreting the rules at this point, given everything that has transpired recently," he said. "The witness may take the stand."

An attractive, professional-looking middle-aged woman walked from the back of the room and took the witness stand. As she was sworn in and took her seat Wyatt crossed to the lectern and smiled at her. "Good morning, Dr. Lynch. Thank you for flying in on short notice."

She smiled but offered no reply.

"You are a medical doctor, Dr. Lynch?" Wyatt led off.

"Yes, I am." She was the kind of witness who would give short, concise responses to everything except her specialty.

"You are a forensic pathologist?"

"Yes."

He recited her credentials into the record: Bryn Mawr College, magna cum laude; Johns Hopkins Medical School; internship at George Washington University Hospital, residency in pathology at Brigham & Women's in Boston. Currently holding the Gladys Schwartz Chair of forensic pathology at Cornell University Hospital. "Impressive résumé," he commented.

"Thank you."

"Have you been favorably cited many times for your work in the field of forensic pathology?" Wyatt asked.

"Yes," Dr. Lynch answered.

"In your extensive work as a pathologist, Dr. Lynch, have you been involved in genetic testing, such as RFLP and PCR?"

"Yes, I have."

Abramowitz leaped up like a cat on a hot tin roof. "Objection!" she screeched. "Genetic testing has not been introduced in this case. Any reference to RFLP or PCR or any genetic testing should not be permitted here. We've already covered that ground thoroughly, with Dr. Ayala."

Grant looked over at Wyatt. "Where is this coming from?" he asked.

"With all due respect to Dr. Ayala, Your Honor, our county coroner may be a forensic pathologist, but not one with expertise in DNA testing." He walked closer to the bench, so that he was standing right in front of Grant. "Genetic testing has been and is being used all over the country, Your Honor, but I'm not planning to try and prove that because my client's DNA doesn't match that of the victim's—all or any of them—that he's innocent, although that proof has been used and accepted in several cases across the country. I have several precedents, if you would care to review them."

Josephine got up and went to the defense table, where several lawbooks and journals, bookmarked with slips of paper, were piled.

Before she could bring them forward, Grant waved them off. "I know most of these cases," he told Wyatt. "I reviewed them prior to the beginning of this trial, in case either you or the prosecution would decide to use genetic testing as an evidentiary tool." He placed his hands together in front of him, as if in prayer. "This is a controversial subject; and while I don't accept the use of it without reservation, it has entered the vocabulary."

He sat back, having made up his mind. "I am going to allow this line of questioning," he announced, "on a conditional basis. If or when it seems to be going in a direction that I feel is irrelevant or not within the jurisdiction of this case, I will stop it." He looked down from the bench. "The objection is overruled. You may continue, Counselor," he told Wyatt.

Wyatt exhaled a deep breath. His entire case, what was left of it, had hinged on this ruling. If Grant had sustained Abramowitz's objection, it would have been over. Now he still had life.

"Thank you, Your Honor," he said from the heart. Turning back to his witness, he said, "Would you briefly explain to the court and the jury what PCR testing is?"

Dr. Lynch nodded. She turned in her chair and faced the jury.

"Every human being inherits DNA patterns from each of their parents," she explained. "They combine to form your own individual genetic 'footprint.' In the same way that no two human beings' fingerprints are identical, each person's DNA makeup is separate and unique. Everyone's DNA—yours and mine, everyone's in the universe—is made up of the same basic amino acids: what determines particular traits or controls various bodily functions, for example, is the order and type of the particular acids in the strands of DNA."

She leaned slightly forward in the chair, drawing closer to the jury box. "All humans have the same number of acid molecules in their DNA strands, but they vary greatly in composition. Each acid component of DNA has a separate and unique weight—which means genes of the same length from two different individuals will have different weights because they contain different numbers of each acid molecule. Even if only a few acids out of hundreds are different, modern technology can tell the samples apart."

Wyatt was watching the jury as Dr. Lynch recited her explanation. They seemed interested; but whether they were getting it, understanding the concept, he couldn't tell. Juries generally didn't like technical stuff. They preferred visual, visceral information. But the framework had to be properly laid in.

"This is where PCR—polymerase chain reaction—comes in," Lynch continued. "PCR allows us, in the laboratory, to identify the particular acids in a sample of DNA and then replicate those particular acids in the same proportions. Hundreds, even thousands of times. Once we have the DNA components in sufficient quantities, we can run tests to separate each sample by its own unique weight."

She paused once again to make sure the jury was with her. They seemed to be.

"PCR test data are comparative," she explained. "We can tell if a particular sample matches another particular sample. Which means that if given a sample from a crime scene, for instance, and if given a second sample from a suspect in that case, we can tell if the two samples came from the same person." She sat back. "Basically, that's it."

Wyatt stepped forward again. "Thank you, Doctor. Would you bring in the projector, please?" he asked the deputy in charge.

An overhead projector and screen were wheeled into the room. The projector was set up by the lectern, where Wyatt could operate it. The screen, as it had been for earlier testimony, was placed near the stand in a way that allowed Dr. Lynch, Judge Grant, and the members of the jury to see it easily. On the cart on which the projector rested was a pile of transparencies in plastic casings. There was also a pointer, which Wyatt picked up and walked over to his witness.

The lights were dimmed. Wyatt maneuvered the top set of transparencies into place on the surface of the projector.

"What we're going to do is very straightforward. We're going to present some basic PCR test samples, and examine them using the criterion Dr. Lynch told us, which is standard in the medical and legal field."

Two side-by-side slides of plastic strips with a line of eight small circles were projected onto the screen. "These are two examples of basic PCR markers?" Wyatt asked his expert witness.

"Yes," Dr. Lynch answered. "The circles inside the plastic strips are called 'window wells.' " She stood up and pointed to the slide nearest her, then to the corresponding slide next to it. On each slide one identical well was stained blue; all the others were clear. She moved the pointer between the two colored dots. "You can see how these two patterns are similar," she pointed out. "That indicates that the DNA on those two wells corresponds."

"So these two samples most likely came from the same person?"

"Yes."

"What could the odds be that two samples looked this identical but didn't come from the same person?" he asked.

"One in five to six hundred, roughly," she answered. "Statistically, those are extremely high percentages."

"Did you extract these samples yourself?" he asked her.

"Yes. These are samples of your blood which I personally took on Saturday."

"Thank you." He put up the next set of transparencies. "Are these samples similar?" he asked.

Having already been briefed, she only had to look at them for a moment. "Yes, they are."

Wyatt picked up an identifying slip from his table. "And again," he said, "these are samples taken from one specimen." He passed the slip on to the jury. "Would you explain where these samples came from?" he asked.

"These are sperm samples taken from victim number four. The first victim from whom sperm samples were taken and preserved."

Abramowitz looked like she was going to object, but after

a quick glance at Judge Grant—who was obviously interested in the information Wyatt was presenting—she held her tongue.

Wyatt left that set of transparencies up and inserted another set alongside them.

"Sperm taken from victim number six," he ID'd them. "Do you see anything interesting, Dr. Lynch?" he asked her.

"The DNA types are the same," she answered. "Identical to the previous ones," she added.

"Does that mean both these women had sex, voluntarily or otherwise, with the same man? The semen source tested the same?"

"Yes."

"Even though it was"—he looked at some notes—"seven and a half months apart?"

"It could have been ten years apart. This sperm almost certainly came from the same man."

As he was about to put up another transparency he saw Josephine frantically waving him over. "Excuse me for a moment," he told the court.

He walked to her and listened while she whispered in his ear. Then he smiled—a big, broad grin—and nodded. Josephine got up and left the courtroom. Wyatt walked back to the lectern.

"We need to have a private conference along with prosecution counsel in your chambers, Your Honor."

"This is insane," Abramowitz objected. "How much more of these hollow theatrics do we have to put up with?"

Wyatt smiled at her. "Not much more." He looked at Grant. "We found Lieutenant Blake's missing computer, Your Honor." He walked to the door that led from Grant's office to the hallway and opened it. Angelo stood on the other side, the computer cradled in his arms. "Come on in," Wyatt said.

Angelo walked in and put the computer on Grant's desk. Abramowitz looked at it like it was a live mortar shell. "Where did you find it?" Wyatt asked his investigator.

"At the bottom of a trash barrel at her condominium complex," Angelo answered. "It was hidden in a crate used to pack dishes, covered with Styrofoam packing. Whoever did it took pains to make sure it wasn't found. But I did anyway," he said proudly.

Judge Grant ordered the computer to be locked up in his office under tight security. Wyatt designated Garrett Green to be his representative in deciphering what was in it. Green and his computer-expert counterpart from the DA's office would go to work on it and see what they could find.

Dr. Lynch took her place on the stand again. Wyatt placed another set of slides of plastic strips on the projector and shone them onto the screen. "Two more samples," he said. "Are these samples identical?"

She looked them over. "Yes."

He consulted his notes. "These are sperm samples taken from the latest victim. One would logically infer that they are the freshest, and most accurate, is that correct?"

"Not necessarily," she corrected him. "The composition of your blood doesn't change with the passage of time. As long as the integrity of the samples is maintained, it would hold constant."

"Okay." Another set of transparencies was placed adjacent to the set already up. "What about these?" he asked.

She looked them over carefully. "This one," she said, pointing to the line on the left, "is identical to these other two."

"From victim number seven."

"Yes."

"What about the other one?"

"It's different. It's someone else's."

"You're right," Wyatt said. "It is. This sample came from blood that was taken from Marvin White." He handed a lab report to Grant. "Here's the affidavit from the lab that did the testing. It's the state-run lab in Washburn, which does all forensic pathology tests for criminal trials throughout the state," he added.

"This doesn't prove anything!" Abramowitz complained. "Dr. Ayala has already testified to all that, Your Honor."

"I'm sure that Dr. Lynch, who is considered more of an expert at this discipline than Dr. Ayala, would disagree," Wyatt said, "but I'm not going to argue that it does. That's not my point."

"What is your point?" Grant asked him with intense curiosity.

"I'm about to show you." He removed the slides of Paula

Briggs's and Marvin White's blood samples and put up two others, again side by side. "What about these two?" he asked his witness.

She looked them over carefully. "They're identical. They're identical to this," she said, pointing to the previous set.

"So they're both from victim number seven," Abramowitz groused from her place. "What is this proving?"

Wyatt walked over to the screen. Taking the wand from Dr. Lynch, he pointed to the strand on the left-hand side of the most recent set of slides. "This is victim number seven," he said. Then he moved the pointer to the slide alongside it. "But this is not."

"What?" Grant interjected loudly, an involuntary response. "Didn't you say the two are identical?" he asked Dr. Lynch.

"They are identical," Wyatt said, "that's true. But they're not from the same sample." He stepped away from the screen. "With your permission, Your Honor, I would like to ask Dr. Lynch to step down for a moment so that I may recall Dr. Ayala to the stand. There's a point in his testimony that applies here, and it would be helpful to go over it again now."

"That's very irregular," Grant said. "Why couldn't Dr. Lynch finish and then recall Dr. Ayala?"

"Because I want to introduce another piece of evidence that ties in to what we're discussing here."

"I'm sorry, Your Honor, but I can't sit here and not object to this farce," Abramowitz said sharply, her voice showing anger mixed with mental and psychological fatigue. "This courtroom has turned into a three-ring circus with Mr. Matthews as the ringmaster."

Wrong thing to say, lady, Wyatt thought.

Confirming his intuition, Grant visibly scowled. "I am in control of this courtroom, Ms. Abramowitz. I'd advise you not to entertain any thoughts otherwise."

"I didn't mean that, Your Honor," she stammered, "but I do think—"

He cut her off cold. "What you think right now is irrelevant, okay? What counts here is what I think." He turned to Wyatt. "As long as this is on point, go ahead. Would you mind waiting outside?" he asked Dr. Lynch.

"Not at all." She gathered herself together and left the room.

"Thank you, Your Honor. Recall Dr. Ayala to the stand, please."

Dr. Ayala had been waiting in the corridor outside. Looking ill at ease, he took his more illustrious colleague's place on the stand. The lights had been turned back on.

"This will only take a moment, Dr. Ayala," Wyatt assured him. He walked to the defense table, dusted his hands with baby powder, put on a pair of latex gloves, and picked up a sealed manila envelope, which he carried to the podium. Holding the envelope up to Grant, he said, "We offer the contents in this envelope, which were taken from the property department of the county jail, Your Honor. As you can see from the seal"—he pointed it out—"it was delivered by a member of the sheriff's department, Lieutenant Myers, who verifies here in writing that no one other than he put the contents in here and sealed it."

Grant looked at the sealed envelope. "I'll accept that."

"Can I see that?" Abramowitz asked, her body rigid with the struggle to keep herself in check.

Wyatt walked it over to her. "You do trust your own people, don't you?" he asked sweetly.

She turned away. "Yes," she bit off.

"Good." Standing at the podium, he opened the envelope and took out the contents: a knife. Holding it up so that everyone, particularly the jurors, could see it, he walked it over to Ayala. "Earlier you testified that the man who committed these seven rapes and murders used a particular kind of knife," he said, refreshing Ayala's memory. "Do you recall saying that?"

Ayala was fixated on the knife. "Yes, I said that."

"Would you mind taking a look at this knife, Dr. Ayala, and telling me if this is the *kind* of knife that would fit your description? Let me get you a pair of sterile gloves first."

Again he walked back to the defense table, holding the knife so that it was clearly visible, picked up a second pair of latex gloves, and brought both back to the stand. He waited while Ayala expertly rolled the gloves onto his hands."

"You do that much easier than I do, Doctor," he complimented Ayala.

"Lots of practice," the doctor answered.

"I'm sure." He handed Ayala the knife. "What do you think, Doc?" he asked. "Could this knife, or one like it, be the murder weapon?"

Ayala turned the knife over in his hands. "Most definitely," he answered without hesitation.

"I'd like to place this knife in evidence, Your Honor," Wyatt said, handing it to the bailiff, who held it with a piece of tissue.

"So ordered," Grant said.

The clerk assigned the knife a number. It was placed into a plastic Baggie.

"Thank you, Dr. Ayala," Wyatt told the coroner. "That's all."

"You are excused, Dr. Ayala," Grant said. He instructed the bailiff to bring Dr. Lynch back in. "You are still under oath," the judge reminded her when she had taken her seat again. Turning to Wyatt: "Proceed, Counselor."

Wyatt had the lights dimmed again. Returning to the screen, he pointed at the slides that were projected. "Earlier, Dr. Lynch testified that these DNA samples were similar, but came from two different sources. This one"—he pointed to the left-hand slide—"came from Paula Briggs, the latest victim. And this one"—he pointed to the right-hand slide of plastic strip—"came from a sample of blood taken from a prisoner currently in custody here in the jail." He walked to the clerk's table and picked up the knife in its protective Baggie. "The same prisoner whose knife was taken from his personal-effects envelope this morning, at the jail across the street."

The courtroom erupted. The buzz among the spectators sounded like a swarming beehive. Jurors scribbled in their notebooks and stared from the slides on the screen to the knife in Wyatt's hand.

"You've got the guilty man in your jail, all right," Wyatt told Judge Grant, the prosecution team, and the jury. He pointed to Marvin. "But he isn't the man who is sitting in this courtroom."

The prosecution immediately requested and was granted a recess to look over this latest development. During the break Wyatt reviewed his strategy with Walcott, Josephine, and Darryl.

"You know what they're going to be coming at you with," Walcott reminded him.

"I'm counting on it," Wyatt said. He was so overflowing with excitement he could hardly sit still. "I'm going to stop at a hardware store on the way back to court and buy them a hammer. Alex Pagano can pound the last nail in his coffin himself."

Judge Grant's chambers were crammed. Alex Pagano had joined the prosecution team. The prosecutors looked remarkably smug; Helena Abramowitz was particularly calm and collected, considering she'd just had a nine-ton safe dropped on her head.

"We've looked into defense counsel's allegations about Elvis Burnside, the prisoner Mr. Matthews claims is the real killer," Pagano told the judge by way of leading off. He was going to handle this personally—his career was on the line. And he didn't want to cut Wyatt's legs off vicariously—he wanted to do the deed in the flesh.

"Mr. Burnside is a despicable character. I agree with Mr. Matthews in that regard. He is a multiple rapist, he has committed numerous acts of violence. He is currently awaiting trial on a rape and assault charge."

Grant was sitting up straight, paying fierce attention. He glanced over at Wyatt, cocking his head as if to say, "How did you manage to do this?"

"But as we all know," Pagano continued, "revelations such as these only take place on television. They don't happen in real life."

He held out his hand. Abramowitz placed a records sheet in it—an orchestrated move.

"We have all agreed that one man committed all seven murders," he said. "I don't think Mr. Matthews has a disagreement with us on that score, do you, Wyatt?" he asked.

"No. I agree that one man did them all," Wyatt said.

"Good. As I said, Mr. Matthews's sleuthing has been nothing short of miraculous, Your Honor. And if I thought that he had uncovered a fresh suspect who really was the killer, I'd be the first to drop all charges against Marvin White and issue him a formal, heartfelt apology. Unfortunately, I can't do that."

He handed Judge Grant the document. "Elvis Burnside was in our own county jail when the fourth rape-murder was committed, Your Honor. That is the record of his incarceration. He couldn't have committed that crime, because we had him locked up. It would have been a physical impossibility." His smile was blinding as he focused on Wyatt. "Sorry, Charlie. Great try, but your hook's come up empty."

Wyatt stared back impassively as Grant read the jail record. Then the judge looked up, an unabashed expression of sympathy on his face. "The district attorney's right, Wyatt," he said, almost mournfully. "I'm sorry." He rose from his chair. "We have to go back into court. Do you have any more witnesses you want to call?"

"No, Your Honor, no more witnesses," Wyatt answered. "However, I do have a document of my own I'd like you to look over. It clarifies and supplements the one Mr. Pagano gave you."

He pulled some papers out of his briefcase. "It's true that Elvis Burnside was in jail when the fourth killing took place. He was serving his time on the county honor farm. I believe the information sheet Alex gave you indicates that."

Grant looked at the record Pagano had presented. "Yes, that's correct," he said. Looking perplexed, he asked Wyatt, "Doesn't that buttress his proposition?"

"That he was in custody of the sheriff, at the honor farm? Absolutely, without question."

The judge was confused. "Then your hypothesis is invalid."

Wyatt smiled. "No, Your Honor." He passed his own papers across the desk to Grant. "Burnside was doing time, all right, but he wasn't in lockup all the time he was doing it."

He turned and looked at Pagano; and he knew that Pagano knew. Not that his adversary had hidden anything—it was that feeling you get when the light suddenly goes on.

"Elvis Burnside was in a daytime work-release program, Your Honor. As you know, it's a commonly used way for the county to make back some of the costs of housing the jail population. An inmate works an outside daytime job, the county garnishees his wages, and they put the money in the till."

"I know about the work-release program," Grant said. "I've assigned prisoners to it."

"I know that, Your Honor. I'm stating the facts for the record." Wyatt continued with his presentation. "Every morning the jail bus would take Burnside downtown to Siskin's Salvage Company, where he worked as a tool-and-die grinder, an occupation he's proficient at. The bus would drop him off at eight in the morning and pick him back up at six in the afternoon. It's right there, on the first page I've handed you."

Grant scrutinized Wyatt's top page. "Yes, I see that," he said slowly.

"Okay," Wyatt pressed on. "In at eight, out at six. Doesn't leave the place. Brings a bag lunch the jail gives him. They don't let him off the property, or out of their sight. It's a condition of his sentence."

He handed Grant another document. "Except for one day. April twenty-eighth, the exact date of the fourth murder. He hands the foreman at Siskin's a note from the jail. He's got a dental appointment and is to be allowed to leave between the hours of three and five-thirty in the afternoon." He walked around to Grant's side of the desk to point out the note. "Obviously a forgery—the officer whose name is on that note will swear he never wrote it, never would write such a note. But our boy Elvis has been on the job a month, he seems like he's a solid citizen, it smells legit. And who from the jail would know Burnside was gone, since when the bus showed up at six, he had already returned?" He pointed to a card stapled to the document. "Left Siskin's at three-oh-seven, returned at five-twenty-six. The foreman had it marked in his records."

He crossed back to his side, standing close to Pagano. Pagano immediately backed away. "The fourth murder was different from the others, Your Honor," Wyatt went on. "All the others were committed at night, when it was dark, between nine at night and three-thirty in the morning." He turned to face Pagano. "But the fourth murder, according to *your* pathologist, Dr. Ayala, whose credibility on judging time of death is considered top-notch, took place between four and seven in the afternoon. The victim's body was found the next day in an alley off Sycamore Drive, which is three and a half short blocks from Siskin's Salvage."

He turned back to Grant. "I'll bet the farm that Elvis Burnside was in that alley between four and five that afternoon, killing that victim with a knife similar to the one I introduced into court. He was working in a metal shop in the salvage yard, Your Honor. There's a million knives like that lying around. He even could have made one."

PART
FIVE

EVERYTHING fell into place, almost instantaneously. The stolen files were found hidden in various places in Blake's computer, along with her altered bar exam scores.

All charges against Marvin White were dropped. A red-faced Alex Pagano stood in front of hundreds of reporters to announce the new suspect in the killings—Elvis Burnside. Along with the indictment of Burnside for the rape-murders of seven people was the parallel indictment of Dwayne Thompson for perjury, theft of government property, illegal tampering with government files, and everything else Pagano could think of to throw at him.

Despite the vow the DA had made to Wyatt, there was no apology to Marvin White. He was still a scumbag as far as Pagano was concerned; now he was an embarrassing scumbag, his Rodney King. And like King, he was convinced, Marvin would be back in the system again.

Wyatt waited at the entrance to the jail. When Marvin came out, still bewildered and grimacing with the not-believing-it-yet smile of one who has been miraculously snatched from the jaws of death, clutching his meager parcel of belongings that had been taken from him when he was booked (minus the gun), he embraced Wyatt clumsily, his voice cracking with relief.

"I knew you was the right lawyer for me," he told Wyatt gratefully, his face lighting up in a huge grin. "From that first day I met you."

Wyatt drove Marvin home. On the way they made a

detour to the hospital, where Dexter was still recuperating from his wounds. The two friends hugged and laughed.

"You did it!" Dexter proclaimed. He was sitting up in bed, looking good—he was wearing silk pajamas and his hair had recently been barbered; his cell phone lay on the covers at his side.

"He did it," Marvin corrected Dexter, pointing to Wyatt. "My man—my *main* man!" he crowed exuberantly.

Wyatt hoped Marvin had learned his lesson. But down inside, not very deep, he doubted it. *The next time you're in trouble, kid, don't call me, he thought. Because I won't be there for you again.*

He didn't say any of what he was thinking. He stood at the edge of the room, watching the two friends celebrate— one for his freedom, the other that he was alive.

They had strung a banner across the street leading into Sullivan Houses: *Welcome Home, Marvin.* Wyatt's Jag was surrounded by scores of kids as he slowly drove down the street to the front of Marvin's apartment. As soon as Marvin got out of the car he was engulfed, his mother leading the charge, leaping bodily into her son's arms, knocking him over.

"Pray thanks to Jesus, you're home!"

"Yeah, I'm home, Mama," Marvin said, picking himself up. "I'm home for good."

Jonnie Rae grabbed Wyatt in a bear hug. "I can't never repay you," she gushed, her heavy body pressed up against his, the smells of her sweat and her kitchen wafting off her. "There's no way I can ever thank you for helping my boy like you did."

"It was my job," he told her. "And I was happy to do it."

He was happy, he realized. Not only for the process, which he had loved; but also for the personal connection. He had saved a man's life.

A man who had tried to kill another man, over money. And might well do so again.

That was the future, over which he had no control. He had to savor what he had now, this moment, because that was his life.

"I'll be seeing you, Mr. Matthews," Marvin promised as they said their good-byes. "I'll be in touch."

"That's good, Marvin. I hope you will."

He drove out of the project, watching the scene recede in his rearview mirror. These people had been the focus of his life for months; but as he turned onto the thoroughfare and headed north, toward the freeway that would take him home, he knew in his gut that he would never see any of them again.

The following day he got a call from the police lab. They had found trace samples of blood from Elvis Burnside's knife.

It would be Paula Briggs's blood on that knife—Wyatt knew that; he didn't have to wait for weeks of testing to confirm it. Burnside was the murderer—finally, after months of chasing shadows, the authorities were going to get it right. And finally, after those shadows had been eluding him, dancing out of his grasp, he had caught them.

He and Josephine closed up their office. The leased computers, copiers, and fax machines were sent back, the beat-up surplus furniture was returned to storage, the phone company took their equipment, leaving bare wires. The photos and charts were taken down from the walls. The space was as bare and barren as it had been the day they'd moved in. All that was left were the ghosts.

Walcott stopped by to say good-bye. "You did a hell of a job," he told Wyatt with sincerity. "Better than anyone had a right to expect."

"We all did a good job," Wyatt answered modestly. "We were a good team."

"We sure were." The career public defender smiled. "I guess I can't talk you into taking another one on? A couple juicy ones came over the transom this week."

"Not this time." Never again, the way he'd done this one. It had been exhilarating, but he was too old to be a rookie again.

They shook hands. "Thanks for the help," Walcott told him. "It was a pleasure watching you work."

Wyatt and Josephine sat in what had become their booth in their local bar. "Cheers," Wyatt said, touching his glass to hers. He didn't sound particularly cheerful.

"Yeah," Josephine responded. She was flat, too.

There was a letdown to all this; they both felt it, the exhaustion. Together they had brought forth a birth, a life, and now an end. The fact that the ending was a happy one instead of a disaster didn't make everything feel all right.

"I got all my paperwork for school in the mail this morning," she told him.

"That's great. You looking forward to it?"

"Yeah. It's going to be a bitch, working a full-time gig and going to school at night, but I'm definitely looking forward to it."

"You'll have to persuade your boss not to work you too hard."

She snorted. "Not a chance."

She was starting law school, at night. During the day she would be working for him as his personal assistant. The job would pay for her schooling and leave her enough money to live on. The unspoken but clear understanding was that she'd be working as a lawyer with him once she got her degree and passed the bar exam.

"When are you going back to work?" she asked him.

"When school starts." Michaela would be home then.

They had a couple of rounds, but didn't talk much. They had talked enough already, all these months, and they would talk again, every day at work. Right now, they both needed some quiet time.

He walked her to her bus stop. "I'll call you in a couple weeks," he said.

"I'll be here."

The bus cruised down the block and slid into the space at the curb. "Bye, Wyatt," she said. "Take care."

"You, too."

They hugged—the strong, reassuring hug two friends give each other. Then she was on the bus, and the bus was into traffic, and he was slowly walking away.

Dwayne Thompson, wearing the same waist chains, handcuffs, and leg-irons he had been brought down in, was returned to Durban State Penitentiary. No more would he be a witness for the state. When his current sentence ended, he would immediately be brought to trial again, and everyone, especially him, knew that he would be convicted and would spend the rest of his life in one prison or another.

He'd given it his best shot. And he had almost pulled it off. He had taken on the entire system and almost single-handedly brought it to its knees. Fuck 'em if they can't take a joke.

As he was being escorted, under heavy guard, out of the jail to the waiting prison vehicle, he saw Helena Abramowitz standing near the sally port he would have to pass through. She was dressed casually, in jeans and a light top. Without makeup on, her hair pinned up in a haphazard bun, she looked ten years younger than she had all the times they'd been together. Her stare at him was intense and unwavering.

Something to take back home, he thought as he was hustled through the locked doors and into the armed car. An image to warm him through the long, lonely nights.

His keepers ducked his head down so he wouldn't bump it against the car's doorframe. As they were pulling away, he looked back at her through the rear window. She was smiling at him—but it wasn't a friendly smile. It was a smile of relief; and the last he saw of her before the darkness took him away was her raised hand, triumphantly giving him the finger.

Wyatt spent the night with Violet. He wanted to take a room at the Four Seasons, the biggest suite they had, a fancy dinner with champagne, but she nixed it. She wanted to spend the night in her own apartment, in her own bed, the bed where they had made love.

They ate in. She cooked for him, a simple meal. Most of the evening was spent on her couch, alternating between talking and heavy kissing. When they went to bed it was the most natural thing in the world, as if they had been doing it for some time, but still with the passion and desire of new love.

The sex was long, slow, sweet. They slept wrapped up in

each other's arms, legs, bodies. At three they woke up at the same time, as if keyed by a mutual, unconscious signal, and made love again. Then they slept until nine, and when they woke from that they made love for the last time.

She had given her two-weeks' notice. She was moving, to Portland, Oregon. "I'm going back into nursing," she told him. She had a job, in a hospital intensive-care unit. They had been thrilled to get her application. "It's what I should be doing. Helping people keep their lives going is better for me than killing animals."

"What about me? Us?"

"There will always be an 'us.' It didn't last forever—" She laughed. "It didn't last hardly at all, did it? But there was definitely an 'us.' More than some people have in an entire lifetime, Wyatt."

As soon as she was settled in, she'd write.

"Promise?" he asked. He was bleeding inside. They were ending before they were beginning.

"I promise."

He knew she meant it. And he also knew, as he had known in a different context with Marvin, that he almost certainly wouldn't see her again.

They said good-bye at her front door.

"I love you," he told her.

"And I you."

He walked down her steps. He was about to turn and say something, one last time—but the door shut behind him, and he was alone.

Summer was coming to an end. In two weeks it would be Labor Day weekend. Same as it ever was. Except nothing would ever be the same as it had been.

He had no idea of where he was going. He'd worry about that later. He didn't know if he was going back to the firm, and if he did whether he'd go back to his old practice or do more criminal defense. He might start a new firm, something smaller, on a more human scale.

His marriage. Where was that? It had been a long run, most of it good. Maybe it didn't have to end.

He stood in front of the empty house. It was late, after

eight—the sun, almost dripping red, was well into its slow western plunge. Taking some deep, cleansing breaths, he closed the door behind him and took off running.

He ran around the back of the house and headed into the woods, the lush, dark trees enveloping him, listening: to the beginnings of night sound, his own breathing, the regular landing and lifting of his stride. Music he would play later came to his mind, Coltrane and Duke Ellington charts, his memory-ear hearing the baritone roundness of his trombone, the fat glissing mournful notes circling around and around the tubing and out the end of the copper bell like blooming flowers. Deeper and deeper into the woods he ran, and as he did women's faces moved across his consciousness like living dreams: Moira, his wife; Michaela, his daughter; Josephine, his comrade-in-arms. Violet, his lover.

The forest was getting denser with every stride. It was dark under the thick branchy canopy, he ran from memory and instinct, feeling the ground give under him. He pushed himself harder, his breathing came harder, he was sweating, dripping with his own cleansing water. On and on he ran, farther than he had ever run in this direction before. His muscles became more and more in tune with his mind and so did his heart, opening like it never had before, in a direction he didn't recognize. And as he looked up over the tops of the trees, seeing shards of moonlight penetrating through, he felt a surge of energy, of hopefulness.

He wasn't sure where he was now—he was on unfamiliar ground. He thought about turning around and heading back, but he didn't, he kept moving forward.

He heard his breathing, he heard the night. He didn't know where he was going, or where he was going to wind up. It didn't matter, because where he was going felt right. He was going in what he knew was the right direction, and that was all that mattered.

ACKNOWLEDGMENTS

David A. Freedman, J.D., was of great assistance in helping me with all the legal aspects of this book. In any cases where legal procedures are not strictly followed the decision was mine alone, for artistic purposes, and is no reflection on his legal acumen.

San Francisco Sheriff Michael Hennessey and his administrative assistant, Eileen Hirst, gave me a thorough tour of their various jail facilities, helping to illuminate for me how a contemporary big-city jail system operates. This story is not set in San Francisco, and does not reflect on the specifics of their program.

Terry Lammers, J.D., Seth Kunin, the pathology department of Santa Barbara Cottage Hospital, and the staff of the Writer's Computer Store in Los Angeles were helpful in their various areas of expertise.

Al Silverman, Elaine Koster, Markus Wilhelm, and Bob Lescher were of great assistance both in helping me shape the form and context of the book and in providing strong emotional and professional support.

Now that you've read
KEY WITNESS

Don't miss J. F. Freedman's riveting new thriller

THE DISAPPEARANCE

Available October 1998 from Dutton

Here's a preview of the opening scene . . .

DAY ONE

The moon, two days past full, hangs low and forbidding-cold, diamond-hard in the late-winter dead-of-night sky. A thirty-knot wind has come out of the northeast earlier in the evening, blowing as hard as the summer Santa Anas. It's brought the temperature down almost to freezing, which rarely happens this late, mid-March; people aren't prepared for it even though they should have been, given the terrible winter this new year has brought forth.

It's late now, well past midnight. Nothing is moving on the streets. All the lights are out in all the houses.

The girl sleeping on the futon hears a noise, a dull thump, like a body bumping into something. The sound is just loud enough to bring her to the edge of consciousness, somnolently turning her head to look up from where it's buried in a pillow.

There are three fourteen-year-old girls sleeping in the bedroom. Eighth-graders having their little slumber party. They have been together most of the day, from mid-afternoon. Emma's mom had dropped them off downtown a couple hours before dark.

They had cruised the Paseo Nuevo mall, bought some tops and shorts at Nordstrom's and the Gap, followed that with dinner at California Pizza Kitchen, and finished off downtown by going to a movie at the Metro 4 down the street (an R-rated movie with Johnny Depp, they brazened their way in with attitude; the movie people let the ID deal slide as long as you don't look like a sixth-grader). Emma bought the tickets. She's fourteen, going on twenty in her head, mature-looking for her age, with an innocent sensuality that oozes from her.

Their parents had just started letting them out at night on their own, as long as they were in by a reasonable hour. They were growing up fast.

Between the time they had dinner and the time they went to the movie they flirted with some older boys who had been in their school before moving on to high school, Bolt or Thatcher or the public high school, but then they danced away, giggling and whispering. They liked the attention, but they weren't dating yet. Except for Emma, and her dates were secrets, except for her very closest friends.

Their parents had given them plenty of money on top of their allowances (these mothers and fathers who comprised various combinations of married, separate, and divorced adults, had their own weekend agendas which didn't include their children; they were all, in their own self-wrapped-up ways, happy the girls could take care of themselves for an entire evening), so they cabbed home and watched *Mad TV* followed by *Night Stand*, which was a stupid-humor take-off on a talk show. The guy who hosted the show lived in Montecito, the same as them. The girls had seen him in Starbucks, hunched over the *News-Press*, nursing a latté. Probably checking out his reviews. He was a minor celebrity, nobody to get excited about, not when there were real celebrities all over the place, John Cleese walking on the beach, Michael Douglas having lunch at Pane e Vino, Michelle Pfeiffer buying wine and brie at Von's.

They'd stayed up way late, past midnight. After they were done watching TV, they went outside and smoked, in a remote corner of the backyard. Emma's house has a huge yard, over two acres of manicured lawn, beautifully trimmed trees, and voluptuous flower beds, you can get lost in it easy, especially at night. Smoking is new to them—they know kids who have been doing it from when they were ten or eleven or even younger, but they were mostly Chicano public school kids. At fourteen, though, eighth or ninth grade, lots of kids smoke, it isn't that big a deal.

Big deal or not, they don't want their parents to find out. They don't want the hassle of dealing with their parents about shit like that.

Glenna, Emma's mom, knows that Emma smokes. She hasn't actually caught her daughter with the burning evidence in her mouth, but she knows the signs. She doesn't like it, but she doesn't hassle Emma too much about it, like other mothers would, so most of the time the girls hang out at Emma's house. Glenna looks the other way about lots of things regular mothers wouldn't—having boys in the house when there aren't any adults around, watching any videos or TV shows they wanted, no matter how R-rated raunchy they are. Glenna is a woman of the nineties; she wants her daughter to be one, too. So she cuts Emma a lot of slack.

The house—it could truly be called a mansion, Montecito is full of houses like this—is all one-story, the bedrooms located in a separate wing from the rest of the house. Emma's bedroom, like her parents' down the hall, has French doors that open up onto a flagstone patio, a path from which leads down the full acre of rolling lawn to the swimming pool and bathhouse.

When they came back to Emma's room they took off their shoes and left them outside.

One of the French doors is open. The almost full moon bathes the doorway, and part of the bedroom in pale yellow shadowy light.

Is something moving in the room? A person?

Whatever it was, it is out the door, it is pulling the door closed behind it, it is across the patio.

The girl is dreaming, a dream within a dream, the kind of dream that feels incredibly real, the kind of dream that if retained at all is always a nightmare in the remembering.

She isn't used to smoking and staying up so late, the way Emma and Hillary, the third girl in the slumber party, are. They're faster than her—she had been tremendously flattered and surprised when Emma had inexplicably decided, at the beginning of the school year, to include her into her circle of friends.

Still, she's the third of the threesome. Which is why she is sleeping on the futon on the floor, while the other two are in the twin beds. Not that she cares. Being in this company is enough; it doesn't matter where you sleep. Futons are fun, it's like camping out.

In her dream the French doors are closed now, the room is tranquil, empty. The moon shines on the carpet, a small, shimmering pool. The figure is gone.

Then nothingness. The girl rolls over in her sleep and her unconscious mind goes blank.

* * *

Hillary and Lisa don't wake up until after ten—normal teenage weekend behavior. Emma isn't there; her unmade bed is rumpled from her sleeping in it. She'd gotten up earlier and gone out, they figured.

They wait in the room for a while, not sure what to do—go out into the house and look for Emma, or wait for her to come back. They watch some television, get dressed, wait.

Finally, hungry and bored, they wander through the house to the kitchen. Glenna—Mrs. Lancaster to the girls—is sitting on a stool at the island, drinking black coffee and reading the *New York Sunday Times Magazine*. Her angular, striking face is devoid of makeup, and her straight black hair is pulled back in a ponytail; her long, slender feet are bare. A tall, athletic woman, she was awake early and played tennis for two hours on her private court with her coach and a friend.

"Emma still sleeping?" she asks, her look going back to her article. "How late were you guys up, anyway?"

The girls look at each other. "She's already got up, Mrs. Lancaster," Hillary says. "We thought she was in here."

Glenna shakes her head. "I haven't seen her all morning." She glances at the clock on the wall. It's almost ten-thirty. "She must be in the shower." She turns a page. There's some great clothing coming out this spring. She needs a trip to New York in the near future.

"We used the bathroom, Mrs. Lancaster," Lisa pipes up. "She wasn't in it."

Glenna cocks her head for a moment, thinking. "Well, she's around somewhere." She lays her magazine aside. Favoring them with a smile: "She isn't much of a hostess, leaving the two of you to fend for yourselves. Do you want any breakfast?" She gets up from her perch, crosses to the refrigerator. "There's fresh orange juice, bagels, croissants. Do your parents let you drink coffee?" Without waiting for a reply, she pours two small glasses of juice. "There's cereal if you want it. In that cupboard." She points across the room.

Lisa hesitates before she speaks. "I had this really weird dream last night. More like a nightmare."

Glenna smiles. "That's what happens when you stay up too late. You're disturbing your biorhythms."

Lisa nods, uncertain. "It was like I woke up in Emma's bedroom, just the way it was when we went to sleep? And the door to the outside was open, and somebody was in there?"

Glenna looks at her more seriously. "Are you sure this was a dream?"

"I thought it was."

"Tell me what you thought you dreamed. Or saw," she says. "What time did you think this was? In your dream."

"I don't know. It was really late. Like maybe morning almost."

Glenna crosses to her. "Did you see something, Lisa?" She cocks her head again so that her eyes lock into the girl's. "Look at me, Lisa. What did you see?"

"What exactly did you see, Lisa?"

They are in the study of Emma's parents' house: Lisa, Hillary, Emma's mother, and a police detective. The detective, a big man with a hairbrush mustache, has asked the question. He's asking all the questions.

Lisa is scrunched up on a couch. Pushing hard up against it—if she could force herself into it, through it, she would.

She's scared. She feels they're all angry at her. Like it's her fault Emma isn't here.

Glenna Lancaster crosses over and sits next to Lisa, taking the girl's fluttering hand. "It's okay, Lisa," she says soothingly, reassuringly. "What can you remember?" she asks the shaking girl.

Lisa shrugs, more of a wriggle. "I—it was really dark. Something was moving, I thought. I mean I thought I saw something. But it was really dark," she ends lamely.

Doug Lancaster arrives at his home like a whirlwind, the braking tire squeal of his turbo Bentley on the circular Italian-tile driveway announcing his arrival. Hair unwashed, clothes hastily thrown on, he charges into the house.

"What?" he asks Glenna, who has jumped up and run toward the door, intercepting him in the front hallway. The entryway to their house is eighteen feet high; the massive ten-foot-high front door was custom-built of imported Hawaiian koa wood, with floor-to-ceiling beveled-glass windows on either side of the doorway refracting the muted rainbow-colored light upon the marble floor. Glenna and her designer had gone to Italy twice before they found a quarry that had the right marble.

She and Doug had built the house themselves when they'd moved to Santa Barbara from Chicago a decade and a half ago. Glenna had supervised every detail of the construction, relentlessly pushing the architect and myriad contractors every day for a year and a half, seven days a week, driving everyone crazy. She went through the three best contractors in the county before she was done, but she got the house the way she wanted it, which is the only way she knows how to do things.

"She's missing," she tells her husband. "Emma . . ."

"You already told me that on the phone," he interrupts her impatiently. "What's the deal? I mean how do you know . . . I mean, what's . . ." His tongue can't keep up with the pace of his anxiety.

"Calm down," she says forcefully. "Come in and talk."

She steers him into the study, where the police detective, a man named Reuben Garcia, has been waiting for over two hours, since they contacted Doug in Santa Monica, no small feat—he hadn't been in his hotel room, and it took forever to get through to him on the back nine at Bel Air Country Club, where he was playing golf with some of the heavies from NBC.

Hillary is gone now. Her parents came and hustled her away. Lisa, the cause for this alarm, is still there—Garcia wouldn't let her leave until Doug Lancaster had gotten home and heard her story, fragmentary as it is, firsthand. Garcia doesn't want any problems later on down the line, such as an irate father with a ton of clout becoming upset because he didn't hear the story himself from the mouth of this small, increasingly terrified four-teen-year-old girl.

Lisa's mother, Susan, is with her daughter. Lisa is her only child. They live alone in a small house in the affordable area of the lower Riviera, in Santa Barbara proper. Susan and Lisa's father have been divorced for a long time—Susan's raised her daughter on her own, and did it while going to Santa Barbara College of Law at night. She's worked for the county for six years now; her salary is decent, enough that she can afford to send her daughter to Elgin, the best private middle school in the area, which is where Lisa met Emma.

Still, Susan makes less in a year than Doug Lancaster draws in salary per month. His salary is for show; he owns four television stations, including the local NBC affiliate, his flagship station. He has a lot of power, and he isn't shy about using it, generally for good reasons—he isn't a bully. But the power is there, and everyone who knows what's going on in this town knows it, including Susan Jaffe, a county employee, and Reuben Garcia, a local cop.

"This is my husband, Doug Lancaster," Glenna says to Susan and Garcia. "Susan is Lisa's mother; you've met her, haven't you?" she asks her husband, whose pulse rate is coming down slightly now that he's finished his bat-out-of-hell drive up the coast and is in his own house.

"I don't think so. Hello," he says, offering his hand.

"We met at Elgin school." Susan Jaffe corrects him. "Last parents' night. Your daughter and mine were in the play together."

"Of course," he responds quickly, diplomatically. "You'll have to forgive me—I'm kind of discombobulated right now, since I don't know what's going on." He doesn't remember the woman at all; she's nice-enough looking in a nondescript, generic way. Much like her daughter, cowering next to her on the couch. "Your daughter was very good in the play, as I recall."

"She had a small part, but she was good, I agree."

"So what's the deal?" Doug says now, having dealt with as much of the amenities as he's going to. "Are we sure Emma couldn't have gone out earlier, with a friend or something? You're positive she hasn't called, and in the rush no one picked up the phone?"

Glenna shakes her head impatiently. "There were no calls. I'm sure."

Garcia cuts to the chase. "Your daughter may have been abducted, Mr. Lancaster."

Doug rocks back on his heels. "What do you mean?" he asks slowly, sounding dumb to himself as the words come out of his mouth.

Garcia extends his hand toward the mother and daughter sitting on the sofa. "Lisa here might have seen something."

Doug looks at Lisa. "Seen something?"

"Sit down," Glenna tells him. She takes his arm and forcefully pushes him into an armchair across from the sofa where the girl sits.

He folds himself into the chair, his eyes fixed on the small girl eight feet across from him, who is shrinking into herself as he stares at her.

"Tell Mr. Lancaster what you saw," Garcia instructs Lisa. "What you think you might have seen," he corrects himself. He isn't committing to anything, not yet.

The sound of the bump brought Lisa out of a deep sleep, the deepest part of sleep that comes about two hours after you first lose consciousness into sleep, where whatever primitive sen-

sors are working make you feel like you're a hundred feet under the ocean, all murky and indefinable.

At first she thought the bump was part of a dream she was having, and yet she wasn't sure; she'd been so deeply asleep, sometimes she had dreams that were like being awake, but were really dreams.

It took her a few seconds to realize where she was; then she knew. She was in Emma Lancaster's bedroom, sleeping on a futon.

She was groggy. From being awakened from deep sleep, and from smoking. She wasn't used to that. Her mouth was dry. She wished she'd brought a glass of water to bed with her; she wouldn't get up and go get herself one, she wasn't comfortable enough in this house yet. This was only her second sleep-over— she wouldn't know how to get to the kitchen from here in the dark anyway; she'd probably trip an alarm and freak everyone out.

She could make her way to Emma's bathroom. She could drink out of the faucet.

She was really tired, exhausted, but her mouth was hot, she had to get a drink. She rolled over on her side, started to push her quilt down off her body.

Someone was in the room.

The door leading to the outside patio was open. Someone was standing in the room, on the floor near the middle, at the foot of the two twin beds. Light was coming in the door from outside, moonlight. Like a dull spotlight shining into the room.

Whoever was standing in the middle of the floor had a bundle in his arms. A large bundle, like a person wrapped up in a blanket.

The person was tall. He seemed tall, anyway, from her vantage point on the floor, looking up. She couldn't tell what he was wearing but maybe a windbreaker, a dark thigh-length jacket.

Her mouth was even drier now, hotter. It felt like the roof of her mouth was burning, like when you eat a slice of pizza that's too hot and the cheese burns your mouth. She really wanted water but she wasn't going to get up, not now.

She lay as still as she could.

The man carrying the bundle moved toward the open door. As he reached it, he turned for a moment, his look back to the room, not a full turn, not enough for her to see a face. She could only see a fragment of an outline.

The figure turned away and walked out the door. He closed the door shut behind him and was gone.

She was suddenly exhausted; her limbs felt like they were bound in cement, and she was scared, too, scared of the unknown, whatever it was. She was too tired to move, and even though her mouth was hot and dry she didn't get up, not even after there was no one standing in the room anymore.

She rolled over again and fell back asleep, almost instantly.

When she woke up hours later, she vaguely remembered it, but she thought it had been a dream.

Garcia prompts her. "What did the intruder look like?" He has already heard it, all she knew or could remember, but he wants Doug Lancaster to hear it himself, from the witness directly. He wants to protect his ass from whatever might come down later.

"Tall."

"Right. You've told us that already. What else?"

"He was . . ."

"It was a man? You're sure of that?" Doug Lancaster interrupts her. He's sitting on the edge of his chair, fidgeting, his knee involuntarily dancing.

"I—I'm pretty sure. I'd say almost sure." She's scared of Emma's father. He is staring at her like he could look right through her.

"Let her finish," Glenna admonishes her husband, putting a restraining hand on his shoulder. "This has been terrible for her. Terrible and terrifying."

He nods, taking a composing breath to calm himself. "I'm sorry, Lisa. Go ahead, please."

"Was there anything else he was wearing you can remember?" Garcia prompts the girl again.

"A baseball kind of hat," she says.

"Could you see his face at all?" the detective asks, getting excited.

"Not really. I could see some of his hair sticking out the back."

His enthusiasm drops. "Dark hair or light?"

She squirms in her place. Her mother has a protective arm around her shoulder.

"I couldn't tell. It was dark."

"Someone, probably tall, probably carrying a bundle that might have been someone wrapped up in a blanket. Hair long enough to be sticking out the back of his hat. Anything else?" Garcia continues his probing. "Could you tell his color?"

"He was white," she answers after a moment's thought.

"Not a black man."

"No."

"Could you tell how old he might be, this intruder? A teen-ager, say, or someone older, like my age, or Mr. Lancaster's?"

She looks from one man to the other. "It wasn't a teenager."

"Can you be any more specific? Twenties, thirties, forties, whatever?"

She shakes her head, eyes averted to the floor. "I hardly saw him. His back was to me. It was dark, and I was asleep, and I was really groggy, you know?" The words are coming out in a scared, scrambled rush. "I don't . . . I wish I . . ." She stumbles to a halt.

"And whoever it was that was wrapped up in this blanket, if it was a person," Garcia goes on. "Was it struggling? Did it look like it was moving or fighting?"

Lisa shakes her head. "It was still. It wasn't fighting. She—" she adds, then catches herself. "I mean . . ."

Doug Lancaster stands up. "I think that's enough for now," he says, coming over and putting a hand on the girl's shoulder. "There's nothing more you can remember, is there?" he says soothingly, a father who has a daughter this girl's age. A daughter no one's seen for over twelve hours now.

"I just have one other question," Garcia says, almost apologetically, now that Doug Lancaster has flexed a little muscle on this girl's behalf. Which is a hell of a nice gesture, considering the man's daughter is missing and may have been kidnapped.

Lisa turns to him, her face a scared-to-death open book.

"What he had in his arms. That looked like it was in a blanket." He doesn't want to ask this question, but he has to. "You think it might have been Emma?"

"It might have been," she answers. "I wasn't thinking anything like that. Not till later," she adds, glancing over at Mr. and Mrs. Lancaster, who look like they've been whacked really hard on their heads with a baseball bat. "But it looked pretty big, the way he had it kind of over his shoulder. So it could have been." She turned her look away, half to her mother, half to the floor. "It was big enough to be a girl."